The Kingswood Book of Fishing

The Kingswood Book of Fishing

Edited by
TONY PAWSON

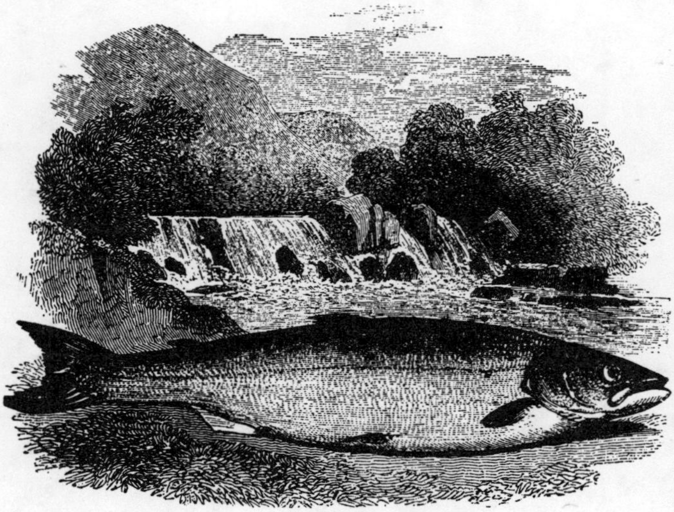

The Kingswood Press

First published in Great Britain
in 1968 as *The Fisherman's Companion*
by Eyre & Spottiswoode (Publishers) Ltd

This second edition published as
The Kingswood Book of Fishing
in Great Britain in 1992
by The Kingswood Press
Michelin House, 81 Fulham Road, London SW3 6RB

A CIP catalogue record for this book
is available from the British Library
ISBN 0 413 65800 7

Printed in Great Britain
by Clays Ltd, St. Ives Plc

Contents

Part 8 – Trout, Salmon and Grayling

Part 9 – Verse

The line drawings in this book are taken from engravings on wood published in Izaak Walton and Charles Cotton's 'The Compleat Angler', edited by Edward Jesse, in Henry Bohm's Illustrated Library, 1856; from 'The Jolly Angler', fifth edition, by J. March; and from 'The British Angler's Manual'.

Introduction

The *Kingswood Book of Fishing* is an updating of Kenneth Mansfield's popular *The Fisherman's Companion*, published in 1968. It remains primarily his work, his inspiration, his personal choice, and a fitting memorial to an angler and writer of distinction.

Mansfield was a natural choice to edit such a book for he was a competent all-round fisherman, well-versed in most methods and with worldwide experience. He had also made a name for himself both as a writer and editor of several fishing periodicals and books. In addition, Mansfield wrote prolifically under the pseudonym Alan Young, which he used in such works as *Sea Angling for Beginners*, and was also editor of *Angling News* and then of *Angling*.

One of his most notable contributions to angling literature was as editor and contributor to the three-volume *The Art of Angling* published in 1957. In listing there the many distinguished fishermen whom he had persuaded to write sections of that comprehensive work this was how he described himself: 'An angler who has wide experience of game, coarse, and sea fishing in the British Isles, Central Europe, the Sudan, and Burma. He is a regular contributor to sporting periodicals and is general editor of the *How to Catch Them* series of angling books, for which he wrote Perch.'

That modest summary does not do full justice to a man whom fellow writers, such as Trevor Housby and Peter Tombleson, recall as a fine angler, an outstanding fishing editor, and a delightful companion. So when the Kingswood Press asked me to revise and update the late Kenneth Mansfield's book they gave me an especially pleasant task. For I share his happy outlook on angling, his respect and fellow-feeling for fishermen of all disciplines.

Mansfield was a true Waltonian, honouring all legitimate anglers and able to share their enjoyment of a variety of method and fish. Not for him narrow-minded 'purisms' or dogmatic assertions about the superiority of some particular specialisms or personal preferences, which is all angling 'purisms' are. That point is neatly made in Caine's *Angler at Large* with his humorous inventions of 'purism' in flounder-fishing.

This was a secondary reason for me to include extracts from that most polished and philosophical of angling writers, Viscount Grey of Fallodon. Clearly he was of like mind in writing, 'The man who has in him no sympathy for the humbler methods of angling, the salmon fisher who despises trout fishing, the dry-fly purist, who cares nothing for other methods of angling, in all these there is something lacking of the greatest pleasure angling can give.'

In like vein are verses from the prestigious Houghton Club's fishing book quoted by Mick Lunn in his most practical and entertaining fly-fishing book of recent years, *A Particular Lunn*. Even among the elite of Test fishermen it appears happily acceptable to poke fun at the dogmatic purists, who only fished dry fly and scorned rainbow trout:

> 'I know the purists always frown
> On any trout that isn't brown
> And furthermore go on to say
> In their authoritative way
> (Which means of course you wouldn't know
> You silly ignorant so and so)
> It's not a trout it's just a char
> That shows what purists really are.'

Kenneth Mansfield seems to me to have settled on the right method of choice for such a book. His selections were made for their entertainment value and for expressing the range and spirit of angling. He favoured too the inclusion of some substantial pieces giving pause for thought rather than filling the book with innumerable snippets designed more to illustrate the author's erudite research than let the reader share the joys of angling.

Approving his method it would have been wrong of me to make more than minor additions and subtractions to his own personal choices. So my main concentration has been on adding more recent material and including some of my own favourites in a new section which I have called 'The Fascination of Fishing', which includes the views of Lord Grey and others on the attractions of angling.

For the rest I have kept to Mansfield's format, merely updating the various Parts, and adding an occasional piece which appeals to me. It also seemed desirable to represent a wider range of overseas authors of the calibre of William Humphrey, Roderick Haig-Brown and Ernest Hemingway (whose *Old Man and the Sea* was instrumental in winning him the Nobel Prize in 1952), or of outstanding angling ability such as Zane Grey, John Sautelle Sr and Dr Robert Sloane. A favourite of mine among fish is the grayling, so highly regarded in Europe, so under-rated in Britain, particularly in the prestigious trout waters of the south of England. I agree its classification as the fourth game fish and have added grayling to the Section on salmon and trout.

Fishing is a happy sport which can give enjoyment in a hundred different ways whether wandering solitary on the wild hills, or sedentary along a crowded canal bank. Where there is happiness there is good humour and that too is reflected in the choices. But fishing also has its trials and tribulations, its moments of despair or boredom, of frustration or even confrontation. Andrew Lang's *Confessions of a Duffer* and an extract from Bruce Sandison's book giving a gillie's-eye view of ungentlemanly gentlemen anglers, depicts these aspects with Lord Byron writing for the few who find it a disagreeable sport in its entirety.

Most important, angling catches the imagination of the young, satisfying in many an inborn primeval instinct. It inspires in them dreams of excitement and triumph. Canada's Tara Robinson, writing (aged eleven) her second book on how to catch the huge Pacific spring salmon, lets such dreams briefly intrude on her technical treatise. 'I am always learning new fishing methods and plan shortly to put out a large book on modern salmon fishing. It will cover all the methods for catching the five Pacific salmon of North America. Dad had my 41½lb salmon from last year smoked and canned. I think that wasn't fair because my Dad caught a 41½-pounder in 1981 and he got his mounted. I'm going to catch a bigger one this year and show him what's what about Salmon fishing. I hope it's a 60-pounder. O.K. enough history and on to fish and fishing.'

Right, that's enough introductory waffle from me keeping you from the expert writing of others. So on to Mansfield's and my selections with the hope they accord with Viscount Grey's recipe for a fishing book: it 'should be written and read, partly perhaps for the sake of hints, information and instructions, but much more that the sense of refreshing pleasure, which has been felt by the writer, may slide into a sympathetic mind.'

For a final reflection I rely on the confident young Tara Robinson: 'If you are reading this book in a store and are not going to buy it, put it down right now. The sales clerk is watching you.'

Winchester
November 1991

Tony Pawson

PART 1

The Fascination Of Fishing

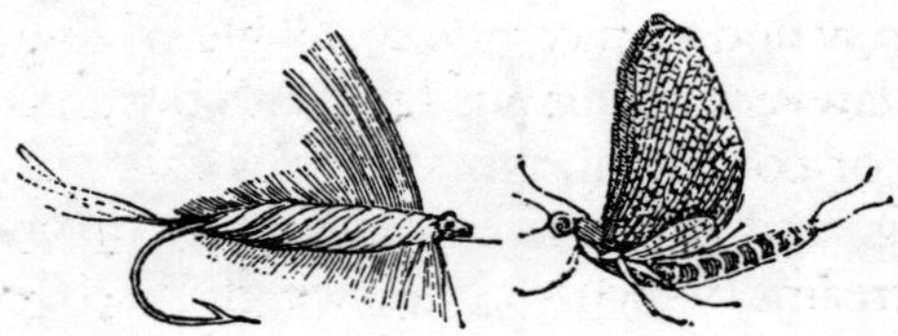

The Happy Life

IZAAK WALTON

No life so happy and so pleasant as the life of a well-governed angler; for when the lawyer is swallowed up with business, and the statesman is preventing or contriving plots, then we sit on cowslip-banks, hear the birds sing, and possess ourselves in as much quietness as these silent silver streams, which we now see glide so quietly by us. Indeed, my good scholar, we may say of angling as Dr Boteler said of strawberries, 'Doubtless God could have made a better berry, but doubtless God never did;' and so, if I might be judge, God never did make a more calm, quiet, innocent recreation than angling . . . But for the practical part, it is that that makes an angler. I once heard one say, 'I envy not him that eats better meat than I do; nor him that is richer, or that wears better clothes than I do: I envy nobody but him, and him only, that catches more fish than I do.' And such a man is like to prove an angler; and this noble emulation I wish to you and all young anglers.

from THE COMPLEAT ANGLER *1653*

The Merry Spirit

Attributed to DAME JULIANA BERNERS

But the angler may have no cold nor no disease nor anger, but if he be causer himself, for he may not lese at the most but a line or an hook of which he may have store [in] plenty of his own making as this simple treatise shall teach him. So then his loss is not grievous, and other griefs may he not have, saving but if any fish break away after that he is taken on the hook, or else that he catch nought which be not grievous. For if he fail of one he may not fail of another if he doeth as this treatise teacheth, but if there be nought in the water. And yet at the least he hath his wholesome walk and merry at his ease, a sweet air of the sweet savour of the mead flowers that maketh him hungry. He heareth the melodious harmony of fowls; he seeth the young swans, herons, ducks, coots and many other fowls with their broods, which meseemeth better than all the noise of hounds, the blasts of horns and the scry of fowls that hunters, falconers and fowlers can make. And if the angler take fish, surely then is there no man merrier than he is in his spirit.

from TREATYSE OF FYSSHYNGE WITH AN ANGLE
c. 1496 (or perhaps earlier)

Earthly Paradise

LORD GREY

Fly-fishing is an earthly paradise, and there is but one quality that is necessary to make us fit to enter into and enjoy it. We must be born with an intense desire to catch fish with a rod and line.

Fly-fishing is but one form of angling, and to enjoy it to the full a man must be born an angler. The passion may be latent, for years it may not discover itself owing to lack of opportunity, but if it is not revealed when opportunity comes, it is not there.

As a boy the real angler will fish for sticklebacks or eels, if he can get nothing better; the watching of a float will be to him a matter of undeviating attention and interest; the bobbing of the float when a fish bites will cause him excitement; the thrill that he will feel when a fish is hooked and is being played is indescribable; and the capture of a fish of relatively large size will produce exaltation; the loss of such a fish after hooking it will afflict him with intolerable anguish. After a successful day, he will be in a glow of beatitude, but blank days will not dull the edge of keenness.

Perhaps only one who as a boy has known the excitement of small experiences can appreciate to the most exquisite degree the pleasure of the highest form of fly-fishing. The angler whose youth has found delight in catching small fish with bait on a short line has a standard of comparison, a measuring-pole of feeling wherewith to gauge the tremendous event of hooking a salmon with fly at the end of twenty yards or more of line. It is well to come through the smaller things to the enjoyment of those that are transcendent, and he who from his earliest youth has had the noblest forms of fly-fishing at his disposal is not necessarily to be deemed the happiest. But without insisting on fine gradations of pleasure, the main point is that for the highest zest and delight in fly-fishing a man must be an angler. He must have a keen desire to fish in the element of water and to capture with rod and line the fish that live there free and at large.

The man who has in him no sympathy for the humbler methods of angling, the salmon fisher, who despises trout fishing, the dry fly purist, who cares nothing for other methods of angling, in all these there is something lacking of the greatest pleasure that fly-fishing can give. Personally, when separated from my own opportunities of fly-fishing, I can never see an angler watching his float on the Thames without feeling a sense of envy, a desire to do what he is doing.

from FALLODON PAPERS *1926*

The Lure of Fishing

JOHN DENNYS

Some youthfull *Gallant* here perhaps will say
This is no pastime for a gentleman.
It were more fit at cardes and dice to play,
To use both fence and dauncing now and than,
Or walke the streetes in nice and strange Aray,
Or with coy phrases court his Mistris fan,
  A poore delight with toyle and painfull watch,
  With losse of time a silly Fish to catch.

Let them that list these pastimes then pursue,
And on their pleasing fancies feede their fill;
So I the Fields and Meadowes greene may view,
And by the Riuers fresh may walke at will,
Among the *Dayzes* and the *Violets* blew:
Red *Hyacinth* and yealow *Daffadill*,
  Purple *Narcissus*, like the morning rayes,
  Pale *Ganderglas* and azour *Culuerkayes*.

I count it better pleasure to behold
The goodly compasse of the loftie Skye,
And in the midst thereof like burning gold
The flaming Chariot of the worlds great eye;

The watry cloudes that in the ayre vprold
With sundry kindes of painted collours flie:
  And fayre *Aurora* lifting vp her head,
  And blushing rise from old *Thitonus* bed.

The lofty woods the forrests wide and long,
Adornd with leaues and branches fresh and greene,
In whose coole bow'rs the birds with chaunting song,
Doe welcome with thin quire the *Summers* Queene,
The meadowes faire where *Flora's* guifts among,
Are intermixt the verdant grasse betweene,
  The siluer skaled fish that softlie swimme,
  Within the brookes and Cristall watry brimme.

All these and many more of his creation,
That made the heauens, the *Angler* oft doth see,
And takes therein no little delectation,
To think how strange and wonderfull they be,
Framing thereof an inward contemplation,
To set his thoughts from other fancies free,
  And whiles hee lookes on these with joyfull eye,
  His minde is rapt aboue the starry skye.

from THE SECRETS OF ANGLING *1913*

The Best Life

O the gallant Fisher's life,
  It is the best of any;
'Tis full of pleasure, void of strife,
  And 'tis beloved of many:
    Other joys
    Are but toys;
    Only this
    Lawful is;
    For our skill
    Breeds no ill,
  But content and pleasure.

In a morning up we rise,
  Ere Aurora's peeping;
Drink a cup to wash our eyes;
  Leave the sluggard sleeping:
    Then we go
    To and fro,
    With our knacks
    At our backs,
    To such streams
    As the Thames
  If we have the leisure.

When we please to walk abroad
  For our recreation,
In the fields is our abode,
  Full of delectation:
    Where in a brook
    With a hook,
    Or a lake,
    Fish we take:
    There we sit
    For a bit,
  Till we fish entangle.

If the sun's excessive heat
  Make our bodies swelter,
To an osier hedge we get
  For a friendly shelter;
    Where, in a dike,
    Perch or Pike,
    Roach or Dace,
    We do chase;
    Bleak or Gudgeon,
    Without grudging;
  We are still contented.

Jo. Chalkhill

Two Poems

Bring the rod, the line, the reel;
Bring, oh bring, the osier creel;
Bring me showers, and clouds, and winds!

All things right and tight,
All things well and proper,
Trailer red and bright,
Dark and wily dropper –
Casts of midgets bring,
Made of plover-hackle
With a gaudy wing
And a cobweb tackle.

Thomas Tod Stoddart

The aeroplane that roars across the world
And back again before the day is out
May still evoke less wonder than the curled
Low ripples that are started by a trout.

T.C. Yelland

True Delight

FRANCIS FRANCIS

I know nothing more pleasant than wandering dreamily away up amongst the hills by the side of some tiny beck, new to the angler, with no sound but the pipe of the plover, or the curlew, or the distant tinkle of the drowsy bell-wether; no encumbrance but a light rod; no bother about what flies will or will not suit; no tackle beyond a yard of gut and two or three hooks in a piece of brown paper; a small bag of moss with well-scoured worms within; a sandwich or a cold mutton chop – the latter for preference – in one pocket, and a flask of the dew that 'shines in the starlight when kings dinna ken' in the other. Far, far beyond all care; away from rates, taxes, and telegrams; proofs, publishers, and printers'-devils; where there are neither division lists, nor law lists, nor share lists, nor price lists, no betting lists, nor any list whatever; where no newspaper can come to worry or unsettle you, and where you don't care a straw how the world wags; where your clients are trouts, your patients worms, your congregation mountain black-faces, water-ousels, and dabchicks; your court, hospital or church the pre-Adamite hills with the eternal sky above them; your inspiration the pure breeze of heaven, far, far above all earthly corruption. Here, in delightful solitude, sauntering or scrambling on, and on, and on, upwards and upwards, from wee poolie to fern-clad cascade; casting or drooping the worm into either, or guiding it deftly under each hollow bank and past each ragged stone, pulling out a trout here and a trout there in the fair summer weather, with now a whiff of wild thyme or fragrant gorse, and now a shaugh of the pipe, and an amazed and charmed gaze at the mountain crags above, and the ever-changing scenery of the hills as the clouds flit over them, with just sport enough to give amusement without enchaining the attention so much as to prevent us drinking in all the delights that nature spreads for us – this is, to my mind, the true delight of angling.

from A BOOK ON ANGLING *1867*

The Nation of Anglers

HENRY RALPH FRANCIS

The enjoyment of these local memories is heightened to anglers by association with the stirring details of what is always an interesting, often a most exciting sport. We remember where the monarch of the brook, long coy and recusant, was at length fascinated by the drop of the tiniest of midges over his very snout; and where, with our gillie's assistance, we contrived to land three lusty trout together, like the elfin in the ballad, 'a' dancing in a string'. We execrate the treacherous stake which had well-nigh robbed us of a good fish and a cast of flies at once, or bless the memory of the smooth sand bank, pleasant to weary feet, where we at last headed, turned, and wound in the salmon who had kept the lead for some three hundred yards down a rocky channel, among stones loose, sharp, and slippery – perilous at once to shins and tackle. How have we enjoyed the early breeze that crisped the stream on a summer morning; the well-earned rest on a mossy bank in the deep hush of noon, and the homeward stroll through the pensive calm of evening.

. . . Mr Balfour's utmost indulgence would hardly admit me to a degree in botany, yet it was with a glow of pleasure that I first found myself throat-deep in a bed of the *Osmunda regalis*, on the banks of the Leven, or gathered the 'pale and azure-pencilled' clusters of the wood-vetch by Greta-side, or discovered the fringed yellow water lily on the Thames, gleaming like the floating lamp of a Hindoo votaress. If a gelogist, the angler may ply his hammer and fill his note-book along the very stream or tarn whence he fills his basket. If an artist, his rambles will acquaint him with every form of the picturesque, from the stern grandeur of Llyn Idwal to the tranquil beauties of Father Thames.

It is this many-sided character of the angler's art which has united so many suffrages in its favour, and has made it attractive to so many distinguished men of such dissimilar tastes and characters. It is this, finally, which has given to the art a literature of its own, abundant and various, in proportion to the number of its votaries and the diversity of their minds, and often highly enjoyable even by the uninitiated.

Writing as long ago as 1856 we were, I remarked, *a* nation of sportsmen, but *the* nation of anglers.

from FISHING *1888 (from The Badminton Library)*

Excitement and Beauty

RODERICK HAIG-BROWN

There is no form of fishing that I cannot enjoy at least for a while and by now I have enjoyed most of them. But I may as well admit that I prefer to fish a river or a stream rather than still water. I prefer to be on my feet rather than in a boat. And I want to catch my fish on an artificial fly whenever there is the remotest chance of doing so – which, for trout and salmon, is practically all the time.

I prefer to fish alone and secret unto myself, and usually do so, though I often enjoy fishing with a friend or several friends. If a stream is crowded I will cheerfully turn to its less productive and less crowded parts, or else go away altogether and come back at some less popular time. For I have come out to go fishing, not simply to throw in a hook and pull out a fish.

When I go fishing I want to be a part of the river and all my surroundings, not a stranger thrusting in upon them. I want to move quietly and at my own pace. I want to see and hear and understand. I want to feel that I know something of where the fish are and what they are doing and why. I want to be able to name the birds I see and take time out to watch them. I want to feel the river about me and to fill my mind with the infinity of lights that break from its surface and its depths. I want to know the trees along its banks, the rocks of the bottom and the creatures that shelter there and feed my fish.

In such participation I cannot be a stranger. I belong there as a man should be able to belong in a setting he has chosen for himself. My claim is as good as that of the heron or the otter or the osprey, even though my efficiency may be less.

As for the fishing, it need not be good. There need only be a chance that it may be good. I do not much want to kill fish – I would rather release them. What I want to find is some classic situation – a good fish rising in a favourable, but not too favourable, place; the perfect lie that one can fish down to with mounting concentration, through a long reach; the difficult place close under the bank, where trouble is certain from the log jam above or the rapid below. These things never grow stale.

I may find them or I may not. It matters very little. In searching I shall certainly find other things, expected or unexpected, and from somewhere among them I shall take home at least one bright picture of excitement or beauty to make the day. After forty years, rivers remain places of enchantment and the fish that swim in them creatures of wonder. Some small share in this is the fisherman's real reward.

from THE MASTER AND HIS FISH *1981*

The Charm of Old Rivers

JOHN WALLER HILLS

Fishing old and famous rivers, rivers which great men in the past have studied and frequented, has always had a peculiar charm for me. I care not for your reservoirs, your newly stocked waters, your made trout streams, however mighty their inhabitants. No. There are two classes of water which make the highest appeal to the imagination and the emotion. There are those which are unknown and unfished, whose mysterious depths may contain anything, and which you are the first to explore. Everyone who has fished such knows with what expectation and awe you draw near. But an emotion equally strong, though different, is given by fishing a river which has been fished for centuries. As I walk its banks, I like to think of those who have walked before me, who have seen the same sights as I see, been faced by the same problems, met with the same disasters and rejoiced in the same triumphs. I like to think that they have been there, those men of the long rod and horsehair line, slow and watchful, crafty men of their hand, quietly studying some great trout as I am studying him, and plotting his defeat as I am plotting it. And after much fishing and much musing over its problems, which are at once always the same and always different, I have turned again to the old writers, and read them with a new light and a new knowledge. Much that was obscure has been made plain and much that seemed archaic or obsolete or even childish has taken on a new meaning. This meaning I have tried to express, and have tried to illustrate it by experience drawn from the noblest of trout streams. It is for readers of this book to say whether the attempt is successful.

But, besides the past, it is well to look to the future. We, too, shall grow out of date. Fishers of a hundred years hence will cast an easy smile on ourselves and on our methods which we think so delicate and so final. Our tackle and our dress, our practice and our appearance, will seem to belong to the dark ages. In the *Chronicles* of the Houghton Fishing Club is an old photograph of members of the club taken outside the Grosvenor Arms at Stockbridge less than a century ago. Look at their immense top hats, white and black, their clumsy square-tailed coats, their whiskers, their fourteen-foot rods, their heavy sea boots. And yet they were great fishers, those old members of the club, and great men too, picked men, the best of their time. Is it possible that we shall ever be like that? Not only shall we be, but we are: we are, to the eye of futurity a century hence. We are just as antique, as obsolete and as far away. A hundred years from now you and your Leonard rod and your fashionable coat and smart wading boots will look as that old photograph looks. Everything will be changed: the rods, the nets, the clothes, the faces, the very figures. Only the Test will be the same, and its trout, and the sport of fishing, and possibly the Grosvenor Arms. The river will remain, so long as a growing town population does not abstract all its pure springs. The trout will be there, until tar poisoning kills the last. And where clear waters and trout are found, there will fishing be found also.

from A SUMMER ON THE TEST *1924*

Angling's Soothing Influence

T. E. PRITT

If one sentence or idea written in this book serves to stimulate a love of angling, the author will be amply rewarded. Alone amongst all field sports success still depends on man's own skill and wariness, and his finny prey are just as wild and untameable as they were ages ago.

But it is not alone the sport of catching fish which constitutes the charm of Angling: there is in every one of us an innate love of Nature in her purest and her simplest phases: the meanest child will stop instinctively to pull the wayside flower. As of old, Angling is still the Contemplative Man's Recreation: the soothing influence of one bright day will linger with us through many a thoughtful hour, and the mind will wander off to the valleys and the hills, to the clear skies and the flying clouds, and memory babbles almost unconsciously of green fields, made musical by the murmuring of a river and the songs of many birds.

from YORKSHIRE TROUT FLIES *1885*

The Great Fascination

FRANK SAWYER

I did not know then that a life on the river would open up for me, that the joys and thrills of my boyhood days would be few in comparison with those I would have in later years.

For this was to come. Five years were to pass. Then, at the age of eighteen, came the chance for which my heart had been yearning, and I started my life as a river keeper.

Today there are other boys at the riverside, boys who are just as full of mischief and fun as I was myself. But they will grow up, even as I did, and in time perhaps their children will come to the valley, too, to have their joys and sorrows. For the old Avon flows gently on. Throughout all the seasons of the year it winds its way towards the sea, gently chuckling now and then as it passes over some gravelly shallow, chuckling, I think, because it knows the great fascination there is beneath those gleaming waters, a fascination which from time to time will clutch at the heart of a boy and hold him captive for evermore.

from MAN OF THE RIVERSIDE *1984*

The Hereditary Passion

ANDREW LANG

The passion, or instinct, being in all senses blind, must no doubt be hereditary. It is full of sorrow and bitterness and hope deferred, and entails the mockery of friends, especially of the fair. But I would as soon lay down a love of books as a love of fishing. Success with pen or rod may be beyond one, but there is the pleasure of the pursuit, the rapture of endeavour, the delight of an impossible chase, the joys of nature – sky, trees, brooks, and birds. Happiness in these things is the legacy to us of the barbarian. Man in the future will enjoy bricks, asphalte, fog, machinery, 'society,' even picture galleries, as many men and most women do already. We are fortunate who inherit the older, not 'the new spirit' – we who, skilled or unskilled, follow in the steps or our father, Izaak, by streams less clear, indeed, and in meadows less fragrant, than his. Still, they are meadows and streams, not wholly dispeopled yet of birds and trout; nor can any defect of art, nor certainty of laborious disappointment, keep us from the waterside when April comes . . .. The gleaming untravelled future, the bright untried waters, allure us from day to day, from pool to pool, till, like the veteran on Coquet side, we 'try a farewell throw,' or, like Stoddart, look our last on Tweed.

from ANGLING SKETCHES *1891*

Refreshing Pleasure

LORD GREY

If, then, a book is written about a pursuit like fishing, it should be not to preach, or to convert, or to dogmatize. Books about sport and country life should be written and read, partly perhaps for the sake of hints, information, and instruction, but much more in the hope that the sense of refreshing pleasure, which has been felt by the writer, may slide into a sympathetic mind.

There remains yet another difficulty, that of expressing pleasure at all. It may be that language lends itself more easily to forms of argument and thought than of feeling. An argument is something which can be caught and held down and strapped into sentences, but after reading an account of a day's fishing, it is continually borne in upon one that, when all has been said, the half has not been told; it is not because there is really nothing to tell, as some cynical and unsympathetic mind may suppose; rather, I think it is because of the nature of joy. Feelings of delight come unsought and without effort – when they are present they are everywhere about and in us like an atmosphere; when they are past it is almost as impossible to give an account of them as it is of 'last year's clouds', and the attempt to analyse and reconstruct the sense of joy that has been and may be again, seems to result in rows of dead words.

It is worth while to consider some of the different ways in which authors of repute have written about angling. Walton, of course, stands first; his book has become a classic, and has been read and remembered now long enough for us to be sure that it will remain so. This, no doubt, is due to his literary skill, and to that distinguished something called style, which Walton had, and without which no book lives long. There is no definition of style which is satisfactory, or which tells how it may be acquired, for when a man has it, what he has is his own and no other's: without him that particular style would never have been, and no one else can produce the same effect of imitating it. It must, therefore, in some way be the result of the man's personality; and the charm of Walton's *Compleat Angler* is at any rate partly due to the simplicity and purity of nature, which find expression in his book. There is a quiet and benign light in his writing, which draws us to it, and makes us choose to linger over it. It must not, however, be forgotten that Walton wrote other books not about angling: these, too, are of literary excellence, and we still have to account for the fact, that it is by the *Compleat Angler* that Walton is best remembered. It may be that the others would not have been forgotten; but unless he had written the *Compleat Angler*, Walton would never have been as well known as he is. It is his best book, and I like to think that it is so, because the happiness of the subject was specially suited to his kind and quiet spirit. Walton took a wide view of the pleasures of angling; he was of too sensitive a nature to neglect what was to be seen and heard around him, and the object of Piscator is at least as much to teach his scholar to enjoy the spirit of places, times, and seasons, as to catch fish. None the less is Walton careful of instructions in the art of angling. In imparting these he had at any rate the advantage of believing that what he had to teach was new, and he enters into details of baits and tackles and methods, with a zest and confident interest which are hardly possible now. There is an impression of freshness and leisure which never leaves us as we read Walton. The delight of days spent by the river is described as if he felt himself to be the teller of good tidings, in which whosoever wished might share. There is a detachment of mind about him, a sense of freedom and length of days, to which it is less easy to attain in these times of trains, letters, telegrams, and incessant news. There were years in Walton's life of civil war, of great disturbance, public misfortune, and excitement, but it was nevertheless more possible in that age to have long intervals undisturbed and to feel remote. With the exception of Gilbert White's *Selborne*, I know no book in which it is so easy for a tired mind to find refuge and repose as in the *Compleat Angler*.

As a contrast to Walton it is interesting to consider Charles Kingsley. He, too, has written delightfully about fishing; there is an onset of enthusiasm in such a piece as 'Chalk Stream Studies', which must stimulate the keenness of any angler, and Kingsley has a good store of knowledge of plants, insects, birds, and all the life about a river. Who would not have kindled at the thought of a day's fishing with Kingsley? Who would not have been the better for it? But any of us might have been somewhat exhausted at the end of it. Kingsley was nobly keen, and he never for one moment leaves us in doubt of the strength and sincerity of his affection for all that was interesting and beautiful out of doors. Everyone should know more and fish better after reading him, but he was a strong mind in earnest, and he wrote so strenuously that in reading him I tremble a little, for fear he may strike too hard, if a big fish should rise. The time, too, in which Kingsley wrote, was so different from Walton's; so much more was known that knowledge seemed to have a sort of completeness. It is never really so. New discoveries are being made as frequently as ever, but for all that, the edges of our knowledge is a border land of mystery, of things left uncertain and still to be revealed. His Fordidge trout belongs to another world than that in which we move: we feel as if, were we in his place, we should long to set out upon our travels to find it. It is not even certain whether a winch should be used, and if so whether it should be placed upon the butt or the middle of the rod. Walton feels that all he has to tell us is visibly leading to some new discovery, which any man with a good will may hope to make in his lifetime. In Kingsley's time, and still more now, this delicious sense of impending discovery has gone. Fish and flies are classified and indexed. We may still argue some points, such as the number of different species of salmonidae, or whether fish have a keen perception of colour; but we know enough to be dogmatic and to make even things which are still uncertain appear not to be open questions. As to rods, tackle, and landing-nets, we are almost weary of the number of inventions, and hardly wish for anything new.

I have taken Walton and Kingsley as two types of appreciative writers about angling; Walton of course, because he is the best of all; and Kingsley, partly for the sake of contrast in time and temperament, and partly because his vigour as a writer makes it interesting to see how he treats the subject which he loved. Of those who preceded Walton, or were his contemporaries, an interesting and excellent account is to be found in *Walton and the Earlier Fishing Writers* by Mr Marston. Of writers in the earlier part of this century there are names to which many of us are grateful, while in later years one instructive book has followed another, showing more and more tendency to deal separately with each special branch of angling. Many men are good all-round anglers, but these are the days of experts and scientific study, and we write not of all that we know, but of what we know best. A chief object of mine will be to express some of this pleasure, to explain some of its qualities and virtues, and to say how it is that we who are anglers congratulate ourselves upon having one of the best and most wonderful recreations that have ever been known to man.

We probably wish our recreation to be not only apart from our work, but in contrast to it, and those who labour with their brain indoors seek for exercise and open air, use for the body as well as freedom for the mind. Youth asks for something more, and finds it in excitement. These are the three great requisites for the recreation of healthy vigorous boyhood – exercise, open air, and excitement. They are to be found in fine quality in games and in sport, and in both it is probably excitement which at first we care for most consciously. As we grow older a change takes place. Let us analyse, for instance, the pleasure in games. At first we desire only to win – we think only of that; we play the game as boys read an exciting story, with a feverish anxiety to know the end. The next stage, as we grow older, is more intelligent, and we begin to understand the qualities of good play. We improve year by year, and take pride in the increase of our own physical prowess, of which the limit is not yet seen. Then from understanding we pass to an artistic admiration of good play for its own sake; we become judges of how the thing should be done, and we are critics of style. Competition is then desired, not solely for the excitement it provides, but as a stimulus to good play; we no longer seriously expect to improve in our own play, but we take pleasure in doing our best. The last stage may be a long one; it begins with the admission that we are past our best. Strength is not diminished, and indeed we may even have more sheer strength than ever, but the effort of using it has become greater. The first sign of deterioration is when our powers seem as great, but it becomes more exhausting to exert them, and when in a hard game we do not last so well. The next symptom follows very soon; we cannot do so quickly what can no longer be done so easily; our performance suggests retrospect; the personal element wanes, and we find satisfaction more and more in contemplation and less and less in excitement and competition; at last we sit among the onlookers, and are advised by our friends to practise golf. There is much that is analogous to all this in the pleasure which is found in sport.

It would be tedious and perhaps invidious to enter here upon a comparison of angling with other sports. Each man sees special advantages in his own favourite pursuit, and possibly pays for this by overlooking some advantages which are to be found elsewhere. One thing I must claim, at any rate for fly fishing, that it involves less pain than is inflicted in any other sport. All experience and observation go to prove that what the fish suffers from most is fright, and this is an objection which may be brought equally against netting, and indeed against any possible method of killing fish except by poison or dynamite, of which the former is repulsive and horrible, whilst the latter causes wholesale and ruthless waste of life. Wordsworth calls angling 'the blameless sport', and with his opinion on such a point any one may be content.

from FLY FISHING *1899*

Every angler, however, has to make up his own mind about his sport and appreciate that in some it rouses feelings of antagonism rather than attraction. Lord Byron was an early and forceful critic, his views succinctly put:

And angling, too, that solitary vice,
Whatever Izaak Walton sings or says;
The quaint, old, cruel coxcomb in his gullet
Should have a hook, and a small fish to pull it.

Anglers, too, have their times of frustration, though this rarely seems to affect their dedication to the sport:

Sometimes ower early
Sometimes ower late
Sometimes nae water
Sometimes a spate
Sometimes ower calm
Sometimes ower clear
There's aye something wrang
When I'm fishing here.

Anon

Confessions of a Duffer

ANDREW LANG

Some men are born duffers; others, unlike persons of genius, become so by an infinite capacity for not taking pains. Others, again, among whom I would rank myself, combine both these elements of incompetence. Nature, that made me enthusiastically fond of fishing, gave me thumbs for fingers, short-sighted eyes, indolence, carelessness, and a temper which (usually sweet and angelic) is goaded to madness by the laws of matter and gravitation. For example: when another man is caught up in a branch he disengages his fly; I jerk at it till something breaks. As for carelessness, in boyhood I fished, by preference, with doubtful gut and knots ill-tied; it made the risk greater, and increased the excitement if one did hook a trout. I can't keep a fly-book. I stuff the flies into my pockets at random, or stick them into the leaves of a novel, or bestow them in the lining of my hat or the case of my rods.

Never, till 1890, in all my days did I possess a landing-net. If I can drag a fish up a bank, or over the gravel, well; if not, he goes on his way rejoicing. On the Test I thought it seemly to carry a landing-net. It had a hinge, and doubled up. I put the handle through a buttonhole of my coat: I saw a big fish rising, I put a dry fly over him; the idiot took it. Up stream he ran, then down stream, then he yielded to the rod and came near me. I tried to unship my landing-net from my buttonhole. Vain labour! I twisted and turned the handle, it would not budge. Finally, I stooped, and attempted to ladle the trout out with the short net; but he broke the gut and went off. A landing-net is a tedious thing to carry, so is a creel and a creel is, to me, a superfluity. There is never anything to put in it. If I do catch a trout, I lay him under a big stone, cover him with leaves, and never find him again.

from ANGLING SKETCHES *1891*

Gillie's-eye View

BRUCE SANDISON

Jim Wallace has spent all his life as a gamekeeper and gillie on Tweed and Till. He was head gillie on the Till for many years and, when asked to return to the Tweed, his father, then aged seventy-five, took over as head gillie.

Jim's father died at the age of ninety-nine, fit as a fiddle to the last.

Jim caught his first salmon as a boy of nine. He remembers it clearly: 'It was in Mill Pool on Whiteadder, on a trout rod – no salmon rods for us lads in those days. An old lade came out of the mill and the river had that sweet evening smell, with water churning through the pool. You just knew you were going to catch fish.

'As light faded, sure enough, there came this great tug. My heart stopped. I would have given a year's pocket-money to have seen that fish on the bank there and then; instead it took damn near an hour. My arms were aching by the time I got it landed.

'There aren't so many fish about these days, what with salmon disease and netting. My gentlemen have to be patient and work hard for a fish, and at times even that isn't enough. But if you know your river, as every good gillie should, where the salmon lie and when they're most likely to take, then your gentlemen shouldn't often go home empty-handed.

'Some gentlemen are very skilful, particularly the younger ones. But just because a man casts forty to fifty yards doesn't mean he is going to catch salmon. Some gentlemen who come here are hardly able to cast at all, but they catch fish with no bother – and very annoying it is for their more able companions.

'I remember two gentlemen who used to fish with me, Mr Robson and Mr Scott. Now Mr Scott was a hard worker and expert caster – up at the crack of dawn, always first on the river, always last to leave. He would cast away non-stop all day, begrudging even a few moments for lunch. If fish were not taking, he would try every fly in his box, and then come to me for more.

'Mr Robson was quite the opposite. He would have a yarn before starting, ask after the family, wander round the garden, as different from his friend as night is from day, and hardly able to put one line beyond his nose.

'Mr Robson always gave his friend first choice of where to fish, and I remember one morning, when Mr Scott had been lashing away in the pool, Mr Robson quietly took three lovely salmon from the run. Nothing would satisfy Mr Scott other than that he should fish the run in the afternoon, so I took him over in the boat and stayed with him. After fishing for an hour or more, my poor gentleman remained fishless, but his friend, in the previously despised pool, had four more salmon.

'We were watching Mr Robson playing the fourth fish when suddenly he staggered backwards and there came a "crack" as the cast broke. Mr Scott was delighted and exclaimed that his friend had been putting far too much strain on the brute anyway, and that it served him right. Then, as we watched, Mr Robson threw down his rod, grabbed the landing-net, dashed into the river, and netted the exhausted fish.

'Mr Scott stood up and shouted: "That's enough. The damn man catches them even when he's lost them!" Picking up his rod, he hurled it into the river and stamped off.

'You'd be surprised how competitive some gentlemen become. I've seen men, friends for years, fall out and argue like children over who should have the right to go down a pool first.

'There's a good lie just up from the cottage, and a fish in it will almost certainly take the first fly offered. Now then, two men, both over seventy, had been fishing here for years. Hearing them in the hotel, you'd have thought them the most considerate creatures on God's earth. But at the river, trying to be first over that lie, they'd act like teenagers pursuing a young lassie, elbowing and shoving, trying to get ahead. And they'd stoop to any device to slow each other down. I've even seen one "accidentally" hide the other's reel or break his cast at the last moment.

'They always used to arrive in the same car, but last time there was such a famous row that it ended with one of them in the river. One drove home and the other took the train. I was there and saw it all, and I'm as sure as certain that the old gentleman didn't stumble into the river as his friend later claimed. But that was the last we saw of them, or, as I understand it, they of each other.

'But it's not only gentlemen who do strange things. Salmon are just as hard to understand at times. I've watched them in the Till, through Polaroid glasses, following a fly. They'll take it into their mouths, spit it out, take it in again, spit it out, and all without the gentleman being any the wiser.'

from A SPORTING GENTLEMAN'S GENTLEMAN *1987*

The Life of a River

RODERICK HAIG-BROWN

I still don't know why I fish or why other men fish except that we like it and it makes us think and feel. But I do know if it were not for the strong quick life of rivers, for their sparkle in the sunshine, for the cold greyness of them under rain and the feel of them about my legs . . . I should fish less often. A river is never quite silent; it can never, of its very nature, be quite still; It is never quite the same from one day to the next. It has its own life and its own beauty and the creatures it nourishes are alive and beautiful also. Perhaps fishing is for me, only an excuse to be near rivers. If so, I'm glad I thought of it."

from A RIVER NEVER SLEEPS *1946*

For some, angling is not just a passion or an obsession. It is the mainstream of their life, and in death the great G.E.M. Skues required his ashes to be scattered beside the river Itchen, which he so loved:

Last Resting Place

RONALD OVERFIELD

And so the final act is carried out. There is no more to be said. The old gentleman lies beside his beloved Itchen placed there by a friend and angling companion of many a long summer's day. To rest where the trout sip down the spinners of late evening and the early night wind rustles the waterside grasses. That all fly-fishers should end their days beside well loved streams would no doubt be George Edward Mackenzie Skues's final wish, while to him we say *requiescat in pace* beside your quiet Itchen for your immortality is assured while anglers cast the fly to chalkstream trout.

from THE WAY OF A MAN WITH A TROUT *1977*

PART 2

Stories

Fiction carries a greater amount of truth in solution than the volume which purports to be all true.

W. M. Thackeray

Two Friends

GUY DE MAUPASSANT

translated by Storm Jameson

Paris was blockaded, famished, at the last gasp. Sparrows were getting scarce on the roofs, and the sewers were depleted of their rats. People were eating anything.

As he was strolling sadly along the outer boulevard on a fine January morning, with his hand in the pockets of his military trousers, and his stomach empty, Monsieur Morissot, a watch-maker by profession, and a man of his ease when he had the chance, came face to face with a brother in arms whom he recognized as a friend, and stopped. It was Monsieur Sauvage, an acquaintance he had met on the river.

Before the war Morissot had been in the habit of starting out at dawn every Sunday, rod in hand, and a tin box on his back. He would take the train to Argenteuil, get out at Colombes, then go on foot as far as the Island of Marante. The moment he reached this place of his dreams he would begin to fish, and fish until nightfall. Every Sunday he met there a little round jovial man, Monsieur Sauvage, a draper of the rue Notre Dame de Lorette, also an ardent fisherman. They would often pass half the day side by side, rod in hand, feet dangling above the stream, and in this manner had become fast friends. Some days they did not talk, other days they did. But they understood each other admirably without words, for their tastes and feelings were identical.

On spring mornings, about ten o'clock, when the young sun was raising a faint mist above the quiet-flowing river, and blessing the backs of those two passionate fishermen with the pleasant warmth of a new season, Morissot would sometimes say to his neighbour: 'I say, isn't it heavenly?' and Monsieur Sauvage would reply: 'Couldn't be jollier!' which was quite enough to make them understand and like each other.

In autumn, as the day was declining, when the sky, reddened by the glow of the setting sun, reflected the crimson clouds in the water, stained the whole river with colour, the horizon flaming, when our two friends looked as red as fire, and the trees, already russet and shivering at the touch of winter, were turned to gold, Monsieur Sauvage would look smilingly at Morissot, and remark: 'What a sight!' and Morissot, not taking his eyes off his float, would reply ecstatically: 'It beats the boulevard, eh?'

As soon as they recognized each other, they shook hands heartily, quite moved at meeting again in such different circumstances.

With a sigh, Monsieur Sauvage murmured: 'Nice state of things!' Morissot, very gloomy, groaned: 'And what weather! Today's the first fine day this year!'

The sky was indeed quite blue and full of light.

They moved on, side by side, ruminative, sad. Morissot pursued his thought: 'And fishing, eh? What jolly times we used to have!'

'When shall we go fishing again?' asked Monsieur Sauvage.

They entered a little café, took an absinthe together, and started off once more, strolling along the pavement.

Suddenly Morissot halted: 'Another absinthe?' he said.

'I'm with you!' responded Monsieur Sauvage. And in they went to another wine-shop. They came out rather light-headed, affected as people are by alcohol on empty stomachs. The day was mild, and a soft breeze caressed their faces.

Monsieur Sauvage, whose light-headedness was completed by the fresh air, stopped short: 'I say – suppose we go!'

'What d'you mean?'

'Fishing!'

'Where?'

'Why, at our island. The French outposts are close to Colombes. I know Colonel Dumoulin; he'll be sure to let us pass.'

Morissot answered, quivering with eagerness: 'All right; I'm on!' And they parted, to get their fishing gear.

An hour later they were marching along the high road. They came presently to the villa occupied by the Colonel, who, much amused by their whim, gave them leave. And furnished with his permit, they set off again.

They soon passed the outposts, and traversing the abandoned village of Colombes, found themselves at the edge of the little vineyard fields that run down to the Seine. It was about eleven o'clock.

The village of Argenteuil, opposite, seemed quite deserted. The heights of Orgemont and Sannois commanded the whole countryside; the great plain stretching to Nanterre was empty, utterly empty of all but its naked cherry-trees and its grey earth.

Monsieur Sauvage, jerking his thumb towards the heights, muttered: 'The Prussians are up there!' And disquietude stole into the hearts of the two friends, looking at that deserted country. The Prussians! They had never seen any, but they had felt them there for months, all round Paris, bringing ruin to France, bringing famine; pillaging, massacre, invisible, yet invincible. And a sort of superstitious terror was added to their hatred for that unknown and victorious race.

Morissot stammered: 'I say – suppose we were to meet some?'

With that Parisian jocularity which nothing can suppress, Monsieur Sauvage replied: 'We'd give 'em some fried fish.'

None the less, daunted by the silence all round, they hesitated to go farther.

At last Monsieur Sauvage took the plunge. 'Come on! But be careful!'

They got down into a vineyard, where they crept along, all eyes and ears, bent double, taking cover behind every bush.

There was still a strip of open ground to cross before they could get to the riverside; they took it at the double, and the moment they reached the bank plumped down amongst some dry rushes.

Morissot glued his ear to the ground for any sound of footsteps. Nothing! They were alone, utterly alone.

They plucked up spirit again, and began to fish.

In front of them the Island of Marante, uninhabited, hid them from the far bank. The little island restaurant was closed, and looked as if it had been abandoned for years.

Monsieur Sauvage caught the first gudgeon, Morissot the second, and every minute they kept pulling in their lines with a little silvery creature wriggling at the end. Truly a miraculous draught of fishes!

They placed their spoil carefully in a very fine-meshed net suspended in the water at their feet, and were filled by the delicious joy that visits those who know once more a pleasure of which they have been deprived too long.

The good sun warmed their shoulders; they heard nothing, thought of nothing, were lost to the world. They fished.

But suddenly a dull boom, which seemed to come from underground, made the earth tremble. The bombardment had begun again.

Morissot turned his head. Away above the bank he could see on his left the great silhouette of Mont Valérien, showing a white plume in its cap, a puff of smoke just belched forth. Then a second spurt of smoke shot up from the fort's summit, and some seconds afterwards was heard the roar of the gun.

Then more and more. Every minute the hill breathed out death, sending forth clouds of white smoke, which rose slowly to the calm heaven, and made a crown of cloud.

Monsieur Sauvage shrugged his shoulders. 'At it again!' he said.

Morissot, who was anxiously watching the bobbing of his float, was seized with the sudden fury of a man of peace against these maniacs battering against each other, and he growled out: 'Idiots I call them, killing each other like that!'

'Worse than the beasts!' said Monsieur Sauvage.

And Morissot, busy with a fish, added: 'It'll always be like that, in my opinion, so long as we have governments.'

Monsieur Sauvage cut him short. 'The Republic would never have declared war –'

Morissot broke in: 'Under a monarchy you get war against your neighbours; under a republic – war amongst yourselves.'

And they began tranquilly discussing and unravelling momentous political problems with the sweet reasonableness of peaceable, ignorant men, who agreed at any rate on one point, that Man would never be free.

And Mont Valérien thundered without ceasing, shattering with its shells the homes of France, pounding out life, crushing human beings, putting an end to many a dream, to many an expected joy, to many a hope of happiness; opening everywhere, too, in the hearts of wives, of girls, of mothers, wounds that would never heal.

'Such is life!' declared Monsieur Sauvage.

'You mean "Such is death",' said Morissot, and laughed.

They both gave a sudden start; there was surely someone coming up behind them. Turning their eyes they saw, standing close to their very elbows, four men, four big, bearded men, dressed in a sort of servant's livery, with flat caps on their heads, pointing rifles at them.

The rods fell from their hands and floated off downstream.

In a few seconds they were seized, bound, thrown into a boat, and taken over to the island.

Behind the house that they had thought deserted they perceived some twenty German soldiers.

A sort of hairy giant, smoking a great porcelain pipe, and sitting astride of a chair, said in excellent French: 'Well, gentlemen, what luck fishing?'

Whereupon a soldier laid at his officer's feet the net full of fish, which he had carefully brought along.

The Prussian smiled. 'I see – not bad. But we've other fish to fry. Now listen to me, and keep cool. I regard you as two spies sent to watch me. I take you, and I shoot you. You were pretending to fish, the better to disguise your plans. You've fallen into my hands, so much the worse for you. That's war. But, seeing that you passed through your outposts, you must assuredly have been given the password to get back again. Give it me, and I'll let you go.'

Livid, side by side, the two friends were silent, but their hands kept jerking with little nervous movements.

The officer continued: 'No one will ever know; it will be all right; you can go home quite easy in your minds. If you refuse, it's death – instant death. Choose.'

They remained motionless, without a word.

The Prussian, calm as ever, stretched out his hands towards the water, and said: 'Think! In five minutes you'll be at the bottom of that river. In five minutes. You've got families, I suppose?'

Mont Valérian went on thundering. The two fishermen stood silent.

The German gave an order in his own language. Then he moved his chair so as not to be too near his prisoners. Twelve men came forward, took their stand twenty paces away, and grounded arms.

The officer said: 'I give you one minute; not a second more.'

And, getting up abruptly, he approached the two Frenchmen, took Morissot by the arm, and, drawing him aside, whispered: 'Quick, that password. Your friend need never know. It will only look as though I'd relented.' Morissot made no answer.

Then the Prussian took Monsieur Sauvage apart, and asked him the same question.

Monsieur Sauvage did not reply.

Once again they were side by side. The officer gave a word of command. The soldiers raised their rifles.

At that moment Morissot's glance alighted on the net full of gudgeons lying on the grass a few paces from him. The sun was shining on that glittering heap of fishes, still full of life. His spirit sank. In spite of all effort his eyes filled with tears.

'Good-bye, Monsieur Sauvage!' he stammered out.

Monsieur Sauvage answered: 'Good-bye, Monsieur Morissot.'

They grasped each other's hands, shaken from head to foot by a trembling they could not control.

'Fire!' cried the officer.

Twelve shots rang out as one.

Monsieur Sauvage fell forward like a log. Morissot, the taller, wavered, spun around, and came down across his comrade, his face upturned to the sky; blood spurted from his tunic, torn across the chest.

The German gave another order. His men dispersed. They came back with ropes and stones, which they fastened to the feet of the two dead friends, whom they carried to the river-bank. And Mont Valérien never ceased rumbling, crowned now with piled-up clouds of smoke.

Two of the soldiers took Morissot by the head and heels, two others laid hold of Monsieur Sauvage in the same manner. The bodies, swung violently to and fro, were hurled forward, described a curve, then plunged upright into the river, where the stones dragged them down feet first.

The water splashed up, foamed, and rippled, then fell calm again, and tiny waves rolled out towards the banks.

A few bloodstains floated away.

The officer, calm as ever, said quietly: 'Now it is the fishes' turn!' and went back towards the house.

But suddenly catching sight of the net full of gudgeons on the grass, he took it up, looked it over, smiled, and called out: 'Wilhelm!'

A soldier in a white apron came running up. The Prussian threw him the spoil of the two dead fishermen.

'Get these little things fried at once while they're still alive. They will be delicious.'

And he went back to his pipe.

from NOVELS AND TALES OF GUY DE MAUPASSANT *1928*

The Little Fishes

H. E. BATES

My Uncle Silas was very fond of fishing. It was an occupation that helped to keep him from thinking too much about work and also about how terribly hard it was.

If you went through the bottom of my Uncle Silas's garden, past the gooseberry bushes, the rhubarb and the pigsties, you came to a path that went alongside a wood where primroses grew so richly in spring that they blotted out the floor of oak and hazel leaves. In summer wild strawberries followed the primroses and by July the meadows beyond the wood were frothy with meadow-sweet, red clover and the seed of tall soft grasses.

At the end of the second meadow a little river, narrow in parts and bellying out into black deep pools in others, ran along between willows and alders, occasional clumps of dark high reeds and a few wild crab trees. Some of the pools, in July, would be white with water lilies, and snakes would swim across the light flat leaves in the sun. Moorhens talked to each other behind the reeds and water rats would plop suddenly out of sight under clumps of yellow monkey flower.

Here in this little river, my Uncle Silas used to tell me when I was a boy, 'the damn pike used to be as big as hippopotomassiz'.

'Course they ain't so big now,' he would say. 'Nor yit the tench. Nor yit the perch. Nor yet the –'

'Why aren't they so big?'

'Well, I'm a-talkin' about fifty years agoo. Sixty year agoo. Very near seventy years agoo.'

'If they were so big then,' I said, 'all that time ago, they ought to be even bigger now.'

'Not the ones we catched,' he said. 'They ain't there.'

You couldn't, as you see from this, fox my Uncle Silas very easily, but I was at all times a very inquisitive, persistent little boy.

'How big were the tench?' I said.

'Well, I shall allus recollect one as me and Sammy Twizzle caught,' he said. 'Had to lay it in a pig trough to carry it home.'

'And how big were the perch?'

'Well,' he said, rolling his eyes in recollection, in that way he had of bringing the wrinkled lid slowly down over it, very like a fish ancient in craftiness himself, 'I don' know as I can jistly recollect the size o' that one me and Arth Sugars nipped out of a September morning one time, but I do know as I cleaned up the back fin and used it for a horse comb for about twenty year.'

'Oh! Uncle Silas,' I would say, 'let's go fishing! Let's go and see if they're still as big as hippopotomassiz!'

But it was not always easy, once my Uncle Silas had settled under the trees at the end of the garden on a hot July afternoon, to persuade him that it was worth walking across two meadows just to see if the fish were as big as they used to be. Nevertheless I was, as I say, a very inquisitive, persistent little boy and finally my Uncle Silas would roll over, take the red handkerchief off his face and grunt:

'If you ain't the biggest whittle-breeches I ever knowed I'll go t'Hanover. Goo an' git the rod and bring a bit o'dough. They'll be no peace until you do, will they?'

'Shall I bring the rod for you too?'

'*Rod*?' he said. 'For *me*. *Rod*?' He let fall over his eye a tremulous bleary fish-like lid of scorn. 'When me and Sammy Twizzle went a-fishin', all we had to catch 'em with wur we bare hands and a drop o'neck-oil.'

'What's neck-oil?'

'Never you mind,' he said. 'You git the rod and I'll git the neck-oil.'

And presently we would be walking out of the garden, past the wood and across the meadows; I carrying the rod, the dough and perhaps a piece of carraway cake in a paper bag, my Uncle Silas waddling along in his stony-coloured corduory trousers, carrying the neck-oil.

Sometimes I would be very inquisitive about the neck-oil, which was often pale greenish-yellow, rather the colour of cow-slip, or perhaps of parsnips, and sometimes purplish-red, rather the colour of elderberries, or perhaps of blackberries or plums.

On one occasion I noticed that the neck-oil was very light in colour, almost white, or perhaps more accurately like straw-coloured water.

'Is it a new sort of neck-oil you've got?' I said.

'New flavour.'

'What is it made of?'

'Taters.'

'And you've got two bottles today,' I said.

'Must try to git used to the new flavour.'

'And do you think,' I said, 'we shall catch a bigger fish now that you've got a new kind of neck-oil?'

'Shouldn't be a bit surprised, boy,' he said, 'if we don't git one as big as a donkey.'

That afternoon it was very hot and still as we sat under the shade of a big willow, by the side of a pool that seemed to have across it an oiled black skin broken only by minutest winks of sunlight when the leaves of the willow parted softly in gentle turns of air.

'This is the place where me and Sammy tickled that big 'un out,' my Uncle Silas said.

'The one you carried home in a pig trough?'

'That's the one.'

I said how much I too should like to catch one I could take home in a pig trough and my Uncle Silas said:

'Well, you never will if you keep whittlin' and talkin' and ompolodgin' about.' My Uncle Silas was the only man in the world who ever used the word ompolodgin'. It was a very expressive word and when my Uncle Silas accused you of ompolodgin' it was a very serious matter. It meant that you had buttons on your bottom and if you didn't drop it he would damn well ding your ear.

'You gotta sit still and wait and not keep fidgitin' and very like in another half-hour you'll see a big 'un layin' aside o' that log. But not if you keep ompologdin'! See?'

'Yes, Uncle.'

'That's why I bring the neck-oil,' he said. 'It quiets you down so's you ain't a-whittlin' and a-ompolodgin' all the time.'

'Can I have a drop of neck-oil?'

'When you git thirsty,' my Uncle Silas said, 'there's that there spring in the next medder.'

After this my Uncle Silas took a good steady drink of neck-oil and settled down with his back against the tree. I put a big lump of paste on my hook and dropped it into the pool. The only fish I could see in the pool were shoals of little silver tiddlers that flickered about a huge fallen willow log a yard or two upstream or came to play inquisitively about my little white and scarlet float, making it quiver up and down like the trembling scraps of sunlight across the water.

Sometimes the bread paste got too wet and slipped from the hook and I quietly lifted the rod from the water and put another lump on the hook. I tried almost not to breathe as I did all this and every time I took the rod out of the water I glanced furtively at my Uncle Silas to see if he thought I was ompolodgin'.

Every time I looked at him I could see that he evidently didn't think so. He was always far too busy with the neck-oil.

I suppose we must have sat there for nearly two hours on that hot and windless afternoon of July, I not speaking a word and trying not to breathe as I threw my little float across the water, my Uncle Silas never uttering a sound either except for a drowsy grunt or two as he uncorked one bottle of neck-oil or felt to see if the other was safe in his jacket pocket.

At that time there was no sign of a fish as big as a hippopotamus or even of one you could take home in a pig trough and all the time my Uncle Silas kept tasting the flavour of the neck-oil, until at last his head began to fall forward on his chest. Soon all my bread paste was gone and I got so afraid of disturbing my Uncle Silas that I scotched my rod to the fallen log and walked into the next meadow to get myself a drink of water from the spring.

The water was icy cold from the spring and very sweet and good and I wished I had brought myself a bottle too, so that I could fill it and sit back against a tree, as my Uncle Silas did, and pretend that it was neck-oil.

Ten minutes later, when I got back to the pool, my Uncle Silas was fast asleep by the tree trunk, one bottle empty by his side and the other still in his jacket pocket. There was, I thought, a remarkable expression on his face, a wonderful rosy fogginess about his mouth and nose and eyes.

But what I saw in the pool, as I went to pick my rod from the water, was a still more wonderful thing.

During the afternoon the sun had moved some way round and under the branches of the willow, so that now, at the first touch of evening, there were clear bands of pure yellow light across the pool.

In one of these bands of light, by the fallen log, lay a long lean fish, motionless as a bar of steel, just under the water, basking in the evening sun.

When I woke up Uncle Silas he came to himself with a fumbling start, red eyes only half open, and I thought for a moment that perhaps he would ding my ear for ompolodgin'.

'But it's as big as a hippopotamus,' I said. 'It's as big as the one in the pig trough.'

'Wheer, boy? Wheer?'

When I pointed out the fish, my Uncle Silas could not, at first, see it lying there by the log. But after another nip of neck-oil he started to focus it correctly.

'By Jingo, that's a big 'un,' he said. 'By Jingo, that's a walloper.'

'What sort is it?'

'Pike,' he said. 'Git me a big lump o'paste and I'll dangle it a-top of his nose.'

'The paste has all gone.'

'Then give us a bit of carraway and we'll tiddle him up wi' that.'

'I've eaten all the carraway,' I said. 'Besides, you said you and Sammy Twizzle used to catch them with your hands. You said you used to tickle their bellies –'

'Well, that wur –'

'Get him! Get him! Get him!' I said. 'He's as big as a donkey!'

Slowly, and with what I thought was some reluctance, my Uncle

Silas heaved himself to his feet. He lifted the bottle from his pocket and took a sip of neck-oil. Then he slapped the cork back with the palm of his hand, wiped his lips with the back of his hand and put the bottle back in his pocket.

'Now you stan' back,' he said, 'and dammit, don't git ompolodgin'!'

I stood back. My Uncle Silas started to creep along the fallen willow log on his hands and knees. Below him, in the band of sunlight, I could see the long dark lean pike, basking.

For nearly two minutes my Uncle Silas hovered on the end of the log. Then slowly he balanced himself on one hand and dipped his other into the water. Over the pool it was marvellously, breathlessly still, and I knew suddenly that this was how it had been in the good great old days, when my Uncle Silas and Sammy Twizzle had caught the mythical mammoth ones, fifty years before.

'God A'mighty!' my Uncle Silas suddenly yelled. 'I'm a-gooin' over!'

My Uncle Silas was indeed gooin' over. Slowly, like a turning spit, the log started heeling, leaving my Uncle Silas half-slipping, half-dancing at its edge, like a man on a greasy pole.

In terror I shut my eyes. When I opened them and looked again my Uncle Silas was just coming up for air, yelling 'God A'mighty, boy, I believe you ompolodged!'

I thought for a moment he was going to be very angry with me. Instead he started to cackle with crafty, devilish, stentorian laughter, his wet lips dribbling, his eyes more fiery than ever under the dripping water, his right hand triumphant as he snatched it up from the stream.

'Jist managed to catch it, boy,' he yelled and in triumph he held up the bottle of neck-oil.

And somewhere downstream, startled by his shout, a whole host of little tiddlers jumped from the water, dancing in the evening sun.

from SUGAR FOR THE HORSE *1957*

Coldstone Mill

NEVIL SHUTE

Coldstone Mill was a tall, factory-like building set in the country-side upon the River Fittel. A lane crossed the river on a stone bridge of two arches; a hundred yards below the bridge the mill stood by the weir, and below that again was the millpool. It was a broad, gravelly pool, scoured wide by the millstream and the weir, overhung by trees at the lower end. It stood in pasture fields, very sunny and bright.

The pilot left his bicycle at the mill and went down to the pool. For a time he walked slowly round the edge trying if he could see a fish; presently he sat down and began to assemble his rod. He fitted a little silvery reel and threaded the fine line, and chose the little trace with the single wire, as the rear-gunner had advised him. He spread out his collection of seven plugs upon the flat canvas of his bag and studied them thoughtfully. Finally he chose a desperate-looking parody of a small fish, more like a septic banana than a fish, and hooked it on the trace. Then, standing up, he began to cast over the pool.

He spent the next ten minutes clearing over-runs upon his reel. He was not a very skilled performer.

He fished for the next hour, supremely happy. The rhythm of the cast, the antics of the plug, delighted him; the warm sunlight, and the very fact of handling a well-designed instrument, made him content. The rush of water from the weir made a murmur that drowned the sound of the many aircraft that were in the sky, except when they passed closely overhead; the water slipping past over the green weed and the gravelly shallows was a thing remote from any of his duties.

He paused after an hour or so, and sat down on the ground, and lit a pipe. He took off the septic banana and fitted in its place a peculiar whirligig designed to represent a lame mouse taking swimming exercise, alleged to be very attractive to a pike. He was still sitting smoking when he turned to a step behind him.

It was Gunnar Franck, carrying his roach-pole and his little stool on his way down to the quieter reaches of the river. 'Phillips, he say you have come here,' he said. 'Goes well?'

'Very well,' said the pilot. 'Marvellous afternoon, isn't it?' He lifted the little steel rod. 'Have a crack with this.'

The Dane took the rod doubtfully, made an ineffective cast, and produced a tangle of line massed and jamming the reel. He handed the rod back to Marshall. 'I shall go catch a roach,' he said. 'When I come back, he will be disentangled, yes?'

The pilot began to unravel the line. 'Just in time for you to muck it up again. Getcha!' He glanced up at the Dane. 'None of those bits hit any of the tanks, did they? I was thinking of that just now. I ought to have looked to see.'

'I looked.' Above their head, in a bare elm-tree, there was a sudden flap and clatter, and a pigeon flew off. They raised their heads to watch it. 'I looked, but there was nothing. Only the bomb doors and the belly and the fabric underneath the tail. It is no damage, really.'

Marshall said: 'It was just as you said "Bombs away". Just after that, wasn't it? We were running-up too long.'

'One minute only. Sixty-five seconds. I had the stop-watch running,' said Gunnar.

'We'll have to get it shorter. I'd hate to get shot up by the Eyeties. I should die of shame.'

'Of shame?' The Dane wrinkled his forehead; there were still points of English manners that eluded him.

The pilot said: 'Did you see that pigeon? This place is stiff with them. You haven't got a gun?'

Gunnar shook his head. 'Seargeant Pilot Nutter, he has a rifle. A little gun, his own. Two-two.'

'Bring it out with you next time you come and let's see if we can't get one or two. They're bloody good eating, pigeons.'

'Oh – oh, yes. Pigeons is ver' good eating. In my country we eat many pigeons.'

'Well, see if you can lay your hands on that gun, and let's have a crack at them.'

'That farmer – it will be all right?'

'I'll see the people at the mill and see if they mind. They ought not to. I'll race around the mess and see if I can borrow a shot-gun. It's a good thing to shoot pigeons. They eat the crops. It says so in the paper.'

'Perhaps the farmer does not read the paper.'

'Get that rifle, anyway.' The pilot wound the last of the line back smoothly on to the reel. He raised the little rod above and behind his head and flicked his arm; the plug went sailing out into the stream smoothly and with no effort.

'Nice,' said Gunnar. He stooped to the bag and picked out a reddish, translucent plug bait. 'I think this one will be the best.' He pointed to the shallows and the backwater between beds of reeds. 'There is the best place for a pike.'

The pilot said; 'Too weedy and too shallow.' He paused. 'Do you think we could get the run-up a bit shorter?'

'I will try.'

Marshall reeled the plug in to his feet and drew it dripping from the water. 'I'll try telling you the evasive action that I'm going to take, down the intercom. Each move, so that you know what's coming. And you can tell me which way to bias it. We'll have to waltz into position before levelling off.'

'It will be ver' difficult,' said Gunnar doubtfully.

'We'll have a stab at it tomorrow on the flight test.'

'Okay.' The Dane picked up his rod. 'Now I will catch a roach for tea.'

Marshall called after him: 'Don't forget about that rifle.'

Gunnar raised his hand, and the pilot stood watching him for a moment as he went away downstream between the trees in the dappled sunshine. He was a damn good chap, Marshall thought. That matter of the tanks – Gunnar never missed a thing. He'd probably get his roach all right.

Marshall turned back to the pool and began casting.

A quarter of an hour later he rested again, thoughtful. There might be something in what Gunnar said; pike liked sunny spots and sometimes came into quite shallow water. He did not think he could cast in among those reeds without catching his plug and losing it eventually; still, if it wouldn't catch a fish what good was it to him? He cast the lame mouse up the backwater into a shallow swim between green beds of weed and drew it fluttering towards him. Was it his fancy, or was there something following behind the bait?

He cast to the same place a second and a third time, without result. Then he changed to the reddish plug that Gunnar had advised, and made an experimental cast or two out into the rough water of the pool. Having got his length he cast again to the same place, the gravelly, weedy shallow, and began reeling in.

In the backwater there was a sudden splashing gulp upon the surface. The line tightened and the little rod bent suddenly; he gripped it with both hands and heard the reel scream as the line went out. He knew at once that it was a bigger fish than he had ever hooked before; indeed, he had only caught two pike in his life, both very small. In the backwater there was a thrashing turmoil in the weeds with quick jerks on the line. He grasped the handle of the reel and got in line. The fish dashed from him up the backwater taking out line as he went; the pilot reeled him in again. Then, in the manner of a pike, the fight went out of him, and Marshall drew him through the swift water of the stream without a kick. He woke up when he saw the pilot and made a short run; then he was finished and came up to the surface as Marshall pulled him in. The great snapping mouth, cream-coloured underneath, was open, the red plug hooked firm in the lower jaw.

The young man breathed: 'God, he's a bloody monster.'

He had neither gaff nor landing-net nor priest. He had too much sense to touch the fish; he towed it with the rod, limp and supine in the water, to a little beach and pulled it up the sandy mud, wriggling and snapping the great jaws. Then with a stone he hit it gingerly upon the head, divided in his anxieties to kill it before it could escape, to kill it without injuring the look of it, and to avoid being bitten. Presently it lay still, and he pulled it up on to the grass.

He was excited and exultant; it seemed to him to be a most enormous fish. As soon as he dared put his hand near it he measured it with his thumb, which he knew to be an inch and a quarter from knuckle to tip; it was thirty-three inches long.

His heart was fluttering with excitement. Mechanically he began to take down his rod and pack up his gear; he would fish no more that afternoon. Anything after this magnificent experience would be an anti-climax; there was a time to stop and rest upon achievement, and this was it. Gingerly and timorously he poked a bit of string through the gills and made a loop. He slung his bag over his shoulder, and with the fish in one hand and his rod in the other went to find Gunnar.

A wet fish thirty-three inches long suspended by a bit of thin string is not a convenient burden if you want to keep its tail from dragging on the ground. Carrying it with his arm crooked Marshall found the muscular exertion quite considerable and it spread its slime all down his battledress trousers; carrying it over his shoulder upon the butt end of the rod was easier, and it spread its slime all down the back of his blouse. In the open air, and while the slime was fresh, this did not seem to matter very much; it became important to him later in the day.

Gunnar saw him coming in the distance and stood up from his little stool, and came to meet him. 'That is ver' good,' he said genially. 'It is a ver' good fish, that one.'

Marshall said: 'Thirty-three inches.'

'So?' The Dane felt the weight of it. 'With which plug?'

'The red one – *and* over in the shallows.'

Gunnar nodded. 'He pull ver' hard?'

Marshall said: 'He gave up pretty soon.' He paused. 'Have you done any good?'

'Two.' The sergeant pilot opened his bag and showed two quarter-pound roach lying upon a bed of grass.

'Coming back to the camp?'

Gunnar shook his head. 'They are feeding well; I shall stay here.' He grinned. 'I think that they have heard the news; so they come out to feed.'

Marshall glanced down at his fish. 'I bet this one's eaten a few roach in his time.'

He left Gunnar and walked up the bank towards his bicycle, carrying his awkward burden. He speculated as he went how much it weighed; his estimates showed a tendency to rise as he went on, so that the buoyancy of his spirits offset the fatigue of his arm. He reached the mill at last and spread the fish, now stiffening, across his bicycle basket and tied it insecurely there with string. Then he rode back to the camp.

The guard at the gate grinned broadly as he rode into the camp with a very large fish drooping at his handlebars, and took occasion to salute him very formally. Marshall returned the salute and rode on to the mess past laughing groups of aircraftmen and WAAFs; nobody in the camp would ever say again that he could not catch fish. He parked the bike and, carrying the fish, went through into the kitchen and induced the WAAF cook to put it on the scales. It weighed eleven and a quarter pounds.

'My!' she said. 'That is a nice bit of fish now, isn't it?' Her words were like music to him. 'Will you have it stuffed, Mr Marshall, like we did the other?'

He agreed, and she gave him a dish for it and arranged it stretched out at full length, and he carried it through into the dining-room and put it on the table for display. Then he went through to the ante-room to see whom he could find to show it to.

'You do any good?'

'I caught the biggest fish in the river.'

'Better not let Ma Stevens see it, if you want to get it cooked.'

Marshall threw down his paper. 'You don't know who you're talking to. When I catch fish, I catch fish.'

Flight Lieutenant Johnson looked at him doubtfully. 'No, really – did you get one?'

Marshall heaved himself up from his chair. 'Come and see.'

He led the way through into the dining-room and snapped on the lights. 'God!' said Mr Johnson. 'What an awful-looking thing.'

'What d'you mean? That's a bloody fine fish. It's eleven and a quarter pounds.'

'Maybe. It looks like something out of the main sewer.'

Marshall glanced at the clock; it was five minutes past six. 'I was going to buy you a noggin,' he said, with dignity. 'Now I shall buy myself two.'

from PASTORAL *1944*

Tom Meets a Salmon

CHARLES KINGSLEY

'Down to the sea?' said Tom; 'everything is going to the sea, and I will go too. Good-bye, trout.' But the trout were so busy gobbling worms that they never turned to answer him; so that Tom was spared the pain of bidding them farewell.

And now, down the rushing stream, guided by the bright flashes of the storm; past tall birch-fringed rocks, which shone out one moment as clear as day, and the next were dark as night; past dark hovers under swirling banks, from which great trout rushed out on Tom, thinking him to be good to eat, and turned back sulkily, for the fairies sent them home again with a tremendous scolding, for daring to meddle with a water-baby; on through narrow strids and roaring cataracts, where Tom was deafened and blinded for a moment by the rushing waters; along deep reaches, where the white water lilies tossed and flapped beneath the wind and hail; past sleeping villages; under dark bridge-arches, and away and away to the sea. And Tom could not stop, and did not care to stop; he would see the great world below, and the salmon, and the breakers, and the wide wide sea.

And when the daylight came, Tom found himself out in the salmon river.

And what sort of a river was it? Was it like an Irish stream, winding through the brown bogs, where the wild ducks squatter up from among the white water lilies, and the curlews flit to and fro, crying 'Tullie-wheep, mind your sheep'; and Dennis tells you strange stories of the Peishtamore, the great bogy-snake which lies in the black peat pools, among the old pine-stems, and puts his head out at night to snap at the cattle as they come down to drink? – But you must not believe all that Dennis tells you, mind; for if you ask him:

'Is there a salmon here, do you think, Dennis?'

'Is it salmon, thin, your honour manes? Salmon? Cartloads it is of thim, thin, an' ridgmens, shouldthering ache other out of water, av' ye'd but the luck to see thim.'

Then you fish the pool all over, and never get a rise.

'But there can't be a salmon here, Dennis! and, if you'll but think, if one had come up last tide, he'd gone to the higher pools by now.'

'Sure thin, and your honour's the thrue fisherman, and understands it all like a book. Why, ye spake as if ye'd known the wather a thousand years! As I said, how could there be a fish here at all, just now?'

'But you said just now they were shouldering each other out of water?'

And then Dennis will look up at you with his handsome, soft, sleepy, good-natured, Irish grey eye, and answer with the prettiest smile:

'Shure, and didn't I think your honour would like a pleasant answer?'

Or was it like a Welsh salmon river, which is remarkable chiefly (at least, till this last year) for containing no salmon, as they have been all poached out by the enlightened peasantry, to prevent the Cythrawl Sassenach from coming bothering into Wales?

Or was it such a salmon stream as I trust you will see among the Hampshire water-meadows before your hairs are grey, under the wise new fishing-laws – when Winchester apprentices shall covenant, as they did three hundred years ago, not to be made to eat salmon more than three days a week; and fresh-run fish shall be as plentiful under Salisbury spire as they are in Holly-hole at Christ-church; in the good time coming, when folks shall see that, of all Heaven's gifts of food, the one to be protected most carefully is that worthy gentleman salmon, who is generous enough to go down to the sea weighing five ounces, and to come back next year weighing five pounds, without having cost the soil or the state one farthing?

Or was it like a Scotch stream, such as Arthur Clough drew in his 'Bothie'? –

> *'Where over a ledge of granite*
> *Into a granite bason the amber torrent descended . . .*
> *Beautiful there for the colour derived from green rocks under;*
> *Beautiful most of all, where beads of foam uprising*
> *Mingle their clouds of white with the delicate blue of the stillness . . .*
> *Cliff over cliff for its sides, with rowan and pendant birch boughs . . .'*

Ah, my little man, when you are a big man, and fish such a stream as that, you will hardly care, I think, whether she be roaring down in full spate, like coffee covered with scald cream, while the fish are swirling at your fly as an oar-blade swirls in a boat-race, or flashing up the cataract like silver arrows, out of the fiercest of the foam; or whether the fall be dwindled to a single thread, and the shingle below be as white and dusty as a turnpike road, while the salmon huddle together in one dark cloud in the clear amber pool, sleeping away their time till the rain creeps back again off the sea. You will not care much, if you have eyes and brains; for you will lay down your rod contentedly, and drink in at your eyes the beauty of that glorious place; and listen to the water-ouzel piping on the stones, and watch the yellow roes come down to drink and look up at you with their great soft trustful eyes, as much as to say, 'You could not have the heart to shoot at us?' And then, if you have sense, you will turn and talk to the great giant of a gilly who lies basking on the stone beside you. He will tell you no fibs, my little man; for he is a Scotchman.

No. It was none of these, the salmon stream at Harthover. It was such a stream as you see in dear old Bewick; Bewick, who was born and bred upon them. A full hundred yards broad it was, sliding on from broad pool to broad shallow, and broad shallow to broad pool, over great fields of shingle, under oak and ash coverts, past low cliffs of sandstone, past green meadows, and fair parks, and a great house of grey stone, and brown moors above, and here and there against the sky the smoking chimney of a colliery. You must look at Bewick to see just what it was like, for he has drawn it a hundred times with the care and the love of a true north countryman.

But Tom thought nothing about what the river was like. All his fancy was, to get down to the wide wide sea.

And after a while he came to a place where the river spread out into broad still shallow reaches, so wide that little Tom, as he put his head out of the water, could hardly see across.

And there he stopped. He got a little frightened. 'This must be the sea,' he thought. 'What a wide place it is! If I go on into it I shall surely lose my way, or some strange thing will bite me. I will stop here and look out for the otter, or the eels, or someone to tell me where I shall go.'

So he went back a little way, and crept into a crack of the rock, just where the river opened out into the wide shallows, and watched for someone to tell him his way: but the otter and the eels were gone on miles and miles down the stream.

There he waited, and slept too, for he was quite tired with his night's journey; and, when he woke, the stream was clearing to a beautiful amber hue, though it was still very high. And after a while he saw a sight which made him jump up; for he knew in a moment it was one of the things which he had come to look for.

Such a fish! ten times as big as the biggest trout, and a hundred times as big as Tom, sculling up the stream past him, as easily as Tom had sculled down.

Such a fish! shining silver from head to tail, and here and there a crimson dot; with a grand hooked nose and grand curling lip, and a grand bright eye, looking round him as proudly as a king, and surveying the water right and left as if all belonged to him. Surely he must be the salmon, the king of all the fish.

Tom was so frightened that he longed to creep into a hole; but he need not have been; for salmon are all true gentlemen, and, like true gentlemen, they look noble and proud enough, and yet, like true gentlemen, they never harm or quarrel with anyone, but go about their own business, and leave rude fellows to themselves.

The salmon looked at him full in the face, and then went on without minding him, with a swish or two of his tail which made the stream boil again. And in a few minutes came another, and then four or five, and so on; and all passed Tom, rushing and plunging up the cataract with strong strokes of their silver tails, now and then leaping clean out of water and up over a rock, shining gloriously for a moment in the bright sun; while Tom was so delighted that he could have watched them all day long.

And at last one came up bigger than all the rest; but he came slowly, and stopped, and looked back, and seemed very anxious and busy. And Tom saw that he was helping another salmon, an especially handsome one, who had not a single spot upon it, but was clothed in pure silver from nose to tail.

'My dear,' said the great fish to his companion, 'you really look dreadfully tired, and you must not over-exert yourself at first. Do rest yourself behind this rock'; and he shoved her gently with his nose, to the rock where Tom sat.

You must know that this was the salmon's wife. For salmon, like other true gentlemen, always choose their lady, and love her, and are true to her, and take care of her and work for her, and fight for her, as every true gentleman ought; and are not like vulgar chub and roach and pike, who have no high feelings, and take no care of their wives.

Then he saw Tom, and looked at him very fiercely one moment, as if he was going to bite him.

'What do you want here?' he said, very fiercely.

'Oh, don't hurt me!' cried Tom. 'I only want to look at you; you are so handsome.'

'Ah!' said the salmon, very stately but very civilly. 'I really beg your pardon; I see what you are, my little dear. I have met one or two creatures like you before, and found them very agreeable and well-behaved. Indeed, one of them showed me a great kindness lately, which I hope to be able to repay. I hope we shall not be in your way here. As soon as this lady is rested, we shall proceed on our journey.'

What a well-bred old salmon he was!

'So you have seen things like me before?' asked Tom.

'Several times, my dear. Indeed, it was only last night that one at the river's mouth came and warned me and my wife of some new stake-nets which had got into the stream, I cannot tell how, since last winter, and showed us the way round them, in the most charmingly obliging way.'

'So there are babies in the sea?' cried Tom, and clapped his little hands. 'Then I shall have someone to play with there? How delightful!'

'Were there no babies up this stream?' asked the lady salmon.

'No! and I grew so lonely. I thought I saw three last night; but they were gone in an instant, down to the sea. So I went too; for I had nothing to play with but caddises and dragon-flies and trout.'

'Ugh!' cried the lady, 'what low company!'

'My dear, if he has been in low company, he has certainly not learnt their low manners,' said the salmon.

'No, indeed, poor little dear: but how sad for him to live among such people as caddises, who have actually six legs, and nasty things; and dragon-flies, too! why they are not even good to eat; for I tried them once, and they are all hard and empty; and, as for trout, everyone knows what they are.' Whereon she curled up her lip, and looked dreadfully scornful, while her husband curled up his too, till he looked as proud as Alcibiades.

'Why do you dislike the trout so?' asked Tom.

'My dear, we do not even mention them, if we can help it; for I am sorry to say they are relations of ours who do us no credit. A great many years ago they were just like us: but they were so lazy, and cowardly, and greedy, that instead of going down to the sea every year to see the world and grow strong and fat, they chose to stay and poke about in the little streams and eat worms and grubs; and they are very properly punished for it; for they have grown ugly and brown and spotted and small; and are actually so degraded in their tastes, that they will eat our children.'

'And then they pretend to scrape acquaintance with us again,' said the lady. 'Why, I have actually known one of them propose to a lady salmon, the little impudent little creature.'

'I should hope,' said the gentleman, 'that there are very few ladies of our race who would degrade themselves by listening to such a creature for an instant. If I saw such a thing happen, I should consider it my duty to put them both to death upon the spot.' So the old salmon said, like an old blue-blooded hidalgo of Spain; and what is more he would have done it too. For you must know, no enemies are so bitter against each other as those who are of the same race; and a salmon looks on a trout, as some great folks look on some little folks, as something just too much like himself to be tolerated.

from THE WATER BABIES *1870*

Plain Fishing

FRANK R. STOCKTON

'Well, sir,' said old Peter Gruse, as he came out on the porch with his pipe, 'so you come here to go fishin'?' . . .

'Yes,' I answered, 'I understood that there was good fishing hereabouts, and, at any rate, I should like to spend a few days among these hills and mountains.'

'Well,' said Peter, 'there's trout in some of our streams, though not as many as there used to be, and there's hills a plenty, and mountains too, if you choose to walk fur enough. They're a good deal furder off than they look. What did you bring with you to fish with?'

'Nothing at all,' I answered. 'I was told in the town that you were a great fisherman, and that you could let me have all the tackle I would need.'

'Upon my word,' said old Peter, resting his pipe-hand on his knee and looking steadfastly at me, 'you're the queerest fisherman I've seed yet. Nigh every year, some two or three of 'em stop here in the fishin' season, and there was never a man who didn't bring his jinted pole, and his reels, and his lines, and his hooks, and his dry-good flies, and his whisky-flask with a long strap to it. Now, if you want all these things, I haven't got 'em.'

'Whatever you use yourself will suit me,' I answered.

'All right, then,' he said. 'I'll do the best I can for you in the mornin'. But it's plain enough to me that you're not a game fisherman, or you wouldn't come here without your tools.'

To this remark I made answer to the effect, that though I was very fond of fishing, my pleasure in it did not depend upon the possession of all the appliances of professional sport.

'Perhaps you think,' said the old man, 'from the way I spoke, that I don't believe them fellers with the jinted poles can ketch fish, but that ain't so. That old story about the little boy with the pin-hook who ketched all the fish, while the gentleman with the modern improvements, who stood alongside of him, kep' throwin' out his beautiful flies and never got nothin', is a pure lie. The fancy chaps, who must have ev'rythin' jist so, gen'rally gits fish. But for all that, I don't like their way of fishin', and I take no stock in it myself. I've been fishin', on and off, ever since I was a little boy, and I've caught nigh every kind there is, from the big jew-fish and cavalyoes down South, to the trout and minnies round about here. But when I ketch a fish, the first thing I do is to try to git him on the hook, and the next thing is to git him out of the water jist as soon as I kin. I don't put in no time worryin' him. There's only two animals in the world that likes to worry smaller creeturs a good while before they kill 'em; one is the cat, and the other is what they call the game fisherman. This kind of fellow never goes after no fish that don't mind being ketched. He goes fur them kinds that loves their homes in the water and hates most to leave it, and he makes it jist as hard fur 'em as he kin. What the game fisher likes is the smallest kind of a hook, the thinnest line, and a fish that it takes a good while to weaken. The longer the weak'nin' business kin be spun out, the more the sport. The idee is to let the fish think there's a chance fur him to get away. That's jist like the cat with her mouse. She lets the little creetur hop off, but the minnit he gits fur enough down, she jabs on him with her claws, and then, if there's any game left in him, she lets him try agen. Of course, the game fisher could have a strong line and a stout pole and git his fish in a good sight quicker, if he wanted to, but that wouldn't be sport. He couldn't give him the butt and spin him out, and reel him in, and let him jump and run till his pluck is clean worn out. Now, I likes to git my fish ashore with all the pluck in 'em. It makes 'em taste better. And as fur fun, I'll be bound I've had jist as much of that, and more, too, than most of these fellers who are so dreadful anxious to have everythin' jist right, and think they can't go fishin' till they've spent enough money to buy a suit of Sunday clothes. As a gen'ral rule they're a solemn lot, and work pretty hard at their fun. When I work I want to be paid fur it, and when I go in fur fun I want to take it easy and comfortable. Now I wouldn't say so much agen these fellers,' said old Peter, as he arose and put his empty pipe on a little shelf under the porchroof, 'if it wasn't for one thing, and that is, that they think that their kind of fishin' is the only kind worth considerin'. The way they look down upon plain Christian fishin' is enough to rile a hitchin'-post. I don't want to say nothin' agen no man's way of attendin' to his own affairs, whether it's kitchen gardenin', or whether it's fishin', if he says nothin' agen my way; but when he looks down on me, and grins me, I want to haul myself up, and grin him, if I kin. And in this case, I kin. I s'pose the house-cat and the cat-fisher (by which I don't mean the man who fishes for cat-fish) was both made as they is, and they can't help it; but that don't give 'em no right to put on airs before other bein's who gits their meat with a square kill. Good night. And sence I've talked so much about it, I've a mind to go fishin' with you tomorrow myself.'

The next morning found old Peter of the same mind, and after breakfast he proceeded to fit me out for a day of what he called 'plain Christian trout-fishin''. He gave me a reed rod, about nine feet long, light, strong, and nicely balanced. The tackle he produced was not of the fancy order, but his lines were of fine strong linen, and his hooks were of good shape, clean and sharp, and snooded to the lines with a neatness that indicated the hand of a man who had been where he learned to wear little gold rings in his ears.

'Here are some of these feather insects,' he said, 'which you kin take along if you like.' And he handed me a paper containing a few artificial flies. 'They're pretty nat'ral,' he said, 'and the hooks is good. A man who come here fishin' gave em to me, but I shan't want 'em today. At this time of year grasshoppers is the best bait in the kind of place where we're goin' to fish. The stream, after it comes down from the mountain, runs through half a mile of medder land before it strikes into the woods agen. A grasshopper is a little creetur that's got as much conceit as if his jinted legs was fish-poles, and he thinks he kin jump over this narrer run of water whenever he pleases; but he don't always do it, and them of him that don't git snapped up by the trout that lie along the banks in the medder is floated along into the woods, where there's always fish enough to come to the second table.'

Having got me ready, Peter took his own particular pole, which he assured me he had used for eleven years, and hooking on his left arm a good-sized basket, which his elder pretty daughter had packed with cold meat, bread, butter, and preserves, we started forth for a three-mile walk to the fishing-ground. The day was a favourable one for our purpose, the sky being sometimes overclouded, which was good for fishing, and also for walking on a highroad; and sometimes bright, which was good for effects of mountain scenery. Not far from the spot where old Peter proposed to begin our sport, a small frame-house stood by the roadside, and here the old man halted and entered the open door without knocking or giving so much as a premonitory stamp. I followed, imitating my companion in leaving my pole outside, which appeared to be the only ceremony that the etiquette of those parts required of visitors. In the room we entered, a small man in his shirt sleeves sat mending a basket handle. He nodded to Peter, and Peter nodded to him.

'We've come up a-fishin',' said the old man. 'Kin your boys give us some grasshoppers?'

'I don't know that they've got any ready ketched,' said he, 'for I reckon I used what they had this mornin'. But they kin git you some. Here, Dan, you and Sile go and ketch Mister Gruse and this young man some grasshoppers. Take that mustard-box, and see that you git it full.'

Peter and I now took seats, and the conversation began about a black cow which Peter had to sell, and which the other was willing to buy if the old man would trade for sheep, which animals, however, the basket-mender did not appear just at that time to have in his possession. As I was not very much interested in this subject, I walked to the back door and watched two small boys in scanty shirts and trousers and ragged straw hats, who were darting about in the grass catching grasshoppers, of which insects, judging by the frequent pounces of the boys, there seemed a plentiful supply.

'Got it full?' said their father when the boys came in.

'Crammed,' said Dan.

Old Peter took the little can, pressed the top firmly on, put it in his coat-tail pocket, and rose to go. 'You'd better think about that cow, Barney,' said he. He said nothing to the boys about the box of bait; but I could not let them catch grasshoppers for us for nothing, and I took a dime from my pocket, and gave it to Dan. Dan grinned, and Sile looked sheepishly happy, and at the sight of the piece of silver an expression of interest came over the face of the father. 'Wait a minute,' said he, and he went into a little room that seemed to be a kitchen. Returning, he brought with him a small string of trout. 'Do you want to buy some fish?' he said. 'These is nice fresh ones. I ketched 'em this mornin'.'

To offer to sell fish to a man who is just about to go out to catch them for himself might, in most cases, be considered an insult, but it was quite evident that nothing of the kind was intended by Barney. He probably thought that if I bought grasshoppers, I might buy fish. 'You kin have 'em for a quarter,' he said.

It was derogatory to my pride to buy fish at such a moment, but the man looked very poor, and there was a shade of anxiety on his face which touched me. Old Peter stood by without saying a word. 'It might be well,' I said, turning to him, 'to buy these fish, for we may not catch enough for supper.'

'Such things do happen,' said the old man.

'Well,' said I, 'if we have these we will feel safe in any case.' And I took the fish and gave the man a quarter. It was not, perhaps, a professional act, but the trout were well worth the money, and I felt that I was doing a deed of charity.

Old Peter and I now took our rods, and crossed the road into an enclosed lot, and thence into a wide stretch of grassland, bounded by hills in front of us and to the right, while a thick forest lay to the left. We had walked but a short distance, when Peter said: 'I'll go down into the woods, and try my luck there, and you'd better go along upstream, about a quarter of a mile, to where it's rocky. P'raps you ain't used to fishin' in the woods, and you might git your line cotched. You'll find the trout'll bite in the rough water.'

'Where is the stream?' I asked.

'This is it,' he said, pointing to a little brook, which was scarcely too wide for me to step across, 'and there's fish right here, but they're hard to ketch, fur they git plenty of good livin', and are mighty sassy about their eatin'. But you kin ketch 'em up there.'

Old Peter now went down towards the woods, while I walked up the little stream. I had seen trout-brooks before, but never one so diminutive as this. However, when I came nearer to the point where the stream issued from between two of the foot-hills of the mountains, which lifted their forest-covered heights in the distance, I found it wider and shallower, breaking over its rocky bottom in sparkling little cascades.

Fishing in such a jolly little stream, surrounded by this mountain scenery, and with the privileges of the beautiful situation all to myself, would have been a joy to me if I had had never a bite. But no such ill-luck befell me. Peter had given me the can of grasshoppers after putting half of them into his own bait-box, and these I used with much success. It was grasshopper season, and the trout were evidently on the lookout for them. I fished in the ripples under the little waterfalls; and every now and then I drew out a lively trout. Most of these were of moderate size, and some of them might have been called small. The large ones probably fancied the forest shades, where old Peter went. But all I caught were fit for the table, and I was very well satisfied with the result of my sport.

About an hour after noon I began to feel hungry, and thought it time to look up the old man, who had the lunch-basket. I walked down the bank of the brook, and some time before I reached the woods I came to a place where it expanded to a width of about ten feet. The water here was very clear, and the motion quiet, so that I could easily see to the bottom, which did not appear to be more than a foot below the surface. Gazing into this transparent water, as I walked, I saw a large trout glide across the stream, and disappear under the grassy bank which overhung the opposite side. I instantly stopped. This was a much larger fish than any I had caught, and I determined to try for him.

I stepped back from the bank, so as to be out of sight, and put a fine grasshopper on my hook; then I lay, face downward, on the grass, and worked myself slowly forward until I could see the middle of the stream; then quietly raising my pole, I gave my grasshopper a good swing, as if he had made a wager to jump over the stream at its widest part. But as he certainly would have failed in such an ambitious endeavour, especially if he had been caught by a puff of wind, I let him come down upon the surface of the water, a little beyond the middle of the brook. Grasshoppers do not sink when they fall into the water, and so I kept this fellow upon the surface, and gently moved him along, as if, with all the conceit taken out of him by the result of his ill-considered leap, he was ignominiously endeavouring to swim to shore. As I did this, I saw the trout come out from under the bank, move slowly towards the grasshopper, and stop directly under him. Trembling with anxiety and eager expectation, I endeavoured to make the movements of the insect still more natural, and, as far as I was able, I threw into him a sudden perception of his danger, and a frenzied desire to get away. But, either the trout had had all the grasshoppers he wanted, or he was able, from long experience, to perceive the difference between a natural exhibition of emotion and a histrionic imitation of it, for he slowly turned, and, with a few slight movements of his tail, glided back under the bank. In vain did the grasshopper continue his frantic efforts to reach the shore; in vain did he occasionally become exhausted, and sink a short distance below the surface; in vain did he do everything that he knew, to show that he appreciated what a juicy and delicious morsel he was, and how he feared that the trout might yet be tempted to seize him; the fish did not come out again.

Then I withdrew my line, and moved back from the stream. I now determined to try Mr Trout with a fly, and I took out the paper old

Peter Gruse had given me. I did not know exactly what kind of winged insects were in order at this time of the year, but I was sure that yellow butterflies were not particular about just what month it was so long as the sun shone warmly. I therefore chose that one of Peter's flies which was made of the yellowest feathers, and, removing the snood and hook from my line, I hastily attached this fly, which was provided with a hook quite suitable for my desired prize. Crouching on the grass, I again approached the brook. Gaily flitting above the glassy surface of the water, in all the fancied security of tender youth and innocence, came my yellow fly. Backwards and forwards over the water he gracefully flew, sometimes rising a little into the air, as if to view the varied scenery of the woods and mountains, and then settling for a moment close to the surface, better to inspect his glittering image as it came up from below, and showing in his every movement his intense enjoyment of summer-time and life.

Out from his dark retreat now came the trout; and settling quietly at the bottom of the brook, he appeared to regard the venturesome insect with a certain interest. But he must have detected the iron barb of vice beneath the mask of blitheful innocence, for, after a short deliberation, the trout turned and disappeared under the bank. As he slowly moved away, he seemed to be bigger than ever. I must catch that fish! Surely he would bite at something. It was quite evident that his mind was not wholly unsusceptible to emotions emanating from an awakening appetite, and I believed that if he saw exactly what he wanted, he would not neglect an opportunity of availing himself of it. But what did he want? I must certainly find out. Drawing myself back again, I took off the yellow fly, and put on another. This was a white one, with black blotches, like a big miller moth which had fallen into an ink-pot. It was certainly a conspicuous creature, and as I crept forward and sent it swooping over the stream, I could not see how any trout, with a single insectivorous tooth in his head, could fail to rise to such an occasion. But this trout did not rise. He would not even come out from under his bank to look at the swiftly flitting creature. He probably could see it well enough from where he was.

But I was not to be discouraged. I put on another fly; a green one with a red tail. It did not look like any insect that I had ever seen, but I thought that the trout might know more about such things than I. He did come out to look at it, but probably considering it a product of that modern aestheticism which sacrifices natural beauty to medieval crudeness of colour and form, he returned without evincing any disposition to countenance this style of art.

It was evident that it would be useless to put on any other flies, for the two I had left were a good deal bedraggled, and not nearly so attractive as those I had used. Just before leaving the house that morning Peter's son had given me a wooden matchbox filled with worms for bait, which, although I did not expect to need, I put in my pocket. As a last resort I determined to try the trout with a worm. I selected the plumpest and most comely of the lot; I put a new hook on my line; I looped him about it in graceful coils, and cautiously approached the water as before. Now a worm never attempts to leap wildly across a flowing brook, not does he flit in thoughtless innocence through the sunny air, and over the bright transparent stream. If he happens to fall into the water, he sinks to the bottom; and if he be of a kind not subject to drowning, he generally endeavours to secrete himself under a stone, or to burrow in the soft mud. With this knowledge of his nature I gently dropped my worm upon the surface of the stream, and then allowed him to sink slowly. Out sailed the trout from under the bank, but stopped before reaching the sinking worm. There was a certain something in his action which seemed to indicate a disgust at the sight of such plebeian food, and a fear seized me that he might now swim off, and pay no further attention to my varied baits. Suddenly there was a ripple in the water, and I felt a pull on the line. Instantly I struck; and then there was a tug. My blood boiled through every vein and artery, and I sprang to my feet. I did not give him the butt: I did not let him run with yards of line down the brook; nor reel him in, and let him make another mad course upstream: I did not turn him over as he jumped into the air; nor endeavour, in any way, to show him that I understood those tricks, which his depraved nature prompted him to play upon the angler. With an absolute dependence upon the strength of old Peter's tackle, I lifted the fish. Out he came from the water, which held him with a gentle suction as if unwilling to let him go, and then he whirled through the air like a meteor flecked with rosy fire, and landed on the fresh green grass a dozen feet behind me. Down on my knees I dropped before him as he tossed and rolled, his beautiful spots and colours glistening in the sun. He was truly a splendid trout, fully a foot long, round and heavy. Carefully seizing him, I easily removed the hook from the bony roof of his capacious mouth thickly set with sparkling teeth, and then I tenderly killed him, with all his pluck, as old Peter would have said, still in him.

I covered the rest of the fish in my basket with wet plantain leaves, and laid my trout-king on this cool green bed. Then I hurried off to the old man, whom I saw coming out of the woods. When I opened my basket and showed him what I had caught, Peter looked surprised, and, taking up the trout, examined it.

'Why, this is a big fellow,' he said. 'At first I thought it was Barney Sloat's boss trout, but it isn't long enough for him. Barney showed me his trout, that gen'rally keeps in a deep pool, where a tree has fallen over the stream down there. Barney tells me he often sees him, and he's been tryin' fur two years to ketch him, but he never has, and I say he never will, fur them big trout's got too much sense to fool round any kind of victuals that's got a string to it. They let a little fish eat all he wants, and then they eat him. How did you ketch this one?'

I gave an account of the manner of the capture, to which Peter listened with interest and approval.

'If you'd a stood off and made a cast at that feller, you'd either have caught him at the first flip, which isn't likely, as he didn't seem to want no feather-flies, or else you'd skeered him away. That's all well enough in the tumblin' water, where you gen'rally go fur trout, but the man that's got the true fellin' fur fish will try to suit his idees to theyrn, and if he keeps on doin' that, he's like to learn a thing or two that may do him good. That's a fine fish, and you ketched him well. I've got a lot of 'em, but nothin' of that heft.'

After luncheon we fished for an hour or two, with no result worth recording, and then we started for home.

When we reached the farm the old man went into the barn, and I took the fish into the house. I found Peter's two pretty daughters in the large room, where the eating and some of the cooking was done. I opened my basket, and with great pride showed them the big trout I had caught. They evidently thought it was a large fish, but they looked at each other, and smiled in a way that I did not understand. I had expected from them, at least, as much admiration for my prize and my skill as their father had shown.

'You don't seem to think much of this fine trout that I took such trouble to catch,' I remarked.

'You mean,' said the elder girl, with a laugh, 'that you bought of Barney Sloat.'

I looked at her in astonishment.

'Barney was along here today,' she said, 'and he told about your buying your fish of him.'

'Bought of him!' I exclaimed indignantly. 'A little string of fish at the bottom of the basket I bought of him, but all the others, and this big one, I caught myself.'

'Oh, of course,' said the pretty daughter, 'bought the little ones and caught all the big ones.'

'Barney Sloat ought to have kept his mouth shut,' said the younger pretty daughter, looking at me with an expression of pity. 'He'd got his money, and he hadn't no business to go telling on people. Nobody likes that sort of thing. But this big fish is a real nice one, and you shall have it for your supper.'

'Thank you,' I said, with dignity, and left the room.

I did not intend to have any further words with these young women on this subject, but I cannot deny that I was annoyed and mortified. This was the result of a charitable action. I think I was never more proud of anything than of catching that trout; and it was a very considerable downfall suddenly to find myself regarded as a mere city man fishing with a silver hook. But, after all, what did it matter? But the more I said this to myself, the more was I impressed with the fact that it mattered a great deal.

The boy who did not seem to be accounted a member of the family came into the house, and as he passed me he smiled good-humouredly, and said: 'Buyed 'em!'

I felt like throwing a chair at him, but refrained out of respect to my host. Before supper the old man came out on to the porch where I was sitting. 'It seems,' said he, 'that my gals has got it inter their heads that you bought that big fish of Barney Sloat, and as I can't say I seed you ketch it, they're not willin' to give in, 'specially as I didn't git no such big one. 'Tain't wise to buy fish when you're goin' fishin' yourself. It's pretty certain to tell agen you.'

'You ought to have given me that advice before,' I said, somewhat shortly. 'You saw me buy the fish.'

'You don't s'pose,' said old Peter, 'that I'm goin' to say anythin' to keep money out of my neighbour's pockets. We don't do that way in these parts. But I've told the gals they're not to speak another word about it, so you needn't give your mind no sorry on that score. And now let's go in to supper. If you're as hungry as I am, there won't be many of them fish left fur breakfast.'

For two days longer I remained in this neighbourhood, wandering alone over the hills, and up the mountain-sides, and by the brooks, which tumbled and gurgled through the lonely forest. Each evening I brought home a goodly supply of trout, but never a great one like the noble fellow for which I angled in the meadow stream.

On the morning of my departure I stood on the porch with old Peter waiting for the arrival of the mail driver, who was to take me to the nearest railroad town.

'I don't want to say nothin',' remarked the old man, 'that would keep them fellers with the jinted poles from stoppin' at my house when they comes to these parts a-fishin'. I ain't got no objections to their poles; 'tain't that. And I don't mind nuther their standin' off, and throwin' their flies as fur as they've a mind to; that's not it. And it ain't even the way they have of worryin' their fish. I wouldn't do it myself, but if they like it, that's their business. But what does rile me is the cheeky way in which they stand up and say that there isn't no decent way of fishin' but their way. And that to a man that's ketched more fish, of more different kinds, with more game in 'em, and had more fun at it, with a lot less money and less tomfoolin' than any fishin' feller that ever come here and talked to me like an old cat tryin' to teach a dog to ketch rabbits. No, sir; agen I say that I don't take no money fur entertainin' the only man that ever come out here to go a-fishin' in a plain, Christian way. But if you feel tetchy about not payin' nothing', you kin send me one of them poles in three pieces, a good strong one, that'll lift Barney Sloat's trout, if ever I hook him.'

I sent him the rod; the next summer I am going up to see him use it.

from AMOS KILBRIGHT,
HIS ADSCITITIOUS EXPERIENCES *1888*

The Sacrifice

SVEN BERLIN

The main river had been like a dragon: turgid, roaring, snarling, at the weeping sky. Even the main stream of the water-meadows was raging now all the sluice gates were open and the meadows were set free. The rain flung spears at us, helmets of water marched in armies down the river. The wind screamed at us, tearing the leaves from the giant ash and elm and willow, flinging them like money into our bankrupt faces. Sudden lightning snatched at my shoulder like a cat's paw and hissed. Gates, brambles, fences, nails, wire, nettles: the hooks that tore at us instead of at the fish, tore at our clothes. The great bull stood against the night, keeping it out: the great fish was hidden beneath the river.

Although we knew it was no good fishing, that in all likelihood we would catch no dace, we had to go on. The cage must be filled. This was part of the law of our great hunt. The cage Cockle had built of wire was strong against the predator and against freedom. We must prison the dace in a small cage of life to make them safe from the zebra of the streams: silver thoughts handed back to preserve them in their own element, just as the eels came up the ditches from the western oceans to shelter and grow. This was the great paradox of eternal preservation: even in some way of one's own life.

Had Cockle known what was going on in my mind I don't think he would have been at all dismayed. His was a natural understanding. He would have smiled at my complicated way of expressing it, but would have taken me seriously; perhaps with a remark about my being a 'darft old bastard'.

The water ran down our faces, cut our cheeks.

'Can't see much of this, Cock. Wonder if the cage is still there?'

We looked down by the little stone bridge.

'Yes, I can see the wor. They'll close the gates after this an' flood the bleedin' medders,' said Cockle. 'The wolter'll lose its force then. Put dace in the cage now and they'll be tore to pieces.'

I thought of the fish in the small cage with hundreds of tons of water being forced through and them trying to keep their noses to the current to save drowning.

'Good job we haven't any fish!' I said.

'No,' said Cockle, 'but we soon will 'ave. I ain't just a pretty face, y'know. We'll go up to that litol pool you calls the Silver Coin Pool. Bit sharpish up there like but sure to be good. Come on.'

The wind ceased suddenly, like a vacuum cleaner being switched off, and the sky was an emporium of rainbows. By the time we reached the Silver Coin Pool we were quite warm. We unskinned our wet clothes, lit cigarettes and started to fish, taking care the newly released sunlight did not cast out shadows or reflections in the waters of the little pool. From under a set of rotting wood sluice gates that were newly closed, just enough water ran to make a gentle stream flow through the centre and out at the other end over a shelf of gravel, into a ditch across the meadows.

'This is *it*, mate!' said Cockle, as though he was experiencing a Sartori. 'Keep quiet and we will catch the dace.'

The stream, running to one side eccentrically through the pool, caused a slow, imperceptible whirlpool under the surface so that when I cast maggots from the palm of my hand they sank like parachutists in the opposite direction. I cast my red float gently by the fringe of bright green weed: it rocked, then glided gently after the maggots like a plane from which they were descending. Without pausing, it dipped once or twice then started to slide slightly sideways. A flick of the wrist and the line tightened, shot backwards and forwards with the powerful little body of a dace guiding it everywhere: a planchette writing its own destiny. Then the fish was flashing in the sun, caught in the tough integument at the side of the mouth. The living creature was in my hand, just as though I had created it out of nothing. That was a delight of fishing.

One after the other we caught these little fish along the edge of the central stream which was the primal life-force of the pool: without it the water would go stagnant, the fish die even though they were in their own element. Sometimes I did not wait for the float to dip, but worked entirely by instinct and precognition, taking, without even a strike, fish from this magic water. Now and then a big stupid roach would bob the float right under and put up a terrific fight before it came to net. Salmon parr attacked the bait, making the float tremble and one would get the gilt hook through its belly or head. If one becomes a fish of that size, a millimetre in length, a twelve hook is formidable: it is wonderful how they survive. Sometimes the gudgeon got caught up in the edge of the wide, greedy mouth. We only kept the dace. Even an occasional chub was put back, whatever the River Board said about their being vermin. Without predators the fish will lose their vitality and strength. Take away the conflict and the artist dies. Roach used as live bait swim to the surface, the parr is too small, the gudgeon dies, the chub pities itself and goes slow, but the dace keeps down, swims actively in circles or against the current without tiring, and if properly hooked will do so for several hours without dying. This is one of the most diabolical forms of sacrifice invented by man, for when the pike approaches the dace cannot get away: an interception of nature . . .

I said, 'What about going up and having a go at Maty?'

'What, the biggun – now?'

'Uh-hur!'

'All right. It won't do much good, but there's no harm trying. I tell yer what though: not to go to the two bridges – the river will be too strong there. Go up to the cut by the whirlpool. The bailiff charges half a dollar if he sees you, but it's worf it.'

We put the dace in the bait and carried it by turns to the little overgrown bridge where the cage was hidden. Cockle was right: Jardine had closed the lower gates and flooded the meadows. Already the water was spilling over the banks, but the fierceness of the stream had done. We got the cage out quite easily, put eighteen fish into it and cast it gently back facing upstream; hid the mooring wire under the rushes. They would be O.K. for another time. We took four fish with us.

The winter sky was high and getting lonely as the afternoon came on. It was beautiful in the pale sunlight to watch the wild geese high up flying south, without the poignancy of having seen them on a Dutch battlefield, upon which my friends had been killed – sacrificed in the great jaws of war: neither could they get away.

We drove round to the whirlpool under the power-station. It was our belief that the great fish – if he had not gone down the tributaries to the Dead Water – would be lying up here in the slack, taking what was expelled to the edges by the churning spirals of water, between a bramble bush and an alder-tree, under a long overhanging bank below the salmon ladder, down which the river slithered like oil. Here the fish of death and the fish of life in the same element swam near to each other, perhaps even without recognition: the salmon passing through the pike's green limbo on his quest into the womb of England. This stretch of inert water seemed divided from the main river where it roared in the whirlpool by an invisible glass wall: quite straight. One side the swirling current, the other almost still water, turning very slowly like a smooth metal drum.

The bailiff appeared: a friendly little man in a huge overcoat, given him by the gentry, and a cloth cap. He had a crafty eye and was not to be deceived. He knew me, and after greetings had been exchanged he allowed me to cross the salmon ladder on a plank bridge to a promontory between the bank and the whirlpool, where he kept a few chickens. Out here it was like being at the axis of this great centrifugal world: the power-station, the houses, making up a private hotel and the bailiff's house on the other side of the river, seemed to swirl round as though on the edges of a roundabout in the brittle sunlight which cracked like barley sugar into a thousand splinters of water; through this and through the revolving tree-tops the wild geese could still be seen flying over, honking and talking to one another. Cockle glided by on the other bank, dreamlike, intent.

I put my hand in the blue bait-can and took hold of a shadowy back: a dace with its jewelled eye gasped: this is the moment when a fisherman comes to terms with himself: he decides whether he can offer this sacrifice. Sometimes, when needles of ice pierce the hands, when the east wind cuts at the head, the pain inflicted on the fish seems more terrible, is close enough to feel sickening to the heart and mind when felt through one's own nervous system and not that of the fish's. This is especially so when the hook slips and breaks the operculum or slips into the great artery by the heart – aorta; or slips too deep into the back and penetrates the spine. Any of these things can happen when the hand rides on the slime coat on a cold day. When larger fish are not being caught as a result the suffering seems pointless. Each stage must be properly faced: the fixing of the fish on two sets of treble hooks, the approach and attack of the pike instilling terror into the dace, the final catching and killing of the pike – a triple murder which, like the bullfight, if done well with precision and with love, is good for one's soul. When these elements of truth are taken out the strength of human life begins to fail and the suffering involved is meaningless.

As I fixed on hooks on that icy afternoon – one in the gristle by the left pectoral fin, because I had broken the operculum and was frightened of destroying the fine gill-rake, and one in the gristle by the dorsal fin – the fish flinched in the sunlight but was unharmed. The moment he entered the water he swam about in all directions until he started to describe a circle round the line, bobbing the great yellow bung which was drifting round on the slowly revolving drum of slack water. As it neared the whirlpool edge it gathered speed until it was caught by the stronger force beyond the invisible division and swept away, disappearing altogether below the water. For a moment I thought the pike had taken it, but before long it reappeared bobbing on the surface. I trotted it down the main stream for some time and then began to wind in. Against the current this was difficult. When the fish reached my hand again it was torn; the hooks were snatched out of its back by the water and the lower group had entered the heart; it was nearly drowned: yet life still remained in the slim silver body. I looked across at Cockle who was watching me.

'What do you think?' I shouted.

'Dead loss. The water's tearin' the poor lil' sods to ribbins. I reckon Maty is down that Dead Water at the side there and he won't come up till this flood goes down.'

The great fish did not move: the water was too heavy. In the failing light we turned the remaining two dace into the water and watched them. After a pause in the mud they seemed suddenly to realize the walls of the bait-can were no longer surrounding them: they were free in their own element. A flash of light and they were gone – back into life whose prison bars are death. We walked up the green lawn by the salmon ladder, along the chalk path over which the river was spilling like water from a basin, to the Bailey Bridge, aching as fishermen do after a long day. The evening air glowed over the water-meadows, the farm in the distance and the Dominie's house, where, the fishermen say, the staff, watching through a hedge, once saw Edward VII on a garden seat having a chambermaid.

We counted two hundred geese going over: the sun had wings.

from JONAH'S DREAM *1964*

The River God

ROLAND PERTWEE

When I was a little boy I had a friend who was a colonel. He was not the kind of colonel you meet nowadays, who manages a motor showroom in the West End of London and wears crocodile shoes and a small moustache and who calls you 'old man' and slaps your back, independent of the fact that you may have been no more than a private in the war. My colonel was of the older order that takes a third of a century and a lot of Indian sun and Madras curry in the making. A veteran of the Mutiny he was, and wore side whiskers to prove it. Once he came upon a number of Sepoys conspiring mischief in a byre with a barrel of gunpowder. So he put the butt of his cheroot into the barrel and presently they all went to hell. That was the kind of man he was in the way of business.

In the way of pleasure he was very different. In the way of pleasure he wore an old Norfolk coat that smelt of heather and brine, and which had no elbows to speak of. And he wore a Sherlock Holmesy kind of cap with a swarm of salmon flies upon it, that to my boyish fancy was more splendid than a crown. I cannot remember his legs, because they were nearly always under water, hidden in great canvas waders. But once he sent me a photograph of himself riding on a tricycle, so I expect he had some knickerbockers, too, which would have been that tight kind, with a box cloth under the knees. Boys don't take much stock of clothes. His head occupied my imagination. A big, brave, white-haired head with cheery-red rugose cheeks and honest, laughing, puckered eyes, with gunpowder marks in their corners.

People at the little Welsh fishing inn where we met said he was a bore; but I knew him to be a god and shall prove it.

I was ten years old and his best friend.

He was seventy something and my hero.

Properly I should not have mentioned my hero so soon in this narrative. He belongs to a later epoch, but sometimes it is forgiveable to start with a boast, and now that I have committed myself I lack the courage to call upon my colonel to fall back two paces to the rear, quick march, and wait until he is wanted.

The real beginning takes place, as I remember, somewhere in Hampshire on the Grayshott Road, among sandy banks, sentinel firs and plum-coloured wastes of heather. Summer-holiday time it was, and I was among folks whose names have since vanished like lizards under the stones of forgetfulness. Perhaps it was a picnic walk; perhaps I carried a basket and was told not to swing it for fear of bursting its cargo of ginger beer. In those days ginger beer had big bulgy corks held down with a string. In a hot sun or under stress of too much agitation the string would break and the corks fly. Then there would be a merry foaming fountain and someone would get reproached.

One of our company had a fishing-rod. He was a young man who, one day, was to be an uncle of mine. But that didn't concern me. What concerned me was the fishing-rod and presently – perhaps because he felt he must keep in with the family – he let me carry it. To the fisherman born there is nothing so provoking of curiosity as a fishing-rod in a case.

Surreptitiously I opened the flap, which contained a small grass spear in a wee pocket, and, pulling down the case a little, I admired the beauties of the work butt, with its gun-metal ferrule and reel rings and the exquisite frail slenderness of the two top joints.

'It's got two top joints – two!' I exclaimed ecstatically.

'Of course,' said he. 'All good trout-rods have two.'

I marvelled in silence at what seemed to me then a combination of extravagance and excellent precaution.

There must have been something inherently understanding and noble about that young man who would one day be my uncle, for, taking me by the arm, he sat me down on a tuft of heather and took the pieces of rod from the case and fitted them together. The rest of the company moved on and left me in Paradise.

It is thirty-five years ago since that moment and not one detail of it is forgotten. There sounds in my ears today as clearly as then, the faint, clear pop made by the little cork stoppers with their box-wood tops as they were withdrawn. I remember how, before fitting the pieces together, he rubbed the ferrules against the side of his nose to prevent them sticking. I remember looking up the length of it through a tunnel of sneck rings to the eyelet at the end. Not until he had fixed a reel and passed a line through the rings did he put the lovely thing into my hand. So light it was, so firm, so persuasive; such a thing alive – a sceptre. I could do no more than say, 'Oo!' and again, 'Oo!'

'A thrill, ain't it?' said he.

I had no need to answer that. In my new-found rapture was only one sorrow, the knowledge that such happiness would not endure and that, all too soon, a blank and rodless future awaited me.

'They must be awfully – awfully 'spensive,' I said.

'Couple of guineas,' he replied offhandedly.

A couple of guineas! And we were poor folk and the future was more rodless than ever.

'Then I shall save and save and save,' I said.

And my imagination started to add up twopence a week into guineas. Two hundred and forty pennies to the pound, multiplied by two – four hundred and eighty – and then another twenty-four pennies – five hundred and four. Why, it would take a lifetime, and no sweets, no elastic for catapults, no penny novelty boxes or airgun bullets or ices or anything. Tragedy must have been writ large upon my face, for he said suddenly, 'When's your birthday?'

I was almost ashamed to tell him how soon it was. Perhaps he, too, was a little taken aback by its proximity, for that future uncle of mine was not so rich as uncles should be.

'We must see about it.'

'But it wouldn't – it couldn't be one like that,' I said.

I must have touched his pride, for he answered loftily, 'Certainly it will.'

In the fortnight that followed I walked on air and told everybody I had as good as got a couple-of-guineas' rod.

No one can deceive a child, save the child himself, and when my birthday came and with it a long brown-paper parcel, I knew, even before I had removed the wrappers, that this two-guineas' rod was not worth the money. There was a brown linen case, it is true, but it was not a case with a neat compartment for each joint, nor was there a spear in the flap. There was only one top instead of two, and there were no popping little stoppers to protect the ferrules from dust and injury. The lower joint boasted no elegant cork hand-piece, but was a tapered affair coarsely made and rudely varnished. When I fitted the pieces together, what I balanced in my hand was tough and stodgy, rather than limber. The reel which had come in a different parcel was of wood. It had neither check nor brake, and the line overran and backwound itself with distressing frequency.

I had not read and re-read Gamages' price list without knowing something of rods, and I did not need to look long at this rod before realizing that it was no match to the one I had handled on the Grayshott Road.

I believe at first a great sadness possessed me, but very presently imagination came to the rescue. For I told myself that I had only to think that this was the rod of all other rods that I desired most and it would be so. And it was so.

Furthermore, I told myself that, in this great wide ignorant world, but few people existed with such expert knowledge of rods as I possessed. That I had but to say, 'Here is the final word in good rods', and they would accept it as such.

Very confidently I tried the experiment on my mother, with inevitable success. From the depths of her affection and her ignorance on all such matters, she produced:

'It's a magnificent rod.'

I went my way, knowing full well that she knew not what she said, but that she was kind.

With rather less confidence I approached my father, saying, 'Look, father! It cost two guineas. It's absolutely the best sort you can get.'

And he, after waggling it a few moments in silence, quoted cryptically:

'There is nothing either good or bad but thinking makes it so.'

Young as I was, I had some curiosity about words, and on any other occasion I would have called on him to explain. But this I did not do, but left hurriedly, for fear that he should explain.

In the two years that followed, I fished every day in the slip of a back garden of our tiny London house. And, having regard to the fact that this rod was never fashioned to throw a fly, I acquired a pretty knack in the fullness of time and performed some glib casting at the nasturtiums and marigolds that flourished by the back wall.

My parents' fortunes must have been in the ascendant, I suppose, for I call to mind an unforgettable breakfast when my mother told me that father had decided we should spend our summer holiday at a Welsh hotel on the river Lledr. The place was called Pont-y-pant, and she showed me a picture of the hotel with a great knock-me-down river creaming past the front of it.

Although in my dreams I had heard fast water often enough, I had never seen it, and the knowledge that in a month's time I should wake with the music of a cataract in my ears was almost more than patience could endure.

In that exquisite, intolerable period of suspense I suffered as only childish longing and enthusiasm can suffer. Even the hank of gut that I bought and bent into innumerable casts failed to alleviate that suffering. I would walk for miles for a moment's delight captured in gluing my nose to the windows of tackleists' shops in the West End. I learned from my grandmother – a wise and calm old lady – how to make nets and, having mastered the art, I made myself a landing-net. This I set up on a frame fashioned from a penny schoolmaster's cane bound to an old walking-stick. It would be pleasant to record that this was a good and serviceable net, but it was not. It flopped over in a very distressing fashion when called upon to lift the lightest weight. I had to confess to myself that I had more enthusiasm than skill in the manufacture of such articles.

At school there was a boy who had a fishing creel, which he swapped with me for a Swedish knife, a copy of *Rogues of the Fiery Cross*, and an Easter egg which I had kept on account of its rare beauty. He had forced a hard bargain and was sure he had the best of it, but I knew otherwise.

At last the great day dawned, and after infinite travel by train we reached our destination as the glow of sunset was greying into dark. The river was in spate, and as we crossed a tall stone bridge on our way to the hotel I heard it below me, barking and grumbling among great rocks. I was pretty far gone in tiredness, for I remember little else that night but a rod rack in the hall – a dozen rods of different sorts and sizes, with gaudy salmon flies, some nets, a gaff and an oak coffer upon which lay a freshly caught salmon on a blue ashet. Then supper by candlelight, bed, a glitter of stars through the open window, and the ceaseless drumming of water.

By six o'clock next morning I was on the river-bank, fitting my rod together and watching in awe the great brown ribbon of water go fleetly by.

Among my most treasured possessions were half a dozen flies, and two of these I attached to the cast with exquisite care. While so engaged, a shadow fell on the grass beside me and looking up, I beheld a lank, shabby individual with a walrus moustache and an unhealthy face, who, the night before, had helped with our luggage at the station.

'Water's too heavy for flies,' said he, with an uptilting inflexion.

'This evening, yes; now, no – none whateffer. Better try with a worrum in the burrun.'

He pointed at a busy little brook which tumbled down the steep hillside and joined the main stream at the garden end.

'C-couldn't I fish with a fly in the – the burrun?' I asked, for although I wanted to catch a fish very badly, for honour's sake I would fain take it on a fly.

'Indeed, no,' he replied, slanting the tone of his voice skyward. 'You cootn't. Neffer. And that isn't a fly-rod whateffer.'

'It is,' I replied hotly. 'Yes, it is.'

But he only shook his head and repeated, 'No,' and took the rod from my hand and illustrated its awkwardness and handed it back with a wretched laugh.

If he had pitched me into the river I should have been happier.

'It is a fly-rod and it cost two guineas,' I said, and my lower lip trembled.

'Neffer,' he repeated. 'Five shillings would be too much.'

Even a small boy is entitled to some dignity.

Picking up my basket, I turned without another word and made for the hotel. Perhaps my eyes were blinded with tears, for I was about to plunge into the dark hall when a great, rough, kindly voice arrested me with:

'Easy does it.'

At the thick end of an immense salmon-rod there strode out into the sunlight the noblest figure I had ever seen.

There is no real need to describe my colonel again – I have done so already – but the temptation is too great. Standing in the doorway, the sixteen-foot rod in hand, the deer-stalker hat, besprent with flies, crowning his shaggy head, the waders, like seven-league boots, braced up to his armpits, the creel across his shoulder, a gaff across his back, he looked what he was – a god. His eyes met mine with that kind of smile one good man keeps for another.

'An early start,' he said. 'Any luck, old fellar?'

I told him I hadn't started – not yet.

'Wise chap,' said he. 'Water's a bit heavy for trouting. It'll soon run down, though. Let's vet those flies of yours.'

He took my rod and whipped it expertly.

'A nice piece – new, eh?'

'N-not quite,' I stammered; 'but I haven't used it yet, sir, in water.'

That god read men's minds.

'I know, garden practice; capital; nothing like it.'

Releasing my cast, he frowned critically over the flies – a Blue Dun and a March Brown.

'Think so?' he queried. 'You don't think it's a shade late in the season for these fancies?' I said I thought perhaps it was. 'Yes, I think you're right,' said he. 'I believe in this big water you'd do better with a livelier pattern. Teal and Red, Cock-y-bundy, Greenwell's Glory.'

I said nothing, but nodded gravely at these brave names.

Once more he read my thoughts and saw through the wicker sides of my creel a great emptiness.

'I expect you've fished most in southern rivers. These Welsh trout have a fancy for a spot of colour.'

He rummaged in the pocket of his Norfolk jacket and produced a round tin which once had held saddle soap.

'Collar on to that,' said he, 'there's a proper pickle of flies and casts in that. As a keen fisherman, you don't mind sorting 'em out. They may come in useful.'

'But, I say, you don't mean –' I began.

'Yes, go on; stick to it. All fisherman are members of the same club and I'm giving the trout a rest for a bit.' His eyes ranged the hills and trees opposite. 'I must be getting on with it before the sun's too high.'

Waving his free hand, he strode away and presently was lost to view at a bend in the road.

I think my mother was a little piqued by my abstraction during breakfast. My eyes never, for an instant, deserted the round tin box which lay open beside my plate. Within it were a paradise and a hundred miracles all tangled together in the pleasantest disorder. My mother said something about a lovely walk over the hills, but I had other plans, which included a very glorious hour which should be spent untangling and wrapping up in neat squares of paper my new treasures.

'I suppose he knows best what he wants to do,' she said.

So it came about that I was left alone and betook myself to a sheltered spot behind a rock where all the delicious disorder was remedied and I could take stock of what was mine.

I am sure there were at least six casts all set up with flies, and ever so many loose flies and one great stout, tapered cast, with a salmon fly upon it, that was so rich in splendour that I doubted if my benefactor could really have known that it was there.

I felt almost guilty at owning so much, and not until I had done full justice to everything did I fasten a new cast to my line and go a-fishing.

There is a lot said and written about beginner's luck, but none of it came my way. Indeed, I spent most of the morning extricating my line from the most fearsome tangles. I had no skill in throwing a cast with two droppers upon it and I found it was an art not to be learned in a minute. Then, from overeagerness, I was too snappy with my back cast, whereby, before many minutes had gone, I heard that warning crack behind me that betokens the loss of a tail fly. I must have spent half an hour searching the meadow for that lost fly and finding it not. Which is not strange, for I wonder has any fisherman ever found that lost fly. The reeds, the buttercups and the little people with many legs who run in the wet grass conspire together to keep the secret of its hiding place. I gave up at last, and with a feeling of shame that was only proper, I invested a new fly on the point of my cast and set to work again, but more warily.

In that hard racing water a good strain was put upon my rod, and before the morning was out it was creaking at the joints in a way that kept my heart continually in my mouth. It is the duty of a rod to work with a single smooth action and by no means to divide its performance into three sections of activity. It is a hard task for any angler to persuade his line austerely if his rod behaves thus.

When, at last, my father strolled up the river-bank, walking, to his shame, much nearer the water than a good fisherman should, my nerves were jumpy from apprehension.

'Come along. Food's ready. Done any good?' said he.

Again it was to his discredit that he put food before sport, but I told him I had had a wonderful morning, and he was glad.

'What do you want to do this afternoon, old man?' he asked.

'Fish,' I said.

'But you can't always fish.' he said.

I told him I could and I was right and have proved it for thirty years and more.

'Well, well,' he said, 'please yourself, but isn't it dull not catching anything?'

And I said, as I've said a thousand times since, 'As if it could be.'

So that afternoon I went downstream instead of up, and found myself in difficult country where the river boiled between the narrows of two hills. Stunted oaks overhung the water and great boulders opposed its flow. Presently I came to a sort of natural flight of steps – a pool and a cascade three times repeated – and there, watching the maniac fury of the waters in awe and wonderment, I saw the most stirring sight in my young life. I saw a silver salmon leap superbly from the cauldron below into the pool above. And I saw another and another salmon do likewise. And I wonder the eyes of me did not fall out of my head.

I cannot say how long I stayed watching that gallant pageant of leaping fish – in ecstasy there is no measurement of time – but at last it came upon me that all the salmon in the sea were careering past me and that if I were to realize my soul's desire I must hasten to the pool below before the last of them had gone by.

It was a mad adventure, for until I had discovered that stout cast, with the gaudy fly attached in the tin box, I had given no thought to such noble quarry. My recent possessions had put ideas into my head above my station and beyond my powers. Failure, however, means little to the young, and walking fast, yet gingerly, for fear of breaking my rod top against a tree, I followed the path downstream until I came to a great basin of water into which, through a narrow throat, the river thundered like a storm.

At the head of the pool was a plate of rocks scored by the nails of fishermen's boots, and here I sat down to wait while the salmon cast, removed from its wrapper, was allowed to soak and soften in a puddle left by the rain.

And while I waited a salmon rolled not ten yards from where I sat. Head and tail, up and down he went, a great monster of a fish, sporting and deriding me.

With that performance so near at hand, I have often wondered how I was able to control my fingers well enough to tie a figure-eight knot between the line and the cast. But I did, and I'm proud to be able to record it. Your true-born angler does not go blindly to work until he has first satisfied his conscience. There is a pride in knots, of which the laity knows nothing, and if, through neglect to tie them rightly, failure and loss should result, pride may not be restored nor conscience salved by the plea of eagerness. With my trembling fingers I bent the knot and, with a pummelling heart, launched the line into the broken water at the throat of the pool.

At first the mere tug of the water against that large fly was so thrilling to me that it was hard to believe that I had not hooked a whale. The trembling line swung round in a wide arc into a calm eddy below where I stood. Before casting afresh I shot a glance over my shoulder to assure myself there was no limb of a tree behind me to foul the fly. And this was a gallant cast, true and straight, with a couple of yards more length than its predecessor, and a wider radius. Instinctively I knew, as if the surface had been marked with an X where the salmon had risen, that my fly must pass right over the spot. As it swung by, my nerves were strained like piano wires. I think I knew that something tremendous, impossible, terrifying, was going to happen. The sense, the certitude was so strong in me that I half opened my mouth to shout a warning to the monster, not to.

I must have felt very, very young in that moment. I, who that same day had been talked to as a man by a man among men. The years were stripped from me and I was what I was – ten years old and appalled. And then, with the suddenness of a rocket, it happened. The water was cut into a swathe. I remember a silver loop bearing downward – a bright, shining, vanishing thing like the bobbin of my mother's sewing-machine – and a tug. I shall never forget the viciousness of that tug. I had my fingers tight upon the line, so I got the full force of it. To counteract a tendency to go headfirst into the spinning water below, I threw myself backward and sat down on the hard rock with a jar that shut my teeth on my tongue – like the jaws of a trap.

Luckily I had let the rod go out straight with the line, else it must have snapped in the first frenzy of the downstream rush. Little ass that I was, I tried to check the speeding line with my forefinger, with the result that it cut and burnt me to the bone. There wasn't above twenty yards of line in the reel, and the wretched contrivance was trying to be rid of the line even faster than the fish was wrenching it out. Heaven knows why it didn't snarl, for great loops and whorls were whirling like Catherine wheels, under my wrist. An instant's glance revealed the terrifying fact that there were not more than half a dozen yards left on the reel and the fish showed no signs of abating his rush. With the realization of impending and inevitable catastrophe upon me, I launched a yell for help, which, rising above the roar of the waters, went echoing down the gorge.

And then, to add to my terrors, the salmon leaped – a winging leap like a silver arch appearing and instantly disappearing upon the broken surface. So mighty, so all-powerful he seemed in that sublime moment that I lost all sense of reason and raised the rod, with a sudden jerk, above my head.

I have often wondered, had the rod actually been the two-guinea rod my imagination claimed for it, whether it could have withstood the strain thus violently and unreasonably imposed upon it. The wretched thing that I held so grimly never even put up a fight. It snapped at the ferrule of the lower joint and plunged like a toboggan down the slanting line, to vanish into the black depths of the water.

My horror at this calamity was so profound that I was lost even to the consciousness that the last of my line had run out. A couple of vicious tugs advised me of this awful truth. Then, snap! The line parted at the reel, flickered out through the rings and was gone. I was left with nothing but the butt of a broken rod in my hand and an agony of mind that even now I cannot recall without emotion.

I am not ashamed to confess that I cried. I lay down on the rock, with my cheek in the puddle where I had soaked the cast, and plenished it with my tears. For what had the future left for me but a cut and burning finger, a badly bumped behind, the single joint of a broken rod and no faith in uncles? How long I lay there weeping I do not know. Ages, perhaps, or minutes, or seconds.

I was roused by a rough hand on my shoulder and a kindly voice demanding, 'Hurt yourself, Ike Walton?'

Blinking away my tears, I pointed at my broken rod with a bleeding forefinger.

'Come! This is bad luck,' said my colonel his face grave as a stone. 'How did it happen?'

'I c-caught a s-salmon.'

'You what?' said he.

'I d-did,' I said.

He looked at me long and earnestly; then, taking my injured hand, he looked at that and nodded.

'The poor groundlings who can find no better use for a river than something to put a bridge over think all fishermen are liars,' said he. 'But we know better, eh? By the bumps and breaks and cuts I'd say you made a plucky fight against heavy odds. Let's hear all about it.'

So, with his arm round my shoulders and his great shaggy head near to mine, I told him all about it.

At the end he gave me a mighty and comforting squeeze, and he said, 'The loss of one's first big fish is the heaviest loss I know. One feels, whatever happens, one'll never –' He stopped and pointed dramatically. 'There it goes – see! Down there at the tail of the pool!'

In the broken water where the pool emptied itself into the shallows beyond, I saw the top joints of my rod dancing on the surface.

'Come on!' he shouted, and gripping my hand, jerked me to my feet. 'Scatter your legs! There's just a chance!'

Dragging me after him, we raced along by the river path to the end of the pool, where, on a narrow promontory of grass, his enormous salmon-rod was lying.

'Now,' he said, picking it up and making the line whistle to and fro in the air with sublime authority, 'keep your eyes skinned on those shallows for another glimpse of it.'

A second later I was shouting, 'There! There!'

He must have seen the rod point at the same moment, for his line flowed out and the big fly hit the water with a plop not a couple of feet from the spot.

He let it ride on the current, playing it with a sensitive touch like the brushwork of an artist.

'Half a jiffy!' he exclaimed at last. 'Wait! Yes, I think so. Cut down to that rock and see if I haven't fished up the line.'

I needed no second invitation, and presently was yelling, 'Yes – yes, you have!'

'Stretch yourself out then and collar hold of it.'

With the most exquisite care he navigated the line to where I lay stretched upon the rock. Then:

'Right you are! Good lad! I'm coming down.'

Considering his age, he leaped the rocks like a chamois.

'Now,' he said, and took the wet line delicately between his forefinger and thumb. One end trailed limply downstream, but the other end seemed anchored in the big pool where I had had my unequal and disastrous contest.

Looking into his face, I saw a sudden light of excitement dancing in his eyes.

'Odd,' he muttered, 'but not impossible.'

'What isn't?' I asked breathlessly.

'Well, it looks to me as if the top joints of that rod of yours have gone downstream.'

Gingerly he pulled up the line, and presently an end with a broken knot appeared.

'The reel knot, eh?' I nodded gloomily. 'Then we lose the rod,' said he. That wasn't very heartening news. 'On the other hand, it's just possible the fish is still on – sulking.'

'Oh!' I exclaimed.

'Now, steady does it,' he warned, 'and give me my rod.'

Taking a pair of clippers from his pocket, he cut his own line just above the cast.

'Can you tie a knot?' he asked.

'Yes,' I nodded.

'Come on, then; bend your line on to mine. Quick as lightning.'

Under his critical eye, I joined the two lines with a blood knot. 'I guessed you were a fisherman,' he said, nodding approvingly and clipped off the ends. 'And now to know the best or the worst.'

I shall never forget the music of that check reel or the suspense with which I watched as, with the butt of the rod bearing against the hollow of his thigh, he steadily wound up the wet slack line. Every instant I expected it to come drifting downstream, but it didn't. Presently it rose in a tight slant from the pool above.

'Snagged, I'm afraid,' he said, and worked the rod with an easy straining motion to and fro. 'Yes, I'm afraid – no, by Lord Bobs, he's on!'

I think it was only right and proper that I should have launched a yell of triumph as, with the spoken word, the point at which the line cut the water shifted magically from the left side of the pool to the right.

'And a fish too,' said he.

In the fifteen minutes that followed, I must have experienced every known form of terror and delight.

'Youngster,' said he, 'you should be doing this, by rights, but I'm afraid the rod's a bit above your weight.'

'Oh, go on and catch him,' I pleaded.

'And so I will,' he promised; 'unship the gaff, young 'un, and stand by to use it, and if you break the cast we'll never speak to each other again, and that's a bet.'

But I didn't break the cast. The noble, courageous, indomitable example of my river god had lent me skill and precision beyond my years. When at long last a weary, beaten, silver monster rolled within reach of my arm into a shallow eddy, the steel gaff shot out fair and true, and sank home.

And then I was lying on the grass, with my arms round a salmon that weighed twenty-two pounds on the scale and contained every sort of happiness known to a boy.

And best of all, my river god shook hands with me and called me 'partner'.

That evening the salmon was placed upon the blue ashet in the hall, bearing a little card with its weight and my name upon it.

And I am afraid I sat on a chair facing it, for ever so long, so that I could hear what the other anglers had to say as they passed by. I was sitting there when my colonel put his head out of his private sitting-room and beckoned me to come in.

'A true fisherman lives in the future, not the past, old man,' said he; 'though, for this once it 'ud be a shame to reproach you.'

I suppose I coloured guiltily – at any rate I hope so.

'We got the fish,' said he, 'but we lost the rod, and the future without a rod doesn't bear thinking of. Now' – and he pointed at a long wooden box on the floor, that overflowed with rods of different sorts and sizes – 'rummage among those. Take your time and see if you can find anything to suit you.'

'But do you mean – can I –'

'We're partners, aren't we? And p'r'aps as such you'd rather we went through our stock together.'

'Oo, sir,' I said.

'Here, quit that,' he ordered gruffly. 'By Lord Bobs, if a show like this afternoon's don't deserve a medal, what does? Now, here's a handy piece by Hardy – a light and useful tool – or if you fancy greenheart in preference to split bamboo –'

I have the rod to this day, and I count it among my dearest treasures. And to this day I have a flick of the wrist that was his legacy. I have, too, some small skill in dressing flies, the elements of which were learned in his company by candlelight after the day's work was over. And I have countless memories of that month-long, month-short friendship – the closest and most perfect friendship, pehaps, of all my life.

He came to the station and saw me off. How I vividly remember his shaggy head at the window, with the whiskered cheeks and the gunpowder marks at the corners of his eyes! I didn't cry, although I wanted to awfully. We were partners and shook hands. I never saw him again, although on my birthdays I would have coloured cards from him, with Irish, Scotch, Norwegian postmarks. Very brief they were: 'Water very low.' 'Took a good fish last Thursday.' 'Been prawning but don't like it.'

Sometimes at Christmas I had gifts – a reel, a tapered line, a fly book. But I never saw him again.

Came at last no more postcards or gifts, but in the *Fishing Gazette*, of which I was a religious reader, was an obituary telling how one of the last of the Mutiny veterans had joined the great majority. It seems he had been fishing half an hour before he died. He had taken his rod down and passed out. They had buried him at Totnes, overlooking the River Dart.

So he was no more – my river god – and what was left of him they had put into a box and buried it in the earth.

But that isn't true; nor is it true that I never saw him again. For I seldom go a-fishing but that I meet him on the river-banks.

The banks of a river are frequented by a strange company and are full of mysterious and murmurous sounds – the cluck and laughter of water, the piping of birds, the hum of insects and the whispering of wind in the willows. What should prevent a man in such a place having a word and speech with another who is not there? So much of fishing lies in imagination, and mine needs little stretching to give my river god a living form.

'With this ripple,' says he, 'you should do well.'

'And what's it to be,' say I – 'Blue Upright, Red Spinner? What's your fancy, sir?'

Spirits never grow old. He has begun to take an interest in dry-fly methods – that river god of mine, with his seven-league boots, his shaggy head and the gaff across his back.

THE RIVER GOD *1930s*

Tide-Head

HENRY WILLIAMSON

Rain fell from grey clouds over the estuary at flood-tide, and Salar leapt for the change in the water. From the hills, clouds in close pack could be seen apparently following the valley which was the estuary; but this was condensation in the colder, windy air above water. Wind from the south-west pressed skits on the waves, and the rain spread to the hills and the moor, and by nightfall every drain and runner and ditch was noisy with falling water. Through pipe and culvert and chute the water hurried, with its differing loads, matter inanimate and suspended, dead leaves, soil, tar-acids from the broken surface of second-class roads, oil, decaying things, and the gases arisen from the disturbance of mud in eddies of the river and its influent streams. Rain poured from a sky without star or moon but luminously stained by the lights of the town under whose ancient bridge the ebb moved heavily and swiftly to the river's mouth: thickly the tide ebbed, overpressed and overweighted by the volume of the spate.

There was no fishing from gravel ridge or sandbank that night. Old tree trunks and roots rode down in the grey-brown water. Far out in the bay the sea was distained when daylight came. The landscape was dissolved in falling grey rain.

Salar had gone up under the familiar piers of the Long Bridge the night before, but, meeting the freshet's thrust, he had turned aside to avoid the thick-water irritations in his gill-rakers. Under the stone wall of the quay there was an eddy of salt water, where with other salmon he rested; but the rising turbid volume of road and field washings swept the eddy away, and the fish turned and swam towards the sea. They gulped unevenly in water which, saturated with carbonic acid gas released from rotting vegetation and silt in ditches and pool eddies, was additionally acid with peat-water run from bog-plashes of the moor. Soon this brown opaque water, loaded with leaves and sticks, was absorbed in the wider waters of the estuary; and into the half-ebb Salar turned, moving across the currents until he found a good stream. Other fish moved with him.

Forward into this they felt their way, turning instantly as they ran into a layer of water which caused them to gulp with choking. This water had been cutting into the mud banks of rotted turf overlaid with sludge below the town's open sewer in the quay wall. Avoiding its acrid taints, Salar found the clearer and faster streams of the secondary freshet which now was coming down. There were no tar-acids or oil-scums in this wide and pleasant water, although leaf-fragments and black twigs were moving thickly over the bed of the fairway. It was runnable water, and he leapt, and drove quickly against its exhilarations. Finding that the good stream continued and broadened, he sought slower water by the edge of sandbank and salting, and moved up faster, but always at the verge of the main or parent stream.

Salar had moved up through this channel many times during the moon's wax and wane; he had drifted with the water, letting the tide take him, slower and slower, until the tidal pool was reached. Here fresh water had lain over the heavier salt, stagnant, chilling, brackish. Roots of trees and rocky juts were slimy with fine mud suspended and settled in the lifeless lake. Disillusioned, he had drifted back with surface flotsam and wreckage and froth which began to return the instant it reached the tide-head: every time the tide-head water had moved back without pause, waveless, assoiled, Salar with it.

But now the stream was alive, and he took life from it. This water was coloured, but not turbid. It was the spate fining down after the first load of drain water had carried away stagnant deposits of used life awaiting recreation. It was not yet water springing from the rock, but it was water enlivened by percussion and repercussion against the living rock and air of earth. A million million bubbles of air had been beaten into it by the force of gravity, a million million fragments of rock had dragged against and resisted its momentum; every swirl and tear and crashing fall had been attended by watchful air. It was saturated with oxygen, sparkling water, life-giving water, faithful to the spirit of Salmon. It was grand running water, and the fish leapt to it, fleeing fast after shadowy companions in play, and, as the spirit sank in them after its exaltation, boring steadily onwards again.

Salar passed under a railway bridge, its tubular iron pillars ringed by marks of old tides. Above, the river ran under sloping banks of mud, gliddery stuff, frittered by castings of ragworms which had their vertical tunnels deep in black sand beneath the mud. This sand was black with the carbon of ancient oak-leaves and twigs and turf covered by salt of tides after the sea-wall had been raised to reclaim marshland otherwise drowned by every spring-tide. At low tide draining water from the marsh gushed through wooden traps hinged above the culverts opening under the wall; the pressure of high tide kept the traps closed, and behind them the water accumulated until the tidal level dropped.

Enclosed and dociled within grassy walls, the river wound eel-like through the marsh. Soon Salar was passing under another railway bridge. He slid forward by a pillar against which the stream was divided and flung out, causing under-water recoil. He was lifted up and back, but swam out of the turbulence, which would have drowned a powerful human swimmer, with three easy sinuations.

The smooth sandy bottom of the estuary was left behind. The water-flow was torn by rocks and boulders of angular and linear shape. They lay between the sea's abrasiveness and the river's smaller polishing. Seaweed grew poorly on the lumps of rock, fretted by alien silt during tidal flows and then swilled by enervating saltless water: enduring alien air while awaiting the sea's brief benison twice every day. And because it was broken water, mud-streaming, unrhythmic, Salar ceased his leaping. To avoid bruise and jar, constantly he had to rise, to swing sideways, to pause and waver before feeling a way around sharp rocks and the rough higgledy-piggledies of the formless watercourse. It was hybrid of sea and river; it was artificial, man-altered, unnatural. The water spirit did not dwell there; its laws and verities were changed and obstructed. Like all hybrids, it was unproductive, outside its cycle established in the great orbit of the sun. The life it created and nourished – except the ragworms which were there temporarily – mullet, bass, flatfish, eels, and shrimps, was tidal-transient. One day the deposits of carbonized leaves and turf, on which the worms fed, would be tunnelled through, assimilated, refined as silt and raised to the surface as castings; then the worms would perish. It was negative land and negative water, belonging not to composition or life, but to dissolution and death.

Salmon, stream-shapen and wave-wrought, were made uneasy, fatigued, in the pill or creek at low water. Many injured themselves, bruising skin and flesh as they hastened to pass through the area. Salar had journeyed here many times before, but always on the flowing tide, in water a fathom deep and more. But this was fresh water rushing in spate over a bed silted by the slower, lesser streams of more than a hundred days.

A small trout was washed past Salar, belly upwards, poisoned by gas bursting suddenly out of a black wad of old leaves in the eddy where it had been resting. Only a small part of the gas had been absorbed as the bubbles wriggled upwards, but it was enough to poison the fish after three gulps.

Salar pressed on, although discomforted and gillstung, because the water cleared as he went forward. He swam around the wider bends, where the current was less strong, and where usually an eddy moved against the main direction of the river. By the roots of the first oak, a massive tree growing in knotted strength out of rock bared cliff-like by a streamlet entering the creek, he rested, hovering near the surface to avoid the silt-drag below.

While he was hovering there he saw a form move beside him which made him turn and swim away at his fastest speed. The form was seal-like, and slightly smaller than himself, but he recognized it instantly as an enemy. This was a young otter, which had been equally startled to see so large an object appear beside it. The otter had come down to play in the water, after hunting rabbits in the hillside oakland; for during a spate it could not hunt in water. Realizing, after the thudding shock of Salar's acceleration, that it was fish, the otter began to hunt around the ledges of rock in which the oak's roots were grown, hoping to surprise fish there. And, groping and peering, the otter came face to face with Trutta the sea-trout, who immediately drove past the otter and knocked it sprawling. Trutta had met otters before, and knew them for slow swimmers who could not hurt him unless they got him into shallow water.

Searching the bed of the eddy, where water turned against shillets at the base of the rocky wall, the otter came upon a smaller fish which was resting there, cowed by the presence of a small river-lamprey which was eating into its side. The fish was one of the six grilse which had travelled from the Island Race and Gralaks at the full of the moon.

The grilse was cowering there, its body curved and taut. The otter sprang sideways off webbed hind-feet with a sweep of its thick tail and as the grilse started off its snapping teeth bit the lamprey, pulling it away from the fish's flank. Swimming up, the young otter crawled out along a root and began to eat the lamprey tail-first, as it had eaten eels with its mother and fellow-cubs during the eel-migration of the previous fall. The taste of the lamprey was unfamiliar, and the otter left it, departing into the wood again to hunt rabbits. Shore rats found the lamprey later, and ate it up.

Meantime Salar had gone up the river, which ran slower through a long pit with rocky side and bottom under the oakwood. Now the water was running slower and clearer, and he swam comfortably through a regular surge of water. The opposite bank was walled, but rough marshy ground was giving way to grassy pasture. Here the first alder grew; the true river was not far away, for alders cannot grow near salt water.

So Salar came at last to the natural river, where it wound widely and was allowed to make its own pools and backwaters to cut into its ancient bed and form its own islets. Its gravel was clean and its music was sharp after the sombrous rythms of the sea.

from SALAR THE SALMON *1935*

Tom Brown and Velveteens

THOMAS HUGHES

Now came on the may-fly season; the soft hazy summer weather lay sleepily along the rich meadows by Avon side, and the green and grey flies flickered with their lazy up and down flight over the reeds and the water and the meadows in myriads upon myriads . . .

Every little pitiful coarse fish in the Avon was on the alert for the flies, and gorging his wretched carcase with hundreds daily, the gluttonous rogues! and every lover of the gentle craft was out to avenge the poor may-flies.

So one fine Thursday afternoon, Tom, having borrowed East's new rod, started by himself to the river. He fished for some time with small success: not a fish would rise at him; but as he prowled along the bank he was presently aware of mighty ones feeding in a pool on the opposite side, under the shade of a huge willow-tree. The stream was deep there, but some fifty yards below was a shallow for which he made off hot-foot; and forgetting landlords, keepers, solemn prohibitions of the Doctor, and everything else, pulled up his trousers, plunged across, and in three minutes was creeping along on all fours towards the clump of willows.

It isn't often that great chub, or any other coarse fish, are in earnest about anything, but just then they were thoroughly bent on feeding, and in half an hour Master Tom had deposited three thumping fellows at the foot of the giant willow. As he was baiting for a fourth pounder, and just going to throw in again, he became aware of a man coming up the bank not one hundred yards off. Another look told him that it was the under-keeper. Could he reach the shallow before him? No, not carrying his rod. Nothing for it but the tree; so Tom laid his bones to it, shinning up as fast as he could, and dragging up his rod after him. He had just time to reach and crouch along a huge branch some ten feet up, which stretched over the river, when the keeper arrived at the clump. Tom's heart beat fast as he came under the tree; two steps more and he would have passed, when as ill-luck would have it, the gleam on the scales of the dead fish caught his eye, and he made a dead point at the foot of the tree. He picked up the fish one by one; his eye and touch told him that they had been alive and feeding within the hour. Tom crouched lower along the branch, and heard the keeper beating the clump. 'If I could only get the rod hidden,' thought he, and began gently shifting it to get it alongside of him; 'willow-trees don't throw out straight hickory shoots twelve feet long, with no leaves, worse luck.' Alas! the keeper catches the rustle, and then a sight of the rod, and then of Tom's hand and arm.

'Oh, be up ther', be'ee?' says he, running under the tree. 'Now you come down this minute.'

'Tree'd at last,' thinks Tom, making no answer, and keeping as close as possible, but working away at the rod, which he takes to pieces: 'I'm for it unless I can starve him out.' And then he begins to meditate getting along the bank for a plunge, and scramble to the other side; but the small branches are so thick, and the opposite bank so difficult, that the keeper will have lots of time to get round by the ford before he can get out, so he gives that up. And now he hears the keeper beginning to scramble up the trunk. That will never do; so he scrambled himself back to where his branch joins the trunk, and stands with lifted rod.

'Hullo, Velveteens, mind your finger if you come any higher.' The keeper stops and looks up, and then with a grin says, 'Oh! be you, be it, young measter? Well, here's luck. Now I tells 'ee to come down at once, and it'll be best for 'ee.'

'Thank'ee, Velveteens, I'm very comfortable,' said Tom, shortening his rod in his hand, and preparing for battle.

'Werry well, please yourself,' says the keeper, descending however to the ground again, and taking his seat on the bank; 'I bean't in no hurry, so you may take your time. I'll larn'ee to gee honest folk names afore I've done with 'ee.'

'My luck as usual,' thinks Tom, 'what a fool I was to give him a black. If I'd called him "keeper" now I might get off. The return match is all his way.'

The keeper quietly proceeded to take out his pipe, fill, and light it, keeping an eye on Tom, who now sat disconsolately across the branch, looking at the keeper – a pitiful sight for men and fishes. The more he thought of it the less he liked it. 'It must be getting near second calling-over,' thinks he. Keeper smokes on stolidly. 'If he takes me up I shall be flogged safe enough. I can't sit here all night. Wonder if he'll rise at silver.'

'I say, keeper,' said he meekly, 'let me go for two bob?'

'Not for twenty neither,' grunts his persecutor.

And so they sat on till long past second calling-over, and the sun came slanting in through the willow branches, and telling of locking-up near at hand.

'I'm coming down, keeper,' said Tom at last, with a sigh, fairly tired out. 'Now what are you going to do?'

'Walk'ee up to School and give'ee over to the Doctor, them's my orders,' says Velveteens, knocking the ashes out of his fourth pipe, and standing up and shaking himself.

'Very good,' said Tom; 'but hands off, you know. I'll go with you quietly, so no collaring or that sort of thing.'

Keeper looked at him a minute – 'Werry good,' said he at last; and so Tom descended and wended his way drearily by the side of the keeper up to the School-house, where they arrived just at locking-up. As they passed the School gates, the Tadpole and several others who were standing there caught the state of things, and rushed out, crying, 'Rescue!' but Tom shook his head, so they only followed to the Doctor's gate and went back sorely puzzled.

How changed and stern the Doctor seemed from the last time Tom was up there, as the keeper told the story, not omitting to state how Tom had called him blackguard names. 'Indeed, sir,' broke in the culprit, 'it was only Velveteens.' The Doctor only asked one question.

'You know the rule about the banks, Brown?'

'Yes, sir.'

'Then wait for me tomorrow, after first lesson.'

'I thought so,' muttered Tom.

'And about the rod, sir?' went on the keeper. 'Master told me as we might have all the rods . . .'

'Oh, please, sir,' broke in Tom, 'the rod isn't mine.' The Doctor looked puzzled; but the keeper, who was a good-hearted fellow, and melted at Tom's evident distress, gave up his claim. Tom was flogged next morning and a few days afterwards met Velveteens, and presented him with half a crown for giving up the rod claim and they became sworn friends; and I regret to say that Tom had many more fish from under the willow that may-fly season, and was never caught again by Velveteens.

from TOM BROWN'S SCHOOLDAYS *1857*

The Lake of the Red Trout

H. A. MANHOOD

The two of us, fisherman and novice, came upon the mountain lake quite unexpectedly in the evening of a long, dusty sunblurred day, and the discovery was as refreshing as ice in the mouth. Trout were everywhere rising with the quiet ripple of earnest feeders, the successive targets having the likeness of eyes widening in merry, welcoming surprise. This was the wine of the mountains for which we searched, we assured each other, as we gazed from a pike-head ledge: a lake of decided character, wonderfully cupped in curiously knotted stone, and sternly different from the greenpan lowland waters in which we had fished for twenty days past.

Since dayspring we had travelled roads without regard for their surfaces or thought for the car, viewing many lakes with critical eyes, questioning warmly interested cottagers (who, at first, misled by our odd clothes and black-sheeted burden of collapsible boat and camping gear, invariably mistook us for journeymen undertakers or outriders of a circus) on the subject of fish and weather, and pondering secretly at times on the wisdom of travelling without maps; fortifying ourselves with promises of a rich discovery, recalling old thrills, old camps found without compass, Rich only hoping always with the strange, illogical faith of the true fisherman who, as it is said, sees fish in every soup-plate, and hatches flies in his armpits when nature fails in her covenants. We crossed sunken bogs veined and fretted like old leaves, where turf had been cut since the Saints were young, and virgin bogs with remote cuttings glowing like the marks of branding irons, all brightly fleeced with cotton-grass upon which melancholy asses browsed as if in the hope of renewing their grey and matted hairs. We searched for the arms of signposts which had fallen from their sockets, but only undecipherable snail-shine marked the bleached wood. Villages blinked awake as we passed, pigs turning in their sleep and fowls skipping from comfortable dust pits in the road with hysterical comment. Heads peered from doorways like flowers drawn in the wind, bright wondering eyes following us in our course . . . The civic guard would pause in the nursing of his infant son to regard us good-humouredly, prepared to advise us minutely, no whit dismayed or affronted when we passed with no more than a choking gift of dust. Sometimes a dog raced with us, and Rich would talk encouragingly, holding the car at level speed. A worthy runner was rewarded with a ship's biscuit and a poor one with a hoot of derision which must have penetrated deeply, if drooping, woebegone head and tail and shambling gait fairly indicated the way of the spirit.

Eight o'clock found us some forty miles west of Cork on a well-graded but peculiarly stony road rising towards a great half-moon range of mountains. A stream ran beside the valley road – a pleasant stream with dark trouty pools and hissing falls. Ruminating on the brink, we imagined a mountain-shadowed lake, a fine oval mirror linked to this handsome splinter necklace. The vision became an enticing fact after conversation with a toothless, bare-footed old dame, who carried a splendid crown of butter on a bit of slate. Approaching nimbly down the road, avoiding flints by enviable instinct, she stood and laughed at the metal rabbit on the radiator cap, and then came and peered shyly round at us, feet deftly shuffling a space clear of larger piercing stones. Was a lake connected with the stream, we asked, and she answered with her eyes on the tobacco with which Rich was filling his pipe –

'Surely! Surely! As grand a lake as the Holy One ever made is away up there in the lap of the mountains. 'Tis called Nam-brach-derg, it is, and 'twill be glad to see ye, for 'tis lonely it must be with only Moriarty and his woman living on the verge and them a little mad with the bleakness of it all.'

And were there fish in the lake?

The old woman smiled and nodded wisely: 'Surely! Surely! for didn't Nam-brach-derg mean the Lake of the Red Trout, and isn't it a pity ye have no Irish to be understanding the country properly. But there, 'tis past understanding entirely we are, and the Irish a dying fire at the back of the world.' She sighed and scratched one foot with the other, eyeing us shrewdly, smiling delightedly when Rich offered his pouch. Adroitly balancing the butter slate in the crook of her arm, she pressed tobacco into her cheek and returned the pouch with a merry wink, blessing us in well-sounding Irish as we climbed into the car. Turning back for a last sight of her we saw her standing with her red skirt folded over the butter to shield it from our dust. She had not yet begun to chew the tobacco, but was saving it for her solitude as a child might save a rare sweet. 'So long!' we called, and she nodded, and, without lowering her eyes, scooped a finger-tuft of butter to her mouth to improve the tobacco. We wished that we had asked her name. 'A fine old Friday Soul,' commented Rich, and so she became for us the Friday Soul, always to be remembered for her mixing of butter and tobacco.

Very soon the road parted with the stream. Hedges dropped away, and only occasional wind-twisted thorns and knuckles of gorse appeared above the cliff edge on our left. We passed a derelict cottage of fire-blackened stone, empty save for a truculent yellow-eyed ram, and a shabby pair of crows nesting in the lichen-patched chimney. Mountain sheep stared down at us from the higher slopes, pausing momentarily in their chewing, the lambs simulating an elderly indifference until an unexpected bumping or slide of locked wheels broke their nerve and sent them panicking in all directions. Already we had climbed two miles. The road could be seen ahead, a dark bristle-edged line swinging in a wide upward curve against the olive-green and rock-littered mountains. Four miles at least to go before we should reach the only basin which seemed at all likely to contain a lake, and from which the stream appeared to drain. The road in its surface and bends reminded us of a river-bed. We recalled the Gap of Dunloe and a particular coast road in Donegal, and endeavoured to make merry over present difficulties. Sometimes a spray of stones would rattle over the edge as we rounded elephant rocks and leaning bastions, and unexpected echoes would rise like brisk laughter at our expense. With a show of carelessness we tried to distinguish a back axle note above the bumpings of the springs, but so many were the squeaks and grunts that accuracy in diagnosis was impossible. 'If she goes, she goes,' declared Rich with philosophic emphasis, adding happily, 'Anyway, the lake can hardly be overfished, even by birds.'

A cold upsweeping wind brought the smell of burning turf to our nostrils, and we saw, far down the valley, a black and smoking strip of bogland. 'It was probably burning long before the Friday Soul was born . . .' The thought occupied us for many minutes and, slowly, the genius of the mountains entered into us, and we were cool and content where we had been fevered and out of humour. A well-rounded green-tinged mass of cloud vanished behind a serrated ridge like a bunch of grapes into a hungry mouth, and it seemed an appropriate nourishment, an explanation of the grape-bloom that was now upon every crag and slope. A distant water-splash sparkled as might wine leaking to waste. Two bell-wethers wrangled together in the valley, making merry jangling music suggestive of convivial occasions. The frenzied boiling of the radiator, and the snatch and lunge of the car over outcropping rocks, seemed but matter for amusement in such a perfect cradle for poetry.

The road ended suddenly, unexpectedly. Driving through tunnelled rocks, we emerged into a quarry-like arena from which sheep-paths only meandered onwards. The place was like the inside of a shell, and as sound is prisoned in a shell, so were our thoughts prisoned. Where was the lake? Evidently we should have to climb. We had cherished hopes of driving to the brink and pitching camp between car and lake. So often had we done this that it had become a habit of mind to anticipate absolute convenience. Still, wasn't this the Lake of the Red Trout, something different and new in our experience? Its inaccessibility was part of its charm. So we argued as we stood there, cut off from the wind, and solemnly regarded by five elderly sheep, who stood like a suspicious reception committee close-grouped upon the path which appeared most likely to lead to heart's desire. Only at the last moment of approach did they turn tail, and we laughed at their undignified flight and were at once silent again, for violent echoes filled the craggy shell, the sounds damping us by their piercing strangeness. Thoughtfully we climbed out of the basin into the wind again, stepping among tufted heath and cotton-grass, casting about for a direction. A magnificent perpendicular cliff-face towered ahead, silvered here and there with slow-sliding water that was like a queer breaking sweat. But the dividing slope that prevented a glimpse of its heels was vividly green, water-nourished, as we discovered after a tentative move.

Time, however, was fast making its round. We were anxious for a sight of the promised water, and camp must be soon fixed. There seemed no way round the treacherous green, so we stepped squarely forward, water bubbling high, the whole slope quaking as we foundered on, loud sucking noises sounding after we had passed. An anxious minute and we were safely across, hurrying over heath and great humped rocks that were like peering heads, to a lichened rampart which barred us from clear vision. Jostling each other in our eagerness, we craned forward, and were together awed and comforted. Stretching downward under our eyes was a great broken slope, toothed with white-bleached tree-stumps and limestone quoins, and gloomy with burnt heather, among which scorched-looking sheep browsed with fatalistic determination. At the foot of the slope was the lake, large and splendid and ringed by breaking trout, walled by the earlier seen cliff which descended straightly into the water the oval length of the lake, dropping in magnificent crags and overlips down to meet the heather slopes on either side. It was as if the seat of a massive straight-backed throne had been made to hold water. A sinister place, Rich thought, in the present light, only redeemed by the breaking trout. We could hear the wind against the cliff, a low defeated sound in the stillness. The rock-face was deep-seamed and creviced, as if anciently scribbled over by a master-graver, splashed with light in curious manner as if someone of lighter soul – perhaps old Moriarty, of whom the Friday Soul had told us – had sought to efface some part of the runic warning. Now a mass of cloud settled upon the cliff-top, and it was as if a great fist were scratching the ragged pate in perplexity at our coming. Distant at the end of the lake, Moriarty's cottage lay like an old lobster-pot, and near it was a boat, a fish to bait the same pot, the Novice thought, then started, for Rich had seen the boat, and was wondering aloud whether we might borrow it. 'Better than the collapsible,' he mused. A wild sad cry, perfectly expressing the dour spirit of the place, surprised us both, echoing as a stone echoes in its bouncing down a well, and we saw a buzzard soar out from the cliff, circling and hovering by a miracle of physical understanding of wind and air, swerving inwards again to its white-splashed roost while echoes of its cry still were flung the length of the gleaming lake.

Sighing a little at the dying light, Rich turned away. 'Time enough for a cast or so before dark,' he said, and lurched and splashed his way hurriedly back to the car.

'But what of the camp?' Practical and with a care for comfort, the Novice followed.

'Pitch it where you like.'

'And supper?'

'Biscuits and chocolate will do if you can't manage to trim a fire.'

'Imbecile!' retorted the Novice lovingly.

Very well we understood each other, the one in his simplicity valuing a good fish well caught far above food and comfort; and the other, being but a novice and with a true English need of snugness, finding utter pleasure in the tight line only when assured that house and belly are in happy order. Quickly but with care, Rich unstraps rods and reaches for the tackle-bags. He will not stop for waders, and hurries off with a length of gut soaking in his mouth and his hands occupied with the screwing of landing net into handle and the fitting of rod joints together.

'Good luck!' calls the Novice as he begins his search for kindling and level tent square, and Rich mumbles a characteristic reply, 'There's no such thing as luck in good fishing – but I know what you mean.'

Within half an hour the camp was fixed for the night, the tent secure against unlikely yet possible wind and rain, sleeping-bags disposed, water brought from a rock trickle fifty yards away, fire burning well, coffee simmering; and a rabbit, killed that morning by a wheel of the car, frying in the pan in butter which we had helped to churn. Enamel plates are propped to heat, food-box spread as table; jam, biscuits, chocolates, and apples piled close to hand, and all is ready. But the Novice hesitates to whistle. He climbs and peers down at the lake, beautiful in the last reflected light, steel-blue and shining in its lapping as if dusted with powdered gems; sees Rich casting from a spoon-point with unfailing artistry. The trout had ceased to rise, but he is reaching for them in their water pockets. Five more minutes and the lake will be dimmed. At the extreme end of the lake, where Moriarty's cottage seems to cower under its ledge, a figure watches; Moriarty himself, it must be, comes like a spider to the edge of his web, waiting and watching without movement. Is he resentful of our intrusion? We should have approached him before fishing, but time was so short. The morning would do as well. After explanation and apology he might, as Rich hoped, offer his boat with true Irish generosity. 'Sure and ye must take she whenever's the fancy's upon ye. 'Tis sorry I am she's untidy a bit, but there, bless ye, I had no feeling at all ye were coming. *Next* year now and I'll have her grand for ye, ladylike enough to mix with the best from Athlone.' So another had promised us and so might Moriarty. Strange and chilling to the soul it must be to live always in the shadow of such a masterful cliff. The Novice sedulously nurses his feeling for comfort, and loudly whistles for the return of the enthusiast, the sound seeming to race round and round that enormous stone cup and curl itself snakily, restrainingly, about the arm of Rich; for he pauses, then waves emphatically and winds in his line, trudging upwards with thoughtful air.

The Novice waits by the camp-fire, toasting a fragment of cheese. He hears Rich cross the quaggy slope, breathing hard, then pause to stamp moisture from his shoes before marching to the fire. 'Smells good!' he declares, and sits to unlace his shoes, pull off soaked stockings, and wriggle his feet perilously close to the glowing turf.

'What luck?' The Novice empties fat from the pan with sympathetic gesture. Already he has seen the empty net and translated the absent-minded expression upon the face of Rich.

'Just one bite.' Transferring a leg of rabbit from one hand to the other, Rich reaches into a pocket and tosses a miserable, muddy-coloured, four-inch trout across. 'And I nearly broke the net in landing him! Happened to slip on some hair weed. Plenty of fish rising, but 'twas a kind of bat and ball they played with my flies. Can't understand it at all.'

'Perhaps the clouds were the wrong shape for good fishing, or maybe the wind was in the wrong key. Did you try the May-bee?' Gently the Novice quizzes and offers excuse, having long ago realized the necessity of excuse to the unlucky fisherman.

But Rich is in no mood for banter. 'Not a bit funny!' He flings a bone from sight and rakes an ember to fire his pipe, gazing reflectively. 'It was queer down there by the water; like trying to fish inside a glass bowl, yourself inside and the fish beyond the glass. I could hear the flies scraping across the water. Trout came and whacked them with their tails, breaking wild, as they say, but not so much wildly as with intelligent sarcasm, it seemed to me. It was just as if someone had told them that those flies weren't good to eat. Fine trout, most of them, well over half a pound. But still, there it is. Tomorrow we'll borrow that boat down the lake and spend all we know, and if we hav'n't enough trout for a reunion supper by night, well, I'll take to prawning!'

The Novice nods over the coffee-pot. Slowly the fire crumbled, surrounding rocks glowing like the great red cheeks of approving giants. Night is fast soaking down upon us. Far down the valley a light swings in erratic dance for several minutes; then blinks out as the cottager, satisfied that cows and fowls are secure, re-enters his dwelling. Now a cold wind drives like a tide across the mountains, filling every niche, whipping sparks from our fire, and shaking heath and gorse until the air is loud with a creaking and sighing as of flailing broken wings.

Rich taps the dottle from his pipe, and carefully damps the fire, hanging shoes and stockings where the wind will dry them. 'To bed, my son.'

Five minutes later we are comfortably relaxed. The winds bumps against the tent, but we are not disturbed. Rich sighs and turns a little. 'We'll try Eagan's Mayflies tomorrow.' The Novice drowsily imagines a great Mayfly swooping like a gull and lifting trout to our ready net. 'Sure, and can't we fly them like kites?' But only a derisive grunt answers him, and presently we sleep.

We awoke late the following morning for all our firm resolves. A great wedge of sunlight seemed to be forcing the tent in two. We rolled over and eyed each other, guessing at the hour, full of amiable blame. Scattering his clothes in a movement, Rich found his watch. 'Half-past nine, mother o'mine!' Hastily he wriggled from the sleeping-bag, snatched a towel, and scrambled out of the tent. But, instead of prancing to the water dip across the way, he stood and stared, hand pausing in its scratching. 'Hello!' A slow voice answered him, 'Good morning t'ye,' said Rich recovered from his astonishment sufficiently to cap the greeting. Intensely curious, the Novice rolled forward, peering between the legs of Rich, seeing no one at first, then meeting the gaze of a ragged old man squatting upon an upturned bucket against the car, his great hands stroking the fishing-rods loosely tied upon the running-board. He was a quaint old fellow, with a white bristling growth of beard upon his brown starved-looking face. Pale blue eyes gazed from sunken sockets, curling lashes looking like old thorns above deep pools.

His sharp nose seemed to sail over the broken waves of his lips. His hat appeared to be the top half of the sleeve of a frieze jacket, roughly folded and stitched. A thick, black, woollen scarf was round his neck, although the day was already hot enough to suggest sunspots. Great varicoloured patches covered his trousers, like crusts of lichen, while his boots were astonishingly like little barrels.

At the sight of the Novice he nodded extravagantly. 'I thought there were two of ye,' he said slowly, and grinned amiably. Producing a stumpy pipe, so burnt that it looked like a cinder raked from the fire, he began filling it with a mixture of tobacco and dust and wool emptied from a pocket. Hastily, perhaps remembering occasions when he himself had been forced to smoke a similar mixture, Rich rummaged for his pouch, forcing it upon the old man. 'Help yourself.'

'Me?' The old fellow scratched his nose in a startled way, examined the tobacco closely, and accepted a meagre pinch. 'I'll try it,' he said, as if uncertain whether it would suit his palate. He stared up. 'I'm Moriarty. I live down there. I saw ye last night.'

'Ah, yes, we were coming to see you.'

'About the fishing? Ye've heard maybe of the monster that is below, and would be catching him and earning fame the world over? Well, maybe ye will, and 'tis Moriarty himself will be helping ye, for 'tis a curse and a terror this beast is. Down below the cliff he lies in a sort of castle under water. 'Twas my sonny did see him first twelve years agone, and 'twas so frightened he was, and him no more than a child, that he fell and was drowned. That's why we must be catching the beast, d'ye understand me? Ye've strong tackle?'

'The strongest there is.' Rich went and sat beside the old man. 'Tell me more. What kind of fish would it be, this monster? And have none fished for it before?'

'God only knows what kind it is, but for sure 'tis of a kind and size ye've never heard of before. One of the priests from the village did fish for him once, but he sickened and died within a week, and I'm thinking 'twas the fish that blackened his soul with its spite and wished him dead. 'Tis as big as a curragh he is, this fish, if fish ye can call him, and him all scarred as if he'd been stabbed and stoned and his teeth all broken with the age of him. Terrible teeth they are still. Often I find trout floating down there, and 'tis bitten in two they are, clean as ye'd slice a stick, and 'tis that is the old devil's idea of fun, to be murdering them gaily.'

'Is it a pike?'

'Nay, 'tis a greater than a pike, but there, 'tis yourselves shall see, and that soon, God willing. Will ye try for him?' The old man eyed us anxiously in turn.

'That we will,' Rich reassured him quickly, 'and be glad of the opportunity. We shall be needing a boat, though.'

''Tis mine ye shall have and myself to be showing ye the place.' The old man flapped his long arms in his excitement. 'Quick now! 'Tis a great day this will be and the end of that great murdering devil if only your gear is strong enough to be holding him. Give me something to be carrying now, and I'll away down below and fix the boat . . .'

'Little enough to be carrying, and that we can manage.'

'But he's a hell of a great beast.'

'The bigger the better. We like them that way, and will come prepared.' Rich's confidence had a calming effect. Moriarty banged his pipe upon a stone with splintering force as if killing a fish, and shambled away, shouting directions.

We watched him go. Rich, still holding the towel in one hand, careless of flies on his naked body, began raking over the contents of a tackle-bag. 'Where did we put the Circus Spoon?'

The Circus Spoon was an enormous spinner bought years before after reading a volume of Irish fishing stories. Never yet used, it nevertheless figures in several excellent tales which Rich tells, preferably by night, when none can see our shudders of amusement. Now it seems that the moment of the Circus Spoon has come. The Novice ponders and names its whereabouts.

'An odd yarn. What did you make of it?'

'It sounds rather like a pike. Logically it can't be anything else. Theoretically pike exterminate trout in a lake, but they've been known to be neighbours before. Whatever it is we'll try for it and pick up some trout by the way.'

'Good. It would be great to be hooked into something quite outside the range of *The Fishing Gazette* – a giant pike or some other entirely outlandish fish. Just think . . .'

'I'm thinking.'

Rich and the Novice imagine great scenes, the one superintending the transport and stuffing of the monster, and the other writing a precise account of the capture with full details of the difficulty in weighing it accurately; how a small boy was seized with convulsions at sight of the fish; of strange things found in its belly. In later years fishermen would visit the lake, row reverently over the spot where it was hooked, recount the long struggle towards the shore, how the gunwale was splintered by a blow of the great tail, of the blood that streamed from its eyes when it was finally killed with hatchet blows . . .

The Novice stared bemusedly as Rich spoke. 'What about breakfast?'

Ah, yes, breakfast! It was soon over, that particular breakfast. Unwashed crocks were piled together, and the tents secured against the beasts of the mountain. Stout sea-rods were tied with dainty split canes and greenhearts for the passage to the lake. The largest of the three gaffs was filed to a needle-point. The Circus Spoon lay with a nine-inch tope reel among wire traces and lesser spoons. Materials for lunch were tossed together. A last survey and we were ready, hardly conscious that we had neither shaved nor combed our hair or cleaned our teeth.

The morning was altogether too perfect from a fisheman's point of view. The light was too strong, shadows too crisp. We could only hope that a little night-gloom remained on the lake. Occasional clouds raced before a strong west wind like scattered hounds upon a scent. A heat shimmer was in the valley and rocks were scorching to the touch. Sheep grazed with dreamy persistence. A hot scent of gorse and heather came in quick breaths. The descent to the lake was quickly made. Together we trotted and stumbled precariously among great bleached rocks and stumps, holding the rods high above our heads for safety, Rich humming softly to himself in happy preoccupation. The lake was magnificent in the full light of morning, the wind breaking it into a silver fleece. The buzzard was waiting high on its pitch, a lonely barb against the blue of the sky. Distant mountains were beautifully furred, and it was as if leopards basked in the stillness of full physical delight. Now the shadow of a cloud strode across the cliff-face like a moth across a wall and was gone. Bright threads of water that trickled over high crags like silver-haired wens on a great brooding face. At one point a stream sprayed outwards in a fine plumy fan which seemed to consume itself.

Now a boat was crossing the length of the lake, impelled, it seemed, by bright tumbling blades, Moriarty bending heroically over the oars. We waited upon the stony shore for him, Rich busy with casts and lines, assembling rods and discussing the merits of flies in loving phrases. As the boat came nearer we could hear the thrust of water, the squeaking of ungreased thole-pins and the wheezy breath of Moriarty himself, all strangely loud and clear in the stillness. At twenty yards he hailed us excitedly, breaking his stroke to peer round and point at a spot directly under the opposite cliff. 'That's where he is!' his shout bumping and echoing explosively.

'The echo might explain why the trout are so shy. They hear too much.' Rich spun the Circus Spoon on its swivel and pulled with all his strength. 'If we do hook Old Mystery he'll have to dance to our tune.'

The boat grounded, Moriarty splashing ashore through two feet of water as if the water were but an illusion. 'Are ye ready?' He seemed younger as he peered closely at Rich as he tied a cast. 'Begob, and that's a gentleman's knot.' Sighting the Circus Spoon he pounced upon it, stroking it and trying the hooks in his horny thumb. 'And is this for *him*? 'Tis the best ye have? Well, we'll be trying it, but, mind ye, 'tis a terrible brute he is, and him with the drowning of my sonny on his soul, and no pity at all inside him.'

Splashing again to the boat, he dragged it ashore, climbed inside, and began bailing out gallons of water with an old saucepan. ''Tis a bit wet she is what with the sun beating on her, and she not tasting water since Holy Thursday; but ye'll not be minding that, for won't our minds be on the catching of that great devil and not on the dampness of our feet? If ye can but make him splash, then 'tis meself will be finishing him!' Proudly he unwound an old sack, revealing a rusted flintlock gun to our astonished gaze. 'One fair shot at him and he'll be finished entirely!'

'And ourselves, too,' Rich murmured, and we resolved privately that never should that gun be fired while we were near. Fishing had ceased to be the quiet meditative pastime that the Novice had once imagined it to be. Doubt had entered his cautious soul. Ever since the day we had ferried a drunken squireen, together with his bicyle and a frantic pig, across Corrib on a day of squalls, and been upset on the way, he had pondered a disclaimer of the popular belief. But now was no time for studied inquiry. All was ready, we were assured, and Rich stepped forward with extreme care into the stern, methodically dampening the flintlock with a handful of water while Moriarty peered at a weakness in the keel. Next, Moriarty himself scrambled aboard, muddling the oars and calling instructions which the Novice, in his own interest, could only ignore. A heave, and an anxious moment balanced upon the bow, and the boat was afloat and the Novice inboard. Two eggs were in the bows together with a litter of old canvas and straw. Search failed to reveal the hen, and the Novice settled down to watch the straining back of Moriarty, wondering whether he should offer to take an oar, but dismissing the thought after a glance at the patched and splintered pair in use. Already, on that trip, he had broken two perfectly sound oars, as they said, and the breaking of another would weigh too heavily on an unreliable conscience.

We crossed the lake at a fair pace, Rich casting in the hope of a trout, somewhat to Moriarty's amusement. 'Why don't ye be trying a worm or a mite of bacon instead of they bits o' feather?' His astonishment was complete when Rich brought to the net a twelve-ouncer. 'Sure and it's just luck! I'm only hoping we'll have the same with him we're after.'

Rich smiled his own sure smile, and, before we had reached the head of the lake, had hooked and missed a second trout, smaller than the first, but sizeable, whereat Moriarty scrubbed his nose on his sleeve. 'Just luck,' he reiterated; 'ye might just as well try and catch 'em with a needle and cotton. Sport? Why yes, I suppose 'tis sport, but 'tis like buying time to waste and an empty belly for your trouble!'

Still, his respect for Rich had increased, and he now did exactly as he was directed, not quite willingly, for he still had the idea of sport in his mind, and thought perhaps that Old Mystery had interested us less than our plans for the capture of him. Rich questioned him again as to the whereabouts of the monster; but Moriarty was compass-sure, and we moved slowly within a dozen yards of the rock-face under the cliff, Rich trolling the Circus Spoon and the Novice casting where he would, Moriarty rowing in a kind of breathless daze, listening, his eyes on the gun beside him. Evidently he was thinking of the moment when he would snatch up the gun and empty it into the head of Old Mystery. The Novice pricked a trout, and muttered in his annoyance, the cliff snatching his words away, rolling them into a deep grumble, which blent ominously with the heavy fall of water-drops from jutting lips.

The grey wall, split and knotted like old oak, was cold and grey and forbidding for all the warmth of sunlight upon it. It seemed apart from the daylight, a bulk out of time, a great face that had outstared all humanity with hardly a change of expression, unaware of sunlight, undisturbed even by the regularity of daylight. Daylight could hardly impress a bulk that could remember the original night in which the world was sunk like a grapeseed in wine . . . the wine of a God's idea. Deep lay the water at its feet, flood-lines marked evenly upon it. Dark glimmered the stone, then vanished. In his reverie the Novice missed a second fish, and Rich chid him gently. 'Better take a button-hook to them. Remember we came for fish and not great thoughts on the nature of things.'

Moriarty judges that we are passing over the deeps private to Old Mystery. ''Tis down there he lies in a sort of castle. On a clear day ye can see him from the top, big as a curragh and ugly as the devil himself when God denied him. 'Twas so my sonny saw him, and 'twas frightened he was and down he fell. The water split his face and blinded him, and he was drowned with his soul all broken, and all the time that big bastard was down there laughing away at the trick. Have I ever seen him on the surface? Ay, surely! Times there are when the trout fly like splinters, and ye'll see the water heave and break and a tail go splash so's ye'd think the world had cracked like a ball of glass! And bubbles go floating along the edge, bubbles big as eggs, and ye'll maybe see black bits of oak and ugly weeds he've loosened in his wandering.' The thole-pins squeaked with suppressed excitement. 'That brass of yours must be moving over him now. Take care.'

But nothing happened. We rowed beyond the stronghold, and the tension relaxed. Rich sighed and felt for his pipe. The Novice cast again with jaunty air, and was astonished when a trout snatched the dropper – so astonished that he struck as if mastering a wild pony, and the fly was left in the mouth of the fish.

'Bad! bad!' came a murmur from Rich, who would make of the Novice an artist like himself, and then he hummed violently, for the match had scorched his fingers, and the Novice was saved further censure.

By now it is time to turn. We judge the lake to be rather more than half a mile from end to end. Again we will tempt Old Mystery with the Circus Spoon. Rich reels in, examines spoon and trace with scientific intentness, and declares himself ready. After prolonged discussion the Novice takes the oars, Moriarty busying himself with the bailing-tin and hammering fast odd nails which have crept from their holes like dark maggots under the strain of rowing. The Circus Spoon vanished astern, and we imagine it spinning seductively. Easily the Novice rows, damping the thole-pins to quiet their plaint, pleased with the smooth progress of the boat and the vigorous chuckle of water; it is as if we are weaving a stout cloth. High above the buzzard watches, perhaps with amusement in its amber-ringed eyes. Without doubt it sees the drowned rabbit floating on our left, but will not relax dignity to pounce while we are close. The Novice imagines the fall of the rabbit from the cliff. Perhaps it had screamed, and then the scream was lost in the wind-whistle of its fall. So must the son of Moriarty have screamed and fallen. Fortunately Moriarty has not seen the rabbit, and is not again reminded of the tragedy. Wasn't it odd that Old Mystery hadn't gulped the rabbit? The Novice watches the trailing line, how it quivers and tears the bubbling water; watches the quiet muscular hands of Rich, waiting like recumbent wrestlers for the moment when they may spend their strength. Moriary has finished his labours with the bailing-can, and is staring overside as if hopeful for a glimpse of the giant. His lips move in constant talk as he examines his thoughts. Now he looks up at the cliff, clearly remembering the flesh that had fallen so cruelly. He spits into the water, peering closely. ''Tis level with that Jesus-crust he lies,' he fumed, and bent past all comfort, his reflection streaming in the water, an appropriate figurehead. By Jesus-crust he meant a reddish-purple cruciform marking upon the cliff, an ironstone eruption which certainly resembled blood-encrusted flesh. An apt name, but then such thoughts were the certain harvest of those who lived in loneliness . . .

The Novice became alert. Rich had felt unusual movement on the line, and was sitting tensed, waiting, prepared to strike and play the monster. Glowing ash fell from his pipe on to his hand, but he did not move to brush it away. Any moment . . . All waited. The spinner would be about level with the Jesus-crust. Had Old Mystery mouthed it experimentally? Maybe now he was moving around it in curiosity, wondering at the impudence of this shining fish-shape which drove so steadily through his domain. Moriarty thought he saw something breaking astern and stamped in his excitement, and that stamping was our undoing. A rotten strake was splintered and water fountained into the boat. Moriarty stared stupidly; Rich nodded as if he had expected as much; and the Novice after one surprised movement, dropped the oars and stuffed the jersey upon which he had been sitting into the splintered hole.

'Better pull inshore.' Rich gave his attention to the line again, but we were now well past the lie of the giant, and there was little hope of a strike. Moriarty was on his knees, holding the jersey into the hole, grumbling in his disappointment.

'But there, 'tis a little job, and ye can be resting while I'm patching her up and then we'll after him again.'

He looked up for our approval, and Rich comforted him. 'To be sure that's what we'll do. We'll hook him yet, and no bother at all.'

The boat scraped on stones, and Moriarty hopped into the shallows, impatiently hauling the boat high, scarcely waiting for us to climb ashore with all our gear before straining to cock the boat. A concerted movement, and the *Diresome*, as we had already named her, was overturned, and we saw how little had divided us from the depths. The entire hull was patched and cross-patched, both with wood and metal, until hardly a square foot of the original timber was to be seen.

'A good boat,' said Rich with gentle irony.

But Moriarty was busy tugging splinters loose, and could only mumble offhandedly, ''E yes, a good boat. 'Twas built by himself, my father that was, but 't 'as been badly used by the weather. Rain driving on it in winter and the sun tearing at it in summer. 'Tis terrible the way weather does destroy a boat.'

It was in our minds to speak of the uses of boat-houses, but we held our peace, remembering poverty and the way it can cramp a mind past all reason. Grateful we settled among heather to enjoy food, calling

Moriarty to join us. For a moment he paid no heed, and then came slowly to see what we had to offer. Trout in vinegar interested him not at all, but baked beans brought an enthusiastic grunt. Slowly he spelt out the label on the tin, begging the tin for use as a patch on the *Diresome*. Tomatoes he had never before seen, and he refused them after long study and questioning on their qualities. Cheese brought a smile, and he remembered cheese that his mother had made from the milk of goats. 'Fine cheese that ye'd never be thinking could be stirred from the crud of a goat.' He accepted ship's biscuits, and thought he would eat them for supper pulped in milk. ''Tis the teeth of me, ye understand. They don't grow good in these parts under the mountains, the good God he knows why.' Our butter angered and amused him. 'For hadn't it been whipped from sour cream by some bitch of a Mary too lazy to be making the scald from day to day . . .' Chocolate delighted him, and he folded the tablet carefully in paper and tucked it into a difficult pocket, ambling ten yards away to eat in comparative privacy.

When, later, Rich tossed an apple and begged a question, he shuffled himself nearer on his backside, face wrinkling, tongue licking the corners of his mouth in search of fragments, hands stroking the apple.

'Have I lived here always? Surely! And my father, too, and the father of him, with no difference in the house except a crust of thatch when the old wears thin. And f'why not, for isn't it a grand place to be living, all peace ye might say, but for that bloody great murdering monster in the lake. A bit cold in the winter, maybe, but what's the harm when the turf is burning well and there's bacon in the chimney and flour in the tub? Sometimes, when the wind runs wild, rocks do bounce down from above, but 'tis what we do expect and no harm at all to us who've nothing to lose. Do I labour? For the foreigners in the valley, d'ye mean? Surely not, and f'why should I when there's me own property to be tending and saving from ruin and the thieves who'd be skinning the very stones of your hearth if ye did but give 'em the ghost of a chance! My woman, she do work a bit, and likes to think she'm propping the house, but there, she's a Philbin, and the Philbins are all cock-heavy and good for nothing but talk.' He sighed and scratched his nose and stared uneasily across the lake, eyes chancing upon the boat, purpose returning. 'Damn we all for wasting time and she waiting to be patched, and that devil waiting and grinning till the lake do boil. D'ye see?'

He pointed with sudden excitement and we stared across the lake, expecting revelation. But it was no more than a gust of wind agitating the waters. We said as much, and he turned fiercely. 'Fools! If ye'd seen what I've seen . . . But there, how can ye be knowing the size and temper of him? Once he came and snatched at my oar, smashing it like you'd break a twig. Another time he whipped water with his tail until it touched a cloud, and the cloud broke and we were damned near drowned with the power of water that fell. That's the spite and temper of him. But I'll not talk. I'll pray that he grabs that brass of yours and then ye'll see.'

He stared down at the apple in his hands and bit at it suddenly, fishily, in illustration; then scrambled to his feet and bolted away down the shore, presently reaching the cottage, careering in and out of it like a wasp in an old apple, gathering tools for the repair of the *Diresome*. After a long time he came slowly back along the shore, stopping once to shake his fist at, perhaps, a cormorant on the lake, stepping on, singing huskily, bringing with him on a half plate 'a toothful of good butter to be tasting', together with many useless tools for our inspection. The butter eaten and justly praised and the tools examined, he crossed to the boat and ceremoniously began the repair, hammering out the tin which had contained the beans, and pegging it awkwardly into place over a wad of canvas. The bulging tin, shining in the sunlight, suggested that the *Diresome* had been badly stung. And then Moriarty tenderly painted the patch with tar, lingering over it, finding other places in need of attention, bending low over them, peering shortsightedly, sweating and muttering to himself.

We tired of watching him, and, rolling our jackets for pillows, fell comfortably asleep, sinking in the honey-scented warmth, the Novice dreaming of a gigantic Moby pursued by a gawky Ahab Moriarty. A dramatic and fitting culmination was prevented by an impatient shout from Moriarty.

'All ready, if you please!'

We stretched and yawned, and became alive again to opportunity. We had wasted time enough. The afternoon was almost gone, and we were no nearer the capture, no nearer to fame. The Novice, yet remembering his dream, visualized a magnificent fish plunging and fighting; himself waiting with the useless gaff, waiting through the hours while Rich played him and to a finish, Rich who was never so sure of hand and mind as when occupied with a good fish. It would be the triumph of his life, and the Novice, too, would he be able to say, 'I was there . . .' We should need the camera. 'Come on, my lad!'

Bundling our gear together we made for the boat, Moriarty beckoning us techily forward. By some untold feat of strength he had managed to refloat the *Diresome*, and was paddling and stamping in the shallows.

'He's on the move, I'm thinking,' he called excitedly. 'Did ye hear the black bishop scream just now? They hate each other I'm telling ye.'

The black bishop was his name for the buzzard. It was possible that the bird could see movement in deep water. Rich settled again in the stern, Moriarty took the oars, and the Novice pushed off. Rich ordered a wide circuit, and Moriarty pulled jerkily, strenuously, straining boat and oars at every stroke.

'Easy! easy!' called Rich, 'else you'll spoil our chances.'

With sober face Moriarty accepted reproof, slowing to an easy trolling speed, straightening the boat for the row down under the cliff.

'Let down the brass,' he begged Rich. 'He moves like a priest when the fancy's on him, and there's no knowing where ye'll touch him.'

In his own time Rich paid out the line. The Circus Spoon vanished. The Novice, with apparent unconcern, assembled a fly-rod and made tentative casts, keeping well down in the boat to avoid warning shadows. An eighteen-ounce fish hooked itself when he turned to look at Rich's hands, and he played it in ungentlemanly fashion, dragging it aboard without waiting for the net, the whole performance earning sharp comment from Moriarty.

'Why the hell can't ye keep quiet instead of jigging about like a frog after flies?'

The Novice apologized, winking at Rich; but Rich's whole attention was on the Circus Spoon. He could not be bothered with trifles. Now we were level with the Jesus-crust. Moriarty peered continually over-side, lips twisting in the intensity of feeling. Once he broke his stroke to reassure himself that the flintlock was to hand. The Circus Spoon must be flashing deep down. But then, if Old Mystery was as big as Moriarty implied, he would scarcely see such a lure. Big and very old, he was probably half blind as well. Did fish become blind with age? Certainly we had caught some elderly specimens whose eyes were queerly coloured and malformed. An interesting point, but . . .

'My God!' Rich struck hard, and his winch screamed. 'Check the boat!'

Moriarty, at the first alarm, had dropped his oars, and was fumbling with the gun. With a warning, 'Drop that damned thing!' the Novice butted him from his seat and got the oars into reverse action. The boat was checked, but not before much line had run out. Moriarty raised himself on his knees, questioning:

'Have ye got him?'

'Got something,' replied Rich shortly, winding slowly. He frowned. 'Not a move. Must be a rock.'

'That's him! That's him! Cunning he is, big and cunning, remember that.' Moriarty dribbled in his excitement and caught his breath painfully.

Rich worked quietly, winding in, never slackening the line for an instant. He was obviously puzzled. His fingers read the vibrations of the line. 'Queer,' he said. Bracing himself, he heaved suddenly, the reel braked against mishap. We saw the rod bend and the line slide slowly to the right. 'He moved then all right! His head seemed to swing, and then he rolled like a pig. The line is quivering . . . you can almost feel something thinking down there. Damned queer! Either he's a monster or it's a turtle we've hooked . . .'

''Tis him! 'Tis him! Drag at him! Make him jump!' Moriarty could not endue calm supposition. He swung from side to side, nursing the flintlock. 'Pull, man, pull, for the love of Mary! Remember, remember . . .!' He could not control himself. 'Damn ye!' Dropping the gun, he made a grab at the rod, half snatching it from the unprepared hands of Rich. The boat rocked. Rich swore and tried to force Moriarty back without breaking the strain. 'Hold the damned fool!' he called, but the Novice could do little. Added weight and motion in the stern would simply cause the *Diresome* to roll over. Moriarty struggled frantically for possession of the rod. A decisive blow sent him sprawling into the bottom of the boat, Rich after him, for he still held the rod. The winch rasped and the line ran suddenly slack. The Novice fell upon Moriarty, and Rich regained the rod. Breathing hard, he wound in, but all strain was gone from the line. Water dropped steadily from the reel. A sudden flickering through the rings and the end of the line came into sight, the Spoon gone, wreched from the trace in inexplicable manner, a topmost happy-chance triangle of hooks only remaining. Rich sat loosely, staring at Moriarty.

'Gone?' whispered Moriarty.

Rich nodded, not trusting himself to speak. Sighing deeply, he felt for his pipe, filling and lighting it with care.

None cared to break the silence. Moriarty sat in the bilge and pulled threads from his jacket. The Novice found a scrap of biscuit in his pocket and chewed hungrily, pondering darkly, all his fine hopes gone. The boat drifted towards the cliff. A vicious gust of wind swept across the lake, and we heard it hiss and whistle like evil laughter against the wall. A cormorant rose from the lake, and the echoing clap of its wings was like mocking applause. We watched it drive steadily from sight, and with it went our last hopes. Now we were in deep cold shadow. Looking up, the cliff seemed to sway over us. The Novice shivered.

'Where to?'

Rich shrugged, puffing steadily at his pipe. Moriarty raised himself to his seat, crestfallen and ashamed. Spitting upon his hands, he thumped the thole-pins tight and balanced the oars, working them slowly, turning the boat towards his cottage. 'Maybe ye'd like some drink, a sip of black cream' He could do no more to compensate us for his folly. We could not hurt him with a refusal. Steadily now he pulled. He looked like one who had been terribly scorched, and yet was without wound or scars. Presently Rich smiled at him. 'Come, man, cheer up! No bones broken and no great loss.'

But Moriarty was sick with disappointment and could only mutter disjointed threats involving dynamite and quicklime. We neared the shore and the ramshackle cottage, and we saw it to be a miserable place indeed, sunk in loneliness. The thatch was rotten, and had been patched with sail-cloth. Mud had been daubed upon the unmortared walls in ineffective attempt to keep out the wind and the rain. The two windows were no larger than biscuit-tins, and were grey with the grime of years. Fowls strutted in and out of the dark interior. An untidy pile of turf was by the door, the crumbs trodden everywhere. In the doorway a figure waited, unseen as yet by Moriarty. The boat grounded in a rough quayway, and we stepped ashore, followed by Moriarty. He waved us towards the cottage, then stopped short with an expression of shame and fear as he saw the woman standing there. Thin and sour-faced she was; toothless, judging by her sunken mouth. Her thin hair straggled untidily, and her boots were laced with twine. A hard worker, but one without grace of body or mind. Rich greeted her with his unfailing courtesy, and she nodded curtly.

'We have been trying for the big fellow under the cliff.'

''Tis great fools ye must be entirely, then, for there's naught there but an old log. *He* told ye 'twas a fish, I suppose, and ye not knowing that 'tis mad he's been since the drowning of our Michael. Always simple and then mad, so that they shut him away for a year and gave me peace of him. But they wouldn't keep him, and now he spends his days like an addled child, not thinking of the hours I must slave to be filling his belly . . .'

'I am sorry.'

'No blame to ye at all!' The woman turned away, picked up a dinted bucket, and went off to milk a sulky cow standing in a threadbare acre beyond the cottage. We looked for Moriarty, but he had hidden himself, and we were glad, for we felt that we had added to his madness by our belief. We called our thanks, but heard no answer. Leaving silver on the window ledge, we hurried away, the woman watching us with her bleak unfriendly eyes. We still felt that she was watching even when we had broken camp and were ready to start. Short had been our talk.

''Tis a great pity to be leaving such trout to play with themselves, but the place is unhappy and not kind to us at all. Foolish to stay . . .' Thus Rich.

'Agreed. And no regrets?'

Not at once did Rich reply. We got under way, and presently, when we were once more in the valley and the lake miles behind, the Novice repeated his question, disturbed by a curious glint in Rich's eyes.

'Regrets?' Rich smiled in a melancholy way. 'Only one.' He hesitated, then felt for a long time in a pocket, producing at last a strange thing, a fish-scale as big as a halfpenny and tough as horn. 'I found that caught on the triangle,' he said sorrowfully, and began to sing softly a song that was like a keen, saying never another word to the Novice for all the understanding that was between them.

from CRACK OF WHIPS *1934*

A Well Poached Salmon

JOHN BUCHAN

In Buchan's novel, John Macnab, *Sir Edward Leithen tries to make good his boast that he can poach a salmon after warning the owner of his intention.*

As he waited, watching the pools turn from gold to bronze, as the sun sank behind the Glenraden peaks, he suffered the inevitable reaction. The absurdities seemed huge as mountains, the difficulties innumerable as the waves of the sea. There remained less than an hour in which there would be sufficient light to fish – Jimsie was immovable (he had just lit his pipe and was sitting in meditation on a big stone) – every moment the Larrig waters were cooling with the chill of evening.

Leithen consulted his watch, and found it half-past eight. He had lost his wrist-watch, and had brought his hunter, attached to a thin gold chain. That was foolish, so he slipped the chain from his button-hole and drew it through the arm-hole of his waistcoat.

Suddenly he rose to his feet, for things were happening at the far side of the haugh. Jimsie stood in an attitude of expectation – he seemed to be hearing something far upstream. Leithen heard it too, the cry of excited men . . . Jimsie stood on one foot for a moment in doubt; then he turned and doubled towards the Wood of Larrigmore . . . The gallant Crossby had got to business and was playing hare to the hounds inside the park wall. If human nature had not changed, Leithen thought, the whole force would presently join the chase – Angus and Lennox and Jimsie and Dave and doubtless many volunteers. Heaven send fleetness and wind to the South London Harrier, for it was his duty to occupy the interest of every male in Strathlarrig till such time as he subsided with angry expostulation into captivity.

The road was empty, the valley was deserted, when Leithen raced across the bridge and up the south side of the river. It was not two hundred yards to his chosen stand, a spit of gravel below a high bank at the tail of a long pool. Close to the other bank, nearly thirty yards off, was the shelf where fish lay of an evening. He tested the water with his hand, and its temperature was at least 60°. His theory, which he had learned long ago from the aged Bostonian, was that under such conditions some subconscious memory revived in salmon of their early days as parr when they fed on surface insects, and that they could be made to take a dry fly.

He got out his line to the required length with half a dozen casts in the air, and then put his fly three feet above the spot where a salmon was wont to lie. It was a curious type of cast, which he had been practising lately in the early morning, for by an adroit check he made the fly alight in a curl, so that it floated for a second or two with the leader in a straight line away from it. In this way he believed that the most suspicious fish would see nothing to alarm him, nothing but a hapless insect derelict on the water.

Sir Archie had spoken truth in describing Leithen to Wattie Lithgow as an artist. His long, straight delicate casts were art indeed. Like thistledown the fly dropped, like thistledown it floated over the head of the salmon, but like thistledown it was disregarded. There was indeed a faint stirring of curiosity. From where he stood Leithen could see that slight ruffling of the surface which means an observant fish . . .

Already ten minutes had been spent in this barren art. The crisis craved other measures.

His new policy meant a short line, so with inifinite stealth and care

Leithen waded up the side of the water, sometimes treading precarious ledges of peat, sometimes waist deep in mud and pond-weed, till he was within twenty feet of the fishing-ground. Here he had not the high bank for a shelter, and would have been sadly conspicuous to Jimsie, had that sentinel remained at his post. He crouched low and cast as before with the same curl just ahead of the chosen spot.

But now his tactics were different. So soon as the fly had floated past where he believed the fish to be, he sank it with a dexterous twist of the rod-point, possible only with a short line. The fly was no longer a winged thing; drawn away under water, it roused in the salmon early memories of succulent nymphs . . . At the first cast there was a slight swirl, which meant that a fish near the surface had turned to follow the lure. The second cast the line straightened and moved swiftly upstream.

Leithen had killed in his day many hundreds of salmon – once in Norway a notable beast of fifty-five pounds. But no salmon he had ever hooked had stirred in his breast such excitement as this modest fellow of eight pounds. '"'Tis not so wide as a church-door,"' he reflected with Mercutio, '"but 'twill suffice" – if I can only land him.' But a dry-fly cast and a ten-foot rod are a frail wherewithal for killing a fish against time. With his ordinary fifteen-footer and gut of moderate strength he could have brought the little salmon to grass in five minutes, but now there was immense risk of a break, and a break would mean that the whole enterprise had failed. He dared not exert pressure; on the other hand, he could not follow the fish except by making himself conspicuous on the greensward. Worst of all, he had at the best ten minutes for the job.

Thirty yards off an otter slid into the water. Leithen wished he was King of the Otters, as in the Highland tale, to summon the brute to his aid.

The ten minutes had lengthened to fifteen – nine hundred seconds of heart-disease – when, wet to the waist, he got his pocket-gaff into the salmon's side and drew it on to the spit of gravel where he had started fishing. A dozen times he thought he had lost, and once when the fish ran straight up the pool his line was carried out to its last yard of backing. He gave thanks to high Heaven, when, as he landed it, he observed that the fly had all but lost its hold and in another minute would have been free. By such narrow margins are great deeds accomplished.

He snapped the cast from the line and buried it in mud. Then cautiously he raised his head above the bank. The gloaming was gathering fast, and so far as he could see the haugh was still empty. Pushing his rod along the ground, he scrambled on to the turf.

from JOHN MACNAB *1925*

A Westerner Looks at Beaverkill

RODERICK HAIG-BROWN

One comes to it as a pilgrim to a shrine, a sacred, shining place, made so by the deeds of the great and passing feet of many generations. And it is just that.

There is sense and no sense in picking Opening Day for the pilgrimage. The noble hills are brown except for scattered conifers; the hardwood trees are brown and leafless and last year's leaf fall is brown under them where it is not whitened by the passing snow flurries. The air is cold, the trout lie quiet in the deep pools, when they are not down in the still deeper pools of the East Branch. It is an unlikely time for good trout fishing.

Yet it is the gathering time for pilgrims old and new, and the time of all times for a new pilgrim to learn the devotion that the little river inspires and to sense its traditions. For the Beaverkill, the Neversink, Battenkill, Willowemoc, and a few others, are surely the nursing waters of American fly fishing.

On Friday night, with the frost tight in the ground outside, the bar at Doug Bury's Antrim Lodge was crowded with fishermen greeting each other for the first time in six months or a year. It was too cold, they agreed, too early, and there were far too many people around. 'Fishing tomorrow, Jim?' 'Naw. Just go out and look it over.' 'Fishing tomorrow, Frank?' 'Drive up and down a bit, maybe, talk to a few guys. Might put up a rod.' Never have so many fishermen driven so far to protest their intention of not fishing. Yet I knew just how they felt. Tomorrow was Opening Day. There would be few lines that did not touch river water, however briefly, and those would mostly be spares.

Bill Naden of the Brooklyn Fly Fishers Club arrived in good time next morning, and he and Ed Zern showed me the river – downstream first, from the Junction Pool at the mouth of the Willowemoc clear to the East Branch of the Delaware. Many miles of beautiful water on a big, bold stream, nearly all of it readily accessible from the road. On

Opening Day, little more than a hundred miles from Manhattan, I had supposed it would be crowded with fishermen. True, they crowded a few favoured spots, lined both banks five or ten feet apart at the Junction Pool and at a slab rock pool by a bridge; but there were miles of water where a man would have found no more competition than on any British Columbia stream within easy reach of a paved road. And fly fishermen, may the Lord sharpen their hooks and guide their wrists, seemed as numerous as spinners.

We drove back, stopping now and then to watch and talk and uncork a bottle, and came to the upper stream above the Willowemoc junction. The shades and living spirits of the great were now with us, their names on our lips: Hewitt with fourteen-foot leaders, La Branche with nine-foot or less – 'That's why he doesn't catch any fish,' said the shade of Hewitt, careless of fact. Sparse Grey Hackle, who will take many more fish from the river on No. 18 and 20 flies; gentle Jack Atherton who, unhappily, will not. And Theodore Gordon: 'For at least a hundred years,' he wrote over fifty years ago, 'the Valley of the Beaverkill has been celebrated for its beauty and the river for its trout.'

Gordon could well write the same words today if he were living. Clear and cold and lovely, the upper stream sparkles down in cascades and runs and trout-loved pools from its spring-fed source in Balsam Lake. We saw fishermen lined again close by Ogden Pleissner's covered bridge. We saw miles of posted water broken by shorter stretches of free water. I thought of Gordon again: 'I fear that in a few years very little water will be free to the public . . . for real sport, give us free water, where the trout are critical, hard to please and highly valued when caught.' Gordon believed that to take large fish when they were shy was the acme of sport.

We wet out lines in the posted waters, working down the Brooklyn Club's Home Pool, through Twin Rocks and on the lip of the dam, where we swung big streamers back and forth in the foaming overflow, while a brief blizzard hid even the nearest bank from sight. We turned back fishless to the big fire in the clubhouse, but tradition had been served and well served, and we were happy as men can be.

Western eyes and a western heart could not ask for more than this. It has all been going on for a very long time. The fathers of the sons and the grandfathers of the grandsons fished here on earlier Opening Days, grew up with the clubs or on the free water. Halford and Skues and Pulman, Walton and Cotton and Berners made spiritual pilgrimage across the ocean to the Beaverkill. Gordon, Hewitt, LaBranche,

Atherton, the Darbees, the Dettes and many others caught the spirit, interpreted it anew, and sent it out across the vast continent. Today it reaches the many millions who seek respite and reward in the fly streams from Atlantic to Pacific, from Mexico to the Arctic Ocean.

I would go again to the Beaverkill when the rhododendrons have opened their buds on the slope above the Home Pool, when the trees are in full leaf and the air hums with warmth and life and the river is low. I would hope for a hatch and a few great trout rising steadily here and there, 'critical and hard to please'. But if there were none, it could scarcely matter. The river would be there and its banks – and all about me the shades of great fly fishers. They would know I searched faithfully, and in an honourable tradition.

from THE MASTER AND HIS FISH *1959*

The Old Man's Great Fish

ERNEST HEMINGWAY

He looked across the sea and knew how alone he was now. But he could see the prisms in the deep dark water and the line stretching ahead and the strange undulation of the calm. The clouds were building up now for the trade wind and he looked ahead and saw a flight of wild ducks etching themselves against the sky over the water, then blurring, then etching again and he knew no man was ever alone on the sea.

He thought of how some men feared being out of sight of land in a small boat and knew they were right in the months of sudden bad weather. But now they were in hurricane months and when there are no hurricanes, the weather of hurricane months is the best of all the year.

If there is a hurricane you always see the signs of it in the sky for days ahead, if you are at sea. They do not see it ashore because they do not know what to look for, he thought. The land must make a difference too, in the shape of the clouds. But we have no hurricane coming now.

He looked at the sky and saw the white cumulus built like friendly piles of ice cream and high above were the thin feathers of the cirrus against the high September sky.

'Light *brisa*,' he said. 'Better weather for me than for you, fish.'

His left hand was still cramped, but he was unknotting it slowly.

I hate a cramp, he thought. It is a treachery of one's own body. It is humiliating before others to have a diarrhoea from ptomaine poisoning or to vomit from it. But a cramp he thought of it as a *calambre*, humiliates oneself especially when one is alone.

If the boy were here he could rub it for me and loosen it down from the forearm, he thought. But it will loosen up.

Then, with his right hand he felt the difference in the pull of the line before he saw the slant change in the water. Then, as he leaned against the line and slapped his left hand hard and fast against his thigh he saw the line slanting slowly upward.

'He's coming up,' he said. 'Come on hand. Please come on.'

The line rose slowly and steadily and then the surface of the ocean bulged ahead of the boat and the fish came out. He came out unendingly and water poured from his sides. He was bright in the sun and his head and back were dark purple and in the sun the stripes on his sides showed wide and a light lavender. His sword was as long as a baseball bat and tapered like a rapier and he rose his full length from the water and then re-entered it, smoothly, like a diver and the old man saw the great scythe-blade of his tail go under and the line commenced to race out.

'He is two feet longer than the skiff,' the old man said. The line was going out fast but steadily and the fish was not panicked. The old man was trying with both hands to keep the line just inside of breaking strength. He knew that if he could not slow the fish with a steady pressure the fish could take out all the line and break it.

He is a great fish and I must convince him, he thought. I must never let him learn his strength nor what he could do if he made his run. If I were him I would put in everything now and go until something broke. But, thank God, they are not as intelligent as we who kill them; although they are more noble and more able.

The old man had seen many great fish. He had seen many that weighed more than a thousand pounds and he had caught two of that size in his life, but never alone. Now alone, and out of sight of land, he was fast to the biggest fish that he had ever seen and bigger than he had ever heard of, and his left hand was still as tight as the gripped claws of an eagle.

It will uncramp though, he thought. Surely it will uncramp to help my right hand. There are three things that are brothers: the fish and my two hands. It must uncramp. It is unworthy of it to be cramped. The fish had slowed again and was going at his usual pace.

I wonder why he jumped, the old man thought. He jumped almost as though to show me how big he was. I know now, anyway, he thought. I wish I could show him what sort of man I am. But then he would see the cramped hand. Let him think I am more man than I am and I will be so. I wish I was the fish, he thought, with everything he has against only my will and my intelligence.

He settled comfortably against the wood and took his suffering as it came and the fish swam steadily and the boat moved slowly through the dark water. There was a small sea rising with the wind coming up from the east and at noon the old man's left hand was uncramped.

'Bad news for you, fish,' he said and shifted the line over the sack that covered his shoulders.

He was comfortable but suffering, although he did not admit the suffering at all.

'I am not religious,' he said. 'But I will say ten Our Fathers and ten Hail Marys that I should catch this fish, and I promise to make a pilgrimage to the Virgin de Cobre if I catch him. That is a promise.'

from THE OLD MAN AND THE SEA *1952*

The Superfish

WILLIAM HUMPHREY

'Closing day,' my small companion met me with at poolside.

'Has come. Aye, Caesar, but not gone,' I rejoined.

'Huh?' My talking in riddles was all that was needed to convince him that I was hopelessly addled.

'Still using them artificial flies, I see.'

'Mmh.'

'Ever get him to bite one of them yet?'

'Can't say I have.'

'Then what makes you think he's going to now at the last minute?'

'Don't think he's going to – just hoping he might. You never know when your luck will change.'

But the truth was, the boy had dashed my hopes. Closing day it was, and that alone would be the thing to make this one different from all the other days I had sunk in this folly of mine. At midnight tonight the Fish and Game Commission of the Commonwealth of Massachusetts would extend legal protection over its most venerable trout, and he would live out his pensionage in this little pool. It was only out of a sense of obligation and to round out the fitness of things that I waded into the water. A sense that, having challenged the fish, I owed him his total triumph over me. It was I who had made today's appointment with him, and there he was.

As often happens, now that I had lost confidence, and, with it, the compulsion to perform, I excelled myself in my casting that day. Four times running I placed my fly – a No. 12 Black Gnat it was, to match the ones that were biting me – over the fish without rousing his suspicions, putting him off his feed and sending him to sulk beneath the bridge. Those repeatedly ignored casts made my young companion smirk; I, though rather ruefully, admire my unproductive accomplishment.

My fifth cast would have alighted in the same spot, some four feet in front of the fish, as the others had. However, it never did. Exploding from the water, the fish took it on the wing, a foot above the surface. Why that cast and not one of the countless others, nobody will ever know. Instantly he felt the barb. Not fright, but fight, was what it brought out in him.

Out of the water he rose again like a rocket – out and out, and still there was more to him, no end to him. More bird than fish he seemed as he hovered above the water, his spots and spangles patterned like plumage. I half expected to see his sides unfold and spread in flight, as though, like the insects he fed upon, he had undergone metamorphosis and hatched. His gleaming wetness gave an iridescent glaze to him, and as he rose into the sunshine his multitudinous markings sparkled as though he were studded with jewels. At once weighty and weightless, he rose to twice his own length. Then, giving himself a flip like a pole-vaulter's, down he dove, parting the water with a wallop that rocked the pool to its edges.

The next moment I was facing in another direction, turned by the tug of my rod, which I was surprised to find in my hand. Nothing remotely resembling his speed and power had I ever experienced in my fishing. Nothing I might have done could have contained him. It was only the confines of the pool that turned him.

Straight up from the water he rose again. Higher than before he rose. It was not desperation that drove him. There was exuberance in his leap, joy of battle, complete self-confidence, glory in his own singularity. Polished silver encrusted with jewels of all colours he was, and of a size not to be believed even by one who had studied him for weeks. I believed now that he had taken my fly for the fun of it. I was quite ready to credit that superfish with knowing this was the last day of the season, even with knowing it was his last season, and of wanting to show the world what, despite age and impairment, he was capable of. Reaching the peak of his leap, he gave a thrash, scattering spray around him. In the sunshine the drops sparkled like his own spots. It was as though a rocket had burst, showering its scintillations upon the air.

Another unrestrainable run, then again he leaped, and for this one the former two had been only warm-ups. Surely he must have a drop of salmon in his blood! Up and up he went until he had risen into the bright sunshine, and there, in defiance of gravity, in suspension of time, he hung. He shook himself down his entire length. The spray that scattered from him caught the light and became a perfect rainbow in miniature. Set in that aureole of his own colours that streamed in bands from him, he gave a final toss of his head, breaking my leader with insolent ease, did a flip, dove and re-entered the water with a splash that sent waves washing long afterward against my trembling and strengthless legs.

'Dummy!' cried the boy on the bank. 'You had him and you let him get away!'

from MY MOBY DICK *1979*

The Big Rainbow and the Huge Brown

JOHN SANTELLE Sr

On the way back to Lake Hawea a sign-posted track on the right leads to the Blue River, at its junction with the Makarora. Here, I fished to two large rainbows, both feeding about twenty feet down. I could clearly see the first one open its mouth and take the nymph; the second one was not interested.

Crossing the suspension bridge over the Makarora, my friend and mentor, Brain Thomson, pointed out what I took to be a large rock. Suddenly the 'rock' swam upstream under the bridge and took up station near the bank we had just left. I hurried back over the bridge and was able to get a nymph in the right spot. The trout turned, took it with great confidence and held on for about thirty seconds but, for some unknown reason, the fly pulled out. Brian, who has caught trout over twelve pounds, put this one down at more than eleven!

On another memorable occasion, in 1985, we fished the Hunter River above Lake Hawea. The Forestry Hut we camped in was not far from the bank of the stream and was most comfortable.

Brian suggested he would walk down river a fair way and fish back up to the hut, whilst I opted to fish a couple of pools upstream from the camp. But it began to rain before I had gone very far, so I made my way back to the hut. After some time Brian returned, very excited, and told me he had seen the biggest brown trout in the river, '*Well over ten pounds!*'

I asked why he hadn't caught it and he said, '*It will take the two of us to catch this one*!'

After a quick snack we walked down to the pool where he had seen the big one. I could understand the problem as soon as we got there. A very large beech tree was growing right on the edge of the steep bank and leaned out over the water. Just below that a fence had been extended to the edge of the bank. About ten yards below the fence there was a small area from which one of us could play the fish and hopefully land it. Below that a line of bushes prevented access, so if the fish did keep going downstream things would be quite difficult.

I crept in behind the beech tree and immediately saw a rainbow of about six pounds. I told Brian to get his eyes checked, but he assured me that he had seen a much larger brown.

Brian insisted that I fish for the rainbow, which was taking nymphs just upstream from the tree. He said he would move to the downstream side of the tree, and agreed to lean around and take my rod if I hooked the fish. I was then to run around the tree and get over the fence. If everything went according to plan, Brian would hand the rod back again and I could then jump down to the flat area and play the fish from there.

Well, everything did go as planned. The rainbow grabbed the nymph which I dangled down to him, then took off downstream flat out. Brian was just able to grab my rod with the tips of his fingers. I negotiated the fence and got down to the flat area without much trouble. The fish swam around in some quiet water just below me and I commented to Brian. '*Looks like he's a gentleman and plans to play fair*'.

I hardly had the words out when an enormous brown trout appeared from the very deep water towards midstream and charged straight at the head of the rainbow. At first I thought he was trying to hunt it out of his territory. The brown hit the leader, but luckily there was enough slack to prevent a break-off. A few seconds later the brownie did exactly the same thing, hitting the leader once more. This time I was ready and threw some slack line. This behaviour went on for quite a while, with the big brown coming within a couple of feet without taking any notice of me whatsoever, even when I raised my arm and jumped up and down trying to scare him away.

Finally I asked Brian to throw a stone at it, and he did just that, but instead of hitting the brown he hit the rainbow on the tail. This caused the rainbow some anxiety and it tore off downstream towards the rapid leading to the pool below. I thought that it would be the end of the battle, but the rainbow turned and swam back to the slow water in front of me.

The big brown then circled around and made another charge. This time Brian was ready beside me with a long stick and he hit the water just above the brownie, causing it to swim away some six yards where it sulked and swam around in a small circle.

The rainbow was duly landed, weighed at just over six pounds and released. Both Brian and I were sure the brown was at least twice as big. When released, the rainbow swam out to the brown and together they disappeared into the deep water. They were apparently good mates and we both felt the big brown had deliberately tried to release the rainbow by hitting the leader. They were both buck fish, possibly 'fishosexuals'.

from 'CHAMPAGNE' FLY FISHING *1990*

PART 3

Flies

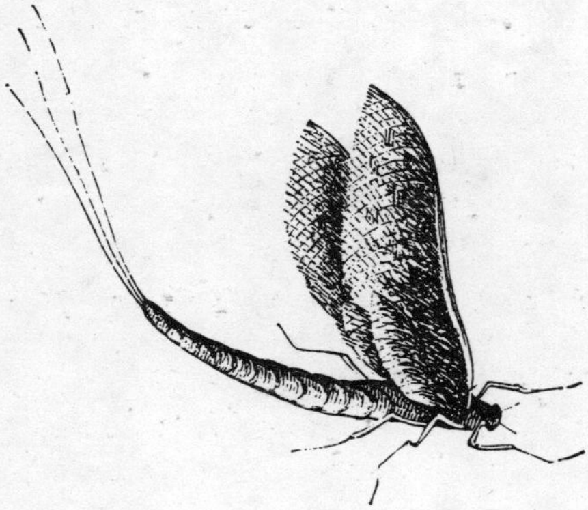

Let Nature guide thee; sometimes golden wire
The shining bellies of the fly require . . .
Each gaudy bird some slender tribute brings,
And lends the growing insect proper wings:
Silks of all colours must their aid impart,
And every fur promote the fisher's art . . .
So just the colours shine through every part,
That Nature seems to live again in Art.

John Gay

Barker and the Fly

THOMAS BARKER

My Lord, I will shew you the way to angle with a flye, which is a delightful sport.

The rod must be light and tender, if you can fit yourself with a hasel of one piece, or of two pieces set together in the most convenient manner, light and gentle. Set you line to your rod, for the uppermost part you may use your own discretion, for the lowermost part next your flye, it must be of three or four haired links. If you can attain to angle with a line made of one hair, two or three links one tyed to another next your hook, you shall have more rises and kill more fish. Be sure you do not overload your self with lengths of your line. Before you begin to angle make a triall, having the wind on your back, to see at what length you can cast your flye, that the flye light first into the water, and no longer, for if any of the line fall into the water before the flye, it is better uncast than thrown. Be sure you be casting alwayes down the stream with the wind behind you, and the Sun before you. It is a speciall point to have the Sun and Moon before you, for the very motion of the rod drives all the pleasure from you, either by day or by night in all your anglings, both with worms and flyes, there must be a great care of that.

Let us begin to angle in March with the flye. If the weather prove windy or cloudy, there are severall kinds of Palmers that are good for that time.

First, a black Palmer ribbed with silver. Secondly, a black Palmer ribbed with an orenge-tawny body. Thirdly, a black Palmer made all of black. Fourthly, a red Palmer ribbed with gold. Fifthly, a red Palmer mixed with an orenge tawny body of cruell. All these flyes must be made with hackles, and they will serve all the year long, morning and evening, windy or cloudy. Without these flyes you cannot make a daye's angling good. I have heard say that there is for every moneth in the year a fly; but that is but talk, for there is but one monethly flye in the yeare, that is the May flye. Then if the aire prove clear you must imitate the Hawthorn flye, which is all black and very small, the smaller the better. In May take the May flye, imitate that. Some make it with a shammy body, and ribbed with a black hair. Another way it is made with sandy hog's hair ribbed with black silk, and winged with Mallard's feather, according to the fancy of the angler if he hath judgement. For first, when it comes out of the shell, the flye is somewhat whiter, then afterwards it growes browner, so there is judgement in that. There is another flye called the Oakflye that is a very good flye, which is made of orenge colour cruell and black, with a brown wing, imitate that. There is another flye made with the strain of a Peacock's feather, imitating the Flesh-flye, which is very good in a bright day. The Grassehopper which is green, imitate that. The smaller these flyes be made, and of indifferent small hooks, they are the better. These sorts which I have set down will serve all the year long, observing the times and seasons, if the angler have any judgement. Note the lightest of your flies for cloudy and dark, and the darkest of your flyes for the brightest dayes, and the rest for indifferent times; a mans own judgement with some experience must guide him: If he mean to kill fish he must alter his flyes according to these directions. Now of late I have found that hogs wooll of severall colours makes good bodies, and the wooll of a red heifer makes a good body, and beares wooll makes a good body: there are many good furres that make good bodies: and now I work much of hogs wooll, for I finde it floateth best and procureth the best sport.

The naturall flye is sure angling, and will kill great store of trouts with much pleasure. As for the May-flie you shall have him playing alwayes at the rivers side, especially against rain: the Oak-flie is to be had on the but of an oak or an ash, from the beginning of May to the end of August; it is a brownish flie, and standeth alwaies with his head towards the root of the tree, very easie to be found: the small black fly is to be had on every hathorn tree after the buds be come forth: your grassehopper which is green is to be had in any medow of grass in June or July. With these flies you must angle with such a rod as you angle with the ground bait: the line must not be so long as the rod, drawing your flye as you finde convenient in your angling: When you come to the deep waters that stand somewhat still, make your line two yards long or thereabouts, and dop or drop your flye behind a bush, which angling I have had good sport at; we call it dopping.

from BARKER'S DELIGHT *1659*

A Choice of Flies

CHARLES KINGSLEY

Look on the soft muddy bottom. You see numberless bits of stick. Watch awhile, and those sticks are alive, crawling and tumbling over each other. The weed, too, is full of smaller ones. Those live sticks are the larva-cases of the Caperers – *Phryganeae* – of which one family nearly two hundred species have been already found in Great Britain. Fish up one, and you find, amid sticks and pebbles, a comfortable silk case, tenanted by a goodly grub. Six legs he has, like all insects, and tufts of white horns on each ring of his abdomen, which are his gills. A goodly pair of jaws he has too, and does good service with them: for he is the great water scavenger. Decaying vegetable matter is his food, and with those jaws he will bark a dead stick as neatly as you will with a penknife. But he does not refuse animal matter. You may count these caddis baits by hundreds of thousands; whether the trout eat them case and all, is a question in these streams. In some rivers the trout do so; and what is curious, during the spring, have a regular gizzard, a temporary thickening of the coats of the stomach, to enable them to grind the pebbly cases of the caddises. See! here is one whose house is closed at both ends – 'grille', as Pictet calls it, in his unrivalled monograph of the Genevese *Phryganeae*, on which he spent four years of untiring labour. The grub has stopped the mouth of his case by an open network of silk, defended by small pebbles, through which the water may pass freely, while he changes into his nymph state. Open the case; you find within not a grub, but a strange bird-beaked creature, with long legs and horns laid flat by its sides, and miniature wings on its back. Observe that the sides of the tail, and one pair of legs, are fringed with dark hairs. After a fortnight's rest in this prison this 'nymph' will gnaw her way out and swim through the water on her back, by means of that fringed tail and paddles, till she reaches the bank and the upper air. There, under the genial light of day, her skin will burst, and a four-winged fly emerge, to buzz over the water as a fawn-coloured Caperer – deadliest of trout flies; if she be not snapped up beforehand under water by some spotted monarch in search of supper.

But look again among this tangled mass of weed. Here are more larvae of water-flies. Some have the sides fringed with what look like paddles, but are gills. Of these one part have whisks at the tail, and swim freely. They will change into *ephemerae*, cock-winged 'duns', with long whisked tails. The larvae of the famous green drake (*Ephemera vulgata*) are like these: but we shall not find them. They are all changed by now into the perfect fly; and if not, they burrow about the banks, and haunt the crayfish-holes, and are not easily found.

Some, again, have the gills on their sides larger and broader, and no whisks at the tail. These are the larvae of *Sialis*, the black alder, Lord Stowell's fly, shorm fly, hunch-back of the Welsh, with which we have caught our best fish today.

And here is one of a delicate yellow-green, whose tail is furnished with three broad paddle-blades. These, I believe, are gills again. The larva is probably that of the Yellow Sally – *Chrysoperla viridis* – a famous fly on hot days in May and June. Among the pebbles there, below the fall, we should have found, a month since, a similar but much larger grub, with two paddles at his tail. He is the 'creeper' of the northern streams, and changes to the great crawling stone fly (May-fly of Tweed), *Perla bicaudata*, an ugly creature, which runs on stones and posts, and kills right well on stormy days, when he is beaten into the stream.

There. Now we have the larvae of the four great trout-fly families, *Phryganeae, Ephemerae, Sialidae, Perlidae*; so you have no excuse for telling – as not only Cockneys, but really good sportsmen who write on fishing have done – such fibs as that the green drake comes out of a caddis-bait, or giving such vague generalities as, 'this fly comes from a water-larva'.

These are, surely, in their imperfect and perfect states, food enough to fatten many a good trout: but they are not all. See these transparent brown snails, *Limneae* and *Succinae*, climbing about the posts; and these other pretty ones, coil laid within coil as flat as a shilling, *Planorbis*. Many a million of these do the trout pick off the weed day by day; and no food, not even the leech, which swarms here, is more fattening. The finest trout of the high Snowdon lakes feed almost entirely on leech and snail – baits they have none – and fatten till they cut as red as a salmon.

Look here, too, once more. You see a gray moving cloud about that pebble bed, and underneath that bank. It is a countless swarm of 'sug', or water-shrimp; a bad food, but devoured greedily by the great trout in certain overstocked preserves.

Add to these plenty of minnow, stone-loach, and miller's thumbs, a second couse of young crayfish, and for one gormandizing week of bliss, thousands of the great green-drake fly: and you have food enough for a stock of trout which surprise, by their size and number, an angler fresh from the mountain districts of the north and west.

And now comes another and an important question. For which of all these dainty eatables, if for any, do the trout take our flies? and from that arises another. Why are the flies with which we have been fishing this morning so large – of the size which is usually employed on a Scotch lake? You are a North-country fisher, and are wont, upon your clear streams, to fish with nothing but the smallest gnats. And yet our streams are as clear as yours: what can be clearer?

Whether fish really mistake our artificial flies for different species of natural ones, as Englishmen hold; or merely for something good to eat, the colour whereof strikes their fancy, as Scotchmen think – a theory which has been stated in detail, and with great semblance of truth, in Mr Stewart's admirable *Practical Angler* – is a matter about which much good sense has been written on both sides.

Whosoever will, may find the great controversy fully discussed in the pages of *Ephemera*. Perhaps (as in most cases) the truth lies between the two extremes; at least, in a chalk-stream.

Ephemera's list of flies may be very excellent, but it is about ten times as long as would be required for any of our southern streams. Six or seven sorts of flies ought to suffice for any fisherman; if they will not kill, the thing which will kill is yet to seek.

To name them:

1 The caperer

2 The March-brown

3 The governor

4 The black alder

And two or three large palmers, red, grizzled, and coch-a-bonddhu, each with a tuft of red floss silk at the tail. These are enough to show sport from March to October; and also like enough to certain natural flies to satisfy the somewhat dull memory of a trout.

But beyond this list there is little use in roaming, as far as my experience goes.

And now to go through our list, beginning with

1 The caperer

This perhaps is the best of all flies; it is certainly the one which will kill earliest and latest in the year; and though I would hardly go as far as a friend of mine, who boasts of never fishing with anything else, I believe it will, from March to October, take more trout, and possibly more grayling, than any other fly. Its basis is the woodcock wing; red hackle legs, which should be long and pale; and a thin mohair body, of different shades of red-brown, from a dark claret to a pale sandy. It may thus, tied of different sizes, do duty for half a dozen of the commonest flies; for the early claret (red-brown of Ronalds'; a Nemoura, according to him), which is the first spring-fly, for the red spinner, or perfect form of the March-brown *ephemera*; for the soldier, the soft-winged reddish beetle which haunts the umbelliferous flowers, and being as soft in spirit as in flesh, perpetually falls into the water, and comes to grief therein; and last but not least, for the true caperers, or whole tribe of *Phryganidae*, of which a sketch was given just now. As a copy of them the body should be of a pale red brown, all but sandy (but never snuff-coloured, as shop-girls often tie it), and its best hour is always in the evening. It kills well when fish are gorged with their morning meal of green drakes; and after the green drake is off, it is almost the only fly at which large trout care to look; a fact not to be wondered at when one considers that nearly two hundred species of English *Phryganidae* have been already described, and that at least half of them are of the fawn-tint of the caperer. Under the title of flame-brown, cinnamon, or red-hackle and rail's wing, a similar fly kills well in Ireland, and in Scotland also; and is sometimes the best sea-trout fly which can be laid on the water. Let this suffice for the caperer.

2 Of the March-brown ephemera there is little to be said, save to notice Ronalds' and *Ephemera*'s excellent description, and *Ephemera*'s good hint of fishing with more than one March-brown at once, viz. with a sandy-bodied male, and a greenish-bodied female. The fly is a worthy fly, and being easily imitated, gives great sport, in number rather than in size; for when the March-brown is out, the two- or three-pound fish are seldom on the move, preferring leeches, tom-toddies, and caddis-bait in the nether deeps, to slim *ephemerae* at the top; and if you should (as you may) get hold of a big fish on the fly, 'you'd best hit him in again', as we say in Wessex; for he will be, like the Ancient Mariner –

long, and lank, and brown,
as is the ribbed sea-sand.

3 The 'governor'. – In most sandy banks, and dry poor lawns, will be found numberless burrows of ground bees who have a great trick of tumbling into the water. Perhaps, like the honey bee, they are thirsty souls, and must needs go down to the river and drink; perhaps,

like the honey bee, they rise into the air with some difficulty, and so in crossing a stream are apt to strike the farther bank, and fall in. Be that as it may, an imitation of these little ground bees is a deadly fly the whole year round; and if worked within six inches of the shore, will sometimes fill a basket when there is not a fly on the water or a fish rising. There are those who never put up a cast of flies without one; and those, too, who have killed large salmon on him in the north of Scotland, when the streams are low.

His tie is simple enough. A pale partridge or woodcock wing, short red-hackle legs, a peacock-herl body, and a tail – on which too much artistic skill can hardly be expended – of yellow floss silk, and gold twist or tinsel. The orange-tailed governors 'of ye shops', as the old drug-books would say, are all 'havers'; for the proper colour is a honey yellow. The mystery of this all conquering tail seems to be, that it represents the yellow pollen, or 'bee bread' in the thighs or abdomen of the bee; whereof the bright colour, and perhaps the strong musky flavour, makes him an attractive and savoury morsel. Be that as it may, there is no better rule for a chalk stream than this – when you don't know what to fish with, try the governor.

4 The black alder (*Sialisnigra*, or *Lutaria*)

What shall be said, or not be said, of this queen of flies? And what of *Ephemera*, who never mentions her? His alder fly is – I know not what; certainly not that black alder, shorm fly, Lord Stowell's fly, or hunch-back, which kills the monsters of the deep, surpassed only by the green drake for one fortnight; but surpassing him in this, that she will kill on till September, from that happy day on which

You find her out on every stalk
Whene'er you take a river walk,
When swifts at eve begin to hawk.

The common tie is good enough. A brown mallard, or dark hen-pheasant tail for wing, a black hackle for legs, and the necessary peacock-herl body. A better still is that of Jones Jones Beddgelert, the famous fishing clerk, of Snowdonia, who makes the wing of dappled peacock-hen, and puts the black hackle on before the wings, in order to give the peculiar hunch-backed shape of the natural fly. Many a good fish has this tie killed. But the best pattern of all is tied from the mottled wing-feather of an Indian bustard; generally used, when it can be obtained, only for salmon flies. The brown and fawn check pattern of this feather seems to be peculiarly tempting to trout, especially to the large trout of Thames; and in every river where I have tried the alder, I have found the bustard wing *facile princeps* among all patterns of the fly.

Of palmers (the hairy caterpillars) are many sorts. *Ephemera* gives by far the best list yet published. Ronalds has also three good ones, but whether they are really taken by trout instead of the particular natural insects which he mentions, is not very certain. The little coch-a-bonddhu palmer, so killing upon moor streams, may probably be taken for young larvae of the fox and oak-egger moths, abundant on all moors, upon trefoils, and other common plants; but the lowland caterpillars are so abundant and so various in colour that trout must be good entomologists to distinguish them. Some distinction they certainly make: for one palmer will kill where another does not: but this depends a good deal on the colour of the water; the red palmer, being easily seen, will kill almost anywhere and any when, simply because it is easily seen; and both the grizzle and brown palmer may be made to kill by adding to the tail a tuft of red floss silk; for red, it would seem, has the same exciting effect on fish which it has upon many quadrupeds, possibly because it is the colour of flesh. The mackerel will often run greedily at a strip of scarlet cloth; and the most killing pike-fly I ever used had a body made of remnants of the huntsman's new 'pink'. Still, there are local palmers. On Thames, for instance, I have seldom failed with the grizzle palmer, while the brown has seldom succeeded, and the usually infallible red never. There is one more palmer worth trying, which Scotsmen, I believe, call the Royal Charlie; a coch-a-bonddhu or furnace hackle, over a body of gold-coloured floss silk, ribbed with broad gold tinsel. Both in Devonshire and in Hampshire this will kill great quantities of fish, wherever furzy or otherwise wild banks or oakwoods afford food for the oak-egger and fox moths, which children call 'Devil's Gold Rings', and Scotsmen 'Hairy Oubits'.

Two hints more about palmers. They must not be worked on the top of the water, but used as stretchers, and allowed to sink as living caterpillars do; and next, they can hardly be too large or rough, provided that you have skill enough to get them into the water without a splash. I have killed well on Thames with one full three inches long, armed of course with two small hooks. With palmers – and perhaps with all baits – the rule is, the bigger the bait the bigger the fish. A large fish does not care to move except for a good mouthful. The best pike-fisher I know prefers a half-pound chub when he goes after one of his fifteen-pound jack; and the largest pike I ever ran – and lost, alas! – who seemed of any weight above twenty pounds, was hooked on a live white fish of full three-quarters of a pound. Still, no good angler will despise the minute North-country flies. In Yorkshire they are said to kill the large chalk trout of Driffield as well as the small limestone and grit fish of Craven; if so, the gentlemen of the Driffield Club, who are said to think nothing of killing three-pound fish on midge flies and cobweb tackle, must be (as canny Yorkshiremen are likely enough to be) the best anglers in England.

from CHALK STREAM STUDIES *1859*

Flies in their Seasons

W. C. STEWART

The time of year when trout begin to take fly readily entirely depends upon the nature of the river and the season. They never rise freely at the artificial fly until they are accustomed to feed upon the natural insect; and the first insects which make their appearance in any quantity are the March browns. It is not until these flies have been a week or ten days on the water, or at a time varying according to the season and district, from the middle to the end of April, that fly-fishing really commences. In that short space of time trout improve wonderfully in condition, and leaving the still water, where they have had their haunts during winter, move up into the stronger parts of the pools, about the sides of which they lie in wait for their prey.

If the weather is mild, which it rarely is at this season of east winds, the end of April is the best fly-fishing time of the whole season. The trout take with a readiness and certainty which they never exhibit at any subsequent period. Flies are still a rarity to them, and they are not yet shy from being over-fed, or from a frequent view of more practical experience of artificial flies. Other reasons why more trout can be captured with the fly at this season than any other are that there are more trout in the water – the summer's fishing and netting not having begun yet – and that the trout are more concentrated in particular places.

As regards the imitation of the March brown, which is held in such high estimation amongst anglers, if the water is heavy, trout will sometimes take it readily, not because they see any resemblance between it and the real March brown – at least we never could – but because it is a good size of fly for the season; any of the flies we have mentioned, dressed of the same size, will be equally killing. The flies used this month should in general be full size; if the waters are coloured, Nos 9 and 10 will be found most effective; but if the waters are small, a size or two less will be advisable.

At this season a warm sunny day is most favourable to the angler. The birth of flies depends in a great measure upon the state of the weather; and when there are no natural flies on the water, trout never rise freely at an artificial one. An east wind or a cold frosty day is a death-blow to the angler's hopes, as in such there are no flies to be seen, and the trout retire to deep water. In this month we have frequently seen, about eleven o'clock in the forenoon a perfect shower of March browns come on the water, which for half an hour or so appeared almost boiling with trout leaping; and then the flies went off and all was quiet again. Till the flies appeared we met with no sport; when they were on the water we got a rise almost every cast, and when they went away we hardly got another trout.

This is what is popularly known as 'the time of the take', and occurs, more or less, at some time of the day the whole season through. The leaping of the trout in all directions at once informs the angler when it commences, and he should make the most of his time. It sometimes happens several times during the day, but rarely lasts more than an hour at a time, and stops as suddenly as it commences. It is only during the take that trout can be caught in very deep water, as it is only then they are hovering near the surface on the outlook for flies. Once it is over they retire to the bottom and there lie; and if the water is very deep they may not be able to see the angler's flies, or if they do, cannot be troubled to rise to seize them; so that when trout are not taking freely, the angler will always meet with most success in comparatively shallow water.

In April the angler must look for sport in the pools, as the trout are not yet strong enough to lie in the streams, and therefore it is of no use fishing in them. There are some parts of a pool in which trout are, at all seasons, more likely to be found than in others. There are always plenty of them lying in the shallow water at the pool foot, which, if there is a ripple on it, will be found the best place of all. Passing up to the deeper portions of the pool, the trout are more congregated about the sides, as it is there that the aquatic insects on which they feed are most numerous. They choose convenient feeding stations below some large stone or tuft of grass, where the river runs beneath the bank, or where a projecting bush affords food and shelter to some finny giant who holds his revels below. Such places are always sure to be tenanted, and what is rather singular, the best feeding station in a pool or stream is generally occupied by the largest trout in it, and if it is captured the next largest takes its place; and we have day after day caught a trout in one spot, each capture being of smaller dimensions than its predecessor.

In cold weather, in the early part of the season, we have generally found the sunny side of the water the best; we suppose because there are more insects there.

Passing from April to May, trout improve greatly in condition, and move into stronger water about the heads of pools, scattering themselves, but not plentifully as yet, through the streams. Of all places where the angler is likely to find trout at any season, the meeting of two streams is the best; there in the quiet water between, and on either side of the strong runs, feeding trout are sure to be lying, watching to seize whatever the stream brings in the way of food. Such places should always be fished with great care.

For fishing slow-running streams, the end of April and beginning of May are the best times, and the trout in such are then in excellent condition; but for rivers in general, the month of May, taking it as a whole, is worth any two months to the fly-fisher. Sport may be more relied upon than in the preceding month. The birth and appearance of flies on the water is rendered less dependent on the weather; a cold day or an east wind does not do the same mischief, and the trout will generally take during the whole day, unless the weather is extremely cold. We have never at this season found it any use to attempt fly-fishing before seven or eight in the morning; the forenoon, from eight till about noon, or an hour or two after, we consider the best time; about two they generally leave off taking, but commence again in the evening, if the weather is mild. In the beginning of the month we have generally met with most success on a warm sunny day; but to tell the most favourable weather with anything like certainty is impossible, as the trout are very capricious, and will sometimes take readily during a hail-storm, while at other times, in such a case, not a trout will rise. Towards the end of the month we prefer a showery day with west wind, or a thoroughly wet one if the weather is warm.

The best condition of water for capturing trout is when there is just sufficient rain to raise the water slightly, and make it of an amber colour. When a large flood occurs, it scatters the trout too much, and they become gorged with food, and do not take so readily; so that more trout can generally be caught in a clear water than after a heavy flood. If the water is only coloured or slightly swollen, trout will be found in the same place as when it is clear; but when the water is large and dark-coloured, it is of no use fishing the streams, as they are too rapid, and in the pools the trout are all congregated about the sides. In such circumstances, therefore, the angler should not waste time fishing the centre of the pool, but merely fish the sides; fishing the side he is on straight up, and as close to the edge as possible, and the opposite side partly across and partly up as usual. The greatest number will frequently be got on the thin side, but the largest and best trout are almost invariably caught on the deep side, and very close to the edge.

The flies used in May should be smaller than those used in April; if the waters are clear, No. 11 or 12 will answer very well, but if the rivers are coloured, a size larger may be used; a good-sized fly will frequently catch the best trout in heavy water.

Towards the end of this month the stone-fly, or May-fly of Tweed-side, makes its appearance – the green drake, to which the name of May-fly is usually applied, not appearing for a fortnight later. These flies give the first great blow to artificial fly-fishing; they are so large, and the trout get them in such abundance, that before they have been many days on the water, the trout become quite satiated with surface food. They are now in prime condition – strong and vigorous – affording excellent play when hooked. They also forsake the deeper portions of the pools, moving up into the strong water at the head, and into broken water and streams, where they choose convenient feeding stations, such as eddies behind stones, below banks, and submerged tufts of grass, and, in short, every place where they can remain unseen, and watch for their prey as it comes downstream towards them; and the angler should neglect no place where he thinks there is a trout.

About the time they begin to act the epicure, becoming exceedingly nice in their tastes, and paying little attention to the angler's lure, and they may frequently be seen following, without making any attempt to seize it. When they are in this mood, which generally lasts till the beginning of August, always use spiders, and reduce their size to No. 12 or 13; a No. 14 midge may also be used with advantage. This, to a certain extent, meets their views, it being more suspicion of the nature of the fly, then want of inclination to seize it, which makes them so nice. On such occasions also, the angler should pass over the pools, and fish the streams, as in them, owing to the roughness of the water, the trout cannot so easily detect the artificial nature of the flies.

From the middle of June to the beginning of August is the worst part of the whole season for fly-fishing. In large rivers, such as Tweed, and all slow-running streams, fly-fishing – at least during the day – is not worth practising. At sunset, however, trout will rise freely, and continue to do so all night, if the weather is favourable. A dry, warm night, with little dew falling, will generally be found most favourable; if there is much dew falling, or a thick mist rising from the water – the surrounding country being free from it – trout will not take freely. At night they leave the streams and pool heads, to cruise about among the pool foots and shallows, and it is in these places that the angler should fish for them. Two flies will generally be found sufficient for night-fishing, and they should be a good deal larger than those used during the day. The largest trout caught during the summer months are usually taken at night, as it is only then that they leave the bottom of the deep pools in search of food.

At this season the fly-fisher, in search of sport during the day, should have recourse to the smaller waters and more backward districts of the country, where the trout are not yet – indeed in some places they never are – satiated with surface food. Fly-fishing at this season is more difficult than at any other, for unless in a very favourable day, the trout will not rise in the pools; the angler, therefore, must have recourse to the streams and rough broken water, and to fish these successfully with the fly is very nice practice indeed. The flies alone should touch the water, and they should never be thrown into the main current, but into nooks and eddies, and all those places where the worm-fisher would look for sport . . . The trout that will take a worm will generally rise at a spider, if thrown lightly over it; but in fly-fishing the angler cannot capture one-fourth of the trout that rise, whereas in worm-fishing he can make sure of one out of two offers, which accounts for the comparatively few trout in the fly-fisher's basket at this season.

In clear sunny days, trout may frequently be seen basking in shallow water, which, at first sight, seems scarcely sufficient to cover them. On such occasions, they will rise greedily at a spider, if the angler keeps well out of sight, and throws lightly over them, he must also take care that the shadow of his rod does not fall upon the water in their neighbourhood. The capture of one will, however, scare away the others, and they will not return for some time.

Trout will rarely, even in the heat of summer, take fly readily early in the morning; they generally commence about six, and continue taking for four or five hours, when they stop for some time; commencing again in the evening, if the weather is favourable. At all seasons, the forenoon is the best time, unless, perhaps, in June and July, when they will take most freely about sunset.

The atmosphere at this season is frequently in a calm thundery state, with heavy white clouds floating about, which is not favourable to the angler. From the end of May to the end of August, a drizzling or thoroughly wet day is the best; next to which is a showery one, and then a bright day with a breeze of wind: a dark day without wind is the worst of all. East wind, which is looked upon with so much horror at the commencement of the season, is not at all objectionable now; being rather favourable than otherwise, as it is generally accompanied with a cool atmosphere.

In July we have always met with even less sport when the water was coloured, than when it was clear, which we can only account for by supposing, that as it is the worm season, the trout are on the outlook for this description of food, and pay no attention to the flies; at least in such circumstances we never see many rises at the natural insect.

In the summer months it is considered a great improvement to hook a maggot to the end of the fly, but this is not fly-fishing, and changes the character of the lure from the most clean and pleasant, to the most disagreeable of all the methods of capturing trout. It has, moreover, at all times a substitute in a fine red worm, which is much more agreeable to handle, and will kill two for one which the fly with the maggot will.

August is a better month for the fly than July, and during the whole of it, but especially at the latter end, trout rise freely. Night-fishing may now be said to be at an end; the nights in general are cold and frosty, and the trout will not rise freely; so that there is little inducement to leave a comfortable bed to shiver at the water-side. By the beginning of September there is a visible change for the worse in the condition of the trout – they are full of spawn, and are fast losing strength, firmness, and flavour. They now commence to leave the streams, and return to the pools and more quiet water; it is worthy of remark, that those which remain in the streams are generally in good condition; if they were not, they would not have strength to keep their place in strong water. The flies used this month, as well as in the end of August, should be a size or two larger than those used during summer; approaching in size to a spring fly. After a flood capital sport may be had; the trout will rise almost as freely as in the month of May, and though in general out of condition, the angler will still meet with some, that will test freely both his skill and tackle. They will continue taking through October, but excepting the small ones, are in such poor condition, as to be totally unfit for use.

The sizes of flies we have indicated are those suitable for southern streams. In highland rivers, where the trout are not so numerous or wary, flies considerably larger than those we have mentioned will frequently secure the best trout.

Fly-fishing in streams inhabited by cunning, cautious trout, when the water is low and clear, is undoubtedly the kind of fishing which requires most science. And for our own part we would rather capture ten pounds weight of trout in some much fished southern stream open to the public, than twice that quantity in some preserved water, or remote highland stream, where the trout seldom see an artificial fly, and are ready to seize anything that presents itself in the shape of food. Fishing in preserved water loses a great part of its pleasure. We like to be free to seek trout where we like, and take them where we can; and as there is more merit, there is more pleasure in filling a basket where all anglers, high and low, rich and poor, are free to do the same, than in a river fished only by a favoured few. All beginners in the art, if they wish to excel, should commence in streams where the trout are remarkably shy, and they will the sooner become skilful. If they commence in highland streams, where the trout are half starved, and where it requires little exercise of skill to capture them, they will get into a careless style of fishing, which they may find it difficult to alter. We have known anglers from the north, who considered themselves, and were considered, good fishers, and who in their own streams could kill seven or eight dozen trout in a day, unable to secure half a dozen small fish in our southern streams. The angler who can kill trout in streams such as Tweed, Gala, or Almond, which are fished by dozens every day, may rest assured that he is quite able to kill them wherever they are to be found.

from THE PRACTICAL ANGLER *1857*

Fly Nomenclature

C. F. WALKER

I wonder how many modern fly-fishermen are conscious of the fact that some of the commonest vernacular names for aquatic insects in use today were unknown a hundred years ago? It is a curious thing that since the earliest days of fly-fishing the angler's names for flies have undergone periodic changes, and I have often speculated on why this should have happened and how the new names came to be promulgated and universally accepted. Supposing, for example, that some pedantically-minded fisherman – not without some justification in this case – decided to call the Mayfly the Junefly. It is hard to believe that we should all soon be using the new name; yet this, or something very like it, seems to have occurred in several cases.

On the face of things it might be supposed that angling books were responsible for this state of affairs, and this was probably so in earlier days. In more recent times, moreover, we have had a good example of this when, in his book, *An Angler's Entomology*, published in 1952, J. R. Harris suggested new English names for some of the flies mentioned and invented names for others which had previously lacked them. This does not, however, account for the changes which occurred towards the end of the last century – at least so far as I have been able to discover. None of the writers of the period whose books I have read laid any claims to the introduction of new names,* but to all appearance were simply following the accepted usage of their respective eras. How, then, did these changes come about?

A number of writers have attempted to identify the flies mentioned by the early angling authors, especially those in the *Treatyse*, but in the absence of any scientific nomenclature before the eighteenth century to act as a guide, this can be no better than guesswork. To complicate matters still further, our remote ancestors did not appreciate that a spinner was the final metamorphosis of its corresponding dun, but believed them to be entirely different species. I do not, however, propose to delve deeply into the history of fly naming, which would, indeed, require a whole book to do it full justice. I am here only concerned with the introduction of our modern names, and for present purposes I shall confine myself to those of the *Ephemeroptera*, or day-flies.

Some of the names in use today are, of course, of quite respectable antiquity, and these may be briefly dismissed before we go on to consider the remainder. So far as my reading goes – and I do not claim to have read everything on the subject – their origins are as follows. The two earliest of these names, by an odd coincidence, are those of flies little appreciated by trout, but in naming flies our forebears were influenced only by the species they saw in the air or on the water,

*Excepting Theakston, whose peculiar system of nomenclature has never been accepted by the angling public. Ed.

without troubling themselves about the trout's reactions to them – the Alder being a case in point. The names in question are Turky-flie and Little Yellow May-flie, which appeared in Cotton's list in 1676 and are, I take it, the equivalents of our Turkey Brown and Little Yellow May dun. Next in chronological order come Little Iron Blue Fly (now abbreviated to Iron Blue) and Red Spinner, both from Charles Bowlker's *The Art of Angling* (*c.* 1758); March Brown and Pale Evening dun from G. C. Bainbridge's *The Flyfisher's Guide* (1816); and Jenny Spinner and August dun from Ronalds's *The Flyfisher's Entomology* (1836). Some of these, no doubt, were the original names, but others were new names for insects already known. Iron Blue, for example, was probably a synonym for Cotton's Violet Flie and Chetham's Little Blue dun, while the March Brown was at one time known as the Dun Drake.

Of the names with no long history behind them Olive dun and its variations are the first to claim our attention. The early writers recognized a number of different-coloured duns, but the first one to notice the olive shade seems to have been Sir Humphry Davy, who in *Salmonia*, published in 1828, wrote:

> Of the blue dun there is a number of different tints, or species, of varieties, which appear in the middle of the day all the summer and autumn long. In early spring these flies have olive bodies; in the end of April or the beginning of May they are found yellow; and in the summer they become cinnamon-coloured; and again, as winter approaches, gain a darker hue.

Next; in the *Handbook of Angling* (1847) 'Ephemera' (Edward FitzGibbon) quoted *The Encyclopaedia of Rural Sports* as saying, 'The early duns are very dark olive', and further on gave the dressing of an 'Olive fly', which clearly represents a dun. This is the first mention of Olive as a name I have been able to find, and seven years later John Jackson, in his book *The Practical Fly-Fisher*, referred to five different kinds of Olive Bloa. Bloa is a north-country term whose precise meaning is somewhat obscure, but from the illustrations in Jackson's book it is evident that the flies referred to were all duns. That the name Olive was not yet in current use, however, seems clear from the fact that it received no mention in *A Book on Angling*, by Francis Francis, published in 1867. Francis was an angler of wide experience, who not only fished many different rivers himself but, as Angling Editor of *The Field*, must have been in touch with fishermen all over the country. We may take it, therefore, that the names of the flies given in his book, which was regarded as a standard work at the time and for many years later, represented those then in common use.

Published in 1882, David Foster's *Scientific Angler* included a list of what the author termed olive dun shades, one of which he specifically called 'the Olive, or April, dun'. Then, in *Floating Flies and How to Dress Them* (1886), we find Halford referring to the Dark, Medium and Pale Olive Quills, all representing duns, without any suggestion that these names were new ones. Finally, in *Dry Fly Entomology* (1897), he gave an actual description of the natural Olive dun, under which name he lumped together five species of the genus *Baëtis*, though in *Modern Development of the Dry Fly* (1910) he separated these into two, which he named Large Dark Olive and Olive duns respectively.

What, then, do these Olives correspond to in the older style of nomenclature? It seems more than a little strange that Halford did not tell us, since the change must have taken place during his lifetime and he was well acquainted with Francis Francis. But it appears that he did not even guess the truth, judging by the following note on the Blue dun which appeared in *Dry Fly Entomology*:

> From time immemorial [he wrote], the existence of such a natural insect (i.e. the Blue dun) has been affirmed, and in the face of so much evidence it must be included in the category of 'Imitations of Natural Insects'. It has never been my good fortune to find or procure a specimen, nor can I find among the lists of British Ephemeroptera any corresponding to it in colour, etc. Two or three friends have sent me what they took to be individuals of this species, but they have on examination all proved to be subimagos of the Olive or Iron Blue dun, or of the Blue-winged Olive.

It was left to J. W. Dunne, in his book *Sunshine and the Dry Fly* (1924), to point out that the Blue dun (or Blue Upright, as it is often called in the West Country) is none other but the fly now known as the Large Dark Olive. In view of Sir Humphry Davy's strong hint of nearly a hundred years earlier, it is surprising that no one seems to have thought of it before.

We are still left with the name Olive, or Medium Olive, to account for, and as this species* often shows a marked tinge of yellow in its make-up I think there can be little doubt that it corresponds to the

*Actually, there are three species of *Baëtis* covered by this name. Ed.

Yellow dun, which appeared in nearly all the early lists of flies. The latter name may also have covered the dun now known as the Yellow Upright, which bears a superficial resemblance to an Olive and was, in fact, rechristened Olive Upright by Harris. I have, however, been unable to trace the origin either of Yellow Upright or Claret dun, both of which I believe to be comparatively modern names.

Most of the duns of other colours observed by our ancestors were presumably no more than versions of the Olives, some of which show considerable variation as the season advances. Those of the paler shades, however, must have been what we should now call Pale Watery duns. The first use of this term I have discovered is in *Floating Flies*, where Halford described the Little Marryat as 'Mr Marryat's imitation of the pale watery dun prevalent in August, September and October'. I fancy, however, that he was here employing it to describe a shade of colour rather than in the specific sense, and that it was not until the publication of his *Dry Fly Entomology* that it first appeared as a name. It was then used to cover four species, two in the genus *Baëtis* and two in *Centroptilum*, which have since been separated, with vernacular names of their own, by later writers.

Amongst the earlier names which in all probability corresponded to one or another of Halford's Pale Wateries were a Whitish dun, a Little dun and a Little White dun (unless the latter was the Pale Evening dun) of Cotton; the Little Pale Blue of Bowlker; the Sky-coloured Blue of Durnford; the Light Bloa of Jackson; and the Sky Blue of Ronalds. Which of them related to which species it is, however, difficult to say, although Harris has seen fit to revive the name Sky Blue for *Centroptilum luteolum*.

Lastly we come to the Blue-winged Olive. It seems hardly possible that such a distinctive fly, and one which plays such a prominent part in the evening rise on so many rivers, can have been overlooked for centuries, yet there is only one fly described before the Halford era which can be identified with something like certainty as the B.W.O. This is the July dun of Ronalds, which from the general colouration and three tails was evidently the female of this species. It is not to be confused with the July dun of Francis and Skues, which was almost certainly *Baëtis scambus*, sensibly renamed Small Dark Olive by Harris. The Blue-winged Olive was first mentioned by name in the list of artificials in *Floating Flies*, while the natural dun, together with its imago the Sherry spinner, were described in *Dry Fly Entomology* eleven years later.

I have not included the Mayfly in my brief survey, as in this case there has been no sudden change of name. Although it was formerly more often called the Green Drake (or Grey and Black Drake in the case of the two spinners), the name Mayfly seems to have been known for a good many years as a synonym, and the older names are still occasionally used today.

From the foregoing it seems that the names Olive, Pale Watery and Blue-winged Olive came into general use at some time during the latter part of the last century; probably between the publication of *A Book on Angling*, by Francis Francis, in 1867 and Halford's first book, *Floating Flies*, in 1886. I cannot, however, find any important work published during these nineteen years which might account for the changes, so as far as I am concerned the whole thing remains wrapped in mystery.

from SALMON AND TROUT MAGAZINE *September 1963*

The Evolution of Fly-Fishing Philosophy in France

MAJOR O. W. A. KITE

Fly-fishing has had a place in English sporting literature for almost five centuries during which the art as we understand and practise it, has been in a state of gradual but constant evolution. Inevitably, perhaps, this has been accompanied by schisms and reformations in our esoteric angling tents, which at times have bitterly divided the main protagonists . . .

But what of fly-fishing in neighbouring France? How has their philosophy evolved, and what have been the principal agencies and contributory circumstances? The first mention of fly-fishing in French angling literature seems to be Kresz Aîné's *Le Pêcheur Français* (1818), in which he described some fifteen artificials: a parallel, so to speak, to the flies for each month offered us by Cotton in the second part of *The Compleat Angler*. At that time, it seems fairly certain, fly-fishing in France was a sport confined to a few relatively early initiates, whereas in England various schools of thought were already beginning to emerge; and in 1834 we find John Rennie taking to task the exact imitators of his day, the 'rationalists', and the fur really began to fly.

Another French book appeared in 1859. Written by Charles de Masses, it was entitled *Le Pêcheur à la Mouche Artificielle*. By this time Pulman had discussed the dry fly; and during the next decade or so, the fly-fishing 'formalists' poured scorn on Cholmondeley Pennell's unsophisticated doctrine of relying on a few sound artificial patterns to take as many trout as a whole range of close imitations of the naturals.

Already, too, the great F. M. Halford, on whom be peace, was at work on his self-imposed task of enlightening his fellow men on what fly-fishing really meant, or ought to mean. In the eighties his first two scholarly and beautifully composed books of the gospel of the dry fly were offered to the angling world. Amongst the illiterate on our island fringes these tablets of stone may have passed unnoticed; but in Wessex, at least, they were accepted as The Word. There are places, I may add, where I suspect they still are!

The reception accorded to the prophet's outpourings was not confined to Wessex. Close on the heels of his first definitive pronouncements there appeared a work which at once brought French fly-fishers into step with the orthodox dry-fly men on this side of the Channel. This was Albert Petit's *La Truite de Rivière* (1897), which familiarized French anglers with the theories and methods of Halford: the concept of the artificial dry fly as exact an imitation as possible of the floating natural insect on which a trout is deemed to be feeding at a particular time.

L. de Boisset, the leading French fly-fishing writer of our time, has said that Petit's book granted the dry fly its French naturalization papers. Certainly, French fly-fishng practice was largely based on Halford's concept during the first two decades of this century, France being rather slower than the United States to formulate her own concepts of the art. This is easy to understand.

The American School, sharing with the French and all other fly-fishing nations a common British heritage, found that in practice their own rivers simply did not lend themselves to Halford's concepts, logical though these may have seemed in the country where they were devised. Indeed, it is interesting to speculate on the course fly-fishing might be taking in all three countries today if Halford had migrated to New York – after the Civil War, say.

On the North American rivers, the natural flies were fewer and of different species and behaviour; the feeding habits of the trout themselves were different, and the nature of the artificials required to deceive them called for considerable differences of approach, if

American and Canadian anglers were to meet with commensurate success on their own waters.

In France the situation was somewhat different. There are in Normandy a number of delectable chalkstreams which, I often think, form an almost exact replica of the famous rivers of Wiltshire and Hampshire: the Risle and its tributaries, the Andelle, Charentonne and Authou, might be likened to the Upper Avon, Nadder, Wylye and Till, respectively; the best of the Avre is reminiscent of the Test, the Orbequier of the Itchen, and so on. The flies which hatch from these rivers are virtually identical; and the flies which catch trout at Bulford or Bossington work equally well at Brionne or Bernay.

At the beginning of the century, then, French fly-fishers were much in accord with their Wessex counterparts, probably more so than the latter were with fly-fishers on the rough rivers of the British Isles where wet fly-fishing was, and is, extensively practised.

There was even a certain amount of direct sporting contact between fly-fishers of the two countries. As early as 1906 we find G. E. M. Skues contributing to *The Field* a somewhat fulsome *Portrait of an Angler*, describing his friend, M. Louis Bouglé, who became a member of the Flyfishers' Club and for many years represented France on the committee.

Skues tells us that with Bouglé,

> Fly-fishing is an intellectual pleasure, and though he does not deny that many fancy patterns catch trout – perhaps even many trout – and that in refusing to use them he is prejudicing his chance of sport, he would rather do that than catch a trout with a fly which either frankly resembled nothing in nature, or which he could not identify with its living counterpart.

For a long time, then, French fly-fishers continued to tread the straight and narrow path of English classicism; while across the Atlantic, La Branche and others steadily and empirically worked out their own very different, if not less effective, salvation.

During the years between the two World Wars, English fly-fishing works proliferated. Dunne put forward interesting if not very convincing theories on fly-dressing; Colonel Harding came up with his painstaking treatise on trout vision, not all of which makes much sense today; Skues hammered away insistently in his plausible endeavours to establish the respectability of the artificial nymph; and there were many other less inspired tomes, some of them long since in limbo, relieved by an occasional literary gem like Plunkett Greene's *Where the Bright Waters Meet*.

The more serious of these works commanded close attention across the Channel where, indeed, the ability to read English rated high among the would-be fly-fisher's accomplishments. But already, in France, moves towards independence were already being made. Up to the twenties, it seems French fly-fishers excused their own lack of originality by saying that the English, having had such a long start, had written so much on the subject that there was very little left for them to say anyway. It was left to A.–J. Gros, in a series of articles published in the magazine, *La Pêche Illustrée*, to point out the fallacies in this contention and thereafter to set his compatriots on the road to formulating their own destiny.

Gros pointed out that the Halford dry-fly series was based mainly on the duns and spinners of *Baëtis* species, flies as common and significant in Normandy as they are in Wessex. But Normandy, he argued, was not France; and the natural flies found on the rivers of the Eastern frontiers, the Massif Central, Savoy and the Pyrénées, differed considerably. Many of the Wessex/Normandy flies are absent from these rivers; while others, unknown in Wessex and Normandy alike, are found there in profusion and are of considerable significance to the fly-fisher.

In some cases, of course, the differences are relatively insignifcant. For example, the Olive dun *B. vernus* is replaced, on many mountain streams by the very similar Olive, *B. melanonyx*. Likewise the Large Olive, *B. rhodani*, is replaced by the Large Dark Olive, *B. gemellus* and/or the Alpine Olive, *B. Alpinus*. But there are in France many other species of *Ephemeroptera* of much importance to the fly-fisher: flies for which no English name yet exists, like the abundant *Oligoneuriella rhenana*, and the well-known laboured swimmer, *Choroterpes picteti*, the artificial of which is the favourite of Charles Ritz.

Note, too, that in France the grayling is held in high esteem as a game fish, a view which I, alone among English fly-fishing writers, seem to share; and the grayling rivers of the Jura and elsewhere have an entomology very different from the gentle and mostly grayling-free chalkstreams of La Belle Normandie.

One of the greatest of European entomologists was the Lyons-born J.–A. Lestage, who in 1921 contributed *Les Larves et Nymphes Aquatiques des Insects d'Europe* to Rousseau's definitive work published in Brussels, where Lestage was director of the Hydrobiological Research Laboratory. He was a scientist; Gros, whom I have mentioned earlier, was a fisherman, an angler-entomologist in the great tradition. In

1925–6, Gros published his articles under the title of *Les Ephémères et le Pêcheur*, the first of a series of brilliant works by French fishermen-entomologists. Significantly, the more they came to know about the natural flies of their own rivers, the less credence they placed on the *necessity* for exact imitation.

In 1927 there appeared a French classic, *La Truite: ses Moeurs et sa Pêche*, by the late Colonel Antoine Vavon; a book notable, among other things, for the excellence of its lithographed reproductions of natural flies. Vavon might be likened, in his outlook, to Gros. He, too, shook his admirers with the blunt statement that 'Faithful imitation of nature is illusory and useless . . . it is sufficient to dispose of a few general purpose patterns'. Already, it would seem, those Frenchmen whose knowledge of natural flies was great were among the first to proclaim their faith in the effectiveness of a few sound artificials. It is a process we observe every year among many, if not all, of our more knowledgeable fly-fishers in this country.

But not everyone is content . . . to fish with just a few patterns. Some would as soon angle for cod! But the difficulty, as far as French fly-fishers were concerned, pre-war, was that no simplified series of dry-fly patterns comparable to Halford's had been worked out for France. This deficiency was remedied in 1939 with the publication of L. de Boisset's *Les Mouches du Pêcheur de Truites, Etude, Imitation, Emploi*, a second edition of which appeared in 1951.

De Boisset described the natural insects of France in great detail and he produced a series of thirty-seven artificials which are understandably popular in that country today, among those whose pleasure is to try to match the natural on the water from their fly-box. Of this number, one is a dry Sedge, one a night Sedge, and the other thirty-five are based on the *Ephemeroptera* (France boasts some sixty species compared to our forty-odd).

De Boisset's method of simplification is interesting. An important insect like the Mayfly rates five artificials: *E. vulgata*, male subimago and female imago; *E. danica*, the same; and a Spent Gnat completes the quintet. The Iron Blue gets three: male dun, female dun and female spinner. The Blue-winged Olive gets a dun and a spent (Sherry) spinner, which is logical, for when trout take B.W.O. duns, in France or in England, they'll take 'most anything, even Orange Quills!

Included in this famous 'Gallica' series are a good many flies unfamiliar to those who do not fish on the continent: *C. picteti*, dun and spent; *Habrophlebia lauta*, a close relative of our Ditch dun, *H.*

fusca; Epeorus assimilis; Ecdyonurus forcipula, E. fluminium and *Rhithrogena aurantiaca*, all stone clingers, of course; *O. rhenana*, mentioned previously, the natural of which is abundant in Franche-Comté; and *Polymitarcis virgo*, one of those fascinating species in which the male has two tails and the female three (I am comforted by the belief that most trout can't count!).

Mention must be made here of the famous French fly-dresser, Gérard de Chamberet, samples of whose beautiful work appear in the coloured plates of De Boisset's masterpiece. It is a characteristic of De Boisset's patterns, and indeed of those artificials favoured by many leading French fly-fishers, that they are dressed with down-turned whisks, first advocated by that conscientious pioneer, A.–J. Gros, way back in 1923.

We must now look back slightly further even than that to trace another great influence on French fly-fishing philosophy, the career of Charles Ritz, a very full account of which is given in his autobiography, *A Fly-fisher's Life* (English version, 1959). For many years Ritz worked in New York, where his interests and aptitudes led to his becoming an expert in fly-rod design. Moreover, his North American fishing experience brought him into contact with the leading anglers of the day and gave him a detailed knowledge of contemporary and progressive transatlantic fly-fishing practice and philosophy, and inevitably had a profound influence on his own approach to the sport.

Ritz returned to France between the wars, an enthusiastic and very experienced fly-fisher, and proceeded to build on these foundations on the Normandy chalkstreams and many other European waters. He continued his work on fly-rod development, in conjunction with the brilliant caster, Pierre Creusevaut, and in due course became technical adviser to the firm of Pezon and Michel, at whose factory at Amboise Ritz's famous 'Parabolic' rods are produced.

It is Ritz's boast that he is always seeking fly-fishing knowledge, and he will travel anywhere in the world to learn at first hand the views and methods of acknowledged specialists. A few years ago he founded the International Fario Club, with headquarters in Paris where, once a year, the members foregather to dine: one or more from most of the fly-fishing countries of the world. The Club is representative, too, in the broad field of fly-fishing activities from which its members are drawn: casters, writers, river keepers, conservationists, entomologists and practising fly-fishers from many lands.

Ritz's views on the artificial fly are summarized in his book. He lists the essential qualities as: good visibility on the water; good quality hackles, again with the emphasis on visibility rather than colour; body to be of the correct colour; optimum outline; hook to be of the best quality; and the dressing to be tight and firm.

This emphasis on visibility is, of course, derived from North America, where such devices as bivisible hackles are much in vogue. Ritz does not stress size . . . as long as the artificials are not too big. Most French fly-fishers of my acquaintance are rather more particular about size, a hangover perhaps from the Halford–Petit era.

The French are perfectionists in some respects. They cast better than we do and are altogether more interested in tournament casting, having a keener appreciation of the advantages improved casting ability confer on a fly-fisher. They are always trying to improve their technique. In a quiet lull before the rise begins, they are less inclined to sit about the river-banks, listening to the birds and admiring the flowers. In these circumstances, I have noticed that men like Jean Chevalier, Yves Rameaux and Alain Crépy constantly practice difficult casts into awkward places; and when the trout do at last move, they attack them speedily and with confidence and finesse. It is a joy to watch; but fishing up behind a good Frenchman would be a very unrewarding experience but for their innate courtesy and sense of fair play.

They tend, on the whole, to know and perhaps to care less about conservation than we do. Certainly they do not have the same deep understanding of fishery management. But there are many exceptions. The expert fly-fishers with whom I fish in Normandy are primarily interested in the manner of taking their fish. Having it, they as speedily release it to fight again another day.

Acknowledged to be one of the greatest fly-fishers of all time is a Comtois cobbler, one Maurice Simonet, who has fished the Ain for most of this century, taking upwards of 100,000 fish in that time. It is doubtful if he ever read Halford; and if he studied Petit he was evidently not unduly impressed, for he is content with just two simple fly patterns, yet is a master of the dry fly in practice. Water sense, casting mastery, precise and accurate presentation, and the quality found in all the contemporary masters of being able to 'magnetize' fish, compelling them to take hold: these are the attributes to this legendary French figure.

French artificial flies, the 'Gallica' series excepted, tend to be general patterns of proved worth, like Simonet's. Another is the Tricolore, with no proper body but a lot of hackle. It floats beautifully. A great favourite on the Risle is the garish-looking Panama. The once-popular

President Billard has lost favour but the Pont Audemer, named after the village of that name, still has its loyal adherents. American flies like the Light Cahill, Quill Gordon and Hendrickson have their protagonists too.

There are a number of keen American fly-fishers living in France. I know several in Paris who fish regularly in Normandy. Then there is George Beall, in the Pyrénées, whose writings are well known both sides of the Channel. Their influence is, I fancy, greater than that of resident Englishmen.

Then there is the ingrained national logic of the French themselves. A typical French sedge pattern is Le Ragot from Brittany. It is dressed with tails, which no natural sedge-fly possesses. But, say the French, it floats better that way!

I have also seen flies dressed from new and exotic materials in use in France. Some of their plastic-bodied Mayflies are remarkable. And it is not just in regard to artificials that the French are abreast of the times. They were quick to spot the possibilities of nymph-fishing in the Netheravon style; and in recent years many of the leading French fly-fishers, and the Americans in their midst, have come to Salisbury Plain to learn the art at first hand, Ritz being among the first.

La Branche, who had much to unlearn before he could begin to propound his own philosophy, likened collecting flies to philately, and thought it an equally amusing and harmless occupation. The supremely simple approach, and undoubtedly one of the most effective, is that of Simonet, in whom we find the fine flowering of the natural genius of France. In Ritz, by contrast, we see the distillation of most of the mainstreams of fly-fishing philosophy from both sides of the Atlantic. Between the two there is a whole range of differing outlooks, as there is in our own islands today.

It is therefore dangerous to try to generalize too much. The English influence is still noticeable in Normandy, where you may still meet those who abhor the nymph and deplore the wet fly. But even there, and to a greater extent elsewhere, the French are increasingly going their own way, founding a school which somehow retains or adapts the best from the older British and North American foundations, drawing also from Central European and antipodean sources, and in so doing, reflecting a process which despite periodic violent interruptions, has been constant and binding amongst civilized peoples down the centuries.

from ANGLERS' ANNUAL *1965*

Advice to the Young

A. H. CHAYTOR

My Dear Boys,

Many fishers, after learning to make a cast, think that the flies are everything. There are some even who think that success is to be had only with double hooks, or with some spinning head or some fanciful 'short rising' hook of monstrous shape. Still more salmon fishers, however, pin their faith to an endless variety of gorgeous flies with charming names – names that plainly speak their real use and object, that is, to catch the fisher, not the fish. These names are themselves a comedy.

Some are truculent, as Butcher, Bull-dog, Thunder and Lightning, Black Dose – carrying in their names the idea of triumphant compulsion brought to bear upon the unfortunate salmon. Others are romantic, as Fairy, Silver Grey, Green Highlander, Golden Eagle, Snowfly, Kate. Others recall the deeds of legendary heroes, such as Jock Scott, Popham, Wilkinson. Their varieties, or supposed varieties, run into thousands, and the whole lot show plainly that the fisher is quite as gullible as the fish.

In a recent book on salmon fishing, there are some really beautiful coloured plates of seventy-two of the best-known salmon flies. For any one who is fond of salmon flies these wonderful plates make the book a delightful possession. But the author, Mr Hodgson, excuses himself for confining his list to so small a number of patterns, and he 'ventures to hope' that these flies would be a sufficient outfit to enable one to fish on any ordinary river in the United Kingdom. But just imagine the fisher hunting through a box containing half a dozen flies of each pattern – or of a quarter of the patterns. And any one who looks at these beautifully coloured flies must see that most of them are of precisely similar type, and dozens of them are for all practical fishing purposes identical – all dressed with the same general type of heavy mixed wing, with its yellow topping of golden pheasant, and a golden yellow tail, and the bodies shrouded by a thick and heavy hackle varying only in shades.

In shape and general design the professional fly tier commonly makes but little variation, and his numberless patterns differ from one another only in a few minor details of their multi-coloured gaudiness. In truth, a good fisher with only half a dozen patterns of really varied flies is, so far as catching salmon goes, not one whit behind the man who arms himself with every fly and angling 'requisite' that Hardy or Farlow or Malloch will so cheerfully sell to him.

But I do not wish to sneer at the possessor of many flies. There are plenty of keen fishers to whom the making or collecting of workmanlike flies is in itself a labour of love, but I think it is generally true that the better the fisher and the greater his opportunities of fishing, the fewer are the flies that you shall find him using – certainly it is so with the most skilful fishers that I have known.

THE CHOICE OF FLIES

In my own opinion, if a fly is neat and workmanlike, well shaped, and with wing and hackle dressed sufficiently lightly to play freely in the water, it is of comparatively small importance after what pattern or of what colours the various parts are composed. There are, of course, points upon which some variety is obviously desirable. In big waters, or in waters stained with mud or with peat from moorland streams, one instinctively feels that the fly should be large and bright in order that it may be seen by as many fish as possible. Salmon have wonderfully good sight at all times of the day and night, and even in stained or muddy water they can see the fly in an astonishing way. Still, if fish are ever to be tempted to take the fly, the first essential is that they should see it; and so one demands some flies that shall be good to see. For this purpose I use either a Jock Scott or a sort of Silver Wilkinson, a silver body dressed with a white or pale blue hackle, and having a turkey wing with two large, bright jungle cocks over it. Then one wants some dark, sober fly as a contrast to the former ones in order to make a change – rather for the fisher than for the fish – when the bright flies have been well tried and have proved for the time being unable to attract the fish. For this purpose I generally use a fly with a rather rough body of claret wool, and with a claret hackle and a mallard wing, or else a very similar fly with a smooth body of port-wine coloured silk and a 'pigeon's blood' hackle, with brown or dun turkey wings. With a few flies of each type – Jock Scott, Silver body, and Claret – I should be well content to tackle a day's fishing, ay, or a week's or a month's fishing on any river whatever, unless it were very low and clear. Then I should like to have the choice of about three more flies – the port fly described above, a sober little fly with dun turkey wing and rough black and orange-brown body, known to me as a 'Gipps,' and a green heckam-peckam.

In the matter of flies I am therefore a heretic who thinks nothing of fishing through a long day without changing the fly more than once, and who would almost equally value his chances of taking fish with any well-dressed fly not excessive in size and gaudiness. But salmon, even on the good days, do not take every five minutes, and it is more satisfactory to be using a fly in which you have full confidence. If the fish will not take a fly with which you have lately done well, you feel confident that it is because they are not in taking humour. But with a new and untried pattern of fly hope soon gives place to doubt, and doubt quickly leads to dismissal – in favour, as Mr Dooley said of the anti-Dreyfus witnesses, of some 'thried and thrusted perjurer.'

You will soon, and often, go through the stage when after some lucky day you pin your faith to, and for long catch nearly all your fish upon, some one fly which later on you have given up, and which now is rarely used and lightly valued. Even now looking at one's fishing-books, one sees that for long periods, or even for a whole season, one fly has been by far the most successful. Then another old favourite has a lucky turn, and for weeks together nearly everything is caught upon that pattern, and for the same reason as before, namely, that you have given it the first trial every day, and have never changed it for another unless the fish were not taking.

I should advise you not to pay overmuch attention to the maxims current among salmon fishers as to what fly you should use or what you should do in this event or in that. For instance, you will be told, 'Always use big flies in spring, small flies in summer and autumn'; 'Never cast again over a risen or pricked fish until you have given him five minutes' rest,' or 'have smoked a pipe,' or 'have changed your fly for a smaller one,' or what not; 'Always use bright flies on a bright day, dark flies on a dark day,' and so on. Now these maxims, and many more like them, are all very well. They are well known and deeply revered amongst anglers, but I often wonder whether the poor misguided salmon is always quite sure of the path of duty thus laid down for him. They remind me of the story of the French visitor who showed some alarm at the prospect of passing a savage-looking dog that stood in the way, barking furiously. 'It's all right,' said his host, 'don't you know the proverb "Barking dogs don't bite"?' 'Ah, yes!' says the Frenchman, 'I know ze proverbe, and you know ze proverbe, but ze question is does ze dog know ze proverbe?' Such maxims may be good rough working rules, but one thing you may be sure of about a salmon, you never can tell either what he will do, or when he will do it, and if the fish doesn't come when invited in what you consider the orthodox manner, don't give him up, but try him in the most unorthodox way that you can think of, and I should suggest, to begin with, an absurdly small fly and fine tackle, and keep your very small flies, unless they have metal eyes, ready on a strand of gut, carefully tied before you go out, so that they may be well tied on and changed the more easily.

from LETTERS TO A SALMON FISHER'S SONS *1910*

Buzz and Kick

'MOC' MORGAN

What about flies? It seems to me that sea-trout anglers often indulge in something of a lucky dip when they choose their flies, yet each must have a principle which governs his choice. In the early 1970s I was privileged to act as boatman for two of the most respected gillies in these islands, Jim Kelly, from Ireland, and Tom Stark, from Scotland. Jim, then in his eighties, had been a gillie on Lough Conn from the age of twelve, and Tom Stark was a 'living legend' on Loch Leven. Between them they had more than 120 years' experience as gillies.

I shall treasure the memory of that day for the rest of my life. I learned a lot about boat fishing, but that wasn't all. In mid-afternoon, when things had become a little slow, I invited them to try some of my flies. From what must have been a few hundred colourful feathered creations, each of them took about a dozen, mainly palmered flies with good-quality hackles.

Jim Kelly picked the flies that he said 'buzzed' in the water, and Tom Stark said his selection had enough 'kick' in them. These may have been somewhat unusual descriptions, but they were certainly explicit. And I have to say that I agreed with their choice. My flies may lack clinical perfection, but I, too, like them to have life. I want flies that are fussy, fidgety, vivacious, frisky, agitated and bustling as they work through the currents in a river. When a fly is retrieved across the river, the current pulls, pushes, presses, opens, lifts and lowers it, and it must react to these pressures. Sea-trout have good vision, and if a fly is not taken, it is not necessarily because the fish has failed to see it. Yet there are times when I believe a fly or lure does go unnoticed, and I like to think that my flies have a presence that makes them more detectable at such times.

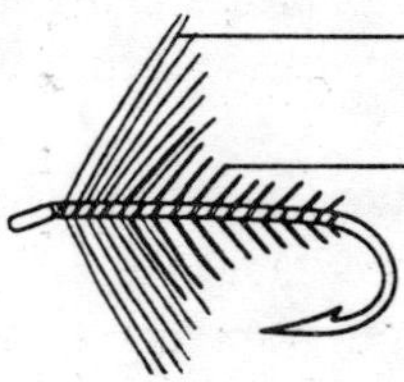

Most anglers develop their own style of fly-dressing, yet there is a tendency for them to retain something of their teacher's influence. My teacher was the great Dai Lewis, of the Teifi, a professional fisher and dresser of flies. His flies had to have the 'kick' he so revered.

It's the hackle that gives a fly its lively qualities. A fly may appear to have bulk when viewed in its dry form, but that's not how sea-trout see it. They see it being worked across or against the current, and all flies dressed with good hackle lose their bulkiness when they are viewed in transmitted light. The qualities that most anglers look for are translucency, glint, gleam and life.

My old teacher, Dai, had an ingenious method of enhancing his flies. He would achieve the necessary gleam and glint in the hackle by adding one or two turns of cree hackle. This had the effect of making the points of the hackle gleam, giving a distinct impression of life and movement. He would also use a turn or two of long, soft hackle as a collar around the normal hackle, adding to the impression of life.

Three seasons ago, on the Camel, I came across the same principle in a Teal, Blue and Silver dressed as a palmered pattern, the teal used as hackle over the shorter blue hackle. It looked good and worked a treat, yet the principle of dressing flies that 'buzz' and 'kick' should be considered not as a Moses-like commandment, but nearer the teaching of the New Testament: blessed are they who give sea-trout things lively and kicking, for they shall be rewarded.

Many anglers like their flies and lures for sea-trout to be dressed on the 'slim-line' principle, with just wisps of wing, a few false hackles, and the hook-shank painted silver. I shared a pool one night on the Coquet with an angler who swore by his very slim flies, and I have to admit that he did much better than I did with my patterns. I suffered similar 'whitewashes' on the Lynher and the Teign at the hands of anglers using 'slim-line' flies. Perhaps we should accept the teaching of my old mentor, Dai, who said that pattern was at times irrelevant. What mattered were the flies' size and the manner and speed of their fishing.

I envy anglers who dress their flies and place them in row upon row in huge purpose-built boxes. I keep my sea-trout flies in four rather old tobacco tins, and my 'filing system' leaves a lot to be desired. But these are the patterns I find most useful.

Box 1 (for floating lines): Zulu, Bumbles, Connemara Black, Green Peter, Black Pennell, Invicta, Teifi Terror, Dai Ben, Teifi Topper.

Box 2 (for sinking lines): Alexandra, Squirrel series, Silver March Brown, Butchers, Red Mackerel, Pryf Llwyd, Haslam, Teal series, Mallard and Silver, Cert, Blackie, Black-and-silver Waddington, Peter Ross.

Box 3 (for surface work): Muddlers, Floating Lure, Surface Lure, Loch Ordie, Wake lures.

Box 4 (for fast-sink lines): Black Waddington Lure, Hover Lure, Tandem Blackie, Peacock-and-blue Lure, Marchogs, Silver Muddler Waddington, Beauty.

from THE COMPLETE FLY FISHER *(edited by Peter Lapsley) 1990*

Basic Rules

MICK LUNN

Halford and his many avid followers were purists and they laid down the basic rules of dry fly fishing, which have survived on our chalkstreams to this day. The only addition – which at the time created a bitter debate and divided the flyfishing world – was the development of the artificial nymph by G.E.M. Skues. He rightly reasoned that a major part of the trout's diet had to be made up of the nymphs of the various aquatic insects found in our chalkstreams. There are still people today who will never use a nymph, believing it to be unsporting. I have to disagree with them.

My earliest recollection of the debate about how to catch fish with the dry fly goes back to the mid-1930s. At that time the talk was about accuracy of presentation with an imitation that most closely resembled the natural insect. To a man, these anglers followed Halford's simple rules: always cast upstream to a fish and only with a single dry fly;

never cast to a trout unless it is rising to the natural fly; never encroach on another's water. Simple though these rules are, my feeling is that whether you use a wet fly, dry fly or a nymph, you should never use a method likely to spoil the sport of other anglers.

Halford died in 1914, and what a great man he was, a 'legend'. His studies of the live insects and his creation of so many artificial fly patterns are represented in his eloquent writings. Even today these stand as great works; I don't think we will ever see the equal of his *Dry-Fly Fishing in Theory and Practice, Dry Fly Entomology* and his *Modern Development of the Dry Fly*, published four years before his death.

My grandfather started tying flies in 1916 at the age of 54, under the tuition of Mr E. J. Power, a Houghton Club member and expert fly tier. In those days, most fly tiers created their artificials the Halford way, making them as accurate to the naturals as was humanly possible with twists of fur and feather. Within a year or two, however, grandfather noticed that beautiful though these creations were, to his mind they did not look as accurate from the trout's underwater point of view as they should.

Halford dressed his flies so that they look as lifelike as possible on the water, evolving in 1910 a set of artificials that were exact to the last detail, right down to differentiating the sexes of the natural. According to grandfather, though, Halford's artificials ignored the trout and how it viewed the fly, so he set about proving the point by creating artificials which looked realistic to the trout's eyes.

To ensure absolute accuracy, he would spend countless hours staring into his aquarium. Here he could observe the way the feet of the mature winged insect dimpled the surface of the water when it emerged and rested, waiting for its wings to become operational. He continued his observations down on the riverside, watching spinners as they either went down in the water to lay their eggs or, like the mayfly, pierced the surface and injected their eggs into the water, shaking and trembling with the effort of ovipositing.

His observations and long hours at the vice created forty patterns, including flies which feature in every dry flyfisher's box today such as the Caperer, Houghton Ruby, Lunn's Particular, Yellow Boy, Sherry Spinner and Hackle Bluewing. As Sir Laurence Dunne once said after trying one of grandfather's new creations, 'I don't know how the old wizard worked that out but he did and it works like a dream'.

He took these notes and observations back with him to his fly tying bench and translated them into a range of quite revolutionary artificial duns, spinners and nymphs, covering the many insects indigenous to the Middle Test. He discovered, among other things, that a hackled artificial fly worked better than Halford's winged patterns, which were accurate right down to the exact wing form and size, but did little to impress the trout. Instead, grandfather created loosely dressed flies, described by John Waller Hills in his book *River Keeper* as 'indefinite and shapeless, without form or modelling, legs and wings mingled in a confused whirl of feathers': these fooled even the most experienced trout.

Since grandfather and father's day there has been a lot of 'jaw' talked about what fly to use and when and the magazines are full of articles about this natural and that, this artificial representation and that. I, however, have devised a much simpler set of rules, designed to take the mystique out of flyfishing, without taking away any of the enjoyment.

These basic, and by no means rigid rules about which fly to use, where and how, are borne out by the way members of the Houghton Club consistently take good fish from their waters. They have proved conclusively over the years that the old and hallowed concept that only an exact copy of the natural will catch a fish is complete rubbish. To those people who argue to the contrary, I show the book in the clubroom, where on a single day every member has taken six fish, and all on different fly patterns.

As far as I'm concerned, it's the size of fly that matters when it comes to that moment when, with furrowed brow, the angler looks into his box and ponders over which fly to tie on the end of his cast. He checks the water, straining his eyes to distinguish the natural on the water that is so avidly being sipped down by the trout. 'So what is that fly?' he asks himself, and 'Do I have an accurate imitation?'

There are a few exceptions to the rule that size is pretty well everything: no matter what you use during a fall of black gnat or hawthorn flies, the trout will be interested only in very small or large black flies. The trout are also highly selective when there is a fall of sherry spinners – the artificial seems to work better than any other small fly – and if you toss a small artificial at a trout who is rising to the mayfly it will be ignored.

Outside of those exceptions the following rules on size of fly rather than pattern seem to work every time. For example, if you see a fish rising consistently, chuck him a small fly. If there's a fish rising to fly you can see hatching on the water, cast it a small, but hackled dry fly. When you see spinners preparing to fall and spot a fish making sipping rises, then use a spinner pattern. Finally, if you come across a fish who rises only occasionally – a 'oncer' – a big fly like a Caperer, Brown Sedge or Wulff will work.

I haven't delved into the entomology of fly fishing because although a knowledge of the natural flies which hatch through the season adds a new and fascinating dimension to flyfishing, it is not absolutely necessary. It is, nevertheless, an absorbing facet of our sport.

The other aspect of dry fly fishing where I disagree with Halford and the purists is in the idea that you should only cast to a visible rising fish. Although I can think of nothing better than fishing for a rising trout, there are plenty of days when you never see a free-rising fish. On such days, particularly from June (after mayfly) to August, when rising fish are hard to find during the daylight hours, a pair of Polaroid spectacles cuts out the surface glare and enables you to search the water for a likely fish feeding below the surface on nymphs. Providing you see it before it sees you, there's every chance you will tempt it with a floating fly or a nymph below the surface. I sometimes wonder if Halford's or my grandfather's flies would have been created differently if Polaroids had been around in their day.

I can remember many July days when I have accompanied an angler during the daytime session and not seen one fish rise. I have, however, spotted several in the water, moving to right and left, as they intercept the nymphs tumbling down to them on the current. Rather than drop a nymph on its nose I have persuaded the angler to try each fish with a large dry fly, only for the fish to rise – perhaps for the first time that day – and confidently grasp the fly in its mouth. It is tremendous sport, and for me there is nothing unsporting or unethical about it. Unfortunately, not all the anglers I fish with are good at what I call 'looking in' the water; young eyes definitely have the advantage here.

Over the past thirty years my simple dry fly rules have worked almost every time. Looking through the book in the clubroom, it is a matter of fact that more fish have been taken on the Red or the Grey Wulff than any other pattern, followed in popularity by the Caperer and the Little Brown Sedge. The Wulff was first introduced to members by Lewis Douglas, the US Ambassador, who arrived in the clubroom one morning, propped his box of Wulffs on the mantelpiece and invited members to try the pattern. It was an instant hit, both with the members and the trout, and I remember my father was inundated with orders from members to tie the pattern on small hooks.

In recent years, fewer fish have been taken on the Houghton Club waters with the kind of tiny artificials recommended by Frederic Halford. Some anglers believe that the success of the larger fly, like the Wulff, has something to do with today's stocked fish being less selective. This can't actually be true because our wild fish fall for the Wulff just as readily as the stock fish. Certainly the tackle we use today is more sophisticated, particularly when you compare today's almost invisible, ultra-fine, double-strength nylon casts with the gut casts of thirty years ago. No, I think that it's the size of fly first, pattern second; after all, my friend Oliver Kite caught hundreds of fish on what he called 'a nymph', which was little more than a bare hook. I even overheard one fisherman – not on our waters, I hasten to add – swear by what he called his Pellet Fly, whatever that was.

My advice to anglers is always to have patience and offer the trout a selection of flies before giving up on it. If it's a really difficult fish and refuses every fly in your box, spit on the fly and see if the trout is prepared to take the fly just under the surface; nine times out of ten it will. Purists may not approve of this method, but it can make the difference between a blank day and fish in the bag.

I think the 'upstream only' dictum laid down by Halford is more a matter of commonsense than etiquette. I must say, though, that I disapprove thoroughly of the 'chuck it and chance it' flyfisher who fishes the water with dry fly, starts off with an upstream cast on the surface and allows the fly to drift downstream before retrieving it as a submerged fly. That, to me, is very definitely unsporting.

Downstream dry fly fishing is in my view allowable when the current and the position of the angler preclude an effective, drag-free upstream cast. In this circumstance, I think it is okay for the angler to stand upstream of the rising fish and cast his line downstream with enough of a belly in the line to allow it to float down to the trout without the current causing drag. The 'downstream drifter', as I call him, is the angler who will pretty well always take fish where there is a mixed current of fast and slow water caused by an encroaching bank of weed or the current-dividing stanchion of a bridge.

from A PARTICULAR LUNN *1990*

Truth about Flies

DR ROBERT SLOANE

Clearly, seeing trout and interpreting the signs (the trout's lie, its depth, speed and direction of movement) leads to a need for correct fly presentation with an obvious skill factor involved in the casting. Presentation involves good judgement, depending on factors such as water clarity, calmness, brightness, drift and flow, wind strength and direction, as well as the behaviour of the fish. A trout may be rising at regular intervals, or returning to a particular spot to take food, or conditions may require that the fly makes a 'splat' on the water, sinks quickly, or slowly, passes a cruising fish at speed, or lies inert on the weeds.

So, seeing the fish and presenting the fly correctly brings us to the final link – the fly itself. I am a great believer in the 'functional' fly, tied as simply as possible so as to behave appropriately in or on the water and to create an impression of suitable shape, size and movement. The quest for perfect imitation is not one which I follow.

Many anglers believe the fly pattern to be all important, but I know too much of trout habits and diet to consider that this is the answer. I have checked too many bags of fish caught on different flies on the same day, during the same rise, to subscribe to this school of thought. The stomach contents of stream or lake trout, taken during a prolific hatch, rarely show that only one size and type of organism has been ingested to the exclusion of all else. This very seldom occurs.

A trout is an opportunistic feeder, generally taking any suitable organism in its path. This is often more evident in stream fish, which will take up station in the current and snatch suitable items from the drift. Stomach contents of lake trout are often more specific, but I believe this to be a function of the trout's feeding depth, area and method, rather than deliberate selection. In general, a trout's diet will reflect the availability of suitable prey in the immediate environment. If a particular item becomes superabundant then this item will dominate the diet, but this does not mean that the trout is actively selecting the item in preference to other suitable prey which may cross its path.

Exact imitation is a particular approach to sport and a challenge to the fly tyer which should not be confused with more successful catching of trout. Of course, it is a great pleasure to develop a near-perfect imitation and to fool a wily fish, but in general such effort is not necessary.

I don't think it matters whether you have the correct number of bristles on the left tarsus of an insect. What seems to be important is the general shape and size of the fly and, in particular, the way it behaves in or on the water. As a consequence a fly box can be developed to provide a small number of multi-purpose, functional fly designs which will serve 95% of requirements during a season. This is how my fly box appears, largely as a result of years of experimental fly tying and fly fishing by my father, close friends and myself.

It is my philosophy that fishing *to* trout is more rewarding than 'blind' fishing and that correct presentation and functional fly patterns are everything.

from THE TRUTH ABOUT TROUT *1987*

PART 4

Mixed Bag

The Trout, the Dace, the Pike, the Breame,
The Eele, that loves the troubled stream,
The Miller's Thombe, the hiding Loach,
The Perche, the ever-nibling Roach,
The shoals with whom is Tavie fraught,
The foolish Gudgeon quickly caught,
And last, the little Minnow-Fish,
Whose chief delight in gravell is.

William Browne

French Interlude

NEGLEY FARSON

It is a hard choice to make, but I almost believe the Frenchman is a more implacable fisherman than either the English or American. We all know de Maupassant's story of the two old comrades who went to fish outside the walls during the siege of Paris, were captured by the Germans and shot as spies, after which the jeering Germans ate their fish. And on the eve of this last war, the very last week before it, in fact, I fished in a slack water behind an island below Strasbourg with an old Frenchman in his rowboat, with the French soldiers climbing up ladders to their lookouts in the trees, staring malevolently at German sentries across the racing Rhine. We were using maggots to catch fish none of which could be larger than a long cigar; but this innkeeper–fisherman had invested his life's savings to buy a pub in this particular spot – so that he could follow his hobby in his off-hours (they were more off than on!) – and now, he complained bitterly, the dirty Boche would one day cross the pontoon bridge and . . . he would never fish again.

'Or perhaps they will merely use a cannon and shoot me where I am!'

He would not move, however, until that day.

I do not know whether anyone else has ever witnessed it, but I have never seen one of those French fishermen catch anything but the bottom where the Seine flows through Paris. Yet think how many businesses were being neglected, how many of those useful French wives were tending shop, while these Frenchmen, by their hundreds, sat on the banks of the Seine with the scantiest hope that they could bring something home that would justify them for a wasted day. I call that courage.

If you drive down across France in the spring, when the streams are full and the leaves are their bright vivid green, you will sometimes think that half of France must be out with rod and grub or worm. You will see (at least, you did one day) the Frenchmen sitting by their poplar-lined canals. Sometimes, with a little lead minnow with a hook in its tail. You will see them leaning over the shore-end of a bridge by some fresh river, jerking their rod up and down, up and down, up and down . . . They are fishing for yellow perch. And many a time I have got out of my car and watched these Frenchmen. I have an affinity with them – and an equal anxiety as to what they might be about to catch. I know the black-barred perch; and the spectacle of one of these Frenchmen always recalled spring days in a canoe on the windy lake back home. Ask them a pertinent question. And the Frenchman, seeing you are a knowledgeable angler, responds with a discourse on local habits.

Finally you are both rewarded; he has got one! '*Eh, bien! M'sieu – demi-kilo!*' And some stocky, jovial Frenchman of the Midi, free from all inhibitions concerning the social values of fishing, will inform you that this monster he is holding up must weigh at least a pound.

I have found, on such occasions, that if you go with this Frenchman (and his trophy) to his favourite little sidewalk café in some sunbaked village square that you will come nearer to his heart – what he really thinks about life and politics – than you possibly could by bribe or guile. He feels, as a fellow fisherman, that he can talk straight with you. You have the common bond. And if you happen to be on a journey in which time is of no importance he will introduce you in the evening to the members of his village fishing club. There is hardly a village in all France which does not have one.

These clubs are not altogether unknown in either England or America, but they are extremely rare. In France they are an institution. Many of them are for more than merely the local coarse fish; they exist in the trout regions where their democracy is just as unblemished. This is particularly true in Haute Savoie, where the swift green rivers race down through the pine forests and grey crags; and where, in most other countries, you would find every foot of such good water owned by some rich proprietor. I had passed in and out of Paris for years, often with weeks to spare, wondering whether it was worth the bother to find where I could buy the right to fish for trout, and then always giving it up because it seemed too complicated. Then by an off-chance I picked a tiny village high up in the mountains of Haute Savoie to settle down in and write my book on South America. And here I found the poor trout fisherman's heaven.

As I drove past Lake Annecy I stopped at the local fishing shop to see what kind of flies they were using, and get some. I was amazed at the 'elegance' of this little tackle shop, its window display, its show-cases, its long line of rods – it might have been in Pall Mall or St James's Street. There was such a professional competence in its air. But what gave me such a start, almost a shock, was that when the proprietor turned round to speak to me from a cast he was tying I found myself looking at the twin brother of the little bicycle-and-tackle shop man I had left only a few days before back in Somerset.

Later, when we were fishing one of the mountain rivers together, I told him about this. But this day when I waited for him to straighten up I found that he couldn't; he was a hunchback. And later, on the river, he told me why he could never stand upright again; he had been 'hunchbacked' on the Somme – shot through the spine. Not only that, but when our acquaintance improved he took me to the fine little hotel he had once owned in Annecy, and had sold so that he could run just his small tackle shop. 'You may think me a fool, M'sieu, but I am a completely happy man. In the hotel I made money – but in my shop I *live*!' On the river one luncheon time, when we ate on the bouldered bank with an eagle soaring high overhead, he told me that he was a member of the Cross of Fire, the Hooded Men, the most violent Fascist organization in all France – and that his brother had just come out from serving three months in prison, because twenty-six rifles had been found in their house.

He was the finest fly-fisher I have ever seen.

'But these flies, M'sieu!' he exclaimed when I went out to my car that first day and brought back my bag, 'are not the ones for here. *Pas ici!* What do you think of these?'

I told him I had never in my life seen the like of those he was showing me. He was immensely pleased. 'They are,' he said . . . half closing his eyes like some composer searching for a chord . . . 'a few experiments that I have made myself . . . I would suggest that you try them.'

I never go into a tackle shop without coming out ruined. But on that day, because I did not know he was so genuine, I bought only three or four casts and a dozen or so of his gnat-like experiments (whose look I did not trust at all), thanking him for mere politeness' sake. When he asked me where I was going to live in the mountains, and I told him about fifty miles up, he again closed his eyes.

'Too far, M'sieu . . . unless you are a goat. The river is full of gorges up there. You will never get down them. Even *I* find it almost impossible.'

I withheld my smile, staring at this satyr-like little creature before me, and listened patiently while he made me write down the names of some villages where, he told me, I should begin fishing lower down.

Then with light sarcasm I asked him how could I fish those stretches of water – when I was not going to live in an hotel or an inn anywhere along the lowest stretch. He replied with amazement: 'The Club!'

He then wrote down the name of a Frenchman in each of some five small villages and wished me good luck. 'Perhaps M'sieu,' he said modestly, 'we might have a day on the river together?'

As this is a more or less accurate account of our conversation that impatient afternoon, for I was anxious to get on, I will merely state that I noticed the name of each Frenchman he gave me was obviously the proprietor of some inn or café (for which I thought he was pimping) and that I lost his own card, which he pressed upon me, even before I reached my own little pub, the Golden Lion.

So much for snap judgements.

A few days later I slid my car down to where the gorges ceased and entered a café. Its proprietor and a hefy daughter were serving what appeared to be the village postman, its policeman, and one or two other non-uniformed gentlemen, with some demi-litres of white wine. I asked if I could speak to the president of the village fishing club. The hairy-armed man behind the bar said that this was he. Could he do anything for me? I replied that I would like to fish this stretch of river; how much would it be? I was asked for how long? I said, possibly a couple of days – maybe more. Were there any fish here?

At that I noticed that the postman, the policeman, and the other non-uniformed gents had stopped speaking since I came in. Now I saw them staring at me intently. I was being appraised. I began to feel uncomfortable . . .

The fat, hairy-armed man behind the bar smiled. Then he shrugged his shoulders. He said – looking at the others – 'There *are* fish . . .' He left the statement hanging in the air; and if ever I have been told more plainly to my face, 'There are fish – providing you know how to catch them,' I don't want to be reminded of it. The others now turned from regarding me and took up their conversation again. It was a bad beginning. I paid fifteen francs a day I think, for a week's fishing, drank a polite demi-litre of white wine, and left the hotel. It required all my courage to ask the proprietor did he mind if I left my car, for safe-keeping before his hotel. He said no, he didn't mind. That was all.

The rivers up there are all snow-fed, many of them are glacial; so that even in mid-summer you will find long, swift stretches where it is hard to wade. Up by the Golden Lion, as the little satyr in Annecy had prophesied, there were gorges. And sides so steep that it was torture to get down to fish the few pools that lay between them. I had tried. I had slipped and slid down through the heavy pine forests (almost breaking my rod) to fish a few of these pools – but there was no way that I could find to get either down or up to fish the next pool. Nothing but a steep climb up the mountain-side, a walk along the mountain road, and then another descent to get down to fish another pool. I found it no good. Not for me. Although the proprietor of the Golden Lion (that excruciating man) did exclaim when I brought home a few fish from my first attempt: 'There! You see I was not lying when I wrote to you that my hotel had kilometres of fine trout fishing!'

But down here was the beginning of orchard country, and alpine wheat. The river was broad, with long beds of grey boulders that now lay bare in the sun. There were farms on one side and slopes of steep pine forests on the other, and grey iron-streaked cliffs. An inspiring country. As I put my rod together and soaked the cast I saw long stickles and channels of water coursing between the islands made by boulders bared by the falling water. There were long broad sweeps where the river was apple-green. And, very wisely, I put on the satyr's cast.

These were light-backed trout with vivid red spots, which struck (when they did strike) with vicious intensity. This river was not a glacial one, and in that ice-clear water I could watch a large part of their fight. In one deep stretch of river, where it was so flat and slow that it was almost like a shallow lake, I got the best fish of the afternoon by putting on an old worn Mayfly. It was a freak attempt, but continuous rises under the branches of some trees on the far side of the pool tempted me. It was about all I could do, wading out till the water seeped over into my waders (and how cold it was!), to get my fly across to them. Time and again I watched it float, unnoticed, down under the branches; then there was a quick splash. I walked backward up on to the island of boulders again. After an exciting few minutes' fight I netted a fine little fish that was over 1½lb.

But although I can say I have scarcely ever seen such fine trout water, I did not touch many trout. The reason explained itself about five o'clock, when I saw a man emerge from the bushes opposite me (I had crossed the river to the opposite side from the village) and fix a wood grub to a reel-less line that was wrapped around an ordinary bamboo rod. He pitched this grub in and let it drift down to a pool that I had been casting over, which began under a leaning tree. Dumbfounded – I recognized him as one of the non-uniformed gentlemen I had seen at midday sitting in the inn – dumbfounded, I say, and a little angry, I saw him pull out a nice nine- or ten-inch trout.

Such competition was too formidable. I watched Frenchman after Frenchman appear, fix on a grub (I learned they got them from Geneva) and pop it into the water. It seemed as if the whole village was down by six o'clock, including the postman. I gave it up. I had eight fish, none of which was up to half a pound, except the one lucky one; yet I felt I could now walk with impunity back to that village inn. And there, tired, I sat down at a table before its arboured door and ordered a litre of white wine.

The hefty daughter came out to serve me, smiling now. *'Et vous? M'sieu – bonne chance?'*

I pulled aside the grass inside my bag and showed her the big one. The next person who came out was the proprietor: *'Bien?'* he asked.

I repeated my performance – with the one big fish. He did not say anything. But, as I had not taken my rod apart – it was leaning against the car – he walked over, and picked it up. He tried it with his wrist. Then (and I watched him do that so carefully) I saw him looking at the flies. He nodded. Then he came back and sat down at the table beside me, tapping it idly with his finger.

'Where did you get that one?' he asked, meaning my one big fish.

So that's the way it began. I was there a couple of months that summer, writing my book; and every afternoon I fished the streams or rivers around me. I have seldom found more congenial, pithy companions than these Frenchmen of the village fishing clubs. The presidency of the club, I learned, was an honour which was supposed to rotate yearly. The proprietors of the village inns or cafés always took it in turn – because it brought such customers! The return from the river always led direct to the café, where the day's luck was discussed. For this it was necessary to have a demi-litre, perhaps several demi-litres of white wine. They were not all grub fishermen. An occasional elderly man (perhaps the village doctor) would amble back with a fly-rod, and make some acid remarks about the rest of the company.

But they all loved fishing. They loved talking about fishing even more, perhaps; but they loved just fishing itself so much that it was not long before I discovered that any stretch of river within an easy walk of one of these villages was simply fished to death. Talk about 'too many rods on the water'; their bamboo poles looked almost like a fence at times.

And so, as his name was like a legend along the river, I called up the little hunchback down in Annecy. Should we, I asked, have a day's fishing on the river together? He asked me to wait a moment. He always called his chubby red-haired little wife '*Mon petit*' (as fat Sacha Guitry used to call his beloved Yvonne Printemps); and I could hear him cajoling her now – the discussion obviously being, would she look after the store? Then his bright voice came back to me.

'Of a certainty! Tomorrow, nine o'clock precisely, I shall meet you at –'

He was at loss for a name, for, he said, 'there is no village there'. But he gave me a rendezvous about fifteen miles below where I had been fishing all the time! 'I shall wait for you by the road,' came his eager injunction; 'I have a little red Citroën coupé – stop when you see it!'

By now I had reached that place in the confidence of M. Vacheron, proprietor of the *Lion d'Or*, to know that he had been the 'fish chef' on the old Olympic. He had cooked in the 'private' restaurant, that *de luxe* dining-room, where millionaires and movie stars gorged themselves across the Atlantic. They had seventeen chefs for, on the average, only thirty-eight people. He was a distinguished man.

'Mr Pierpont Morgan,' said M. Vacheron, '*always* ordered oysters *au gratin* and lobster Newberg.'

This night, learning that I was to fish with the celebrated M. Croisier, he wondered if it might not be possible for me to bring some of my trout back alive – as some of the Frenchmen did in these parts with a little barrel or tin can of water on their backs. I firmly told him no; we would have to continue in our usual way. I did not intend to burden myself in these rough streams with any additional pounds of wobbling water.

'Very well,' sighed M. Vacheron; 'I would like to cook you the true *truite au bleu*. But for that I must have them alive. I cook them alive and then clean them afterwards. If you cannot bring them back alive, then you must mark the two or three you have caught last – the last to die – and I shall do with these. These I shall cook. The colour will not be *truite au bleu* – but they will taste almost as good.'

M. Vacheron lived over his past, with the aid of many cognacs, every night; and now, dejected because of my refusal to provide him with live trout, he declared: 'The golden age of cooking is over, M. Farson. It is the sauces. Truffles and cream and butter – even the big restaurants aren't so free with these any more. From our point of view (the chefs') probably the finest restaurant in the world was the old Café Royal in London when Mrs Nobel owned it . . . Ah . . . everything! . . . hundreds of truffles . . . and the butter you wanted . . . if a dish was not precisely correct . . . you threw it in the fire . . .

'And some of the dishes we used to prepare . . . The *Crêpes Veux-tu* . . . ! They were pancakes cooked in apricot brandy . . . with lizards done on them in meringue . . . with cherry eyes . . . and then little piles of fresh peaches and pineapple piled up all around . . . !'

As we sat in his kitchen, where he held these nightly reminiscences, the rain ran in rivers down its window-panes. There had been a cloud-burst that day. And we had seen a staggering thing – a farmhouse up on the Alpine meadow behind us struck by lightning. It was one of those Swiss-chalet affairs, with broad stones holding down the shingles of its roof. It went up in one grand blaze as if a high explosive had hit it. We had watched it from our balcony.

Its owners were away, having just taken their cattle to graze on a higher alpine slope. 'And now,' said the sophisticated M. Vacheron, 'they have lost all their money – it is burning there now – for, M. Farson, you know a French peasant never puts his money in a bank. He doesn't trust banks.'

I, selfishly, was only worried about this rain; would it spoil my day tomorrow with M. Croisier? I awoke early to a clear blue sky over the glistening pine forest, drank my bowl of coffee, leapt into the car – and swerved and slithered down the slippery mountain road to where I found a little red Citroën almost lying on its side in a ditch in a deep forest twenty-five miles below. M. Croisier was in an exultant mood: 'We shall have a fine day!'

The only habitation we passed that day was a saw-mill. For mile after mile the river sides here were too steep for farming. That is why there were no villages. That is why there were so many trout. But M. Croisier fished in a peculiar way: he fished with a wet fly, upstream, throwing the fly *directly* ahead of him. He got thirty-seven trout and I got, I think, seventeen.

But what fishing!

We cast with lines not much longer than our rods. We fished behind every rock, boulder, ledge. And M. Croisier even took fish from dead against the bank. Tap-Tap-Tap went M. Croisier.

'But!' I protested at first, 'you don't leave your flies on the water long enough for any fish to touch them!'

The little hunchback man smiled: 'Do not worry, M. Farson. If the trout are there – I shall get them.'

The point was, he explained, that where the stream was so swift, and especially after this cloud-burst in the upper mountains, the trout just *couldn't* leave any lee they had found – that was why, he said, we would find so many of them right up against the bank. And again, if we let our lines rest on the water for more than an instant, we would have our casts swept back against our own waders. 'No! – it must be like that!' – and he put his flies behind a rock before us just as if they were on the end of a wand.

I had never seen anything like it.

Nor have I ever seen anything like his eagerness. There were one or two fairly large pools or riffles that we approached. But before I could get up to them the little satyr raced on ahead of me. He couldn't resist it. '*Pardon, M'sieu!*' he always said, apologizing for his selfishness – then raced me to the next pool just the same. The forest, rocks, glistening, racing water, were all so fresh that sun-filled morning, with the white clouds scudding across the blue sky overhead, that I felt too full of the sheer joy of living to mind much what he did – but, I decided, the next time M. Croisier and I went out *I* would put on running shoes.

There was a pool by the saw-mill, with some logs in it which were waiting to be cut. Here M. Croisier put his fly-rod down and took a short little rod, about the size of a section of trout-rod, from his back. It was a stout little piece, with an off-cast wire loop at its tip. This, said the satyr, was a 'Dandinet'. He then took from his bag a wooden spreader very similar to those you see in tackle shops around which are wound hand-lines for sale. But on this one was nothing but yards and yards of stout gut – just, let us say, some sixty or a hundred yards of a cast. And on the end of this M. Croisier slid a little lead minnow – after which he attached a hook to the end of the gut.

'You see,' he said, giving it a flick, 'I can cast this anywhere.'

The little lead minnow shot through the air . . . the gut unwound off the spreader as easily as a thread-line off a Silex reel, and *plunk*! the minnow fell into the pool, say, about forty yards from us. The instant it hit the water M. Croisier was already winding it in with a swift revolution of the wooden spreader. And this he did with the speed with which you would bring back your Devon with a bait-casting reel.

A fish took the minnow. When it jumped I saw the lead minnow shoot yards up the gut-line. 'You see,' exulted the expert M. Croiser, 'when the minnow shoots up the line they have nothing to shake against . . .'

It was purely for my amusement, he said, that he had brought the 'Dandinet' along. And then to show me what he really could do with it, he shot the minnow upstream where the river entered the pool. And again he retrieved it. 'But this, M. Farson . . . is not like fly-fishing!'

I still had a lot of my two months to go, and this was the beginning of a friendship. M. Croisier told me that – and very plainly.

The way it came about was that at the end of the day, before we began the long walk back to our cars, for we had been fishing up-river all this time, we reached a village. Here, after a stiff climb up the river-bank, M. Croisier and I rested ourselves in its small inn's yard. We had a few litres of white wine. And during this I attempted to pay him for some casts and flies I had borrowed from him on the river. He held up his little hand in dismay:

'M. Farson! No! In my little shop in Annecy, I shall charge you for *everything – beaucoup!* But on the river, M. Farson . . . on the river we are comrades!'

It was a gesture from *la belle France* I shall never forget.

from GOING FISHING *1932*

The Fishing Hotel

L. R. N. GRAY

An hotelier
Stood at the Golden Gate, his head was bent and low,
He meekly asked the man of Fate which way he had to go.
'What have you done,' St Peter said, 'to seek admission here?'
'I kept an hotel on earth,' said he, 'for many and many a year.'
St Peter opened wide the gate, and beamed on him as well.
*'Come in and choose a harp,' said he, 'you've had your share of Hell.'**

*Author unknown to me. Ed.

What an implied libel on the average guest the above verse is! As far as fishing guests are concerned I most definitely take the opposite view. Ninety-nine per cent of them are a pleasure to have around, and the odd miserable, selfish trouble-maker can always be 'induced' to leave before he or she spoils the atmosphere of the house . . .

When it comes to fishing hotels, the fact that salmon, trout and sea-trout fishing is usually far from any large town and difficult to get in other than small stretches (if it is any good) and then only at an uneconomic price, tends to make catering for fishing guests the sideline of a country pub. The exceptions are the all-round sporting hotel of fair size, and licensed of course, and the small town hotel with the usual commercial and family trade, and fishing as a seasonal attraction. In Scotland, of course, conditions are different.

Before I had my own fishing I stayed at several of these pubs or hotels with fishing in the West Country, caught plenty of salmon at times, and enjoyed myself. I had more than my money's worth, but I should hate to think what they would have to charge for fishing if they had to buy their fishing rights at today's prices. Luckily, almost all I know have held their fishing for very many years; otherwise the charges would have to be doubled or twice the number of rods allowed on the water, and usually there are too many already.

In recent years a third class of fishing hotel has appeared – the country house which had fishing rights or could acquire some within reasonable distance. At present, outside Scotland, their number is few, but almost every year, as large country houses become more difficult to live in privately, and fewer are needed for prep. schools, convalescent homes, etc., some mug opens one up as a country house hotel with fishing. I am of this number (but I had the fishing before I bought the house). Our ranks are headed by a Duke who now runs his West Country seat as a fishing hotel.

After five seasons at this game I now feel sure that it is not a business proposition. It is worth something to live in a lovely place, have staff and overheads paid for by the business, a little fishing yourself now and then and nice people to talk to if you feel like it – real 'brothers of the angle', who, while on holiday at any rate, think and talk of little but fishing. Unfortunately I have to earn my living apart from the hotel, so I never get as much of it as I should like, but it is a lovely life if you can afford it. Even if you can't fish when you have time, because all the beats are taken, you can always gillie for the guest with the lowest score and help him to even it up. Making someone else fish the water as you know it *should* be fished is not only interesting to them, but to you, too. If you have someone who can fish reasonably well but doesn't know the water, it is almost as good as fishing yourself.

Of course I get called upon to prove my theories and demonstrate them in practice. To fail is a serious matter, so if conditions are not reasonably good it is necessary not to put yourself in a position where you have led the guests to believe they ought to be catching fish if they could fish well enough. If you do, and a fish is not forthcoming, it is certain that you will be handed the rod, and told to do your stuff in no uncertain terms. Your prestige will be valueless unless you can succeed where the guest has failed. There are other, and more frequent, occasions when it is hard to restrain yourself from snatching the rod uninvited, especially when your pupil is a novice and slow at following instructions!

It makes such a lot of difference to the catch if those fishing know the river well. Two average local rods would catch twice as many salmon here as half a dozen good visitors. The record of the water therefore suffers very badly. I issue a detailed guide to my water with instructions how to fish each lie. It helps a little and saves me a lot of trouble, but I can usually still go down for half a day and beat the total catch of the other five rods. I think it is their tactics which are at fault, rather than lack of knowledge of the river. They concentrate on the right pool, perhaps, but at the wrong time; and so on. Guidance on tactics and the planning of the day's campaign are usually more valuable than exact knowledge of lies, which only experience of the water can teach.

The question of allotment and rotation of beats used to annoy me at times when I depended on fishing hotels for all my fishing. Some hotels take as many guests as they can get, and let them all fish where and how they can. Naturally there is a rush to get breakfast first and dash to the best pool. Others arrange individual beats, but change them at lunch-time or after an even shorter period. In one case I know, the beats are very small and changed every three hours from 6 am till dusk; consequently guests fish the hours allotted to them on the best pools, and tend to skip their times on the less likely waters. Ten rods means two to each beat, and fifteen rods three at a time, but I believe that little if anything is charged for fishing, and the hotel keeps all the fish except the second, or something like that. These systems allow twice as many rods on the water as I (as a guest) liked, unless the water was in good order and on the high side. You cannot feel very hopeful, starting to fish a pool with fly when you know it has been flogged with prawns, spoons, plugs, worms, and various 'poppers' and doodlebugs from America. If the rods are not doubled up on a beat you can rest the pool for an hour or two before starting to fish, but in low water that is often not long enough.

Having experienced this sort of thing as a guest and thereafter gone elsewhere, I determined to have exclusive daily beats on my own water, with the change-over at 2 pm and an inflexible rule of moving down one beat every day. It saves time and trouble, and makes any suspicion of favouritism impossible. If rods want to swop amongst themselves that is up to them, but I strictly enforce one rod to one beat. My four miles of bank, divided into six beats, have two portions where neighbours have the opposite bank, and if two friends on adjoining beats 'gang up' opposite one of them, it is likely to force them to retaliate and put two rods on opposite us. This policy means that I can only take half the rods usual on hotel water, and consequently the overheads per guest in the hotel are double what they might be, and the same applies to the fishing charges. (The fish belong to the angler.) I thought, however, that there were plenty of people willing to pay the extra for a generous and exclusive beat all to themselves, and plenty of room and service in the hotel. It probably works out cheaper per fish, and (what would count heavily with me) they know that, apart from a little opposition from my neighbours on a couple of pools on two beats, they have a stretch completely to themselves to rest or fish as they wish. It is a very comforting feeling to be first down the water that day, but with fishing rights worth a minimum of £5,000 per mile per bank and rates of around £50 per mile, plus the expenses of bush trimming, ladder-making, bridges over ditches, stiles, huts, a cable bridge, bank repairs, etc., it can't be cheap fishing.

As one's overheads are constant and irreducible, extra guests are the answer, for their extra cost is little more than their food and laundry. But few men bring their wives fishing, even when the weather is warm and the countryside lovely. I think they like to escape completely on their fishing holiday. Britons seem to leave their wives at home. Americans, on the other hand, either bring them or send them to Paris to look at dresses . . .

Another minor trouble in the management of a purely fishing hotel is the difficulty of getting guests in to meals – particularly if it is a long walk to some of the beats. One popular small pub I used to go to had all its water running alongside roads, and nowhere had you to walk more than 300 yards to your car or the pub. They warned everyone that hot meals were served bang on time. They would give you a maximum of fifteen minutes grace, and then it was put on your table whether you were there or not. If you were 'in' a fish, then it was just too bad that your meal was cold when you arrived. It was surprising how punctual everyone became.

They were lucky to have all their water so accessible. It was unnecessary for them to provide sandwiches, etc., for those who could not be bothered to come back to lunch. Except in drought conditions, when midday fishing does more harm than good, everyone wants a packed lunch, and that means a rush while guests are having breakfast – especially on the first day of the new intake, when they are eager to get down to the river. Incidentally, few people realize that a good packed lunch costs more than a hot cooked one; and it is very difficult to give variety all through the week.

Getting guests in to dinner in the evening in March is fairly easy, as it is dark early enough to force them home, but by early April they trail in at dark and after and it is impossible to keep dinner and staff hanging about. At this time of year, except on dull days, the sun is shining straight down most of our pools between noon and 3 pm and it is better not to fish then because of line shadow. We therefore switch over to dinner between 1 and 2 pm and solve the problem of the evening meal by leaving a cold supper which they can have as and when they want it. It is on the table by 7 pm (covered of course) and often in summer is not eaten until 1 am. Soup and coffee are in thermos containers and guests help themselves . . .

Fishermen with the right temperament to be successful are happy, pleasant, 'normal' people. You get none with peculiar phobias or who need the services of psychopathic specialists. A large number of doctors seem to fish, and they ought to know what is good for them to counteract the strain and stress of modern times. Enforced exercise and unconscious concentration on the fishing is all that the average tired businessman on the verge of a breakdown needs to put him right. There is nothing like salmon- and seat-trout-fishing to make people forget all their worries, and the exercise gives them an appetite and tires them out so that they sleep well. Mind and body are therefore rested without drugs, and recovery is swift. If I were a Harley Street 'nerve' specialist I should invariably prescribe a month's fly-fishing where the finer points can be learnt, and plenty of walking and wading are necessay . . .

So many guests are so nice to have in the house that one hates to have to give them the bill when they have struck a bad week; but they know that all fishing, and salmon-fishing particularly, is a gamble, and the luck evens out over two or three visits.

Very occasionally you get a new guest who just does not fit in. They are the selfish, conceited types who consider none but themselves, usually can't fish for toffee (but think they are the 'cat's' whiskers') and behave as if they have bought up the whole place and you and all your staff were their slaves. They would make very bad commissars or dictators, but would greatly enjoy such positions. They are invariably very jealous fishermen, who sulk if others catch fish and they don't, and attempt to use prawn or worm when these baits are barred to give themselves an advantage over the other rods. Such people are best spotted early and 'induced' to leave before they spoil it for the other guests. They always have hides like rhinos, but, even so, they soon become so unpopular with the other guests that they are unlikely to enjoy themselves and come back again, so you don't really lose much. Some I have managed to cure by giving them a straight 'down-to-earth' talk, but where I see no hope of reform I ask them to leave after twenty-four hours' trial. Usually they react rather violently. One said, 'Good God! I've never been so insulted in my life.' I replied, 'Well, if you don't go you'll learn what I really think of you, but of course I don't want to be rude.' He went.

A bossy woman is the worst of all offenders. She often has a patient, peace-loving husband, and takes full advantage of it. Over the years she dominates him more and more, and attempts to do the same to anyone who has the misfortune to serve her. In her own home she can never keep any staff – even a char – and she never realizes how 'impossible' she has gradually become. Usually she is rolling in money and must 'swank' and throw her weight about . . . the only thing to do is to tell such women that your establishment is obviously not up to their standard and that you recommend them to go to a six-star place in Hades. The vials of wrath really break when you tell her poor husband that he can come alone whenever he likes!

If you don't induce such people to go you will lose your other guests or your staff, so you must tackle the job as soon as you see it is going to be necessary.

The general management and care of hotel water is important, and can make a lot of difference to the pleasure and comfort of guests, many of whom are either getting on in years or suffering from a shameful lack of exercise. (I admit to being in the latter class during most of the 'off' season.) If I kept my water to myself I should have left it much more bushed than it is, and it would then undoubtedly hold more fish – particularly sea-trout – than it does now; but if I did, much of it would never be fished by guests, either because few of them can execute any cast other than the overhead, or because, not knowing that our wading is dead easy, they would be fearful of deep wading to avoid high bushes on the bank. Therefore most of the bushes have to be kept trimmed to make casting easy. Even though this means fewer fish, it ensures more fishable water, and with fishing rights worth at least £2 per yard per bank we can't afford to leave productive water virtually unfished.

Many improvements can be made in the way of bridges over ditches and ladders down the banks where wadable pools should be entered and left. They act as a certain guide and don't cost much to make. Never use anything but oak, however, as the effect on a really fat man of falling through several rotten rungs of a ladder and landing wallop in a couple of feet of water has to be seen and heard to be believed.

Much can also be done (slowly and bit by bit in order to avoid mistakes) to improve pools by small groynes and projections in the bank, low weirs to increase the depth of water in the pool above, or to scour out a channel in a shallow run, and, of course, by the manufacture and correct placing of actual lies for fish . . . For almost all these jobs I am a strong advocate of large stones, rather than concrete.

All this sort of work is endless, and will keep an owner busy and interested for the rest of his life. Sometimes on hot summer days a bathing party of guests can be organized to help, and many hands make light the work. It is all good exercise for them.

In short, one can sum up the life of the proprietor of a fishing hotel in a very few words – 'Never a dull moment!'

from TORRIDGE FISHERY *1957*

Killarney in 1830

ANON

From the concurrent testimony of all the old fishermen, there was formerly most superior salmon-fishing in Killarney; but the erection of stake-nets and the constant hauling on the river Laun have very much injured it. Still, a considerable number of salmon come up in the winter and spring floods, many of which remain during the summer; and at other seasons, whenever the water is high enough for them to pass, there is sure to be a fresh supply. But they are no longer caught of that immense size which they are said to have been thirty or forty years ago.

Wherever the angler goes, he is sure to hear these same complaints of the diminished size of the salmon of the present day. Every fisherman he meets will tell him of the enormous monsters which he or his father killed in former times. Great allowances must doubtless be made for the exaggerated medium through which Age ever contemplates the deeds of its youth. The old man has always, since the days of Nestor, been a '*Laudator temporis acti, se puero*'.

But, independently of this natural tendency to look back upon everything connected with the days of our prime as intrinsically superior to present objects, I think there is sufficient ground for believing that the salmon formerly, if not more numerous, were at least, in all probability, larger than now. Until within late years, the market for this delicate fish was confined to a circle of a few miles round the place where they were caught, and they were therefore of comparatively little value. But, latterly, from the improvements in the means of conveyance, and especially since the invention of steam, it has been found practicable and profitable to send salmon from the extreme north of Scotland, and from the farthest west of Ireland, to Glasgow, Liverpool and London.

The respective fisheries have consequently become infinitely more valuable, and their lessees much more attentive, as well to the capture of those which enter the rivers before the fence months.

The rivers are incomparably better protected during the breeding season than formerly; and, such is the extraordinary fecundity of this department of the animal kingdom, that a few fish, if suffered to spawn in safety, will suffice to stock a stream. But, then, if this increased care, during the period when the salmon are the most exposed to the ruthless attacks of the rustic poacher, insure an increased number of young fish; on the other hand, the improved methods which the prospect of gain has taught the legal fisherman to use prevent their reaching any great age.

In every river where there are stake-nets or salmon-boxes, it is almost impossible for the fish to escape for many successive seasons: few, therefore, attain their natural size. At the same time, those that do pass, either in the fence months, or in very high floods, being much better protected than formerly, while they are rendered helpless and worthless by the process of spawning; the numbers, on the whole, are not diminished, although the size of the individual fish is much inferior to what is recorded of the aged Leviathans of old, which for many succeeding years had been permitted to frequent their native stream.

Almost every stream or lake in Ireland, that I have seen or heard of, contains more or less brown trout. These vary very much in size and in appearance, some being short and thick, with small heads, and hog-like backs, as, for instance, those of Westmeath Lakes, and others distinguished by huge heads, and long, lanky bodies, as the 'gubba-hawns' of many of the Connemarra Loughs.

But the fish which perhaps afford the most sport are the white or sea-trout – the salmo trutta – and which are found in most rivers and lakes that communicate by any considerable stream with the sea. These are, in their habits, very similar to the salmon; mounting, like them, into the fresh water, to spawn; after which they return, also like them, into the salt water.

There are few or no white trout in the Lakes of Killarney, but great quantities of brown trout, generally small, though occasionally of good size. There are also, fortunately, no pike.

Upon asking for the best fisherman, I was universally referred to one James Doherty; and finding that he had a convenient small boat of his own, I engaged it and its master, most days during my stay, in preference to one of Lord Kenmare's boats. I had every reason to be satisfied with him and his crew. They were invariably civil, ready and anxious to do anything and everything that I wished; and, what is no slight recommendation at Killarney, I had not to complain of a single instance of drunkenness.

Doherty is an extremely good fisherman, and a sensible, intelligent man. He is perfectly acquainted with his lake, which is of the utmost consequence; as without his knowledge one might fish the whole day without once casting the fly in any spot where a salmon ever lies. It is only in certain places where the depth of the water is from five to twelve feet that the angler has the least chance of rising a fish. These spots are often over isolated rocks, in the very middle of the Lake, which could never be guessed by one unacquainted with the place, but which Doherty knows to an inch by certain landmarks. These are what he calls courses, and are the only part of the Lake that there is the slightest use in trying.

The summer had been so uncommonly dry that the water was lower than had been remembered for many years, and the salmon were consequently driven off some of their usual courses. This was much against our sport. I have had ten or twelve rise at my fly, but never succeeded in killing more than two in any one day, although it was seldom I did not take at least a single fish. They were small, the largest that I killed weighing only seven pounds and a quarter; but we certainly saw some much larger. Having been long in the fresh water, they had all a dark, reddish appearance, and their flesh was softer and less flavoured than of those fresh from the sea. Many of them, however, played with great strength and vigour, and the whirlpool they made in the water, when dashing at the fly, was very fine – enough to cause the heart of the young tyro to jump to his mouth.

Doherty used invariably plain flies, of a smallish size, with dark turkey wings, and brown olive bodies, ribbed with narrow gold twist. I in general preferred my own more gaudy Limerick flies; and it was difficult to say which on the whole were the most successful; sometimes his proving the most killing, and, at others, mine. I am, however, perfectly convinced that flies somewhat handsomer than his, and with a richer mixed wing, but not so gaudy as mine, would succeed much better than either.

The greater part of the boats belong to Lord Kenmare, who established them in order to put a stop to the system of extortion formerly practised on visitors. Their prices are regularly fixed; and are, I think, seven shillings for two oars, eight shillings and six-pence for three oars, and ten shillings for four oars; besides which there is *always* a coxswain, or guide, for whom two shillings more are paid; and *generally* a bugler, who expects at least five shillings. By far the best of the buglers is Spillane; he is, moreover, a very respectable, intelligent and well-conducted man.

In addition to this first cost it is always expected that dinner and whiskey should be provided for the crew. The former is charged at the inns one shilling a head; the latter is *ad libitum* of the employer, but cannot be reckoned at much less than half a bottle for each, on a long day's expedition. The boating excursions at Killarney are therefore expensive pleasures, unless you are with a large party.

Most of the boatmen are, I fear, a sad drunken set. While out with their company they get a great deal to drink; and, making double the common wages of the country, too often spend most of their money in whisky at night. They have, consequently, as might be expected, an habitually muzzy, half tipsy, half drowsy, look and manner. I must, however, add, that I scarcely heard of a single instance of their impertinence or incivility, although they have not infrequently most extraordinary characters to deal with.

from THE ANGLER IN IRELAND *1834*

The Trout by the Bridge

RICHARD JEFFERIES

Just below the shadow of the beech there is a sandy, oozy shore, where the footprints of moorhens are often traceable. Many of the trees in the plantation stand in water after heavy rain – their leaves drop into it in autumn, and, being away from the influence of the current, stay and soak, and lie several layers thick. Their edges overlap, red, brown and pale yellow, with the clear water above and shadows athwart it, and dry white grass at the verge. A horse-chesnut drops its fruit in the dusty road; high above its leaves are tinted with scarlet. It was at the tail of one of the arches of the bridge over the brook that my favourite trout used to lie. Sometimes the shadow of the beech came as far as his haunts, that was early in the morning, and for the rest of the day the bridge cast a shadow. The other parapet faces south, and looking down from it the bottom of the brook is generally visible, because the light is so strong. At the bottom a green plant may be seen waving to and fro, in summer, as the current sways it. It is not a weed or flag, but a plant with pale green leaves, and looks as if it had come there by chance; this is the water-parsnip.

By the shore on this, the sunny side of the bridge, a few forget-me-nots grow in their season, water crows-foot flowers, flags lie along the surface and slowly swing from side to side like a boat at anchor. The breeze brings a ripple, and the sunlight sparkles on it, the light reflected dances up the piers of the bridge. Those that pass along the road are naturally drawn to this bright parapet where the brook winds brimming full through green meadows. You can see right to the bottom; you can see where the rush of the water has scooped out a deeper channel under the arches, but look as long as you like there are no fish.

The trout I watched so long, and with such pleasure, was always on the other side, at the tail of the arch, waiting for whatever might come through to him. There in perpetual shadow he lay in wait, a little at the side of the arch, scarcely ever varying his position except to dart a yard up under the bridge to seize anything he fancied, and to drift out again to bring up at his anchorage.

If people looked over the parapet that side they did not see him; they could not see the bottom there for the shadow, or if the summer noonday cast a strong beam, even then it seemed to cover the surface with a film of light which could not be seen through. There are some aspects from which even a picture hung on the rail close at hand cannot be seen. So no one saw the trout; if anyone more curious leant over the parapet he was gone in a moment under the arch.

Folk fished in the pond about the verge of which the sedge-birds chattered, and but a few yards distant; but they never looked under the arch on the northern and shadowy side, where the water flowed beside the beech. For three seasons this continued. For three summers I had the pleasure to see the trout day after day whenever I walked that way, and all the time, with fishermen close at hand, he escaped notice, though the place was not preserved. It is wonderful to think how difficult it is to see anything under one's very eyes, and thousands of people walked actually and physically right over the fish.

However, one morning in the third summer, I found a fisherman standing in the road and fishing over the parapet in the shadowy water. But he was fishing at the wrong arch, and only with paste, for roach. While the man stood there fishing, along came two navvies; naturally enough they went quietly up to see what the fisherman was doing, and one instantly uttered an exclamation. He had seen the trout! The man who was fishing with paste had stood so still and patiently that the trout, reassured, had come out, and the navvy – trust a navvy to see anything of the kind – caught sight of him. The navvy knew how to see through water. He told the fisherman, and there was a stir of excitement, a changing of hooks and bait. I could not stay to see the result but went on, fearing the worst. But he did not succeed; next day the wary trout was still there, and the next, and the next. Either this particular fisherman was not able to come again, or was discouraged; at any rate he did not try again. The fish escaped, doubtless more wary than ever.

In the spring of the next year the trout was still there, and up to the summer I used to go and glance at him. This was the fourth season, and still he was there; I took friends to look at this wonderful fish, which defied all the loafers and poachers, and above all, surrounded himself not only with shadow over the minds of passers-by, so that they never thought of the possibility of such a thing as trout. But one morning something happened. The brook was dammed up on the sunny side of the bridge, and the water let off by a side-hatch, that some accursed main or pipe, or other horror, might be laid across the bed of the stream somewhere far down.

Above the bridge there was a brimming broad brook, below it the flags lay on the mud, the weeds drooped, and the channel was dry. It was dry up to the beech-tree. There, under the drooping boughs of the beech, was a small pool of muddy water, perhaps two yards long, and very narrow – a stagnant muddy pool not more than three or four inches deep. In this I saw the trout. In the shallow water, his back came up to the surface (for his fins must have touched the mud sometimes), once it came above the surface, and his spots showed as plain as if you had held him in your hand. He was swimming round to try and find out the reason for this sudden stinting of room. Twice he heaved himself somewhat on to this side over a dead branch that was at the bottom, and exhibited all his beauty to the air and sunshine. Then he went away into another part of the shallow and was hidden by muddy water. Now, under the arch of the bridge, his favourite arch, close by, there was a deep pool, for, as already mentioned, the scour of the current scooped away the sand and made a hole there. When the stream was shut off by this dam above, this hole remained partly full. Between this pool and the shallow under the beech there was a sufficient connection for the fish to move into it.

My only hope was that he would do so and as some showers fell, temporarily increasing the depth of the narrow canal between the two pools, there seemed every reason to believe that he had got to that under the arch. If now only that accursed pipe or main, or whatever repair it was, could only be finished quickly even now the trout might escape! Every day my anxiety increased, for the intelligence would soon get about that the brook was dammed up, and any pools left in it would be sure to attract attention.

Sunday came, and directly the bells had done ringing, four men attacked the pool under the arch. They took off shoes and stockings and waded in, two at each end of the arch. Stuck in the mud close by was an eel spear. They churned up the mud, wading in, and thickened and darkened it as they groped under. No one could watch these barbarians longer.

Is it possible that he could have escaped? He was a wonderful fish, wary and quick. Is it just possible that they may not even have known that a trout was there at all; but had merely hoped for perch or eels? The pool was deep and the fish quick – they did not bail it, might he have escaped? Might they even, if they did find him, have mercifully taken him and placed him alive in some other water nearer their home? Is it possible that he may have almost miraculously made his way down the stream into other pools?

There was heavy rain one night, which might have given him such a chance. These 'mights' and 'ifs' and 'is it possibles' even now keep alive some little hope that some day I may yet see him again. But that was in the early summer. It is now winter, and the beech has brown spots. Among the limes the sedges are matted and entangled, the sword flags rusty; the rooks are at the acorns, and the plough is at work in the stubble. I have never seen him since, I never fail to glance over the parapet into the shadowy water. Somehow it seemed to look colder, darker, less pleasant than it used to do. The spot was empty, and the shrill winds whistled through the poplars.

from NATURE NEAR LONDON *1883*
(reprinted from the Standard)

Record-Breaker

BRIAN VESEY-FITZGERALD

If you live in Ireland and fish for pike, you will sniff at our pike. If you live in the Gaeltacht and fish for pike you will not sniff at our pike, you will snort; for fish that provide an English angler with after-dinner stories to last him the rest of his life are regarded as pretty ordinary hereabouts. Did not the *Limerick Chronicle* of 9 May 1862 report the capture in Lough Derg, on rod and line, too, of a pike that weighed 90½lb, and measured 5 feet 8 inches in length? That (no one accepts it as a record by the way) remains the master pike. And then there are two Irish pike of over 70 lb, both caught on rod and line: the County Clare pike of 78 lb, taken in 1830, and the Kenmure pike of 72 lb, which was taken on a fly. Neither of these fish find acceptance in the record books. The record Irish pike, rod caught, weighed 53 lb and was taken on Lough Conn in 1920 (a sixty-pounder was reported to have been taken in the same lough in 1942) by Mr John Garvin. These are exceptional fish, but pike of over 30 lb, fish that would instantly find their way into English record books, are common enough in the Irish Lakes, and there have been more than a few of over 40 lb taken in recent years. So, if you live in Ireland and fish for pike, you will sniff at our pike, and small blame on you.

You will sniff, too, if you set store by the Cheltenham pike or the Whittlesea pike. But you should not do so. The Cheltenham pike did undoubtedly weight 60 lb, but it was not caught. It gave itself up. It was seen floating on the surface by the caretaker of the reservoir, who put out in a boat and hauled it aboard by the tail. It was very, very old, and quite blind, and it was dying of old age and starvation. The Whittlesea pike did undoubtedly weigh 52 lb. But the poor thing was not caught. It was stranded when the mere was drained. No, you should not sniff at our pike in relation to either of these fish. Our pike at least was caught. It did not weight 60 lb or even 52 lb, but it was caught and it remains the heaviest English pike that was caught. You will not find it in the record book, because it was not caught by fair angling. And you can sniff at that if you like.

Caught by fair angling or not, the fish was caught. And it is more than just the heaviest pike to be caught in England. It *is* the heaviest yet caught in England, but it holds two further records, records that are, I imagine, extremely unlikely to be broken. It is the only pike, so far as I am aware, to be caught on a croquet mallet. And it is the only record fish, so far as I am aware, to be hooked by a child three years of age. Our pike, you see, holds three records. It occupies a position of honour in the study now, looking very fierce in its glass case. Below it, in letters of gold, are its measurements: weight 40 lb, length 4 feet 1 inch, girth 25 inches; a noble fish.

It was caught in 1865 in the big pond in the grounds of Upton House, Edgehill, in Warwickshire. It was actually caught by the late Colonel R. Purefoy Fitzgerald, but it was 'hooked' by his son, then aged three, and later a famous admiral. And it came about in this wise. The little boy, as befitted a future Admiral of His Majesty's Navy, was playing boats. His boat was a child's croquet mallet, and to the handle was attached a length of stout string in order that he might not lose control of his fleet. The pike took the croquet mallet and made at full speed for the centre of the pond. The small boy, showing already signs of that tenacity for which he later became famous, did not immediately relinquish hold of the string, and so followed the pike into the water. He then let go of the string, and the pike made off. The water in the pond was low (1865 was a very dry year) and the fish, no doubt rather upset by the strange feel of the prey it had seized, grounded itself at high speed on a mudbank. It was not itself visible, but floating on the surface was the tell-tale string. Colonel Fitzgerald waded out, took hold of the string, and after a short but severe tug-of-war, hauled the pike ashore. It was weighed almost immediately, and it was weighed again within a few hours by no less an authority than Frank Buckland, a friend of the family. He found also that the fish was starving. But he was very excited about it, and exhibited it in London on several occasions shortly afterwards.

Not a fish to be proud of, you say?

from THE FISHERMAN'S BEDSIDE BOOK *1945*

The Art of the Tiddler

F. W. HOLIDAY

The mystique of the dry fly has been described by many graphic pens; but the pure art of tiddler-fishing goes neglected. Despite the current pose of certain Principal Anglers who would have us believe that they are experts at everything from bullheads to barbel, it remains a fact that at heart many of us are specialists. This can only be the result of a grubby, misspent childhood by the waterside.

With small children, as I remember it, the value of a small happening often bulks astonishingly large. A tiddler is a wonderful fish. A gudgeon is a whale. Six inches of squirming eel can be converted – presto! – into the Goliath struggles of a tropical moray encountered in a shady lagoon. Glass jars and small boys have a close affinity. They draw together like magnetized particles and the jars are full of pond-water and tiddlers before you can say wink!

A tiddler is one of numerous small common fishes. A loach is a tiddler, and so is a minnow. Sticklebacks are tiddlers to be highly prized because they sport colour. Into jars with tiddlers you can also put newts; and these animals will give fascinating displays by clapping with white human hands against the restraining glass.

The first tiddlers I remember were exhibited in jars tied with string around the neck and swung on sticks. Various big boys of eight or nine had gathered into a conspiratorial gang in order to invade the private property of a mill.

Here was a sheet of greenish water with a faint sheen of steam over the upper end which was used to cool the mill engines. Large notices said sternly: TRESPASSERS WILL BE PROSECUTED; indeed, there was a very limber caretaker on the property whose sole function appeared to be the pursuit and capture of tiddler-poachers. As if this deterrent was not enough, there was, in addition, a formidable barrier of spiked railings flanked at either end by an old brick wall whose top was liberally covered in broken glass. These obstacles only whetted the appetities of tiddler-poachers of true worth. Fish snatched under such conditions were as desirable a prize as Jason's Golden Fleece.

A fellow urchin showed me how to do it. First, one prised a railing from its bed in which it lay slackly after assault from many generations of small boys. A distant whistle from a dirty little gnome wearing glasses signified that the coast was clear. Quickly, through the gap with you, sliding on your behind down the embankment, and never stop for breath. Fling into the water with the tackle and sharp about it.

This was the tiddler-fishing in all its purity. Bent pins are a fiction of writers. We used size 18 roach hooks, discarded by our betters, with the frayed gut cut away. Cotton was tied direct to the hook with a bunch of grannie-knots. Bait: a scrap of worm, sections of which were kept in a boot-polish tin. I remember the wicked odour of that tin even now.

The fish fed eagerly, starved of food in that parody of a lake. Multitudes of tiddlers appeared around the worm, dabbing at it furiously. Finally, one would gulp the morsel, only to be jerked skywards in an energetic parabola as one or other of the rabid anglers flung up the garden-cane rod.

It was largely a communal asault – one or two cane rods, and many willing fingers as yet more anglers crawled through the railing gap to see how we were faring. The jam-jar took on depth and mystery as captured tiddlers prowled its murky interior. Sport became hectic. It became necessary to limit a man to one fish – sometimes not even that – before the rod changed hands. Yet a distant howl of: 'He's coming!' was enough to send the well-drilled team through the railing gap as one man.

Needless to say, such pleasures were frowned on by parental authority. The illicit tiddler became a thing to conceal with guilty shame under one's jersey. All too soon the season passed and it became 'winter' – a period of cold, you discovered, when fishing ceased and one year changed into another. When I was eight the family moved to Canada and stayed for four years.

. . .Walking five miles to a village school was a small chore when fishing-tackle from the store lay at the end and money burned a hole in the pocket to buy it. But it was crude stuff, this: a hand-line wound on a wooden frame with big japanned hooks. The frame was discarded in disgust and a thin stick was cut from the nearest grove. Thus equipped, it was time to plan a trip. At the tender age of nine I was ready to fish on my own without the aid of distracting advisers.

Beyond the farm where we lived beyond the virgin woodland, lay a creek. In Canada all streams are called 'cricks'. It was not easy to fish. Gentians and golden rod grew in a thick jungle. Milkweed threw sappy branches in every direction, and the air was heavy with warmth and the lazy drifting wings of swallowtail butterflies.

The swallowtail has a most delightful smell – though few works on entomology record this interesting fact. It also has a superb poetry of motion. Beyond the milkweed and the swallowtails lay the water. But it was an alien world.

True, a preliminary peer, hanging head-first over the bank, revealed some old favourites. A stickleback fanned agitatedly beside its completed nest. But there were more menacing things. Great crayfish – yellow, black and green – crawled evilly between the stones. Round the bend of the creek floated an object like a black raft which quickly sank. This was a snapping-turtle – and people said they could take off your finger. Before starting to fish I armed myself with a supply of rocks!

That first afternoon's fishing produced a sucker-fish, a creature of barbel-like profile, which weighed about a pound and sent me running breakneck to exhibit this first game wrested from the wilderness. By association of ideas the capture was crammed head down into a jam-jar where it gasped out its wretched life, tail flapping feebly. A major triumph, this, indeed.

After a month sucker-fish were not enough. Despite the attraction of a colony of grey cranes which lived near the sucker-pool I journeyed farther afield, equipped now with food. Lunch-time drinks, of course, came from the creek; and how strange water tastes after flowing between the warm roots of cress and marsh-marigolds. A bigger creek was discovered and a smallmouth bass took the worm. The day's fishing produced a mixed bag of bass and sunfish, which are as splendid as their namesake. Sunfish, with their gorgeous scarlet-rimmed eyes, soon became the prime quarry.

Sunfishes were made for small boys. Several species are found in Southern Canada – White Crappie, Black Crappie, Bluegill and Pumpkinseed. They are deep, frilly-finned, pugnacious little fish; some of them are not so little, since Crappies up to 5 lb are reported. They feed freely on anything offered.

In due course a neighbour took on himself the onerous duty of filling his old Ford with rods, boys and bait, and drove this odd cargo to Lake Ontario. But here creek-tactics failed lamentably. A cold wind blew the 6,500 square miles of fresh water into sea-like billows into which my baits plopped in vain. Muskellunge, pickerel and heavy trout inhabit the lake. I never caught one. Nor did I catch a Walleye or even a Great Northern Pike. The art of the tiddler has its limitations.

It was soon after this trip that I was weaned away from tiddler-fishing for ever. How did that boyhood metamorphosis take place? I don't remember. Quite suddenly, at the age of about twelve, I owned an old steel rod, a wooden float and no less than two fishing-lines. The jam-jar had gone; and only in retrospect does its passing seem sadly symbolic. The art of the tiddler is a thing of beauty brought about by the sheer wonder of new life surveying new life. Inevitably, it must always be brief.

In later years, to most of us, come all the gilded trapping of expertise: the dry-fly box, the Sheffield match outfit, the tope rod. Line-rafts and old tweed hats loom at status symbols guaranteed to crush all with less than twenty years of experience. Pundits arise and are cast down. There are esoteric cults relating to the capture of carp on crusts and the throwing of mighty lines. Principal Anglers strut the stage, bowing to their fans with puffy pride. The biggest fish have been caught and the best fishing books have been written. The world turns on, like a great wheel . . .

Maybe the enchanted moments can never be recaptured; the delirious moments of looking at those little fish in the jar. Many attempt the impossible. Aquaria, microscopes and biological tomes, with names like 'British Species of Ephemeroptera', are only half the story. When a senior Army officer spends New Year's day up to his thighs in a chalkstream studying the hatch you know he is searching, too!

Grubby fingers, a stickleback and a little green pond-water are unlikely materials with which to construct small, private heavens. But, as someone said, eleven is infinity to the cannibal who counts on his fingers and thumbs; and there are no degrees in the quality of Heaven!

from ANGLERS' ANNUAL *1963*

A Tale of Two Boxes

E. L. MATTHEWS

Tom Trevor was the oldest of the full-time professional fishermen working from the village. He was a man with a very strong sense of the consideration due to men who made their living by fishing, as against those who merely did it for fun. He had a perpetual complaint about the box we kept floating at anchor outside the harbour, where we maintained a stock of live sand-eels for those anglers who wanted them; this did not prevent him from emptying the box any time one of his customers wanted bait.

He came up to me one morning on the quay. 'You amateurs are all the same,' he said. 'Fast asleep in your beds when you ought to be out fishing, and getting in everybody's way, like that box of yours making a hazard in the fairway, when the fish have gone off feed. Every morning there have been bass feeding around that box, and nobody there to catch them.' A couple of nights later, for no reason that I know of, I woke up just after three o'clock. Fishing had not been much good recently, so before I could have second thoughts I put on some clothes and went out. It was a very dark night, with a heavy overcast, no wind and the tide about an hour up the flood. I picked up the minimum amount of tackle from the loft and waded down the harbour to a dinghy that was just afloat. I had left a basket courge of sand-eels tied to the harbour wall the previous evening, picked up that and paddled very quietly out of the harbour. It was so dark that I could not see my rod point over the stern of the boat.

My tackle was as simple as it could be. A light rod, a Nottingham reel, a six-foot trace with a biggish hook tied to the end and nothing else. Outside the harbour I sat in the stern, baited up, and pulled ten feet or so of line through the top ring, intending to row forward and let the line run off astern. But by the time I had got back amidships, line was running off the reel although the boat was stationary. I tightened up and it was a good bass. He ran well and I was most careful with him, to prevent any splashing. I got him inboard safely, a nice fish between four and five pounds, and repeated my paying out tactics. This time I felt the fish take right underneath the boat. He was just about the same size as the first. The third one took me as quickly and ran me round the anchor line of the bait-box and broke me up. It took me some time to get retackled in the dark and I had drifted a long way down the bay before I was fishing again. I had no bites out there, but as soon as I paddled back past the sand-eel box I had another fish. The smell of the eels must have attracted them and there were probably enough sand-eels escaping to keep them interested. They kept feeding hard for the next couple of hours, but I wasted a lot of time by getting broken twice more. The sky was just beginning to lighten in the east when the first of the fishing-boats came out from the harbour and as soon as their engines started up the fish stopped feeding. It started to rain and the wind got up with the sun. As I had not taken an oilskin, I decided that the best of the morning was over, went back in, put the fish in a box and left them in the fish loft. It was a nice catch, nine even-sized bass, all around four and a half pounds, and a small one.

The cook had just come in when I got back. She was surprised to see me about so early and made tea for me, so I promised her a bass to take home that afternoon. While I was having my tea the fish lorry came in to take the previous day's catch of mackerel into the market at Newlyn. I offered the driver tea, but he was late and would not stop.

I was finishing my breakfast later on when Tom came in to telephone the market prices. I never knew why he bothered to phone, he only had to shout a little louder and they could have heard him at Newlyn, twenty miles away. 'Seventy-six stone of mackerel at seven shillings,' he bellowed, 'and three stone of bass at forty bob.' Whose were the bass, then? I did not have any bass yesterday. I went quickly out of the dining-room and over to the fish loft. My catch had gone, taken into market with the mackerel. Tom looked at me very hard, when I explained. ''Tis easy to happen,' he said, 'but the fish in Trevor boxes is Trevor fish. It always has been so. It must be so. But you chose the right day, forty shilling a stone is a good price. I'll buy you a pint out of it one of these mornings.'

I went out into the increasing wind and rain to catch the fish I had promised the cook. It took me all the morning.

from CREEL *December 1965*

Fish taken in the Thames and on our Coasts

WILLIAM HARRISON

THE RIVER THAMES

Thus we see the whole tract and course of ye Thames by whose head and fall, it is euident that the length thereof is at the least, one hundreth and eighty miles, if it be measured by ye iourneys of the land. And as it is in course, the longest of the three famous riuers of thys Isle, so it is nothing inferiour vnto them, in abundance of all kinde of fishe, whereof it is harde to say, which of them haue eyther most plentie, or greatest variety, if the circumstāces be duely weighed. What should I speake of the fat and sweete Samons, dayly taken in this streame, & that in such plentye, as no ryuer in Europa, is able to exceede it, but what store also of Barbelles, Troutes, Cheuins, Pearches, Smelts, Breames, Roches, Daces, Gudgins, Floūders, Shrimps, Eles. & c. are commōly to be had therein, I referre me to them, that knowe the same by experience. And albeit it seemeth from time to time, to be as it were defrauded in sundrye wise, of these hir large commodities, by the insaciable auarice of ye fishermen, yet this famous ryuer cōplayneth of no wante, but the more it looseth at one tyme, the more it yeeldeth at another. Onely in Carpes it seemeth to be scant, sith it is not long since that kynde of fishe was brought ouer into Englande, and but of late to speake of, into this streame by the violent rage of sundry Landfloudes, that brake open the heades and dammes of dyuers Gentlemens pondes, by which meanes it became pertaker also of this said commoditie, whereof earst it had no portion that I could euer heare of.

OF FISHE TAKEN VPON OUR COASTES

As our foules haue their seasons, so lykewise haue all sorts of fish, whereby it cometh to passe that none, or at the leastwise very few of them are to be had at all tymes . . . I finde fiue sorts, the flat, the roūd, the long, the legged & shelled, so the flat are deuided into the smoothe, scaled & tailed. Of the first are the Plaice, the Butte, the Turbot, Dorrey, Dabbe, & c. Of the seconde, the Soles, & c. Of the thirde, oure Chaites, Maidens, Kingsones, Flathe and Thornebacke, whereof the greater be for the most parte eyther dryed and caryed into other countries, or soddē, sowsed, & eaten here at home, whylest the the lesser be fryed or buttered, sone after they be takē, as prouision not to be kept long for feare of putrefaction. Under the round kindes are commonly comprehended Lumpes an ugly fish to sighte, and yet very delicate in eating, yf it be kindlye dressed. The Whighting, (an olde waiter or servitor in the Court) the Rochet, Gurnard, Hadocke, Codde, Herring, Pilchard, Sprat, & such like. And these are they whereof I haue best knowledge and be commonly to be had in their tymes vppon our coastes. Under this kinde also are all the great fishe contained as the Seale, the Dolphin, the Porpasse, the Thirlepole, Whale, and whatsoeuer is round of body, be it neuer so great and huge. Of the long sort are Cungres, Eles, Garefishe and suche other of that forme. Finallye of the legged kinde we haue not manye, neyther haue I seene any more of thys sort then the Polipus, called in Englishe the Lobstar, the Craifish, and ye Crabbe. As for the little Craifishes, they are not taken in the sea, but plentyfully in our fresh ryuers in banckes and vnder stones where they kepe themselues in most secret maner, and oft by lyknesse of coulour with the stones among which they lye, they deceiue euen the skilful takers of them, except they vse great diligence . . . As touching the shelly sorte we haue plentie of Oysters, Muscles and Cocles. We haue in lyke sort no small store of great Whelkes, and Perewincles, & eache of them brought farre into the land from the sea coast in their seuerall seasons.

from HOLINSHED'S CHRONICLES *(Black Letter)* 1577

Regulations Concerning Fishing in the Thames

ACTS OF PARLIAMENT

1099–1100 13 WIL. 2 CAP. 47, L, I. No Salmons to be taken, from the nativity of our Lady, unto S. *Martins* day, in all points. Nor none to be taken in Millpooles, from the midst of *April* untill Midsummer.

1. Offence, burning the Nets and Engines.
2. Imprisonment for a quarter of a yeere.
3. For a whole yeere.

1558–9 I ELIZ. CAP. 17. None shall with any maner of Net, Weele,

But-eayning, Kepper, Lymercreele, Raw Fagnet, Trolnet, Trymnet, Scalboat, Weblister, Sturlamet, or with any other device or engines, made of cheare, woollbine, canvas; or shall by any heeling-Nets, or Trimbleboat, or any other device, engine, cautelles, wayes or means soever, heretofore made or devised, or hereafter to bee made or devised, take and kill any yong brood, spawne, or frie of Eeles, Salmon, Pike or Pickerell, or any other Fish, in any floudgate, pipe or the taile of any Mill, Weare, or in any straites, streames, brookes, Rivers, salt or fresh.

Secondly, none shall take and kill any Salmons and Trowts, not being in season, being kepper Salmons, or kepper Trowts, or shedder Salmons or shedder Trowts.

Thirdly, none shall take and kill any Pike or Pickerell, not being in length ten intches Fish, and more; nor any Salmon, not being 16. intches fish, and more; nor any Trowt, not being eight intches; nor any Barbell, not being 12. intches, and more.

Fourthly, none to fish with any Nets, Tramels, Keep, Weare, Helme, Creele; or by any other Engine, device, wayes or meanes; but onely with Net or Tramell; whereof every mesh or mash shall be two intches and an halfe broad; Angling excepted.

A Proviso, that this shall not extend to Smelts, Roches, Minoes, Bulheads, Gudgeons or Eeles, in place where the same have beene used to be taken.

The Offenders to lose for every offence 20. shillings, and the fish; and also the unlawfull Nets, Engines and Instruments.

The Maior of *London (inter alia)* shall have full power and authority by this Act, to enquire of all offences committed contrary to this Act, by the oathes of twelve men or more, and to heare and determine all and every the same.

The paines and forfeitures to be at the use of every such person and persons (being no body politick nor corporate, or head of the same) before whom such conviction shall be had: and to the use of every body politicke and corporate, that hereafter have lawfully had any fines, & c. upon such conviction.

reprinted from THE SURVEY OF LONDON
by John Stow, revised 1633

Elmbury Memories

JOHN MOORE

A LIBERAL EDUCATION

A professional fisherman called Bassett was another of our holiday schoolmasters. He got well paid by the gentry for taking them out in his boat and showing them the likeliest places for sport, yet he would often sacrifice the chance of earning ten shillings to spend the afternoon with us and to teach us what he knew. He taught us one thing that nobody else could: he taught us to be quiet. Chatter and sudden movement he abominated; he was the *stillest* person I have ever known, as still as the cat waiting for the mouse, as the stilt-legged heron fishing in the shallows. When he rowed the boat you could not hear the splash of the oars or the creaking of the rowlocks; whenever he moved his action was slow, calculated and completely silent. He was a hard taskmaster; he would never let us rest our rods on the side of the boat – 'Birmigum fishing', he called that: the city dwellers' Sunday afternoon out. Always we must hold them, although they were much too heavy for us, in aching arms until we got a bite. If the float bobbed, there must be no exclamation, no schoolboy's yelp of delight when the fish was hooked. And when we caught one it must be killed silently and swiftly – 'kill it as if you were a murderer', was his grim and blood-chilling instruction – lest it flap about on the floorboards and drive the others away. He had never read *The Compleat Angler* but old Izaak's motto, 'Study to be quiet', was his also . . .

Bassett taught us the hard discipline of angling: Mr Chorlton soon taught us its beauty, when he took us up the river on calm summer evenings and showed us how to throw a fly. He was careful not to suggest to us that this method of fishing was necessarily superior to any other, so we grew up without any silly snobbery about floats and worms: instead we took the sensible view that the purpose of fishing is to have fun. We were equally happy, therefore, whether we were catching bleak with houseflies, or watching the long black porcupine-quill when we fished for tench and bream, trolling for pike in winter, or sitting, oh! so quietly, in the sternsheets of Mr Chorlton's boat, while with exquisite grace he swished his shining split-cane rod and sent out the cob-webby line towards the dark eddy under the overhanging willows. It was Mr Chorlton's custom (anathema to Bassett) while fishing to talk. He would chide the reluctant fishes with a quotation from Shakespeare, ask the favour of the immortal gods in Latin, curse a broken cast in Homeric Greek. He never talked down to us. If we didn't understand what he said we would always ask the meaning of it. And so we did, with the result that we learned a great many wise sayings in a far more pleasant way than if we had been sitting at a schoolroom desk . . .

THE RIVER-GOD

He was – even at sixty-five – the best shot I have ever seen, the best stalker, the best naturalist, and incomparably the best fisherman. Yet his fishing-tackle was almost as primitive as a schoolboy's. His greenheart fly-rod, which must have been as old as himself, had a kink in the middle joint and two kinks in the top joint; it was nearly as crooked as an apple bough, or its owner's legs. But in his hands it was a magic wand with which he would conjure up fishes when nobody else could catch anything. In the little brook which ran through his farm, a mere runnel overgrown with reeds, bushes and willows, he discovered a few trout where lesser men would have found only bull-heads, gudgeons, and eels. He caught two or three every season in the mayfly time, using only the top joint of his rod and dabbling a fly between the branches. The biggest was two and a half pounds, and he got it out from between the roots of a great willow. I swear that no other man could have landed it in such circumstances.

The Colonel didn't mind what he fished for so long as it swam, what he hunted so long as it ran, nor what he shot so long as it could fly. There were eels in his brook as well as trout and it was his custom to fish for them on Sunday afternoons, an otherwise barren time when there was no hunting and no shooting and the pub was shut. His method of fishing was original (for the Colonel was nothing if not experimental in his approach to every kind of sport). He used no less than six cheap cane rods, which he distributed at intervals along the bank. His lines were baited with lobworms. To each rod-point he fixed a small bell, such as might hang round the neck of a cat. He sat down in the middle of the line of rods, smoked his pipe, and took an occasional swig out of his flask of whisky. Whenever the *tinkle-tinkle* of a bell called him from this pleasant occupation, he strolled leisurely to the appropriate rod and landed his eel. He said that the bells, besides being useful, made the sport more exciting. The tinkling sound, now coming from one rod, now from another, now from two or three at once, gave to the pastime a sense of urgency which eel-fishing generally lacked.

Having caught his basketful of eels, and eaten them for supper, the Colonel nailed up their skins on his barn door and when they were thoroughly cured he oiled them and cut them into narrow strips and used them for bootlaces. I still possess a pair; and they are stronger and more supple than any other laces I have ever seen.

from PORTRAIT OF ELMBURY *1945*

A Tench called Diana

D. G. CAMERON

'Let's face it,' said Fred. 'On your money you can't afford to cast one of your fancy flies within fifty miles of London. Swallow your pride. Come with me and catch a tench.'

So I went. And if it seemed slightly ridiculous to be going fishing on a rush-hour tube train, fresh from the office in city suit and Italian suède shoes – well, that just showed how unimaginative I had been on all those occasions when I set off for the Eden.

'Now then, isn't it lovely? Isn't it peaceful?' Fred beamed as the dappling water of the gravel pit reflected in his spectacles. I admitted that after its fashion, the pond had a certain peace.

Boeings, Comets and Viscounts from the Airport crossed over every five minutes; trains on the line behind us were only a little less frequent; pylons reared up along one bank; a fairground two fields away sent bumper car noises and amplified rock 'n' roll drifting down the summer breeze.

But the wavelets lapped as soothingly as sleep, and in one corner, a row of fine elms coloured magnificiently in the golden evening sun. Reminding my sensitive soul of other places, of the world outside London – of real fishing.

'You're striking too fast,' complained Fred. 'You can't take liberties with tench as if they were trout, you know. That float may go bob-bob, bob-bob for twenty minutes, but you don't strike until it goes right under. And even then you ought to wait a while.'

He had given me a 12-ft split-cane rod which felt as if it could kill a barracuda. Attached to a No. 10 hook of 5 lb b.s. nylon was a lump of bread as big as a golf ball (English size, of course). It was the sort of tasteless, snow-white stodge that comes ready sliced and wrapped in wax-paper: Fred said tench liked it better than brown. Plebeian, mud-clogged creatures.

The fairground boomed out a song which went: 'Please-wait-for-me, DIANA.' Judging by the number of times it rent the air, it was somebody's very favourite tune. The row of elms turned to russet gold, and at what seemed intervals of twelve hours or so the little float would go bob-bob, bob-bob, and I would strike too fast.

Dusk came and with it a chilled cramp. The planes and the trains became fewer; the float, which didn't even bob-bob any more, was a tiny greyness suspended in mist. 'Perhaps we'd better pack up and have a beer while there's still time,' muttered a subdued Fred.

I turned to take a last look at my comforting elms, now almost invisible against a deep lilac sky. How long they held my mooning gaze I don't know, but it was just long enough.

For when I turned back, realized the float was gone, and made a panic-stricken upward lunge with the rod, I was into a fish. A fish with the quietly determined power of a dynamo and the immovable weight of a sack of cement.

It cruised out into the darkness, back and forth, from side to side. Fred was screaming something about weeds. I was in a timeless tug-of-war, butterflies in my stomach, heart in my mouth, knowing I must give an uncaring little laugh when, as must happen, the nylon gave.

Then it was lying in a lamplight, in the landing-net, among the crumpled grass, pink eye glaring indignantly – beautiful, bronze, brave, enormous tench.

'Can't find the balance,' Fred had a tremor in his voice. 'Not bad. Go about four and a half.'

As I tilted the net to let her go, my hands were shaking badly. The fairground amplifier was bellowing 'Please-wait-for-me, DIANA'. I hope she does: I want very much to go back one night, on the tube, to the pond, the pylons and the elm-trees, and catch Diana again.

from ANGLING *September 1960*

The Prickly Cohort

KENNETH MANSFIELD

Damp cotton wool, stuffed with pins and served with a mud sauce is a description thought by many to apply to freshwater fish on the table.

This raises the question: 'What is a freshwater fish?' Common sense would reply: 'A fish that swims in fresh water'; but in the English language, if in no other, this is not so. Trout, char and whitefish, for example, normally swim in fresh water, and salmon spend, perhaps, a quarter of their lives in it, but in strict English (and in law) they are not freshwater fish, for this term is reserved to the species which anglers have sensibly but unflatteringly called 'coarse fish'. The principal coarse fish are barbel, bream, carp, chub, dace, eels, gudgeon, perch, pike, roach, rudd and tench.

A goodly array, it may seem, but from the culinary viewpoint several of them can be dismissed with a few words of disapprobation.

It may be going too far to say that barbel are actively poisonous: on the other hand, it is safe to say that many people are allergic to barbel's flesh and that their roes should never be eaten by anyone. It is said that an otter will not eat a hen barbel, though it may catch and kill one.

Bream, dace, roach and rudd merit the description which starts this article. Three hundred years ago bream caused a Frenchman to write: 'He that hath Breams in his pond, is able to bid his friends welcome'; but bream must then have been different fish, or French cooking triumphed over difficulties insuperable to the modern English cook, whose opinion of bream may be summed up by the parodist thus:

Sing a song of Norfolk,
Broads full of fish.
Five-and-twenty bronze bream
Baked in a dish.
When the pie was opened
What a lack of taste!
Rows of eyeless needles
Served in cotton waste.

Roach and rudd join bream in the mud-and-needle class, and though dace are more palatable they have even more small bones than the others. Chub must also go into the discarded class, for they are only just edible when cooked within two or three hours of capture, a condition which puts them out of court and kitchen for any but anglers who cook their kill at the waterside.

There are at least two dictionary definitions of 'edible'. One is: 'fit to be eaten', and the other: 'that which can be eaten'. The five species of fish so far reviewed belong to the second definition, for they can be but are not fit to be eaten. In spite of this there are several recipes for their preparation, but every one of these shares an elaboration of method and a wealth of ingredients which prove that the basic material is inferior. With the same treatment stock-fish would become appetizing.

Carp and tench are full-fleshed, relatively boneless fish that are eaten with the greatest appreciation in many parts of Europe, where their raising in fish ponds to supply the market is a considerable industry. Carp form a traditional Christmas Eve dish in parts of eastern Europe, and a form of caviar made from their roes, once generally appreciated, is even now eaten by those of the Jewish faith to whom the scaleless sturgeon is an unclean fish.

Curious experiments were made which resulted in the successful castration of carp, a process which resulted in abnormally quick growth and, it was claimed, an increase in gastronomic excellence. A certain Samuel Fuller discovered this possibility in the early eighteenth century, and he passed his observations to Sir Hans Sloan, founder of the British Museum of Natural History and then President of the Royal Society, under whose direction large numbers of carp were treated in this way.

In America, carp were introduced into the Hudson River about one hundred and fifty years ago. European carp had been put into a lake which burst its banks and released the fish into running water. They were given a good start by protective legislation. Now they are vermin, infesting the waterways and lakes of the eastern states. Astronomical numbers in pounds are caught every year, most of the fish going to the canning factories.

Carp and tench have been unduly neglected in this country in recent years, but they were once a mainstay of the county dinner-table. Whenever Parson Woodforde expected some important guest for dinner he cast (according to his diary) his nets in his tench pond in the morning.

Carp of from 3 lb to 8 lb are considered the best size for cooking, and monsters such as the 44-lb British rod-caught record (taken last year) [1952], which now swims in a tank at the London Zoo aquarium, are better seen than eaten.

Conversely, eels are better eaten than seen. Perhaps it is the fact that eels are unpleasing to the eye and, alive or dead, gruesome to the touch, that has led to their being neglected in England and abhorred in Ireland – though snakes and St Patrick may have something to do with the Irish case.

Whatever the cause, that triumph of simple cooking, a dish of jellied eels, is left to Londoners east of Aldgate Pump and to those that eat at stalls on Epsom Downs in Derby week. Smoked eels, too, stand high on the roll of cured delicacies, yet the few that are to be found in England are imported.

Eels are of excellent flavour and (to drift into the jargon of dietetics) they have the highest number of calories per pound of all fish, flesh and fowl. If neither taste nor calorific value appeals they can be used as an excuse for other things, for it is said that he

Who know not physic should be nice in choice
In eating Eels, because they hurt the voice:
Both Eels and Cheese, without good store of wine
Well drunk with them, offend at any time.

The days are past, but not very long past, when gudgeon could be bought alive from tubs at any fishmongers, but he who would taste gudgeon today must catch his own. In late Victorian and early Edwardian days gudgeon-fishing from punts on the Thames attained the status of a Society amusement, and platters of these little fish appeared as one of the many courses that went to the making of a normal dinner in those days.

Like most other freshwater fish, pike were appreciated more in the past than they are now. In Edward I's time they sold at the same price as porpoise, 6s 8d a pound, as against 5d for salmon and 6d for turbot, the next highest priced fish. Yarrel wrote: 'Pike were so rare in the reign of Henry the Eighth, that a large one sold for double the price of a house-lamb in February, and a Pickerel, or small Pike, for more than a fat capon.' A Billingsgate price list for 1804 shows pike and carp at 1s a pound, salmon 1s 6d, tench 1s 6d – and roach 2s to 3s a hundred!

In spite of some loss of popularity, pike today are considered one of the better freshwater fish. They can be baked whole, and comparatively bone-free cutlets can be taken from behind the head. Exceptionally pike attain weights of 50 lb or more, but this accomplishment entails a long lifetime of predatory feeding in which cannibalism takes a part, and fish from 6 lb to 10 lb are infinitely more numerous and undoubtedly better on the table, especially from October to March, when there is a distinct curd between the flakes of flesh. As the *Haven of Health* has it, 'the pikerell or pyke is of firm and hard substance, yet giveth clean and pure nourishment'.

Like the best morsel on a plate, the perch has been left until last. Here is a fish so full of flabour that only the minimum of concomitants is desirable. Any trout recipe will serve for perch, and the resulting dish will equal if not exceed the merit of the trout themselves – but anyone preparing perch should remember that they cannot be scaled.

Ausonius was in tune with modern taste when, 1,600 years ago, he wrote:

Nor let the Muse, in her reward of fame,
Illustrious perch, unnoticed pass thy claim;
Prince of the prickly cohort, bred in lakes
To feast our boards, what sapid boneless flakes
Thy solid flesh supplies! though river fed
No daintier fish in ocean's pastures bred
Swims thy compeer; scarce mullet may compete
With thee for fibre firm and flavour sweet.

Ausonius let himself go like this over the perch of the Moselle, but Dr Badham added: 'Aelian speaks in equally high terms of those of the Danube; and Platina of the Po and Lake Maggiore. The River Rhine and the Swiss lakes were early known to produce very fine ones; but perhaps the perch of our Norfolk Broads are as good as any.' Badham wrote that in 1853. Nothing truer has been said in the intervening hundred years. An indication of the perch's gastronomic excellence can be seen in the 1804 Billingsgate price list already quoted. Perch then sold at 2s 6d a pound, a price far above that of any other fish, from either fresh or salt water.

There are several other species of coarse fish that have received no mention – minnows, sticklebacks, miller's thumbs, bleak and ruffe, for instance – but they are all small and are of no culinary importance, though at one time they had their uses.

There was no frozen fish in the shop round the corner in 1650 and Thomas Barker (combining the arts of chef and angler in his *Barker's Delight*) gives a recipe for roasting trout that would appeal to few in these hurried days.

There is one good trout of a good length [he says], some eighteen or twenty inches long, we will have that roasted.

You must take out the intrails of this trout with opening the trout one inch at the upper end of his belly, as nigh the gills as you can; then open the trout within one inch of the vent, so you may take the intrails clean out: then wash the trout very clean, keeping the belly whole: then take half a pound of sweet butter, some thyme, sweet marjoram and parsley chopt very small, mix the butter and herbs together and put them into his belly, with half a dozen of oysters, sew up the two slits with a needle and thred as well as you can: there are broches made to rost a fish, for want of that broch you must take an ordinary broch and spit the fish on; take four or five small laths full the length of the fish, tie those laths on about the fish with a piece of packthred from one end to the other, make the fish fast on the spit, set the fish to the fire.

The first thing you bast the fish with must be a little claret wine, next you must bast with butter, with an anchovas beaten together, then bast with the liquor that falleth from the fish until the fish is rosted; when the fish is rosted take a warm dish; and cut the fish off into that dish; then beat that sauce that came from the fish very well, and pour it on the fish, and serve it up.

Old Barker – he was in the seventies when he wrote his book – summed up his chapters, whether about cooking fish or catching them, in doggerel verse. He finishes his trout-cooking chapter thus:

Restorative broth of Trouts learne to make:
Some fry and some stew, and some also bake
First broyl and then bake, is a rule of good skill
And when thou dost fortune a great trout to kill,
Then rost him, and baste first with good claret wine
But the calvor'd boyl'd trout will make thee to dine
With dainty contentment, both the hot and the cold,
And the marrionate Trout I dare to be bold
For a quarter of a year wil keep to thy mind,
If covered close and preserved from wind.
But mark now good brother, what now I doe say,
Sauce made with Achoves is an excellent way,
With oysters and lemmon, clove, nutmeg and mace

When the brave spotted trout hath been boyled apace
With many sweet herbs: for forty years I
In Ambassadours Kitchins learn'd my cookery,
The French and Italian no better can doe,
Observe well my rules, and you'l say so too.

About a hundred years later another book appeared which is full of quaint recipes, though they are not quite so exotic as those in *Barker's Delight*. This was William Verral's *Complete System of Cookery*. Both books and their recipes may seem quaint now, but in their day they were practical guides whose instructions were faithfully followed in the kitchen. Here is one of Verral's recipes for cooking carp – '*Des carpes à la cour*; carps done the court fashion'.

A brace of carp is handsomest for a dish. Place your fish in a stewpan that they just fill, upon two or three slices of bacon or ham, that you may turn them the easier; pour in as much wine as will just cover them, a ladle or two of cullis, season with a bunch of onions and parsley, some cloves and mace, pepper, salt, and three or four bay leaves, and two or three shallots and mushrooms, an anchovy or two; and let your melts or soft rowes stew with the fish about half an hour; but the spawn or hard rowes boil separate, and when your sauce is ready cut it in pieces, and put in, for it is very apt to crumble to bits and spoil the comeliness of it. For the sauce take about half of what the fish are stewed in, and as much cullis added to it. For a *sauce hachée* a little burnet, pimpernel, a mushroom or two, and some parsley, all minced very fine; take your melts or spawns and cut in small pieces, and boil a little while in your sauce; dish up your fish, add the juice of a lemon, and pour upon 'em; Garnish with parsley only.

Tench may be done in just the same manner.

My last recipe, though hardly practical, conjures up visions of smiling fields through which Izaak Walton, whose recipe it is, once carried his rod:

And in the spring they make of them excellent Minnow-tansies; for being washed well in salt, and their heads and tails cut off, and their guts taken out, and not washed after, they prove excellent for that use; that is, being fried with yolk of eggs, the flowers of cowslips and of primroses, and a little tansy; thus used they make a dainty dish of meat.

from WINE AND FOOD *Winter Number 1953*
(revised by the author)

Anglers' Weather

DAVID BOWEN, F.R.MET.S.

The scope of the public weather service has widened considerably since the war and can be of use to us, as anglers. Thirty-day long-range outlooks have been issued, twice monthly, by the Meteorological Office since December 1963 and the standard twelve-hour bulletins (each with a 'further outlook' covering another twelve hours) are, of course, still available. If we wish, we can telephone our nearest local 'met' office for extra information on the weather in any of the main regions.

But do these types of forecast give us all the information we require; are they sufficiently localized?

I should be surprised if more than just a handful of anglers felt completely satisfied on this point. First of all, weather conditions in Britain vary fantastically from place to place – so much so that in a single region one watershed may be saturated, and another almost dry, at exactly the same time. Secondly, if it is long-range weather with which we are concered it is unlikely that the forecast we are given will given any indication of timing. In the third place, the forecast is not always presented in the form we require, for diurnal temperature changes are seldom given, and no attempt is made to prophesy amounts of rainfall for a given period or from a given depression, storm, or front. Fourthly, we are generally left to make our own interpretation of each forecast in terms of river, lake, or sea conditions. Finally, there is no guarantee that any given forecast will be within a stated bracket of accuracy; if we are left to assume an accuracy of anything between 0 and 100 per cent, then, clearly, it is time we entered the forecasting business ourselves!

I am not suggesting that we should turn a blind eye to 'official' weather pronouncements; but, rather, that we should supplement these offerings by judging future weather for ourselves whenever we can.

On what information shall we base our own forecasts? Experience, of course, is a great thing: few, if any, anglers find themselves unable to judge the mood of the weather if they study any local area. But it is worth considering how we form our judgements on future conditions, and with what degree of success. It is only fair that we examine our own forecasts with the same impartiality as those of the Air Ministry.

In this country the weather systems that affect our fishing (and personal comfort) move either from west to east or from south-west to north-east on approximately seven days out of ten: but that calculation is based on a year's records. Within any one year, and especially in the spring, there are times when easterly or northerly airs can be very persistent, and who wants to fish in an easterly wind? To overcome this difficulty, a brief glance at the daily weather maps published in the press is well worth while. Some newspapers publish charts of the whole of the North Atlantic and denote, by means of arrows, the anticipated future movements of the weather systems affecting Great Britain.

In general, it is true to say about our weather that it has a tendency to get into a rut; so that, up to a certain point, the longer any one spell has lasted, the longer it is likely to continue. A change, when it does come, will probably be shown by a change in barometric behaviour, either from quick movement to slow, or from frequent 'see-sawing' to a steadier performance giving a level or almost level trace.

The barometric tendency, as we have all discovered, is important; for the steadier the needle, the better the fishing – always provided that the weather does not become too hot. Our hottest summer (and frequently the coldest early spring and winter) spells are associated more often than not with a steady barometer needle at or around the 'High' position. But the barometer will do more for us than tell us, immediately, whether or not fish will bite or lie dormant. It will tell us, too, something about the complicated sequences of weather that, if not absolutely certain, are more likely than not to follow in the next few days. For our weather systems are governed very largely by barometric pressure, and rises and falls of pressure control windflow; this, in turn, controls cloud cover, rainfall and temperature patterns, according to the particular season. If we can discover the key to the working of this barometric weather machine, then we have only to superimpose our knowledge of what happens locally in a given situation to obtain a reliable, if comparatively short-term, forecast.

Working on the suggested seasonal basis, I would suggest an angler's weather guide on the following basic formulae:

Spring. High pressure from Azores or Biscay direction: barometer steady; little wind, clear skies, warm day temperatures, possibly cool nights. Mainly dry. Fishing conditions mainly good, subject to sufficient water and other local effects.

Periods of low pressure from south-west or west: barometer variable; fresh winds alternate days; no very warm days but considerable temperature variations between one day and another. Rain or showers, short, dry intervals. Fishing conditions good on approximately alternate days, subject to local effects.

Periods of low or comparatively high pressure from north-west, north or north-east: winds moderate to fresh; variable cloud, cool or cold day and night temperatures. Some rain, but probably not heavy or continuous. Fishing poor to moderate, subject to local effects.

Summer. High pressure from Azores or Biscay: barometer mainly steady; little wind, mainly clear skies, warm or hot day temperatures and warm nights. Mainly dry, but chance of local thunder-showers. Fishing conditions becoming sluggish in southern counties due to heat, but varying according to type of angling and water conditions; best conditions generally during early evening.

High pressure from the south-east or east: barometer mainly steady; little wind, very clear skies, hot day temperatures and warm nights. Mainly dry, but chance of local thundershowers. Fishing conditions generally only poor to moderate, but depending on water available and other local effects; best conditions during early evening.

High pressure from north-east, north or north-west: barometer steady for a time; moderate winds, clear skies in south, otherwise cloudy. Low to moderate day and night temperatures. Mainly dry in south; occasional showers elsewhere. Fishing conditions averaging at moderate and depending very much upon local effects. It should be noted that high pressure from this direction gives way to low pressure more readily than when it originates from the south-west or east.

Periods of low pressure from south, south-west or west: winds moderate to fresh, occasionally strong; frequently cloudy periods with rain or showers. Variable day and night temperatures, but mainly on cool side of average. Fishing conditions poor to moderate, but moderate to good during temporary finer days or half-days – which occur in this type of situation – subject to local effects.

Periods of low pressure from north or north-east: winds moderate to fresh, occasionally strong; frequently cloudy except in south. Rain in many districts, and temperatures colder than average. Fishing conditions poor to moderate in most districts, but better (comparatively) in south during temporary breaks in the weather, subject to local effects.

Autumn. High pressure from Azores or Biscay: barometer mainly steady; little wind, mainly clear skies, warm day temperatures and cool nights. Mainly dry. Fishing conditions moderate to good, subject to local effects.

Periods of low pressure from south or south-west: winds varying considerably from day to day, moderate, fresh or strong; frequent cloudy periods, with rain or showers. Variable day and night temperatures, but fairly mild on the whole. Fishing conditions poor to moderate, but moderate to good during temporary finer days or half-days, subject to local effects.

Periods of low pressure from north-west or north: winds often very gusty, moderate, fresh or strong; mainly cloudy apart from sunny breaks in south at times. Cool or cold day and night temperatures. Fishing conditions mainly poor, but perhaps moderate at times in the south, subject to local effects.

By this table I have, I believe, covered most of the typical weather situations that we experience time and again, year after year, in these islands. The wind direction for each forecast is, of course, directly related to (and the same as) the directon from which the high or low pressure systems are approaching; and for this reason I referred to the strength of the wind only. In each section it has been necessary to refer to 'local effects' – not simply as a safety factor, but, rather, to emphasize that the relationship between weather and fishing conditions can vary from area to area, and between one season and another. Even two apparently similar spring or summer seasons can differ widely in their potential for angling, due to the difference in preceding weather in each case. Thus, if we are to anticipate the odds for or against a good season for trout or salmon (and who doesn't?), we must look at the weather on a world-wide basis, seeing that so much of it is imported over the run of weeks, months and even years. In this way we can get the feel of the climate and the likely changes in temperature and rainfall that are of such paramount importance to us . . .

For a knowledge of what any approaching summer season will be like, we must look to the situation over Greenland and the southern Arctic during May and about the first ten days of June. If, at this time, there has been a persistent high pressure region, a wet summer over Britain is far more likely than not. This is because a northern high pressure area that builds up during the late spring is likely to persist into the summer, and, more and more, it will block the progress of northward-moving Atlantic storm centres. These will then turn south-eastwards towards our own coasts and the near Continent. And it is fact, not fiction, that if June is wetter than average, July is far more likely to be wet than otherwise, and the odds are three to one on a wet August, or at least a mainly wet one, following a long wet period in July. It is little wonder that the Swithin legend persists so stalwartly in spite of evidence that the original saintly deluge is entirely without historical documentation. But the tale serves to underline an important and often unpleasant scientific truth! . . .

The early evening television weather forecasts of the B.B.C. are useful to anglers, for they show a good deal of the northern hemisphere weather conditions. So, for that matter, do the charts published in certain daily newspapers, including *The Times,* the *Guardian,* the *Scotsman* and the *Daily Telegraph.*

When winter, according to the calendar, is almost over, we are all well aware that 'as the day lengthens, so the cold strengthens'. At least this is often the case, not only during January and February, but right up to the middle or end of May. What are the signs of a late winter, and a cold, unwelcome spring? I find that a building up of high pressure over the Continent (either to the East or to the North) is likely to take place every year at some point between winter and spring, and if it persists for four to six weeks, then add at least another four to six weeks before expecting the cold to give way, and for east winds to be replaced by friendly westerlies. Once again, it is a case of having to put up with our good old English weather getting into a rut. Despite day-to-day variations, this happens every year in one respect or another . . .

There is hardly any aspect of weather forecasting that will fail to pay dividends to the patient angler who is prepared to devote some of his time to its study. And despite the trend towards more scientific forecasting, now apparent, there is still good use to be made of some of those old weather sayings that have helped us all (and perhaps occasionally misled us!) in the past. Some of these have even been verified by scientists as being tolerably accurate and to be based on scientific truths. Included in this category are: 'Red sky at night, angler's delight' (if I may be permitted to leave the shepherds out of the picture for the present), although the red must be a pinkish glow and not an angry crimson hue reflected under rainclouds. 'Rain before seven, clear by eleven' is another fairly reliable saying, but more so in eastern and southern counties than in the west and north. Morning and evening mists, whether over rivers, lakes, marshes or hills, are fair weather signs; but inland mists during the day, particularly over high ground, indicate that rain and high winds are imminent.

The list of old-time weather signs that can be useful is in fact a long one; but some need to be adapted to meet the prevailing weather conditions of individual local areas. Lack of scientific proof for any particular maxim is not necessarily a sign of its failure to be of use. Many of them deal with the behaviour of fish, insects and birds, and even if these are merely responding to existing conditions, they are doubtless so sensitive to even minute weather changes that they can act, on our behalf, as prophets. According to one saying, we can expect rain or wind (but cold weather in winter) when pike lie on the bed of a stream. But if, during damp rainy weather, fish bite readily and swim near the surface, an improvement is likely. Alternatively, if it remains cloudy, it will remain quiet rather than windy.

In Victorian days it was customary for weather prophets to put leeches into a jar and to deduce a great variety of changes from their behaviour. For my own part, I prefer to take a weather hint from creatures in their natural habitat.

from ANGLERS' ANNUAL *1965*

By Foreign Streams

SIR ROBERT BRUCE LOCKHART, K.C.M.G.

I passed my examination for the Consular Service and in December, 1911 was appointed Vice-Consul in Moscow . . . the Russians are great fishers although neither their angling methods nor their fish are ours. The Moscow countryside, flat with wide horizons, has a beauty of its own and its leisurely rivers and streams invite that melancholy contemplation of immensity which appeals to nearly all Russians. But their waters contain only what we call coarse fish, mistakenly, I think, for many of them are game and some, like orfe, noble and aristocratic in appearance. In the European Russia of those days trout and salmon has to be sought in Finland and Lapland.

Neither my purse nor my duties permitted me to go so far afield. During the spacious days before the First World War, I tried my skill and luck for pike in the upper reaches of the Moscow river, and in August fished for perch and roach in the lake at Cosino where I shared a dacha with my chief. The lake, larger than the average Highland loch, also contained pike, but I found perch-fishing more suited to my mood and I would lie back in the boat and, with an occasional glance at my float, watch the wide vista of cornfields shimmering in the heat . . .

In Novemenber, 1919 I was offered and accepted the post of Commercial Secretary at our Legation in Prague, and a month later, with two rod-cases in my luggage and a heart filled with hope, I set out for Czechoslovakia.

Although I was only dimly conscious of it, I was on the threshold of a fishing paradise. It was, too, a paradise to which I had a golden key. In Russia I had already seen something of the Czechs and had helped them in their negotiations with Trotsky for the free exit of their army. On my arrival in Prague they were eager to show their gratitude. I liked trout-fishing. The teeming lakes and streams of their country were at my disposal. Moreover, I had a protector and an ally in my Minister, Sir George Clark, who shared my love of angling and of solitude, and who, until the shooting season began, took me with him on many week-ends to the attractive Bohemian countryside.

Within an hour's run by car there were delectable pleasaunces: a dry-fly stream on the Lobkowicz estate at Melnik which ran through lush meadows and where only the old castle on the hill with its vineyards lying to the sun reminded me that I was not in Hampshire, and a plashing burn ending in a little lake at Dobřiž, the country seat of Prince Colloredo Mansfeldt. Here I caught on fly my largest Czechoslovak trout, a plump and over-fed cannibal of three pounds. Within less than three hours' reach were the rivers of the Riesengebirge, the Erzgebirge, and the Bohemian Forest; fast-running mountain streams not unlike the Spey and set in scenery which recalled Scotland but was warmer and richer in vegetation. In turn I explored them all with a zest unimpaired by the extravagance and late hours of my life in an over-gay post-war Prague until I had established favourites to which I came back again and again.

Never shall I forget my first fishing expedition in Czechoslovakia. My first three months in the country had been over-festive with numerous victory banquets and subsequent late hours and much champagne in Nacht-lokals. An ancient state was being reborn, and its renascence was being celebrated with the same delirious enthusiasm and extravagant hospitality with which the Bohemians had welcomed the birth of Prince Rupert three hundred years before. Then with the first warmth of spring came the repentence of repletion, and I turned my back on the city to seek spiritual comfort in the running streams and pure air of the mountains.

My destination was Jachymov or Sanct Joachimsthal, the famous Kurort in the Erzgebirge . . . Within half an hour of my arrival I was on the best of the three Joachisthal lakes. I do not think that until then it had bever been fished with fly, for the trout were both greedy and innocent. I caught a good fish almost with my first cast, and a minute or two later I hooked and landed three trout at once. Their combined weight was four and a half pounds, and each fish was over a pound.

More alluring were the streams near Jachymov, and I spent many a happy day on a moorland burn on the high plateau close to Gottesgab. The trout were small, but the vista of mountain and forest was peaceful and pleasant, and one never saw a living soul for the whole day long. The whole district was near the German frontier and was drained by numerous trout streams. I fished them all either from Carlsbad or Marienbad . . .

My dream-river, however, was the Otava which flowed through the Bohemian Forest amid bewitching scenery of mountain, fir-clad hills, and woods of silver birch. Before the scientists devastated the countryside to make life easy for the city, it had been a famous salmon-river. Even in the first years after the war a few salmon survived the long and perilous journey up the Elbe from Hamburg, through Dresden and Prague, until they reached the spawning beds in the upper reaches of the Otava. They never took a fly, but one or two were captured on a minnow, and the rest, I suspect, fell victims to the spears and nets of local poachers. Today the new locks of Prague have put an end to this remarkable Odyssey.

In my time, the Otava contained good trout that were not easy to catch and, above all, it could be fished from May till November, for it abounded in grayling. And let it be said that the grayling of the mountain streams of Bohemia and Bavaria is in every respect a nobler fish and worthier foe than our own sluggish grayling, playing as well as the liveliest trout and sweeter to the taste if cooked soon after capture. Indeed, in all my angling life I have enjoyed nothing better than a November day on the Otava, when the midday sun had warmed the water after a sharp night frost, and gentle breaks in the long pool opposite the castled hill of Raby, where Žižka, the Czech Cromwell, lost an eye, show that the grayling are on the rise and that each fish worth keeping will weigh a pound or more . . .

It was from Prague, too, that I made the luckiest fishing discovery of my life. I had been reading a German book on fishing by Professor Heintz, the great Bavarian angling expert and, enraptured by his account of the Bavarian streams, I took seven days' local leave and set out for Munich. It was only a night's journey from Prague, and, although I had no right to go outside the frontiers of Czechoslovakia, I have always regarded regulations as barriers to efficiency and therefore always breakable if broken discreetly.

I had no plan beyond a vague intention of calling on Professor Heintz and seeking his aid. He was away in Berlin. In despair I went to the fishery branch of the Munich Department of Agriculture, saw a long-bearded official who shook his head, talked much about angling licences and finally, after much prompting on my part, gave me the address of Herr Schuessel, a local businessman who had some private fishing. Herr Schuessel, then honorary Consul-General for Japan, was charming, and after some hesitation not only allowed me to fish, but there and then took me out to his river.

In this manner I came to know the Sempt, a dry-fly river not unlike our Hampshire chalkstreams, but set in more majestic surroundings. Its smooth, clear waters flow evenly through rich meadow-land carpeted with wild flowers. Wild birds abound, for the lush grass on the banks provided a safe sanctuary and the river-weed succulent food for wild duck of all sorts. Kingfishers dart downstream like a blue flash . . . The stream holds large brown trout which rise best to a dry-fly and is richly stocked with rainbows which, in Bavaria, thrive and grow to a size of two pounds or more. And in the distant background is the clear-cut prospect of the snow-crested Alps from which in the evening deer and even golden eagles descend to this warm-scented valley.

My first day on the Sempt was sheer murder, for, fishing wet-fly on a cold May morning, I landed twenty-seven trout weighing twenty-three pounds. Ever afterwards I confined myself to dry-fly, concentrated on the big fellows, and had more leisure to enjoy the charms of my surroundings. My biggest catch was a piece of unpardonable exhibitionism. Some English friends who were staying in Munich were rash enough to doubt my stories of the large Sempt trout and to make jokes on the theme of seeing is believing. By this time I had mastered the art of thread-line fishing with a small minnow and a quarter ounce lead, a legitimate form of attack against salmon in a stony Scottish river, but indefensible in a dry-fly stream.

Vanity, however, and a small bet demanded that I should produce at least one big trout by dinner-time; so taking my tiny spinning-rod, I set out for the Sempt. Fortune was kind, for from a long, deep pool fed daily by scourings of a slaughter-house immediately above it, I took out six large trout. They were in beautiful condition. Their combined weight was eighteen pounds, and each fought like a tiger. I was back in time to have them cooked for dinner. Their flesh was as pink as a clean-run salmon's and my friends declared with zest that they had never eaten such succulent trout. I have an instinctive dislike of eating fish that I catch myself. On that evening I contented myself with cold ham . . .

At the end of 1923, I resigned my post at the Legation . . . I joined the staff of the Anglo-International Bank which, supported by the Bank of England, conducted its business in Central Europe and the Balkans. I have never discovered whether banking is made for man or man for banking. I soon realized that it was not made for me or I for it, but I have never regretted the experience, for it gave me a first-hand knowledge of all the Central European and Balkan capitals and took me to new streams. I served my apprenticeship in Vienna, but was too busy mastering the mysteries of banking to have much spare time for angling expeditions.

On holidays and Sundays, however, I went abroad in search of trout, and I remember one delightful week-end at Edlitz-Grimenstein where . . . I stayed at a modest but scrupulously clean Austrian inn and fished the local stream, little bigger than a burn, with a peace of mind and cheerful contentment that had little to do with the catching of trout . . .

A little later in my short banking career I was sent to Yugoslavia to unravel the sinister tangles of a fraud which had cost the bank over a hundred thousand pounds. I was enchanted, for my job took me not only to Belgrade and Zagreb but also to the Dalmation coast, then unspoilt by tourists, and to Montenegro. No banker can have had a more delightful assignment. I was more or less my own master . . . Best of all, I had long spells of freedom, for there were many vexatious delays while our lawyers wrestled with the Yugoslav Minister of Finance.

I put my enforced leisure to my own good use. My headquarters were in Zagreb, for my bank had an interest in the Croatian Discount Bank on whose manager, Dr Stanko Šverljuga, I relied for advice . . .

He introduced me to the Slovenian Krka, a fairy stream in a land of dreams. It flows through a broad fertile valley on the fringe of the Julian Alps. Through the fields which line its banks its limpid waters pursue a slow and gentle course offering golden opportunities to the dry-fly fisher. But at almost every bend there is a waterfall down which the river, gathering strength, hurls itself into a torrential pool where a wet-fly or a minnow brings the best reward . . .

The river fished best after a slight rise of water, but even in a drought the evening rise never disappointed. A Slovene gillie, a magnificent weather-beaten mountaineer, tall, slim, and straight as a guardsman at attention, always followed me with dog-like devotion. Never before had he seen dry-fly fishing, and to him it was a kind of magic which he had to recount to the simple Slovene villagers with much stretching of the hands to illustrate the size of the monsters which fell to this floating fly. *The Times* published his photograph which I had sent them. I gave him the cutting from the paper, and he treasured it ever afterwards.

At night when I came back to the primitive wooden inn where I stayed, there were fresh trout, delicious new potatoes, and home-made bread and butter to be washed down with the excellent local white wine. Then, lighting a pipe, I would sit at the window and listen to the serenade of shepherds' pipes and singing voices. The moon would rise, showing the outline of the mountains in sharp and steely relief, and casting a ghostly light on the dancing waters. The casement window of my bedroom overhung the river, and I would go to bed to the soft plash of rising trout.

from MY ROD MY COMFORT *1949*

Christmas Eve, Naples 1850

DR C. DAVID BADHAM

Nothing can exceed the bustle and noise of the streets today; all the way up the Toledo is one vast scene of excitement: the beggars whine for alms in stronger accents; the cries of itinerant salesmen are perfectly terrific; the vociferation of buyers who will not be sold, and of sellers who will not be bought, rise high above the shrilling of the children, the lashing of whips, the yelling of dogs, the chanting of processions, the bursting of petards, the rolling of drums, and the crashing of wheels. The battle of hard bargains is fought with spirit today, and the subject of contention is – eels; every favourite Italian bonbon, frittura, and dolce is on sale as well, but these certainly form the staple commodity, and carry off all the honours of the day, holding the same place in the affections of the lazzaroni, and being as indispensable a standing-dish for his Christmas, as roast beef and plum-pudding are to an Englishman . . .

Fish-stalls everywhere predominate: here giant lobsters expand and flap their fan-like tails, and bound off the board as if they already felt the hot water. Thousands of 'uongli', piles of 'fruitti di mare', and every other species of bivalve, with fish of all shapes and hues . . . lie in confused heaps upon the street flags; but the predominating delicacy, the fish most in request, is, as we have said, eels. This is indeed 'All-eel day'; not a biped of our race in Naples but hopes to eat them in some fashion or other; the very paupers consider it hard if no friendly Christian furnish them with the means of procuring a taste at least of 'capitoni', though these expensive luxuries fetch not less six carlini a rotolo, or about a shilling a pound. The dispersers of the delicacy occupy either side of the Toledo from end to end, and there display the curling, twisting, snake-like forms of their slippery merchandise, in every possible pose . . . some, suspended over the booths, wriggle round the poles to which they are attached; others undulate their slimy coils by thousands in large open hampers; and while some are swimming, but in vain, for their lives in wooden troughs of cold water, others are fizzing and sputtering in the midst of hot grease in huge frying-pans over the fire; customers are incessant in their demands, and every man, woman and child carries home eels, cooked or uncooked, for breakfast, dinner, supper, and many an intermediate meal besides.

These eels come principally from Comacchio, the low country below Venice; they are almost as large as the conger, but far more delicate in flavour; when first taken, they are kept in brackish stews, and from thence sent to all parts of Italy, sometimes, as here, alive, but more commonly chopped in pieces, grilled, and preserved in a pickle of salt and vinegar, shrouded in bay-leaves, and served out to customers on the point of a porcupine's quill.

from PROSE HALIEUTICS *1854*

Fish out of Water

KATHARINE WHITEHORN

Other people's organization always looks the most indescribable confusion to the outsider. The men in white coats, the wooden boxes in apparently haphazard heaps, the metal containers that looked like giant lidless sardine tins – all this, I was assured, represents MacFisheries' brand-new up-to-date scheme for by-passing Billingsgate and getting its fish directly from trains on to vans.

Eskimo men, their heads in fleece-lined helmets, their duffle coats concealing onion layers of jersey, moved in and out of the deep freeze with fish not due to be distributed that day: to walk into it was like walking into solid glass, clear, horrifying, sharp. We stayed in perhaps thirty seconds, and the bitter dawn outside was a puff of warm air when we came out. A man in a white coat, his clogs shifting on the wet concrete, showed us salmon after magnificent salmon: 'I defy anyone to tell a Scotch one from an Irish one,' he said. We examined lobsters – red ones already boiled for shops with a small demand and no boiler, dark blue ones aggresively alive. The man in charge casually picked up two waving monsters and showed us how to tell a cock from a hen by, of all things, the corns on its underside.

'Look at that,' said the marketing director, showing us a box of carefully interlayered Danish plaice finely shrouded in powder ice. 'They may be three days old, but look.' The plaice's spots were bright, the blood in their gills even brighter. Keen journalists do not, of course, feel sick at having to peer down a fish's gills at six-thirty in the morning; but a sight I could have done without was a metal chest of drawers, the drawers filled with a coiling mass of live eels. After them, even the carp, scaly and revolting, seemed easy work.

Carp, apparently, are sold only in districts with a proportion of Jewish or West Indian people in the neighbourhood (Jewish people, too, insist on fish with heads on, so that they can tell how fresh it is). I was told that you could practically work out where you were by looking at the fish-slab. Haddock implied Scots, hake the West Country or Wales, gurnard the north-east of England, red mullet either West Indians or people who had visited the Mediterranean. The marketing director, a fanatic fish-eater from the east coast himself, says they have an uphill task with psychology, regional and otherwise: women have a feeling that fish are too white and flabby to be fed to their men (like the mistaken idea that the worm in the raspberry is all raspberry, anyway); what fish people eat depends on what was available where they grew up.

Fish, it seems, are a lot more international than one might think. Squids from Aberdeen end up in quantity on the Côte d'Azur; red mullet, fished in the warm waters off Cornwall or the coast of Spain, go *via* London to Paris. MacFisheries buy perhaps twenty-five per cent of their fish abroad – even, though it makes them unpopular in the trade, from Iceland. But the MacFisheries view of the British fish trade is not conducive to popularity anyway.

After our Dawn Ordeal at the distribution centre at Finsbury Park, we visited what felt like a very large number of the 236 branches it serves. It was interesting to see that in the Brompton Road they take the skins off the soles before the customer meets them, that in Mount Street there is a man who knows how to bone a turkey, that as managers are allowed to vary their prices to suit the neighbourhood, sprats were 1s 6d in Knightsbridge, 1s 3d in Swiss Cottage and 1s in Muswell Hill. It is all the same fish, however; and even if you are the only bream-eater in Cheam you can order it for the next day – a flexibility that does not always go with modernization.

One point on which I was inclined to take issue with them was on standardization. If even rifles come variably off the production line then so must chickens and herrings, and although I see the point about enforcing general standards, I still feel they would get further with the discriminating if as well as MacChickens and MacDucks they had, as it were, Supermacs – they do, after all, buy pheasants from Mr Macmillan.

I was also deeply unimpressed by their reasons for refusing to consider live trout tanks: they say the trout do not feed once they are tanked (who does), but they still stay infinitely fresher than dead. It seems a sad pity that whereas Geneva (I am told) has only one fish restaurant without a *vivier*, London hasn't a single one.

But what appealed to me about all this was that it seemed, at least to my untutored eye, to be enlightened streamlining; and since we cannot very well go back to getting our fish out of the stream at the bottom of the garden, it is somehow more heartening to see something modernized intelligently than to find a small untouched corner where a dying process continues unspoiled. The discussion rages worst, of course, around the question of frozen fish.

All the branches get delivery before nine o'clock, and at that hour the fish that has been deep-frozen is rock hard. But by noon, it will all look 'fresh'; and MacFisheries feel that at least some of the views people hold about frozen fish are wide of the mark – granted that no fish will ever taste as marvellous as one that was alive ten minutes ago, the concept of freshness has changed somewhat by the time we are talking in terms of fish that has already been on the trawler ten days before it hits the Humber. The marketing director felt that the *way* in which something was deep-frozen was all-important: if it was frozen slowly, allowed to get even very slightly unfrozen at the 'handling points', then it would taste quite different from and infinitely worse than a fish dealt with correctly. He may be right: until we have a panel of really respected food experts to decide and comment on such things – brand by brand, process by process – we shall just have to keep on by guess and buy cod, as now.

from ROUNDABOUT *1962*

A Blagdon Day

CHRIS OGBORNE

Just as a precaution, the alarm was set for 7.30 am, but by that time it has already been switched off, the coffee has been made, and I am now looking out on what any angler would term a perfect morning. A short drive, with more than an occasional glance at the high, but unbroken cloud cover, and then the turning down to the Lodge. It is still early for a boat day, barely 9 am, but Tony is already here, looking, as I am, in disbelief at a gentle but persistent southerly ripple.

Even as we watch, there is a good hatch of midge taking place, and beyond the reed there are the tell-tale humps and fins of rising fish. The normal anticipation prior to any fishing expedition changes to barely concealed excitement at the thought of the day to come, for in conditions like these the morning sport, at least, should be assured.

Part of the formalities – part of the pleasure – is the brief chat with David at the Lodge, and the boat number is allocated. But today, even Dave senses that it is time for fishing rather than words, and urges us to be on our way. The gear is stowed, the wine immersed in the lake to chill for lunchtime, and the painter is untied. This last act severs not only the physical connection with the bank, but seems also to release the fishermen from normal conventions; we are beyond the reach of telephone, and of other people, insulated yet not isolated, released from all other concern, at least for a day.

The temptation on a morning like this is to row a few strokes into Pipe Bay, and start fishing without further delay. But even if the long haul up to Top End seems longer than usual, it is well worth it, as the classic drift from Wood Bay to Rugmoor is available with a southerly wind. The delay is a bonus in another way, as it allows a more careful study of this prolific midge hatch, it anything thicker now than when we first looked. Close inspection confirms the large red midge, which means only one thing – Grenadier. I stop rowing just off Wood Bay, and we hastily change flies; Grenadier on the bob, size 10 Red Buzzer in the middle, and long shank Pheasant Tail on the point. This covers the obvious choice, but also includes a degree of 'hedged bets', in that the general Pheasant Tail Nymph will probably be taken in view of its overall rather than specific appeal.

At most, the ripple is only about a three-inch chop, and here in the shelter of the trees, we are right on the edge of the calm water – a perfect place to start the drift. It is just after 10 am, and although heavily overcast, there is a warmth to the day that we have not seen yet this year. Spring is in full cry all around, and swallows are touching the water around us, sharing the insect hatch with the trout. The season has a smell of its own, breathing a vitality into the day, and seeming to heighten our sense of anticipation.

No sooner are we into the ripple than the first rising fish are seen. They are moving quickly and, as so often happens when feeding on the red midge, they seem to be taking the insect at the point of hatching, right in the surface film. We are barely twenty yards into the ripple when I lift into the first fish, predictably to the Grenadier. No sooner is he in the boat, a good rainbow of 2 lb, than Tony is being followed by a big fish; his Grenadier bob is working back towards the boat and a huge bow wave follows it, closing but not taking. He speeds up the retrieve, but still the fish only follows, until finally it turns away with a swirl within feet of the boat. Glances are exchanged – part smile, part wistful and part excitement. The next five casts see two more bow-waving follows, obviously from good-size fish, but no contact is made.

We are well into the ripple by now, and a fairly quick retrieve is needed to keep in touch with the flies. The occasional dorsal fin and nose is showing, but mostly the signs now are of fish feeding savagely just below the surface. I change the top dropper to Red Buzzer and there is a crashing take, within seconds of the fly touching the water. A rainbow of well over 3 lb leaves his element, hurling spray into the air as he lands, and makes an immediate run for the boat. Before I am really in touch he is behind us, which is just as well as Tony is also – a bow waver finally said yes to the Grenadier. Adrenalin flows as two big fish are played, one on each side. The fish tire together, but Tony nets his first, and we compare information from the Marrow Scoop; Red Midge it almost certainly is, the two fish are packed with them, both pupae and hatching insect. So, in terms of fly, it's 'either or'. I settle for Grenadier on bob, Pupa on dropper, and a big, bushy Soldier Palmer on the point – all angles should be covered. And so they are it seems, as fish come to all three flies before the drift is over. In no time, we are at Rugmoor, and as the water shallows we move out of rising fish, but a ten-minute row takes us back across to the Withies. Iron nerve is needed to ignore the moving fish during the trip back, especially as some of them look really big, and if anything, they are feeding even harder than before.

Already, it looks like being one of those days, and if limit bags are to be avoided too early, then some kind of standard is needed. We agree – anything below 2 lb goes back to fight another day, and thus the next four fish are returned. This drift sees pulls, follows and takes – superb fishing. Blagdon at her glorious best. Again we row back, and turn to move out of Bell's.

Even before the drogue has opened, a muttered exclamation from Tony rivets attention on something big moving across our line, forty yards away; one moment unreachable, but in the next he has changed direction and moves directly towards us, pointing at the middle of the boat. My line is out and Tony's isn't, so it's his fish, and he drops the tail fly exactly right, a yard in front of the huge nose. A surge in the water, and before slack is taken up the fish is on: the explosive take is followed by a headlong run away from us, and the reel screams its beautiful tune. A full flyline and another twenty yards of banking are gone, and the curve of the rod says that pressure will become terminal if he doesn't stop soon. He does, and for a second things go slack as he reverses course towards us. Tony is only just in control when the fish leaps across our drift, and I clear my own line behind the boat so as not to interfere. The fish is back on the reel now, and quality Orvis engineering is stretched by another twenty-yard run. By now, we have some measure of his size, and Tony is handling the very best of Blagdon's progency – a 4 lb-plus rainbow, fin perfect, that has almost certainly been in the lake since last year, and has no intention of coming anywhere near the net that I optimistically wield. Time and again the fish bores deep; time and again he wallows on the surface, testing the 5 lb tippet with a flap of his great tail, until finally he is spent. Who can say how long it has been, or indeed whether time has any meaning at all at such moments. Certainly, we must have drifted half way across Top End before the pink and silver flanks are cased, so very gently, over the rim of the landing net. The fish will later turn the Lodge scales at 4 lb 8 oz.

So the wonderful morning runs its course, holding us in a grip that defies the intrusion of any thoughts other than fishing, and its attendant pleasures. A celebratory glass of wine after Tony's fish, a lunch taken at anchor off the Withies, and an afternoon break for ourselves and the trout. A quiet stroll around Wood Bay, with the quarrelsome coots chastising one another, the grebes performing their enchanting nest ceremony, and the swans proudly, regally, patrolling their designated stretch of bank. The song of the chaffinch, surely the purest distillate of an English spring, is all about us. The world outside has slowed, and perhaps for today it does not exist – such is the therapy of fishing.

At 4 pm the cloud cover is still with us, the ripple holding up well, and another good hatch of midge. We opt for a longer drift, from Rainbow across to Ash Tree, where we saw some good fish on our way down this morning. But the wind has other ideas, and the southerly breeze now has a touch of west in it, pushing us towards Pegs instead of Ash Tree. The afternoon fish are harder to tempt, and on this drift we take only one brown, returning two smaller ones. As we pull back across Rugmoor Point, the first sedges of the year are in evidence, and I wonder whether a Pupa may be the answer. A little early in the season perhaps but who knows how quickly the fish can adapt.

A cup from the Thermos at 6 pm and by 6.30 the evening is already here. The cloud has broken at last, and a pale pastel sunset marks the beginning of the end. The ripple is dying, but in doing so is breaking into wind lanes; not content with a wonderful daytime, Blagdon is giving us her very best, in a classic evening. A lull in the fishing only precedes the storm to come, as the green midge begin to hatch in profusion. Fish are everywhere, and we cast selectively to the better fish. Tony hooks a small Brown, but his buzzer dropper is seized by a 3 lb rainbow – chaos ensues, during which time he loses the bigger fish and finally nets and releases the smaller. Our smiles are genuine, not rueful, for who could deny fish their freedom after the earlier bounty.

As the soft evening finally closes, shrinking visibility, and reducing awareness to within fifty yards of the boat, we row quietly back to the Lodge. The ebbing ring of a rising fish still shows, but we have had our fill. After the excitement comes the quiet, and the balm of darkness closes the day. The stroke of the oars slows, and the landing stage lights, with their attendant clouds of flies, take us almost by surprise.

The final rituals are performed – the weigh in, the happy smiles of fellow anglers who have shared the lake with us yet have remained unseen till now. The real ale at the pub never tasted better, and conversation trails into silence. The other world will return tomorrow, but long after its return, the memory of today will linger, cast in the mind as a retreat when insanity threatens. A classic day. A perfect day. A Blagdon day.

from BLAGDON *1985*

Taupo's Picket Fence

SIDNEY VINES

The Maoris call Lake Taupo 'The Sea of Taupo'. This is a fitting name, for the rainbows treat the lake as the salmon treats the ocean. They spend the summer feeding in the lake, and in autumn they run up the many rivers and streams that flow into it to spawn. In spring they fall back, spent, to begin the cycle again.

Taupo is both a civilized and a wild place. Taupo town (population 20,000) is geared to the needs of tourists. It offers plenty of accommodation of all kinds. Good guides, boats, and a variety of aircraft are available. A tackle shop contains everything the visiting angler could want, including local advice and the hire of chest waders – which are essential.

Despite the civilized comforts, there is a wild side to Taupo. Sudden storms spring up. Wading can be dangerous. Every year, there are a few accidents – caused invariably by those who venture out into wild places without a guide. Beyond the north shore there is a screen of steam about a mile wide from the thermal geysers of Wairakei. The whole vast lake of 240 square miles was formed by an earthquake 1,400 years ago – only yesterday in geological terms. Minor tremors are common. They are said to help tourists suffering from constipation.

In company with that stalwart fly-fisher Tom Stuart-Menteath (who emigrated to New Zealand in the sixties) I set out one sunny March afternoon to explore the lake, and especialy to see the famous 'picket fence' at the mouth of the Waitahanui, 8 miles south of Taupo town. We parked our car, and walked through the bushes on to the shore, where the scene was revealed. About twenty anglers stood in water up to their chests, in a half-circle, casting out into the lake with heavy, powerful rods. Flies whizzed through the air. It looked a trifle dangerous and irresistibly comic.

While we watched, a Maori angler hooked a fish, played and lost it. 'You've come half way round the world for this,' said Menteath. 'You had better have a go.' I was not all that keen, but Menteath was right. The picket fence was by no means the only reason for my visit to New Zealand, but it was certainly a major one.

So, equipped with what Menteath said was an infallible local lure called a Red Setter, I joined the half-circle and began to fish with my little graphite rod. One braced oneself against the water and cast out into the edges of the current. For some reason, this varied. The water of the Waitahanui flowed out hosepipe fashion, moving by ten or so degrees. The good anglers watched this, and always aimed for the edges, where the fish were running up.

On my left was a venerable Maori with a battered black sombrero and a grey beard. His name was Barney Northcroft and he was deferred to by the other Maoris. He courteously made room for me, and they were all most friendly. But I sensed from their smiles that they did not have too high an opinion of the Poms.

After about twenty minutes I felt my line check and instinctively tightened. Suddenly the rod was almost torn from my hands. The reel screamed and far out a huge silver shape leapt. The Maoris were greatly amused. What would the Pom do now? I heard Menteath on the beach giving instructions. 'Lift your rod and walk behind the line. They will stop fishing while you do it. Then wade back up to the beach.' This was accomplished while the fish leapt several times. I reached the beach and saw to my horror that almost all my 80 yards of line and backing had gone. I cursed my own foolishness. In the tackle shop at Taupo they had warned me that at the lake I would need at least 125 yards.

With great care, I played the fish out and drew him in. A Maori shouted, 'Bring out the landing net' – which was greeted with general merriment. The Maoris regard landing nets as effete. They let the fish flap up the beach, helped with a few kicks. 'Let them laugh,' said Menteath. 'We're taking no chances.' Skilfully he netted the fish. It lay on the beach, and I gazed at it in awe – a six-pound rainbow of perfect proportions, as silver as a fresh-run salmon. 'A noble fish,' said Menteath.

Barney Northcroft called out, 'You can't get them like that in the Serpentine', which caused another outburst of mirth. Then another called, 'You're not giving up are you?' Indeed I was not, and they allowed me to resume my place in the line. Another twenty minutes, another check to the line, another fish – only three pounds this time, but another beauty – and all this time not one of the local experts had touched a fish. Barney shouted to his friends, 'It takes a Pom to come out here and teach us how to fish.'

A typically generous remark, but I would have been foolish to believe it. The Maoris are fine anglers, with a natural rhythm to their casting. Over a fisherman's life the luck averages out, and that afternoon my luck was in. I was in the right place at the right time, with the right fly. Such occasions are rare.

Not much skill is required at the picket fence. It is a sort of comic-opera fishing, made memorable by the charm of the Maoris and the quality of the fish. Experienced American anglers from Colorado, who have fished for the rainbow in its home – the Red River – say that the Taupo rainbows are in better condition. The environment is ideal for them. There are many places around Taupo where there is better fishing than at the picket fence, though not better fish. Its popularity is due to its accessibility and its safe wading – a level shingle.

My abiding memories are of that magnificient six-pounder and Barney Northcroft. He may feel now that not all Poms are whingeing, and sometimes they may even catch a fish or two. I like to think so.

from FLYFISHING AROUND THE WORLD
(edited by Tony Pawson) 1987

Tactics for Tailers

DR ROBERT SLOANE

The general absence of the mention of 'tailing' trout in the overseas trout literature doubtless sets Tasmania aside, because in this country fishing to tailing trout is 'bread and butter' to local fly men. 'Tailing' is a general term which is applied to the foraging activity of brown trout in shallow lake and backwater margins. Often the trout are quite conspicuous in the shallows, which may be only inches deep. Frequently the dorsal fin, back and tail become visible as the fish feeds; or a swirl, disturbance, sudden lunge and splash, a rustle of tussocks or movements of rushes will give the trout's position away.

This activity peaks in Tasmanian lake margins and stream backwaters early in the season, in September and October, as the fish feed on spawning frogs, worms, caterpillars and other small creatures which have been flushed from the earth and vegetation by rising water levels after spring rains.

Trout may often feed on tadpoles in this manner during November and December and may be found tailing around lake margins well into the summer, feeding on snails and small crustacea. There is a chance of finding a tailing fish at any time of the season, particularly at dawn and dusk, but often they can be found during the middle of the day along untrodden shores if conditions are overcast.

It must be a combination of conditions, in particular the nature of the lake margins, which favour this type of feeding pattern in Tasmania; many lakes flood over shallow grass and sedge land and some spill into extensive swamps and marshes where fish will tail freely. Water levels, food availability, light intensity, water temperature and angling pressure are all critical factors which affect such activity. Obviously deep, clear, stone-sided lakes and artificial impoundments with steep, barren shores do not encourage marginal feeders.

I am reminded of an American visitor I took fishing to Bronte Lagoon early one season. When we came to a flooded canal backwater full of logs, bushes and tussocks, he stood aghast, not believeing that the water could hold trout. After several hours sneaking around the margins fishing to tailers he freely admitted that I had in fact not given him a 'bum steer', and commented, 'If we had water like this in the States we would stock it with bass, we wouldn't dream that it could be a suitable trout water'.

Another experience which comes to mind also involves an American who is in fact a prominent international trout writer and expert fly fisherman. When he visited Tasmania I went fishing with him to the Western Lakes area, accompanied by an experienced friend with much local knowledge. After a short walk we came to a series of shallow, flooded lagoons where a number of large brown trout were tailing.

We put the visitor on to one of the fish, after my companion had demonstrated the local art. Alas, he was so overcome with excitement that he could not present the fly properly. At no stage did he know whether to cast with his rod or click his camera or vice versa! Anyway, to cut a long story short, in his vast experience he had never encountered anything quite like it and virtually could not cast to the tailing monsters. Such can be the excitement of this type of fishing.

Naturally, the type of fly used under these conditions is extremely important, but more in its *function* than in its appearance. The main requirements are that the fly should make a small 'splat' as it enters the water, to attract the attention of the foraging fish. The fly should then sink very slowly so as not to become lost in the weeds and as it is retrieved it should rise towards the surface and swim in the clear water between and above the weeds.

We have developed a type of fly which serves this purpose to perfection. We call it the Rabbit Fur Fly. Variations on the theme are infinite in terms of colour, size and optional extras, but in its simplest and most effective form the Fur Fly is tied from natural grey-brown wild rabbit fur. A narrow strip of dried rabbit skin with fur attached is folded and tied round a suitable hook (a round bend, size 8 Mustad 9980 is ideal for the purpose). After the fur is tied down the skin is snipped off, and a few turns of black ostrich herl are added as a head. That's all there is to it! A coloured wool or silk body can be laid on the hook shank; the fur type and colour, the bulk of fur used, the hook size and the head colour and shape can all be varied to suit the tyer's own whims.

The fly can be landed with a 'splat', and on entering the water the fur flares out, covering the hook completely as the fly slowly settles to the bottom. If it is drawn forward it will rise towards and bulge the surface and the fur will contract; when stopped the fur will again flare out. It thus progresses with a pulsing movement as it is twitched gently and hesitatingly along. Needless to say, the trout love it and I rarely use anything else early in the season to tailing fish in river backwaters or on lake shores.

For frog feeders the plain grey-brown Rabbit Fur Fly is deadly. It should be cast several feet in front of the fish or into a suitable gap in the tussocks, gutter or other lie. Invariably the trout will detect the initial shock waves and move over to pick up the fly as it settles in the water. Of course, when the fish takes the bulky Fur Fly it finds little more than a bare hook and the strike is a mere formality.

The ability of trout to detect the source of a disturbance in the water is remarkable. This was brought home to me strikingly one day when I cast a fly with a 'splat' into a gap in the tussocks on the Long Shore at Bronte Lagoon. A trout immediately reacted from several metres away, bow-waved around two tussock clumps and picked up the fly from the bottom; the fly was not moved and the trout's view had been totally blocked by the tussocks.

The Rabbit Fur Fly, although not bearing any natural resemblance to a frog or related beast, has nevertheless come to hold the pride of place in my fly pouch and though I have often tied more complicated variations I always conclude that the simplest tie is the best and most effective. I do have specific preferences for particular furs and colours for certain places, but much of this is purely psychological and a bit of an indulgence on my part.

from THE TRUTH ABOUT TROUT *1986*

Oola on the Alta

CHARLES RITZ

I had taken bigger fish on the Alta, while fishing as Tony Pulitzer's guest on the Jöraholmen farm, but never under circumstances as bizarre as the day I found myself being ghillied by a girl.

This came about by chance, as it was my day to fish a very fine salmon pool, adjoining a great rocky point, which is ordinarily fished by boat. But I had offered my boat to a friend who was leaving for home that evening. His fishing had been unlucky and we all wanted to give him a last chance. My host concurred, and suggested that I try fishing the pool from the rocky promontory, as long as I would have no boat at my disposal until after 2 pm when the other guest would have to leave.

This was challenging, as if I did succeed in hooking a fish, casting from the rocks, the only possible gaffing place would be on the lower part of the rocky point, where the footing for gaffing is on a narrow ledge, about three feet wide and twelve feet long and some three feet above the water level.

I pondered the problem through a late breakfast and at 11 a.m. decided to go look at this difficult landing spot, to see if I could figure out a way to cope with a fish there with nobody around to gaff it for me.

The cook was busy in the kitchen, the Jöraholmen family was out on the farm, the chauffeur had left with Tony Pulitzer, and I was about to give up the idea when suddenly I remembered that in passing the house I had seen somebody hanging up the laundry out in back. That would be Oola, I realized, the young Lapp girl who had only a few days before begun working as kitchen helper and laundress.

Nobody knew much about Oola, who was short and stocky and very round, except that young as she was she already had several children, back in the village of Kaiteno, from lumberjacks, village boys and slate quarry workers. She had explained, in applying for the job, that she needed money to send back to the Lapp woman who was taking care of her kids, the result of her too great kindness to mankind. Oola was high in the front and low in the rear, with a very round face, dark but extremely smooth skin and Asiatic eyes. She was a very sweet girl, with a most comprehensive viewpoint, always looking at us men hungrily, I thought, and we all felt sorry for the poor creature.

'Hello, Oola, how would you like to go fishing with me for an hour?'

She jumped up in the air saying, 'Yes, yes.'

I picked up my rod and the gaff and we started for the trail, of about half a mile, that led to the pool, Oola following along behind me until we reached the first barbed wire fence.

I snaked under it, as it was too high to climb over, and when I reached the other side Oola passed me the rod and the gaff and started to imitate me. She stopped with a yell, as the barbed wire caught in her skirt. I managed to get her loose and urged her on and just as she started to crawl again there was another, louder yell, reflecting a more serious problem. This time the wire was taut and stretching almost to the limit across that area of Oola which resembled two honeydew melons. After several failures I finally succeeded a second time in giving her full freedom of movement and Oola was at last able to pass and join me.

This she did, however, in such a confused and excited state that she threw her arms around me and I had to explain with many gestures that this was not part of salmon fishing and I almost told her I did not want to increase her little tribe. So off we went again towards the pool through the mossy grass and the birch trees.

When we reached the top of the rock, I decided to show Oola what I expected her to do and exactly how to use the gaff. She became more and more excited and I stepped away from her so as to keep clear of her weapon which she was waving frantically. We went to the rocky point and I started casting. 'Oola, all you have to do is to hold the gaff and keep away from my line while I am casting and always stay a reasonable distance behind me until I have the salmon at the foot of the rock, ready for gaffing.' She was holding the gaff and started to dance around me, again waving her weapon dangerously. I somehow managed to calm her and get her back to normal. After a few minutes I located two salmon just where the slack and fast waters met. This was a very good sign. I decided to use a medium size Arctic wolf hair tubefly and started casting.

All of a sudden I thought my fly had caught in a tree and when I turned I noticed the leader wrapped around the gaff and Oola standing close behind me. I stared at her and said: 'Now, Oola, come and sit on the rock and leave the gaff on the ground and if you don't obey, you will have to go back to your chores.'

On the third cast, I was into a good fish. He immediately jumped twice and made for deep water and then up again for another jump as he tried to reach the current and swim downstream. He succeeded in doing this and took out a lot of line. I had to follow him trying to prevent the line from breaking on the jagged edges of the rock. I finally managed to stop the fish, then heard some wild yells, just as I had a slack line and the fish turned upstream. Suddenly I saw Oola, gaff in hand, doing some kind of wild Lapp dance. By that time, my nervous system had almost reached its peak and I had the hardest time to control myself, the fish and Oola. At the end, in despair, I threatened to throw Oola in the pool. She began to cry and, gaff still in hand, started to return to the camp.

'Oola, came back at once, otherwise I will have to send you home to Kaiteno.'

She stopped, came back and sat down on a big stone. I was then able to concentrate on the salmon. Three more runs, then he started to show signs of fatigue and I began to think that my usual luck was back. The fish tried twice to swim downstream and reach the current, but without success. He was finally almost still. I could start to bring him close enough for the gaffing. Then the great tragedy of my fisherman's life happened. I had decided I could not trust Oola with the gaff and the only solution was to hand her the rod realizing that any additional delay would increase the chances of the fly tearing loose. I could see it on the edge of the mouth. Now I explained to Oola how to handle the rod.

'Oola, here is the rod, hold it high with both hands one on the reel and don't move. Remain as still as a statue!'

I took the gaff and immediately had it fast into the fish and lifted him out of the water, on to the rocky ledge. But the salmon was still lively and got off the gaff while I was trying to grab him with my hands. Oola then pulled on the rod with all her strength and broke the leader which had already been frayed on the rocks.

As I was scared of losing him, I did the only logical thing that came to mind. I flopped down on the salmon. All of a sudden, I felt a tremendous weight on me. Oola was so excited and wanted to be so helpful that she lay on top of me. When the fish had quietened down and I managed to get Oola off me, I looked around for a stone to kill the poor salmon but not seing one, I sent Oola to find a suitable stone. She soon returned with a rock of about twenty pounds which she wanted to drop on the salmon and probably on me also. I ordered her to lay it down and succeeded in making her understand the need to find a small stone. Soon she returned with a smaller stone, but still too heavy. On the third trip she brought the right sized stone. I killed the poor salmon and finally he was ours! We were shaking and then looked at each other and I felt like giving her a brotherly kiss, but at the last moment I changed my mind because she was looking at me with such spawning eyes.

The salmon tipped the scales at twenty-nine pounds. From that day on every time I saw Oola she gave me such a hungry look that I always had to tell her to stick to her laundry and that I had a French Oola waiting for me in Paris.

Upon my return to Paris, Ludwig Bemelmens was staying with us at the Ritz and when I told him Oola's story, he said: 'Charles, if you write about it, I will gladly make a sketch for you,' which he very kindly did.

But all my friends could say was: 'Oola indeed. Ooh-la-la, you wicked old Frenchman!'

And what kind of remark is that to make to a Swiss?

from A FLYFISHER'S LIFE *1972*

PART 5

The Spring Spawners: Coarse Fish

O let me rather on the pleasant Brinke
Of Tyne and Trent possesse some dwelling place
Where I may see my Quill and Corke downe sinke,
With eager bite of Barbill, Bleike, or Dace . . .

John Dennys

The Record Carp

RICHARD WALKER

Although I was brought up on roach-fishing by a fine roach-fisher, of course I caught other fish too, and one species I have always found fascinating is the carp. During my schooldays and for some years after the Second World War, the carp was the subject of more misconceptions than any other fish. It was supposed to take a hundred years to grow big; to be nearly impossible to catch, biting only if the tackle was ultra-fine and then breaking away; to prefer complicated pastes laced with aniseed or honey; and to reach a maximum weight of not much over 25 lb. A noted ichthyologist, Dr Tate Regan, gave that figure; a noted angler stated that one might expect to wait a thousand hours before catching one's first carp; a noted editor said that life was too short even to contemplate carp fishing!

If I hadn't caught several large carp, and seen much larger ones, before I read or heard all this, I might have believed them.

From 1946 onwards I made an intensive study of carp. I had taken over fifty double-figure carp before 1940, but from 1946 till 1953 I fished for little else each year, from mid-June to mid-October. I wrote to, talked with, I fished with other anglers who were interested in carp.

This is not the place to relate the history or the conclusions of those days. Here I shall include only the stories of my two biggest carp. Both came from Redmire Pool, and the first of them set a new British record.

I first fished Redmire on 16 June, 1952. On that visit I caught two carp of 5 lb apiece; Peter Thomas had one of 28 lb 10 oz. For me, that opening day was the commencement of a series of visits that totalled 460 hours before I hooked the fish for which I was hoping and which I knew could be caught. I slept on the bank; I was often soaked, often hungry, often tired. I had only weekends and one week's holiday in which to fish, and to reach the water I had to travel a hundred and thirty miles each way. I went by train, I cadged lifts.

In July, having by then hooked and lost two monster carp, I saw Maurice Ingham catch one of 24¾ lb. That night I caught an eel and a rat.

On 12 September, 1952 Peter Thomas and I went again to Redmire.

We left home in a downpour, but by the time we had reached our destination the sky had cleared and the stars were shining brightly. It was very cold indeed, but we fished until about 2 am, when we noticed a bank of black cloud coming from the north-west, and decided to pitch our tent before it began to rain again.

We chose a spot on the west side of the lake, in deference to the theory I have that when carp have been driven into deep water at night by falling temperature, they usually move out of it again in the early morning on the side which first catches the morning sunshine. Here we camped, pitching the tent with its open end about three yards from the water and directly facing it. Between the tent and the water's edge a large groundsheet was spread.

Looking across the lake, about a hundred yards wide at this point, we could see a line of trees, which appeared as black shadows. To the left, ten yards along the bank, was a clump of weeping willows, whose branches trailed in the water, and beyond them was tough pond-weed. This extended about twenty yards out into the lake, as did another bed of the same stuff on the right of our position. Beyond that, forty yards away, was the dam at the end of the lake, which runs at right angles to the bank from which we were fishing. Half-way along the dam were once some alder-trees, which have long since been felled, but their stumps still live and a tangled mass of writhing roots trail in the water. Immediately to our right, on the bank from which we were fishing, was a mass of brambles hanging in the water and extending to the bottom, concealing an undercut bank hollowed-out to a depth of between three and four feet, a favourite haunt of moorhens and rats.

Having arranged our week-end home, we baited our hooks and cast out to the edge of the deep water, a few yards beyond the pond-weed; Peter's to the left and mine only a few yards to the right of where his bait landed. Both baits consisted of balanced paste and bread-crust on number 2 hooks which had been carefully sharpened beforehand; mine was whipped direct to a 12 lb-breaking-strain nylon line, of which I had a hundred yards on a fixed-spool reel. Rods were the usual MK IV carp-rods, which have never failed us yet – ten ounces of hardened split-bamboo can be made to do surprising things. Electric buzzers were clipped to the lines between butt-rings and reels, and all was ready for the carp to bite; to attract them mashed-bread ground-bait was thrown out. By this time, the sky had clouded over completely, and instead of rain there was a decided increase in temperature, but the darkness was intense. I cannot remember ever being out on a blacker night. It was so dark that even the rats were less active than usual, and all I could see were the silhouettes of the trees opposite. The lake was completely still, its surface unbroken by either wind or the movement of fish; and so it remained, except for one heavy splash far out, and a brief spell of 'flipping' by very small fish on the surface, until some time between 4.30 am and 5 am. About that time one of the buzzers sounded, and we were both at our rods at once.

'It's yours,' said Peter. I raised the back of my hand under the rod to feel if the line was being taken, and felt it creep slowly over the hairs, an eerie but satisfactory sensation. In went the pick-up; a pause to make sure the line had been picked up properly, and then I struck hard and far back. I encountered a solid but living resistance, and Peter, needing no telling that a fish was hooked, reeled up his line out of the way. I crouched so that I could see the curve of the rod against the sky – even that was difficult in the extreme darkness – and waited on events. I did not want a fresh lively fish brought too soon into the fifteen-yard-wide channel between the weed-beds, and I determined that if possible the battle should be fought in the deep water beyond.

The fish moved slowly and solidly towards the dam. Every few seconds came a tremendous tug; it felt as if the rod had been struck by a sandbag. As the fish neared the dam, I remembered those alder roots. Four pounds or forty, it must not get among them, or all would be lost, so I increased pressure. At first it had no effect; then as I bent the rod more, the efforts of the fish became intensified. I knew only a few yards separated it from disaster, and hung on grimly. The rod bent as never before – I could feel the curve under the corks in my hand; but everything held for the two or three minutes that the fish continued to fight his way towards his refuge. Then, suddenly, he gave it up. He turned and forged into the weed-bed between me and the roots, and I was only just able to keep the line taut. Presently he stopped, and all was solid and immovable.

Peter said 'Take it easy. Wait and see if he'll move.' I did. Nothing happened. I said, 'I'll try hand-lining.' Peter said, 'All right, but take it easy. That's a big fish, you don't want to lose it.'

I had no idea how big a fish it was. I knew it was a good one, but all I could think of then was: 'Maybe another twenty-pounder – I hope!' I pulled off a couple of yards of line, so as to be able to get the rod up quickly if the fish bolted suddenly; then I pointed the rod straight at the fish and began tugging. The first few tugs made no impression; then came a frantic pull, up went the rod, and out went the fish into the deep water again. I let him go well out, and then tightened up firmly again, praying for him to move left; and he did. When he was opposite, I gave him the butt and crammed on pressure to the limit; and in he came, grudgingly, pulling and boring every inch of the way, but always losing ground, until at last he came to the surface and rolled three or four yards out.

Peter was ready with the net, and as I drew the fish towards it, he switched on the electric lamp. We saw a great expanse of golden flank as the fish rolled. 'Common carp,' said Peter. The fish rolled again, then righted itself, and suddenly, with a last effort, shot towards me and to the right. I could do nothing to stop it, and to my horror it crashed through he fringe of trailing brambles; in the light of the lamp I could see the swirls as the fish tried to thrust even farther under; but though I put the rod-point under water and strained it as hard as I dare, nothing would shift the fish, which eventually settled down into an immovable sulk.

Peter climbed out to the edge of the overhang and put the big net, thong down, over the hole in the brambles where the fish had gone in. Then, feeling carefully down the line with his free hand, he reached the fish's nose and pulled it round, steering it into the net. I saw vaguely a commotion; then Peter began to lift. He stuck half-way and called for me to take his lamp. I slackened line, put down the rod and went to his assistance. Once I had the lamp, he could grasp the mesh of the net, and with a tremendous heave he swung net and fish up and over the brambles and on to the bank.

We knelt side by side looking at it. I knew it was big, and suddenly it dawned on me it was more than that. It was tremendous! I cut a stick, notched its end, and with this Peter extracted the hook which was only lightly lodged in the roof of the mouth. Then we put the fish in a sack and lifted it on my spring balance, which goes up to 32 lb. The pointer came up against the top with such a thump that we both knew at once that here was a new record; but we could tell no more; so we tied up the mouth of the sack and lowered it into the water.

Then we rebaited out hooks and cast out again. Peter went into the tent; but I knew I could never sleep, and sat smoking and thinking till dawn. It was then that I resolved that, record or no record, that fish should not be killed. Many, many times I had wondered what I should do if ever I caught a record carp; now I had to decide, and kill it I could not.

At about 10.30, I was able to telephone Mr H. F. Vinall, then curator of the aquarium at the London Zoo. To cut a long story short, a van containing a vast tub, and two good fellows who gave up their Saturday afternoon for the purpose, came and fetched it; and it arrived alive and well. I asked that it should be accurately weighed on arrival, which was done, and the weight recorded at 44 lb. I thought the sack must have been included at first, but the matter was investigated, and it has now been established that the weight was 44 lb to the dot, without the sack or anything else.

It is now living at the aquarium at the London Zoo – ten years older at the time of writing and, I think, a good deal lighter in weight!

One of the reasons why we look forward to the first weekend of a new season is that it will be the first chance to try new theories and ideas that we have thought up when we couldn't try them out.

Very often we find they don't work out as well in practice as we had hoped, but sometimes they answer surprisingly well. As far as the first week-end of the 1954 season was concerned, they worked out very nicely for me. Before I tell you what happened, I'd better explain what some of these ideas and theories were.

First of all there was the question of losing big fish at Redmire, not because they broke the tackle but because, somehow, they got rid of the hook. Maurice Ingham and Bob Richards have both hooked monster fish, only to have the hookhold give after playing them for a time. I had lost no fewer than four whoppers in the same way during the previous two seasons.

Pete Thomas suggested that this was due to the peculiar shape of the mouths of the big Redmire fish. Their mouths are very much 'underslung', and Pete pointed out that a hook struck upwards could scarcely help coming up against bone, into which it would penetrate only a little way, and come out again very easily. So we decided it would be a good idea to use a running lead, stopped a few inches from the hook. The pull on striking would then be downwards and the hook would penetrate the bottom lip. This had happened to the 22¾-lb and 17½-lb carp I caught at Dagenham in 1952, using sunk crust and an Arlesey bomb.

Secondly, there was the idea that fish can become preoccupied not only with foods of certain kinds, but with particular sizes. This led us to think that lumps of groundbait ought to be about the same size as hookbait.

Thirdly, there was an idea for circumventing the craftiness of a big carp that was in the habit of feeding along a sort of shelf at the dam at Redmire. This dam is about a hundred yards long, squarely across the end of the lake, and about five yards out from its middle is the deepest part of the lake, about twelve feet. But close to the dam itself is this shelf, about four feet wide and five feet below the surface. There are dense weed-beds along the sides of the lake, and I had found that a big carp would come out of the weed-bed at the east end of the dam and feed on groundbait along the shelf.

I hooked and lost him in June 1952 and from then on, groundbait along that shelf was never eaten by next morning if I or anyone else sat anywhere along that dam, no matter how quietly we sat behind bushes. But if we went off and fished somewhere else, morning found the groundbait along the shelf all gone. So here was a problem to solve.

Pete and I arrived at Redmire at about 10 pm on 19 June. The weeds along each side of the lake were very, very thick, and packed together with algae and scum. The only open water was a strip down the centre of the lake, forty to fifty yards wide and ending at the dam.

We groundbaited along the shelf of the dam and fished till about 4.30 am, then we gave it up, removed our baits and went to sleep. The groundbait was untouched then, but when we looked again at about 7 am, it was all gone.

The next evening, I chose a position on the west bank about forty yards from the dam, and cast diagonally to the right, so that my lead fell on the dam itself about fifty or sixty yards away. The tackle consisted of a James number 3 carp hook, carefully sharpened, tied to the end of two hundred yards of 9 lb-breaking-strain perlon monofil, dyed deep chestnut in silver nitrate solution. A 1 oz Arlesey bomb was stopped by a small shot about six inches from the hook. Rod and reel were the usual MK IV and Mitchell.

I walked round to the dam, found the tackle, baited with a piece of new flake the size of a pheasant's egg, squeezed it so it would sink and dropped it in so that it sank to the shelf. Then I scattered about twenty similar pieces around it. Returning to the rod, I put it in its bite-alarm rests and wound in the slack. But my line was now lying across a dense weed-bed, through which it seemed impossible to drag a big fish. I could not get back to the dam after hooking a fish, because trees and brambles made this impossible. So we fetched the boat over and moored it in a little bay a few yards to the left of my rod.

Bob Richards, holder of the king carp record with a 31 lb 4 oz fish, had joined us that evening, and he, Pete and I sat talking till after midnight. Then Bob went off to fish a gap in the weeds on the east side, while Pete cast out over the weeds to my left. Our long vigil had begun. It continued until daybreak, and after. The sun rose deep orange, its beams making the lake steam. Nothing moved; I was lost in a quiet world of green and grey and gold.

Then, at 5 am, the bite alarm, which I had not troubled to switch off, sounded, and the line slithered and snaked away through the rings. Sixty yards away, under the mist and the still green water, something had picked up the bait and was making off with it, fast. I cannot tell you how I picked up the rod, dropped in the pick-up of the reel, and struck, because I don't remember. But I must have done it right, for there I was with the rod arched and the slipping clutch snarling as something big and powerful shot up the lake and then turned into the weeds, still going fast, on the far side. It went into those weeds and kept going, but when it stopped at last it remained stopped. Nothing I could do, not even fierce hand-lining, shifted it an inch. Pete unhitched the boat and paddled it past the jutting piece of grass bank on which I stood. I jumped in, and across to the other side we went, following the line. Up it came, with festoons of weed and green slime which slid down it back into the water.

Presently it ran straight up and down. I bent the rod more and more, and something down below began to rise. Then it began to move, very slowly, up the lake. I kept the pressure on, and up to the top came the fish, beating the water in rage and flinging the festooning weeds off the line. Then he rolled over and went down, away and out into the open water. Pete paddled the boat after him for dear life.

Once in the clear, we made sure he stayed there, and eventually after a slogging struggle, he came up, rolled, and plunged down again; but this time it was into the bottom of the great net. I dropped the rod and heaved him into the boat, and there was the hook, right through the bottom lip.

Bob Richards was waiting for us, all smiles, when we reached the bank, and he had the spring balance ready. The weight was 31 lb 4 oz, the same as his own big fish, and the length 31 inches. After we had taken some photographs, I slid the fish back to grow into a fifty-pounder, which I hope Bob will one day catch.

from STILL WATER ANGLING *1953*

Europe's Biggest Grayling

WILLIAM B. CURRIE

One of the things which took me to Finland to fish was the suggestion that in Lapland waters there were grayling of enormous size to be taken by rod and line. Eric Taverner had a fascinating reference in his book, *Anglers' Fishes and their Natural History*. 'Very little is known of the conditions that govern the size grayling can attain. In Test, Avon, Wylye and Nadder a 3 lb fish is exceptional, but not rare. The heaviest example of this fish taken in these waters are 4 lb 8 oz and 4 lb 12 oz. Whereas in the waters of Finland and Lapland grayling are known to attain a weight of 7 lb or even 8 lb.'

During my Lapland trips I have been lucky enough to see several hundreds of large grayling and to take, on fly, at least fifty over two pounds, including several around the four-pound mark. The taking of these fish was a very thrilling episode in my Finnish fishing. It taught me reverence for the big grayling in fast water, and it made me think again about how and when big grayling take the fly. The Finnish grayling were the biggest in Europe and that is another way of saying that they were the biggest in the world.

When I first went to Finalnd in 1958 the record grayling taken by rod and line stood at 3½ kilos (7.7 lb) but during the summer of 1958 the record was broken in no uncertain manner. From a southern Finnish lake a grayling was taken weighing 7 kilos (15.4 lb), doubling the existing records to give an astonishing new record. For years Finns had said that in their waters were grayling far bigger than any recorded officially. The big fish of 1958 proved this beyond all shadow of doubt. It also gives biologists a new yardstick on grayling size, and to anglers it gives a keener edge to their fishing for grayling, since such fish exist.

Quite the most fabulous grayling fishing I had in Lapland was on Poroeno river, which makes up the headwaters of the Lätäseno river system which, for many miles, marks the boundaries of Norwegian and Finnish Lapland in the extreme north-west of Lapland. This is an area of fells and tundra, and the river flows crystal clear over sand and gravel and it is the home of the biggest grayling in the biggest numbers I have ever seen. To reach Poroeno river, one must fly to Rovaniemi, capital of Lapland, and from there travel some ten hours by bus over the sandy road leading to Norway. One leaves the bus at

Kilpisjärvi, where there is an excellent tourist inn, and from there one must set out into the hills to strike the headwaters of Lätäseno river. It took us seventeen hours' walking to reach the river. We took food and tackle for a fortnight's camping in the open, three fish barrels and about twenty pounds of coarse salt. This, my Finnish friends assured me, was to preserve the big catch. I thought we must surely fail completely by tempting the gods in this way. In fact, we filled these barrels in three days, catching over two hundred pounds' weight of big grayling and trout and char in one marvellous burst of fishing activity.

I realized what I was up against in the first stream I fished. I mounted a trout-rod and a normal trout cast, and began to fish the most attractive stream, purling down over gravel and easing into a marvellous deep pool over silver sand. I had to take at once and lost a fly. I re-cast and had another take, only to lose the remainder of my cast. This was rectified in a moment. I replaced my four-pound cast with a eight-pound sea-trout cast and No. 8 flies which I cast down and across and had the satisfaction of taking a fish at once and feeling the great power of these heavy grayling in the fast water. That fish weighed about two and a half pounds and it was quickly followed by several others of similar weight.

Later in the day when the angle of the twenty-four hour Arctic sun had lowered sufficiently, I fished dry fly for these big fish and took them on light tackle, but the time taken with a three-pounder hooked at one in the morning in bright sun convinced me that although it was fun to play a three-pounder for twenty minutes on light stuff, it was pointless after repeating the performance a time or two. I resorted to my sea-trout tackle and made hay.

Some miles farther down the river we camped beside the most attractive rapid I have ever fished. Its top run was fan-shaped with thirteen streams chuckling down over a bar of stones to form a deep and very wide pool below, over the same bright sand. I began wading out over the stones at the head of the stream and casting a two-fly sea-trout cast with a No. 8 double Grey Monkey on the tail and a Hardy's No. 8 Brown Turkey on the dropper. In the hour which followed I took nine fish weighing twenty-seven and a half pounds. Between wading and fighting and carrying my very heavy bag, it became excessively tiring, but the sport was quite out of this world.

At one point I was on my eighth stream out from the bank, and wading was becoming fairly difficult. I had seven fish in the bag weighing some twenty pounds when I felt my fly being taken with a very heavy double thump. I tightened, and the fish immediately took line and fought heavily and deeply down into the pool below me. The weight in my hand told me that this was no three-pounder. This was something really big.

I played the fish hard, bending my ten-foot rod well in the fight and soon, after several alarming runs across and down stream, the fish began to tire. I eventually caught sight of the fish firmly hooked on the dropper and was astonished to see that it was only a fish of some three pounds. In a flash I realized that I had, in fact, two fish on – a three-pounder on the dropper and what appeared to be something much bigger on the tail fly.

Running over in my mind how the tail fish should be netted first and then the dropper fish scooped up, I drew the fish near me. After some struggle I managed to get my net under the large tail fish which was somewhat less exhausted than the smaller dropper fish. I netted the big one and was in the process of scooping the dropper fish into the net when the big one splashed out and, horror of horrors, the fly firmly through the lip of the smaller fish in the net snagged the mesh. There I was, a hundred yards from the bank with a millstone of a bag round my tired shoulders, a three-pounder snagged in the net and, struggling out into the stream, a not-so-dead big grayling on the end of an anchored yard-and-a-half of nylon.

In a very quick piece of action I tucked rod and net handle under my left arm, and with my right whipped out my sheath knife and severed the dropper of the cast. After that it was comparatively simple to play out the remaining fish and net it beside the still-snagged smaller fish. The smaller fish weighed three pounds and the tail fish four pounds. Seven pounds of grayling in fast water, both fish with dorsal fins erect and pectorals extended and fighting in the stream with great power. This was one of the greatest fights I have ever had with any species of fish at any time.

These big grayling, I discovered, wanted a good-sized fly fished deeply. In fact I used salmon tactics for these fish. I fished small doubles, No. 8 usually, and these flies on the tail took the cast down very quickly. At times I allowed the flies to trundle down on the sand and this proved to be a deadly method of taking the bigger grayling. If flies were fished near the surface and were moved fast, smaller grayling or trout came to the cast but not the big fish. In fact it was a sort of nymphing, with the flies looking very much live some form of large larvae rolling down with the stream.

In Lapland, also, I had grayling leap during the fight and this was quite a spectacle. On a river in northern Lapland, the Utsjoki, I fished dry fly for grayling and had a two and a half-pounder take a No. 16 Butcher. That fish leaped five times before it was netted. The leap of a big grayling is not the high arc of a sea-trout nor the lunge of a salmon. It is a heavy twisting flop which can break tackle very easily unless one is careful. In home waters I have not had grayling leap. Perhaps it was the temperature of the Arctic waters which made the grayling leap so.

These Lapland grayling were delightful eating, with pink flesh of firm texture. Often they were roasted whole on green sticks driven in beside a glowing birch fire. The sides of the fish were cut with a series of slits by our knives and the fat collected in these cooked the fish in its own oil. The fish was taken in the hands, salted and eaten straight off the bone. With memories like this of Lapland and its fishing I have every motive for a return visit as soon as it can be arranged.

from GAME FISHING *1962*

The Perch

FRANCIS FRANCIS

The perch is usually described as a bold biting fish, and so he may be where he is not much fished for, or where perch are over-plentiful and small, or when, like other fish, they have a hungry day; but if by the above character it be meant that good perch were deficient in wariness, then I contradict it. Where they are at all fished – and my remarks apply to rivers and lakes where they are well and regularly fished for – there are few fish more capricious or careful in biting than large perch; small ones may often be taken in any quantity, but not so when they gain experience. I have known places haunted by numbers of good perch – perch from a pound and a half to three pounds in weight – and yet, season after season, there are seldom more than one or two of them caught, and these nearly always at the starvation part of the year, i.e. after the heavy winter floods, when the small fish are all driven up the brooks, and the perch are driven into the few still eddies that exist. Here, while the river is tearing down outside in a spate, from one or two hundred, and sometimes more, perch will often be congregated in a space of some ten or twenty square yards, perhaps.

After these fish have battled with the frosts of winter, on short rations for weeks, what chance has a minnow among such a host, or what chance even a hundred minnows? No wonder, then, that you pull them up two or three at a time, one for each minnow; the only wonder is that they do not, in their eagerness, swallow the plummet of your paternoster in its descent, by mistake. In truth and faith, January and February are deadly months for poor Perchy. Cabined, cribbed, confined in a black hole of an eddy, they are pulled out not in braces, dozens, or even scores, but often to the tune of hundreds. I have seen and helped to catch ten dozen and over out of one hole, and have heard of twice ten dozen being taken. But catch Master Perch on a fine summer's day, in this way, if you can. Often have I, through the crystal-clear water, watched the proceedings of a dozen perch at the worm or a minnow on my hook, some twelve or thirteen feet below. How they come up to it with all sail set, their fins extended, their spines erect, as if they meant to devour it without hesitation! and how they pause when they do come to it, and swim gently round it, as if a worm or a minnow were an article of vertu, which required the nicest taste, and the consideration of a connoisseur to appreciate it properly. At length one of the boldest, taking hold of the extreme tip of the tail as timidly as a bashful young gentlemen takes hold of the tip of his partner's finger when he leads her to the festive quadrille, will give it a shake. Now, if you are curious, watch your float; see how it bobs down, after a fashion that would make you think the perch must not only have swallowed the bait, but half digested it; whereas, in fact, they cannot make up their minds about it. Is it a safe investment or is it not? Is it real old Chelsea or only a modern imitation?

There are various ways of catching perch. The first, and most common, is with the live minnow, or, if minnow cannot be had, any other small fish, or fry of gudgeon, dace, or roach, will do; but these should only be used when the angler has no other alternative, as, although the perch is infinitely the more desirable and valuable fish, fry should not be wasted. There are four ways of using a minnow, all of which will take perch: viz, with a float and either one or two hooks, or a paternoster with two or three, with a loose line and roving minnow, or by spinning.

With the float, the lowest hook (if two are used) should be two or three inches off the bottom, and the next one should hang between mid-water and the bottom. The best way of baiting the minnow is to pass the hook tenderly and carefully through the gristle of the upper lip; some choose the back fin, but a minnow so hooked neither lives so long nor moves so freely as when hooked by the lip. When a perch takes the float down, do not strike directly, as the tackle used for this fishing being usually fine, it is as well to make sure of him; for, in spite of anything that some sceptical anglers may say to the contrary, the scratching and losing of one or two perch *does* most indubitably very often – I won't say always, because there may be exceptions, but does very often – drive the shoal away. I have noticed it scores of times, and have heard many good and experienced anglers verify the fact. Therefore rather give him a little time, and even let him leave the bait, or cut if off, in preference to being too hasty and scratching him.

The paternoster is simply a gut line, a yard or four feet long, with hooks about a foot apart, and weighed at the end with a bullet or pear-shaped plummet. Some anglers use three hooks, and some two, a necessity which is more often regulated by the depth of the water to be fished. But the lowest hook, unless the bottom is unusually foul, should be almost on the ground, as it is the habit of the minnows to strike up towards the surface in their efforts to escape, just as it is the habit of all fish when pursued by an enemy; fear causes them to seek the surface, and even to jump out of the water. Therefore if the minnow be not kept down, it will be much above the head of such perch as are lying at the bottom; and, if the water be at all coloured (as is best for perch-fishing), this will not only be a fault, but a great one; whereas if the hook be kept close down to the lead, it will catch two or three fish against either of the other hook's one. The second hook should be fixed nine inches above, and must hang clear of the tie of the lower hook. This is the best form of paternoster made.

Some people make a paternoster by tying their hooks on to coarse hog bristles, and these again on to a piece of perforated bone, through which the main line runs, a shot above and below it keeping the bristled hook in its place. This is done in order to keep the minnow clear of the main line (bristles being stiffer than gut) and to permit him to swim freely and unnaturally round and round like a mill-horse – a very clever contrivance, and very exquisite fooling, but an abomination of abominations in practice. It is the paternoster of tackle-makers – made to sell, not to catch fish. Paternostering properly followed is a very skilful and not particularly easy branch of angling, and as far as my experience goes, not one angler in a thousand knows how to make or fish a paternoster properly. You cannot fish too fine for the perch in season; and the finer you fish, the more and better fish you catch. To put a great coarse hog's bristle, with a cumbrous paraphernalia of shots and bone, under a perch's nose, is a downright insult to his common sense of self-preservation; and, if he condescends to take your minnow at all, he will take it probably *without* the hook.

To use the paternoster, first be sure your baits are alive, and then commence at the top of the eddy or stream, and fish the eye, or first eddy, carefully, for there the best fish lie. Drop the tackle to the bottom, keeping a tight line, so that the lead touches the bottom, but with no slack line; let it rest a minute, and if no bite comes, lift it, and move it from left to right, or vice versa, round about you, until the immediate neighbourhood is fished; then, lifting the tackle out of the water, swing it out a yard or two farther downstream; let it rest a minute, and then draw it towards you, a foot or so at a time, until the tackle comes home, when repeat the cast, lengthening the distance each time, until the place is fished out, or you have to move lower down. If you get a bite, do not strike at the first nibble, but drop the point of the rod so as to yield a little line; but when you feel a quick 'pluck, pluck, pluck', strike firmly, but not too heavily, and remember that *the heavier the fish you expect to catch, the more time you must give them*, as they are slow and cautious, and if the hook be not well in their mouths, you will lose them to a certainty – when good-bye to sport. I always use a landing-net if the fish is over half a pound; if under, I lift him in at once, as it saves so much time, from the other hooks often getting hung up in the net.

The localities in which to look for perch vary with the season. Early in the summer the angler will find them in the streams, as in gudgeon-swims, into which they come when the ground is raked or disturbed, and here they often take the angler's gudgeon worm ravenously; indeed, perch occasionally take a worm almost as well, and in some cases even better than they do the minnow. They are often taken on the ledger, and these are frequently the best fish too. Some time since I was fishing with a friend on the Thames; we were dace-fishing, with the float-line; he had a paternoster out on his side of the boat for perch; I had a ledger on my side for barbel; I had at least a dozen bites, and caught two or three nice perch, while he never got a touch, with a choice minnow and a small gudgeon not four or five yards off, and the perch were feeding all round us. As the summer advances, the perch seek the deeper and stronger streams, the quiet eddies and deep holes near piles, lock-gates, piers of bridges, corners of weirs, and by heavy weed-banks. At this time they are well fed and cautious, and will try the angler's skill to make a good dish of them. As the season advances, and the winter floods sweep down, they all draw into the great eddies, or still corners, particularly after a sharp frost, and here they will be found in great numbers; and when the water is a little coloured, they may be taken in from three to seven or eight feet of water, or deeper, in any quantity, and they are then hungry, though in good condition. As March comes on, they get heavy in spawn, when they should not be disturbed. By the middle of April they get amongst the weeds, rushes, or fibrous roots of trees, in still backwaters, and here they deposit their spawn in long ropy glutinous masses. It is astonishing what a vast number of eggs the female perch will void; they are very small, and about the size and appearance of little seed pearls. Perch spawn about the end of April, and get into fair season again by the end of June.

Perch may often be caught with a spinning minnow, but it is not a very common method of angling for them, though the best fish are usually so caught; and I have known good execution done in lakes by spinning, either with a minnow (real or artifical) or a spoon. Indeed, I almost think, from my experience, that I am justified in saying that they take a spoon better than almost any other spinning bait; but I have found them prefer the triangular spinner made of spoon metal (commonly called the 'otter') to the regular spoon, the only reason I can give for it being that it spins better and more evenly than the spoon, which wobbles a good deal; and though this is liked by pike, and not always objected to by trout, particularly lake trout, it would seem that it is not a strong recommendation to perch.

A handful or two of gentles or broken worms will be found useful as groundbait, when float-fishing with worms. But whatever you do, do not take your wife's or sister's gold-fish globe out with the muslin cover on it, and a stock of lively minnows inside, under the supposition that the perch will rub their noses against the glass, like cats at a dairy window, according to the old superstition.

Perch in this country seldom exceed four pounds in weight, but one of three pounds is a rarity, while a two-pound perch is a fine fish. They have been known to reach nine pounds weight, and in the large lakes of Germany and Scandinavia they occasionally reach a very large size. A dish of half-pound perch, however, is not in our less favoured land to be despised. The best day's perch-fishing I ever had was on the Kennet, a capital perch river. I fished with a friend, and we took home thirty-seven perch which weighed sixty pounds – many of them weighed two pounds, and some were over that weight. My companion had three large perch on his paternoster at the same time: he bagged two of them: one was two pounds, the other two pounds and a quarter, and the one which got away was the larger than either of them. We lost a great many fine fish in the course of the day, I in particular losing nearly as many as I caught. I had another excellent day's sport on the Kennet subsequently, though of a mixed character, consisting of pike and perch.

from A BOOK ON ANGLING *1872*

Finding those 10 lb Tench

JOHN ELLIS AND MAURICE INGHAM

Very few anglers today will deny the existence of tench far heavier than the 8½lb fish which holds the record for the species.*

Experience and observations made generally known over the last ten or twelve years are the reason for this belief. There is, in fact, no doubt at all that tench of at least ten pounds exist in many waters in Great Britain; that in some places they are fairly numerous; and that in a few waters tench of this size, and bigger ones, occur in shoals.

In 1957 Dr Otto Schindler expressed the view that the *average* weight of European tench is eleven pounds. I am sure that we can apply this figure to British tench in the most favourable conditions, and that not only are these fish present now, but that fish of similar size have always been in our waters.

I cannot explain why none of these big tench has been caught in the five hundred years of the recorded history of British angling, but here are some general observations that may be partial answers.

1. Even though these big tench may be much more numerous than most anglers believe, they will always be vastly outnumbered by smaller tench and be much more difficult to locate.
2. Because they are apparently capable of subsisting mainly by eating micro-fauna throughout their lives, we cannot expect to select the biggest tench by varying the size of our baits.
3. In some waters they seem hardly ever to leave the shelter of the dense weed-beds which are an essential feature of their habitat if they are to reach great size.

*The record tench now is one of 9 lb 1 oz caught at Hemingford Grey, Huntingdonshire in 1963. Ed.

4. Most of their activity takes place at night.
5. They are so powerful that they can break with little difficulty the kind of tackle used by most anglers.

I am totally unable to advise anyone on how they may be caught, but I have been sufficiently fortunate to fish in several waters which undoubtedly contain such tench, and an account of what happened on one of these trips may be of some value and interest.

From 23 to 26 July Norman Woodward of Leicester, Maurice Ingham of Louth and I fished a certain Midlands lake with the specific intention of getting to grips with some of the very big tench it was known to contain. Their existence had been established beyond any doubt by Norman, and he had actually hooked several, all of which had avoided capture, usually by breaking his line in devastating fashion. Since most of these encounters had taken place whilst Norman was fishing from the dam which contains the three-acre lake, it was from here that we started to fish, spaced out, and fishing in five or six feet of water with lobworms in pitches which had been well baited up with soaked bread and worms. Anxious to make the most of our trip, we fished right through the night of the 23rd although conditions were not very favourable and the night was a chilly one. There was little tench activity during the night and, although we all had occasional inconclusive bites, only one tench was caught, a three-pounder by Maurice.

The following day was much better. The sky was well clouded and we had a quiet, warm day with occasional light showers of rain, the water temperature being in the mid-sixties on the Fahrenheit scale. We spent most of the day walking round the lake or rowing over it in Norman's boat, trying to find evidence which would lead us to some sensible conclusions on the whereabouts of the big tench.

Eventually we decided that at least some of them were in a jungle of reeds, rushes and weeds which grew close to the bank on the right-hand side of the lake as we saw it from the dam. We decided that Maurice, because of his superior experience of very big fish and because he had with him the most suitable tackle for the purpose, should fish in a pitch at this point, whilst Norman and I stayed on the dam to provide some sort of control against whatever Maurice encountered. What happened to him is best told in his own words.

> The water was shallow close in to the bank and twenty feet out there was a depth of only about five feet, but from there the bottom

fell away quite steeply into deep water. At the foot of the gently sloping bank was a belt of burr-reeds about six feet wide which extended away to the left. To the right, about thrity feet away, the reeds ended in a dense patch of bulrushes – the true bulrush with dark green circular stems which grow to a height of six feet to eight feet – which extended out into the lake for a distance of about twelve feet.

With the help of a double-bladed scythe, a double-sided rake and a length of rope John and I cleared out some of the pond weed – *Potamogeton natans* – which was growing profusely in the shallow water. It was not a complete clearance by any means, but we thinned out the weed sufficiently over a fairly extensive area to give me, as I thought, a reasonable chance of playing and landing a big tench, if I was fortunate enough to hook one.

By late afternoon I had completed my preliminary preparations, and scattered a few handfuls of soaked bread and a score or so of lobworms along the edge of the patch of bulrushes, which was where I had decided that my bait would lie.

Norman had already had experience of the tremendous strength of the very big tench in this lake and so I chose tackle which I felt would weigh the balance of power heavily in my favour. My rod was a Mark II Carp-rod, which is nearly twice as powerful as its famous offspring, the Mark IV. The line was brand new soft braided black Terylene of twelve pounds breaking strain on a Pfleuger Skilcast multiplying reel. To the end of the line I whipped a No. 2 carp hook. I used no float and the line was unweighted.

As dusk was falling I baited up with the biggest lobworm I could find and cast out almost parallel with the bank to my right so that the bait was lying in about three feet of water just beyond the edge of the patch of bulrushes. The Pfleuger reel has a very light audible check and I relied on this to give me warning of a bite.

Gradually the light faded until the night became velvety black as heavy clouds began to pile up in the west. The air was still and oppressive and a thunderstorm seemed imminent. Over on the far side of the lake John and Norman were catching fish but my pitch seemed quite dead and I began to have doubts about the wisdom of my choice. Then, suddenly, I became aware of the quiet ticking of my reel. I lifted the rod gently off the rests, took up a few turns on the reel as I lowered the rod tip, and then I struck – hard!

The effect was rather shattering: the resistance was quite unyielding, and for a split second I wondered if my hook was fast in some underwater snag, but I was not left long in doubt. Anyone who has ever caught a tench will be familiar with the rhythmic tugging as it bores away with great thrusts of its powerful tail. It is unmistakable. That is what I now felt, except that the strength of the tugging was far greater than anything I had ever experienced or imagined.

I knew I must not yield any line or my fish would become inextricably entangled in the bulrushes or in the jungle of weed beyond, but I was confident in the strength of my tackle and I hung on grimly. For a while I was content merely to hold on but then I decided that more positive action was needed and I began to apply side-strain to try to draw the fish away from those menacing bulrushes. I gradually increased the strain until I was fairly heaving the rod over to my left, but I made absolutely no headway. Still that remorseless rhythmic tug-tug-tug – just as if someone were beating the end of my rod with a sandbag.

I have no idea how long this went on – it seemed an eternity, but I suppose it could not have lasted longer than thirty seconds. Then there was a loud 'twang' as my rod whipped back, and I wound in to find an empty and slightly misshapen hook.

John and Norman tell me that they heard my blasphemies from across the lake. I don't remember. I only know I was too shaken to fish any more that night.

Many people have asked me how I can be sure it was a tench when I did not see it. But I am quite certain it was – it could have been nothing else.

As we had fished all the previous night and been active all day, we decided at this point to have a meal, sleep until dawn and then fish from the dam again until the tench went off the feed. The weather was still favourable the following morning, being warm and overcast, and the dusk and dawn sessions on the dam produced seven tench between us, three each for Maurice and me and one for Norman, all in the 2½-3 lb range. This tended to confirm our opinion that the big tench were not, at this time, in the region of the dam.

In spite of the disappointment we all felt at the loss of Maurice's big tench, there did seem hope now that what could be done once might very well be done again, that another of the big tench might be induced to take a bait and that this time there might be a different result. In the event the rest of the trip went bad on us. During the evening of the 25th a cool rain started to fall and became progressively cooler and heavier. We did some fishing in these unpleasant and unfavourable conditions, and Norman picked up another tench similar to the others we had caught. But by morning conditions were so adverse that we decided to pack up and go home.

Looked at unimaginatively the results of the trip are not impressive. The statistics reveal that three anglers spent four days tench-fishing and that, at the end of that time, they had caught only nine fish of a very modest size.

But we came near to making angling history.

from ANGLING *June 1963*

A February Pike

H. T. SHERINGHAM

So terrible was he, said one, that when he left his lair the river retreated before him, fleeing impetuously over its banks and taking refuge in the water-meadows; so ravenous was he, said another, that moorhens and ducks shunned the spot, herons dared venture no nearer than half a mile, and even an otter had been seen in the grey of the dawn hastening away with every sign of consternation in its countenance. The great pike of the previous year, said a third with conspicuous candour, weighed the better part of nineteen pounds; but even that creditable magnitude had not secured for it untroubled repose, for the unhappy fish had lived in a state of constant panic, ever dreading the time when it should be its turn to be devoured.

Only death indeed, intimated the candid one, had resolved its doubts, and that barely, for its nineteen-pound struggles had been misinterpreted as the seductions of a wee timorous bait. The monster had come forth from the depths to take advantage of the situation, and had only been driven off by the heroism of angler and keeper, who would not submit tamely to the insolence that regarded nineteen pounds of hard-earned pike as no better than four ounces of dace. Therefore they repelled the giant with shoutings and splashings, landed their nineteen-pounder, and took it away to the taxidermist; in fact, if evidence of the story were needed, the fish might now be seen in a glass case with gold letters on it.

These Gargantuan fables were, even to an intelligence enfeebled by recent influenza, obviously but the persiflage of the club, the imaginative flights that every honest angler takes from time to time into the unknown. Nevertheless, they chimed in wonderfully with the convalescent mood that suggested a holiday and a pike or so to end the season, and next day I put myself with my tackle into a cab, and then into an express train, little dreaming that I was about to enjoy the only week of spring weather that graced the year 1903, insinuated by a stroke of pleasing humour into the middle of February, where none but I could find it. When, an hour and a half afterwards, I got out at the station for which I was bound, the sun shone and the air was like wine, the wine of the South with the chill taken off. And when, yet an hour later, I reached the river-bank, I sat on a stile, reflected that the world is indeed good, and looked round for May-flies.

But, be the sun never so warm and an overcoat never so embarrassing, it is not given to mortal angler to see May-flies on the Kennet in February; if it were they would be in vain, and a salted dace was more appropriate to the season. There was no wind, but he triver was of good height and colour, so the chance of a fish or two was not so bad. It remained a chance, however, for neither by spinning nor trolling with snap-tackle was a run gained in the whole length of water as my disposal, though, it must be confessed that I did not overwork myself. I was a convalescent, after all, conscience admitted, and had a perfect right to enjoy this miraculous gift of spring as I would. The keeper, who appeared with the frugal midday repast, was politely of the same opinion, but there was a small pike in the adjacent brook, and he would esteem it a favour if it could be removed, as it harried his trout and vexed his soul. To be brief, it was removed, and it weighed three pounds and a half. This was the only fish that greeted the spring on the first day.

The second day was like unto the first, and every whit as perfect – more perfect in fact, for the keeper had procured some live baits, and the salted dace could be discarded. His mind was not, however, quite free from care, for it appeared that there was another small pike in the adjacent brook, which harried his trout and vexed his soul hardly less than the first. This also was removed with the help of a gudgeon on a paternoster, and it weighed two pounds and a quarter; but the Kennet yielded nothing, though the keeper, cheered by slaughter, talked in somewhat Gargantuan strain of a big pike seen occasionally by himself and others. Asked if this fish had been known to cause floods, eat ducks, moorhens and herons, alarm otters, and wrestle with anglers for a live bait weighing nineteen pounds, he confessed that these accounts bore the impress of exaggeration; the fish he meant would be somewhere about sixteen, and it lay just opposite the second hatch-hole in the middle field. This exactitude of detail made the fish seem a possibility, but neither spinning nor live-baiting induced him to move, and the second day ended with little done, but much enjoyed.

On the third day there was a soft vernal air after a crisp, frosty night, and I awoke to the joyful consciousness that I was fully restored to health. Sunshine had been too much even for the notorious after-effects of influenza, and there was now no reason why I should not fish as though I meant to catch something. The masters of the gentle art inform us that good intentions are not enough of themselves to bring about success; in these days of over-fishing one must also use science and fine tackle. I pondered over the matter during breakfast, and afterwards looked through my tackle-box for a trace that should satisfy the requirements of science and the remarkable weather. Eventually I picked out a rather fine Thames trout trace of single gut, soaked it, and tested it up to a dead weight of five pounds. To match it there was a flight of live-bait hooks tied on similar gut, and I observed to myself that any moderately skilful angler ought to be able to land anything with such excellent material.

Then in a state of considerable elation I went off to the river, to find it the least bit ruffled by the breeze, and very suitable for the testing of my theories. I began with a live dace on float-tackle, casting it out almost to the other side of the river and allowing it to swim downstream, while I kept pace with it along the bank. And, sure enough, as it reached the spot pointed out by the keeper there was a check, the float went under, and a vigorous strike just revealed the fact that the fish was a heavy one before the trace parted at an upper knot.

Then was it borne in upon me that the sun was too hot, the breeze too mild, the season out of joint, and science a wicked delusion. Had there been a snoring breeze, had the white waves been heaving high, as even a convalescent has a right to expect when fishing for a pike in February, had the still small voice of science been drowned by a conflict of the elements, I should never have thought of using a ridiculous gut trace (on which Izaak Walton himself could scarce have landed a minnow), and that sixteen-pounder would have been mine.

Besides, I was no longer convalescent, and boisterous weather was what I needed – was no less than my due. In a word, my meditations were supremely ungrateful, and I was justly punished when the wind dropped altogether, February became more like May than ever, and not another fish moved for the rest of the day.

On the morrow, however, there was a real south-westerly wind and a fine ripple on the water. Pike, I reflected, as I mounted an eight-inch dace on a Pennell spinning-flight, have been known to run at a bait twice in a day, twice even in an hour, almost, even, twice in a minute. It was therefore logical to expect the sixteen-pounder that morning. Yet, by the time a third of the water had been carefully spun over without a touch, the edge of enthusiasm was to some extent blunted, and the keeper, who appeared about midday, was asked somewhat petulantly to explain the wrong-headedness of the fish under his charge. This, of course, he could not do, but, willing enough to tell of past triumphs, he furbished up the tale of the nineteen-pounder anew, and dwelt on the labour of carrying it home, accompanied as it was by two other of fourteen pounds and thirteen pounds respectively, both caught by the lucky fisherman on the same day.

Having done his duty by the triumphs of history he departed and somewhat cheered I returned to my spinning, determined to give the sixteen-pounder another chance. Opposite the hatch-hole of which mention has been made, the river was deep and some thirty yards wide, but a few yards above was a shelving shallow. Spinning across and upstream I thoroughly searched the deep water and worked up towards the shallow, making casts of about thirty-five yards. At last, in some four feet of water, I had that blessed sensation only obtained in spinning for pike, the sensation that something which suggests a stout post has come into collision with the bait, but something that sends a thrill up the line and obviously is not a post. In a second or two it became obvious that the fish was a heavy one, and I cast a hurried glance over my shoulder to see if the keeper was still in sight. He was – a microscopic figure in the distance – and I whistled with all my breath to recall him. Fortunately the sound carried, the retreating figure stopped, recognized the signal of distress, and returned at a run.

Meanwhile it was as much as I could do to play the fish and attract assistance at the same time. At first the pike moved steadily upstream for fifty yards or so; then he came back again at a great pace, and I had to run with him, winching in line for all I was worth – a vain proceeding, as the fish immediately took it all out again. After a while, however, it became evident that the main battle was to be in the deep water, and by the time the keeper arrived proceedings had become more dignified and sedate.

'That's him,' gasped the keeper, as a thick olive-green back showed for a moment close to the bank.

'Twelve pounds,' I commented. 'He's making a good fight for his size.'

The sight of the fish suggested that it was nearly time for the net – a big grilse net – and it was not long before the gradual application of the butt told. The pike was brought in and the net was slipped under it. 'He's a big twelver-pounder!' I exclaimed, when it became obvious that the net was too small, a point emphasized by the fish, which rolled out of it and hurried away to the other side of the river, fortunately still hooked. Thrice this happened, but the fourth time the quarry, utterly beaten, allowed himself to be packed inartistically into the inadequate receptacle and dragged ashore in triumph. As net and fish were carried safely out into the meadow I enlarged my estimate of him to sixteen pounds.

'More,' said the keeper, and it became apparent that he was right when, each holding one end of a sack, we were traversing the mile that lay between the river and a weighing-machine. By the end of the mile the more moderate estimate (the keeper's) was forty pounds.

As a matter of fact, the fish weighed twenty-three pounds and a few ounces, though, as I still fondly imagine, in the glass case it looks more. The triumph was not Gargantuan, perhaps, but in such marvellous spring weather it seemed so. It is seldom that one has everything that one could desire, and that holiday was perfection. It made the influenza quite worth while.

from AN ANGLER'S HOURS *1905*

Rudd and Tench Records

E. C. ALSTON

As I expect you know, any water in which the level alters usually contains big fish. In the mere where I caught my record tench and rudd this was the case. The mere is at Wretham, Norfolk, and is called Ring Mere, and this water goes dry every twenty years or so. When I first went to Wretham there were no fish in the mere. I restocked it with fish from Standford Water, a few miles away. I put in rudd, tench, and a few pike and an odd roach or two. I suppose I put in about fifty rudd and fifteen tench. The rudd were about ¾ to 1 lb in weight, the tench 2½ to 3 lb.

After putting the fish in I did not bother about them at all and the first intimation I had of the success of my experiment was when a village lad caught a rudd of 3¼ lb.

I at once went over to the mere and I think I must have had about the best catch of rudd on record. I do not exactly remember the number I caught, but it was in the neighbourhood of thirty fish, ranging from 2¼ to 4¼ lb, the largest weighting 4½ lb, which I had mounted by Cooper.

I paid a village lad to carry the rest to a small mere close by but when I went to look at it I found the stupid fool had thrown most of them on the mud and they were all dead. The fishing remained good at Ring Mere until it was 'found out'. People came from all quarters, some from great distances, towing boats behind their cars. I do not think these visitors did much, as I fear I had taken the cream of the fishing and the fish soon became very shy. I stocked many places round with them and I think that some people had some fun with the tench. They gave great accounts of being broken by large fish, probably tench.

I used to see some monster tench in Ring Mere when I was fishing for rudd, some were very big, from 7 lb to 10 lb. I caught one of them, a seven-pounder, which was also mounted for me by Cooper, and this fish was one of the *smaller* ones that I saw. I used to see them turning over in the weeds when I was fishing.

The following summer Ring Mere went dry, and I went down with a landing-net to see what I could save. The tench were there but thin as rakes. I saved as many as I could. They were very thin and gaunt and weighed from 5¼ lb to 5½ lb. I forget how many I rescued. There were also a lot of rudd up to 2½ lb and I saved all I could. The pike did not grow to any size, the largest I had was 11 lb.

from a letter to 'B.B.' (1933) published in
THE FISHERMAN'S BEDSIDE BOOK *1945*

The Chub beneath the Bridge

PETER WARD

The crystal-clear stream curled and eddied softly beneath the old wooden bridge. The water on either side was thick with lush green fronds of rununculus and willow-moss. Great willow-trees lined the banks, their branches reaching down to trail vee patterns on the water surface. Through a chink in the moss-grown planks, warped by time, it was possible to peer down into the depths below. There, when the eye had become accustomed to the shadow cast by the bridge, a wonderful sight unfolded.

No weed extended into this area. Instead there was a big hollow, scoured in the river-bed by the action of the water. Moving over the yellow gravel, and gradually resolving from shadows into well-known shapes, were fish. What fish they were! Long, grey barbel hugged the bottom in tight formation; an anxious-looking grayling fanned steadily, its huge dorsal curling in the current; there were hungry spotted trout, sleek red-finned roach and fleeting dace. Then the pulse quickened and the mouth dried a little as a shoal of chub swam into view.

In the middle of the shoal was the biggest chub I have ever seen. The portly grey-brown form, surrounded by smaller brethren, reminded me of a battleship with its attendant fleet of lesser craft. I put the weight of the big fellow at 7 lb to 8 lb, an estimate that was later supported by several angling colleagues. My first sight of this fellow, on a misty October morning, spelt the beginning of an obsession; a determination that he should grace my net.

I studied the situation with care.

The clearance beneath the bridge was insufficient to allow a float to be watched for any distance. Equally, the proximity of the trailing weed ruled out the use of standard legering techniques. The only suitable method seemed to be a leger with a longer than usual trail, 4 ft to 5 ft from weight to hook. In theory, if the weight were lowered slowly on the upstream side of the bridge, the bait should drift fairly naturally to within range of the fish. The tackle decided, it remained to make a choice of bait. With an eye glued to the crack I flicked morsels of food upstream so that they filtered down through the weed-bed into the swim. Maggots, bread, redworms and lobs. All were accepted as they arrived in the eddy. It became obvious that my quarry, along with others in the swim, was catholic in his tastes. The only thing left to rule out the smaller fish was to gauge the size of the bait, so that only his huge gape could encompass it.

I settled myself behind a small bush on the upstream side of the bridge and attached a large piece of crust to the hook. Gently the baited tackle was lowered between the weed and the woodwork. Hardly had the line tightened when the rod-tip went down. Trembling with excitement, I snatched the strike; but was relieved to feel the familiar plunge of a heavy chub. Several anxious moments followed. The fish ran hard downstream, made a sideways lunge for the bridge-pilings and then a headlong dive into the weed. Then it was over and the brassy-scaled fish slid across the rim of the landing-net.

I knew at once that this was not Leviathan; and the spring balance confirmed my fears by registering just over 5 lb. A fine fish on any other day, but on this occasion the subject of a baleful glare. A few hurried paces to the bridge and a glance showed that Leviathan was still there, apparently unruffled by all the commotion. Another cast. This time the hook, carrying three large lob-worms, was under strain; and the rod was soon bucking again. The taker was a smaller chub, not quite making the 4 lb mark.

There were to be no more takes that day. Eventually I moved on to pastures new.

Sleep came with difficulty on the night before my next visit to the water, two weeks later. During the fitful rest, however, the answer came to me. A crayfish, the biggest that I could find. That would do it.

Arriving at the waterside next morning, I feverishly assembled my tackle and almost ran through the dew-wet grass to the bridge. There he was, slowly opening and closing his great white mouth.

Out went the crayfish to be grabbed by an invisible fish as though it had fasted for a month. A hard strike drove the hook home and all hell broke loose under the bridge. Whatever had taken me broke water with an echoing smash and bolted, the reel screaming in protest. The fight was a short and vicious one that stirred the whole stream. Finally a red-hued rainbow trout lay gasping on the bank. Just on 4lb, a real Dead Sea apple in more ways than one.

I fished on as the sun climbed in the sky to warm my back; but the disturbance caused by the trout had been enough to put down the other fish. Later in the day the pangs of regret were eased a little, when I took some nice barbel from another swim.

Soon it had become part of a regular pattern to start my day on the water by fishing the bridge swim. Many were the fish that I took from it, some of them fine specimens; but always the big chub remained aloof. Others tried, better anglers than myself; and enjoyed the same success, or lack of it.

Then one morning, bending to the bridge, I saw that my old adversary was no longer there. I was to wait for his return in vain. I like to think that his end, if indeed it had come, was a peaceful one; and that he had not fallen victim to a marauding otter.

Whatever the means, the result was the same. He was gone; and with him, so had part of my angling life. For a long time I was to miss the eager anticipation followed by the wave of pleasure at seeing him there; the scheming and plotting to bring about his downfall; the excited tackling-up, thinking each time that this would be the day.

Most of all, however, I shall miss the sense of humility that he was able to bestow; the way that he treated my every effort with lofty disdain was the perfect antidote to any conceit that tended to grow from too much success.

I hope one day soon another 'great uncatchable' will come along to take his place.

from ANGLERS' ANNUAL *1967*

The Trout's Sister

FREDERICK MOLD

To the all-important question, 'Wilt thou have this woman to be thy lawful wedded wife . . .?' once came the unexpected reply, 'Oh, yes, I'll 'ave 'er, but I'd rather 'ave 'ad 'er sister!'

In the spring and summer we fish for the trout. In the autumn and winter we angle for her sister – the grayling, and I want here to make the plea that she is not to be thought of as a poor compensation but a very exciting prospect indeed.

What does she look like? Something like a dace – silvery, metallic blue – hence the name 'Grayling' – but easily distinguished from the dace by an enormous dorsal fin, unusual eyes, a small mouth and protruding upper lip. Oh dear, you would rather have her sister? Read on. She has been called the 'Silver Lady of the Stream' and in the pure water essential to her existence she is as graceful and clever as any of her rivals. Despite the fact that Izaak Walton said 'she grows not to the bigness of trout; for the biggest of them do not usually exceed eighteen inches', she nevertheless grows fast. If she is twenty-four months old by the autumn, she will probably be a foot long and, to my mind, reign as the most interesting fish until the approach of the next trouting season.

Where does she swim? Where does she *not* swim would be a shorter question to answer for she is to be found in clean, swiftly flowing water – preferably where the bottom is stony – from the South of Scotland through England and Wales, and in all parts of the river except where the water is very shallow or rough.

What does she eat? Insects of all kinds, worms, caterpillars, grasshoppers, maggots – the possibilities are legion. For the sake of brevity I will therefore confine methods of fishing for this species to two – fly-fishing and worming.

When fishing for grayling with a dry fly it is important to realize that, unlike trout, which rise to the near surface of the water when inclined to feed, this 'sister' lies near the bed of the river and rises almost perpendicularly to take the fly. This is followed by an instant descent and if the target is missed – which often happens – the grayling will try, try and try again.

Water of about a yard in depth will give good sport, preferably the glide of a river, and in such places the fisherman must look for the characteristic 'rise form' which is nothing more than a dimpling of the surface. Under such conditions fish a small dry fly – the fancy ones are generally the favourite patterns, perhaps because it is argued that they are the more easily seen by the low-lying fish, but I have proved that you need not be too fussy about pattern. Always try to imitate the natural fly on the water first. This will possibly be a pale watery imitated by a Ginger Quill. You might then try something with a twist of gold on the body or a red tag, but far more important than pattern is the method of casting which must be done with extreme finesse, dropping the fly upstream of your quarry on a leader tapered to at least 4x and a small hook – No. 14 or 16 old scale, 1 or 00 new scale.

A classic method of fishing the dry fly for grayling is to fish downsteam, allowing the fly to drift over the rising fish and avoiding surface drag by aiming the fly a few feet above the surface and pulling it back as it begins to fall, thus allowing the fly to fall lightly on the water and at the same time preserving a yard or two of precious 'slack'.

When no rise forms are to be seen try wet fly fishing. Here the method differs from that of trout fishing in that *downstream* fishing is the order of the day for drag does not alarm the lower *feeding* grayling as much as it does the near surface trout.

Naturally the wet fly method comes more into its own later in the season – in, say, November – when the grayling is probably at her best. The most likely time of the day for sport will be in the early afternoon.

It is essential now to get your flies or nymphs well down to the fish. In clear water a single nymph of the Sawyer type, weighted with copper wire, tied with a pheasant tail body and devoid of hackle, fished on an extremely fine leader, can provide excellent sport often enabling you to watch the whole drama of the 'take'. You may break the rule here and fish upstream but in coloured water your flies, weighted with lead bodies if necessary, must be cast across to sweep down with the stream and the least indication of a rise must be rewarded with an instananeous yet delicate strike.

I am not fond of spending valuable fishing time in the constant changing of fly patterns and have found that in most conditions it is sufficient to fish a couple of wet flies on a leader. Let one be a combination of black, red and silver, and the other a choice between a Gold-ribbed Hare's Ear and a wet Wickham's Fancy.

With the onset of real winter you can swim the worm – a small red worm – as did the late J. H. R. Bazley. His float was the famous tiny cork kept in place by a plug just over an inch long. Place a single shot about a foot from the round bend hook and with – preferably – a free-running centre-pin reel trot your delicate morsel down the eddies, under the banks and in the longer glides. Again you must use fine tackle – about 2 lb breaking strain nylon – to take the bait to within a few inches of the bottom. The art here is to keep the float moving as fast as the water and to strike gently at the slightest sign of 'float-falter'.

Dry fly, wet fly and worm are equally attractive, on their day, to as interesting and edible a fish as graces our streams during the autumn and winter months. Some even prefer the grayling to her sister!

from ANGLING *November 1962*

Pike of the Reservoirs

FREDERICK J. WAGSTAFFE

Among the big-pike waters in England are some which, although they produce specimens from time to time, never earn the attention their potential deserves. I am thinking of some of the Midland reservoirs, waters ranging in size from something under fifty acres to well over a hundred acres. Perhaps they are ignored because they present such a vast number of problems to the few big-pike specialists who fish them that it is difficult to capture better-than-average fish consistently, even though the quality fish are present in numbers.

Unlike the concrete-sided monstrosities of the London area, most of the Midland reservoirs were formed by building a dam across a valley fed by one or more streams. They appear as vast, featureless waters to the newcomer, and, indeed, to many who have fished them for years. But they are not. Study them carefully and you find that within the shelving sides are streambeds, thickly-weeded shallows, and mysterious deeps.

The type and density of the weed growth varies considerably from reservoir to reservoir. Of the three I fish regularly, one is virtually weed free; the others are densely weeded in parts only. In all of them, though, the major problem is finding where the pike are feeding.

To the beginner it is just a matter of casting out and hoping. The average angler takes things a little further. He thinks a little, and then decides that early in the season, if the weather is mild, the shallows are the place to fish, but that after the first few frosts, the pike will have moved to the deepest part of the water. Certainly most of them assume that by the end of November the shallower areas will be completely devoid of fish. To the reservoir pike angler who thinks, however, this annual mass migration to the deep water off the dam is a much less certain thing.

The truth is that locating pike in these waters is far more complex than either the beginner or the rather more experienced angler realizes.

On the face of it one could be excused for thinking that with the onset of winter it would be natural for the pike to drop back to deeper and deeper water along with the roach and other food fish. This is stated as fact so often by angling writers that it is hardly surprising that most people believe it.

Experience tells me that it is not so. While there may be some movement by the pike as water conditions change, there is no mass migration. I have caught too many pike from shallow parts of the reservoirs throughout the winter months – in a wide range of conditions and water temperatures – for that to be true.

I am not suggesting that the shallows are always most likely to produce pike – far from it. There are occasions when no feeding pike can be discovered in the shallows, and the only offers one gets then come from the deeper areas and channels, well away from the banks. Days like this occur both in the comparatively mild autumn period and in the bitter depths of winter.

Conversely, even in periods of extremely low water temperatures, the shallows often produce pike while the medium-depth areas and deeps produce nothing, and I believe that the supposed mass movements to the deeps by the pike – and their principal winter food fish – is a fallacy, something dreamed up many years ago and blindly repeated and accepted.

What are the factors influencing pike movement? Water temperature must play a part, but it is difficult to determine to what extent. Distribution of the roach and perch shoals in these reservoirs must also be a factor.

I have a feeling that weed decomposition may have a bearing on fish movements from shallows to deeps at times, but this is something that is difficult to anticipate, because there are so many variables to be taken into consideration at any one time. The rate of decomposition of predominant weeds at varying water temperatures; possible dispersal of the effects of this decomposition by winds and currents; weed-free areas where fish may move to, while decomposition is taking place – those are just some of the variables.

In effect, then, the difficulty of pike location on large waters cannot be solved by generalisations. By trying to take into account all the relevant factors, one can get a rough idea of the most profitable lies to try, but one can still be wrong quite often. Therefore, it pays to adopt roving tactics for much of the time, searching the area thoroughly.

Early in the season, and occasionally later on when the pike are feeding well, lures can be extremely successful because of the ease with which the water can be properly searched with them. A variety of spoons and plugs and the 'know-how' for using them can be a deadly combination.

As the season progresses, however, a wobbled deadbait is generally a more effective method. A slow sink-and-draw retrieve with a deadbait on wobbler tackle will often induce a pike to take, even when conditions are such that they are not particularly inclined to do so. As with spinning, each swim within casting distance can be covered with ease, and deep and shallow water fished at almost any speed to suit the mood of the pike.

The main problem with a wobbled deadbait is that when a pike takes and turns it, the hooks are the wrong way round for striking home. Couple this with the occasional necessity for long-range fishing and it is obvious that some pike will be merely pricked and lost, or not even touched at all by the hooks on the strike. However, despite the problems, this is one of the most effective methods of taking reservoir pike.

A deadbait mounted on some sort of spinning flight has its uses, but the action doesn't seem quite so killing as a wobbled bait. Generally, I use a spun deadbait only when nothing but tiny baits, such as sprats, gudgeons or very small dace, are available.

The legered herring is a method favoured by many big-pike hunters, and it is used a good deal on my reservoirs, but comparing the rod-hours per man with the average number and size of pike caught, it doesn't seem to me to be one of the more effective methods.

Using herring, I catch, on average, only one pike for every six or seven trips, and I have yet to take one of over 6½lb. Compare this with my results with spun or wobbled deadbaits. I catch pike most times I use them and I have taken a twenty-pounder with each method, and plenty of double-figure fish.

The chances of casting a herring on leger tackle close to a pike on such vast expanses of water are too slim for the method to be more than occasionally rewarding.

One trick I find useful when my deadbaits are too soft for continuous casting is to 'bob' them under a float, but it is a method which can be used only when there is a strong wind and plenty of wave action. By hooking the deadbait in the middle of the back it bobs up and down as it is carried along. Used with a greased line it can be made to cover a wide area, so it has the advantage of searching a water quite well. As an alternative, it is certainly worth bearing in mind, and it has accounted for many a good pike . . .

The tackle needed to meet the demands of reservoir piking is often as specialised as the method. For example, a range of rods to cover various types of artificial lures is an asset. For deadbait spinning, a rod built almost to beachcaster specifications is useful. Again, hooking arrangements for deadbaits mounted on wobbler tackle have been devised so that the bait can be cast with maximum force without being ripped to shreds by the hooks after a couple of casts . . .

One method of locating the pike is to watch for the roach shoals leaping and rolling on the surface. Very often, particularly early in the morning and between sunset and nightfall, huge shoals can be seen covering large sections of the deeper water.

Every now and then pike scatter them, and it is then that one must forget about fishing slow and deep and fish slowly just under the surface instead. It appears at times that although roach are not active on the surface by choice, they are sometimes forced there by large numbers of pike all coming on feed at once and converging on them from all directions, leaving them only one escape route – upwards!

Sighting a roach shoal is no guarantee that you will catch pike – the shoal may be well out of casting range – but if you can reach it, then it is often worth the effort, because any feeding pike are unlikely to be far away.

I have fished reservoirs for some years and I have fished them hard and often, but I feel I am still a long way from discovering any real pattern of pike movement and behaviour. Sometimes a series of events has led me to believe that a pattern was coming to light, but then an apparently inexplicable change in feeding habits has completely contradicted my interpretation of the events and I am back where I started.

from FISHING *October 1966*

I want Fun in my Pike Fishing

FRED J. TAYLOR

It always used to be thought that cold frosty weather was the best weather for pike. Our grandfathers were emphatic that the pike really began moving then, but today we are mostly agreed that mild weather, especially if it follows a long cold spell, provides the best conditions for pike-fishing. I believe that more pike are caught in mild weather conditions than are caught when the banks are hard with frost; but this does not mean that frosty mornings are no good at all for pike fishing.

Very often those white, frosty mornings are followed by bright sunshine later in the day, and anyone who has read J. H. Bazley's *Art of Coarse Fishing* will know that he preferred a 'summer's-day-in-winter' for his pike fishing.

There is a lot to be said for sunshine on a winter's day and the effect it can have upon pike is especially noticeable. I do not believe that its effect upon the weather is enough to increase the temperature of the river in general. I do not believe that any slight increase in the water temperature which the sun *might* bring about is sufficient to cause the pike to start feeding. But there is no doubt in my mind that it is often the sunshine alone which, directly or indirectly, brings about a change in the pike's behaviour.

For a start the sun almost invariably causes the dace to become active on the river. It can also cause the small roach and rudd of the lake to prime and sport on the surface. Therefore, on both river and lake, the sun often starts something moving; and where there is continued movement, the pike are often stirred to go and investigate. Once they have begun to move around, it is not long before they follow their natural instincts and begin to feed. The fact that small fish are active is sufficient to whet their appetites, despite the fact that a few hours previously they were apparently not interested in food.

I have never believed that moving baits were necessary to catch pike and it has been proved in recent years that dead baits, lying still on the bottom, are often just as effective as live baits. But when the sun is shining there seems to be an association between pike and movement of one sort or another.

This does not mean that dead baits will be refused and live baits taken, however, for the dead bait is often preferred, even in bright sunshine. Sometimes it is necessary to attract the pike by some sort of movement and you can do this in several ways. The reason for the need of movement on sunny days is somewhat obscure, but it is possibly because the pike are hunting mainly by sight and swimming perhaps nearer the surface. A dead bait, lying on the bottom, will often be overlooked as a pike swims over it, high in the water. A live bait fished near to the bottom is even more likely to be overlooked if it remains still, which it often does. A live bait, swimming on a level keel, is much less visible than a dead bait, which lies on its side. An active live bait is, of course, less likely to be overlooked than either a dead bait or a torpid live bait. Even so, I have known times when a pike has glared balefully at a live bait for as long as twenty minutes and then, finally, accepted a stationary dead bait. This does not prove anything except that I think the movement of the live bait attracted the pike originally. Movement of the actual bait was nil; but there was movement in its vicinity, which was the important factor.

Many times I have spun across my stationary dead baits with spoons and other dead baits without any of them being taken. They have been *followed*, however, and once the pike were in the vicinity of the stationary dead baits they began to take them. It is a well-known fact that pike seldom take spoon baits in bright conditions but they will often follow them time and time again. If a real fish, live or dead, is encountered on the way, they will often take it first time despite their refusal of the spinning baits.

The question is, of course, would they have found the dead bait if they had not been stimulated into action by the movement of the spinner? And would they have been so keen to follow the spinner if the day had been cold, bleak and sunless?

I have put spinners and dead baits across the noses of a good many pike in my time and I have never known them react so well at any time as they do when the water is clear and the day sunny. I do not suggest that these conditions are the best nor that the pike *feed* better in these conditions. Obviously a pike which is moving around slowly in search of food on a dull day is more likely to be caught than one which has merely been stimulated into moving by some means or other. What I do suggest is that, if you can get a pike to move, it will be more likely to feed afterwards; and that one of the best times to get it to move is when there is some sun on the water.

If the sunshine makes the small fish prime and move around, and this in turn makes the pike sit up and take notice, all well and good. If not, it is possible to bring it about by other means. I have already mentioned two ideas, lively live baits and spinning baits, but there are others.

Probably one of the methods is to start roach-fishing in earnest. The business of working up a swim with maggots and cloud bait often brings pike into the swim, but the thing to remember if you're attracting pike into the swim, the pike bait has got to be there too – not twenty yards downstream. All too often the pike bait outfit is regarded as a second string and is left to fend for itself while the angler concentrates on roach-fishing; but this is not the way to catch pike.

I think you have to regard the roach outfit as the second string and the means of starting the pike feeding. A roving live bait in a roach swim is a menace, of course, but a stationary dead bait gets in no one's way, even if it is cast plumb into the centre of the swim. Quite often the first warning comes when a pike attacks one of the roach as it is being played in.

Sometimes the keep-net itself will be attacked and I have seen more than one pike lifted clear of the water with its teeth tangled in the keep-net mesh. A friend of mine caught a number of pike one day by lowering a bait alongside his keep-net and giving the keep-net an occasional shake. Once again the bait was still but the movement attracted the pike to it. The day was bright and sunny.

Where the roach-fishing is hardly worth pursuing because the fish are small, it is possible to start some sort of activity in the vicinity of the pike bait by throwing cloud bait at the float or into the water above the place where the dead bait is lying.

Peter Stone, my brothers (Joe and Ken) and I caught a round dozen pike in one day by applying this technique. We lost a lot more because the hooks came adrift but it was noticeable that, while our baits remained still most of the time, the pike took them readily enough if we livened them up. The ground had been white with frost as the sun rose. The water was very clear, but the pike remained active until the sun set, as long as we kept them on the move.

We did this by periods of spinning, roach-fishing and ground-baiting around the pike baits. One particular pike struck several times over one of the stationary dead baits but did not take it until we 'made' it. While the dead bait remained still, Peter threw a live bait over it, Joe cast a wobbling dead bait and I cast a spoon. Ken threw groundbait at Peter's float every few minutes. We were determined to get this pike or scare it stiff in the attempt and we finally got it. In the midst of this commotion Ken's line, which was holding the stationary dead bait, began to run out, and he caught the pike. Only 11¼ lb and by no means a specimen, but certainly the best of the batch we caught that day. The dead bait had been lying in about six feet of water and had been untouched all day until we went to work in the area.

I have always believed that pike react to vibrations in the water and that water disturbance often causes pike to move even in coloured water but of late I have had reason to think that their reactions are even more noticeable in sunshine. This probably explains the reason why members of my club have caught more pike an hour or so either side of midday in the winter months. As I have said, I believe this is due to a chain of circumstances beginning with the sunshine which stirs the lesser creatures and makes them easy to be seen . . .

Plenty of people still fly to their pike-rods when the ground is hard with frost; others stay in bed and wait for a milder day because they are convinced that they will be wasting their time. No one can lay down any hard and fast rules about pike-fishing; we can only generalise, but I believe it is a very poor day when no pike at all can be induced to move. I have caught them in the worst of conditions and when I have expected nothing. Just as often I have failed to catch them when conditions have seemed perfect.

I am not expert enough to be able to choose whether I catch a big pike or a small one; the waters I fish do not hold enough big pike for that. If I want a big pike I am prepared to use a big bait, to take my chance and wait during a spell of mild weather. But if I want really good pike-fishing fun, I prefer to be at the water between 10 am and 2 pm on a 'summer's-day-in-winter' and to try to start them moving. Once they start moving they can be caught.

from ANGLING *February 1962*

Barbel by Sight and Sound

PETER STONE

Of all the fish that live in our rivers none gives me greater pleasure than the barbel. I have taken a great number of these grand fighters from various rivers, yet every time I land one it is an 'occasion'.

I can go chub-fishing and curse a two-pounder for taking my bait. Bream do not create much interest until they top the 4 lb mark, yet no matter how small a barbel may be I still get a lot of pleasure from catching it.

Strangely enough, you don't catch many small ones – at least where I live – and a record-breaker is always a possibility. I am convinced that the 14 lb 6 oz record* will be broken, and that the new record will come from the Hampshire Avon, the Dorset Stour or the Thames.

Comparatively few anglers fish for them. Many, of course, don't have the opportunity to do so, for only a dozen or so rivers hold them. Even so, far more barbel would be caught if more anglers on the barbel rivers were interested in them.

*Three anglers share the barbel record, all having caught 14 lb 6 oz specimens. They are: Mr T. Wheeler (Thames at Molesey, 1888); Mr H. D. Tryon (Hampshire Avon, 1934); Mr F. W. Wallis (Hampshire Avon, 1937). Ed.

The first thing to do, of course, is to find your barbel, but this isn't easily done. If it were, more fish would come to net. Chub cruise on the surface, bream roll, pike swirl, but barbel rarely show themselves. How, then, do you find them?

Very occasionally you may see one jump clear of the water, re-entering it tail first; or you may see a swirl and a big red tail as the fish goes down. In narrow, shallow streams you may see them on the bottom.

When I am fishing this sort of water I spend an hour or so looking for them – without rod and tackle. It is best done when the sun is high, and polaroid spectacles are a great help. Peer down and look hard.

At first you may see nothing, but when your eyes become accustomed to their new focus you may see two small orange dots on the river-bed, two or three inches in diameter. The inexperienced eye is apt to mistake these for stones but if you see them, keep your eyes fixed on the area. Gradually the shape of a fish will appear, the two orange pieces being the barbel's pectoral fins. If you continue watching, the fish may suddenly turn over quickly on to its side – 'flashing' as we call it – and when it does this the whole bronze shape of the barbel can be seen. This way of locating the fish is possible only in fairly shallow water, but in deeper water, too, the 'flashing' can sometimes be seen. The outline of the barbel cannot be detected beforehand, of course, and all you see is a great golden flash.

One of the best places to look for them is where masses of streamer weed cover the water surface. Only recently I returned from a day on our Kennet fishery when the barbel had not been going. I had taken only one, and with the sun beating down I took a walk. I came to a dense patch of streamer weed and as it looked promising I fetched my tackle. I cast out alongside the nearest clump and waited. After a time a pair of orange fins came from under the weed close to my bait. The barbel 'flashed' and retired again to the weed. In all, three fish emerged while I was there, returning at once to the weed, not in the slightest bit interested in my bait. But barbel were there all right. If you see them like this in the streamer weed, fish alongside as darkness falls and you should get results. I wasn't able to stop on that occasion, but I am positive I could have caught one once the sun was off the water.

If you can't locate them by sight you *may* do so by ear. They often give their presence away by making a sucking noise in the streamer weeds, especially at night. We often hear this on the Kennet and the noise they make is unbelievable. The last time I heard it, it sounded as if several courting couples were having a kissing session! Why they make this noise I don't know, but it seems pretty obvious that they are surface feeding on something in the weed. I hope to discover the answer, for there is no doubt that the right bait cast on top of the weed would produce results.

If your water has a weirpool it is worth watching the shallows during the early morning and late evening. If you notice some miniature waves, often accompanied by a dorsal fin, you have found your barbel. You are especially likely to see this in the early weeks of the season, but towards August they tend to keep to the deeper pools. Do not, however, make the mistake of keeping to the weirs, but search the open river. I take many more barbel from the latter than the former, and they are usually the biggest. It's worth investigating any nice streamy run, providing the bottom is a gravel one.

Of one thing you can be sure; where you see or catch one barbel, there are several more. They keep in shoals, though unlike bream these do not run to terrific numbers.

The fish making up a shoal are not necessarily of the same size. The first one you catch may be 2 lb and the next 10 lb, so keep plugging away once you catch one.

Find your barbel and you are half-way home, for despite what many anglers imagine, these fish can be caught by anybody who is prepared to put his mind to it. In most waters they are not easy, for they have quite rightly been called the 'river carp'.

They are a challenge, and one that I have always enjoyed accepting.

from ANGLING *November 1962*

The Roach-Fishers

PATRICK R. CHALMERS

The roach is a small fish, a man may go through a long angling life and never see a two-pound roach at all, probably never a one-pound roach . . .

And yet the roach occupies a niche by himself among the fishes and before him the lesser candle unceasingly burns. If the salmon is 'the fish' the roach is the roach, and where the salmon is, and has been, the enkindling joy of hundreds, the roach has been, and is, the recreation of tens of thousands, which is perhaps the better part after all . . .

The roach, small and insignificant, can yet exercise over some angling natures a charm and balm that even the trout fails of. When I first fell in love with the Thames it was at Shiplake, and it was not long before I was noticing that a stout man, dressed entirely in black and topped by a black billycock hat, sat upon a camp stool every Sunday above Marsh Lock and fished, reaching with a roach-pole out and over the rushes, for roach. I learned that he was a Londoner, an attendant during the week in a lavatory on the underground railway. And that he locked up on Saturday night and caught the theatre train to Henley. That, arrived there, he walked up to the Marsh and sat down and waited until the by-laws bade him begin to fish. And that there he sat fishing till it was night and time to catch the nine something up to London again.

I did not learn all this from the angler himself, nor do I know if he caught many roaches, for he had a gloomy and taciturn soul (a depression of spirits I dare say, engendered by his dismal calling), and he disliked to be talked to. And I cannot find it in my heart to blame him. For I myself hate the chatty person who asks a total stranger, 'Had any sport, sir?' . . .

After spawning roach are the most dwalmy of all fish and so weak and foolish that they may, almost, be taken by hand. It is for this, perhaps, that the roach has been called the river-sheep. He cannot be called silly-sheeplike at any other time, though in herds he goes and in companies he feeds, indeed an October roach is, next to the barbel, the cunningest commoner in the Thames. And if I were my Conservancy lords I'd have no line wetted for Thames roach till the first of August; let the roach come in with the mallard, say I, when he is as fit to eat as he ever is and to catch as he can be . . .

I have seen in September, big catches of roach made on weed, on silk weed, fished upon a tiny triangle. Fished off the weir (where you have located the companies of the roach) in exactly the same way as that to which the barbel succumb. But even with a big bag of roach so taken, you will still not be a roach-fisher.

Who then *is* a roach-fisher? Why, Walter Coster used to tell me that the London roach-fishers who, in pre-war days, sat on a fine Sunday from Quarry Hole to Stone House were, many of them, swell mobsmen taking their leisure in the most delightfully lazy way in the world. And if you come to think of it you will agree that nothing is so sedative as a roach-angler's Sabbath and that no man's nerves are more important to him than the nerves of the cracker of swell cribs.

But of course there are many men who fish for roach who have never robbed a duchess of her diamonds in all their unenterprising lives. These are the dull fellows like myself. But there is another class of roach-fishers who may be called the professors of the art, the supermen, the men to whom there are but two sorts of fish, the roach and the rest.

These men are not common on the Thames, they are generally the sons of lesser rivers, Ouse, Arun, Colne and Lea, and a score more provincial waters, where *Rut lus Rutilus* is Caesar. But your Thames enthusiast exists and he is invariably the artist of the roach-pole. And a very good artist he is, even though that loved cliché of our kind, 'the merry music of the reel', means nothing to him. For of course the roach-pole has no reel attachment . . .

I will try to give you a picture of the expert himself as he steps out of the train and on to Goring platform this October Sunday morning.

He is a lean, elderly fellow and he is dressed in dark clothes. His face is lined and a little weatherbeaten but not with the tan of the countryman. He has not shaved since yesterday and his cheeks show the dark grizzle of a strongly growing beard . . . He has neglected the razor because he has been up since 5 am . . .

And here I will stop to say that this early habit of the roach-fisherman was once an asset of high legal importance to Mr Marshall Hall in one of his forensic triumphs. Anyone interested in criminology will remember a trial for murder of twenty years ago . . . The prisoner's acquittal depended on his being able to prove to the satisfaction of my lord and the gentlemen of the jury that he was within doors at four-thirty of a September morning when, in the grey light of dawn, a beat constable had seen a man leave a house in a mean street where, even then, in an upper room, lay the naked body of a young woman murdered by means of a razor 'or some sharp instrument'. It was not disputed that the young artist in the dock had been in the girl's company till after midnight, it was not disputed that he had the habit of associating with the flotsam of pavements and public-houses. He went into the box and swore that he had left the deceased alive and well at 1.30 am and that he was home by 2.30. But he was a bachelor in lodgings. Who was to prove his return at 2.30 of a Sunday morning and all the world asleep?

In the room above the prisoner's room lodged an elderly man who came forward and swore that he was out o'bed and dressed at 2.30 and that he had heard the prisoner come in, seat himself on a creaking bedstead, remove his boots and drop them, first one and then the other, on the floor.

'Why,' asked his lordship from the bench, 'were you up and dressed at two o'clock of a Sunday morning?'

'I am a roach-fisher, my lord,' explained the witness with simple dignity. What could be more satisfactory? . . . Half an hour later the prisoner was, thanks to Mr Marshall and to roach-fishing, a free man . . .

And so we will go back to our roach-angler . . . He wears a black, blanket-lined 'oil' and a scarf of red tartan. His pole and folding net are packed compactly in a waterproof cover. These he carries over his shoulders at, what a rifleman calls, 'the slope'.

But his gait is not soldierly, for, slung upon his packed pole, he bears over his shoulder the box without which there would be no roaching . . . It contains tackle of all kinds, but its real use and excuse is to be the throne of the bank angler. It is as much a symbol of roach-fishing as the pole itself . . .

And presently our angler is by the swim that he intends to fish. He walks quietly, he puts his pole together with discretion. No threading of the reel line through the rod's rings for him. And for that I pity the angler, for to hear the short *staccato* sounds of the reel, 'like the call of a corncrake', Mr Bromley-Davenport* says that they are, prior to a day's fishing is a jolly and a hopeful thing.

Now he makes his depth-soundings without splash or hurry. He attached to the ring at the end of his cane top-joint a short length of fine line. Then the gut, the quill, a shot or so, and then the small hook. The whole attachment equals the length of the pole. The angler throws in groundbait. He puts his long-handled net where he hopes it may be handy presently. The actual net, like the net of other roaches, is made just big enough to take a two-pound roach. The true roachman declines to admit that fish other than roach are in the river and that even if there *are* others he does not want to have any ado with them.

And so, conservatively, he sits down on his box and, baiting his angle, makes his cast upstream. The line is weighted so as to allow

*Colonel William Bromley-Davenport, M.P., author of 'Fox-hunting, Salmon-fishing, Covert Shooting and Deerstalking' (1885). Ed.

the quill float to ride deeply in the water. The hook must trip daintily along the floor of the Thames.

The pole is laid upon the open palm of the left hand as lovingly as though it were a Christmas box. With the angler's right hand it is guided and controlled. The rod point follows the bait until the quill dips ever so slightly. The angler strikes. The roach is hooked. The roach-angler is not as others are. He shows no emotion, he makes no sign. He remains *in situ*. He unships the pole from its butt. Left-handed he reaches out his net; right-handed he draws the roach over it. There is no splashing, there is no hurry.

And so the October day wears to evensong and to the train to town. Methodically the fisherman packs up and trudges stationwards. Over Streatly Hill the west is clear and golden, low to the hilltop leans the silver sickle of the young moon.

from AT THE TAIL OF THE WEIR *1932*

Tench Methods

RICHARD WALKER

For the last two years I've been worrying about a curious difference between my tench fishing methods and those employed so successfully by Fred, Ken and Joe Taylor at Wotton Lakes. I'd found that in most of the waters where I fish for tench, it pays to have the lead on the tackle a good distance from the hook. I've watched tench feeding in several of these waters and seen them standing on their heads to pick up a bait.

When they're doing that, they're liable to brush up against a line running from float to shot, or leger-lead, if the bait lies close to the hook. This not only causes a lot of false alarms to be registered by the float, but it can result in the tench actually pulling the bait away from his own mouth, by brushing against the line or washing the line sideways by fin and tail movements. I'm not guessing that this happens; I've seen it, quite often.

The Taylor brothers, however, fish more often than not with one shot, a big swan-shot, about an inch from the hook, and a peacock quill float attached by the bottom end only. They catch plenty of tench, too. They call it the lift method, because the float registers a bite by lifting upwards. It isn't new; it's been used on the Lea for tench, and also big roach, for many years, but it never seemed to claim much interest elsewhere until the Taylors began catching vast numbers of tench with it, as well as other kinds of fish.

I tried the lift method at Wotton, and it certainly works well; but in other places I fish, it isn't very successful, and I'm wondering why. Possibly the nature of the bottom and of the bait may provide some clue.

At Southhill Park, one of the places where the lift hasn't seemed to work so well, the bottom is for the most part quite large stones. A bait like a worm or a piece of paste probably rests in a hollow among the stones, and a tench has to stand on his head and try to suck it up. A line rising vertically above the bait would make that difficult.

On the other hand, fishing with crust on a flat bottom, using the lift technique, means that the crust floats up an inch above the shot. A tench need not stand on his head at all to take it. Consequently, he won't be nearly as likely to touch the line. Crust or flake on lift tackle often seems to work better than worm on the same gear; possibly because the worm will try to bury itself in the mud, and a tench would have to dig it out – banging up against the line in the process.

When tench are shy, as they often are by August or even earlier in waters that are heavily fished, you can often catch fish on a level bottom by using the lift method, with smallish baits, and striking at small float movements, when ordinary methods fail. I think it pays when fixing up the tackle, to have a soft shot, pinched on fairly lightly. Then you can put it close to the hook or bread baits, or slide it a foot or so away from the hook if you decide to try worm – or if you get a lot of niggling bites with which you can't connect by striking early, but which never develop into a more definite pull however long you wait.

Any mug can catch tench when they're feeding well and boldly in a straightforward swim; but to catch then consistently means finding where they are at any given time and using the right technique to suit the swim they're in and the behaviour of the fish themselves.

Many an angler says: 'The tench aren't on today' when, had he known enough, he might have had a good bag. It is true there are times when fish won't feed – but they aren't nearly so common as the times when we anglers are too ignorant to catch fish.

from FRED J. TAYLOR'S FISHING FOR TENCH *1979*

A Beginner's Day

H. T. SHERINGHAM

He has breakfasted early in the August morning, and is making his final disposition before starting. His clothing is of sober hue (the trunk of an old willow tree is a good model for angling fashions), his tackle, bait, and lunch are in the creel, with a small piece of soap and a duster; his rod and landing net are tied together for the journey; his tobacco, pipe, matches, and knife are in his pockets; his mackintosh is on a chair, his broad-brimmed, grey felt hat on his head – he is ready? No, he is not ready. He must go carefully through both creel and pockets to see that the necessaries of the expedition *are* where he supposes them to be; otherwise he may later awake to the fact that he is in the country, while his reel or tackle-book is on a table in London. This, I can assert from personal knowledge, is a very unpleasing discovery to make. Also to find yourself at the waterside with tobacco and without matches is a disaster of the first magnitude. Therefore, let the novice make a practice of overhauling his luggage before he starts.

The journey needs no comment, except that it is a blissful thing to see London gradually giving way to green fields; and to step out onto the platform of the wayside station, with its restful country activities, and into the sweet air of a summer morning. Let not delight in his freedom, however, cause the novice to leave his rod or basket or mackintosh in the rack of his railway carriage, lest his joy be turned to mourning. Here also I speak out of a full heart; there is a blankness about the world when one stands on a country platform, a silly basket in hand, watching the distant train which is carrying one's rod away to alien climes. The novice, however, makes no such fool of himself, but bears his goods proudly, and so arrives at the mill where he is to fish. Here he shows the miller his card of permission, is assured by that honest man that Mr Jones had rare sport with the chub last Friday, makes no comment on this circumstance, and hurries off to the mill-pool, where I advise him to begin his fishing career.

While we have been gossiping the novice has caught another, ½ lb this time, which has joined its fellow in the creel, and now he is face to face with a new situation. His float got into the main stream, and so worked further out into the eddy about four yards from the wall. Then, without warning, it vanished, drawn under as by a firm hand. The rod was raised smartly after the due interval, and a solid weight was encountered. This suddenly changed into an active and violent resistance, and the fish bolted into the strong stream, swimming with or being carried by it right out into the pool. Taken aback by these events the novice has been perforce content simply to hold the rod up and let the fish pull line off the reel. Now, however, it is twenty yards away, where the current is more diffused and less strong, so he can begin to wind in again, working the fish sideways into the eddy. It comes back fairly quietly until it is almost under the rod, but it is deep down and invisible. Then it makes another dash for the stream, but the fisherman puts on more strain and stops it. There follows a solemn and sulky circling round and round in the depths, and once or twice a gleam of silver is seen as the fish turns on its side. At last it comes to the top and lies there beaten, looking very big and imposing. The net is under it, and it is landed in triumph. It is a handsome fish, with big silver scales, shading into golden brown on the back, red fins, and a big blunt head; it might be own brother to that chub or cheven which Master Izaak's pupil was so happy to catch, and the spring balance shows it to be 2½ lb, that is to say, almost a big one. A 3-pounder is a big chub in most rivers, and a fish of 1½ lb worth taking in many. But the novice will have more to do with chub later; at present he is lucky to have begun so well, and he may be justly proud of himself even if he does no more to-day, as seems possible, for during the next hour he gets never a bite, though he tries the eddy on both sides of the stream with care and patience.

from ELEMENTS OF ANGLING *1909*

The Fisherman in Winter

BERNARD VENABLES

To many fishermen the end of the season comes about 30th September. In a fine year, it might perhaps be prolonged until the end of October. In any case they think of it as an occupation for the leafy months. It is associated in their minds with the hum of bees and the drowsiness of warm days.

This is certainly a very lovely part of the fisherman's year, but it is very far from being all of it if he is to get from it all that there is to be had. The winter can give him such an extension of his pleasure as he had no conception of until he has tried it.

I think that for most anglers an appreciation of landscape and a delight in the sounds of nature are bound up with their pleasure in angling; and for a great many this means leafy banks, the scent of hay, birdsong and the charm of seeing animals about their business. And all this, they feel, is something that passes with the summer. In winter, they think of everything as being held in a deep cold sleep.

This is far from being true, as any winter fisherman can tell you. In winter the otter may still be seen by the lucky fisherman. The heron still stalks about the shallows in search of little fish. The kingfisher and the dipper have not departed, and in fact the dipper sings more sweetly from December on than it does at any other time. Many others of the waterside animals are still abroad, even the squirrel that so many believe sleeps the winter through. It can be seen in all but the hardest weather. There is no dead stop to nature as the town dweller seems to suppose. When the very last of the bloom and leaf has left the banks, it is only quite a short pause before catkins and the earliest blossoms bestrew it again.

And in that pause there is no real stop. A fox has jumped from beneath my very feet in the dried sedges on an iron hard day in December. The weather has as lovely a procession of change as it has at any other time. Mild, pale blue skies give way to inky threatening ones, and those in turn to the crack and glitter of sharp frost. Any weather but a steady downpour is a pleasure on the river bank. The leaves may have gone from the trees, but they are none the less beautiful for that. However familiar your river bank, if you know it only in summer its winter loveliness will be a revelation to you. Then your eye can dwell on the clean and massive strength of oak and ash and beech, and see the pale clear colours of them. You can find pleasure in the brilliant crimson of the osier, and in the elegant lean and droop of the willows over the water.

But of course you do not come to the water merely to find a gentle pleasure in landscape and birds and trees. Nor need you do so. You have come to fish and you can do this to very good purpose. Some of your fishes of summer will no longer be feeding and therefore ready to be angled for, but of the others some will show you better sport now than ever they did in summer. And of those properly regarded as summer fish, there are days throughout the winter that will bring them from their torpor unless it be a very hard season.

The tench and the carp are most justly regarded as fish of summer, but there are many of them that have found their way to the fisherman's keep-net on a mild day in winter. In the south particularly, the middle hours of a warm day will bring them all on feed. Of bream too this is true. On these days, large catches have been made in the heart of winter. As for the barbel, in recent years they have flouted every rule that is said to govern them, by feeding lustily almost throughout the winter. These winters, it is true, have been mild, but it is something that it has been well worth while to set out specifically to catch barbel at the end of December.

But though all these fishes may provide occasional sport to vary the fisherman's days, it is not on them that he relies. In most places they are no more than windfalls and it is not for them that a man becomes a convinced winter fisherman. It is for those fish that in the winter reach their full prime, and only then give the angler the whole sport of which they are capable.

The roach, I suppose, is the most popular fish of all. It is a good fish to fish for in the summer. Its subtlety, the difficulty of its deception, ensure that. But it must be admitted that as a fighter it does not rank very high. In winter, however, it is another fish. Its shy cunning is not in the least blunted, and it develops as well a muscular power unknown in the summer fish. A roach then, of a pound and a half, will show its mettle.

The rudd of winter is equally improved. In fact its showing at the end of a line will be even better than that of the roach. For this is a deeper fish, a more solid and weighty fish. A day with rudd in the closing months of the season can be a red-letter day.

As for the chub, between that of summer and that of winter there is just no comparison. Let us admit that the chub of summer is too often a lank and spiritless thing that gives way with scarcely a struggle. But how different it is in winter. Then a chub of over three pounds will give you all the fight you can want. I have seen many on the Wye, that, seeming irresistible, have plunged to freedom in the roots.

But of all the fishes of winter, there is none perhaps that so comes into its own as the pike. The limp and flaccid fish of summer becomes a fierce and powerful fighter that inspires thousands of fishermen to its pursuit, whatever the weather.

Now let's join Mr Crabtree and Peter, and see what winter sport we can have in their company.

from MR CRABTREE GOES FISHING *1989*

PART 6

Conversation Pieces

Tenth-century Fisher-boy

ABBOT AELFRIC

Note: Aelfric's Colloquy was a Latin-English (Anglo-Saxon) phrase book for scholars. It dealt with several trades and pursuits, and the following covers fishing. M is the master, P the fisher-boy.

M: What craft do you follow? P: I am a fisher.

M: What do you get from your work? P: Food, clothes and money.

M: How do you catch fish? P: I get into my boat and cast my nets into the river, and throw out my hook and my rods, and whatever they catch I take.

M: What if the fish be unclean? P: I throw the unclean away, and take the clean for food.

M: Where do you sell your fish? P: In the town.

M: Who buys them? P: The townspeople. I cannot catch as many as I could sell.

M: What fishes do you catch? P: Eels and pike, and minnows, and eel-pouts, trout and lampreys, and whatever else swim in the river.

M: Why do you not fish in the sea? P: I do so sometimes, but not often, because rowing in the sea is difficult.

M: What do you catch in the sea? P: Herrings and salmon, dolphins and sturgeon, oysters and crabs, mussels, winkles, cockles, plaice, and flounders, and lobsters and many more.

M: Do you not wish to catch a whale? P: I do not!

M: Why not? P: Because it is a dangerous thing to catch a whale. It is safer for me to take my boat on the river than to go whale-hunting with several ships.

M: But many do catch whales, and escape the dangers, and get good money by it. P: You are right, but I dare not do so, because of my sluggishness of spirit.

from AELFRIC'S COLLOQUY *c. 1000*
translated by Walter W. Skeat
in 'The Angler's Note-Book', 15-3-1880

The Angler at Home

ANON

Piscator. Here must we stay. Now is supper come.
Viator. I am the more sorry, for your talk is meat and drink to me.
Pi. Yea, but meat and drink is fitter for me that have not eaten today. Well, let us have grace.
Vi. Have ye not a fish grace?
Pi. Yes, that I have, and that for an angler.

Almighty God, that these did make,
As saith his holy book,
And gave me cunning them to take,
And brought them to my hook;
To him be praise for evermore,
That daily doth us feed,
And doth increase by spawn such store
To serve us at our need.

Vi. A very good grace, and a fit. Now, I pray you, let your Cisley come in.
Pi. Call your mother in, maid.
Vi. What fish call you these?
Pi. Gudgeons.
Vi. They be very good, indeed, well dressed. How take you these?
Pi. These are as fit for a young beginner as may be, for one bait doth serve them at all seasons, and you may make them to bite all day if you have sundry places. Come, wife, come! Thou thinkest that nothing is well done unless thou be at the one end of it. Sit down and eat, for I am hungry.
Cisley. I believe well. How like you your broth?
Pi. Hunger findeth no fault.
Vi. But I pray you, teach me to kill these pleasant fishes.
Ci. I pray you, sir, let my husband awhile alone until he have eaten, and then you cannot please him better at meat than to talk of angling, though for my part I would he had never known what angling meant.
Vi. Why, I pray you?

Ci. I think he had never known what the colic had meant, if he had not known what angling had meant.
Vi. Is it even so?
Pi. Soft, dame!
Vi. Nay, I pray you, let us two alone, and eat you awhile, for I believe that your wife is not fasting, no more than I. Now, mistress, is it true that your husband hath caught the colic with fishing?
Ci. Surely I suppose so, with his long standing, long fasting, and coldness of his feet, yea, and sometimes sitting on the cold ground, for all is one to him, whether he catch or not catch. Yea, and sometimes he cometh home with the colic, indeed, and is not well of two or three days after, so that I hope he will give it over shortly.
Vi. Is this true?
Pi. Yea, what then?
Vi. Then I say, *Faelix quem faciunt aliena pericula cautum.* Happy is he . . .

[Four pages of the book are missing here. When the text resumes, Piscator is speaking of fishing from a boat.]

. . . stand you beneath him as the water runneth, so that you may angle in the thick water, and you shall have trim sport. And if he that doth stir the water have in a bag of linen some ground malt, and now and then cast in as much as he may hold between his three fingers where he stirreth, that it may fall just where you angle, it is the better. And you may put on two hooks at this sport and so have a good mess quickly. Land when you see the bite die, then remove to another place, and so on, as your store of fish, plats, and speeding is.
Vi. Now cometh your wife again, and I shall be shent for keeping you from eating.
Pi. No, no, she knoweth this talk to be meat and drink unto me. Now, wife, come and sit down.
Ci. We have brought you all.
Vi. All, quoth ye? Indeed, here is store. Oh, here is the great perch that you took in the morning. It is so, indeed. But what are these lying about him?
Pi. Ruffes.
Vi. What fish is it?
Pi. Oh, excellent.
Vi. I pray you, how take you them?
Ci. Good sir, let him eat his meat.

Pi. My wife counteth me like the instrument of Lincolnshire. But now that I have somewhat stayed my hunger, I can both eat and talk. The ruffe is the grossest at his bite of any fish that biteth, and is taken with the red worm on the ground, and where he lieth, there is he commonly alone. He is envious, bristled on the back as the perch, in each fin a sharp prick, his gills sharp at the end, and swalloweth the bait at the first, great goggle-eyed, and cometh up very churlishly, and will hold his lips so hard together that you shall have much ado to open them, and commonly you must rend the gills asunder to get out your hook. He is full of black spots and like to rised bacon, and therefore we call them little hogs. But surely an wholesome fish! With two hairs you may fish for him, he is so gross in his feeding and cometh not up gently. Hold you, there is one of them. Taste of him and tell me.

Vi. A very good fish.

Pi. There cannot be a better, and chiefly for a sick body. I count him better than either gudgeon or perch, for he eateth faster and pleasanter. The worm is his only bait that ever I did know. My master that taught me to angle could not abide to catch a ruffe; for if he took one, either he would remove or wind up and home for that time, he did know them so masterly among other fish. But for my part, I have been well content to deal with them, for this property they have, as is seen among the wicked; that though they see their fellows perish never so fast, yet will they not be warned, so that you shall have them as long as one is left, especially a little before a rain or in the bite time. And if you close some small worms in a ball of old black dung or earth, and cast it in where you angle for them, you shall have the better sport, for at that will they lie like little hogs, as is aforesaid. You so listen to my talk that you eat nothing.

Ci. You men say that women be talkative, but here is such a number of words about nothing, as passeth.

Pi. Why so I say, all is nothing with you and your kind unless it be about pins and laces, fringe and guards, fine linen and woollen, hats and hatbands, gloves and scarves; and yet I marvel that you should say that my talk hath been of nothing. For one part of the attire that now is of no small charge among you, we have a fish to father it called a ruffe, of whom I spake even now, unless you will have it the diminutive of a ruffian. But it may be that the name doth come from the ruffe, the fish, for surely the greater part that use the long gut gathered together of this fish, they may well be said to be in their ruff and like unto the ruffe in disdain.

Vi. Well now, I pray you, to the taking of the perch.

Pi. The perch is a gross fish and easily taken. A red worm is his common bait, but the quick minnow is the best, putting your hook through the corner of her lip, and so let her swim alive an ell in the water, with plummets to keep her down; and strike not over soon when you see the bite, but let him go as far as the length of your line, that he may swallow it, or else his mouth is so wide and so full of bones, and also he will many times gape for the nonce and cast out hook and minnow. The minnow, the minnow also will somewhat bear off your hook, but when your fish is in his gullet, then all is safe, so that your hook bend not or your line break.

Vi. I may fish with more hairs for him than one or two?

Pi. That you may, with four or six, and a good, handsome, compassed hook. He will also in winter bite at a good gentle or a ball of bread. A ravenous fish it is also, and liveth for the most part by eating up of his fellows, as the covetous enclosers do. And if you come to the lair of great perches, let your line be strong, for when you have struck one the residue will come and make such a stir about your line and him, with their bristles up, that they will deliver their fellow if you have not a good line and very good hold.

from THE ARTE OF ANGLING *1577*

Chub Lore

IZAAK WALTON

Piscator. I doubt not but at yonder tree I shall catch a *Chub*: and then we'll turn to an honest cleanly Hostess, that I know right well; rest our selves there, and dress it for our dinner.

Venator. Oh Sir, a *Chub* is the worst Fish that swims, I hoped for a *Trout* to my dinner.

Pisc. Trust me, *Sir*, there is not a likely place for a *Trout*, hereabout, and we staid so long to take our leave of your Huntsmen this morning, that the Sun is got so high, and shines so clear, that I will not undertake the catching of a *Trout* till evening; and though a *Chub* be by you and many others, reckoned the worst of *fish*, yet you shall see I'll make it a good Fish by dressing it.

Ven. Why, how will you dress him?

Pisc. I'll tell you by and by, when I have caught him. Look you here, Sir, do you see? (but you must stand very close) there lye upon the top of the water in this very hole twenty *Chubs*. I'll catch only one, and that shall be the biggest of them all: and that I will do so, I'll hold you twenty to one, and you shall see it done.
Venat. Aye, marry Sir, now you talk like an Artist, and I'll say you are one, when I shall see you perform what you say you can do; but I yet doubt it.
Pisc. You shall not doubt it long, for you shall see me do it presently: look, the biggest of these *Chubs* has had some bruise upon his tail, by a Pike or some other accident, and that looks like a white spot; that very *Chub* I mean to put into your hands presently; sit you but down in the shade, and stay but a little while, and I'll warrant you I'll bring him to you.
Venat. I'll sit down and hope well, because you seem to be so confident.
Pisc. Look you Sir, there is a tryal of my skill, there he is, that very *Chub* that I shewed you with the white spot on his tail: and I'le be as certain to make him a good dish of meat, as I was to catch him: I'le now lead you to an honest Ale-house where we shall find a cleanly room, *Lavender* in the Windows, and twenty *Ballads* stuck about the wall; there my Hostess (which I may tell you, is both cleanly and handsome and civil) hath drest many a one for me, and shall now dress it after my fashion, and I warrant it good meat.
Ven. Come Sir, with all my heart, for I begin to be hungry, and long to be at it, and indeed to rest my self too; for though I have walk'd but four miles this morning, yet I begin to be weary; yesterdays hunting hangs still upon me.
Pisc. Well Sir, and you shall quickly be at rest, for yonder is the house I mean to bring you to.

Come Hostess, how do you? Will you first give us a cup of your best drink, and then dress this *Chub*, as you dressed my last, when I and my friend were here about eight or ten days ago? but you must do me one courtesie, it must be done instantly.
Host. I will do it, Mr *Piscator*, and with all the speed I can.
Pisc. Now Sir, has not my Hostess made hast? and does not the fish look lovely?
Ven. Both, upon my word, Sir, and therefore let's say grace and fall to eating of it.
Pisc. Well, Sir, how do you like it?
Ven. Trust me, 'tis as good meat as I ever tasted: Now let me thank

you for it, drink to you, and beg a courtesie of you; but it must not be deny'd me.

Pisc. What is it I pray Sir: you are so modest, that methinks I may promise to grant it before it is asked.

Ven. Why, Sir, it is, that from henceforth you would allow me to call you *Master*, and that really I may be your Scholar, for you are such a companion, and have so quickly caught, and so excellently cook'd this fish, as makes me ambitious to be your Scholar.

Pisc. Give me your hand; from this time forward I will be your Master, and teach you as much of this Art as I am able; and will, as you desire me, tell you somewhat of the nature of most of the Fish that we are to angle for; and I am sure I both can and will tell you more than any common *Angler* yet knows.

Pisc. The *Chub*, though he eat well thus drest, yet as he is usually drest, he does not: he is objected against, not only for being full of small forked bones, disperst through all his body, but that he eats watrish, and that the flesh of him is not firm, but short and tastless. The *French* esteem him so mean, as to call him *Un Villain*; nevertheless he may be so drest as to make him very good meat; as namely, if he be a large *Chub*, then dress him thus:

First scale him, and then wash him clean, and then take out his guts; and to that end make the hole as little and near to his gills as you may conveniently, and especially make clean his throat from the grass and weeds that are usually in it (for if that be not very clean, it will make him to taste very sour) having so done, put some sweet herbs into his belly, and then tye him with two or three splinters to a spit, and rost him, basted often with Vinegar, or rather verjuice and butter, with good store of salt mixt with it.

Being thus drest, you will find him a much better dish of meat than you, or most folk, even than Anglers themselves do imagine; for this dries up the fluid watry humor with which all *Chubs* do abound.

But take this rule with you, That a *Chub* newly taken and newly drest, is so much better than a *Chub* of a days keeping after he is dead, that I can compare him to nothing so fitly as to Cherries newly gathered from a tree, and others that have been bruised and lain a day or two in water. But the *Chub* being thus used and drest presently, and not washed after he is gutted (for note that lying long in water, and washing the blood out of any fish after they be gutted, abates much of their sweetness) you will find the Chub being drest in the blood and quickly, to be such meat as will recompence your labour, and disabuse your opinion.

Or you may dress the *Chavender* or *Chub* thus:

When you have scaled him, and cut off his tail and fins, and washed him very clean, then chine or slit him through the middle, as a salt fish is usually cut, then give him three or four cuts or scotches on the back with your knife, and broil him on Char-coal, or Wood-coal that are free from smoke, and all the time he is a broyling baste him with the best sweet Butter, and good store of salt mixt with it; and to this add a little Time cut exceeding small, or bruised into the butter. The Cheven thus drest hath the watry tast taken away, for which so many except against him. Thus was the Cheven drest that you now liked so well, and commended so much. But note again, that if this Chub that you eat of, had been kept till to morrow, he had not been worth a rush. And remember that his throat be washt very clean, I say very clean, and his body not washt after he is gutted, as indeed no fish should be.

Well, Scholar, you see what pains I have taken to recover the lost credit of the poor despised *Chub*. And now I will give you some rules how to catch him; and I am glad to enter you into the Art of fishing by catching a *Chub*, for there is no fish better to enter a young Angler, he is so easily caught, but then it must be this particular way:

Go to the same hole in which I caught my *Chub*, where in most hot daies you will find a dozen or twenty *Chevens* floating near the top of the water, get two or three grasshoppers as you go over the meadow, and get secretly behind the tree, and stand as free from motion as is possible, then put a Grasshopper on your hook, and let your hook hang a quarter of a yard short of the water, to which end you must rest your rod on some bough of the tree, but it is likely the Chubs will sink down towards the bottom of the water at the first shadow of your Rod (for a Chub is the fearfullest of fishes.) and will do so if but a bird flies over him, and makes the least shadow on the water: but they will presently rise up to the top again, and there lie soaring till some shadow affrights them again: I say when they lie upon the top of the water, look out the best Chub, (which you setting your self in a fit place, may very easily see) and move your Rod, as softly as a Snail moves, to that Chub you intend to catch; let your bait fall gently upon the water three or four inches before him, and he will infallibly take the bait and you will be as sure to catch him; for he is one of the leather-mouth'd fishes, of which a hook does scarce ever lose its hold; and therefore give him play enough before you offer to take him out of the water. Go your way presently, take my Rod, and do as I bid you, and I will sit down and mend my tackling till you return back.

Ven. Truly, my loving Master, you have offered me as fair as I could wish. I'll go and observe your directions.

Look you, Master, what I have done, that which joys my heart, caught just such another *Chub* as yours was.

Pisc. Marry, and I am glad of it: I am like to have a towardly Scholar of you. I now see, that with advice and practice you will make an Angler in a short time. Have but a love to it and I'le warrant you.

Venat. But Master, what if I could not have found a *Grasshopper*?

Pisc. Then I may tell you, that a *black Snail*, with his belly slit, to show his white: or a piece of soft *cheese*, will usually do as well: nay, sometimes a *worm* or any kind of *Flie*, as the *Anti-flie*, the *Flesh-flie*, or *Wall-flie*, or the *Dor* or *Beetle* (which you may find under a Cow-tird) or a *Bob*, which you will find in the same place, and in time will be a Beetle; it is a short white worm, like to and bigger than a Gentle, or a *Cod-worm*, or a *Case-worm*, any of these will do very well to fish in such a manner. And after this manner you may catch a *Trout* in a hot evening: when as you walk by a Brook, and shall see or hear him leap at flies, then if you get a *Grasshopper*, put it on your hook, with your line about two yards long, standing behind a bush or tree where his hole is, and make your bait stir up and down on the top of the water: you may, if you stand close, be sure of a bite, but not sure to catch him, for he is not a leather mouthed Fish: and after this manner you may fish for him with almost any kind of live flie, but especially with a *Grasshopper*.

Venat. But before you go further, I pray good Master, what mean you by a leather-mouthed Fish?

Pisc. By a leather-mouthed Fish, I mean such as have their teeth in their throat, as the *Chub* or *Cheven*, and so the *Barbel*, the *Gudgeon*, and *Carp*, and divers others have; and the hook, being stuck into the leather or skin of the mouth of such fish does very seldom or never loses its hold. But on the contrary, a *Pike*, a *Pearch*, or *Trout*, and so some other Fish, which have not their teeth in their throats, but in their mouths (which you shall observe to be very full of bones, and the skin very thin, and little of it:) I say, of these fish the hook never takes so sure hold, but you often lose your fish, unless he have gorg'd it.

Ven. I thank you, good Master, for this observation; but now what shall be done with my *Chub* or *Cheven*, that I have caught?

Pisc. Marry, Sir, it shall be given away to some poor body, for I'le warrant you I'le give you a *Trout* for your supper; and it is a good beginning of your Art to offer your first fruits to the poor, who will both thank God and you for it, which I see by your silence you seem to consent to. And for your willingness to part with it so charitably, I will also teach more concerning Chub-fishing: you are to note that in *March* and *April* he is usually taken with wormes; in *May*, *June* and *July* he will bite at any *fly*, or at *Cherries*, or at *Beetles* with their legs and wings cut off, or at any kind of *Snail*, or at the black *Bee* that breeds in clay walls; and he never refuses a Grasshopper on the top of a swift stream, nor at the bottom the young *bumble-bee* that breeds in long grasse, and is ordinarily found by the Mower of it. In *August*, and in the cooler months, a yellow *paste*, made of the strongest cheese, and pounded in a Mortar, with a little butter and saffron, (so much of it as being beaten small will turn it to a lemon colour.) And some make a paste for the Winter months, at which time the Chub is accounted best, (for then it is observed, that the forked bones are lost, or turned into a kind of gristle, [especially if he be baked]) of Cheese and Turpentine; he will bite also at a Minnow or Penk, as a Trout will: of which I shall tell you more hereafter, and of divers other baits. But take this for a rule, that in hot weather he is to be fisht for towards the mid-water, or near the top; and in colder weather nearer the bottom. And if you fish for him on top, with a Beetle or any *fly*, then be sure to let your line be very long, and to keep out of sight. And having told you that his spawn is excellent meat, and that the head of a large Cheven, the Throat being well washt, is the best part of him, I will say no more of this Fish at the present, but wish you may catch the next you fish for.

from THE COMPLEAT ANGLER *1653*

A Day on the Dove

CHARLES COTTON

Pisc. Good morrow *Sir*, what up and drest so early?
Viat. Yes *Sir*, I have been drest this half hour; for I rested so well, and have so great a mind either to take, or to see a Trout taken in your fine River, that I could no longer lye a bed.
Pisc. I am glad to see you so brisk this morning, and so eager of sport;

though I must tell you, this day proves so calm, and the Sun rises so bright, as promises no great success to the Angler: but however we'l try, and one way or other we shall sure do something. What will you have to your breakfast, or what will you drink this Morning.

Viat. For breakfast I never eat any, and for Drink am very indifferent; but if you please to call for a Glass of Ale, I'me for you; and let it be quickly if you please: for I long to see the little Fishing-house you spoke of, and to be at my Lesson.

Pisc. Well *Sir*, You see the Ale is come without Calling; for though I do not know yours, my people know my diet, which is always one glass as soon as I am drest, and no more till Dinner, and so my Servants have served you.

Viat. My thanks, and now if you please let us look out this fine morning.

Pisc. With all my heart. Boy, take the Key of my Fishing-house, and carry down those two Angle-Rods in the Hall window thither, with my Fish-pannier, Pouch, and landing Net, and stay you there till we come. Come *Sir* we'l walk after, where by the way I expect you should raise all the exceptions against our Country you can.

Viat. Nay *Sir*, do not think me so ill natur'd, nor so uncivil, I only made a little bold with it last night to divert you, and was only in jeast.

Pisc. You were then in as good earnest as I am now with you: but had you been really angry at it, I could not blame you: For, to say the truth, it is not very taking at first sight: But look you, *Sir*, now you are abroad, does not the Sun shine as bright here as in *Essex*, *Middlesex*, or *Kent*, or any of your Southern Countries?

Viat. 'Tis a delicate Morning indeed, and I now think this a marvellous pretty place.

Pisc. Whether you think so or no, you cannot oblige me more than to say so; and those of my friends who know my humour, and are so kind as to comply with it, usually flatter me that way. But look you *Sir*, now you are at the brink of the Hill, how do you like my River, the Vale it winds through like a Snake, and the situation of my little Fishing-house?

Viat. Trust me 'tis all very fine, and the house seems at this distance a neat building.

Pisc. First then of the natural Flie; of which we generally use but two sorts, and those but in the two months of *May* and *June* only, namely the *Green Drake*, and the *Stone-Flie*; though I have made use of a third that way, called the *Chamblet-Flie* with very good success for *Grayling*, but never saw it angled with by any other after this manner, my

Master only excepted, who did many years ago, and was one of the best Anglers, that ever I knew.

These are to be angled with, with a short Line, not much more than half the length of your Rod, if the air be still; or with a longer very near, or all out as long as your Rod, if you have any wind to carry it from you, and this way of Fishing we call *Daping*, *Dabbing* or *Dibling*, wherein you are always to have your Line flying before you up or down the River as the wind serves, and to angle as near as you can to the bank of the same side whereon you stand, though where you see a Fish rise near you, you may guide your quick Flie over him whether in the middle, or on the contrary side, and if you are pretty well out of sight, either by kneeling or the Interposition of a bank, or bush, you may almost be sure to raise, and take him too, if it be presently done; the Fish will otherwise peradventure be remov'd to some other place, if it be in the still deeps, where he is always in motion, and roving up and down to look for prey, though, in a stream, you may alwaies almost, especially if there be a good stone near, find him in the same place. Your Line ought in this Case to be three good hairs next the hook; both by reason you are in this kind of angling, to expect the biggest Fish and also that wanting length to give him Line after he is struck, you must be forc't to tugg for't; to which I will also add, that not an Inch of your Line being to be suffered to touch the water in dibling; it may be allow'd to be the stronger. I should now give you a Description of those Flies, their shape and colour, and then give you an account of their breeding, and withall shew you how to keep and use them; but shall defer that to their proper place and season.

For the length of your Rod, you are always to be govern'd by the breadth of the River you shall chuse to angle at; and for a Trout River, one of five or six yards long is commonly enough, and longer (though never so neatly and artifically made) it ought not to be, if you intend to Fish at ease, and if otherwise, where lies the sport?

Of these, the best that ever I saw are made in *Tork-shire*, which are all of one piece; that is to say, of several, six, eight, ten or twelve pieces, so neatly piec't, and ty'd together with fine thred below and Silk above, as to make it taper, like a switch, and to ply with a true bent to your hand; and these are too light, being made of Fir wood, for two or three lengths, nearest to the hand, and of other wood nearer to the top, and a Man might very easily manage the longest of them that ever I saw, with one hand; and these when you have given over Angling for a season, being taken to pieces, and laid up in some dry place, may afterwards be set together again in their former postures, and will be as strait, sound, and good as the first hour they were made, and being laid in Oyl and colour according to your Master *Waltons* direction, will last many years.

The length of your line, to a Man that knows how to handle his Rod, and to cast it, is no manner of encumbrance, excepting in woody places, and in landing of a Fish, which every one that can afford to Angle for pleasure, has some body to do for him, and the length of line is a mighty advantage to the fishing at distance; and to fish *fine, and far off* is the first and principal Rule for Trout Angling.

Your Line in this case should never be less, nor ever exceed two hairs next to the hook, for one (though some I know will pretend to more Art, than their fellows) is indeed too few, the least accident, with the finest hand being sufficient to break it: but he that cannot kill a Trout of twenty inches long with two, in a River clear of wood and weeds, as this and some others of ours are, deserves not the name of an Angler.

Pisc. There *Sir*, now I think you are fitted, and now beyond the farther end of the walk you shall begin, I see at that bend of the water above, the air crisps the water a little, knit your Line first here, and then go up thither, and see what you can do.

Viat. Did you see that, *Sir*?

Pisc. Yes, I saw the Fish, and he saw you too, which made him turn short, you must fish further off, if you intend to have any sport here, this is no *New-River* let me tell you. That was a good Trout believe me, did you touch him?

Viat. No, I would I had, we would not have parted so. Look you there was another; this is an excellent Flie.

Pisc. That Flie I am sure would kill Fish, if the day were right; but they only chew at it I see, and will not take it. Come *Sir*, let us return back to the Fishing-house; this still water I see will not do our business to day; you shall now, if you please, make a Flie your self, and try what you can do in the streams with that, and I know a Trout taken with a Flie of your own making will please you better than twenty with one of mine. Give me that Bag again, *Sirrah*; look you *Sir*, there is a hook, tought, silk, and a feather for the wings, be doing with those, and I will look you out a Dubbing, that I think will do.

Viat. This is a very little hook.

Pisc. That may serve to inform you, that it is for a very little Flie, and you must make your wings accordingly; for as the case stands it must be a little Flie, and a very little one too, that must do your business. Well said! belive me you shift your fingers very handsomely; I doubt I have taken upon me to teach my Master. So here's your dubbing now.

Viat. This dubbing is very black.

Pisc. It appears so in hand; but step to the doors and hold it up betwixt your eye and the Sun, and it will appear a shining red; let me tell you never a man in *England* can discern the true colour of a dubbing any way but that, and therefore chuse always to make your Flies on such a bright Sun-shine day as this, which also you may the better do, because it is worth nothing to fish in, here put it on, and be sure to make the body of your Flie as slender as you can. Very good! Upon my word you have made a marvellous handsom Flie.

Viat. I am very glad to hear it; 'tis the first that ever I made of this kind in my life.

Pisc. Away, away! You are a Doctor at it! but I will not commend you too much, lest I make you proud. Come put it on, and you shall now go downward to some streams betwixt the rocks below the little foot bridge you see there, and try your Fortune. Take heed of slipping into the water as you follow me under this rock: So now you are over, and now throw in.

Viat. This is a fine stream indeed: There's one! I have him!

Piat. And a precious catch you have of him; pull him out! I see you have a tender hand: This is a diminutive Gentleman, e'en throw him in again, and let him grow till he be more worthy your anger.

Viat. Pardon me, *Sir*, all's Fish that comes to' the' hook with me now. Another!

Pisc. And of the same standing.

Viat. I see I shall have good sport now: Another! and a Grayling. Why you have Fish here at will.

Pisc. Come, come, cross the Bridge, and go down the other side lower, where you will find finer streams, and better sport I hope than this. Look you *Sir*, here is a fine stream now, you have length enough, stand a little further off, let me entreat you, and do but Fish this stream like an Artist, and peradventure a good Fish may fall to your share. How now! what is all gone?

Viat. No, I but touch't him; but that was a Fish worth taking.

Pisc. Why now let me tell you, you lost that Fish by your own fault, and through your own eagerness and haste; for you are never to offer to strike a good Fish, if he do not strike himself, till first you see him turn his head after he has taken your Flie, and then you can never strain your tackle in the striking, if you strike with any manner of

moderation. Come throw in one again, and fish me this stream by inches; for I assure you here are very good Fish, both Trout and Grayling, lie here; and at that great stone on the other side, 'tis ten to one a good Trout gives you the meeting.
Viat. I have him now, but he is gone down towards the bottom, I cannot see what he is; yet he should be a good Fish by his weight; but he makes no great stir.
Pisc. Why, then, by what you say, I dare venture to assure you, 'tis a Grayling, who is one of the deadest hearted Fishes in the world, and the bigger he is the more easily taken. Look you, now you see him plain; I told you what he was, bring hither that landing net, Boy, and now *Sir*, he is your own; and believe me a good one, sixteen Inches long I warrant him, I have taken none such this year.

from THE COMPLEAT ANGLER PT II *1676*

Coquetdale

STEPHEN OLIVER

Bell. One might suppose that you have been born in Coquetdale, you are so ready with the 'Hyntynge of the Chyviot'. But I should like now to hear a little of your fishing. I suspect that you have returned with an empty creel, or we should have heard something of your exploits before this; for anglers are not accustomed to be silent on their success. I should like to see your take – a couple of thorney-backs, perch par courtesie; half a dozen minnows, and an eel; but not a single trout, except the dozen which you would buy in coming home, to save yourselves from being laughed at.
Oliver. Thorney-backs and minnows! – I should like much to catch a few of your trouts. But you shall see. Waiter, let the hostler bring up that hamper of trouts and the pike which we caught this afternoon. A pike – it is a halbert of a fish – a very weaver's beam!

Enter Hostler, with a tolerably well filled basket of trouts and a pike.

Bell. Well done! These are something better than thorney-backs, after all. I dare say you have nearly a stone and a half of trouts here, and some of them really prime ones. You have been lucky in hooking the skeggers today; if you continue as you have begun you will rouse the jealousy of your brother anglers.

Oliver. Skeggers! Why surely you do not call those fine trouts, of from two to three pounds weight, skeggers? I do not think there is a single skegger amongst them.

Bell. There you are wrong - and prove that you are better acquainted with Izaak Walton than with the trouts of the Coquet, notwithstanding the numerous visits you have paid to this part of the country. The trout which Walton describes as the samlet, or skegger, is the small brandling trout of the Coquet; but the trout which we here call the skegger is a large one, almost like a bull trout, and the name is derived from an old word, 'to skug' - to seek cover or shelter; for these trouts are mostly found under the shadow of a bank or projecting rock, and they are by some called alder or alter trouts, in consequence of their haunting the roots of alder-trees, that grow by the side of the stream. Since I have alluded to etymologies, I must go one step farther to notice that 'skug' is most probably derived from the Moeso-Gothic 'Skygda', to shadow or cover; and that the mountain Skiddaw, in Cumberland, probably owes its name to the same source. Skygddha - the dark shadow - is admirably expressive of its character when seen from the foot of Withop, before the sun has illumined its south-western side, and when its dark shade is extended over the vale of Derwent. But what a famous pike you have caught; I have seldom seen such a one taken in this part of the country. What weight is he?

Oliver. Ten pounds three ounces; length from eye to fork, two feet seven inches and three sixteenths, by the exiseman's rod.

Rev. J. T. That is not a Coquet-bred fish; he must have escaped from some pond or loch during the late rains. Pray where did you take him?

Oliver. In the deep pool a little above Brinkburn. I observed him lying at his ease near the surface of the water, and tried him first with a small trout, which he would not look at. I then put on an artificial frog with a double snap, which I had among my baits, and he seized it in a moment. I struck as soon as he turned, and luckily hooked him; and directly that he felt himself pricked, swoop! he was off like a whale. I let him have about forty yards of line, though not too gently, before I attempted to check him. I then was obliged to put my tackle to the test, as he was likely to gain, had I allowed him more line, a rocky part of the stream. When I found that my tackle would hold him, I began to wind him gently back, and had got him, after a good deal of manoeuvring, within twenty yards of the end of the rod, when off he went again. He repeated this three or four times, growing weaker every sweep he took, till at last I got so far master of him as to draw him to the shore, where Burrell landed him with a gaff.

Rev. J. T. But how did you come by the trouts? I was out myself this morning, and only caught half a dozen which were scarcely worth bringing home; and yet I ought to know something of Coquet, and I am persuaded that you could not have more suitable flies, for I always make my own.

Oliver. We began at Piper-haugh, and fished down to Weldon Bridge. At first we had only indifferent success till we tried a fly recommended by our landlord, the red-hackle, and afterwards we had no reason to complain. We got the greatest number between Brinkburn and Weldon. At the commencement I was inclined to blame my friend Burrell for our want of success; for the trout is a sly fish, that appears to be instinctively aware of the danger that awaits him when a scientific angler is in company, and carefully keeps himself out of harm's way.

Burrell. You practical anglers always claim the privilege of laughing at the novice, until he perceives that your pretended mystery is a mere bag of smoke, and becomes as wise as one of yourselves. You have been winding a long reel about that pike, Oliver, but you do not relate the most interesting part of the feat – that the fish at one period of the contest had the better of the angler. I was a short distance up the stream, attending to my own sport, when I heard a loud splash, and on running towards the place, there was this simple fisherman floundering about in the water, holding his rod with both hands, and the pike making off with him, when I luckily dragged him out. In strict justice, the merit of taking the pike belongs to me.

Oliver. I do not deny it. I only wish that you had made a little more haste, and not laughed quite so loudly.

Burrell. Who could help laughing? – And then the hubbub and the loud ha! ha! brought out the miller's wife to see if any of her live stock had fallen into the water; and when she found that it was neither calf nor pig, she sent down – kind, motherly old dame – to offer the poor gentleman who had got such a ducking a change of her husband's clothes. Had you only accepted the offer, you had made me your bondman for ever. I think I see you in the honest miller's corduroy small-clothes, rig-and-furrow stockings, and grey coat, of the cut of the last century, with white metal buttons about the size of a crown piece. Dominie Samson in all his glory!

Oliver. You are really excellent at a sketch, Burrell. You are 'whipping it up' in your own style. Put the bottle about, Mr Bell, and favour us with a song, if you please.

Bell. Willingly – I am too bad a singer to require much inviting. Singers, whether good or bad, should only annoy a company once; either by their obstinacy in refusing to sing, or by their miserable performance. My subject must be about fishing, I suppose; and though my 'Piscatory Eclogues' are neither choice nor numerous, you shall have one such as it is.

THE FISHER'S CALL

The moor-cock is crowing o'er mountain and fell,
And the sun drinks the dew from the blue heather-bell;
Her song of the morning the lark sings on high,
And hark, 'tis the milk-maid-a-carolling by.
Then up, fishers, up to the waters away!
Where the bright trout is leaping in search of his prey.

O what can the joys of the angler excell,
As he follows the stream in its course through the dell!
Where ev'ry wild flower is blooming in pride,
And the blackbird sings sweet, with his mate by his side.
Then up, fishers, up! to the waters away!
Where the bright trout is leaping in search of his prey.

'Tis pleasant to walk at the first blush of morn,
In spring when the blossom is white on the thorn,
By the clear mountain stream that rolls sparkling and free,
O'er crag and through vale, its glad course to the sea.
Then up, fishers up! to the waters away!
Where the bright trout is leaping in search of his prey.

In the pools deep and still, where the yellow trouts lie,
Like the fall of a rose-leaf we'll throw the light fly;
Where the waters flow gently, or rapidly foam.
We'll load well our creels and hie merrily home.
Then up, fishers, up! to the waters away!
Where the bright trout is leaping in search of his prey.

Oliver. Thank you, Mr Bell – a good subject, and a good song. Your toast, if you please.
Bell. All honest anglers.
All. All honest anglers!

from SCENES AND RECOLLECTIONS OF FLY FISHING IN NORTHUMBERLAND, CUMBERLAND AND WESTMORELAND *1834*

PART 7

Sea Angling

THIRD FISHERMAN. *Master, I marvel how the fishes live in the sea.*
FIRST FISHERMAN. *Why, as men do a-land: the great ones eat up the little ones.*

William Shakespeare
PERICLES, *II.i.*

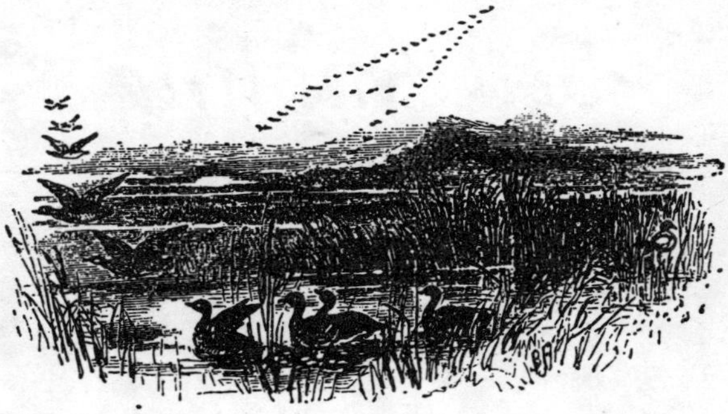

Sea Fishing – 19th Century

STANLEY KNEALE

In Ramsey Bay, where most of my sea-fishing experience was gained, if you want a big day, long-line fishing does it, especially in winter, when the cod is in its prime. You want four or five lines of about eight hundred hooks each, a smart stiff sailing-boat of about twenty-five feet keel, not too high in the gunwale, so that the lines may be taken in more easily, plenty of beam and ballast, and three or four men who know what they are doing; for, at that time of the year, you may see some nasty weather between the start to Bahama Bank (the best cod ground) about seven miles distant, and the return to harbour. As the cod-boats there are not decked, or only partially so, they require very careful handling; in rough seas very often one man steers and three bale. It is marvellous how some of the regular fishermen manage those boats; going out in all kinds of weather, they handle them with a skill which only comes from long experience and knowledge of boats, tides, currents, and winds. They are good companions, can spin long yarns and tell good fish stories, and are always ready to instruct an amateur. There is something very fresh and exhilarating on a bright winter's morning in starting off with a nice breeze, bounding from crest to crest of the short curling waves, everything light and buoyant, dancing in the sunlight, with your lips salt with the showered spray from your boat's rude contact with some large wave.

Arrived at the bank, down comes the sail, and mast too, if there is much sea or ground swell on; and over go the lines, shooting across the tide, and buoyed at the ends. Then comes two or three hours' waiting, which can be filled in by pollack, bream or bass fishing, the tide carrying out a light-leaded line and trace, to which are attached flies, spinning-baits, or, best of all, sand-eels. If the fish are in the humour, and the tide right, which is the most important thing (neap tides are the best), you may have some capital sport with pollack, although they are not quite so large here as in other parts of the bay. The bass and bream are scarcer and more uncertain. Then comes the time for lifting the long lines; cod, skate, flounders, plaice, halibut, red and grey gurnet, congers, dog-fish, and many other kinds coming tumbling into the boat, but, of course, principally cod. Occasionally a halibut or skate bigger than usual requires two or three gaffs to bring him over the side. I have seen halibut five or six feet long brought in by the cod-boats. Buckland mentions one caught in Ramsey Bay as among the biggest captured round the coasts of the British Isles. With two or three hundredweight of fish in the bottom of the boat, the lines neatly coiled in the baskets, off you start home again with the freshening breeze, and generally a good bit of beating, as the prevailing winds are off-shore, westerly or sou'-westerly; and, unless you have a good suit of oils on, you will not have many dry garments by the time you get back to the harbour.

But from a sportsman's point of view, by far the most fascinating fishing is with rod and fly or spinning tackle, for pollack, cod-fish, codling, and occasionally, mackerel. This sport was ably and charmingly described in the first series of *Anglers' Evenings*, in a paper entitled, 'Rod Fishing off the Isle of Man', where the whole art of pollack-fishing is so fully discussed that there remains little to say. The most important thing is to get the right tides, weather, and time. I have always found the flood-tide much the best, the fish coming in with it closer to the rocks, except when the sea is rough. Then, of course, they keep to the deeper water, are more scattered, and have to be fished for with much heavier leads. The best time for pollack-fishing, as for most sea-fishing, is in the early morning about sunrise, or in the evening after sunset; they come nearer to the surface then and rise more readily to the fly. The autumn is the best season, although in some years I have known them to be very plentiful in May and June.

As in any other kind of fishing, the finer the tackle the better the sport. Single salmon gut is quite strong enough for your traces or flycasts; you may lose some flies or spinning tackle now and then (generally in the weed) but in the long run it will repay you. The tackle sold on the spot is made of twisted gut or gimp, and would pull a whale out; as a rule, the tackle used by the boat fishermen is very clumsy, but of course they do not use it with a rod, but simply a hand-line. They very rarely fish for pollack, as it is not a good eating fish and there is no market for it; and they consider you are rather idiotic to waste your time on the 'kelleig', as they call them, when you might be more profitably employed long-lining, bottom-fishing, or mackerel-fishing. Undoubtedly, the heaviest fish are taken by trolling with the sand-eel with a fairly heavy lead, say three or four ounces, so as to sink the spinning sand-eel two or three fathoms below the surface, according to the tides and time of day. The fish always lie nearer the surface in the evening.

On a fine calm night, as you are rowed in and out of the little bays, overshadowed by the great towering rocks looking dark and mysterious against the sunset sky, with the quiet dip of the oars, or a disturbed cormorant slipping into the water from his resting-place or now and then the splash of a fish as he rushes to the surface in pursuit of some small fry, breaking the quietness of the scene – suddenly there is a tug and a splash, followed by the delightful screech of the reel, as away goes a good pollack to his home among the weed. You follow, giving him all the butt you can to prevent his going down – their tendency is generally down; they scarcely ever rush to the surface, as salmon or trout sometimes do when first hooked, but seem to know by instinct that their safety lies in the long dark tangle, in and out of which they endeavour to thread your line. They often take eighty or ninety yards of line off your reel, and you have to follow them with the boat. I remember one day, after a long rush, following up in a boat, winding in as I came along until I got right over my fish with a big strain on all the time, as much as a strong salmon gut would bear; but not an inch would it budge; however, patience hath its reward, and knowing the sulking habits of my friends the pollack, I continued to keep a steady strain on, fearing all the time that he had fastened me in the long brown weed at the bottom. After about ten minutes I felt a slight stir, and he came to the surface quite played out; the gaff quickly transferred a good pollack of fifteen pounds into the boat. It is a fish that caves in very quickly after the first rush or two; very unlike the mackerel, which, for its size, is the hardest fighting fish I know, either in salt or fresh water. But if the fights in pollack-fishing are not very hard or long they are frequent. On a good day you have not to be content with one fish, as in salmon-fishing, but can count them by the dozen. Then there is the delightful pull home – if the evening is chilly you are only too pleased to take a turn at the oars; if not, comfortably settled in the stern, puffing away at your favourite pipe, a goodly array of shimmering fish lying in front of you, and, in the distance, the town and harbour lights guiding you home to a good supper to which you feel you can do full justice, you begin to think there are many less enjoyable sports than pollack-fishing. Of course there is another side to the picture, when, minus fish, a stiff wind offshore and a choppy sea making it rather difficult and dangerous work, you are glad to pull into the friendly shelter of a headland, beach your boat on one of the little gravelled bays, high and dry out of the reach of the tide, and tramp home trying to dry your soaked clothes in the five or six miles between you and a good fire and refreshment for the inner man . . .

The biggest day's sea-fishing, in point of numbers, that I ever had was a fine day in June, a good many summers ago, in Ramsey Bay. L–, who was not a rod-fisherman, but was very keen and always worked hard and successfully with the hand-lines, two cousins, myself and the boatman made up the crew of the *Snaefel*, a small open schooner of about twenty-five feet keel; a very handy fishing-boat, and much more convenient than the larger partly-decked sailing-boats you now get there for hire. She was also a fast boat in her time, and many are the races we have had going or returning from the fishing ground with the lug-sail or cutter-rigged fishing-boats. On this particular afternoon we had not much chance of trying her sailing powers, as it was almost a dead calm. Starting about three, we drifted out to the whiting ground, about a mile from the end of the pier, where the whiting come right into the bay. They are generally very numerous, although perhaps not so large as those caught off Manghold Head, which is about five miles from the habour mouth, and, taking it all round, is much the best ground for whiting and other bottom-fishing. As the tides run strong, and the water is deep, you require heavy leads, about 3 lb, to keep your line on the bottom. This evening we had not wind enough to take us out there, and since it is no joke rowing two or three tons of ballast along, we dropped our anchor in about five fathoms of water so clear that we could see all the fish on the sandy bottom. Whiting, unlike the pollack, are never found on a rocky bottom, and are generally enticed in-shore by the sand-eels or other small fry. To lower the sails and make ready the lines was the work of a very short time. The whiting lines generally used have a cross-bar of whalebone or stiff wire about a foot above the lead, to the ends of which the hooks are attached by a couple of feet of fine water cord. As the hooks and snooding are coarse, we used to put on a large trout hook, say No. 9, and a couple of strands of fairly strong gut, the greater penetrating power of the fine-wired hooks and invisibility of the gut telling a tremendous tale at the end of a day's fishing. Having our supply of fresh sand-eels on board, we cut them up in small pieces and bait our hooks, taking care to leave the point of the hook uncovered; over go the lines, and we begin in real earnest to pull in the fish. They were so thick that we very often had a couple of whiting on before the line reached the bottom. You generally find the bottom with your lead, and fish about a foot or two off, but this evening it did not seem to make much difference where, or how, we fished – up came the lines with two fish on each time, until it really became hard work lowering and drawing in. At last L –, who was very keen on a big catch, noticed that the boys' lines were down twice as long as ours. The fact was that they had got tired of bending over the gunwale pulling fish in, so they let their lines remain on the bottom, knowing that there were sure to be two fish on each line; after that L– kept a sharp eye on them and held them steadily at work. The bay was literally alive with fish that evening; we caught whiting, cod, skate, sand-soles, plaice, mackerel, red and grey gurnet, dog-fish, and even herrings. It is a very rare thing for the latter fish to be taken by line in Ramsey Bay; however, that evening we had about a dozen of them, and finished up by catching a fine lobster on a hook which had got entangled in its claws.

About eleven o'clock, after seven hours' fishing, the bottom of the boat was so thick with fish that it rather hampered our movements, and we thought it time to start for home. Then began the business of counting our spoils, and we found we had six hundred fish of one kind and another. The local paper referred to the catch afterwards as not the charge, but the death of the six hundred. I think it was the record catch by hand-line that season.

But, of course, there are blank days in sea-fishing as well as in river-fishing. There are many agents at work to make the day good or bad – tides, winds, fish moving in shoals over a very extended water, shoals of dog-fish chasing and frightening them out of the usual fishing grounds, and dozens of little things which make sport uncertain. But if you are on the spot and have plenty of fishing time, winter and summer, as was my good fortune some ten or eleven years ago, you are bound to find the right day sometimes and have big catches which you remember, while the blank days are forgotten. Lately, in my brief visits to the island, I never seem to get the big days I used to have, either on the river or on the sea. On the rivers, or rather streams, the trout are getting great epicures, and much more particular about the way the flies are presented to them, as they are more fished for; but on the sea it is harder to account for. I think the only solution is that you are not on the spot at the right time, or it may be that the continual scraping and disturbing of the breeding beds by steam dredgers and other trawlers has something to do with the scarcity of fish. Again, the beating and churning of the sea by the largely increasing number of steamers which pass in and through the bay no doubt scares them to other feeding grounds.

Mackerel-fishing is best in the months of July, August and September. These fish vary very much in size, and round the coasts of the Isle of Man are, as a rule, much smaller than on the south coast of England and Ireland. In Ramsey Bay they are fished for almost entirely by whiffing or railing. One fisherman, sailing and managing his boat and a couple of lines with heavy leads of about 3½lb, often gets thirty to forty dozen of mackerel in a good morning's fishing; but, as you may imagine, it means very hard work, and non-professional anglers are, as a rule, contented with a few dozen. The biggest catch I ever had was twenty-five dozen. This kind of fishing, although very much followed and enjoyed by visitors, to me gets rather monotonous; the slow sailing through the water at about four knots an hour, and the constant heaving and drawing in of the line, with a mackerel or simply your spinning bait at the end, lacks the variety one gets, for instance, in bottom-fishing. The leads also are heavy, and the strain caused by the lines being dragged through the water often makes it difficult to decide whether one has a mackerel on or not, especially with a lumpy sea, when the motion of the boat gives the line sharp jerks very easily mistaken for the tugging of a fish. I have tried numbers of different kinds of spoon and spinning baits, but have found nothing equal to the bait generally used over there – a thin strip of skin cut with a very sharp knife from the under side of the mackerel. It is very bright, and if properly cut and put on the hook three or four dozen fish may be killed without changing the bait.

In pollack-fishing in Ramsey Bay the mistake most people make is in fishing along the rocks. They are of course nearer at hand, and not so far from the harbour if bad weather comes on, and occasionally give some fair sport. But for a good evening's fishing, the weather being favourable, you should go right round the Manghold Head into Port Moar Bay, and fish along the rocks and rocky shores there. It is about seven or eight miles' pull from the harbour. The pollack are much more numerous, and larger. The south of the island is a still better rod-fishing ground, the bottom being principally rocky. A friend of mine, while staying at Port Erin a couple of summers ago, killed from fifty to a hundred pounds of pollack and bloggan each evening, though the weather was not as fine as it might have been. Boating is very dangerous there, on account of the strong tides and currents, wich frequently run five or six knots an hour.

from ANGLERS' EVENINGS *c. 1890*

Sharks from the Shore

JACK SHINE

At the mouth of Kiscannor Bay, on the west coast of Ireland, some five miles from the seaside resort of Lahinch, is Green Island. It is an island only on the top three hours of the tide when the rocks which join it to the mainland are covered. The water is deep and when the tide is out access can be gained to numerous rocks outside the island which drop away straight into six fathoms. There are twenty fathoms of water no more than a quarter of a mile offshore and the bottom is extremely foul. Wrasse are plentiful and there is good fishing for pollack, mackerel, bull huss, conger, tope and porbeagle shark.

The last species is an extraordinary addition, surely, but nevertheless quite true. Porbeagle sharks can, and have been, taken by anglers shore-fishing from this area. Regularly? Well, in July and August of 1963 I had five. The weights in the order of catching were 106 lb, 130 lb, 90 lb, 101 lb and 138 lb. In 1962, a mere novice at this game I had three, 77 lb, 75 lb and 91 lb. I am told that fishing of this kind from the shore is unknown outside Australia and South Africa. Plenty of deep-sea sharks, of course, but definitely not from the shore. My own conviction is that sharks can be taken at other points. A likely place would be where mackerel and sprat shoals frequent fairly deep water offshore. I say sprat shoals because porbeagles feed on them. As an incentive to any angler, prepared to try this very thrilling form of fishing, I relate here some of my own experiences with these powerful fighting fish.

In June, 1962 I had my first experience of a shark from the shore. Whilst spinning some fifty yards out, my mackerel flies (home-made of white goat's hair) were taken with a tremendous bang. After a strong run of forty yards I lost contact and on retrieving I found that only the top fly of a five-fly trace remained. I felt an urge to find out at any cost what manner of fish this was. The only wire traces available were two feet long with 6/0 hooks. On these I had taken tope from time to time. One was quickly baited with a small mackerel slice and cast out about fifty yards with float attached.

Seconds after it had settled on the water it was taken, porpoise fashion, by a porbeagle shark. The tail and dorsal fin could be seen clearly. During the following ten minutes that shark gave some terrific runs. It was in the 120 lb class and on mackerel tackle (13 lb breaking strain line, etc.) hardly any pressure could be applied. Finally close in it bored down and vibrations through the rod told that it was slashing with its tail. The inevitable happened – the tail or rough hide came in contact with the nylon monofilament and the shark was gone.

But what seemed to be a dream up to now, of catching something really big from the shore here, became a very distinct possibility. Hopes soared still higher when it transpired that on that same evening another angler over a quarter of a mile away had lost his mackerel flies to a shark, and on mounting a German Sprat had that taken also. So the shark I had contacted was not an isolated one and there were probably a good number close inshore. With the right equipment I was convinced one could be caught and landed and so I began a shark-fishing expedition, much to the amusement of my fellow anglers.

During the ensuing weeks several more anglers lost mackerel traces to sharks. This was encouraging as sooner or later I felt that one of the species would surely take my mackerel bait, now more properly mounted on a seven-foot wire trace. I didn't hook the first two takers as I did not give them enough time to swallow the bait properly, but at last, on 27 June the first porbeagle was hooked and landed. It weighed only 77 lb but had put up a tremendous fight on 19 lb breaking strain line. On 5 August two more were taken on the same tackle, one of 75 lb and one of 91 lb. I found it interesting to see that the smaller shark, when close in and nearing exhaustion, was followed about by another of its brethren. Immediately after gaffing I cast another bait which was taken at once by the ninety-one-pounder which was probably the other fish I had seen.

My first shark of 1963 was hooked towards the end of May. This one stripped an almost complete four hundred yards of 19 lb b.s. line off the reel before turning. After a forty-five minute battle it was lost because a 90 lb breaking strain wire trace gave way. This was either sawed through by the shark's teeth or cut on underwater rocks. After this I decided that since really big sharks were not only possible but very probable, my tackle required some changes.

The tackle I now used is as follows: a medium-heavy 8 ft solid glass fibre rod, an Alvey side cast reel loaded with 300 yards 32 lb breaking strain nylon monofilament, plus 60 yards backing; a 7 ft 250 lb b.s. cable-laid wire trace with 10/0 hook. The trace is swivelled at the top and joined to a further 7 ft stout courlene line also swivelled at the top. This last is well-nigh essential, as it withstands abrasions from underwater rocks, when sharks bore down as they normally do, especially when close inshore at the end of the struggle. Instead of the courlene line an additional length of cable-laid wire is sometimes used.

For bait I generally use the tail half of a fresh mackerel. This is tied to the hook firmly with white cord. A small float completes the tackle. This is tied on direct to a swivel either 7 ft or 14 ft from the hook. The bait itself provides sufficient weight for casting and the 14 ft overall trace presents no difficulty with the Alvey reel as the bait can be swung out by hand to 60 yards or more. If an offshore wind is blowing I usually tie on a balloon in place of the float. In this way the bait can be floated out long distances.

Porbeagles can also, of course, be taken using artificial spinning baits. Using a large goat's hair fly on spinning tackle I did contact one but lost it after a struggle, as I had only a 3 ft wire trace. Judging by the many mackerel flies lost here to sharks, and from the numerous occasions when sharks can be seen in clear water, close in, actually taking these flies, it is evident they can be taken by spinning methods.

This sort of fishing can surely be done from other centres and to anglers wishing to experiment I offer the following suggestions:

A very high degree of patience and perserverance is required. There are very many blank days and it may be more true to say blank weeks or months. A shark from the shore cannot be compared with one from a boat, and if you use deep sea heavy tackle from the shore you are unlikely ever to have success.

Line capacity is a vital factor from the shore. You will probably make contact fifty yards out and a long run seawards can be expected immediately you have set the hook.

Give the shark plenty of time to take the bait well into its mouth. It will probably set the hook by its own munching action and the risk of the hook being deflected by its many rows of teeth is avoided.

It is essential that the shark be played almost to a standstill. The farther out from shore he fights the better. You will have, inshore, numerous underwater ledges, and, maybe, obstructions on both sides of you. Should the shark come in here in its full or near-full strength you can expect trouble.

Carry at least one really strong gaff, and do not underestimate a porbeagle's weight. It may be only 5 ft in length, but many have a girth of over 3 ft and weigh over 100 lb.

Finally, a porbeagle shark is edible. Indeed its steaks are a rare delicacy. All that is required is that it should be bled, and the best way is by lancing its gills.

from ANGLING *February 1964*

Conger Fishing – Before 1914

F. V. MURMANN

I have fished a conger, both by day and night, and I have caught much bigger fish in deep water during the daytime than ever I have caught at night. For instance, at Valentia, in 1911, I landed a conger of 43 lb from somewhere near the coastguard patch, and my wife, fishing at Deal in November, 1913, hooked and landed a fish just over 40 lb in weight in the middle of the day.

During August, 1912 I had a night's fishing off Kirk Michael, Isle of Man, during which I landed many congers, but nothing exceeding 25 lb in weight. Unless I am mistaken, Mr Harrison caught his record conger in May, 1914 [62 lb] during daylight fishing on the coastguard patch at Valentia.

In July, 1911 the coastguard officer at Valentia, who accompanied a party of us to Port Magee, at the southern end of Valentia Island, about two o'clock in the afternoon on a very bright day, hooked and brought to the side of the boat one of the largest congers I have ever seen. Unfortunately, owing to the anxiety of the boatman to get this fish on board, he, in his eagerness, took a wild dab at it with the gaff, which severed the line, and we lost fish, gaff, and the whole bag of tricks, excepting the rod.

I might say that this particular day's fishing was one of the most exciting of my experience. We had arranged with the Port Magee people for a boat, and some men, to take us out at that end of the island, and we left the Royal Hotel, Valentia, between nine and ten in the morning, looking forward to a good day's sport.

The party consisted of Dr Marrett and a friend, Chief Officer Blundell, Mike, a very useful and obliging boatman, attached to the Royal Hotel, Valentia, and myself. It will be remembered that the summer of 1911 was particularly hot, and this particular Thursday morning in July I should imagine was one of the hottest. However, that has nothing to do with the subject beyond the fact that the Port Magee fishermen had not used their boats to any great extent that summer, and they had been left high and dry on the beach, with the natural result of 'gaping seams'. There were not a great number of suitable boats at Port Magee on this occasion, but we chose what was considered to be the most serviceable, to the best of my recollection a 30-foot whaler which perhaps was in better condition than the rest, which isn't saying a great deal. We got our gear and provisions on board and having embarked ourselves we started out with four of the Magee men, and the fisherman Mike, the latter rowing stroke. Apparently, there was a competitive spirit between the Valentia man, Mike, and the other men from Magee, as the former set a very good pace, which was maintained for the four or five miles along the channel to the fishing-ground.

We had not gone more than a quarter of a mile before we discovered what we were in for, as the bottom of our boat very much resembled a sieve, and all spare hands were kept busy baling to keep the water down. During the excitement of fishing, the water gained, as the balers were more interested in the size of the fish than in keeping the leak down, the result being that we were at times well over feet and ankles in a mixture of sea water and blood, which was anything but pleasant.

I remember that the journey out to the fishing-ground was also somewhat exciting, on account of half-submerged rocks, upon which we nearly found ourselves on more than one occasion. Owing to a late start, it would be somewhere about one o'clock before we reached the sea entrance to the Magee channel. We had taken an old fellow with us who apparently knew all about the marks, and we anchored at the spot indicated by him, but with no great success. Leaving that, we pottered about to one or two other places, finally dropping anchor off a ridge of rocks running for some distance from the land – a sort of a natural breakwater. Keeping at a respectable distance from these rocks, the fishing was excellent, for with the exception of halibut we caught pretty nearly every kind of sea fish. We had some very decent congers, but, as mentioned above, we lost our best. There is an old saying amongst fishermen that 'the best fish is never landed'; and this conger of Mr Blundell's – who by the way was fishing for the first time with a rod – was really a fine specimen.

I had good opportunity of seeing this monster close to the boat; it had a fine broad head and good shoulders, tapering down gradually to the middle and tail as a conger should do, and I should say was about six feet in length, perhaps a little more. I was sorry that this fish was not brought on board, as it was a real novice's catch, and most of us know that beginners have encouraging luck.

All who have fished for conger are aware that immediately it is taken out of the water the sea eel is fairly quiet and remains so for some little while, until it gets a second wind, and then the fun begins. One of the first good-sized conger I caught was at Deal in 1909 or 1910, the latter year, I think. I was out with William Stanton; we had caught a few small conger, never much over 15 lb or 16 lb when I managed to get hold of one somewhere about 27 lb in weight; she was placed into the bottom of the boat, and remained quiet until another small conger was dropped on top of her; this apparently enlivened her, and for quite five minutes the larger conger took charge. Wriggling and twisting she came for both of us at once, with her jaws wide open, a fearsome subject. Bill Stanton got to work with a thole pin whilst I went for the fish with the gaff. We did eventually quieten it, and then hobbled the little beggar with a hook in her jaw and a length of line tied up in the bows of the boat . . .

My first experience of all-night fishing for conger was some years ago in the Isle of Man; a party of four of us, consisting of a doctor from Leeds, another friend from Blackburn, a local gentleman, and Mr William Cubbon, left the harbour about half past seven one evening. It was not a long sail, perhaps five or six miles, but in those pre-daylight-saving times we had to get away early in order to pick our marks whilst there was sufficient light. We made for a spot off the Point of Ayre Lighthouse and anchored just as it was getting dusk.

Fishing was rather quiet to begin with, but we gradually got amongst the big ones. I believe there was some sort of a sweepstake amongst us for the biggest fish, which was won by the local gentleman with a conger of 40 lb. Whilst we were fishing, the weather, which at first was fair, began to freshen up and the water became very lively . . .

I have always found the conger eel a very dainty feeder, taking no bait unless absolutely fresh; there have been times at Deal, when, for some reason or other, fresh bait was not procurable on setting out in the morning, and we were, perforce, obliged to use 'yesterday's left over', but without any success beyond a dogfish or two. Sometimes we were able to obtain, whilst at sea, fresh caught herring and sprat from inshore fishermen returning home with their catch, and as soon as this was used fishing was good.

I remember other occasions, in the Isle of Man and at Valentia, when the absence of fresh bait completely stopped our fishing.

There is one instance that comes to my memory which occurred in the Isle of Man – we had been fishing all day at Kirk Michael – perhaps a fifteen-mile sail from Ramsey, where we were staying.

We had caught plenty of mackerel on going out, and we had, as we thought, a sufficient supply to last six of us throughout the day, our intention, of course, being to return with daylight. However, we had scarcely picked up our moorings and anchored when a fog settled down, which continued with us throughout that day and the better part of the night. By about six in the evening the bait was exhausted, and one of our company, presumably in a fit of absent-mindedness, suggested to the boatman that 'we might as well take up the anchor and make for home'. The fisherman's reply was very much to the point: 'Yes, sir,' said he, 'if you will just whistle for some wind we will get home as quickly as possible.' We remained there all night, and a slight breeze coming up about three in the morning we started for home, but only landed at Ramsey just in time to get to the hotel for lunch.

That was my second all-night's fishing in the course of three days, and I was so tired that I went to sleep over my dinner that evening . . .

When fishing for conger I use a wire trace with no more than two fairly large hooks attached. I do not think that my home-made trace is any different from the accepted pattern.

I use a nickel-plated piano wire in three lengths, each joined to the other by a swivel; the hooks being also swivelled.

The lead runs free on the line, and I usually use some form of what I think is known as the Clement's boom, as I consider this method of attaching the lead enables the bite of the fish to be felt with more certainty.

from a paper read to The British Sea Angling Society and published in its QUARTERLY JOURNAL *March 1921*

Bass over Splaugh Rock

DES BRENNAN

It was a wonderful July morning, bright, warm and sunny with the lightest of sea airs as I waited for Clive Gammon to disembark from the Fishguard steamer at Rosslare. We had arranged a week's bass fishing together on the Dingle Peninsula and we were both eagerly looking forward to it. As we packed the fishing gear into the back of my old 'Commer' I could feel the heat burning through my shirt and I thought, 'what a lovely morning for the Splaugh'. I had but to mention it to Clive and we both set off looking for a boat.

We found John Ferguson with his boat already in the water waiting for two anglers who had engaged him for 9 am. John is a great character, an angler himself who knows every inch of the famous Splaugh grounds. He explained that he was already booked but if his clients were agreeable we could come along as the other boats were already out. As chance would have it one of the anglers turned out to be my dentist who was on holiday with his family, and in less time than it takes to tell we were all abroad and heading for the Splaugh.

Ten minutes later we rounded Greenore Point and our eyes anxiously scanned the horizon for signs of fowl working over the shoals. Not a gull in sight. 'There they are,' said John, 'at the southern end of the Splaugh'. Our eyes were not as keen as his for five minutes passed before we were able to spot them. Yes, they were there all right. Thousands of them like flakes of snow fluttering against the sky. Another quarter of an hour's motoring against the strong tide that flows over the shoal grounds that is the Splaugh Rock brought us abreast of the gulls. Getting uptide of them John cut the outboard motor so as not to disturb the shoal and we drifted slowly down on them.

As we drifted we saw an indescribable sight. The calm surface of the sea was, over a large area, thrashed to foam by literally thousands of bass ravaging the shoals of small fry. The confusion was added to by hordes of gulls, terns, gannets, guillemots and razorbills all joining in the slaughter and filling the air with their shrieks. One after another we cast and four German Sprats (the favourite local lure) hit the water in quick succession. The fish were so thick that it seemed impossible not to foul-hook them, yet the first retrieve was fruitless. We cast again and again into the shoal but there was no great 'take' on. Time after time as we reeled in our lures half a dozen or more bass would follow them in until they saw the boat and then they would shear away without taking.

Soon we drifted out of the shoal and as John brought the boat back uptide of them I changed my lure, putting up a Lemax spoon while Clive tried a Toby. We both had fish on the next pass. Stubborn, hard running, fighting fish that took us all our time to land, but soon they were safely in the bottom of the boat, scattering tiny fry all over the boards, so glutted were they with fish. My friend was also in a fish and by the time it was brought to gaff we had drifted out of the bass.

As we looked around us we saw fowl working all over the Splaugh, so John decided it would be best to anchor in the run of fish and let the tide bring them to us instead of chasing after each shoal. As shoal after shoal passed within casting distance a lively little private competition developed between Clive and myself with John exhorting us to greater efforts. Two to one, four all, seven-six – with fortune changing with each cast and never more than one fish between the two rods.

Soon all count was lost as both of us were suffering from aching wrists and arms from our efforts to bring the surging, fighting bass to the gaff. Riding to an anchor as we were the bass could make full use of the tide. On the light spinning gear and 10 lb b.s. line each fish was a real battle, and we were never sure of him until he was in the boat. This was bass fishing at its exciting best.

My friends had brought their two young sons with them and they were kept busy unhooking the fish for us. As I tired I could no longer resist the wish in the younger's eyes and after casting out my spoon I handed the rod over to him for the retrieve. There was a sudden snatch at the line, the rod arched over and line screamed off the reel. The next ten minutes were hectic as I coached the boy in fighting the bass. I was more nervous than he was. It was his first fish and it was important that he should not lose it. Soon it was alongside. One swift, sure stroke of the gaff and it was in the boat.

The look on the lad's face gave me more satisfaction than half a dozen fish on my own rod. He turned round, handed me the rod and said, 'Throw it out again, please.' And while the fishing lasted that's just what I did, and I have seldom enjoyed myself more. Suddenly it was over. The tide had turned and both fish and fowl vanished as if by magic. The four hours since we left Rosslare Harbour had simply flown and for the first time since we started fishing we had leisure to enjoy a cigarette.

When we got ashore we sorted out the catch. Our share came to twenty-six gleaming beauties averaging a little over 5 lb each. Our best fish was 7½ lb. It was, as Clive said, a great start to our week's holiday.

from ANGLING *June 1963*

The Heaviest Rod-caught Fish

HAROLD W. McCORMICK

Neither the Basking shark nor the Whale shark is a game fish, but their sheer enormousness attracts fishermen interested in landing something larger than anyone else has ever landed.

Hooking into a Whale shark is not a guarantee of a thrilling ride or several hours of a mighty tug-of-war. The Whale shark's inertia is often as massive as its bulk. For some reason, however, stories of exciting Whale shark encounters have a way of becoming more widely told than the dull ones.

Zane Grey, for instance, once hooked a Whale shark off the tip of the peninsula of Lower California. He snagged its tail with a gaff hook. Grey later vividly described how the Whale shark tried for five hours to fight off capture, towing Grey's boat for miles. Finally, it plunged into the depths, running off some 1,600 feet of line before it tore out the hook. During the chase, or rather, the tow, harpoons were hurled at the shark. Grey said they bounded off the shark's thick hide or bent under the pressure exerted by harpooners trying to thrust them into the shark.

Writing about effortless captures of Whale sharks and their 'entirely inoffensive . . . sluggish' habits, E. W. Gudger, the outstanding authority on the Whale shark, dryly remarked, 'Mr Grey's fish seemingly was the most active of any of which we have accounts.'

It must be said for Zane Grey, however, that he did go after real fighting sharks. And he probably did more to establish the shark as a game fish than any other angler. Like the four-minute mile and the seven-foot high-jump, the 1,000-pound shark stood for years as a seemingly unattainable goal for game fishermen. Gradually, as tackle and fishing techniques improved, the records went higher and higher: 800 pounds . . . 900 pounds. Then, on 11 March, 1936, a 996½-pound Tiger shark was caught off Australia. The record stood but a month, for Zane Grey had arrived in Australia determined to land a 1,000-pound shark. He got one – a 1,036-pound Tiger shark.

Since then, the records have been tumbling regularly, especially in Australian waters. One Australian shark fisherman extraordinary, Alf

Dean, has caught the four largest fish ever taken on rod and reel – each a Great White* and each weighing more than a ton.

Dean, a genial, burly man who runs a small vineyard when he isn't shark-fishing, caught his first shark in 1939. It weighed 868 pounds. In the years that followed, Dean's prowess as a shark-fisher increased, and so did the weight of his sharks. His fishing ground had been the Great Australian Bight, that huge, crescent-shaped curve along the southern coast of the continent. Great schools of fish sweep through the Bight, and, savagely competing for food among them, are innumerable sharks, including some of the largest found in any sea on earth.

In 1951, Sir Willoughby Norrie, governor of South Australia, caught a 2,225-pound Great White shark, at that time the largest fish ever landed with rod and reel. Dean was determined to beat Norrie's record, and, in 1952, he did.

Dean's encounter with his first record shark began at two o'clock one morning when his hired boat was riding at anchor in the Bight after a futile, all-day search for sharks big enough for Dean's taste. A banging on the hull of the boat awakened him; he rolled out of his bunk with a flashlight, went on deck, and in the flashlight's beam caught the dorsal and tail fins of the biggest shark he had ever seen. The shark was violently nuzzling the boat, intoxicated by the scent of whale oil dripping from a tank in the stern. (Using the whale oil, and an occasional bucketful of steer's blood, Dean lays down an alluring, provocative slick that sharks pick up miles away. They trail his boat, ravenous for food promised by the savory scent of the wake.)

All night long the great shark banged noisily against the side of Dean's boat. The maddening scent of food so excited the shark that once it grappled the propellor and shook the boat, as if to awaken the occupants to get the meal it yearned for. Soon after dawn, Dean dropped his line off the stern, and the shark took it, racing off 250 yards. The shark writhed and rolled. Once it leaped almost fully out of the water. But, by fighting on the surface instead of sounding, the shark soon tired. It was all over in about forty-five minutes. The shark, a Great White, weighed 2,333 pounds and was sixteen feet long. The world's record belonged to Alf Dean! Less than a year later, he topped his own record by landing a 2,372-pound Great White.

On 10 April, 1955 Dean caught a 1,600-pound shark, lashed it to the side of the boat, and went off looking for something more worth

*Great White shark – *Carcharodon carcharias (Linn.)* – known also as White Shark, Man-eating Shark, White Pointer, White Death. Ed.

while. Suddenly, a huge shark began to attack the captured 1,600-pounder. Oblivious to Dean, who clouted it with the handle of a gaff, it kept ripping big chunks out of the dead shark. Finally, the mate aboard the boat threw a set of baited hooks to it. The shark lunged for the line, but somehow managed to hook itself in the tail. Dean fought to land the shark, tail-hooked or not. It was impossible. He cut the line. Again, a set of hooks was cast out, and the shark grabbed for the bait, this time hooking itself in the mouth. Dean struggled for half an hour to set the hooks. They tore out, and the shark disappeared.

The boat had gone about a mile from the spot where the shark first struck. Dean decided to head back to the spot and anchor. As soon as the boat anchored, the same shark – the cut line still hooked in its tail – reappeared. Dean tried again, and this time, after a fight for an hour and a half, he landed the persistent shark. It weighed 2,536 pounds. Dean had once more broken his own record.

Dean broke the world record a fourth time, in 1959, when he landed a 2,664-pounder. But Dean's biggest fish, like the biggest fish of all fishermen, was the one that got away.

In Australia they call Alf Dean's biggest fish Barnacle Lil, for she is a female and she has broken the heart of many a shark fisherman. Dean met her one moonlight night in the Bight when she banged his boat and broke off a seal carcass, a *pièce de résistance*. Dean often hangs over the stern of his boat to lure sharks that follow his piquant wake. He got a look at her as she lingered near the surface a few yards from the boat, munching on the seal. He looked her over avidly and estimated her measurements: more than twenty feet long and at least 4,000 pounds.

He lowered a new seal lure over the side. Near it he dropped his line with his favourite shark bait, seal liver, skewered on two great hooks. Barnacle Lil charged for the hooks, the lure, the liver – everything, including part of the boat's transom. Through the spray churned up by her explosive lunge, Dean could see that she had the hooks in her mouth. He put his reel in gear and set the hooks. Time after time, she fought the hooks by rocketing to the surface, lifting her huge, graceful white body nearly out of the sea. Then she settled down, pitting her 4,000 pounds of controlled fury against Dean's straining arms and ever-taut line. For two solid hours she fought. Then, slowly, foot by foot, turn by turn, he began reeling her in.

He got her to the side of the boat. A crewman reached his gloved hands down to the wire leader attached to the end of the line. (Under game fishing rules, in order to claim a record, the fisherman cannot be aided until he brings his fish to gaff. At that time, another person can grasp the leader, but not the line. During a fight, no part of the fishing tackle may be touched by anyone except the fisherman.) But Barnacle Lil was not through. She suddenly found new strength and whirled seaward again, tearing the leader out of the boatman's hands. 'Twenty men could not have held it,' Dean later reported.

Dean's hands were turning to mush. Blisters erupted and broke on his palms. His fingers, chafed raw by the constantly bobbing rod, were stiff with pain. His legs were knotted with cramps. The aching muscles in his back and arms seemed ready to burst. And the fight went on. One hour . . . Two hours . . . Three times Dean brought the shark to the boat. Three times the glistening leader cleared the water, and three times Barnacle Lil dashed out to sea with new strength!

As the fight went into its fifth hour, Dean was seized by a new torment, stomach cramps. Still in the bolted-down tractor seat he used for his fishing chair and still fighting the shark, he relieved the cramps somewhat by urinating in a can, a feat he never could figure out how he performed.

After five and a half hours, Dean knew he could hold out no longer. But some tremor in the line, some mysterious signal he felt almost intuitively, told him that Barnacle Lil was tiring. Once more, with aching hands, he began to reel in. He got her to the boat, and the boatman began pulling up the leader. About ten feet of the thirty-foot leader were in the boat when Barnacle Lil made her last, wild try for freedom. She dived, straight down. The leader, snagged on the boat's pipe railing, followed the shark down, and, in a flash, tore out seven feet of railing, then snapped. The indomitable Barnacle Lil was free.

Several big-game fishermen had sighted and pursued her before Dean had his frustrating affair with her; others have since given chase, but she has not yet been vanquished.

from SHADOWS IN THE SEA *1963*

The Haven

CLIVE GAMMON

It is more than that, of course, this drowned river valley that merges with the estuary of the two Cleddaus miles from where it meets the Atlantic at St Ann's Head. At its mouth there are wide, shallow beaches protected from the destroying force of the seas outside, so that they harbour a fantastic wealth of small marine life. There are tiny covers cut out of the soft Old Red Sandstone, dark with bladder-wrack and surrounded by low, fern-covered cliffs. There is the deep course of the channel, where the tide races at eight knots on the big springs. There are the harbours of Milford and Pembroke Dock and the Pembroke River, and farther up still the maze of creeks and sub-creeks that cut into the hinterland of the county. At Llangwm, miles from the open sea, herrings shoal, and the bass and mullet travel almost to Haverfordwest, where in the thirteenth century, merchant ships brought wine from Spain and took back grain and butter to Bristol.

The birds and fish are a strange mixture, true sea-birds and estuary birds, deep-water fish and estuary fish. I have seen gannets far up the Haven where the mudflats are dense with curlews, and sea-trout, mullet, and bass are in company with skate and ling and conger.

What follows is, perhaps, discursive, with many digressions. In that respect, it is like the Haven itself.

In 1865 HMS *Warrior* was the mightiest ship in the world. She was ironclad, the first of her kind, though she fired her broadside through gun-ports as Nelson's ships had done. In spite of fears that she would sink immediately upon launching, on the grounds that iron did not float, she steamed and sailed for years as a notable ornament to the British Battle Fleet until she became obsolete without having fired a purposeful shot, except in salute. But she remains in service, as part of the command of the Queen's Harbour Master in Milford Haven, a sheer hulk, anchored for ever in the deep water channel above Pembroke Ferry, used as a jetty to which naval craft tie up to be fuelled from the Admiralty storage tanks on the hill above. She has little superstructure now, and her decks are a maze of piping that carries the oil. Huge anchors hold her, and wooden constructions, catamarans and dolphins, connect her with the shore. Two years ago she was towed down to Milford for cleaning, but it seems unlikely now that she will ever move again.

The tides in the Haven are very fierce, reaching six or seven knots at times. One current is channelled into the fifty yards between the *Warrior* and the shore, and at certain times of the year this patch of water is the scene of immense activity by thousands of bass who trap shoals of brit between ship and shore and in the intricacies of the wooden construction. This usually happens at the time of the big September tides especially if the water has been warmed by strong sun. Numbers of brit are marooned on the woodwork when they fling themselves from the water to escape the predatory bass, and the angler who is lucky enough to be there at the right moment has no need of any other bait. He simply hooks one on and flicks it out, with no lead on his trace, into the ruck of feeding fish. There is no doubt, as they say, of success. The bass are as easy to catch as summer mackerel, and huge bags can be taken.

The fishing is done from the woodwork itself and one needs Admiralty permission to be on board. The Navy is notably more generous of permission than the Army is under similar circumstances, but they insist, with some reason, that there be no smoking. This can be extraordinarily trying when the fishing is good, and indeed when the fishing is slack. But it is worth putting up with for there cannot be very many places where you can catch more than a hundred bass on a single tide, as John Lindenbergh has done. My best bag didn't come near this, but I have had more than fifty once or twice. This is, of course, nothing to boast about because the fishing was easy, and it must sound rather slaughterous. In extenuation I had better say then firstly that all the fish I caught were eaten; and secondly that I am now strong-minded enough to have abandoned the practice. I do not think it would have been possible to do this until I had experienced a *Warrior* bass carnival, and I am sure that no bass fisherman could resist the temptation to do it at least once, considering the meagre rewards he has to accept usually.

There is, in fact, a more precise and enjoyable alternative. On normal tides, there are usually some bass present, or at least passing through. Then it is possible to catch them on a small Swedish artificial spinner, casting into the channel from the shore. The method has a lot to recommend it. The kind of light fixed spool outfit that could be used for sea-trout, five- or six-pound breaking strain line with no lead attached, is all that is necessary. The bass can be seen swirling on the surface as they move through with the current so that it is possible to cast to an individual fish, and with the weedy anchor chains and the woodwork a constant hazard, the fight is likely to be very even.

This does not convey the special atmosphere of bass-fishing at the *Warrior*, I suppose. Immediately behind one's back is a precipitous, heavily wooded slope, reaching so close to the sea that at high water on a strong spring tide it is impossible to cast overhead from the shore because of the beech boughs that overhang. There is never very much light, and the rocks, blackened shale and red sandstone, are thickly covered with dark bladder-wrack. On the other side the hulk itself shuts out the light, and the dipping anchor chains add to the claustrophobic effect. There is no tide-noise either, so that the sudden plash of a feeding bass behind the catamaran can be nerve-shattering.

Such a context seems more suited to conger, and there are undoubtedly great conger in the deep hole beneath the *Warrior*. Fish up to seventy pounds have been *landed*, with no prejudice to the even mightier fish that have broken away, as they are bound to do in such difficult circumstances. (It is almost impossible to prevent a big conger going downtide and under the woodwork, even though he may have been pumped up from amongst the rocks in the first place, a thing not easy to achieve.) Fifty pounds is of course an extraordinary size for so close inshore, and it was probably a fish in this category that provided the basis of the local legend of Billy Brooks and the Mighty Conger of Hazelbeach (it always assumes capitals in my mind). Billy was fishing from a dinghy at the time, it is said, and the conger took his bait near the *Warrior*. The ebb was flowing at its fastest, and he had to up-anchor and follow his fish down tide. By the time darkness fell he had been towed as far as Hazelbeach, almost as far as Milford, and he saw its head break the surface, 'as big as a seal's, it was'. It is no discredit to Billy that he took the Roman way out, and cut the line. I must confess that I did not have this story at first hand but by way of those assiduous chroniclers of huge bass, vast skate and extraordinary mullet, John Lindenbergh and Roy Haggar. Conger do not appeal very much to my own fishing temperament, for multiple reasons, but I can understand the fascination they exert on some sea-fishermen. They are obviously very powerful fighters, although so dour that the battle tends to resolve itself into a tug-of-war. I suppose they have a certain beauty of strength and evil, but they are not beautiful to me, although they do not repel me in the way that skate and dogfish do.

Skate are not very commonly taken at the *Warrior* on rod and line, though they are often harpooned by workmen on board as they swim very slowly with the tide just below the surface. Dogfish are an ever-present nuisance though, and this seems a good opportunity for me to give way to one of my more strongly-held prejudices and denounce them here. I should not have thought it necessary, if it were not for the fact that a few months ago I was astonished to read in the angling press of a man who had allowed himself to be proclaimed Dogfish King of some South Coast resort or other, and appeared holding one of the creatures in a photograph. It seemed that he fully intended to catch it and was anxious to catch more. Only once have I intentionally fished for them, and that was to provide specimens for the zoology department of a school where they were needed for dissection. If the Dogfish King had such an excuse, he did not give it. Dogfish are so indiscriminating that they will continue to chase a bait and seize it after they have been hooked on it once and have kicked free – even while the line is being retrieved for re-baiting, I mean. Dogfish put up no perceptible fight, to the extent that on some occasions I am not sure whether the unresisting weight I am winching to the surface belongs to one of them, or a spider crab, or a clump of bladder-wrack. I hate the way they writhe about when they are landed. I hate their dry, horribly unfish-like skins and the harsh rubbing sounds that their squirmings produce. Above all I hate their evil, winking eyelids. No fish should have eyelids.

I am firmly prejudiced in favour of fish looking like fish. For that reason I do not care much for skates and rays, monkfish, angler fish, gurnard, john dories, sunfish, and hammer-headed shark. Conversely I love bass, mackerel, pollack and tope for being streamlined and beautiful, as well as certain of the other sharks like the blue and the thresher. I have never been quite sure about cod, and I confess to being inconsistent over true flatfish of which I approve even though they are undeniably odd-looking. They are cool, wet, healthy looking, and familiar, and though I do not fish for them specially as a rule, I am always pleased when I catch one by accident. A plaice fresh from the sea, especially a big one, is undeniably a handsome fish. The bigger flats – brill, turbot, and halibut – are worthy opponents, particularly the last-named. I have an unfulfilled ambition to catch a halibut on rod and line. They are not commonly encountered in British waters, except off the south-west coast of Ireland and possibly off Scotland. Not long ago I saw a film that portrayed the voyage of a fishing-boat from Aberdeen that set long lines for halibut in the Arctic Circle. They baited the hooks with frozen herring and the sight of those great, brown, formidable predatory flatfish being hauled over the sea haunted me for days.

There are no halibut at the *Warrior*, so far as I know, but there are a great variety of species. The commonest fish there are small pollack that provide excellent training for newcomers to sea-fishing, and these can be caught in great numbers by using 'the feathers', a trace armed with as many as fifteen feathered lures. This tackle is not particularly to be recommended, and I feel that its legitimate use is confined to catching bait and giving encouragement to novice sea-anglers, since by using it they are able to catch numbers of small fish, which gives them confidence. Its real abuse is amongst shoals of mackerel and school bass, but more of that later. Herrings sometimes shoal at the *Warrior*, and it is unfortunate that the tide race is so fast that fishing for them with delicate float-tackle is impossible. They, too, will take the feathers, even though the hooks are large and herrings are regarded in some quarters as plankton feeders who are unlikely to take even a tiny bait.

Fishing with the bait on the bottom is a hazardous business because of the weedy rocks, but if the risk is taken there are large pouting and ballan wrasse, and in the winter whiting, and sometimes cod. Right through the year very big bass feed around the *Warrior*, but there cannot be very many more difficult places in which to play a big fish, and a drop net is essential for the last stages. More often than not, the angler, who did not expect to encounter anything so large, loses all sense in the last stages and tries to haul the fish up on to the catamaran by the line. A break is then quite inevitable. Even experienced anglers are prone to this kind of mental blackout. A month ago Lindenbergh hooked a bass and played it until it was quite beaten. It was clearly a fish of ten or twelve pounds, but he was alone and there was no one to climb down with the gaff. There was not really very much he could have done, I suppose, except wait until someone *did* arrive, and there was no certainty that anyone would. He tried to lift it out, of course. The *Warrior* is one of the few places where it is possible to fish the deep, main channel of the Haven. Except at slack water, the tide is too fast for a small dinghy to be anchored and the kind of fishing platform that the *Warrior* provides is essential. Many creeks branch off the Haven, though, and these can be easily fished from the shore. At low water they are often no more than tiny trickles running between high mud banks where there are lugworm and crab for bait. (Locally they are called *lakes*, not out of perversity, since the term recurs in south-west Ireland and is plainly cognate with Anglo-Saxon *lacu*, running water. It is there again in Frainslake and Swanlake, two beaches that have tiny freshwater streams running over the sand.) As soon as the tide comes nosing in a few inches deep, bass arrive, tiny school bass as a rule that steal the bait and give the rod-top the kind of ferocious jerk that one learns to recognise after a while, but not until the idea that one has successively missed several ten-pounders is dispelled by hooking one of the basslings.

Better fish arrive later, and have the disconcerting habit of running towards the shore when they pick up the bait, so that the line, instead of tightening and giving warning, falls slack. Lindenbergh once had an eight-pounder that took him like this. He started to reel in, thinking that the current had shifted his lead, and was pulled on to his knees as the bass changed direction. In a way, he was lucky to hook it. Usually a sharp strike is necessary to set the hooks and one cannot really afford to put the rod down in a rest.

This tends to be a counsel of perfection, I suppose, especially when there has not been a bite for a long time and concentration starts to wane. I remember an Easter Monday when there was a black wind that froze my hands so much that I could not hold the rod any longer. It blew so hard that it was impossible to keep the line tight, and in the end I gave in and put my rod down on the rocks that ran down to the high-water mark. Devan was with me and we huddled down in the scanty shelter that there was. It would have been more logical to go home, I suppose, but we didn't. After a very long time I saw a disturbance amongst the marginal wrack that the tide was lapping, fifty yards perhaps, upstream. It was a bass of two or three pounds, apparently hopelessly entangled in the weed, head down and tail up, thrashing about a good deal. In the natural order of things, bass do not allow this to happen to them, for if they did there would soon be very few bass. It then occurred to me to try and get it in the landing-net, since it was within easy range, but an ill-judged prod provided all the stimulus it needed to bury itself much deeper in the weed, out of sight and out of reach. I was thinking about the letter I would send to the *Angling Times* about this foolish and ill-adjusted fish as I began to reel my line in, but instead of it coming from somewhere in midstream it was coming downstream. And then everything stuck. I suddenly realised that somewhere in the middle of bushels of shoreweed was that bass *with my hook aboard*, seventy or eighty yards away from where I had cast in the first place. I did not land it, of course, and I did not deserve to. Like any ditter, I had thrown out and left my bait to fish for itself, and I can only urge that the weather was truly terrible.

I must explain 'ditter', since the term first came into use in the neighbourhood of the *Warrior*. Devan and I once saw a man fishing from the stern of a dinghy using what appeared to be a roach-rod with a pike float set about eighteen inches above the hook. We could not see what he was using as bait, but since it was being whirled along the surface at something like six knots and the depth there was not much short of eight fathoms, it hardly mattered. When it had travelled thirty yards or so, he retrieved it, then sent it on its course again. 'What's he trying to do, Devan?' I said, and, without taking thought, he replied 'He's ditting for wrasse!' Since then the term has broadened out in meaning; early on Bernard Venables suggested that it should imply he-who-goes-fishing-in-shiny-black-shoes, and indeed, this is within its scope. However, its general application is to those fishermen who will never learn anything and who fish in such a way as to frustrate the man who has mastered at least the basic principles of his art. They are common on piers, where they tend to cast over at least two of their neighbours' lines each time they try. The ditter on the beach is notorious for using heavy cutty-hunk line that produces so much tide resistance that it is swept inshore, laterally, of course, and tangles with every other line in its path. Ditters are not to be confused with beginners, who are forgiven their trespasses. Indeed they sometimes boast of having fished for forty years or more. They are a sub-branch of the genus that never gives signals in traffic. Members of the freshwater fishing branch are called 'neddies', a term that originated in Hampshire.

But ditters are rarely to be found on the muddy shores of the Haven creeks since they nearly always prefer to fish within a hundred yards of a car park or bus stop. Few men fish the creeks, in fact, for the going is hard and often treacherous. Lindenbergh once came very near his end one hot summer's day when he was collecting lugworm. He knew the mudbanks well, but the strong sunlight and the constant bending to bring out the worms must have combined to put him in a fainting fit. He fell face down on the mud, but by good fortune Devan was only a few yards away and was able to prevent him suffocating. I have a horror of the mud myself, and I prefer to dig bait the hard way, with a fork in the sand. I don't mind fishing over it from the shore, but I hate going into it.

Very often, on calm evenings in the summer, the creeks are full of mullet that swim near the surface and create oily, V-shaped ripples. Some are quite enormous but they seem to be impossible to catch on rod and line. Travelling mullet like these ignore all baits, though when they find their way into one of the tidal mill ponds, they seem to change their habits and will sometimes take a ragworm quite freely especially when they have remained in the pool for some time. But only fish of up to three or four pounds seem to take up residence in this way, and the monsters drop back with the tide. The biggest mullet I have ever seen were in the Docks at Milford, but unfortunately, no fishing is allowed there. It is possible that a policy of massive ground-baiting, if it were continued over several days, might hold the travellers in one place long enough for them to be conditioned into taking a bait, but I have never tried to do this. The best time for mullet

– August and September – is also the best time for bass and tope and other fish, and I have never been sufficiently single-minded to drop everything and concentrate on them for the fortnight or more that might be necessary.

The mullet leave in October, but there are bass in the creeks the whole year round, although the winter and spring fish tend to be small. However, they fill the gap in the year's cycle of sea-fishing in South Pembrokeshire, for between January and April there is a slack period on the coast when few fish come in, though there are sporadic visitations of codling and whiting. Very occasionally a big bass is taken in this springtime pause, and in each case that I have heard of, the fish has apparently just spawned and is in poor, lank condition, another mysterious and unsatisfactory piece of evidence in the difficult business of deciding where and when bass spawn.

Bass and mullet travel up the Haven to the extreme limit of the tidal water, up to Haverfordwest on one branch of the Cleddau, and to Blackpool Mill on the other, where inexperienced sea-trout fishermen have spent fruitless hours casting a fly over shoals of the latter. Even such deep water species as skate find their way up at least as far as Garran Pill, which is miles above the Haven entrance at St Ann's Head. The Pill itself is undoubtedly one of the most frustrating places I have ever fished. Never have I seen so many fish moving as I saw there one Sunday morning, and I have never fished with less result. Many of the fish were sea-trout, and throughout the morning salmon leapt. The majority were mullet, and I expected nothing of them, but there were bass as well that were just as indifferent.

from A TIDE OF FISH *1962*

The Sport that Died

ERIC HORSFALL TURNER

On 27 August, 1930 Big Game fishing was born off the coasts of Britain. Mr L. Mitchell Henry caught a tunny of 560 lb on rod and line, about fifty miles into the North Sea from Scarborough. The news was headline stuff. Big Game fishing had come to Britain. No more looking at films of Zane Grey doing the job at £70,000 an expedition – go and do it yourself, off Scarborough.

In 1932, Colonel E. T. (now Sir Edward) Peel caught a North Sea tunny weighing 798 lb. This broke Zane Grey's world record for tunny, made off Nova Scotia with a fish of 758 lb. In 1933, Mr Mitchell Henry caught a tunny of 851 lb, which still remains the biggest fish taken from the North Sea.

Tunny fishing became 'fashionable' in August and September. The tunny fleet of expensive cruisers was a picturesque sight in Scarborough Bay. A diversity of the anglers they contained caught well over a hundred tunny in the years before war broke out. One angler even caught two tunny on the same trace!

The war ended. In 1949, seventeen anglers caught forty-seven tunny between them. One or two anglers went out in the succeeding years to 1955; and caught a few fish. Since 1955, not a single tunny angler has put out from Scarborough.

Why this sudden and spectacular flash in the angling pan of Britain?

News that the North Sea contained tunny is popularly supposed to have come from a local zoologist, who based his 1928 deductions on fishermen's stories of 'big fish that cruised about the herring nets during the haul'. But the presence of tunny in the North Sea was known before that. In 1923, Captain D. K. Wolfe Murray, FZS, made considerable investigations. Later, he wrote a paper for a French scientific journal. Writing of the Continental trawler fleet he said: 'Every trawler has an escort of fish (tunny) varying in numbers . . . during 1923 I frequently counted as many as thirty fish swimming alongside.'

There are various species of tunny. These were the big Blue Fin, *Thunnus thynnus*, of the Atlantic, averaging about 600 lb apiece in weight. They were of the mackerel breed, as fine fighters as any fish in the world – and 600 lb of bone and muscle to fight with! There is no record of other types of tunny in the North Sea: nor have any of the Blue Fins been caught, or even seen, south of a line roughly drawn from Flamborough Head to Denmark. Why did they come down the North Sea? Some said they followed the mackerel; others that they followed the herring shoals. The Lowestoft sea research staff think that water temperature, or salinity, are the more likely influences. The fact is that nobody knows – and until anglers want to catch them again, nobody but the biologists will have much urge to find out.

Anglers' news of tunny soon reached the Continental fishermen: but at that time there was no market. Anglers had the shoals to themselves. The flesh of the Blue Fin is not very tasty. But the flesh of the smaller Yellow Fin of the Mediterranean is tasty, as many an *hors d'oeuvres* gourmet knows. The Italians found out how to put tunny in tins so that the contents came out firm, and not in an oily mess; then they found how to mix the flesh of the big Blue Fin with that of the little Yellow Fin and make the combined product appetizing. The Continental fishermen found their market. By 1950, the price they got was equal to 1s a 1 lb gross weight – £30 for a 600 lb fish. The Danes, in particular, kitted up and went for tunny. Four or five floats, with baited hooks on steel traces, were put over the side. On deck lay boxes of herrings or small fish. When the electric fish-detection apparatus showed the tunny below, the crew shovelled over a few small fish to bring them to the surface and round the baited hooks. When a float dipped, an electric current was passed down the steel trace. The great stunned fish was hoisted on deck, gutted and slid below into the ice.

In 1953 we invited one of the Danish skippers aboard our keelboat, chartered for a week's tunny fishing. Over the bottled beer, he said that he was catching 120 to 140 tunny a year in this way. He was only one of many. At a rough guess, 3,000 to 4,000 tunny were being taken every year from the seas around the Dogger. The trawlers' escorts of tunny vanished. By 1955, the British herring crews rarely saw a tunny, where they had seen many in the days before the war. Even in those days, it was hard enough, and pretty expensive, for anglers to find tunny. By 1955, the game was up for the angler.

There was talk, for a time, of international control. It ended like all such talk – in whispers, then silence. Just as the nylon nets are bidding fair, today, to exterminate the salmon of British waters with a devastating, thoughtless rush of commercial frenzy – so the fishermen of the Continent stripped the North Sea of its tunny.

from ANGLING *October 1961*

Conger, Tope and Bass

TREVOR HOUSBY

The best-ever inshore boat fishing trip I can remember was off Brook ledges on the Isle of Wight. The ground in this area is made up of peaks and ledges fissured by deep, narrow cracks – ideal territory for a multitude of conger. July and August tends to be the time to fish

Brook, and a rising tide with no moon provides the perfect conditions. Under these circumstances air and water temperatures are high and the local conger go on a feeding spree that is hard to match. These conditions have given me many good nights on Brook, but one stands out from all the rest.

Reaching Brook at 9 pm, with just about an hour to go before dark, we stopped short of the extensive ledges to feather two boxes of bait mackerel. It seemed enough at the time but later I wished we had thought to catch more. With plenty of light to pick out shore marks we set the anchor in about 40 ft (12 m) of water. The echo sounder showed we were in a gully surrounded by walls of vertical rock. Brook ledges are swept by heavy tides. Even neap tides can be strong here, and so we had brought along several buckets of assorted leads. As always the end tackle consisted of a simple running leger and 100 lb (45 kg) breaking strain wire trace. Long-liners' nylon is now used in preference to the rather stiff wire, but at that time it was not readily available. End-tackle losses were expected to be high and the six anglers aboard had made up enough traces to last the night.

On arriving at slack water we had chopped up a dozen prime mackerel and dropped them over the side. By twilight we were all baited up and ready to go, expecting to catch conger and bull huss. Brook is one of those areas that often produce a few surprises. The trip was an 'invitational', all the anglers having been chosen for their ability. One of our top rods was Carlo, an Italian long-time resident in Britain. It was going to be his night, although at that time none of us knew it. As darkness increased I had a strong pull of a bite which turned out to be a 16 lb (7.3 kg) bull huss. Two more of similar size were soon boated but as yet there was no sign of the conger.

Twenty, thirty, forty minutes passed with nothing else to show for our efforts. Suddenly, my rod was almost ripped put of my hands by something that tore off down-tide at high speed. Five minutes later it was still fighting hard. A tope, I thought, yet that seemed unlikely for I had never caught or heard of a tope being caught at night or from such a rugged piece of ground. A tope it was, however, and a big one. It was not weighed but was estimated to be around 40 lb (18.1 kg) before being released. Shortly after, the conger came on the feed. Not just the odd fish, but waves of them. At times it seemed that everyone on the boat was into a fish at the same time. In fact, I stopped fishing and became gaffman. As each conger was swung inboard I cut the trace and dropped the eel into a plastic dustbin, for conger slime can turn an already wet deck into a skating rink. The dustbins kept both the decks clean and the eels quiet.

By 1 am I was onto the last and fifth dustbin and still the eels kept coming. Most were on the big side, stocky fish in the 25–30 lb (11.3–13.6 kg) class with the odd 40-pounder (18.1 kg) thrown in. It is amazing how many eels a dustbin can hold. They pack themselves in nose to tail and never move again. By my estimate we had close to 1,000 lb (454 kg) of eels in the boat and the fishing was still hot. Carlo, who had been doing better than most, suddenly let out a grunt. When I reached him his rod was doubled over as somewhere below us a very big eel fought a vicious battle for its freedom. Suddenly it started to swim up and as its head broke surface I struck with the gaff and heaved it inboard.

It went berserk, tore off the gaff and fell writhing and slapping against the dustbins. So great was its strength, it sent the dustbins flying, dumping a mass of live eels on the deck. One minute I was operating on a clean and tidy boat, the next I seemed to be up to my knees in angry, slimy eels. No sooner did I get a dustbin half full of eels than it was knocked over again. Finally, I had to use a special forked eel knife to chop through the spine of each eel.

Last back into the bin was Carlo's monster. It was clearly over 50 lb (22.6 kg) and I was anxious to see it weighed. With the decks clear, all hands got to work with brush and deck hose. Once it was safe to walk about we swung the big eel up on the scales where it swung the pointer to 58 lb (26.3 kg). Everyone was anxious to start again, but it was only an hour until dawn and as it turned out the conger had just about finished feeding. We got a couple more before Carlo was suddenly back in action. At first the fish fought hard: a dashing, different sort of battle that kept us guessing. But in the end the strong conger tackle wore it down and as it surfaced I was amazed to see a 12½ lb (5.7 kg) bass on the line. How a normally finicky fish like a big bass came to pick up half a mackerel on 100 lb (45 kg) trace wire I shall never know. But it did and I could see that Carlo was delighted. What a night! More conger than we could have imagined plus a tope and a monster bass.

from SUCCESSFUL SEA ANGLING *1990*

Flounder Fishing as an Art

WILLIAM CAINE

In an ANGLER AT LARGE *Caine describes how, after failing to catch sea-trout, he was diverted by watching a small boy spear flounders. He and his friend were intrigued enough to try their hand, but decided to develop purer sporting methods of flat-fishing.*

To the true purist all things are pure. In every angler, however, the purist lurks. In one he is predominant, in another he is subordinate to the hunter. When I see a trout, for instance, a beast of prey rises within me. I want to catch, not to fish. But when I see a bull-head, the lust of slaughter is less fierce – I cannot say why – and I am ready to be an artist for art's sake. The fact is I have not the skill to be a purist in trout-fishing, and I know that there are many anglers who are in a like situation.

Let it be understood that I do not address the purist of the chalk-stream. That which follows is intended for those whose purity is equal only to the strain attendant upon the pursuit of flat-fish (*Pleuronectes Flesus*). Necessity is the mother of purism. The trout-fisher, having no worms, imagines the artificial fly. The flounder-fisher, having no spear, imagines a landing net. To catch a flounder in a landing net is not as easy as it sounds. To begin with, your flounder is a very fearful and crafty fish. He is so fearful that he has made himself exactly like the sand and weed on which he lives. It is therefore very difficult to find him, unless one has exceptional eyesight. He is so crafty that when you disturb him by treading about in the water he flits imperceptibly to a new spot, where a single shiver of his body – a feat of *leger-de-corps* in which he has no equal – he covers himself with sand. His little horrid eyes alone remain visible, and these he fastens upon you with a cold stare, full of malevolence.

The first step in puristic flounder-fishing must now be taken, the hypnotism of the quarry. The practitioner will fix his eyes on those of the flounder, and will approach him cautiously from behind. On reaching the flounder he will lower his landing-net until it is upright in the water, touching bottom a few inches in front of the flounder's nose. This manoeuvre can be executed only if the angler maintains the hypnotic gaze. If his eye wavers for an instant the flounder will see the descent of the landing-net and dart away. All being ready, the purist will advance the right foot and tread heavily on the tail of the flounder.

The flounder will then dash into the landing-net. This is the crude form of the sport.

MacAlister and I soon tired of such simple work, and began to refine it. We allowed the puristic part of our natures full play. We raised flounder-fishing to the dignity of what it is – an art. First of all we ruled out all spears, baits, and hooks. Then we made a law that no flounder should be touched except on clean sand. This was necessary, because MacAlister had shown symptoms of wishing to take his hands to them among the weed. The man who would guddle *Flesus* would be capable of any infamy. Thirdly, we decided that any fish which should bolt into the net before he should actually be trodden on, should be considered 'foul started' and return to the water. We fixed a size limit – a two-and-threepenny French fire-proof frying-pan. Then we made any but round-mouthed landing nets unlawful and impure. A V-shaped net, owing to the large space of sand which it straddles when inverted, gives the quarry little or no chance. We agreed that any fish which should evade the net once should be let alone, for after he has been driven from place to place for some time a flounder loses heart, and allows himself to be taken with ridiculous ease. Even a good sportsman will respect a gallant and skilful antagonist, and rejoice in his escape: but as purists we are actuated by a still higher principle. With the purist it is first time or not at all. The proper exercise of his skill is to him of such moment that one bungle disqualifies him in his own eyes from proceeding further in the matter.

from ANGLER AT LARGE *1911*

Broadbill Swordfish

ZANE GREY

Morning came, still, soft, rosy, balmy, colorful. Larks, up with the break of day, poured forth their perfect melodies. The grass was heavy with dew. Mullet and garfish were breaking the surface of the still water near the beach. Wide circles waved away and disappeared.

Beyond the bay the ocean, placid and smooth, resembled a mill pond. There was, however, a long low scarcely perceptible swell, which my watchful eyes detected. We ran out to the rocks for bait, and caught half a dozen kahawai in as many minutes. I saw a huge kingfish, so the boatman called it. He came up and lunged for a kahawai on the trolling line, making a sousing splash at the boat. If he was not a regular old yellowtail, belonging to the family *seriola*, then I missed my classification. The boatmen call this species kingfish; but kingfish belong to the mackerel family, and there was no mackerel about this fish. He looked to weigh close to a hundred, and made me keen to catch one.

Outside of Cape Brett we found the sea one vast, glassy expanse. What a day to hunt for broadbill swordfish! I had not seen a better day in all my swordfishing at Catalina. Moreover, the air was pleasant, the shore line strikingly clear. I did not expect to see a broadbill swordfish, but I certainly could not help looking for one on such a sea as that. Birds were scarce. There was no sign of small fish on the surface. We ran out several miles, and all the while I perched on the deck, scanning the sea near and far. All at once I saw fins. I called out and stood up. We thought the fins belonged to a Marlin. Then we saw two more fish farther on, and formed the same conclusion about them. Suddenly the one nearest came up higher, showing his dorsal fin. I stared. I could not believe my eyes. Surely that brown-hooked rakish leathery dorsal could not belong to a broadbill swordfish, one of my old gladiator friends way down here in the Antipodes! But it did.

'Broadbill!' I yelled in wild excitement. 'Look! . . . *Three broadbills*!'

Leaping for my tackle, I called for Arlidge to run around in front of the nearest fish. 'Careful!' I warned. 'Not too close!' At that he got close enough to scare a Catalina broadbill out of a year's growth, but the consequence was not so dire here. Williams threw a hook baited with an eight-pound kahawai hooked through the back. I deplored that, but it was too late. I let out a hundred feet of line. The swordfish came on at my left, not quite an equal distance away. We glided ahead of him, and I dragged the bait fairly close to his path. Suddenly he saw it. He dove. I waited tensely. Indeed, the others on board were tense, too. Nothing happened. I thought he had passed us by. Then he swirled up, showing half his bronze body, huge, glistening. I thrilled all over. He had lunged for the bait. I knew he would hit it, and so I called out. Did he hit it? Well, he nearly knocked the rod out of my hands. How that peculiar switching up of the line made me tremble! No other fish in the sea can give a line that motion.

The swordfish struck again, again, and the fourth time. It was great. I could scarcely realize the truth. Then he took the bait and made off slowly at first, then increasing his speed until he was going fast and my line was whizzing off the reel. When we had half of it off, two hundred and fifty yards, I shut down on the drag, and as R.C. would say, 'handed it to him'.

In a moment more I new I was hooked to a real old *Xiphias gladius*. He came up and showed his enormous shoulders, his high dorsal and half of his tail. Then he sounded.

The fight began, and, as I wanted to excite these boatmen who had scarcely ever heard of a broadbill, I performed rather violently and strenuously, which soon told upon me. I got out of breath and slacked up, until the fish ran out the line. He went down deep, which was disappointing as I wanted him to do some surface stunts. He never showed again. In half an hour I was wet with sweat and thoroughly warmed up. I fought him hard. Long before the hour passed I knew I had on a very heavy swordfish. I could not do much with him, though sometimes it appeared I had the mastery. At the hour-and-three-quarters mark I shut down on the drag and let him pull. Here I found to my surprise that he could tow the boat. It was not a small boat, either. That, I knew, would be hard on him; and thereafter, when I needed a rest, I let him drag us a bit. Three-quarters of an hour of this sort of thing wore him out to the extent that I was soon getting line back and daring to hope for the best. He was so enormously heavy that I could not lift him more than a foot or so at each pump of the rod. He had been down a thousand feet. All this fight had taken place with the fish at a great depth, which was new in my experience. But every broadbill teaches you something new. Finally I was lifting this swordfish, beginning to feel assured that I might get him, when the hook began to rip. I felt it rip – rip – and come out! I reeled in the long line without saying a word. The boatman felt the loss even more keenly than I.

from TALES OF THE ANGLER'S ELDORADO, NEW ZEALAND *1926*

Thrashing the Herring

DAVID NUTTALL

To my certain knowledge Spring deliberately thrash through herring to stun them, then turn to feed on the cripples. I don't think that the Coho thrash a school of herring. They do feed in among them and they will herd them and circle them and they will follow behind another Coho to pick up what he leaves, but they don't thrash or barge the herring.

The Spring, on the other hand, barges his way through the school then circles to pick off those that are stunned. Sometimes a Coho, because of its aggressiveness, will reach the stunned herring before the Spring does, but it's the Spring that does the thrashing, not the Coho. This might explain why the Spring 'take' is so delicate and careful as opposed to the Coho's frantic pulling at the bait.

To see a Spring salmon thrash a school of herring is a rare, awe-inspiring, sight, seldom seen but once seen, never forgotten. It will awaken in you the realization that these magnificent fish really have to work hard for their feed.

The Spring will sometimes hit a single herring with the object of stunning it so that he can return to eat it. Moochers often experience a single hit on their line and then moments later the Spring will mooch the bait. If your hooks are sharp enough you will sometimes catch the Spring when he hits your single herring.

When thrashing a school, the Spring starts from the bottom of the school driving up and whipping his body as a man would whip a handsaw. His rush ends when he bursts through the school at which time he circles and sinks to pick up those he has killed, stunned or otherwise maimed. His mouth is shut tight for this thrashing with no thought of grabbing a herring on the way through the school. I have observed this thrashing clearly on two occasions, both early in the spring; the salmon were clearly recognizeable as large Springs, both because of their huge size and because there just weren't any Coho that big around. On the second occasion when I observed the thrashing, I set my two rods, one at thirty feet and the other at forty-five feet. There were four big Springs that I could see thrashing and I was so excited that my fingers were trembling. Something bumped my herring hard, really hard, then nothing. Quickly I stripped off six feet of line, leaving the rod in the holder, trying to simulate a stunned herring dropping to the bottom. Sure enough, my line went completely slack but not until a good long minute and a half had passed after the initial bump. So much time had elapsed that I was actually reaching for the rod to strip off another ten feet or so when he took. Moochers are continually amazed at how long it can take for a Spring to finally take a bait. I grabbed my rod, set my feet and reeled as fast as possible; he was there for a split second but before he could be struck, he let go. The herring was badly slashed on both sides where it had been pulled from his mouth. I threw it back over to lower it to forty-five feet again but before it reached that depth the line again went slack. This time the frantic reeling paid off; the rod bent double and I hit him, driving in both sets of hooks, as it proved later. The salmon was plainly visible to me at the moment the hooks were set; he had paused in his upward journey to shake his head, trying to free it of the weight of the sinker or perhaps because my reeling had taken the weight of the sinker away from him as my line caught up to the sinker so that he thought he was free. The moment my hooks set he raced the last few feet to the surface and scooted along the surface at top speed, his dorsal showing. He seemed to be still trying to outrun the weight as I gave him absolutely slack line without even my ratchet on to see what he would do. He weighed an even seventeen pounds.

from MOOCHING: THE SALMON FISHERMAN'S BIBLE *1980*

The Young Expert

TARA ROBINSON

All right, all you fisherpersons. I hear that most of you have read my first booklet and think that you know as much as me. But you are wrong. I have learned a lot since I did my first booklet. I've been to Seattle, Port Angeles, Neah Bay, Sekiu, Ucluelet, Tofino, Barkley Sound, Alberni, Nanaimo, Campbell River, as well as lots of little spots along the way. I even went to Fanny Bay. I am now eleven and I learned a lot in my travels. Also, my Dad invented a lot of new lures. My biggest fish last year was a 41½ pound (19 kilograms) Spring salmon.

This new book includes some of the details from my first booklet but I've added more big fish lures and stories. Besides my Dad's lures, it covers Tomic Plugs, Hot Spots, Riptide lures, Reef Raider lures and Buzz Bomb lures. I've also put in a small section on motor mooching strip and cut plug.

I hope that by reading this book you will be catching lots of big fish like I do. The hardest fish to catch is the salmon so most of the book will deal with salmon fishing.

Once you know all about catching salmon in salt water you can use this information to catch all types of large fish.

I have lots of fishing experience and I'm going to share a lot of my stories and secrets with you. I may also tell a couple of funny stories.

If you are reading this book in a store and are not going to buy it, put it down right now. The sales clerk is watching you.

Over the past four years Dad has put on a lot of fish shows and I always go. When we do a fish show we bring along a big frozen salmon and my job is fish-keeper. I have to keep it iced and make sure nobody steals it. Last year we showed a 54¼ pounder (25 kilograms) which was caught by Mr Carmen Angus of Sooke. He caught it at Otter Point on June 11. At these shows I meet a lot of interesting fisherpersons and many share their secrets with my Dad and I. I am always learning new fishing methods and plan to shortly put out a large book on modern salmon fishing. It will cover all the methods for catching the five Pacific salmon of North America.

Dad had my 41½ pound (19 kilogram) salmon from last year smoked and canned. I think it wasn't fair because my Dad caught a 41½ pounder in 1981 and he got his mounted. I'm going to catch a bigger one this year and show him what's what about salmon fishing. I hope it's a 60-pounder (27 kilograms).

from HOW TO CATCH REALLY BIG FISH *1983*

PART 8

Trout, Salmon and Grayling

Glory be to God for dappled things –
For skies of couple-colour as a brindled cow;
For rose-moles all in stipples upon trout that swim.
Gerard Manley Hopkins

Salmon Through the Looking Glass

ARTHUR OGLESBY

Shortly after eight o'clock on the evening of 18 June, 1966, a 46½ lb salmon took my bait in the Upper Bolstad pool of Norway's river Vossa. After a quite fantastic forty-minute struggle, during which the fish took me down the violent rapids into the fjord below, it came to the gaff.

I strolled back to the superb anglers' lodge with my host, Odd Haraldsen. He is a salmon-angler of great competence and experience; and our chat was about various points which showed during the play of the fish. But behind this discussion I had the feeling in my mind, 'That was the fish of my life. Now I shall be content for ever . . .'

In a day or so my reactions had changed completely. During the three weeks before the catch, eight salmon of over 50 lb had been taken from the same beat. One of them was over 60 lb. Why should a 46½ lb fish, in these circumstances, be the fish of a lifetime? I am still on the right side of forty-five; and if the good Lord spares my bones for another twenty years, must I spend those years with the thought that I *have* caught my largest salmon? Thomas Jefferson once said: 'The dreams of the future are more likeable than the history of the past; and for all the merit of thrilling memories of the past, a man is finished if he accepts them as an end-all'. It is more than likely that I shall never catch another salmon of such dimensions. But should that fish be accepted casually as the fish of a lifetime?

I think not.

E. R. Hewitt said he proposed to write of the three ages of the fisherman:

When he wants to catch all the fish he can;

When he strives to catch the largest fish;

When he studies to catch the most difficult fish he can find, requiring the greatest skill and most refined tackle, caring more for the sport than the fish.

I accept this philosophy to a large extent; and I certainly accept it in trout fishing. In trout fishing the largest trout is often the most difficult to catch. But there can be no denial of the fact. I have yet to meet the angler who is so blasé about being in Hewitt's third category that he does not stick his chest out a little when, instead of getting the most difficult fish, he gets the biggest.

In many cases the capture of large fish is a matter of accident. Unless the angler can see his quarry, as in dry-fly fishing for trout, or has knowledge of the whereabouts of a whopper, he is just as likely to get a small one as he is to get a big one. I am not talking of the techniques used by specimen hunters of coarse fish. They often bait up pools and swims deliberately, and then fish with baits which are too large for the small fish to take. But in most types of fishing the taking of a really big fish is very much of a lottery; and this is particularly applicable to salmon fishing. On reflection, my 46½ lb salmon, taken from a beat that had given anglers eight fish of over 50 lb during the three weeks prior to my catch, was little more than a mediocre performance.

There are requirements in such affairs, of course. The angler must fish correctly, with the type of bait, lure or fly that he has chosen. Only the hard, and often bitter, school of experience will teach him the finer points in the game, and how to make the best choice in these things. But once he is aware of these requirements and puts them into practice, it is ninety per cent luck whether he ties into a big one – or into just another salmon.

There are no specimen hunters in the specialized sense, so far as I know, in the ranks of salmon anglers. If there are any, they will not be taken very seriously by those who really know the game. In most instances the angler is quite content to catch a salmon; and it is only when it is safely knocked on the head that he worries about the weight. If the river is reputed to hold a good head of 30 lb fish, a 20 lb fish is just another salmon; but if the angler caught the same 20 lb salmon on say, Tweed in February or March, he would be envied by all anglers on the river. Don't be fooled, however, into thinking such a catch would make him a better angler. He would have been *lucky*: nothing more.

Fishing methods have great relevance in these things. They can have considerable influence on the angler's sense of satisfaction with his catch. On at least one river I fish, it is almost impossible to catch a salmon on fly. I have caught the odd one with fly at times; and after taking a 5 lb or 6 lb fish in this way, I have felt a distinct air of superiority over the successful wormers and prawners with their 20 lb fellows from the same water, in the same conditions. But is it the method – or the fish? For me, the fish always predominate – but with definite reservations. It might be well to consider these reservations and their development.

Frankly, I dislike prawning and worming for salmon; but not from any stupid, sophisticated arguments that such methods are not 'the done thing'. I dislike the messy business of putting the damned baits on the hook; damaging them on rocks, or the bottom; and having to bait up again frequently within five minutes. This dislike originated, no doubt, from practice of the cleanest and possibly the easiest way to fish for salmon: fly on the greased line. The fly is small and easily presented; the line floats; and the thrill of hooking and playing a salmon on such tackle is the greatest I know.

When we consider the intermediate methods between these extremes, there is the sunk fly, and the spinning or wobbling artificial bait. Dyed-in-the-wool greased liners will cringe, I have no doubt, at any suggestion that such methods have merit; but in many ways, with great respect, the angler who uses the sunk fly or active lure has to think in a sort of third dimension – with method adjusted to thought. A veritable novice can catch the odd salmon with modern spinning tackle; but to be consistently successful with this method there is a much broader canvas to be covered than is the case with fly on the greased line. In the case of the fly on greased line, the salmon must rise deliberately and take the fly; and this reaction is entirely at the volition of the fish itself. In fishing the sunk fly and the spinner, there is some element of luck in whether the fly or lure hits the salmon on the nose, so to speak, and causes it to take – when in fact it is not really a 'taking' fish. Fly on the greased line, for this reason alone, must retain a primary place among methods – and perhaps rightly so.

Until I began fishing the Lune, some three or four years ago, I had been content to catch salmon by any sporting method I could devise: spinning, prawning, worming – anything: just to catch salmon. Those days were successful enough in terms of fish caught. I recall several occasions when I came home with between five and eight fish. Slowly, this approach began to pall a little; and since I began to fish some lovely fly pools on the Lune, my approach has changed from predominant interest in sheer numbers of fish caught, to interest in fewer fish caught by a more satisfying method.

There are many times, of course, when the fly on greased line is useless: early spring; late autumn; water at low temperatures, dirty, or with prevalent acidity. These factors have a very positive influence on the inclination of salmon to take the high-swimming fly of the angler. In such circumstances, with me, it must still be the fish. If other methods pay the greatest dividends, regardless of their comparative lack of interest, other methods it must be. I see no rhyme or reason for plodding along with what is regarded as the 'done thing' when my experience tells me that such a method is useless on the day. If it has to be the Toby, or a big Black and Gold Devon – on they go. Let us set about getting fish!

Samuel Johnson commented that our brightest blazes of gladness are commonly kindled by unexpected sparks. The big salmon of the Vossa was something in the nature of such a spark. When I began to fish the river, I desperately wanted to catch one of its monsters with fly. I have yet to catch a salmon of 20 lb with fly on the greased line. But greased line was out of the question: hot sun; a river fed with the melting snows of the great mountains, inland; low water temperature; and bank-top water level. Even the sunk fly was almost certainly a waste of time. I gave it a trial with a heavy line and brass tube-fly; but I was well aware that the method was not getting the lure anywhere near the deep-lying fish. I turned to a big copper spoon, with additional lead weighting to get it down. The method resulted in the hooking of one fish, but it got off minutes afterwards.

By the evening of our first day, the ghillie was urging me to turn to the prawn. Who was I to argue? If it meant the hooking of one of their big fish, and the ghillie went through the messy business of mounting the blessed thing on the tackle, why not? Better a big fish by any methods than no fish at all.

The rest you know already. The fish took the prawn; fought as valiantly as a combination of any two fish I have ever taken; and gave me forty minutes of great excitement. It was exactly twice the weight of the biggest salmon I have taken from British waters; and very much heavier than two fish of 27 lb and 31 lb I had previously taken from Norwegian rivers. The former of those, incidentally, was taken from the upper beats of the Vossa when I fished it some years before; and the latter from the superb Jolstra, near Forde. But where was the real achievement? As I have said, eight fish of over 50 lb had been taken from the beat during the short open period of the season before I fished it. It may be of interest to add that during that short period, eighty-seven salmon had been taken from the six-rod beat; of which thirty-nine were over 30 lb, eighteen over 40 lb, and one of the eight over 50 lb was over 60 lb. We are back to my opening point. Should this fish of mine have been accepted casually as the fish of a lifetime?

The truth is that the challenge still remains; and remains in a much more complex form than mere ambition to take a bigger salmon. The challenge is there, for instance, to take a 20 lb salmon on fly with the greased line; then, perhaps, a 30 lb fish with the same method; then, again, a 40 lb fish with spinner; and, if life and opportunity give the chance, a fish of the same weight on the fly. Ultimately, the challenge is to achieve what Richard Waddington described as his lifetime ambition when he hooked a 51 lb fish on a salmon fly of his own design, and beached it without assistance on the bank of the Norwegian Aaro river.

Goethe was undoubtedly right: the best thing we get from history is the enthusiasm it rouses.

from ANGLERS' ANNUAL *1967*

The Evening Rise

JOHN WALLER HILLS

The jealous Trout, that low did lie,
Rose at a wel-dissembled Flie.
Sir Henry Wotton 1651

from 'On a Banck as I sate Fishing'

Some time after mid-May the evening rise starts, and lasts till the end of the season. There is a great difference between different rivers. On the Test and Itchen you do not get it before May is well on its way, and the same on the Hertford and Dorset streams: on Driffield Beck not till June. On the Kennet, on the other hand, you get it from earliest times. I have known it in April, and on cold nights, too. But it is nowhere in full swing until June, and one part of it, the sedge rise, till July. It is an unsatisfactory thing, this evening rise. You get fish, certainly, but you seldom get as many as you feel you ought. And the mind is weighted with an unpleasant apprehension of finality. Daylight has a definite end which nothing can prolong. A morning rise, starting at eleven, may last an hour or it may last five. It has the charm of uncertainty and of hope. But an evening rise has fixed limit. There is no scope for imagination or fortune, and the pleasures of fishing are mental. The trout, too, during an evening rise are always difficult and often exasperating.

But before discussing that, it is necessary to analyse the rise in rather more detail. When the hay has been cut, and wet places are golden with mimulus, and the pomp of high summer is reigning, there are three evening rises. The first begins some time between six and seven (ordinary, not summer time) and lasts till shorty before sunset. This I call the casual rise. The second starts after the last edge of the sun has sunk below the actual horizon and ends when it is too dark to see a small artificial on the water. This is the small fly rise. The third rise then opens and runs for something under half an hour, rarely longer. This is the sedge rise. The casual rise may begin any time after six. Trout move languidly, often taking spinners, but sometimes indecipherable insects. They are difficult, because at no time in the twenty-four hours are they so readily put down. A cast which would past muster in the stillest noon sends them off like a shot. I suppose this is due to the slanting light. And it is not easy to see what they are taking. Altogether they are a high test of skill. But they can be caught. Try them with the prevailing spinner, or a fancy fly such as the pheasant tail. A blue upright sometimes kills.

The small fly rise has a very different appearance indeed. If it be a good one, trout rise not languidly but eagerly, sometimes madly. And it starts with all the unexpected suddenness of the morning rises of early May. I recollect particularly 25 July, 1918. I was strolling up the bank on a quiet, warm evening. A stile had to be crossed, and I remember stopping a minute or so before crossing it and watching the aquamarine sky and its reflection in the opal water. The stile lay a little back, behind a bushy willow, which shut out the water. Before crossing, not a ring was to be seen: when I had crossed, and cleared the willow, the surface was boiling. The movement had started as though on the stroke of a clock. And often this sudden beginning will come immediately after the last rim of the sun has disappeared.

During the casual rise fish are usually taking spinners, if spinners there be. On warm, still evenings, when the female fly can get back to the river to lay her eggs, there will be spinners. But if it be cold, and particularly if it be windy, the females are driven away, and none of them fall as spinners. Smuts, too, are often on the water at this time, or you may have a hatch of small sedges. If so you will find that trout take the artificial very well. During the small fly rise, trout may want either duns or spinners, or occasionally nymphs. It is often very difficult to see whether they are rising or bulging; or, if they are rising, what they are rising at. During the casual rise, too, the fish, though picksome and hard to please, are not particular about pattern: but during the small fly rise they settle down to one article and refuse everything else. Your fly must be exactly right, or you get nothing till dark. During the casual rise fish are often unapproachable; during the small fly rise they are easy to approach and hard to put down, but hard to catch. You no longer need crawl or kneel, you can stand up. As the dusk deepens, you can get nearer and nearer. Your hook can be a size or two bigger, your gut thicker: though, if you take my advice, you will never, even for mayfly or sedge, use stronger than finest natural, for on that you can kill the biggest trout that swims. But in spite of the advantage of ease of access, larger flies and heavier gut, trout are harder to get: harder than they are in the heat of noon, with 4x points and 000 hooks. They are hard because they take only one kind of food and because they demand a higher standard of imitation. You must copy what they are eating and you must copy it in a way they like.

As I look back over many evening rises, I get the impression of more failures than successes. Not absolute failures, perhaps, but relative; one brings away the sense of not having done as well as one ought. Fish rise so confidently and so often: there are so many: you do not put them down, for they go on rising: but though they are taking winged fly, you they will not take. Rivers differ greatly in the ease with which fish are caught in the evening, and so do different parts of the same river. The Test is easier than the Itchen, and the Kennet a good deal harder than either. But the Test can be difficult enough.

Even if you see what the trout are gulping down, your troubles are not over. A typical summer evening fly is the blue-winged olive, and the best artificial is the orange quill. By the by, never be afraid of a large orange quill, up to No.1. But sometimes they will not look at the orange quill or at the coot-winged imitation, or at any olive or red or ginger quill that man's wit devised. Then you have an extremely difficult choice to make: are you to go on trying fly after fly, losing precious time in changing, and rattling your nerves, too, or are you to stick to what you think the best pattern? This is to say are you to change your fly or change your fish?

Before answering that, let me ask you if you are sure that you know what trout are taking. Blue-winged olives are floating down, certainly, and fish are breaking the water: but are they feeding on the nymph or the winged fly or the spinner! It is wonderful how hard it is to tell this, in the lessening light. Anyhow, if the winged fly is refused, do not hesitate. Try the hackle blue-wing first, then the sherry spinner, and then the nymph sunk . . . However, since fishing books should be definite or nothing, I will tell you exactly how I do behave, not how I should. I try first an orange or red quill, according to river, then a hackle blue-wing unoiled and awash, and then probably a sherry spinner. After that, I should think it useless to go on changing, and certainly at some time or other I should go back to the fly I thought best. Whether my final choice were an orange or red quill would depend on the river: at Driffield a red, on the Test, Itchen or Kennet an orange. In streams where you do not get much blue-winged olive, such as those of Dorsetshire or Derbyshire, my final selection, if all else failed, would be a ginger quill. I kill more fish nowadays on the ginger than on the red quill, whatever may have been the case twenty years ago.

Hitherto, I have been talking of nights when the blue-winged olive alone comes down: but they are rare, for you usually find a mixed mass of pale watery and medium olive as well, and also their spinners, and perhaps that of the iron blue. You can tell if the trout are taking pale watery, for their rise to it is very different from the boil that they make at the blue-winged olive, and you can act accordingly. Again, you can sometimes tell when they are taking spinners, but in the dusk you cannot tell which. So you must try the sherry, yellow boy, Houghton Ruby and Lunn's Particular, all of them. But often you are beaten, and then, as I say, at some time of the night, if nothing will induce them to rise, go back to one fly and stick to it. Carry an electric torch, and then you can change your pattern easily on the darkest night.

But here I must interpolate. On some evenings, and indeed some seasons, you get an early hatch of small sedges, and after them come the blue-winged olive and sherry spinner. The ordinary procession is reversed. Thus on the 14 and 15 July, 1928 there was a hatch of small sedge early and a fall of sherry spinner after dark. On each night I killed on a sedge at about eight o'clock and then on a sherry spinner and 3x gut after eleven o'clock had struck.

But now for the sedge proper. When it gets too dark to see a No. 0 fly on the water, you can try a good-sized sedge. It is little use before this, and little use after complete darkness. Do not change to sedge too soon, and if your orange quill is killing well, stick to it. The time during which a sedge is taken rarely exceeds half an hour and is usually only a quarter. Of all fishing the sedge rise is the most uncertain. Not only may you have bad days, but bad years. I am not sure, too, whether success is caused by the presence of sedges themselves. Sometimes they are swarming in the reeds like bees and you cannot get a rise, while at others you may kill fish when there is not a natural fly to be seen: but you do not usually do much with the artificial until the time has come for the natural to hatch out, and it does not hatch in full force until July. A warm, windless night is almost essential. The easiest fish to catch is one lying close under the other bank, provided of course that it is within your reach. Get straight opposite him, and cast two feet above him. Be quite sure that you are reaching him; the tendency in the dusk is to cast short, particularly when you are throwing into the liquid reflection of the reeds. If he does not take, try this: when your fly is about to come over his nose, pull six or eight inches of line sharply through the rings with your spare hand: this has the effect of causing the fly to scutter over the water, and often makes the trout come at you with a glorious smashing rise like a sea-trout. Pattern is not important, though size is. In the early part of the season do not go beyond No. 2: in July and August you can get up to No. 4 or 5. Always fish the sedge dry. I myself do not carry more than four patterns: small dark sedge, coachman, large hare's ear sedge, and cinnamon sedge. Of late I have unconsciously dropped the silver sedge, which I used to use greatly: I killed on it the biggest trout I ever got on the dry fly.

Sedge fishing is not scientific, though a good man will always beat a bad one. But fish are often simple-minded, and anyone can catch them, those great cunning creatures which defied the most skilful in daylight. You catch trout by throwing across, or across and down, and either pulling the fly intentionally, or letting the stream cause it to drag. This, though it looks like clumsy fishing, actually reproduces most accurately the path of the natural sedge. But curiously enough it only answers at night, for never have I known shy fish take a dragging sedge by day. Some fishers despise the sedge: others regard it as the best part of a summer day. I express no opinion one way or another, but only mention three qualities which the sedge rise possesses. First, you may get hold of heavy fish quickly one after another, which is great fun. Second, you can redeem a bad day, and get even with those contemptuous, supercilious trout who have defeated you. Third, you have a chance of getting a real monster. On still summer nights, when not a leaf stirs, and in the pearly shadows you cannot see where the reeds end and their reflection begins, when the ghost moth is rising and falling over the damp meadow, and if you are lucky you may catch a glimpse of the graceful pink elephant hawk moth flying at the yellow iris flowers: when the great red sedge is flopping about in his feeble and aimless flight, and clouds of smaller sedges are flickering tirelessly up and down over the unbroken surface, perchance some dim memory begins to stir in the slow mind of the old trout. All the season through he has fed at the bottom, grubbing on shrimps and caddis and water-snails and minnows and even on his own relatives. But he recalls seasons such as this, far back in former years, when all was quiet and warm and peaceful, when the fat sedges would tumble clumsily on to the water, and in their efforts to escape would make a ripple and commotion spreading far over the placid pool, and he remembers how fresh and fair they were to eat. Then he forsakes his lair under the arched willow roots and rises to the top and takes up his old station in the shadow of the tussock, where he used to lie long ago in his active middle age, when he weighed a bare two pounds. Aye, he weighs more than twice two pounds now, perhaps three times or more, he is the prize of a lifetime – and perhaps as your sedge comes over him you will see a break like that of a big raindrop, a little circle like the palm of a man's hand, and when you strike you will think you have hooked the trunk of a tree. That possibility always gives an excitement to sedge-fishing. You are on the edge of the mysterious and the unknown, and you feel as you do when fishing a salmon river in which forty-pounders are not an impossibility.

For sedge fishing you must have a warm, still evening, and this is best for the small fly rise, too: but do not be driven home either by mist or cold rain or wind. If it is cold and wet, spinners will not get on the water, what I call the casual rise will be blank, and you will do nothing till the winged fly hatches; but there is often a good show of this on inclement, tempestuous nights. Do you recollect that typical summer evening, 14 June, 1907? It was shiveringly cold, there was a wild wind and pelting showers. When I reached Winchester by the evening train, the weather looked so bad that I only went out because I was too restless to stay in: and yet I got a brace before being driven in to the fireside. Or 13 June, 1922 on the Kennet, a vile day which got viler, until the rain hammered down and the bitter wind blew in your teeth? Yet blue-winged olives hatched from eight to half past nine and I landed ten takable fish, of which I kept two brace. Or again, that other day in the same year, cold and wild and wet, 15 July, 1922? There was a mighty hatch of the same fly just before dark, and I got six fish weighing nine pounds. Or 23 May, 1924, wintry and wet, with half a gale? There was a splendid evening rise at Mottisfont right up to half past nine. And perhaps the worst night I ever was out was 9 June, 1928 at Stockbridge. So cold and wet was it, that two or three of us sat before the fire in the keeper's house debating whether we should go out. Yet there was a good hatch and we all got fish. I landed one of 3 lb 7 oz and broke in another which assuredly was bigger, on the sedge, too. No, never let weather keep you indoors, even on English summer nights. However, warm clear nights are of course the best. Black thunder clouds are very bad, in fact light is of great importance, and fish are often shyer on a cloudy than on a cloudless night. Fog is generally bad, but sometimes, if it is light and silvery, fly will hatch and trout will swallow them.

Many a bad day has the sedge redeemed. My most notable recollections of it, however, relate, not to the Test, but to the Kennet, which is the greatest of all sedge rivers. On 28 June, 1914 a friend and I were fishing there. It was clear, summer weather, fair and hot, with an indeterminate breeze varying from south to west. Working hard till dark I got four fish of no great size, none of them on the sedge. Some time between nine and ten at night I reeled up and went in search of my friend. He had caught nothing till the last quarter of an hour; however, in that short space he had beaten my whole day's efforts, for he had taken four fish which weighed a great deal more than mine, all on the coachman. That is no usual incident. On 26 July in the same year I toiled all day till tea-time for two fish which were only just over the pound limit, and at the small fly I failed to rise fish after fish: but in ten minutes with a coachman I rose all the six fish I tried for and got two brace. Again on 2 August, 1914, the last day's fishing before the war, I laboured unceasingly against a gusty wind for three fish, and once more made an utter mess of a hatch of blue-winged olives; whilst in the magic fifteen minutes during which trout take the sedge I landed four out of the six I found rising, and kept three which weighed only a fraction under six pounds. That year, 1914, was a good sedge year, and such years are scarce and should not be missed.

A moon behind your arm, especially a full moon, makes fish nearly impossible to approach. They are put down far more easily than by the brightest sun. You may be rising trout regularly, when suddenly the first cast stops them, because the unnoticed moon has risen. It is an immense advantage to be ambidextrous, and fish underhand with the inshore hand.

Those who fish rivers where mayfly come will agree that, though with it you get a higher average weight, yet actually the biggest fish are killed on the sedge. In 1903 on the Kennet was a great mayfly season for heavy fish, and a friend of mine who had the Ramsbury water got the truly remarkable bag of six fish in one day which weighed over ninteen pounds: and yet the two heaviest fish of the year were got on the sedge. I got the heaviest. It was 26 July, 1903, a cloudy, gusty day, with a downstream wind, and I was on the water from eleven till five without seeing a rise. My friend and I then had tea and walked up the river at a quarter past six. Olives began to appear and trout to move; and suddenly a really large one started rising. We stood and watched, with growing excitement. He was taking every fly, in solid and determined fashion, and the oftener he appeared the bigger he looked, and the faster beat our hearts. It was settled that I was to try for him. I was nervous and uncomfortable. He was very big: it was a long throw and the wind horrible: I could not reach him, and like a fool I got rattled and pulled off too much line: there was an agonised groan from my friend behind me when a great curl of it was slapped on the water exactly over the trout's nose. We looked at each other without speaking, and he silently walked away up the river, leaving me staring stupidly at the spot where the trout had been rising. Of course he was gone.

The next two hours can be passed over. The small fly rise came and went. I caught a trout on a No. 2 silver sedge and finally, at about a quarter past eight, found myself gazing gloomily at the place where I had bungled. The wild wind had blown itself out and had swept the sky bare of cloud. Silence had come, and stillness. The willows, which all through the long summer day had bowed and chattered in the wind, were straightened and motionless, each individual leaf hanging down as though carved in jade: the forest of great sedges, which the gusts had swept into wave after wave of a roaring sea of emerald, was now calm and level, each stalk standing straight and stiff as on a Japanese screen. There had occurred that transition, that transmutation from noise and movement to silence and peace, which would be more wonderful were we not so accustomed to it, when a windy summer day turns over to a moveless summer night: when the swing, and clatter and rush of the day is arrested and lifted from the world, and you get the sense that the great hollow of the air is filled with stillness and quiet, as with a tangible presence. They are peaceful things, these summer evenings after wild days, and I remember particularly that this was one of the most peaceful; more so indeed than my thoughts, which were still in a turmoil. I stood watching mechanically, and then, tempting fate to help me, made a cast or two over the spot where the fish had been. How easy it was to reach it now, how lightly my fly settled on the water, how gracefully it swung over the place. All to no purpose, of course, for nothing happened, and I was about to reel up when a fish rose ten yards above, close under my bank. It was one of those small movements, difficult to place. It might be a very large fish or a very small one. A wild thought swept through me that this was my big one: but no, I said to myself, it cannot be. This is not where he was rising. Besides, things do not happen like that, except in books: it is only in books that you make a fearful bungle and go back later and see a small break which you think is a dace, and cast carelessly and hook something the size of an autumn salmon: it is only in books that fate works in such fashion. Why, I know it all so well that I could write it out by heart, every move of it. But this is myself by a river, not reading in a chair. This is the real world, where such things do not happen: that is the rise of a half-pound trout.

I cast. I was looking right into the west, and the water was coloured like skim milk by reflection from where the sun had set. My silver sedge was as visible as by day. It floated down, there was a rise, I struck, and something rushed upstream. Then I knew.

Above me was open water for some twenty-five yards, and above that again a solid block of weed, stretching right across. My fish made for this, by short, irresistible runs. To let him get into it would have been folly: he must be stopped: either he is well hooked or lightly, the gut is either sound or rotten: kill or cure, he must be turned, if turned he can be: so I pulled hard, and fortunately got his head round and led him down. He played deep and heavy and I had to handle him roughly, but I brought him down without a smash, and I began to breathe again. But then another terror appeared. At the place we had reached the only clear water was a channel under my bank, and the rest of the river was choked with weed. Should I try to pull him down this channel, about three of four yards wide, to the open water below? No. It was much too dangerous, for the fish was uncontrollable, and if he really wanted to get to weed he would either get there or break me: even with a beaten fish it would be extremely risky, and with an unbeaten one it was unthinkable. Well, if he would not come down he must go up, and up he went willingly enough, for when I released pressure he made a long rush up to the higher weed-bed, whilst I ran up the meadow after him, and with even greater difficulty turned him once more. This time I thought he was really going right through it, so fast and so heavy was his pull, and I think he was making for a hatch hole above: but once more my gallant gut stood the strain and, resisting vigorously, he was led down. This proceeding was repeated either two or three times more, I forget which: either three or four times we fought up and down that twenty-five yards of water. By then he was tiring, and I took up my station in the middle of the stretch, where I hoped to bring him in: my hand was actually on the sling of the net when he suddenly awoke and rushed up. He reached the weed-bed at a pace at which he was impossible to stop, shot into it like a torpedo, and I had the sickening certainty that I should lose him after all. To hold him hard now would be to make a smash certain, so I slacked off: when he stopped I tightened again, expecting miserably to feel the dead, lifeless drag of a weeded line. Instead, to my delight, I found I was still in contact with the fish, and he was pulling hard. How he had carried the line through the weeds I do not know. To look at it seemed impossible: and if he had reached them earlier in the fight, when he played deep in the river, before he tired and the pressure brought him near the top, I should have been jammed hopelessly. But the line was clear, and the fish proved it by careering wildly on towards the hatch, making the reel sing. I believe he meant to go through into the carrier, as fish have done before and after, but I turned him. However, we could not stay where we were. The hatch was open at the bottom, there was a strong draw of water through it, and if a heavy, beaten fish got into this, no gut could hold him up. At all risks he must be taken back over the weed into the clear water. I pulled him up to the top and ran him down. Then, for the first time, after so many perils, came the conviction that I should land him. He was obviously big, but how big could not be known, for I had not had a clear sight of him yet. He still pulled with that immovable, quivering solidity only shown by a very heavy fish. But at last even his great strength tired. He gave a wobble or two, yielded, and suddenly he was splashing on the top, looking huge in the dusk. There ensued that agonising time when you have a big fish nearly beat, but he is too heavy to pull in, and nothing you can do gets him up to the net. At last I pulled him over it, but I lifted too soon, the ring caught him in the middle of the body, he wavered a moment in the air and then toppled back into the water with a sickening splash. A judgement, I thought, and for a shattering second I believed he had broken the gut, but he was still on. I was pretty well rattled by then and, in the half light, made two more bad shots, but the end came at last, he was in the net and on the bank.

How big was he? Three pounds? Yes, and more. Four pounds? Yes, and more. Five? He might be, he might. My knees shook and my fingers trembled as I got him on the hook of the steelyard. He weighed a fraction over 4 lb 8 oz. I walked up to find my friend and asked him to weigh him, too. He made him a fraction under 4 lb 9 oz. And that is my biggest fish on the floating fly.

from A SUMMER ON THE TEST 1924

The Skill of the Fisherman

MORLEY ROBERTS

Do we catch the trout that we do catch by quickness or cunning? I wonder. Often it seems to me that all we basket are the mere accidents of the day. Not our skill but the hasty folly or accidental slip of the rush among trout fills our creels. Some trout get overconfident. They play tricks. As it were they 'jay-walk' and get run over. To take this view seems humiliating, but when I am humble in spirit I have to take it. It is for this reason that I am at times in conflict with my fellows. We all recognize the necessity of speed in striking when we see the rise or note the suddent disappearance of the oiled fly. But we often miss seeing it, and yet find a trout on. Ought we to strike then? It is a fine question. Some do and lose the trout. Others hook it still more securely. My own feeling is that it is best to go very delicately, remembering that the trout is probably very lightly hooked. Best to chance what was the result of chance.

This predestinate view of fishing is disliked by many. Their pride is up in arms. They have so long credited themselves with surpassing skill and wisdom that to withdraw those credits, and place them with destiny, greatly disturbs their self-esteem. Is not this the case with many in life? . . .

Not for an instant would I deny that there are cases in which a moderate pride in achievement on our waters seems pardonable, even justifiable. Those who are persistently the favourites of destiny must in the end believe in their skills as the prime factor of success. Whether Dagon himself, or perhaps some Sumerian fish goddess whose name I cannot now remember, backs them, they do not know, perhaps do not care. But I must ask how it is that such men do not wonder a little why even they cannot now catch in the Barle what they did. For D., certainly our greatest fisherman, could not nowadays back himself to equal my greatest catch, though it is a favourite thesis of this that there are just as many trout in the river as there ever were. This I shall disprove presently. But D. still catches many there, and convinces many that this is due to his skill. Far be it from me to maintain that he is not skilful, though I believe his enthusiasm is what has moved the heart of the fish god or goddess, whichever it may be, to watch over his fortunes. Of him I must speak at some length, for if there was ever an enthusiast for fishing on modern lines, D. is the man. I know that the ascetic dry-fly purist may smile. Let him who will measure success and glory with a foot-rule and the scales. Let those whose fishing is, after all, but a sedentary occupation, come and see the thin, tall, eager 'Captain' as we still call him, leap into a car to drive miles to every difficult stream on Exmoor, where he works till dusk comes down or even later, to come home at last with thirty trout of 'say' five to the pound, far beyond our average. Few of us can return with more than seven- or eight-inch fish. D. can and does. There were times when I suspected him of taking everything, sorting out those calculated to reduce his average, and giving these to hungry villagers, while he retained those fit for our hall table and the surprise of strangers. I am now sure I wronged the man. His skill, if it is skill which avails, is assuredly great, as great as his perseverance, which continues in philosophical study on his return. Though most good fishermen when on the water are solitary-minded, slow-moving eremites or pilgrims, for the most part they do, on returning home, take on the aspect of social common humanity. Not so D. It is true that when you meet him in the hall he will answer your salutation, and when you praise his dish of deeds, which to diminish the glory of your own poor platter, he will say that they are not so bad considering. But then he retires to his own sitting-room where his light burns till midnight or even later. Does he rest? Does he lie down or even sit and read? By no means. D. owns every gadget, contraption and contrivance which the ingenuity of man and his own brain have evolved to aid in the capture of trout. At night he studies these, pondering gravely. This may be observed through his window. You may see the very wrinkling of his thoughtful brow as his mind works on the past and the morrow. His rods are perfect and kept in perfect order. His reels continuous polishing keeps with their native lustre. Some he has himself invented. In nothing is he careless. If I cannot dry my line by stretching it between the two alien Araucarias which have viciously intruded themselves on Exmoor, I hang it precariously over picture-frames in the public sitting-room. But D. has a fine patent affair like a gigantic skeleton reel on which to wind his line. It is very pleasant to watch him at work. His air is always sweetly serious when fishing is concerned. I would not have any infer that he cannot joke about the world at large if he is incapable of joking about rods, or reels, or lines, or flies. His favourite fly is a pink or yellow Tup, though he has flies of all kinds. I believe that D. combs and brushes the wings and hackles of his flies every night before he puts them to bed. Perhaps he brilliantines them. His aim is perfection and, if he does not attain it, he comes ever nearer, like the asymptote to a curve. Not easily could he be imagined doing anything illegitimate. Some might almost think of him as capable of taking a foolish trout by accident and returning it to the river even if it weighed half a pound.

However much I admire him, and the destiny which is his, certain grave suspicions as to the way he is aided by that destiny have at times occurred to me. Does he in that secret place sacrifice to Dagon? Dagon was powerful and may yet be. Is not a bishops's mitre directly descended from the head-dress of Dagon's priests? What is the open gap of the mitre but the ritualistic head of a fish? There is, not far from Simonsbath, that secret pool hid in its gloomy wood which is well suited for diabolic rites, a blue and sombre pool, scarcely visited by the sun. There are stones thereby that might serve as altars. Is it not curious to think that D. himself, in a rash moment, owned that he had placed two trout there? Why? I have crept in and seen them. Year by year they grow. No one dares to catch them. Are they sacred to Dagon? Does D. in some awful 'rose of dawn' sacrifice to him in secret? The smell of ritual frying is sweet to the god's nostrils. If these suspicions have any real foundation, is not D.'s apparent skill as nothing to the directions of this dread deity?

And yet, however that may be, what would we not give to be so much in favour? I am the more inclined to believe in fishing fate when I recall the few strangely careless, ill-equipped men – whose reels are rusty, whose rods are whipped with string, whose flies never have their hair or feathers oiled or curled, whose line is never dried, whose very waders leak – who get just as many fish as D. The gods are good to those they love. Not all die young. Who knows what may happen? I can imagine D. some day being confronted, in the very hall and atrium of his triumphs, the hall in which his catch out-numbers, out-weighs and out-shines the catch of all the rest of us combined, with the mightiest dish from Mrs Elworthy's kitchen full to the slippery brim of trout beyond the dreams of avarice, trout caught by some half-ragged, unenviable fellow whose gear would shame poverty itself. Like things happen. Most sincerely I hope they will never happen to D. Such calamities are unendurable. They embitter the heart of the most stoical, the most callous, and are all the harder to endure because the man who has brought them on any of us is mostly so fearfully, so damnably modest as to suggest to the whole crowded hall that he could, of course, do better if he really tried. This is all the more bitter because it is possibly true. There are splendid fishermen who, for all their skill, patience, learning and science, lack the rare grace which is poured, as it were from heaven itself, on some who have the gift and the glory and know not why.

Though there are other elegant exponents of the fishing art who come to Exmoor, there is none like D. When he is not at real work, that is when he is not fishing, I understand he has something to do with Persia. I do not know what fish they catch in Persia as I have never been there and do not mean to go. There are, I am aware, sharks in the Persian Gulf, and there is pearl-fishing at Bahrein. Perhaps D. catches pearls and sells them for a great price so as to be able to support himself in adequate glory and armament on Exmoor. But we fishermen care very little about what others do for a living in their spare time. We judge a man on his fishing, not on account of his wealth. If a rich man with all the appurtenances of a complete angler comes and shows that he is inclined to pride himself on his tackle rather than his trout, we turn away from him, though he were as rich as any legendary Jew from Frankfurt. Better a poor man with a whole cane rod who can catch trout than a purse-proud Plutus fitted out for disaster and disgrace by Farlow himself.

There are others among us besides D. who are great, though I have, in my discretion, chosen him as a most notable example and type of a true fisherman. There are some who say Tom M— is a greater man. I respect him highly, but have lacked close opportunities for studying him. I will, therefore, speak of K. the Doctor. Him I regard with something not far removed from affectionate admiration. It may be that he takes the art in a rather lighter spirit than D., but he is a very deep fellow, and yet can chat with us in the smoking-room of Africa and its animals, birds and insects either in a biological or zoological spirit, which are very different spirits indeed. He is, as a doctor should be, very thoughtful at times, and not least so when presented with the problem of a large, wary and very difficult trout. He does not pass on as D. does after about three casts. For D. says as he goes, 'There are days to come, so look out.' K., however, sits on the bank and falls into a deep study. For what is this trout but a 'case'? I imagine him saying, 'I look on this fish, for the purposes of the day, as a "foreign body" in the Barle. It is my duty to extract it.' There are few of the minor operations of surgery which present such charming opportunities of sporting skill as foreign bodies, and there are few trout in the Barle on which K. sets his mind that do not in the end come out.

I am, as it were, an addict of doctors. I know so many and am, though I say it myself, a great credit to them and at least two or three great surgeons. I am not one of those whom Harley Street depresses . . . I would class good doctors, yes, and surgeons too, 'terrible and dear' as any such may be, with Dr Barle himself when the trout are on the rise. Ah, how often I have gone forth, in hope and gloom mingled with many aches and pains and forebodings, and have come back cured, and laden! Is it not wonderful that that awful aching in the back, which at evil times afflicts so many of us, disappears utterly with the first trout? Even a rise ameliorates it. These Barle cures surpass the miracles of healing shrines, for they come with certainty. The magic of a medicinal river makes new men of us. The youthful become mere boys, and we older men resume our youth. Dr Barle is a great specialist for old age and premature, aye, even natural and looked for decay. I would that K. were a rich consultant in Harley Street, with even greater rivers at his command that he would share with me. I think he would do so, even though he so greatly disappointed me this year by fishing at Withypool and never coming to see me on the rarer waters of the upper Barle. If this occurs again I shall take serious notice of it and strike hard.

from A HUMBLE FISHERMAN *1932*

Battle on the Ythan

G. F. BROWNE

It is now half past three o'clock, and we are rapidly approaching Newburgh. The change of tide seems to make the fish frantic. We are never still for half a minute, and never cease wondering what his size must be if his strength is so enormous and so untiring. Finally, he decides on going up with the tide. The waves become embarrassing, and the boat is no longer easy to manage. A new fiend enters the fish, and makes him play the maddest pranks imaginable. We have for some time discussed the probability of his being a strong fish hooked foul, which would account for some part of his power; but just when the waves are at the highest and the boat is blowing up the river close upon the fish, out he springs two feet into the air, a monster as large as a well-grown boy, with the line leading fair up to his snout. 'Never land that fellow with a couple of trout-lines, or any other line,' is the fisherman's verdict; and as if to confirm it a cry comes the next minute, 'The line has parted!' Sure enough one strand has gone, owing to the constant friction of the wet line running through the rings for so many hours, and within twenty yards of the end of the line there is an ugly place two inches long, with only two strands out of three remaining. There is no longer a moment's safety unless that flaw is kept on the reel; and the necessity of pressing close on the fish leads Jimmy such a life as he will probably not forget. We are hungry and cold and somewhat wet; it is growing very dusk, and if we would not land him with 120 yards of line, how can we with twenty? We have caught a Tartar indeed.

And now night comes on in earnest . . . The clock at home strikes seven, and we hear our passenger groaning over the fact that they are just going in to dinner. Lights peep out on the hillsides . . . At length a measured sound of oars is heard, and a black pirate-like boat comes down upon us. We state our need. Can he take this gentleman down to the pier, and bring us back some food? 'Na!' And that is all he will vouchsafe to say as he sheers off again. Soon, however, a more Christian boat appears, and with many complicated manoeuvres, to keep the line clear of the boat in the dark, we trans-ship our friend about eight o'clock, loaded with injunctions to send off food and a light. The light would be of the greatest service, for a frozen finger and thumb are not sufficiently certain indicators of the passage of the frayed portion of the line from the reel; and as the fish has never ceased to rush from one side to the other, frequently passing sheer under the boat, and requiring the utmost care to keep the line clear of the oars, we think almost more of the coming lantern than of the sorely needed food. It is an hour before the boat returns, with an excellent lantern, a candle and a half, a bottle of whiskey, and cakes and cheese enough for a week. Before setting to work upon the food we attempt to put in execution a plan we have long thought of and carefully discussed. A spare rod, short and stiff, is laid across the seats of the boat, with the reel all clear, and a good salmon-line on, with five or six yards drawn through the rings. We wait till the fish is quiet for a moment or two under the boat, and taking gently hold of the line he is on, pass a loop of it through the loop at the end of the salmon-line. As if he divined our intention, off he goes at once, running the flaw off the reel, and costing us some effort to catch him up again. This is repeated two or three times. At last we get the loop through, get a good knot tied, snap the old line above the knot, and there is our friend careering away at the end of a hundred yards of strong salmon-line, with some seven or eight yards only of the thinner line. When we examine the now innocuous flaw, we find it is seven inches long, and half of one of the remaining strands is frayed through.

Time passes on as we drift slowly up the river towards Elcho. Ten o'clock strikes, and we determine to wait till dawn, and try conclusions with the monster that has had us fast for ten hours. The tide begins to turn, and Jimmy utters gloomy forebodings of our voyage down to the sea in the dark. The fish feels the change of tide, and becomes more demoniacal than ever. For half an hour he is one incessant flurry, and at last, for the first time, he rises to the surface, and through the dark night we can hear and see the huge splashes he makes as he rolls and beats the water. He must be near done, Jimmy thinks. As he is speaking the line comes slack. He's bolting towards the boat, and we reel up with the utmost rapidity. We reel on; but no sign of resistance. Up comes the minnow, minus the tail hook. Jimmy rows home without a word; and neither he nor the fisherman will ever get over it.*

from OFF THE MILL *1895*

A Day on the Chess

JAMES ANTHONY FROUDE

A day's fishing at Cheneys means a day by the best water in England in the fisherman's paradise of solitude.

Such a day's privilege had been extended to me if I cared to avail myself of it, when I was coming down to see the chapel, and though my sporting days were over, and gun and rod had long lain undisturbed in their boxes, yet neither the art of fly-fishing, nor the enjoyment of it when once acquired and tasted, will leave us except with life. The hand does not forget its cunning, and opportunity begets the inclination to use it. I had brought my fishing-case along with me. Shall I stay at the inn over the day and try what can be done? The rain and the prospect of another such breakfast decide it between them. The water-keeper is at the window – best of keepers – for he will accept a sandwich perhaps for luncheon, a pull from your flask, and a cigar out of your case, but other fee on no condition. The rain, he tells me, has raised the water, and the large fish are on the move, the

*A large fish was taken in the nets at Newburgh the next year which was popularly recognised as the fish of the above account. It had a mark just where I saw the tail hook of the minnow when the fish showed itself once in the strong water above Newburgh. It was the largest salmon ever known to be taken, weighing 74 lb as weighed at Newburgh, and 70 lb in London the next day.

Mayfly has been down for two days. They were feeding on it last evening. If the sky clears they will take well in the afternoon; but the fly will not show till the rain stops.

The Cheneys fishing is divided in the middle by a mill. Below the mill the trout are in greatest numbers, but comparatively small; above it is a long still deep pool where the huge monsters lie, and in common weather never stir till twilight. The keeper and I remember a summer evening some years ago, when at nightfall, after a burning day, the glittering surface of the water was dimpled with rings, and a fly thrown into the middle of these circles was answered more than once by a rush and scream of the reel; and a struggle which the darkness made more exciting. You may as well fish on the high road as in the mill-pool when the sun is above the horizon, and even at night you will rarely succeed there; but at the beginning of the Mayfly season these large fish sometimes run up to the rapid stream at the pool head to feed. This the keeper decides shall be tried if the fly comes down. For the morning he will leave me to myself.

Does the reader care to hear of a day's fishing in a chalk stream fifteen miles from London? As music to the deaf, as poetry to the political economist, as a mountain landscape to the London cockney, so is a chalk stream trout-fishing to those who never felt their fingers tingle as the line whistles through the rings . . .

Breakfast over, I start for the lower water. I have my boy with me home for the holidays. He carries the landing-net, and we splash through the rain to the mill. The river runs for a quarter of a mile down under hanging bushes. As with other accomplishments when once learnt, eye and hand do the work in fly-fishing without reference to the mind for orders. The eye tells the hand how distant the bushes are, how near the casting-line approaches them. If a gust of wind twists it into a heap, or sweeps it towards a dangerous bough, the wrist does something on the instant which sends the fly straight and unharmed into the water. Practice gives our different organs functions like the instinct of animals, who do what their habits require, yet know not what they do.

The small fish take freely – some go back into the water, the few in good condition into the basket, which, after a field or two, becomes perceptibly heavier. The governor, a small humble bee, used to be a good fly at Cheneys, and so did the black alder. Neither of them is of any use today. The season has been cold and late. The March brown answers best, with the never-failing red spinner. After running rapidly through two or three meadows, the river opens into a broad smooth shallow, where the trout are larger, and the water being extremely clear, are specially difficult to catch. In such a place as this, it is useless to throw your fly at random upon the stream. You must watch for a fish which is rising, and you must fish for him till you either catch him or disturb him. It is not enough to go below him and throw upwards, for though he lies with his head upstream, his projecting eye looks back over his shouders. You must hide behind a bunch of rushes. You must crawl along the grass with one arm only raised. If the sun is shining and the shadow of your rod glances over the gravel, you may get up and walk away. No fish within sight will stir then to the daintiest cast.

I see a fish close to the bank on the opposite side, lazily lifting his head as a fly floats past him. It is a long throw, but the wind is fair and he is worth an effort – once, twice, three times I fail to reach him. The fourth I land the fly on the far bank, and draw it gently off upon his very nose. He swirls in the water like a salmon as he sweeps round to seize it. There is a splash – a sharp jerk, telling unmistakably that something has given way. A large fish may break you honestly in weeds or round a rock or stump, and only fate is to blame, but to let yourself be broken on the first strike is unpardonable. What can have happened? Alas, the red-spinner has snapped in two at the turn – a new fly bought last week at —'s, whose boast it has been that no fly of his was ever known to break or bend.

One gumbles on these occasions, for it is always the best fish which one loses: and as imagination is free, one may call him what weight one pleases. The damage is soon repaired. The basket fills fast as trout follows trout. It still rains, and I begin to think that I have had enough of it. I have promised to be at the mill at midday, and then we shall see.

Evidently the sky means mischief. Black thunder clouds pile up to windward, and heavy drops continue falling. But there is a break in the south as I walk back by the bank – a gleam of sunshine spans the valley with a rainbow, and an actual Mayfly or two sails by which I see greedily swallowed. The keeper is waiting; he looks scornfully into my basket. Fish – did I call these herrings fish? I must try the upper water at all events. The large trout were feeding, but the fly was not yet properly on – we can have our luncheon first.

How pleasant is luncheon on mountain-side or river's bank, when you fling yourself down on fern or heather after your morning's work, and no daintiest *entrée* had ever such flavour as your sandwiches, and no champagne was ever so exquisite as the fresh stream water just tempered from your whisky flask. Then follows the smoke, when the keeper fills his pipe at your bag, and old adventures are talked over, and the conversation wanders on through anecdotes and experiences, till, as you listen to the shrewd sense and kindly feeling of your companion, you become aware that the steep difference which you had imagined to be created by education and habits of life had no existence save in your own conceit. Fortune is less unjust than she seems, and true hearts and clear-judging healthy minds are bred as easily in the cottage as the palace.

But time runs on, and I must hasten to the end of my story. The short respite from the wet is over. Down falls the rain again; rain not to be measured by inches, but by feet; rain such as has rarely been seen in England before this '*aestas mirabilis*' of 1879. It looks hopeless, but the distance by the road to the top of the water is not great. We complain if we are caught in a shower; we splash along in a deluge, in boots and waterproof, as composedly as if we were seals or otters. The river is rising and, as seldom happens with a chalk stream, it is growing discoloured. Every lane is running with a brown stream, which finds its way at last into the main channel. The highest point is soon reached. The first hundred yards are shallow, and to keep the cattle from straying a high iron railing runs along the bank. Well I knew that iron railing. You must stand on the lower bar to fish over it. If you hook a trout, you must play him from that uneasy perch in a rapid current among weeds and stones, and your attendant must use his landing-net through the bars. Generally it is the liveliest spot in the river, but nothing can be done there today. There is a ford immediately above, into which the thick road-water is pouring, and the fish cannot see the fly. Shall we give it up? Not yet. Farther down the mud settles a little, and by this time even the road has been washed clean, and less dirt comes off it. The flood stirs the trout into life and hunger, and their eyes, accustomed to the transparency of the chalk water, do not see you so quickly.

Below the shallow there is a pool made by a small weir, over which the flood is now rushing – on one side there is an open hatchway, with the stream pouring through. The banks are bushy, and over the deepest part of the pool the stem of a large ash projects into the river. Yesterday, when the water was lower, the keeper saw a four-pounder lying under that stem. Between the weir and the trees it is an awkward spot, but difficulty is the charm of fly-fishing. The dangerous drop fly must be taken off; a drop fly is only fit for open water, where there is neither weed nor stump. The March brown is sent skimming at the tail of the casting-line, to be dropped, if possible, just above the ash, and to be carried under it by the stream. It has been caught in a root, so it seems; or it is foul somewhere. Surely no fish ever gave so dead a pull. No; it is no root. The line shoots under the bank. There is a broad flash of white just below the surface, a moment's struggle, the rod springs straight, and the line comes back unbroken. The March brown is still floating at the end of it. It was a big fish, perhaps the keeper's very big one; he must have been lightly hooked, and have rubbed the fly out of his mouth.

But let us look closer. The red-spinner had played false in the morning; may not something like it have befallen the March brown? Something like it, indeed. The hook has straightened out as if, instead of steel, it had been made of copper. A pretty business! I try another, and another, with the same result. The heavy trout take them, and one bends and the next breaks. Oh! — ! Well for Charles Kingsley that he was gone before he heard of a treason which would have broken his trust in man. You, in whose praise I have heard him so often eloquent! You who never dealt in shoddy goods. You who were faithful if all else were faithless, and redeemed the credit of English tradesmen! You had not then been in the school of progress and learnt that it was the buyer's business to distinguish good from bad. You never furnished your customers with cheap and nasty wares, fair-looking to the eye and worthless to the touch and trial. In those days you dealt with gentlemen, and you felt and traded like a gentleman yourself. And now you, too, have gone the way of your fellows. You are making a fortune, as you call it, out of the reputation which you won honourably in better days. You have given yourself over to competition and semblance. You have entered for the race among the sharpers and will win by knavery and tricks like the rest. I will not name you for the sake of the old times, when C.K. and I could send you a description of a fly from the farthest corner of Ireland, and by return of post would come a packet tied on hooks which Kendal and Limerick might equal, but could not excel. You may live on undenounced for me; but read C.K.'s books over again; repent of your sins, go back to honest ways, and renounce the new gospel in which whosoever believes shall not be saved.

But what is to be done? Spite of the rain the river is now covered with drowned Mayflies, and the trout are taking them all round. I have new Mayflies from the same quarter in my book, but it will be mere vexation to try them. Luckily for me there are a few old ones surviving from other days. The gut is brown with age – but I must venture it. If this breaks I will go home, lock away my rod, and write an essay on the effects of the substitution of Political Economy for the Christian faith.

On, then, goes one of these old flies. It looks well. It bears a mild strain, and, like Don Quixote with his helmet, I will not put it to a severe trial. Out it shoots over the pool, so natural-looking that I cannot distinguish it from a real fly which floats at its side. I cannot, nor can that large trout in the smooth water above the fall. He takes it, springs into the air, and then darts at the weir to throw himself over. If he goes down he is lost. Hold on. He has the stream to help him, and not an inch of line can be spared. The rod bends double, but the old gut is true. Down the fall he is not to go. He turns up the pool, he makes a dart for the hatchway – but if you can stand a trout's first rush you need not fear him in fair water afterwards. A few more efforts and he is in the net and on the bank, not the keeper's four-pounder, but a handsome fish, which I know that he will approve.

He had walked down the bank pensively while I was in the difficulty with my flies, meditating, perhaps, on idle gentlemen, and reflecting that if the tradesmen were knaves the gentlemen were correspondingly fools. He called to me to come to him just as I had landed my trout. He was standing by the side of the rapid stream at the head of the mill-pool. It was as he had foretold; the great fish had come up, and were rolling like salmon on the top of the water gulping down the Mayflies. Even when they are thus carelessly ravenous, the clearness of the river creates a certain difficulty in catching them in ordinary times, but today the flood made caution superfluous. They were splashing on the surface close to our feet, rolling about in a negligent gluttony which seemed to take from them every thought of danger, for a distance of at least three hundred yards.

There was no longer any alarm for the tackle, and it was but to throw the fly upon the river, near or far, for a trout instantly to seize it. There was no shy rising where suspicion balks the appetite. The fish were swallowing with a deliberate seriousness every fly which drifted in their reach, snapping their jaws upon it with a gulp of satisfaction. The only difficulty was in playing them when hooked with a delicate chalk stream casting-line. For an hour and a half it lasted, such an hour and a half of trout-fishing as I had never seen and shall never see again. The ease of success at last became wearisome. Two large baskets were filled to the brim. Accident had thrown in my way a singular opportunity which it would have been wrong to abuse, so I decided to stop. We emptied out our spoils upon the grass, and the old keeper said that long as he had known the river he had never but once seen so many fish of so large size taken in the Chess in a single day by a single rod.

How can a reasonable creature find pleasure in having performed such an exploit? If trout were wanted for human food, a net would have answered the purpose with less trouble to the man and less annoyance to the fish. Throughout creation man is the only animal – man, and the dogs and cats which have learnt from him – who kills, for the sake of killing, what he does not want, and calls it sport. All other animals seize their prey only when hungry, and are satisfied when their hunger is appeased.

Such, it can only be answered, is man's disposition. He is a curiously formed creature, and the appetite for sport does not seem to disappear with civilization. The savage in his natural state hunts, as the animals hunt, to support his life; the sense of sport is strongest in the elaborately educated and civilized. It may be that the taste will die out before 'Progress'. Our descendants perhaps, a few generations hence, may look back upon a pheasant *battue* as we look back on bear-baiting and bull-fighting, and our mild offspring, instructed in the theory of development, may see a proof in their fathers' habits that they come of a race who were once crueller than tigers, and will congratulate themselves on the change . . . We blame our fathers' habits; our children may blame ours in turn; yet we may be sitting in judgement, both of us, on matters of which we know nothing.

The storm has passed away, the dripping trees are sparkling in the warm and watery sunset. Back, then, to our inn, where dinner waits for us, the choicest of our own trout, pink as salmon, with the milky curd in them, and no sauce to spoil the delicacy of their flavour. Then bed, with its lavender-scented sheets and white curtains, and sleep, sound sweet sleep, that loves the country village and comes not near a London bedroom. In the morning, adieu to Cheneys, with its red gable-ends and chimneys, its venerable trees, its old-world manners, and solemn memories of its mausoleum. Adieu, too, to the river, which, 'though men may come and men may go', has flowed and will flow on for ever, winding among its reed-beds, murmuring over its gravelly fords, heedless of royal dynasties, uncaring whether Cheney or Russell calls himself lord of its waters, graciously turning the pleasant corn mills in its course, unpolluted by the fetid refuse of manufactures, and travelling on to the ocean bright and pure and uncharged with poison, as in the old times when the priest sung mass in the church upon the hill and the sweet soft matins bell woke the hamlet to its morning prayers.

from CHENEYS AND THE HOUSE OF RUSSELL *1887*

Tussle with a Salmo-Ferox

R. MACDONALD ROBERTSON

We were sitting lazily chatting and striving to combat the delightful lassitude induced by hard exercise on a stormy loch, followed by the luxury of a change to the skin, a hearty dinner and a crackling log fire. It was mid-September, and the equinoctial gales appeared to have set in permanently, accompanied by lashing rain, which was causing the loch to rise rapidly. To us was announced Nichol Macintyre, our boatman, who for more than forty years had materially assisted in thinning the piscine inhabitants of Loch Awe, and who could never be induced to lay down his oars until all hope of 'adding a fin to the gentleman's creel' had vanished. We were in the dining-room of Auchnacarron Lodge, on the north shore of Loch Awe, when Macintyre, our boatman, entered. He suggested that we should next day try the river; we must start about eight o'clock, as we had seven miles to pull, and, if the gale held from the west, it would take all we knew to pull the three miles to the Pass.

Next morning I was awakened by a shower of gravel. Tumbling into my clothes, I hurried downstairs, and put up a substantial lunch, while breakfast was being prepared. By eight o'clock we were ready to start.

Wet work it was getting an offing, but when once clear of the shore, we had the wind dead aft, and a clear run of four miles before us. I sent Nichol forward to trim the boat, and then, with the sheet in one hand, and an extemporized tiller in the other, our little craft, with the aid of a tiny lugsail, performed the run in half an hour. Having reached the entrance to the Pass of Brander, we crept up the weather shore with a minnow on my salmon-rod and an ordinary loch trout cast and flies on my trouting-rod. On reaching the last sheltered point I took in my minnow, but allowed the flies to remain out with a very short line. We then settled down to a hard pull.

When we had gone about another mile and had reached the part of the pass where the shale comes sheer down to the edge of the loch – I believe the locality is pronounced Schloch'n ewer – a heavy squall was causing us to lose way and my flies must have sunk six or eight feet, when whir-r-r-r went my reel; the water parted close to the boat, and a great thick rosy-brown fellow leapt three or four feet into the air. I had just time to lower the point of my rod, ease the line, and so frustrate the obvious attempt on the part of the fish to break my fine trout cast by a slap of his great tail. Nichol had gained possession of my oar by this time, and was straining every sinew to hold the boat. Which way would he go? Thank goodness he was off downwind. Had he gone the other way Nichol could not have followed him; a few seconds' run would have exhausted my short line, and the first salmo-ferox that I had hooked in my life would at this moment have probably been enjoying life in the deep, dusky recesses of the weird and rocky pass, instead of undergoing a course of mummification in the garret of a taxidermist.

On we went, our friend steering an almost straight course for half or three-quarters of a mile . . . I had then only about one-fourth of the requisite length of line on my reel, small flies, and correspondingly fine gut. I thanked my stars it was a fine-drawn four-yard cast, which had been specially made for me a fortnight before, and the soundness of which I had carefully tested. If I was severely handicapped in many points, I had at least the advantage of the services of one of the most experienced boatmen the countryside could produce. It was quite a treat to observe the dexterous manner in which he followed and seemed to anticipate, the movements of our spotted antagonist.

On went the fish with never a check, utterly ignoring the two or three pounds of pressure I steadily maintained, the bit fairly between his teeth. Soon I found myself trying experiments based on the assumption that our spotted hero had stubbornly made up his mind to prevent me from having my way even in the smallest detail of the fight; hence, when we began to swerve slightly out of his straight course, I turned the point of my rod to that side, as if to assist him, when he would immediately change his mind and go the other way. Can I have been mistaken in this? I think not, for we enacted the same game over and over again, until apparently our friend found the occupation of towing pall upon him, and he straightway sounded and sulked.

Nichol held the boat while I 'pumped' as strongly as I dared, but without result. My antagonist lay sullen and motionless, in the highest of dudgeons. After trying every means of civil persuasion in vain, and after expending every epithet in the vocabulary, both sacred and profane, and fairly driven to desperation, I ultimately decided to bombard the perverse brute with stones until I should succeed in dislodging him.

As we had been skirting the shore all the way, I told Nichol to edge the boat against the precipitous shore, only some five yards distant, where, without landing, we were able to gather a few large stones; then, pulling out again to windward of old brownie, we fired one missile after another. At the fourth discharge, his scaly majesty made a slight movement, then rushed forth like a boy discharged from school, and nearly emptied my reel before Nichol could get into his wake; and, if we might judge from the pace, he had fairly gained his second wind. This time he made for the opposite shore obliquely downwind, but just before reaching it, made up his mind to return, and back we had to go.

All this time I had been sitting huddled up in the bottom of the boat, so as not to make pulling harder than necessary by exposing my surface to the wind. Now for the first time, I took a hurried glance to see how Nichol was standing the strain, and when I saw his exhausted but game-to-the-last look, I longed to give him a dram from my flask, though this was impossible under existing circumstances. Nichol seemed to read my thoughts, for he exclaimed: 'Dinna tak' your eyes off him. I'm doing fine!'

The mad rushes now ceased, and our good boat was steaming at half speed, with an occasional slow down. As if to favour us, the wind lulled somewhat, and we could follow, when it was necessary, upwind. It must have been at the end of three-quarters of an hour that I first brought the quarry to the surface, where he came grudgingly, tugging and straining intermittently; but sight of us seemed to give him new life, which it took some ten minutes to exhaust. During a quiet interval I said: 'Get the gaff handy, Nichol.' No answer.

'Nichol, have you got the gaff?'

Then he replied: 'No, sir, we've left both gaff and net. I took everything out of the boat last night when I hauled her up out of reach of the waves, and must have forgotten to put them back. I remembered it all the moment you hooked him, but I daren't tell you for fear it would upset you and spoil your hand, whereas if he broke away without your knowing the gaff was left behind I wouldn't have felt so bad.'

I suppose I must have ejaculated something, for Nichol said: 'Yes, sir, that's just how I felt, but I gave it up, as I couldn't find words to do the subject justice.'

'What shall we do?' I asked.

'When he's not able to sit upright, we'll slip ashore, sir.' By this time the hardy warrior's strength was almost spent and as he came again to the surface, lying on his side, the keen pleasure of seeing him almost ours was momentarily marred by observing him once more open his mouth and gasp heavily before he once more gave a sweep of his powerful tail and dived nearly to the bottom.

'Poor beggar, he's hard up. I almost thought I heard him sob that time he opened his mouth,' remarked Nichol, who, by this time, was edging the boat towards the shore. The fish, having again surfaced was following quietly, lying on his side. Our difficulties were not yet ended, for the shale on the steep hillside afforded very insecure footing. I managed, however, to scramble up a few feet, and, reclining with my feet well buried among the loose stones, I began to wind up slowly.

'He'll come now, sir,' said Nichol, as he lay crouched at the water's edge. In he came, inch by inch, till he touched the stones.

Contact with them, however, seemed to infuse new life into him, and I could not check his efforts, feeble as they were, though I put on all the pressure I dared. It looked like having to make a hasty run for the boat – no, he was turning; the strain that he scoffed half an hour ago was too much for him now.

Lying on his handsome broad side, he allowed me to tow him gently towards Nichol who lay motionless. Almost before the stones were reached Nichol's right hand was buried under the great spotted gills, and the possessor of them was high and dry, struggling under Nichol's prostrate form. Neither would the latter move until I had put down my rod and passed a string through the still gasping gills.

'Don't take the fly out, sir,' said Nichol. 'Cut the gut and leave it in his mouth when you get him stuffed.'

Still embracing the fish, I followed holding the string, we scrambled back to the boat and laid out the trophy tenderly.

'Well, I've never seen a trout in grander condition, or finer marked,' said Nichol, as I poured him out a good stiff dram . . .

'What is he – fifteen pounds?' I asked.

'More than that, sir. He's as near twenty as fifteen,' was the reply.

When the fish was cosily wrapped away in Nichol's oilskin in the prow of the boat, we rowed on to the river and landed at the little red shelter where luncheon was quickly disposed of and work recommenced, but neither minnow nor fly elicited any response, and at 5 pm we made for home.

Great were the rejoicings that night at Carron Lodge, and many a toast drunk. Nichol, getting the scales, said: 'You hold him up, sir, your arms are stronger than mine. Now, towards the right. Fifteen and a half pounds! But I had thought he was more, and so he was when he first left the water. I'll pack him early tomorrow morning, and send him off from Taychreggan Hotel by the boat to the stuffers for you, sir.'

When pipes were finished and glasses emptied, candles were called for and I, for one, slept none the worse for my eighty minutes' exciting tussle. When shall I have such another I wonder?

This specimen was carefully stuffed and is preserved in a glass case at North Berwick, the identical fly with which it was caught being still deeply embedded in its jaw.

from IN SCOTLAND WITH A FISHING ROD *1933*

With Axe and Auger

W. C. PRIME

There is a lake over the mountains, some forty miles from the Rookery, which I had long desired to see; but I could never persuade a friend to go with me on an exploring expedition. A recent extension of the railway had made it somewhat more accessible, if I was to give credit to the information given me by a baggage-master, who assured me that the railroad crossed an old wood-road which led in three or four miles to the lake.

There is, I think, a love of novelty in all anglers. We prefer to fish new waters when we can, and it is sometimes pleasanter to explore, even without success, than to take fish in familiar places. New and fine scenery is always worth finding. But I could not beat these ideas practically into the brain of either Steenburger or Doctor Johnson, and I resolved therefore on a solitary expedition to the lake.

I had not then, what I now possess, and strongly recommend to roving anglers, a patent India-rubber raft, made in two cylinders, with a light frame to sit on. This boat or raft, packing in a small compass when not 'blown up', weighs less than fifty pounds, and can be carried on a man's shoulders to any lake or pond. I have frequently used it on water never before fished, and to reach which it was necessary to climb hills so steep and so covered with alternate rock and under-brush that two men would have found it quite impossible to carry up safely any boat, however light. An axe and an auger wherewith to build a raft were therefore essentials to my equipment, and these, with some hard bread and sandwiches, and one heavy and one light fly-rod, made up the sum total of my luggage.

Taking the forenoon accommodation train up the road, I went forward to find my old informant, the baggage-master, or, if not him, some other one who could supplement my scanty knowledge of the locality I was seeking.

Luckily there was a man who said he knew all about it, and, after riding forty miles or so, the conductor stopped his train at a road-crossing in the woods, I tumbled out, and civilization at once departed from me, drawn by the power of steam.

It had been a sudden idea, and the realization was somewhat discouraging. Alone in the woods, with sundry traps in the way of luggage, and with no other guide than the words of the confident individual I had met on the cars, who said that the lake lay at the foot of a hill to which he pointed across the forest, I set out, and after a half-mile tramp came on the traces of a clearing, and, soon descending into a hollow, found a saw-mill. Two men who were running it were evidently astonished at the appearance of a traveller, but they very good-naturedly offered advice, to wit, that, if one wanted trout-fishing, he could find it then and there in the mill-dam, but that if he went to the lake he would find no trout, for nobody ever could take trout there except through the ice in the winter.

'What size do they take them?'

'Oh, sometimes five or six pounds.'

This was the same story I had heard at a distance, and it confirmed my hopes. I chatted a while with the sawyers, and tried the contents of their pond. A few casts brought up some small trout, and at length a very decent fish, perhaps a pound in weight, rose to the scarlet ibis. Landing him, and leaving him with the others for the use of the men, who had never before seen fly-fishing, and were astonished at the process, I pushed on in the afternoon towards the unknown lake or pond. The road became less a road and more a path as it ascended hill after hill, winding and pleasant, but always tending upwards. At last it opened on a large clearing where stood a ruined log-house, deserted long ago, and a tolerably decent barn, in which there was a small quantity of dry hay. This was an unexpected luxury, for I had calculated on a night in camp. I took possession of the only tenantable end of the log-house, deposited my packages, and resolved to make this my headquarters, since it was evident the lake was distant not over a mile at most. Then taking a light rod I plunged into the forest, and in less than half an hour emerged on the banks of the lake. It lacked an hour of sunset, and there was but little time for the examination of the shores. Boat there was none. The unbroken forest surrounded the sheet of water. There was no time this evening to construct a raft, and if I was to have trout for supper, it must be by casting from the shore, and so I went to work at once.

In visiting a new lake like this, the chances are always against the fisherman. He knows nothing of the special haunts of the trout, and can form no opinion of the shape of the bottom of the pond – an idea of which is generally necessary to guide one in looking for this fish. The safest rule is therefore to seek for the main inlet, and, if the water is here found shoal, to wade out far enough to get a cast over deeper water. Beginning on this rule, I had a long hunt for the inlet, and it was after sunset before I found it. It happened fortunately that there was an accumulation here of old driftwood, well packed together, which supported me, and I had a good clear back cast. For ten or fifteen minutes it was all vain work. Nothing broke the surface which had life. The gloom began to settle on the lake. It grew cold withal, and the wind was sharp. I frankly confess that by this time I wanted fish because I was hungry. If supper were to be confined to three or four pieces of hard bread, it was not to be regarded with any earnest longings and joyous anticipations. If, on the other hand, I could look to the rich salmon-coloured meat of a trout as waiting me in the old log-house, it was something worth thinking about.

And as I thought about it, he rose with a heavy rush, and slashed the tail-fly with his own broad tail and went down again. Cast after cast, and he would not rise again. So I fell back at last on the old white moth, and taking off all the other flies, cast this alone, in the twilight which was now almost darkness. He came up at it at the first cast, and took it, head on, following the fly from behind. It is not often on still water that a trout takes a fly with his mouth before striking it with his tail; but they sometimes do it on a white fly in the evening, and from this fact it seems likely that they regard it as an animal moving in the water and not as a fly at all.

He took it and turned down; then, as he felt the hook, swayed off with a long, steady surge, and circled half around me. Supper was tolerably certain now, and my appetite at once rose. In less than five minutes I had him, a good, solid three-pounder, in the landing-net, and at once struck a bee-line for the log-house in the clearing.

The cabin was nothing to boast of as a shelter. The roof was tight over the end opposite the chimney, but the windows were destitute of glass, and the breeze, which had sprung up freshly before I left the lake, was talking loudly to itself inside of the place as I approached it. There was plenty of wood around the old hut, and in ten minutes I had the chimney blazing at a terrible rate. Firelight is as much a polisher indoors as moonlight outside. It smooths down all the roughness of an interior. It reddened the walls of the cabin and covered them with dancing images. I had nothing in the way of eatables except the trout, hard bread, and some salt. The salt was the great article. It was on the faith of that salt that I had ventured on the expedition. With a few pinches of salt and a good rod or gun, one may live luxuriously for a while, if he have luck. Without the salt – only imagine it. You may not think much of it as a thing to possess, but just reverse the picture and imagine fish and game in abundance without it, and you may thereby find in some measure what it is worth.

I recall oftentimes a scene at Wady Haifa where the palms of Ethiopia bear golden fruit, but where salt is worth more than golden dates. There I have bought bushels of luxurious fruit for a single handful of the condensed brine from the far-off sea.

One half of the trout was turning before the blaze, hung on the small end of a birch sapling; the other half was reserved for breakfast, for it was by no means certain that any other food was to be found. A pile of hay from the barn made a soft bed in the sheltered end of the room. While the fire burned I mused, and before the musings had assumed form the trout was cooked, and then my supper was ready and eaten, the bed looked more and more inviting, and by nine or ten o'clock I was sound asleep in the corner.

Morning found me sleeping. The sun and air were streaming in at the window-frames innocent of sash or glass. But while the question of breakfast was under discussion, a voice came in by the same avenues with the sunshine and wind, singing a cheery song, and I saw the tall form of one of the sawyers of the mill swinging along towards the wood in the direction of the lake. He pulled up at a hail and turned to the cabin.

'Glad to see you lively this morning,' he said in a hearty voice. 'I thought I'd come over and bring you suthin' to eat; expected to find you in camp, down along the pond.' Then, entering the cabin and seeing the half of the last night's trout hanging before the fire – 'Well, you seem to ha' taken care of yourself. You don't say you got that feller last night with one of them little poles o' yourn?'

We made a substantial meal together at once, and the best thanks that could be given my friend were visible in the justice done to his corn-bread and hard eggs. He had come three miles across the country on this hospitable errand, and was delighted when I proposed to him to spend the day on the lake, and promised to go home with him in the evening.

The first work was the building of a raft. To the uninitiated it is often a puzzle how rafts are constructed by fishermen in the forests, and possibly there are not many sportsmen who have regarded an axe and an auger as parts of an outfit. The two things are essential to a forest expedition, and in going to fish an unknown sheet of water one might almost as well leave his rod behind him as these tools. There are ways of getting on without the auger, but a raft lashed together with withes is a dangerous craft. I had had such a one part with me in mid-lake, while I swam ashore with my rod in my hand, losing even the fish I had taken. In the present case I had both tools. The construction of the raft was very simple. Two pine-trees supplied six logs, each about a foot in diameter, which were rolled into the water and floated side by side, a few inches apart. Across these, smaller timbers were laid, the axe shaping them down flat where wooden pegs were driven in auger-holes through them into the heavy logs. It was but little over an hour's work to complete it, for the timber was at hand in good size and quantity. Then we covered the raft with balsam boughs, to stand or sit or lie down on, and a couple of long poles finished the furniture of the vessel on which we pushed out at the inlet of the lake. The day was so much more beautiful than the previous one that the lake appeared like a new place, and the trout were rising on the surface here and there in a way which indicated that the warm sunshine had brought out some small flies, invisible to the eye at a distance, but satisfactory as indicating that the fish were on the feed. It was nearly ten o'clock when I began casting. But nothing rose to my flies till I had changed them twice or oftener, and had on at length three small gnats, a dun, a yellow, and a black, and then came the first strike at the yellow, a half-pound fish soon killed. Another at the yellow again, a somewhat larger fish, gave me some slight work, and a third took the yellow once more, and thereupon I changed: the dropper yellow, the tail-fly yellow, and intermediate a small scarlet ibis. The first cast made with this new bank, as some men call the arrangement, cost me the scarlet fly. A large fish took the dropper, and at the same instant another struck the ibis. They headed in opposite directions, and the very stroke of the two parted the slender thread. I landed but one of that cast, and only once after that had two at the same time, and then saved them both.

The sport continued good till about one o'clock, and then ceased. The breeze rippled the water, the flies were increasing in number in the warm sunshine, but feeding-time was over and the fish went down. I have seen the same thing often on other waters.

The object of the expedition was accomplished. There were trout in the lake – they would rise to the fly. Over a dozen beautiful large fish, and nearly another dozen which ran below a half-pound each, were fair evidence of the contents of this water. Six of the smaller fish had been taken with bait by my friend, the sawyer. He had cut a birch rod, and with hook and line which I supplied, and the fin of a trout for bait, which he kept constantly moving near the bottom of the lake, he had captured a half-dozen fair-sized fish.

So we left the raft to drift towards the leeward side of the lake, and started for the log-house in the clearing; and thence, carrying heavy weight, we trudged over the hills to the home of my friend of the mill.

from I GO A-FISHING *1873*

Whose Trout?

G. E. M. SKUES

I have already expressed my views on the growing tendency in the little syndicate of four members that fished the stretch of Itchen of which I write to restrict the admission of guests to fish the water, and ultimately, in the middle 'thirties, much to my disgust, the only way in which it was possible to entertain a friend on it was to invite him to share one's rod. I had, and thank goodness still have, a friend (C.L.C.) to whom this restriction was not wholly a penance, because he was a devout admirer of my rod – a lovely little 9 ft 5 oz Leonard, dating back to 1905, which he styled W.B.R., which, being interpreted, means World's Best Rod, and so it fell to him one Saturday in June to motor over from a neighbouring valley and a village which had sheltered Izaak Walton in his old age, and to meet me on the middle of our two-mile stretch. I had entered the meadows from the bottom of the length and had been detained for a while at a bend known as Mac's Corner, where the trout had the exasperating habit of proving nearly, but *very* seldom quite, 3 lb – and on the occasion in question each of the brace I extracted from that curve ran true to from – 2 lb 15 oz.

However, that was good enough to reconcile me, when I met my friend on the middle of the stretch about eleven o'clock, to surrendering my W.B.R. to him, with the cast and the midget nymph which had done the trick with my brace – and I soon had the satisfaction of seeing my friend leading by the nose to my ready landing-net a quite pleasant two-pounder. Then I was able to tell him that a few yards farther upstream at a bend there was suspected to be a quite impossible three-pounder: and not long after I was privileged to see the W.B.R.'s top go up and the W.B.R. make the curve of beauty and to hear my friend exclaim, 'Got him!' It was some minutes before he got a glimpse of his fish and exclaimed, 'By George, I believe he's a four-pounder!' It was some minutes more before he could turn the trout and persuade him to head downstream. All, however, seemed to be going well till the trout was brought close under our bank, when he took a scare and tore the line off the shrieking reel and, with a wrench under the far bank, kicked free.

I do not recall that anything outstanding marked the rest of our day together.

Two or three weeks later I was on the river about a hundred yards below the scene of the tragedy narrated, when, near the top of a straight run of about 300 yds of river, I saw under the far bank (the left) a small raft of cut weed collected by some underwater obstruction. Watching the spot as a likely one, I presently observed the surface broken by a tiny swirl which I had no difficulty in attributing to the absorption of a nymph. Taking the hint, I dropped my nymph with an 00 Pennell sneck in it an inch or two below the raft of cut weed and had the immediate satisfaction of seeing the floating gut drawn under as by some adhesion and, on raising the tip of the W.B.R., finding that I was into something solid. My usual experience with trout hooked under that far bank (and I had had them up to and just over 3 lb) was that they could generally be persuaded to cross over and come under my bank and be played and killed there. But this fish was not having any. Nothing I could do would bring him across, and for the entire three hundred yards to Mac's Corner, though he came downstream, he bored stubbornly under the left bank. At Mac's Corner, however, there is a right-angled turn of the river to the east with the push of the current across to the right bank, and here, with the aid of that push, I succeeded at length in bringing that stubborn trout under my bank. But he turned upstream immediately and forced his way, still under my bank, for a hundred yards or more before I could again turn him and lead him foot by foot to a little bare patch at the top of Mac's Corner, when for the first time I got a view of his proportions. From that point I resolved that the battle *must* be finished there. But again and again, as I led him towards the waiting net, he sheered off, still keeping his balance. But at last, at the umpteenth shot, I had the net under him and drew him ashore.

Was he, could he be a four-pounder? It was years since one had been taken on that stretch. The priest having performed his office, I fixed the hook of my spring balance into the trout's jaw, and was delighted to see it pull down to 4 lb 3 or 4 oz. But, alas, it thought better of it and reverted to 3 lb 14 oz., where it stayed. Still, it was the biggest trout I had ever had from the Itchen in over fifty years, though I had two or three times seen and twice had hooked bigger. But the regretful reflection assailed me, 'Was it my friend's lost fish?' Hooked a short stretch below the spot where C.L.C.'s loss had occurred, it was unlikely that another fish of that size would have been so near.

A curious feature of the kill was that though the trout was hooked in the upper jaw the hook had worn through that jaw and secured a tight grip on the lower jaw.

from ITCHEN MEMORIES *1951*

Shocks and a Lesson

G. E. M. SKUES

In early September 1891, having gone through a pretty strenuous time, I was badly run down when I started with an angling friend from the British Museum to spend ten days of my three weeks' annual holiday on the upper waters of the Yore; and at the expiration of that ten days I was not a little surprised to find that, thanks to the bracing moorland air and the good feeding provided by the good-natured landlady of the inn at which we stayed, I had put on no less than 13 lb in weight. From there we planned to proceed to Winchester and to spend the remainder of our three weeks upon the Abbots Barton stretch of the Itchen immediately above Winchester by the kind permission of the client who was the lessee of the water. I had been presented in 1887 with a copy of Halford's *Flies and How to Dress*

Them, and in 1889 with Halford's first edition of *Dry Fly Fishing in Theory and Practice*, and both of us, relatively inexperienced, looked on these immortal works as revelation from on high with all the authority of gospel truth.

We had heard on the day of our arrival in Winchester that the great man was putting up at The George and was nightly welcoming his worshippers at that hotel to hear him expound the pure and authentic gospel of the dry fly – which no one would dream of questioning. So that evening found us, after our meal, among the humble listeners. It came to our ears on that occasion that we were to have the great man's company on the Abbots Barton water, the lessee having invited him for a week. With becoming reverence we listened to his words of wisdom until it became necessary that the session be broken up.

On the following day we were on the water a quarter of an hour or so before our mentor's arrival – taking the side stream, my friend above in the Ducks' Nest Spinney, I a couple of hundred yards farther downstream, thus leaving the main river, the fishing of which was reputed the better, to the great man. He was not long behind us and presently we saw him casting on Winnel Water, the main river. Soon afterwards he crossed the meadow which divided the two streams and accosted me from the left bank of the side stream to advise us kindly on the fly to put up, and to make his advice clearer he cast his fly to light on the right bank of the side stream, having first ascertained that I had mounted a fly of George Holland's dressing, known as the quill Marryat. He insisted that his fly, which was an india-rubber olive, was the right fly. My selection was based on little pale duns seen on the water. I took a look at his fly and was not a little shocked to see how coarse was the gut on which his fly was tied, but I was also too polite or timid to venture on such a comment.

We met at lunch-time and he inquired how I had done. I said two and a half brace. He had one trout only, but congratulated me civilly and offered to put me up for the Flyfishers' Club, then recently formed. Not expecting, despite my additional 13 lb in ten days, to live long enough to make it worth while, I declined and did not in fact seek membership till the autumn of 1893, when a voyage to the Cape and back had gone a long way to re-establishing my health.

Halford only fished the Abbots Barton length for three more days of this week, but just as I had been profoundly shocked to do better than the great master did on the first day, I was fated to be similarly shocked on each of his three other days. Yet it encouraged me to rely most on my own observations and not to attach undue importance to authority. My friend, by the way, caught the biggest fish of the week (1 lb 13 oz), but it was his only catch.

At this period I had had little Itchen experience – perhaps three or four days each year since 1883, but for years afterwards I looked back on those four days whenever I was faced with the alternative of letting myself be guided by authority or going on my own wilful way, and I have seldom had grounds for regretting the lesson September 1891.

from ITCHEN MEMORIES *1951*

Per Ardua . . .

A. P. GORDON CUMMING

The upshot was, he shot down the narrows, and went rolling head over heels down the foaming 'Meux & Co's Entire' (this being the usual colour of summer floods). To stop him was impossible. I held on above the rapid till I thought my good Forrest rod would have gone at the hand, and certainly the fine single gut I had on earlier would have parted with half the strain.

All I could do was to give him what line he required until he found a resting-place behind some rock – this he did after rattling off fifty yards of line. Waiting some minutes till he seemed quiet, I threw off some ten yards more line, and turning the top of the rod upstream, I darted it down to my man on the gravel below, having cautioned him not to alarm the fish by letting the line get taut. To scramble up the rocks and down again to the gravel bed, to resume my possession of my rod, was two or three minutes' work, and just as I seized hold of it, the fish, having ventured from his shelter, was, in spite of his efforts, hurried down at racing pace, taking more line than I liked, while I followed, crawling and leaping along some impassable-looking country, such as I would not have faced in cold blood. By this time he had nearly reached the Essor fall, and all seemed lost. I do not think he really intended going over, for when he felt himself within the influence of the strong smooth water he tried his best to return, but in vain; over he went like a shot, and long ere I could get round some high rocks and down to the lower part of the fall, I had 80 or 90 yards out, and to follow him farther on this side of the water was impossible, owing to the steep rocks rising beside the stream. To add to the embarrassment of my position I found, on raising the point of my rod, that in going over the fall the fish had passed beneath some arch deep under water, thus making my case appear very hopeless. But, determined not to give it up yet, I sent my man up to the house of Relugas, where he found an old three-pronged dung-fork and a garden line, with which we managed to construct a grapnel, and at the second throw in I got hold of the line below the sunken arch, then fastening it to my right hand, I made my man throw the whole line off the reel and through the rings, and having drawn the remainder of the line through the sunken arch, and clear of the impediment, I formed a coil, and with my left hand pitched the end of it up to him, when he passed it through the rings again from the top of the rod, fixed it to the axle of the reel, and handed me down the rod to where I stood. From the long line out, and the heavy water, I could not tell whether the fish was on or not, but the line looked greatly chafed all along.

I now tried the only plan to end the business; leaving my man holding the rod, I went to a bridge some distance up the river, and having crossed to the other side and come down opposite him, he pitched the rod over to me. I felt that if he was still on I was sure of him, and reeling steadily up the 80 yards which were out, I followed down to the big round pool below, where, to my surprise, I became aware that he was still on. He made but a feeble resistance, and, after a fight of two hours and forty minutes, we got the clips into as gallant a fish as ever left the sea – weight 19½lb and new run. The last hour and a half was in a roaring white flood. The fly was, as you may imagine, well 'chained up'.

from A LETTER *1848*

Dry Fly on the Earn

A. R. B. HALDANE

For several years the Earn trout almost entirely defeated me. Except on rare occasions, the only fish I got were small ones in some of the more rapid streams, the larger ones in the deep pools continuing to disregard the wet flies which I offered them, no matter how carefully I fished, casting the longest line of which I was capable; but the time came when having learned in Hampshire the use of the dry fly, I came back to Aberuthven to put to the test the growing conviction that now I would have some chance with the big trout in the quiet water.

Morris, the keeper, is one of those who regard trout-fishing as a child's but innocent occupation with which those who care, may, on rivers where the salmon run late, pass the time till the real fishing starts. While I do not share his view, I cannot feel surprised at the good-natured contempt with which he regarded my early efforts, and after so many weary fruitless days when he watched me fishing down the Aberuthven streams, he had reason to bless the day I first used a floating fly.

Our first real success came on a day in the middle of May many years ago. Public holidays are not as a rule happy in their coincidence with good fishing conditions, but this one was the exception, a fresh day of late spring following rain in the night which had raised the river a few inches and given it a touch of colour. The air was mild, and a light breeze blew upstream. The Earn has a chronic habit of changing its course, cutting into the sand and clay of the banks first on one side and then on the other. As Morris and I walked down the river that morning we came towards a part where the stream had for the last few seasons been at work eating its way deep into the deep rich soil on the near side. So a steep bank of clay and gravel fell almost sheer to the edge of the water and from the top of the bank great lumps of turf, undercut by the water, had fallen off into the stream. These lay along the edge of the current and some, more recently fallen, lay only half-submerged, making behind them tiny bays of quiet water at the very edge of the fast current. As we came nearer, we saw that the sand martins, which nest in the face of the broken bank, were flying backwards and forwards low over the stream, constantly sweeping to the surface as they picked off the water the olive duns which now we could see rising in quantities from the water or blowing from the bank above.

A few small fish out in the stream were taking the flies with eager splashing rises, but what pleased us most was that trout were feeding quietly and steadily in the smoother patches of water close to the foot of the bank. We made a wide and hurried detour, coming back to the water's edge some yards below the lower end of the stream. Lowering myself over the bank I got a precarious footing at the edge of the current and faced upstream, while close at my shoulder the sand martins flashed in and out of their nesting holes. For fifty yards above me, it seemed that each little backwater behind each lump of turf held a trout, and as we watched we would see a nose come quietly up and then a tail appeared as the fish sucked in the olives caught by the eddies and drifted into the quiet water. I had no olives, but a Greenwell did just as well. The light breeze gave all the help one could have wished and if the fly floated even for a few seconds in the smooth water before the current caught the line and dragged it away, it was generally taken. Each trout on being hooked dashed out into the stream and down past me. I could not move back to get below them and some were lost as they were with difficulty brought back against the current; but most were well hooked, and in the end came to the net which Morris, for once reconciled to trout-fishing and as eager as I, handed down from the top of the bank. By the time the top of the stream was reached we had caught nine trout, of which the smallest was not under half a pound, several of them being over one pound.

from THE PATH BY THE WATER *1944*

Scottish Memories

SIR EDWARD DURAND

Owing to a disgusting and eminently unfair shortage of the necessary means I have not had one quarter of the opportunities with regard to salmon that I have had for trout-fishing, and that is possibly why I have only twice, plainly and distinctly, seen the occurrence with the bigger fish.

The first time was many years ago on the Wye. I was fishing with fly, off the bank, and was accompanied by the river-keeper as gillie. Much to the surprise of the latter, who had told me that fly was quite useless at that time of the year, I had quite a successful morning, rising three fish and landing two. I had just worked up a nice bit of water without moving anything when I found further progress barred by an abrupt rise in the bank, which for some distance up the river rose sheer out of the water to a height of ten or fifteen feet. The keeper told me it was a good bit of water to fish, and that the owner of the other bank caught plenty there, but owing to the height above the water on our side, it was usually neglected.

I thought I would give it a try however, and clambered up to the top to have a look. What struck me immediately was the clearness of the water as I looked down into it, and it was at once apparent that no salmon were lying near our bank though there seemed to be some likely places in mid-stream and over on the other side where the main current was flowing.

I fished the centre of the river and gradually lengthened out my line to the full extent of my ordinary casting abilities, without any result at all, and then moved upstream for a few yards to cover fresh water. On repeating the performance I noticed that with my longest cast I was still many yards short of the other bank, and just beyond my fly was a smooth hump of water, evidently flowing over some submerged rock. I walked up a few paces and lengthened out my cast to try to reach the place, which looked like a very good lie for a salmon.

I was now throwing a longer line than I could really manage, and lost one fly by touching the ground behind me. After knotting on another, I nearly gave it up, but the place looked so likely that I had one more try to get the fly out. I succeeded at the first cast and, shooting as much line as I could, got the fly to light well above the hump of water and swing down to it in the current.

A fish was there and he had it first time, with a big swirl and a heavy jar as I pulled the steel home in his jaw.

For a moment or two he stayed where he was, tugging at the restraint, but to my joy he then went upstream like a torpedo with the taut line throwing up spray as it cut through the current. I manoeuvred him out into mid-stream and got a shorter hold on him by following up as fast as possible, but I was careful not to put on enough strain to turn him downstream, as I feared trouble if I had to clamber down the end of the steep bank to a lower level. He made several good runs and fought hard, but I gave him no rest and he shortly began to tire.

We then had to think of gaffing him; the bank where I was standing was far too steep for the keeper to get near the water, and we decided that the best chance was to lead the fish downstream to the edge of the plateau and, letting him drop down a short way, draw him up again close to the bank, where the keeper could gaff him from the lower level, while I stayed on the top. I cautioned the man to keep out of sight as much as possible, as I thought the fish might have another run or two still left in him, and I was again mindful of the difficulty I would have in scrambling down to the lower level if he made a bolt downstream. However, this luckily did not happen.

The first part of the manoeuvre was successfully accomplished, and I turned the salmon in the river below us and started to reel him in. As he came in sight into the clear water below the bank I had one of the shocks of my life. Had I got into a tunny or a swordfish by mistake? Or what was this thing about three yards long doing on the end of my line? And then I realized it was another and bigger salmon following the hooked one with his nose almost touching its tail.

The keeper from his lower level could not see what was going on, but the fish saw him and dashed off again, luckily for me up and across stream; but from the swirl the two of them made as they turned, the keeper also thought it must be the grandfather of all fish that I had on the end of my line.

I soon regained control, and allowed the salmon to drop slowly down the river again, while the keeper changed his position to a place where he could better conceal himself. This time there was no mistake and he gaffed his fish cleanly, but the bigger fish had been following closely all the time, as I could see plainly from my exalted position on the bank above them. The man very nearly dropped his gaffed salmon when the other and bigger fish swirled away in a mad rush as his friend and companion was lifted, kicking and struggling, from the river. A fish on the gaff is worth two in the water.

When they were safely up on the bank I scrambled down, while the priest was performing the final rites, and then, only, had time to tell what I had seen. The keeper was rather disappointed in the size of the fish, although it turned the scale at 22 lb; he had expected something colossal.

He had seen a following fish once or twice before in his life, but never such a really pertinacious one as this had proved himself to be, but he could give no definite reason for their behaviour. We were a long way from any spawning beds and it was early in the season for the fish to be thinking of such things. Was it merely curiosity aroused by the struggles of the hooked one? Or was it the prompting of that law of nature which makes every injured or crippled animal a fit object for immediate destruction, even by his own kith and kin? I had watched the bigger fish closely for some time, but I had seen no signs of any attack being made.

As I said before, I have noticed much the same sort of thing happen while trout-fishing, but then it is usually the case that the follower is markedly bigger than the hooked one, and I think his behaviour is undoubtedly due to his hopes of a free meal. Also I have had trout scarred and bitten in the course of the fight, after they had taken my fly, and even in one or two instances have had them entirely removed, but in all probability this was the work of pike, and that is quite another story.

But I did see the same thing happen once again with salmon, and this time it had a very different ending.

I was up in Scotland in late autumn, and after a wet, misty morning which had driven us down off the hill in despair, I appropriated one of the stalkers to act as gillie and, after struggling into my waders, tramped down to the sea pool below the lodge to see if I could do anything with the sea-trout. I was earnestly requested by my hostess to catch something quickly and send it up to the house, as the fish for dinner had not been delivered that day.

I was not expecting salmon as the river had been running low and clear, but I thought that the wet morning might have put some colour into the water, and that the sea-trout might be taking in the sea pool in the evening. I took down a venerable old rod, inherited from my father, a Hardy's ten-foot split cane that is now well over fifty years old and is still as good as on the day it was made. I had a nearly new sea-trout line on the reel with plenty of backing, and put up a 2x cast with a team of three flies.

Donald, the gillie, went down to look at the river while I was making preparations, and his solemn, austere countenance was almost cheerful when he came back to report. 'There was-ss some watter since the morn, and she was-ss moving.' From which I deduced that there was a bit more water in the river than had been the case latterly.

Donald advised me to fish down the long pool first, before I waded in at the tail-end, because there were some good lies in the deeper water above. I had to do this from the bank, and again I found myself poised rather high above the water; also, in spite of the very slight stain caused by the morning's rain, I could see clearly to the very bottom of the river below me.

I had not been casting five minutes before a boil at my tail fly, in the centre of the river, made me lift the rod-point, and I knew at once that I was into something big. The gallant little rod bent like a hoop as the fish made his first rush up and across stream. I clumped along after him as fast as my waders and brogues would allow, and after some time succeeded in getting him into the smoother water near my bank. As soon as he came in sight I could see that my first guess had been right and that I was fast in a salmon, also that my fish was being closely followed by another, again a slightly larger one.

Even Donald's imperturbability was not proof against the excitement of my having hooked a 'fush' and not one of the 'wee bit trooties', and if I had obeyed all the advice and anxious entreaties which he hurled at me in rapid succession, I should have lost my fish ten times over. Luckily I realized my only chance was to keep a light strain on the salmon and let him tire himself out completely before I tried to take control in any shape or form.

I did not look at the time and do not know how long the fight went on, but I *do* know that I was getting quite weary of making repeated runs up and down the bank to the head of the pool. Luckily the side strain turned the fish each time before he got into the fast water above, and each time, as I led him downstream towards the centre of the long calm stretch, there was that other fish following every movement close behind him.

After what seemed like hours to me the fight began to slacken a bit and I had a faint hope of gaining some sort of control, though I was fearful of putting on any real strain. I noticed there was a deep and narrow channel under my bank and I thought that if I could only get the fish into that, and lead him up it, I might give Donald a chance to use his gaff. There was a convenient little point of bank jutting into the stream just below where I was still playing my salmon, and I told Donald to scramble down to the water's edge and hide himself there until I led the fish upstream past him, but I warned him he must make sure of his first stroke because he was unlikely to get a second, as the cast would probably break.

I let the fish drop downstream, well out from the bank, with the bigger one still following closely, until I got below where Donald was hiding at the water's edge. I then put on all the side strain I dared until he came round, head upstream and close to my bank, but some yards below me. Then, keeping as steady a strain on the line as I could, I walked upstream backwards. I passed above the crouching stalker and could not now see my fish as it was hidden by the jutting bank. Slowly I stepped backwards, farther and farther, until I felt almost sure the salmon had got past the ambush in safety. Suddenly Donald straightened up, there was much splashing for a second, and then he was stumbling up the bank, with a triumphant shout of 'I haff her, sir-r-r', and a goodly salmon was kicking on his gaff.

Thankfully I was just about to drop my rod-point, when the reel screeched as the line was torn off it, and the rod bent into a hoop again under the strain. I yelled back to him: 'Ye have not, she's still on.' I had not time to look, but Donald said afterwards that he nearly dropped his 'fush', gaff and all, into the river in his surprise. However, he recovered himself sufficiently quickly to get the salmon safely up the bank and to do the necessary with the priest, but when he got back to me I had to laugh at his face of complete bewilderment.

I explained to him what had been clear to me, after the first shock of surprise, that he had let my fish pass him and had gaffed the follower. He had not been alongside of me all through the fight, and had not seen how closely it had followed its leader the whole time.

My hooked salmon had evidently got a bad scare, as he put up another good fight, but my tackle held and I was soon able to lead it up close to the bank again, and the hidden stalker made no mistake this time. Thankfully I laid my rod down and went to gloat over the two fish. Donald was busy with the spring balance and declared the hooked fish to be a good 9 lb, and the unhooked one 12 lb and 'a bittock'.

It then flashed across my mind that I could have a bit of a joke with my hostess, remembering her strict instructions about sending in an early supply of fish.

I looked at my watch and was surprised to see that I had been away from the lodge only an hour and a quarter. I swore Donald to secrecy and, tearing a leaf out of my note-book, scribbled a short note to the effect that I was obeying orders in sending in early my catch up to date, and hoped it would be enough for dinner, but if not I was still trying to catch more. As I wrote I could see Donald handling the rod with reverential awe, and murmuring to himself that it was 'a grand wee thing'. He chuckled appreciatively when I told him what I had written, and that I was going to allow the party at the lodge to think that I had killed these two fish in under an hour, but that he was to give no details and come back to me as quickly as he could. He walked off with his burden, still chuckling.

I snipped off the tail fly of my cast and some two inches of gut which looked frayed and doubtful, and after fastening on another fly made my way down to the shallow water at the tail of the pool, and waded in to try for sea-trout. Donald appeared on the bank again very quickly and said he had handed in the note and the fish at the back door, and had come away without seeing any of the party.

It was barely ten minutes after this, while I was standing in mid-stream playing a nice lively sea-trout, that I became aware of a small crowd of onlookers on the bank, watching the fun. I scrambled ashore for Donald to net out a good 3 lb fish, and was immediately assailed with questions.

My host and another of the party armed with salmon-rods had rushed down to the river, quite convinced that there must be a big run of fish coming up from the loch. Several others had come down to look on, and all were anxious to know where I had caught the fish and why I was not still fishing for salmon.

I told them I did not wish to be selfish and had left the rest for them, and besides, I had really come down to the river for sea-trout, and had caught the salmon only for my hostess's sake, as she has asked me to do.

My canny host looked at the trout-rod and said: 'You never landed a salmon on that toothpick?' I assured him that I had done so. How had I managed to get them both so quickly? Oh, that was quite easy: Donald had gaffed them within a few minutes of each other. Which, when you come to think of it, was quite true in every respect!

Still thoroughly unbelieving, they went off upstream to try their luck. Some of the party went with them, while others stayed to see if I would provide any more thrills, and as the dusk fell the sea-trout began to take well and I had quiet a nice basket when the time came to knock off and go home to dinner.

I had to stand a hot fire of questions at that meal, and found it very hard to keep up the deception without telling actual lies. I could see that my shrewd host was still very unconvinced and eventually I had to let out the whole truth. Even that was strange enough to be hard to swallow, and it was only the corroborative evidence of Donald next morning that finally cleared me of the suspicion of having deliberately 'stroke hauled' the two fish. I can even hear a faint echo of 'fisherman's yarns' from readers of the story, but in the words an uncle of mine always used to quote to us as children: 'He who is not strictly accurate is of no value to his fellow creatures.'

from WANDERINGS WITH A FLY ROD *1938*

Dry Fly Fishing

LORD GREY

Anglers differ as to how late the evening fishing should be prolonged. Night fishing with a large wet fly should not be allowed on good dry fly water. It is poor fun to haul out of the river by main force in the dark, on thick gut, a trout that might give good sport in daylight. Before it gets dark, however, there is a half-hour in which it is just possible to see where a fish is rising, but just not possible to see one's fly. It needs both skill and judgement to put an artificial fly properly over a fish in these conditions, but during this half-hour a skilful angler may expect to get a brace of good trout with a floating sedge fly. This is perfectly fair fishing, but it has not the same interest as the finer fishing in better light; it needs skill, and yet it is comparatively clumsy work. The angler strikes at sight of a rise without being sure whether it is to his fly or not. He can, and indeed must, use stronger gut, because, when a trout is hooked, he cannot tell accurately what it is doing, or follow its movements adjusting the strain carefully to the need of each moment as he would do in daylight. In short a great part of all that happens, both before and after he hooks a trout, is hidden from him, and he has in the end to rely more upon force, and less upon skill to land the fish. All this takes away much of the pleasure, and if the day has been a fairly good one, I would rather forgo the last brace than kill them under inferior conditions. On the other hand, if luck has been very bad, or the trout have been particularly exasperating and successful in defeating the angler, or have refused to rise all day, then the sedge fly in the last half-hour of perceptible twilight gives a very satisfactory opportunity of trying to get even with them. After a fair day, however, it seems to me better to leave off when I cease to be able to see a medium-sized quill gnat upon the water at a reasonable distance.

Very pleasant the evening is after a successful day in hot, bright weather in June. Let us suppose that the angler has caught some three brace of trout in the day, and a brace and a half in the evening on good water. He will then have had plenty of interest and excitement, moments of anxiety, and even of disappointment, but all contributing in the end to give a delightful satisfactory feeling of successful effort. Some great events, some angling crisis there will have been during the day, to which his thoughts will recur often involuntarily. Some incidents will seem to have been photographed upon his mind, so that he can recall clearly not only the particular things done or seen, but his own sensation at the time. What he thinks about in the evening will not be only of angling, but of the scenes in which he has spent the day. I am often ashamed to think how much passes unnoticed in the actual excitement of angling, but the general impression of light and colour, and surroundings is not lost; some is noted at the time, and some sinks into one's mind unconsciously and is found there at the end of the day, like a blessing given by great bounty to one who was too careless at the time to deserve it. May is the month of fresh leaves and bright shrubs, but June is the month in which the water meadows themselves are brightest. The common yellow iris, ragged robin and forget-me-not make rough damp places gay, and the clear water in the little runnels amongst the grass sparkle in the sun. Of wild shrubs which flower in June, there are two so common that they seem to possess the month and meet the eye everywhere. One is the wild rose, and the other is the elder, and great is the contrast between them. The commonest sort of wild rose is surely the most delicate of all shrubs in spite of its thorns. It is exquisitely delicate in the scent, colour, form and character of its flowers, and there is nothing more graceful in nature than the way in which a long spray of wild rose in full blossom offers its beauty to be admired. I am not so fond of the elder; when one is close to it there is a certain stiff thickness about the bush, and a deadness of colour both of leaves and flowers, and the scent is heavy and spiritless. But masses of elder flower at a distance have a fine foamy appearance, and I always feel that they are doing their best to honour the season. Though the sun may be as hot as midsummer, everything in the first half of June seems young and fresh and active. Birds are singing still, and for a week or two it seems as if the best of spring and summer, warmth and songs, luxuriance and freshness, were spread abroad so abundantly that it is almost too much. The cup of happiness is full and runs over. Such may be one's last thoughts in the quiet of approaching night after sounds have ceased, and in the perfect enjoyment of 'that still spirit shed from evening air'.

As June draws to a close, and during the whole of July, the rise during the day becomes more uncertain and feeble. There are many days in July when the dry fly angler spends more time in watching and waiting than in active fishing. His best chance before the evening will be between ten and one o'clock, and though he must be prepared for very light baskets, yet there are mornings in July when trout are to be found feeding slowly and quietly here and there, and when they will take a red quill gnat if it is put to them attractively. I have known days in July, when the result of a morning's fishing has been unexpectedly good, equal in total weight to that of the very best days in other months, and equal also in regard to the size and condition of the individual fish.

In August I have only once had a morning's fishing which could fairly be compared, as regards the total weight of trout landed, with the good days of earlier months, and it always seems to me that the condition of the trout in this month ceases to be quite first-rate. Of September, on dry fly rivers, I have had no experience. Anglers who write of it agree in saying that the trout rise better, but that their condition has fallen off, and that an unduly large proportion of female fish are killed.

from FLY FISHING *1899*

A Warwickshire Trout

'B.B.'

I have never captured a record fish but I have caught two 'notable fish', one a trout and the other a tench. The trout came out of a brook in Warwickshire where no trout were supposed to be, but I afterwards found out this supposition had been cleverly bruited abroad by those whose lands adjoined the brook. The stream was certainly unprepossessing to the uneducated eye. It was very narrow, much overgrown with bushes and the banks patrolled by bulls. The latter, I have no doubt, had been placed there by riparian owners. But what are such trifles to a small boy? Any active and healthy boy is a match for a bull if he keeps his head and as for keepers and farm bailiffs . . .

When I was about thirteen years of age I went to stay one spring with my grandfather, who, in his day, had been a keen fisherman. He had a coachman named Dickon, who wore a glass eye, always an object of morbid fascination to the young. Dickon had lost his eye one winter afternoon when he was chopping wood, a chip flying up had almost gouged it out.

But I digress. One spring morning I was with Dickon in his harness-room watching him polishing the brass fittings to a collar. . . . The conversation turned to fishing. 'Ah,' said Dickon, polishing away at a buckle, 'there *are* trout if you knows where to look for 'em. Didn't Mr Free used to get up at five in the morning when he stayed here, and go out and catch them?'

'Trout?' I asked incredulously.

'Aye, trout. Good 'uns too!'

'Where did he go?' I asked.

'Why, Peddar's Mill, of course.'

'But the Commander told me there were *no* trout there!' I exclaimed. (The Commander being the chief 'riparian owner'.)

Dickon smiled and went on polishing. That was enough. I would go to Pedder's Mill as soon as I could get my tackle together.

The next day I developed a roaring cold in the head. But despite this, and managing to conceal my malady from adult eyes, I set off soon after breakfast with my trout-rod, neatly dodging my grandfather who was talking to Dickon by the coach-house.

It was a wild April morning, grey and blowing hard, with occasional showers. Though the wind was cold it was one of those days when you feel the spring everywhere, you hear it too, and smell it.

I reached Pedder's Mill and had barely rigged up my tackle in the shelter of the hawthorns by the old mill (they were speckled all over with bursting green buds and a thrush had built a very new emerald green nest in the heart of one of them) when the miller up at the mill opened the hatch and the still water at my feet became alive with thundering turmoil, dead leaves appeared and drowned sticks turned over and over in the muddy maelstrom.

Then came the miller and ordered me off. I went out on the road, walked down it for a quarter of a mile and rejoined the brook.

I lay low under a willow stump until I saw the Commander come down the drive in his neat trap, complete with cockaded coachman, and then began to fish. Soon a man appeared up by the Dower House kitchen garden fence, and bawled at me at intervals. I took no notice for a time until he began to purposefully climb the fence. Bailiffs and bulls are best left to themselves. He meant business so I stood not upon the order of my going.

These interruptions were tiresome and this latest interference made me impatient. I made another détour and came upon the stream again. Here, under a pallisade of alder-trees I at last got my fly on the water and fished the brook down for some two hundred yards without the sign of a rise. Then the stream took a sharp turn to the left in a sort of elbow.

Under the far bank, the current was swift and the fly tittupped round on the ripples and was engulfed. The reel sang as a big fish made upstream and I had to follow. He made for a biggish pool some twenty yards above and there we fought it out for twenty minutes. I had no net (the very young do not carry nets) and I had to play my fish right out and beach him on the shingle at the pool head.

He was a beauty and I took no chances with him, he was practically drowned when I towed him ashore and fell upon him, a trout of three and a half pounds.

The battle won I wrapped it up in dock leaves and put it in my pocket, though the tail flapped under my right arm. I regained the road and almost at once heard the sound of a fast-trotting horse. It was as I had feared, the Commander was returning.

I raised my cap respectfully, and then I heard the clatter of hooves mingle and stop as the trap was pulled up. The Commander was a red-faced man, clean-shaven, of course. He glowered at my rod. I endeavoured to keep my right side turned from him lest he should see the 'tell-tale tail'. I wished the ground would open and engulf me but at that moment Providence took a hand. There came again the sound of trotting hooves and just as the Commander was about to cast aside his carriage rug and descend upon me, no doubt with the object of searching my small person, there swept round the corner my grandfather, likewise in his trap, with Dickon beside him. Under the confusion of the meeting I bolted through the hedge and ran all the way home.

Now, by hook or crook, I had made up my mind to have that fish 'set up'. As bad luck would have it my grandmother met me in the drive and I foolishly showed her my trout, telling her I was going to have it stuffed.

She said nothing, probably because she knew I was a determined young devil, but when my grandfather returned, having calmed the Commander, she told him I was going to have my big trout 'stuffed'.

'That trout will be eaten here!' he thundered, and, as I was afraid of my grandfather, I said no word. Next day I was due to leave for home and without saying anything to anyone I raided the larder, procured my trout and wrapped it up in paper, posting it off from the post office 'ere I left for the train.

In the queer way grown-ups have, the trout was forgotten in the business of seeing me off to the station and on the way thither I confided in Dickon what I had done, and he gave his unqualified approval. That is why that three-and-a-half pound brook trout still surveys me as I write these lines, superbly mounted in an ebony-framed case, a pleasant reminder of boyhood's triumphant victory over elders and betters, and an aldermanic fish.

First published in THE FISHERMAN'S BEDSIDE BOOK *1945*
(from 'Fisherman's Folly', an unpublished MS.)

When All Else Failed

V. J. ROBINSON

The June weather was hot and the river was very low and very clear. For ten days we had been praying for rain. It was the upper part – forty miles from the sea – of one of Scotland's (shall I say) second-class salmon rivers.

That the fish were 'there' had been established: on a recent day when the Crooked Pot was being fished for the umpteenth time (with a small tube fly) a fish of about 15 lb had rolled quietly on the surface – one could not claim it as a rise, belike the fly had no bearing on the matter. Also in the same pool a smaller fish had been seen. Fifty yards upstream, at the bottom Ardgully, Angus and Bill had stationed themselves on a high bank above the pool and, with polaroid glasses, had spotted seven fish in the deeper water at the head of the Pool. How to catch them? . . . it was a testing problem.

Large and small flies had been ignored, a tiny minnow, spun delicately, had produced no result. Trout flies and, as a last resort, something really big and offensive had been offered: no good. It became a matter of honour and prestige that we caught and ate a salmon. We had fished early and late but all to no avail.

There came to dinner one evening a neighbour and his wife. This neighbour, though he owned a mile or so of fishing, was not very keen on the salmon but let his friends have free of his water. I was discussing the situation when he said: 'You should try the worm – we always do.'

I recoiled, regretting deeply the Bollinger he was enjoying . . . but the seed was sown and next morning I found myself in conference with Angus, whose eyes glistened as I expressed my wishes.

Ten-thirty found us on our way to the river. I must now introduce the members of the party. Firstly my daughter-in-law, Ann (to use that vivid expression of Patrick Chalmers's), 'keen as knives' on the fishing. She had no knowledge or experience, but was unable to pass a river, a loch or indeed *any* water without stopping to look at it, a born fisher in the making.

The only other member, apart from myself, was Bill. A young fisherman of considerable skill and experience where trout were concerned, but his tally of salmon was small. He was the true son of his father in that he was a confirmed and inveterate poacher and, as such, endeared himself to me. His philosophy could briefly be summed up in, 'Try everything legitimate and try it well: if all else fails, "give them the works".'

And so we came to the Crooked Pot and made our preparations. There was no nonsense of flies or spinners today. The Garden Ranger was the stuff and Angus proceeded to mount a large and attractive specimen. The rod was an astonishing affair of mixed parentage. Where Angus obtained it I know not, but it was about 12 ft long and constructed of cane, greenheart and hickory.

By virtue of my seniority I was urged to have first go. Now it must be clearly realised that the river was dead low, the water quite clear, the pool comparatively small in width (an easy cast across) and about 25 yds long, and the banks sloped down to the water's edge. It was essential to keep out of sight.

Angus, having dealt with the ranger, handed me the rod. I crept down to the head of the pool dragging the thing behind me (I swear it weighed as much as a 12-bore). Backwards and forwards I swung the bait and dropped it well out in the rush of water at the very head of the pool. Slowly the line was paid out, yard by yard, until the ranger was 15 yds down the pool. Nothing happened and the line was wound in and the bait raised.

Again I swung it out and paid out line – kneeling and crouching to keep out of sight. Four, five, ten yards of line out and then a check . . . the rod-top jerked and jerked again. Then it stopped and I waited a second. There was no further result, so I raised the bait to the surface. A splash behind it and a fish of about 7 lb swirled up behind the worm.

Loud cries from the gallery and Ann, in a voice like a peahen screamed, 'Did you see it? Did you see it?' A foolish question, but excusable under the circumstances. Once more the ranger went out – down again yard by yard – and then it stopped. Two or three violent jerks came to the rod-top . . . I could stand it no longer and, jumping to my feet, I struck hard.

Then things really did begin to happen. The fish was fairly hooked and immediately leapt from the water and started madly to career round the pool. Loud cries of excitement and encouragement from the male members of the gallery. Ann gave a choking sob and burst into tears. Meanwhile the fish gave of his best. Several determined but fruitless efforts were made to leave the pool.

Downstream was broken water for 20 yds and then the Island Pool, a long, rather narrow place (most excellent fly water) for 40 yds, then more very broken and rocky water and another pool. I had no wish to have to follow a fish downstream as the banks were covered with hidden rocks and gorse and there were many concealed holes. However, all was well and in about seven or eight minutes I led a very gallant fish to the gaff which Angus used so well after his years of experience: 7½ lb and fresh as paint. Many were the exclamations of satisfaction. Much back-slapping took place and all was merry. The fish was hooked under the chin.

And so to lunch, fresh baps (or softies) with ham and butter and hard-boiled eggs, tomatoes and lettuce topped up with cheese and biscuits and beer. What more could be desired?

After lunch a further plan was discussed, and Bill went 100 yds upstream to bottom Ardgully. The objective was the salmon already spotted there by polaroid glasses from the high bank. Angus climbed the bank and reported that 'the fleet was in'. Bill crawled up and presented the 'ranger'.

For half an hour he attempted to contact a fish. Angus kept up an agonised and agonising running commentary. There were five fish all close to each other, one big one of, say, 15 lb and four all about 7 lb or 8 lb. Every time the worm came near the big fish he turned and closely examined it. The others were unresponsive. Eventually, white and shaking, Bill gave it up and returned to the seat above the Crooked Pot. The Pool had had a good rest and we urged Bill to see what he could do. He had refused to use Angus's rod and preferred his own, a good 10 ft dry fly rod well suited to the present occasion.

There was the usual cautious approach and presentation of the ranger. We had not long to wait for results. It was the fourth or fifth swim down when the check took place. Again the rod-top was bent and twitched. Then the line moved steadily off and Bill struck. The response left the efforts of the previous fish nowhere. This was obviously something much larger.

First the fish ran three times right round the pool – showing itself for all to see in a succession of noble leaps. The gallery cheered. Again Ann wept. Then the fish decided to go down and Bill had no option but to follow straight through the broken water to the Island Pool and 40 yds down to the bottom. Bill pursued with great gusto, falling several times as he found concealed holes and tripped over rocks he could not see.

The instant the fish arrived at the end of the Island Pool it turned and made up at full speed and back to the Crooked Pot. Round this again and then off once more to the Island. I am not clear what Bill was doing but somehow he kept in touch and was not left too far behind. This time the fish decided it had had enough of the Island, and before we knew what was afoot, he was out of the bottom of the pool and into rougher water towards the Green Mounds.

At last it was showing signs of tiring. Then, horror of horrors, the cast became caught round the top of a rock which projected three feet out of the water some two yards from the bank. With great presence of mind and notable agility, Angus sprang on to the rock, swept the cast clear with the gaff and was back with us on the bank. The end was near and in a backwater 10 yds lower down the fish was gaffed.

Sixteen pounds and a noble fighter. Great indeed were the congratulations and exclamations of praise for Bill for his agility, and for Angus for saving the situation in a dreadful moment.

Half an hour later Bill had another fish – from the bottom Ardgully – and we went home to dinner. The Bollinger on this occasion was both proper and inevitable. After dinner Bill, with the enthusiasm of youth, went again to the river and caught a fourth fish – a little chap of 4 lb. And so we had four fish in the day, an event almost unknown on this stretch.

The next day I spoke seriously to my companions. I would allow them just one fish each, we must not overdo this business. We went after breakfast to the water below the house. We fished pool after pool, we caught a number of eels but of salmon we saw no sign. Did we strike a lucky day? I think so. The conditions were the same the day following but the fish were not prepared to play.

Thus the Garden Ranger came into its own. Many anglers will deride this method of catching such a wonderful fish as a salmon. And yet . . . under conditions of low clear water, where a slip in presentation of the bait or an incautious move as one approaches the water makes success out of the question, I do maintain that far more skill is required to catch a fish than is called for in throwing a minnow into a high, coloured water and just winding it in.

As Bill is wont to assert – 'When all else fails, give them the works'.

from THE FIELD *18-11-1965*

Christmas in Tasmania

MAX CHRISTENSEN

A nice fat lake trout is, I have found, a very welcome Christmas gift here in Tasmania. Being midsummer the lowlands start feeling the heat and the high country offers better opportunities for the angler to catch a trout for Christmas.

A mayfly hatch on lakes at the 3,000 ft level starts early December. At 4,000 ft anything may happen but generally the hatch is later, being delayed or totally disrupted by snowfalls. Colonel Yaul and I were discussing these matters and as we had had an early spring we decided to make a trip by Land-Rover and camp at the Julian Lakes, a beautiful spot at 4,000 ft . . .

We arrived at Julian before sundown and after pitching camp on the shore of a small bay we soon had a cheerful log fire going in front of the tent. The day's hardships are forgotten, the dog is fed and the Colonel looks after the glasses while I make preparations for the evening meal. A glorious sunset paints the lake in changing colours and an occasional rise dimples the surface, luckily too far out to disturb our peace. When filling the billy at the water's edge I dislodged a nymph and farther along the shore a couple of spinners were disporting themselves.

The next morning I posted the Colonel on a comparatively shallow bay which sloped into deep water, and where I thought the beginning of a hatch was most likely. Being the wandering type myself I set off to explore other possibilities. When I returned things were happening. The mayfly duns (*Tasmanophlebia lacustris*) were popping through the surface and slowly drifting out into deeper water; trout one after the other made no mistake about them. Under a shady bush the corgi proudly stood guard over five beautiful fish. The Colonel made a couple of casts to dry his fly, then landed it nicely in front of a good fish. Bang . . . it is on . . . .

I stayed with him for a while and caught a couple of fish. The trout were rising a good way out. This did not bother the Colonel unduly, as he had found a bit of a shelf which brought him closer to the fish. I find continuous long casting rather a bore when standing in water to within an inch of the top of the boots. We therefore decided that the Colonel should stay and try to catch his limit (twelve) and I would fish my way round the shore back to camp. By three o'clock in the afternoon and carrying eight fish I arrived back in camp. Much to my surprise I saw a lot of washing on the line, a very wet and semi-dressed Colonel in the tent, and only eleven fish.

If you cast for a long time in the same spot the trout, though still rising, retreat a little, you stretch a little, and eventually you have no more stretch left. Invariably you take that fatal little step forward and find no bottom. At four thousand feet there is nothing to be said for total immersion.

We fished for a further two days in this area and caught more fish than the average mortal deserves.

from JOURNAL OF THE FLYFISHERS' CLUB *Winter 1965*

The Finest Trout in the River

HARRY PLUNKETT GREENE

It might naturally be supposed that if one had the fishing of a trout-stream like the Bourne one would not leave an inch of it unexplored, but it was a fact that up to this time none of the rods had ever taken the trouble to investigate the top quarter-mile of the water. Savage and Sharkey had somehow got it into their heads that there was nothing worth troubling about above the 'lagoon' immediately beyond the viaduct, and as they lived close to the top of the fishing, all the rest of us, myself included, had tacitly accepted this as a matter of fact. Nowadays the whole of this region is a vast watercress bed, and anyone looking out of the window of the train, when passing over the viaduct, would never realise that there was, or ever had been, a river there at all; but in those days there were two streams above, as well as below the bridge, meeting a little way up and stretching as one for a quarter of a mile to the end of the fishing.

We had all of us come on occasions as far as the hatch below this final stretch, but, in the belief that the water above was a blank, had always turned back when we got there.

On 31 August of this year (1903), the last day of the season, I found myself at this hatch at about six o'clock in the evening. I had got four fish averaging 1¼lb, but it had been a bad rising day, cold and windy. At six o'clock it suddenly turned warm and calm, and I was sitting on the hatch smoking a pipe before going home, when I thought that, just for fun, I would walk up to the end of the water. I expected nothing, and had half a mind to leave my rod behind and saunter up with my hands in my pockets. I got over the fence and strolled up on to the bank unconcernedly, and, as I did so, from one weed-patch after another there darted off a series of two-pounders racing upstream like motor-boats. I dropped like a stone, but the damage was done. I just sat there cursing the day I was born and myself, not only for having lost the chance of a lifetime – but for having left his goldmine undiscovered and untouched for two years – for today was the last day of the season! . . . Every fish was under the weeds long ago, and I might just as well pack up my traps and clear out.

There was an old broken-down footbridge about a hundred yards above me, and I thought that I would go up to it and explore the reach beyond, more with a view to the possibilities of next year than with any hope for the present. I got down from the bank and circled round through the meadow till I got to it, and was just picking my way across its rotten planks when under my very feet I saw a small nose appear, followed by a diminutive head and the most enormous shoulder I ever remember to have seen in a chalkstream. I froze stiff where I stood, except that my knees were shaking like aspens, for there right underneath me was gradually emerging the fish of my life. I do not mean to say that I have not caught bigger fish before and since, but this was a veritable star in the dustheap, a Cinderella stealing out of the kitchen that we had all despised, and the romance of the thing put him . . . on a pedestal of fame from which I have never taken him down.

It was agonising work, for he swam up in the most leisurely way at a rate of about an inch every five seconds, while I was straddled across two rotten planks, either of which might have given way at any moment, and had to pretend that I was part of the landscape. He was immediately under me when he first showed up and I could easily have touched him with my foot. What fish will see and what they will not see will ever remain a mystery! It was then about half past six (old time), the time of day when one's visibility is most clear, and yet he took not the smallest notice of me. He just strolled up the middle of the stream contentedly as though he were having a smoke after dinner. I can still feel my joints creaking as I sank slowly to my knees and got my line out. It fell just right and he took no more notice of it than a water rat. I tried again and again, lengthening the cast as he moved up, and at last he rose towards it, examined it carefully and, horror of horrors! swam slowly after it downstream through the bridge under my feet! It would have been laughable if it had not been so tragic. There was I pulling in the slack like a madman, and leaving it in wisps round my knees, scared lest he should see my hand move; and he passed my by without a word and disappeared into the bowels of the bridge.

I just knelt there and swore, trying to look over my shoulder to see if he had gone down below. There was no sign of him, and the situation was painful in the extreme, for my knees were working through the rotten woodwork, and if I tried to ease myself I should either bring the bridge down with a crash or anyway evict Cinderellum for good and all.

I bore it as long as I could, and was just going to give it up and scramble out anyway, when I saw that nose slide out again beneath me, and my old friend started off on his journey upstream once more.

I began on him with a shorter line this time, and he took the fly at the very first cast like a lamb. If he was a lamb as he took it he was a lion when he had it. Instead of running upstream, as I hoped and expected he would do, he gave one swish with his tail and bolted down through the bridge, bending the rod double and dragging the point right under. It was done with such lightning speed I had no time to remonstrate. I threw myself flat on my stomach and got the rod sideways over the bridge, and then the fight began. I was on one side of the bridge and he was half way to Southampton on the other. He got farther and farther downstream, going from one patch of weeds to the next, and digging and burrowing his nose into the middle of it, while I just hung on, helpless, waiting for the end. He quieted down after a bit, and finding that he could not rub the annoying thing out of his nose on the south side he determined to explore the north, and he began to swim up towards me. I must have been a ridiculous sight, spread-eagled on the rotting planks with splinters digging into my legs and ants and spiders crawling down my neck, vainly endeavouring to hold the rod over the side with one hand, to wind in the line with the other, and to watch him over my shoulder all at the same time. Fortunately I must have been invisible from below, but the moment he got under the bridge he saw the rod and tore past me upstream with the reel screaming. But now we were on even terms and there was a clear stretch of water ahead, and I was able to play him to a finish. I was really proud of that fight, for, in addition to the cramped style which I was compelled to adopt, it took place in a stream ten feet wide, half-choked with weeds, and I got him on a 000 Iron-blue at the end of a 4x point. He weighed 3¾ lb when I got him home, and I have always bitterly regretted that I did not get him set up, for, with the exception of an 11¾-pounder in the hall of Longford Castle, caught in the Avon by one of the family on a 'local lure' (the name of which neither fork nor spade would dig from me), he was the most beautiful river-trout in shape, colour and proportion I ever saw.

from WHERE THE BRIGHT WATERS MEET *1924*

A Spring Day

A. H. CHAYTOR

I had to go north for a good sportsman's burying to-day – my cousin Bill. On Friday evening I found myself free, so after wiring to know what the river was doing, I started off by the night train to get one day at the salmon.

On Saturday morning I found the river still in flood and very high – a foot above the rails, but reported to be clearing and falling quickly. There was a wretched, foggy east wind, but on a one-day fishing, if only the water will let me fish, I shall never waste time in grumbling at the weather.

In the fourth pool I got a good yellow trout of 2 lb. I saw a fresh fish in the level dub of the A pool opposite the stone jetty, and in the evening saw a second lying above him by the fence. Twenty yards above the railings in the Thorns stream there was another fish splashing every now and then in the heavy stream, but none of them would take a fly, or even a minnow, though I pegged away at them until about four o'clock. Then I went to the hut and fished down. The stream below that was far too heavy to fish, but when I got to the pool below the Stakes it grew suddenly dark. About five o'clock a gentle, misty rain began, and just below the neck of the stream, to my surprise – for the Devil's Water coming in just above was still in muddy flood – a good fish took on the edge of the stream and almost under my bank. First he rushed me about and then I hustled him about, but took the very greatest care in doing so, as I felt sure that it was my only chance of the day, and I was anxious to get him thoroughly 'done' before bringing him up to that ugly, bushy bank, in the high water that was running. Even when he got tired he kept out of reach for some time, but at last he swirled round just above me and began boring under some willows. He was swimming almost straight downwards in deep water with his head out of sight, but against the roots of the willows, and his tail slowly waving in the dark red water about six inches below the surface. I reached over the willows below him and, to lessen the great risk of gaffing the line, I gaffed him in the 'tummy', near the tail – greatly fearing another bungle such as that by which I lost a fish in the same place when we were last fishing together. This time all went well, and he proved to be a clinking good fish, a perfect little pig in shape, and he weighed 18 lb.

I fished that pool over again and then hurried off to give a last trial to my friends of the morning, but though the water was clearing and looked quite good enough for them, yet my eighteen-pounder remained the only taker of the day.

That, my dear boys, is spring fishing all over. Pool after pool, looking perfect, and certain, as you feel, to hold fish, you fish over without a sign. Your high hopes are growing faint or have gone altogether, when, often at the most unlikely place, jump in your arm goes an electric thrill, and the one rise of the day has come and the fish is gone: or else, hardly knowing how it has happened, your nerves are found wanting, and the half-raised rod is twitching and quivering with the line tight upon a plunging, splashing, rolling salmon, beginning a battle of anxious, growing hope, ending with a noble, glittering prize.

As far as catching fish goes, you may now go home. Unless your lines are, indeed, cast in pleasant places you have had your only fish of the day, and you will catch no more. The memories of many days of spring fishing tell us so, and in our hearts we know it as we admire this shapely, shining fish. But, go home! do you say? Hang it, man, the day is only just begun. Go home! Don't you know that every cast that I make after this I shall feel certain that I am going to take another fish. I shall be fishing better than I have ever fished to-day. I've got one; nothing can make it a blank day now, and, with a little luck, I shall certainly get another.

Well, this is called patience by those who don't know. But it is nothing at all like patience. It is hope, undying, unquenchable, the heart and soul of salmon fishing.

TO A SALMON RIVER IN SPRING

Springing in the moorlands
In a thousand rills,
Each a tiny torrent
That the rain-storm fills,
Here a mighty river
Pouring from the hills.

Brown rushing river
Swirling round our knees,
Running here so broadly
Through the lowlands leas,
But hiding lusty salmon
Fresh from wintry seas!

Yield up these monarchs of thy peat-stained streams!
Show us each fastness where a salmon gleams!
Make us the dreamers of thy fairest dreams!

from LETTERS TO A SALMON FISHER'S SONS *1910*

Grafham: Britain's Greatest

BOB CHURCH

Grafham's regular trout fishers are very good and it is here that many new methods are being developed. Some of these were at first scoffed at by the old traditionalists, but now these modern techniques are accepted by anglers and management alike, and they help to catch a lot of trout even on difficult days. All this is far removed from the old chalk-stream approach which is so unsuitable when fishing the large new reservoirs.

Probably the greatest modern invention of all is the drift control rudder device. This was the brainchild of my genial old friend, Dick Shrive. The rudder allows a boat to be drifted bow-first down the wind instead of the traditional broadside drift. The rudder is a simple affair which is G-clamped to the centre of the transom. The angler in the stern position operates the tiller to point the boat virtually in any downwind direction. This operation does not interfere with his fishing.

The method is obviously ideal for sinking-line fishing with a lure. Instead of continuously running your fly-line over and ending up with nothing but slack as in traditional drifting sinking-line methods, now you can fish properly. Each angler casts out from different sides of the boat. At 30 yd each, a 60 yd strip of water is being covered right down to the bottom for the entire drift. Naturally this searching technique catches fish, especially as the rudder takes you where you want to go and not merely where the wind blows you. For example, you can go in and out of bays keeping 60 to 70 yd from the bank. This method has really caught on at Grafham since I first wrote about it in 1973, and the catch rate has improved with it.

When the same drifting is required in very strong winds, naturally the boat travels too fast, so I then use a large 48 in square drogue. This has four strong cords attached to each corner of the rot-proof, heavy duty nylon material. These corners are reinforced with leather and punched with sail eyelets. The four cords are of equal length, about 1 yd each, and these are collectively tied to a large sea swivel. Finally, a 3 yd length of much stronger nylon rope is tied from the other eye of the swivel to the boat. This drogue is lowered from the central stern position and secured by a 4 in G clamp.

While other boats drift too fast, and out of control as far as sensible fishing is concerned, my drogue allows me to continue to fish deep and slow. This style of drifting does not have to be sinking-line fishing and, in fact, some of my best results come when fishing for rainbows with a sink-tip fly-line.

As the fish cruise upwind just a few feet or so down, feeding on daphnia, they appear to become reckless and to attack almost any lure if it is pulled 'across' their path. Lures like Black Chenille, Missionary, Appetizer, Church Fly, Whisky Fly, Leprechaun, Sweeney Todd and Jack Frost catch a lot of fish at these times.

A large proportion of the trout caught from the bank during late May through to July fell to some kind of nymph. The normal Buzzer patterns in black, green, orange, brown, claret, grey and red catch plenty of fish. These are fished on hook sizes 14, 12 and 10.

Another type of nymph fishing has really begun to catch on this season. This can be described as the 'Cove' style. Arthur Cove, from Wellingborough, is known as the Pheasant Tail nymph man. He likes to use them large on No 8 or 10 long-shank hooks. These give him a very consistent catch rate. He uses a variation with a grey wool thorax which I feel is even more of a killer.

Arthur always uses a full double-tapered floating fly-line to get a perfect presentation. His line is coloured white so he can see the slightest movement at the tip. He strikes early, long before the take is felt at the hand. I caught a number of good fish on Cove Pheasant Tail variations, using thorax colours of yellow, green and orange, as well as the grey and original.

During mid-July fish come well to the sedge in calm evenings – the calmer the better. For the past two seasons I have really taken advantage of this fishing and have caught some large fish on sedge pupa patterns. Fish that can be seen rising and boiling near the surface are rarely taking the adult sedge; more often than not they will be on pupa in the surface film, taking it just prior to emergence.

At this time my favourite fly is a Brown and Yellow Seal's Fur nymph. This has a couple of turns of yellow hackle at the head too. It can be fished as a centre dropper with an Invicta or Standard Sedge on the top. The Standard Sedge, by the way, is a very effective deer-hair pattern invented by Terry Thomas. I have witnessed take after take coming to it when anglers nearby using Invictas have failed to get any, so bear this in mind. The Brown and Green nymph, also in seal's fur, and the Amber nymph are certainly worth trying at this time.

from STILLWATER TROUT FISHERIES *1976*

Traun Trout and Grayling

TONY PAWSON

We were not to see any pike, but the most expert of the Traun fishermen, Roman Moser, takes forty or more a year on his special pike streamer flies. The information leaflet also includes the helpful comment: 'If desired the fishmaster will advise the fisherman.' It is certainly sensible to take advice. As Reinhard commented to me, 'Those who don't know how to fish the Traun may come here and catch only three small fish in a week. But if you fish it right it is the best grayling river in Europe, with the largest grayling you will ever catch, and the wild rainbows are the fiercest fighters you can hook.'

By the riverside Reinhard was soon demonstrating the technique which brings daytime success. It is a peculiar mixture of traditional nymph fishing and coarse-fishing skills. 'Most of the fish lie in the darker, deeper water. You must go as close as your trouser waders will take you, then use these full-function, fast-join casts to work your leaded nymph right down on the bottom. If you let it drag, or rise a few inches too high, you won't catch a thing.' The full-function casts are of the braided type, to which Rafael had also introduced me in Spain. The particular version for this method of fishing had thin slivers of copper wire inserted within the braid to ensure fast sinking. The fast join aided rapid change of leader, which needed to be down to 0.16 mm, or even finer. A tiny red wooden indicator was slid up the line to be positioned at the estimated depth of the water. Reinhard then demonstrated the casting method – one false roll cast, then the operative one, checked like a parachute cast so that it fell loosely coiled close to the indicator. This allowed the nymph to sink deep before the fast current dragged it. At once the line had to be mended and paid out, and then you had to keep mending and paying out so that the red indicator went bobbing down without drag, the nymph bumping the stony bottom. It looked easy enough as Reinhard demonstrated with fluent casting and sure control. But two hours were enough to convince us that plenty of practice was needed for reasonable competence.

Nor was there any success to encourage, with not even Reinhard or Peter provoking any reaction. So we moved to a new area near the Steyermuhl weir where a channel of water streamed back to the main river. 'This is often good for grayling,' said Reinhard. Like myself, John had not appreciated just how large those grayling would be. When his indicator checked in the swift current his instant strike seemed to have caught the bottom. Looking across, I saw him yanking the rod to free it. But suddenly the bottom moved, and he was playing a grayling, whose sail-like dorsal fin gave it great power in the racing water. It played like an autumn salmon, now holding deep, now running purposefully, now jumping. When it gave up we measured it at 51 centimetres before returning it, a remarkable fish close to the UK record of 3½ pounds. At least, we thought it remarkable. How were we to know it was just average? At once Reinhard hooked a couple of similar fish and I had one much smaller before the sidestream was fished out. Higher up in the main river son John had a brown trout of about a pound to confirm his growing confidence in a method which I still found difficult.

A late and protracted lunch back at the inn ended with Reinhard saying: 'The morning has not been good. The evening will be better.' From my point of view it was. On the leaded nymph I had a small rainbow before changing to a Sedge for the evening rise. It was almost dark when the river around me began to boil with rising rainbows. One of around a pound and a half gave me a fierce fight. I then hooked one which played so hard that after ten minutes I was only just on terms when Reinhard came to inquire what was wrong. 'It must be six pounds or more,' I told him, 'but it's under control now.' It wasn't, and it got off before I had a proper view of it. Reinhard was too polite to challenge my opinion of its weight, but I thought he smiled knowingly. He had caught a lot of the Traun's wild three-pound rainbows, and I hadn't as yet any experience of their awesome power. Blagdon's rainbows are renowned for their fighting qualities, but these were to prove twice as strong, twice as active. So perhaps that fish would merely have proved to be my first three-pounder, and not the great trout I imagined.

The next day's pattern was much the same, with John catching a couple of good grayling on the nymph in a delightful stretch of water round some islands, while Peter and I caught numbers of very small rainbows, and one of about a pound, fishing dry fly in the shallow runs near the bank. That evening John had two good rainbows while fishing with a Sedge Pupa before the main rise, much of which Peter spent locked in battle with an immense grayling. We measured that at 63 centimetres or about 25 inches – surely about six pounds and the largest Peter had caught in the Traun.

That was one turning-point for me. Peter took it on a Buck Caddis, and in future I was to fish that dry by day with growing success, as I found the nymph method difficult to master, and for me not as enjoyable as dry fly. Then at dinner Reinhard had a long talk with an immensely tall thin man said to have an unfair advantage in fishing the Traun, since his high chest waders enabled him to go in much deeper than anyone else. He told us of a place close to Gmunden, below the power station, where there was 'super' fishing. We hurried there the following morning and super it was. At the head of the first run my Buck Caddis caught me a grayling of a couple of pounds – 'Tony has a *small* grayling,' I heard Reinhard call. Lower down John continued to fish the nymph method, having learnt by now how to trot it down thirty or forty yards without drag. More than a dozen times his red indicator checked, and though the strike still gave him problems he had won battles with seven big grayling and rainbows, before switching to dry fly to catch another five. His three best grayling measured 59, 57 and 56 centimetres as he revelled in this fishing with the bright sunlight and lovely setting.

Meanwhile the Buck Caddis had brought me half a dozen. With few rises to cover it was a question of searching the water, casting now upstream, now across, now floating the fly over areas I had just waded. The grayling took no fright as you waded quietly over them. One rose a few feet from John in water he had just passed and I hooked and lost it by floating the fly down towards him. Traditionally grayling are difficult to hook, but have a reputation of being silly fish that will rise again and again if you miss them. Not so the big ones on the Traun. They gave you one chance and one chance only; and after some of the most confident head-and-tail rises there was inexplicably no touch at all as you lifted the rod in happy expectation.

There was still the evening to enjoy and this time Reinhard and another very experienced Traun angler, his Dutch friend Gerard Tegelaar, undertook to complete our education by standing by us and talking us through the subtleties of the brief sedge rise. The water they had chosen seemed shallow and deserted as we fished it in muted anticipation from six to seven, standing four in a row knee-deep in fast water and casting back to the bank. It was in that period that we had our briefing:

'At seven o'clock you will see the occasional rise, and may take some fish on the Sedge Pupa. Float it down, but fish out the cast letting it drag. With the Sedge Pupa the drag sometimes provokes a fierce take.

At 7.25 change to a dark Sedge, while it is still light enough to see. At 7.30 precisely the bats will wheel in, the sedges rise in clouds, the water erupt with rises. By 8 all will be over. Your maximum possibility is four fish [Gerard was in fact to catch five on our final evening in that furious half-hour], because each will take over five minutes to land. Your leader should not be less than 0.20 mm to play them hard enough to give you that chance. You must also cut your cast short, and it is right that you have a white line. For much of that half-hour it will be too dark to see your fly. You must judge its position in relation to the end of your white line and strike whenever you see a rise in that area. Once the rise is on you can wade in close to your fish and it is best to fish only for those within a few yards of you.'

It all happened exactly as described. Nothing stirred for an hour. A couple of swans sailed majestically by. A glider soared noiselessly above our heads. The waters murmured on with unbroken surface, the myriad olives drifting down untouched. A few large sedges began to wing past. Then came the first few rises and my first mistake. I was convinced I could see my pupa drifting towards where a fish had shown and with iron control ignored a rise a few feet away. 'Why do you not strike?' inquired Reinhard. And, when I tightened too late, the rainbow was touched but not hooked. The fly I had thought was mine was in fact a natural floating by, and the trout had indeed taken my small artificial. However, I soon had one nice rainbow, which took me down to the backing twice. A few yards below, John, in even faster water, had even fiercer fights with a couple more, and was then busy for a time with his torch. When a grayling gave up it could be released with ease. But the rainbows never gave up. Even when played out the touch of the hand would send them jumping away again to renew the fight. This one had leaped from John's grasp as he tried to unhook it and broken away with his fly. That was to happen to each one of us over the three nights.

Reinhard stood at my back urging me to fish close. 'Why don't you have a go?' I asked him. 'Look and see,' he replied. Turning round, I found him already fighting a rainbow. 'What did I tell you? It kept rising within a yard of us so I just dibbled my fly over it, and it took it at once.'

from FLY FISHING AROUND THE WORLD *1987*

Three Grayling

G. E. M. SKUES

One autumn day during the 1914–18 War I met with my late friend, Hugh T. Sheringham, and discussed grayling and grayling flies with him. He, like me, was kindly provided by Mr Irwin Cox with a season ticket on the Abbots Barton stretch of the Itchen and he told me that in a small length I called the 'Trait d'Union' (because it broke away from the side stream just below Kingsworthy Mill and in 100 yards or so joined the main Itchen) he had spotted, but failed to catch, a small shoal of biggish grayling that occupied a deepish hole a long cast above Cart Bridge, which served the carting of hay crops from the meadows to the east, and he recommended me to have a shot at them. The Cart Bridge in question was barred to unauthorised passengers by an iron gate some 15 feet high with a *chevaux de frise* of spear-pointed spikes radiating in a half circle across the entire top of the gate and impossible to climb round, and when not in use the gate was kept studiously locked.

On a sunny Saturday afternoon a few days later I stood by the west side of the Cart Bridge and studied the bottom of the Trait d'Union – here 5 or 6 feet in depth, and, sure enough, on the bare chalky bottom of a deep hole in the centre I espied a small shoal of three grayling approaching – 2 lb apiece. I accordingly knotted on my cast a fly I had prepared experimentally for the occasion. This was the tie:

Hook	No 2 Pryce-Tannatt's round bend
Tying silk	Crimson
Hackle	Soft blue (dark) hen
Body	Peacock herl dyed claret.

I had not begun to fish when I became aware of three khaki-clad figures crossing the meadows towards the far side of the iron gate. I called to them that the gate was locked and impassable. Did that stop them? Not much! One after another, like three monkeys, they scaled that fiendish gate – got over the spear spikes at the top (which I would not have attempted for £100) and came down on to the Cart Bridge on my side.

They then waited to see what I was doing, and I pointed out to them the little clutch of three grayling in the deep hole in mid-stream. They then stood aside to let me cast and looked on for a few minutes, then turned to make their way westward to cross the side stream, when I called, 'Any of you like a grayling?' They came rushing back to be first to get a grayling and I was able to net out and hand to the winner a grayling not far from 2 lb. The three then turned and were making off, when I called, 'Anyone else like another?' and two came rushing back to get a similar fish out of my landing net.

Before they reached the bridge to the west again, I called, 'Who's for number three?' and the third man came back to receive his similar fish. 'No good to wait for any more – that's the lot.'

As it turned out, it was so, for, though each of these three fish took the fly directly it was offered, not another fish did I get that afternoon.

from ITCHEN MEMORIES *1951*

The Virtues of Grayling

ROBIN MULHOLLAND

It is from September onwards that grayling begin to show their real virtues and the angler who pursues them quickly realises that he is fishing for truly wild fish. When they are rising to surface fly they are usually very specific and an effective imitation or representation is required to deceive them. Even then they will frequently rise but not take the fly. At that time of the year of course small flies are needed. The naturals available include reed smuts, caenis, the small dark olive and various pale wateries. When the *ephemeroptera* hatches are heavy then grayling can usually be caught on the popular patterns such as Beacon Beige and Tup's Indispensable. Often, however, at that time the reed smuts and caenis are the most plentiful and then deception is more difficult. Grey Dusters in the smallest size, Black Gnat patterns and the Janus, a fore-and-after fly with cocked-up tails, are the most likely to be effective. A fine point helps to ensure that fish do take the fly and do not turn away at the last moment. The use of fine points is a feasible proposition, because unlike trout, grayling do not head for the weed when hooked and it is possible therefore to fish for them with points of 2-pound breaking strain or less. As the shoal often lies out in shallow water the use of a long leader is also an advantage. The chalk streams are at their lowest levels in the autumn; frequently the sun is bright and the fish are easily disturbed by line and cast flashing overhead.

Herl-bodied flies are successful on the chalk streams just as they are everywhere else. Rolt developed his Witch on the Wylye as both a trout and grayling fly and it is still successful there as it is on the Avon. The explanation for the success of such flies as Rolt's Witch, Red Tag, Treacle Parkin, Terry's Terror and the various Bumbles seem to lie in the combination of herl body and bright tag. My conclusion is that this combination and many of these flies that are just as attractive to trout as grayling are good representations of a hatching nymph. The rough body produces the furry effect of occlusion and the bright tag at the red/orange/yellow end of the spectrum creates the effect of the haemoglobin in the nymph's body.

Rolt mentions his Witch as being particularly effective close to or under the bank and in rough weather. It may be that fat herl bodies are fair representations of a wider range of miscellaneous insects, some water-borne and some land-borne, which fall on the water particularly on a windy day. I prefer the former explanation, however; it is more logical and has greater appeal than the latter. The theory is also supported by the success of the Gold-ribbed Hare's Ear as a grayling fly. This fly is perhaps the most successful all-round fly on the chalk streams for both trout and grayling and can be fished as an emerging nymph or just below the surface as a nymph that has failed to emerge. Again, the rough body creates the impression of a hatching nymph and the selective grayling are much more likely to rise to that than they are to rise to a dun imitation which could well take off as they are on their way up. I have always found it difficult to understand why grayling lie on the bottom and rise from what is often a considerable depth. Nevertheless that is what they do and I feel sure that it influences their reaction to duns. It's a long way to go for something that might fly away before they arrive! When they are lying in very shallow water or on the top of weed, as they do when weed covers most of the river, then they are lying much closer to the surface and their behaviour in the rise is more like that of a trout.

from GRAYLING: THE FOURTH GAME FISH
(*edited by Ronald Broughton*) 1989

The Deserving Grayling

HENRY RALPH FRANCIS

I have thus far spoken almost exclusively of trout. The grayling, however, deserves more than a mere casual notice, and Cotton's ghost might haunt me if in writing of 'fine and far off' I ignored the fish he loved so well.

And, indeed, 'for my own particular', I greatly admire the grayling, who, I think, is less prized than he deserves. His beauty is the least of his merits – yet how beautiful he is! Taken out of season – in June, for instance, or early July – the dull yellow brown of his back and sides is not attractive; but when he has recovered his condition, and adds the charm of colour to his always graceful shape – when he shows a rich dark tint down to the mesial line, and silver mail as bright as that of the salmon in level lines below, while his lofty back fin, like some 'storied window, richly light', transmits the sunshine through purple, red, and gold, no lovelier prize, save the rarely caught red char, can grace an angler's creel. The curious vegetable fragrance, again, whence he draws his name of *Salmo Thymallus*, contrasts agreeably with the ancient and fish-like smell which clings to other finny captives.

For the table, I should place a well-grown grayling in autumn or winter above the average of river trout, while the 'shetts,' or two-year-olds, are in season all the summer through, and if judiciously fried are nearly equal to a smelt in flavour.

Cotton is in a measure right when he calls him 'the deadest-hearted of fishes', making 'no great stir' on the hook. He bores steadily down toward the gravel, working mostly up stream, but rarely making a sudden rush or attempting to weed himself. Yet even this dispraise needs some qualification. In small streams I have several times encountered grayling who fought for their lives with all the dash as well as the doggedness of lusty trout, though I have never met with the like in a large river. I might make a fair guess at the cause of this difference, but prefer to record the simple fact.

I have seldom fished for grayling with any lure but the artificial fly. To me, indeed, the crown of all fly fishing is a bright breezy day on the Teme or Lug about the middle of August, when the grayling are coming on and the trout not yet gone off. The sport is varied but almost continuous; there is seldom a reach to be 'skipped' on your river-side beat. From the dashing rapid haunted by trout you ascend to the steadily running ford, from two to four feet deep, in which you know that the grayling lie thick – 'not single spies, but in battalions'. At the top of this again you come on a deep pool with foam-flecked eddies where the trout reassume their sway, while on the confines of these different reaches you may hook either trout or grayling or both together. A brace of the former with one of the latter, or *vice versa*, make rather an exciting complication.

from FISHING *1888* (*from The Badminton Library*)

PART 9

Verse

The Fat Fellow

. . .I
Sat watching for the fish – so eagerly!
And from the reed the tripping bait did shake
Till a fat fellow took it – no mistake . . .
He hugged the hook, and then his blood did flow;
His plunges bent my reed like any bow;
I stretched both arms, and had a pretty bout,
To take with hook so weak a fish so stout.
I gently warned him of the wound he bore;
'Ha! will you prick me? You'll be pricked much more.'
But when he struggled not, I drew him in;
The contest then I saw myself did win.

Theocritus 284 BC

Come live with me . . .

Come live with me and be my love,
And we will some new pleasures prove,
Of golden sands and crystal brooks,
With silken lines and silver hooks.

There will the river whispering run,
Warm'd by thy eyes more than the Sun;
And there the enamored fish will stay,
Begging themselves they may betray.

When thou wilt swim in that live bath,
Each fish, which every channel hath,
Most am'rously to thee will swim,
Gladder to catch thee than thou him.

If thou, to be so seen, beest loath,
By sun or moon, thou dark'nest both;
And if mine eyes have leave to see,
I need not their light, having thee.

Let others freeze with Angling-reeds,
And cut their legs with shells and weeds;
Or teach'rously poor fish beset,
With struggling snares, or windowy net.

Let coarse bold hands, from slimy nest,
The bedded fish in banks outrest;
Let curious traitors sleave silk flies,
To 'witch poor wand'ring fishes' eyes.

For thee, thou need'st no such deceit,
For thou thyself are thine own bait:
That fish that is not catched thereby,
Is wiser far, Alas! than I.

John Donne

Dapping

See where another hides himself as sly,
As did Acteon, or the fearful deer;
Behind a withy, and with watchful eye
Attends the bit within the water clear,
And on the top thereof doth move his fly,
With skilful hand as if he living were.
  Lo how the Chub, the Roach, the Dace and Trout,
  To catch thereat do gaze and swim about.

His Rod, or Cane, made dark for being seen,
The less to fear the wary Fish withal:
His line well twisted is, and wrought so clean,
That being strong, yet doth it show but small,
His Hook not great, nor little, but between,
That light upon the watery brim may fall,
  The Line in length scant half the Rod exceeds,
  And neither Cork nor Lead thereon it needs.

John Dennys

Angler's Song

Man's life is but vain, for 'tis subject to pain
  And sorrow, and short as a bubble;
'Tis a hodge-podge of business and money and care
  And care and money and trouble.

But we'll take no care when the weather proves fair,
  Nor will we now vex though it rain;
We'll banish all sorrow, and sing till to-morrow,
  And angle and angle again.

Anon c. 1620

St James's Park

Beneath, a shole of silver fishes glides,
And plays about the gilded barges' sides;
The ladies, angling in the chrystal lake,
Feast on the waters with the prey they take:
At once victorious with their lines and eyes,
They make the fishes and the men their prize.

Edmund Waller

The Fisher

In genial spring, beneath the quivering shade,
When cooling vapours breath along the mead,
The patient fisher takes his silent stand,
Intent, his angle trembling in his hand:
With looks unmov'd, he hopes the scaly breed,
And eyes the dancing cork and bending reed.
Our plenteous streams a various race supply,
The bright-eyed perch with fins of Tyrian dye;
The silver eel, in shining volumes roll'd;
The yellow carp, in scales bedropp'd with gold;
Swift trouts, diversified with crimson stains;
And pikes, the tyrants of the watery plains.

Alexander Pope

On Worms

Far up the stream the twisted hair he throws,
Which down the murmuring current gently flows;
When, if or chance or hunger's powerful sway
Directs the roving trout this fatal way,
He greedily sucks in the twining bait,
And tugs and nibbles the fallacious meat:
Now, happy fisherman, now twitch the line!
How the rod bends! behold, the prize is thine!
Cast on the bank, he dies with gasping pains,
And trickling blood his silver mail distains.
You must not every worm promiscuous use,
Judgment will tell thee proper bait to choose;
The worm that draws a long immoderate size
The trout abhors, and the rank morsel flies;
And if too small, the naked fraud's in sight,
And fear forbids, while hunger doth invite.
Those baits will best reward the fisher's pains,
Whose polish'd tails a shining yellow stains.
Cleanse them from filth, to give a tempting gloss,
Cherish the sullied reptile race with moss;
Amid the verdant bed they twine, they toil,
And from their bodies wipe their native soil.

John Gay

On Flies

But when the sun displays his glorious beams,
And shallow rivers flow with silver streams,
Then the deceit the scaly breed survey,
Bask in the sun, and look into the day.
You now a more delusive art must try,
And tempt their hunger with the curious fly.
To frame the little animal, provide
All the gay hues that wait on female pride,
Let Nature guide thee; sometimes golden wire
The shining bellies of the fly require;
The peacock plumes thy tackle must not fail,

Nor the dear purchase of the sable's tail.
Each gaudy bird some slender tribute brings,
And lends the growing insect proper wings:
Silks of all colours must their aid impart,
And every fur promote the fisher's art.
So the gay lady, with expensive care,
Borrows the pride of land, of sea, and air;
Furs, pearls, and plumes, the glittering thing displays,
Dazzles our eyes, and easy hearts betrays.
　Mark well the various seasons of the year,
How the succeeding insect race appear;
In this revolving moon one colour reigns,
Which in the next the fickle trout disdains,
Oft have I seen a skilful angler try
The various colours of the treacherous fly;
When he with fruitless pain hath skimm'd the brook,
And the coy fish rejects the skipping hook,
He shakes the boughs that on the margin grow,
Which o'er the stream a waving forest throw;
When, if an insect fall (his certain guide),
He gently takes him from the whirling tide;
Examines well his form, with curious eyes,
His gaudy vest, his wings, his horns and size.
Then round his hook the chosen fur he winds,
And on the back a speckled feather binds,
So just the colours shine through every part,
That Nature seems to live again in Art.

John Gay

The Monarch of the Brook

Just in the dubious point, where with the pool
Is mixed the trembling stream, or where it boils
Around the stone, or from the hollow'd bank,
Reverted plays in undulating flow,
There throw, nice-judging, the delusive fly:
And, as you lead it round in artful curve,
With eye attentive mark the springing game.

Straight as above the surface of the flood
They wanton rise, or urged by hunger leap,
Then fix, with gentle twitch, the barbed hook:
Some lightly tossing to the grassy bank,
And to the shelving shore slow-dragging some,
With various hand proportioned to their force.
If yet too young, and easily deceived,
A worthless prey scarce bends your pliant rod,
Him, piteous of his youth and the short space
He has enjoy'd the vital light of heaven
Soft disengage, and back into the stream
The speckled captive throw. But should you lure
From his dark haunt, beneath the tangled roots
Of pendent trees, the monarch of the brook,
Behoves you then to ply your finest art.
Long time he, following cautious, scans the fly;
And oft attempts to seize it, but as oft
The dimpled water speaks his jealous fear.
At last, while haply o'er the shaded sun
Passes a cloud, he, desperate, takes the death,
With sudden plunge. At once he darts along,
Deep-struck, and runs out all the lengthen'd line;
Then seeks the furthest ooze, the sheltering weed,
The cavern'd bank, his own secure abode;
And flies aloft, and flounces round the pool,
Indignant of the guile. With yielding hand,
That feels him still, yet to his furious course
Gives way, you, now retiring, following now,
Across the stream, exhaust his idle rage;
Till floating broad upon his breathless side,
And to his fate abandon'd, to the shore
You gaily drag your unresisting prize.

James Thompson

To a Fish of the Brooke

Why flyest thou away with fear?
Trust me, there's naught of danger near;
I have no wicked hooke
All covered with a snaring bait,
Alas to tempt thee to thy fate,
And dragge thee from the brooke.

O harmless tenant of the flood,
I do not wish to spill thy blood,
For Nature unto thee
Perchance hath given a tender wife,
And children dear, to charm thy life,
As she hath done for me.
Enjoy thy stream, O harmless fish;
And, when an angler for his dish
Through gluttony's vile sin,
Attempts, a wretch, the full thee *out*,
God give thee strength, O gentle trout,
To pull the raskall *in*!

John Wolcot

Go, Take Thine Angle

Go, take thine angle, and with practised line,
Light as the gossamer, the current sweep;
And if thou failest in the calm still deep,
In the rough eddy may a prize be thine.
Say thou'rt unlucky where the sunbeams shine;
Beneath the shadows, where the waters creep,
Perchance the monarch of the brook shall leap –
For fate is ever better than design.
Still persevere; the giddiest breeze that blows,
For thee may blow with fame and fortune rife;
Be prosperous – and what reck if it arose
Out of some pebble with the stream at strife,
Or that the light wind dallied with the boughs?
Thou art successful; such is human life.

Thomas Doubleday

The Fisher's Call

The winter blast's dead and the spring breezes blow;
If the haughs are patch'd white, 'tis with daisies, not snow;
The earth for foul sleet drinks the bright glancing rain;
Then, my boys, let us off to the Coquet again.

Down the hills leap bright feeders released from their chains;
The very dry heather feels blood in its veins;
All nature is stirring, strong lamps on the lea,
Blithe birds on the bough, show how backward are we.

The primrose peeps out on the edge of the burn,
With a doubtful pale face lest old Hyems return;
Whilst the delicate perfume betrays it as clear
That her purple-frock'd playfellow hides herself near.

The bloodhounds of glory, unkennelling now,
Are taking the field, as we fishers will do;
But with fly-rods, not muskets, we march to attack,
And no knapsack for us, but the creel at the back.

The skylark and blackbird our bugles shall blow,
And the roll of our drums be the river's hoarse flow;
Our flags are unfurling on every tree;
And I think we all guess where our quarters shall be.

The waters curl freely beneath the west gale,
And come down from the moors like the berry-brown ale;
Unfish'd are the slacks and unthrash'd are the streams,
And we'll make our exploits beat our sanguinest dreams.

We'll tempt them with black, and we'll tempt them with gray;
Ay, the skeggers shall yield if they come in our way;
We'll raise them in shallow, we'll raise them in deep,
In the pool's smoothest stretch and the stream's roughest sweep.

There's not a rude brae which the current makes wroth,
Nor an angry eddy, bewhirling in froth,
Nor a single old stone with a white beard of foam,
But shall pay for our visit before we win home.

Our flies will sweep here and our flies will float there,
As we try all the sleights of hook, feather, and hair;
Quick jerking out small and slow leading out great;
Nor cease till gall'd shoulders complain of the weight.

The minnow in summer its monsters can kill,
And the worm loads your pannier when nothing else will;
But give me the spring-time, the light-dropping hackle,
And the masterly cast with the finest of tackle.

Like a sensitive nerve is the long taper line,
That doth from the tenuous fly-rod decline;
And the leap of the fish, with electrical start,
Strikes swift through the hand, on the high-bounding heart.

When the gods deign to hear our petitions of bliss,
Though we frame each a first, our joint second is this,
In the sweet-flowing waters of Coquet to stand,
With the creel on the back, and the rod in the hand.

William Greene

The Pirate of the Lakes

Gaily rock the lily beds
  On the marge of Lomond lake;
There the wandering angler treads,
  Nature round him – all awake,
  Mountains ringing,
  Fountains singing
Their sweet secrets in the brake.

Swiftly from the water's edge
Shoots the fierce pike, wing'd with fear,
To his lair among the sedge,
As the intruding form draws near;
All elated,
Primely baited,
Seeking solitary cheer.

Throbs aloud the eager heart,
And the hand in tremor moves,
When some monster, all alert,
Round the tempting tackle roves;
Boldly daring,
Or bewaring,
While the gleamy lure he proves.

Then at length each doubt subdued,
Turns the lake-shark on his prey;
Quickly gulp'd the fatal food,
Suddenly he sheers away
All enshackled,
Firmly tackled,
Out into the deep'ning bay.

But with steady caution school'd,
Soon his boasted vigour fails;
By the angler's sceptre ruled,
Maim'd the sullen pirate sails;
Shoreward wending,
Uncontending,
Him the joyous captor hails.

And along the margin haul'd,
All his fretful fins a-spread,
Though by ruthless iron gall'd,
Still he rears his cruel head
Uncomplaining,
Death disdaining –
See him as a trophy led!

Thomas Tod Stoddart

The South Wind

O blessed drums of Aldershot!
O blessed south-west train!
O blessed, blessed Speaker's clock,
All prophesying rain!

O blessed yaffil, laughing loud!
O blessed falling glass!
O blessed fan of cold gray cloud!
O blessed smelling grass!

O bless'd south wind that toots his horn
Through every hole and crack!
I'm off at eight to-morrow morn
To bring such fishes back!

Charles Kingsley

Hiawatha and the Sturgeon Nahma

Forth upon the Gitchee Gumee,
On the shining Big-Sea-Water,
With his fishing-line of cedar,
Of the twisted bark of cedar,
Forth to catch the sturgeon Nahma,
Mishe-Nahma, King of Fishes,
In his birch-canoe exulting
All alone went Hiawatha.

Through the clear, transparent water
He could see the fishes swimming
Far down in the depths below him;
See the yellow perch, the Sahwa,
Like a sunbeam in the water,
See the Shawgashee, the crawfish,
Like a spider on the bottom,
On the white and sandy bottom.

At the stern sat Hiawatha,
With his fishing-line of cedar;
In his plumes the breeze of morning
Played as in the hemlock branches;
On the bows, with tail erected,
Sat the squirrel, Adjidaumo;
In his fur the breeze of morning
Played as in the prairie grasses.

On the white sand of the bottom
Lay the monster Mishe-Nahma,
Lay the sturgeon, King of Fishes;
Through his gills he breathed the water,
With his fins he fanned and winnowed,
With his tail he swept the sand-floor.

There he lay in all his armour;
On each side a shield to guard him,
Plates of bone upon his forehead,
Down his sides and back and shoulders
Plates of bone with spines projecting.
Painted was he with his war paints,
Stripes of yellow, red, and azure,
Spots of brown and spots of sable;
And he lay there on the bottom,
Fanning with his fins of purple,
As above him Hiawatha
In his birch-canoe came sailing,
With his fishing-line of cedar.

'Take my bait,' cried Hiawatha,
Down into the depths beneath him,
'Take my bait, O Sturgeon, Nahma!
Come up from below the water,
Let us see which is the stronger!'
And he dropped his line of cedar
Through the clear, transparent water,
Waited vainly for an answer,
'Take my bait, O King of Fishes!'

Quiet lay the sturgeon, Nahma,
Fanning slowly in the water,
Looking up at Hiawatha,
Listening to his call and clamour,
His unnecessary tumult,
Till he wearied of the shouting;
And he said to the Kenozha,
To the pike, the Maskenozha,
'Take the bait of this rude fellow,
Break the line of Hiawatha!'

In his fingers Hiawatha
Felt the loose line jerk and tighten;
As he drew it in it tugged so
That the birch-canoe stood end-wise,
Like a birch-log in the water,
With the squirrel, Adjidaumo,
Perched and frisking on the summit.

Full of scorn was Hiawatha
When he saw the fish rise upward,
Saw the pike, the Maskenozha,
Coming nearer, nearer to him,
And he shouted through the water,
'Esa! esa! shame upon you!
You are but the pike, Kenozha,
You are not the fish I wanted,
You are not the King of Fishes!'

Reeling downward to the bottom
Sank the pike in great confusion,
And the mighty sturgeon, Nahma,
Said to Ugudwash, the sun-fish,
To the bream, with scales of crimson,
'Take the bait of this great boaster,
Break the line of Hiawatha!'

Slowly upward, wavering, gleaming,
Rose the Ugudwash, the sun-fish,

Seized the line of Hiawatha,
Swung with all his weight upon it,
Made a whirlpool in the water,
Whirled the birch-canoe in circles,
Round and round in gurgling eddies,
Till the circles in the water
Nodded on the distant margins.

But when Hiawatha saw him
Slowly rising through the water,
Lifting up his disc refulgent,
Loud he shouted in derision,
'Esa! esa! shame upon you!
You are Ugudwash, the sun-fish,
You are not the fish I wanted,
You are not the King of Fishes!'

Slowly downward, wavering, gleaming,
Sank the Ugudwash, the sun-fish,
And again the sturgeon, Nahma,
Heard the shout of Hiawatha,
Heard his challenge of defiance,
The unnecessary tumult,
Ringing far across the water.

From the white sand of the bottom
Up he rose with angry gesture,
Quivering in each nerve and fibre,
Clashing all his plates of armour,
Gleaming bright with all his war paint;
In his wrath he darted upward,
Flashing leaped into the sunshine,
Opened his great jaws, and swallowed
Both canoe and Hiawatha.

Down into that darksome cavern
Plunged the headlong Hiawatha,
As a log on some dark river
Shoots and plunges down the rapids,
Found himself in utter darkness,

Groped about in helpless wonder,
Till he felt a great heart beating,
Throbbing in that utter darkness.

And he smote it in his anger,
With his fist, the heart of Nahma,
Felt the mighty King of Fishes
Shudder through each nerve and fibre,
Heard the water gurgle round him
As he leaped and staggered through it,
Sick at heart, and faint and weary.

Crosswise then did Hiawatha
Drag his birch-canoe for safety,
Lest from out the jaws of Nahma,
In the turmoil and confusion,
Forth he might be hurled and perish.
And the squirrel, Adjidaumo,
Frisked and chattered very gaily,
Toiled and tugged with Hiawatha,
Till the labour was completed.

Then said Hiawatha to him,
'O my little friend, the squirrel,
Bravely have you toiled to help me;
Take the thanks of Hiawatha,
And the name which now he gives you;
For hereafter and for ever
Boys shall call you Adjidaumo,
Tail-in-air the boys shall call you!'

And again the sturgeon, Nahma,
Gasped and quivered in the water,
Then was still, and drifted landward
Till he grated on the pebbles,
Till the listening Hiawatha
Heard him grate upon the margin,
Felt him strand upon the pebbles,
Knew that Nahma, King of Fishes,
Lay there dead upon the margin.

Then he heard a clang and flapping,
As of many wings assembling,
Heard a screaming and confusion,
As of birds of prey contending,
Saw a gleam of light above him,
Shining through the ribs of Nahma,
Saw the glittering eyes of sea-gulls,
Of Kayoshk, the sea-gulls, peering,
Gazing at him through the opening,
Heard them saying to each other,
''Tis our brother, Hiawatha!'

And he shouted from below them,
Cried exulting from the caverns:
'O ye sea-gulls! O my brothers!
I have slain the sturgeon, Nahma;
Make the rifts a little larger,
With your claws the openings widen,
Set me free from this dark prison,
And henceforward and for ever
Men shall speak of your achievements,
Calling you Kayoshk, the sea-gulls,
Yes, Kayoshk, the Noble Scratchers!'

And the wild and clamorous sea-gulls
Toiled with beak and claws together,
Made the rifts and openings wider
In the mighty ribs of Nahma,
And from peril and from prison,
From the body of the sturgeon,
From the peril of the water,
They released my Hiawatha.

He was standing near his wigwam,
On the margin of the water,
And he called to old Nokomis,
Called and beckoned to Nokomis,
Pointed to the sturgeon, Nahma,
Lying lifeless on the pebbles,
With the sea-gulls feeding on him.

'I have slain the Mishe-Nahma,
Slain the King of Fishes!' said he;
'Look! the sea-gulls feed upon him,
Yes, my friends Kayoshk, the sea-gulls;
Drive them not away, Nokomis,
They have saved me from great peril
In the body of the sturgeon,
Wait until their meal is ended,
Till their craws are full with feasting,
Till they homeward fly, at sunset,
To their nests among the marshes;
Then bring all your pots and kettles,
And make oil for us in Winter.'

And she waited till the sun set,
Till the pallid moon, the Night-Sun,
Rose above the tranquil water,
Till Kayoshk, the sated sea-gulls,
From their banquet rose with clamour,
And across the fiery sunset
Winged their way to far-off islands,
To their nests among the rushes.

To his sleep went Hiawatha,
And Nokomis to her labour,
Toiling patient in the moonlight,
Till the sun and moon changed places,
Till the sky was red with sunrise,
And Kayoshk, the hungry sea-gulls,
Came back from the reedy islands,
Clamorous for their morning banquet.

Three whole days and nights alternate
Old Nokomis and the sea-gulls
Stripped the oily flesh of Nahma,
Till the waves washed through the rib-bones,
Till the sea gulls came no longer,
And upon the sands lay nothing
But the skeleton of Nahma.

Henry Wadsworth Longfellow

The Breeze is on the Heron-Lake

The breeze is on the Heron-lake,
   The May-sun shineth clear;
Away we bound through the ferny brake,
   With our wands and angling gear.

The birch-wreath o'er the water edge
   Scatters sweet flies about;
And around his haunt of whisp'ring sedge,
   Bells up the yellow trout.

Take heed! take heed! his eye is bright
   As falcon's in the sky;
But artful feather hove aright,
   Will hood a keener eye.

Beware, beware the water-weed,
   And the birch that weeps behind,
And gently let the true line speed
   Before thee on the wind.

Oh! gently let the good line flow,
   And gently wile it home:
There's many a gallant fin I trow
   Under the ribbéd foam.

A merry fish on a stallion hair
   'Tis a pleasant thing to lead
On May-days, when the cowslip fair
   Is yellowing on the mead.

When the breeze starts up, and the sun peeps out,
   And grey flies two or three
Hold merry frolic round about,
   Under the green-wood tree . . .

Thomas Tod Stoddart

A Lay of the Lea

Up i' the early morning,
Sleepy pleasures scorning,
Rod in hand and creel on back, I'm away, away!
Not a care to vex me,
Nor a fear perplex me,
Blithe as any bird that pipes in the merry May.

Oh, the Enfield meadows,
Dappled with soft shadow!
Oh, the leafy Enfield lanes, odorous of May blossom!
Oh, the lapsing river,
Lea, beloved forever,
With the rosy morning light mirrored on its bosom!

Out come rod and tackle –
Out come midge and hackle –
Length of gut, like gossamer, on the south wind streaming –
Brace of palmers fine,
As ever decked a line,
Dubbed with herl and ribbed with gold, in the sunlight gleaming.

Bobbing 'neath the bushes,
Crouched among the rushes,
On the rights of Crown and State, I'm alas! encroaching;
What of that? I know
My creel will soon o'erflow,
If a certain Cerberus do not spoil my poaching.

As I throw my flies,
Fish on fish doth rise,
Roach and dace by dozens, on the bank they flounder;
Presently a splash,
And a furious dash –
Lo! a logger-headed chub, and a fat two-pounder!

Shade of Izaak, say,
Did you not one day
Fish for logger-headed chub by this very weir?
'Neath these very treēs
Down these sedgy leas –
Where's the nightingale that should be singing here? . . .

Oh, the pleasant roaming
Homeward through the gloaming!
Oh, the heavy creel, alack! Oh, the joyful greeting!
Oh, the jokes and laughter,
And the sound sleep after,
And the happy, happy dreams, all the sport repeating! . . .

T. Westwood

The Octopus

Strange beauty, eight-limbed and eight-handed,
Whence camest to dazzle our eyes?
With thy bosom bespangled and banded
With the hues of the seas and the skies;
Is thy home European or Asian,
O mystical monster marine?
Part molluscous and partly crustacean,
Betwixt and between.

Wast thou born to the sound of sea-trumpets?
Hast thou eaten and drunk to excess
Of the sponges – thy muffins and crumpets,
Of the seaweed – thy mustard and cress?
Wast thou nurtured in caverns of coral,
Remote from reproof or restraint?
Art thou innocent, art thou immoral,
Sinburnian or Saint?

Lithe limbs, curling free, as a creeper
That creeps in a desolate place,
To enrol and envelope the sleeper
In a silent and stealthy embrace,

Cruel beak craning forward to bite us,
  Our juices to drain and to drink,
Or to whelm us in waves of Cocytus,
  Indelible ink!

O breast, that 'twere rapture to writhe on!
  O arms 'twere delicious to feel
Clinging close with the crush of the Python,
  When she maketh her murderous meal!
In thy eight-fold embraces enfolden,
  Let our empty existence escape;
Give us death that is glorious and golden,
  Crushed all out of shape!

Ah! thy red lips, lascivious and luscious,
  With death in their amorous kiss!
Cling round us, and clasp us, and crush us,
  With bitings of agonized bliss;
We are sick with the poison of pleasure,
  Dispense us the potion of pain;
Ope thy mouth to its uttermost measure
  And bite us again!

A.C. Hilton

A Gallop of False Analogies

There is a fine stuffed chavender,
  A chavender or chub,
That decks the rural pavender,
  The pavender or pub,
Wherein I eat my gravender,
  My gravender or grub.

How good the honest gravender!
How snug the rustic pavender!
From sheets as sweet as lavender,
  As lavender or lub,
I jump into my tavender,
  My tavender or tub.

Alas, for town and clavender,
  For business and my club!
They call me from my pavender
To-night – ay, there's the ravender,
  Alas, there comes the rub!

To leave each blooming shravender,
  Each spring-bedizened shrub,
And meet the horsey savender,
  The very forward sub,
At dinner in the clavender,
And then at billiards dravender,
  At billiards soundly drub
The self-sufficient cavender,
  The not ill-meaning cub,
Who me a bear will davender
  A bear unfairly dub,
Because I sometimes snavender,
  Not too severely snub,
His setting right the clavender,
  His teaching all the club.

Farewell to peaceful pavender,
  My river-dreaming pub,
To bed as sweet as lavender,
To homely, wholesome gravender,
And you, inspiring chavender,
  Stuffed chavender or chub.

W. St Leger

The Oldest of Crafts

I propose to invite
Your attention to-night
To a claim that as anglers we hold,
To take the first place
In the sports of our race,
As I'll show from the records of old.
And if I've no case
I will gladly give place,
But at present I hav'n't a doubt
That the earliest dish
That man ate was a fish,
And, in all probability, a trout.

Ichthyologists tell
Of a panic that fell
On the fishes some ages ago,
When with terror benumbed
Many thousands succumbed
To a sudden and terrible blow.
The professors declare,
With that sapient air
Wherein learned professors delight,
That the fossils they find
Make it clear to their mind
That this death was begotten of fright.

But, taking to task
Our professor, we ask,
'Can you tell us the cause of this fear?'
Then he looks very grave,
And his answer is suave
As he says 'Well, it's not very clear';
But the angler steps in,
And he says, with a grin,
'If you cannot explain it, I can:
'Twas some wag of a trout
That had let the cat out,
And announced the arrival of Man.'

In the matter of streams,
It undoubtedly seems
That Eden was very well off;
And that angling began
With the very first man
We assert – though the critic may scoff;
For how to kill time
In that beautiful clime
Must have bothered old Adam, no doubt,
Till he hit on the plan,
Like a sensible man,
Of tickling the Paradise trout.

In the days of the Ark,
When the heavens were dark,
And the waters had covered the earth,
The jolly old trout,
Who was cruising about,
Must have thought it a matter of mirth.
For there, at his ease,
In the tops of the trees,
Regaling on excellent food,
He said, 'To my mind,
'Tis a very ill wind
That serves to blow nobody good.'

Now the patience of Job
Is the theme of the globe,
And that he was an angler is sure;
For he says in his book
That you can't with a hook
The wily leviathan lure.
As to Jonah's ill fate,
Though it's sad to relate
How he to the fishes was thrown,
Yet we see in this act
The remarkable fact
That ground-baiting wasn't unknown.

Then we'll drink as we ought
To so ancient a sport –
Let your glasses be filled to the brim:
What sportsman can boast
Of a heartier toast
Than 'The trout, and for aye may he swim!'
May he rise in his might,
And with energy fight;
And when his last struggle is o'er,
May he never regret
'Twas an angler whose net
Brought him safely at last to the shore.

R. Godby

The Fish

In a cool curving world he lies
And ripples with dark ecstasies.
The kind luxurious lapse and steal
Shapes all his universe to feel
And know and be; the clinging stream
Closes his memory, glooms his dream,
Who lips the roots o' the shore, and glides
Superb on unrelenting tides.
Those silent waters weave for him
A fluctuant mutable world and dim,

Where waving masses bulge and gape
Mysterious, and shape to shape
Dies momently through whorl and hollow,
And form and line and solid follow
Solid and line and form to dream
Fantastic down the eternal stream;
An obscure world, a shifting world,
Bulbous, or pulled to thin, or curled,
Or serpentine, or driving arrows,
Or serene slidings, or March narrows.

There slipping wave and shore are one,
And weed and mud. No ray of sun,
But glow to glow fades down the deep
(As dream to unknown dream in sleep);
Shaken translucency illumes
The hyaline of drifting glooms;
The strange soft-handed depth subdues
Drowned colour there, but black to hues,
As death to living, decomposes –
Red darkness of the heart of roses,
Blue brilliant from dear starless skies,
And gold that lies behind the eyes,
The unknown unnameable sightless white
That is essential flame of night,
Lustreless purple, hooded green,
The myriad hues that lie between
Darkness and darkness! . . .

And all's one
Gentle, embracing, quiet, dun,
The world he rests in, world he knows,
Perpetual curving. Only – grows
An eddy in that ordered falling,
A knowledge from the gloom, a calling
Weed in the wave, gleam in the mud –

The dark fire leaps along his blood;
Dateless and deathless, blind and still,
The intricate impulse works its will;
His woven world drops back; and he,
Sans providence, sans memory,
Unconscious and directly driven,
Fades to some dank sufficient heaven.

O world of lips, O world of laughter,
Where hope is fleet and thought flies after,
Of lights in the clear night, of cries
That drift along the wave and rise
Thin to the glittering stars above,
You know the hands, the eyes of love!
The strife of limbs, the sightless clinging,
The infinite distance, and the singing
Blown by the wind, a flame of sound,
The gleam, the flowers, and vast around
The horizon, and the heights above –
You know the sigh, the song of love!

But there the night is close, and there
Darkness is cold and strange and bare;
And the secret deeps are whisperless;
And rhythm is all deliciousness;
And joy is in the throbbing tide,
Whose intricate fingers beat and glide
In felt bewildering harmonies
Of trembling touch; and music is
The exquisite knocking of the blood.
Space is no more, under the mud;
His bliss is older than the sun.
Silent and straight the waters run.
The lights, the cries, the willows dim,
And the dark tide are one with him.

Rupert Brooke

Heaven

Fish (fly-replete, in depth of June,
Dawdling away their wat'ry noon)
Ponder deep wisdom, dark or clear,
Each secret fishy hope or fear.
Fish say, they have their Stream and Pond;
But is there anything Beyond?
This life cannot be All, they swear,
For how unpleasant, if it were!
One may not doubt that, somehow, Good
Shall come of Water and of Mud;
And, sure, the reverent eye must see
A Purpose in Liquidity.
We darkly know, by Faith we cry,
The future is not Wholly Dry.
Mud unto mud! – Death eddies near –
Not here the appointed End, not here!
But somewhere, beyond Space and Time,
Is wetter water, slimier slime!
And there (they trust) there swimmeth One
Who swam ere rivers were begun,
Immense, of fishy form and mind,
Squamous, omnipotent, and kind;
And under that Almighty Fin,
The littlest fish may enter in.
Oh! never fly conceals a hook,
Fish say, in the Eternal Brook,
But more than mundane weeds are there,
And mud, celestially fair;

Fat caterpillars drift around,
And Paradisal grubs are found;
Unfading moths, immortal flies,
And the worm that never dies.
And in that Heaven of all their wish,
There shall be no more land, say fish.

Rupert Brooke

The Pike

From shadows of rich oaks outpeer
The moss-green bastions of the weir,
Where the quick dipper forages
In elver-peopled crevices,
And a small runlet trickling down the sluice
Gossamer music tires not to unloose.

Else round the broad pools hush
Nothing stirs,
Unless sometimes a straggling heifer crush
Through the thronged spinney where the pheasant whirs;
Or martins in a flash

Come with wild mirth to dip their magical wings,
While in the shallow some doomed bulrush swings
At whose hid root the diver vole's teeth gnash.

And nigh this toppling reed, still as the dead
The great pike lies, the murderous patriarch
Watching the waterpit sheer-delving dark,
Where through the plash his live bright vassals thread.

The rose-finned roach and bluish bream
And staring ruffe steal up the stream
Hard by their glutted tyrant, now
Still as a sunken bough.

He on the sandbank lies,
Sunning himself long hours
With stony gorgon eyes:
Westward the hot sun lowers.

Sudden the gray pike changes, and quivering poises for slaughter;
  Intense terror wakens around him, the shoals
    scud awry, but there chances
  A chub unsuspecting; the prowling fins quicken,
    in fury he lances;
And the miller that opens the hatch stands amazed
    at the whirl in the water.

Edmund Blunden

The Wild Swans at Coole

Although I can see him still,
The freckled man who goes
To a grey place on a hill
In grey Connemara clothes
At dawn to cast his flies,
It's long since I began
To call up to the eyes

This wise and simple man.
All day I'd looked in the face
What I had hoped 'twould be
To write for my own race
And the reality;
The living men that I hate,
The dead man that I loved,
The craven man in his seat,
The insolent unreproved,
And no knave brought to book
Who has won a drunken cheer,
The witty man and his joke
Aimed at the commonest ear,
The clever man who cries
The catch-cries of the clown,
The beating down of the wise
And great Art beaten down.

Maybe a twelvemonth since
Suddenly I began,
In scorn of this audience,
Imagining a man,
And his sun-freckled face,
And grey Connemara cloth,
Climbing up to a place
Where stone is dark under froth,
And the down-turn of his wrist
When the flies drop in the stream;
A man who does not exist,
A man who is but a dream;
And cried, 'Before I am old
I shall have written him one
Poem maybe as cold
And passionate as the dawn'.

W.B. Yeats

The Cream of It

'Twixt the primrose and the dog-rose,
   'Twixt the March-Brown and the Drake,
Till young rooks, in gollywog rows,
   Hold the windy elms awake,
Lie the paths that Ariel flits on
   When we dream, in cities mean,
Easter waters, streams at Whitsun,
   And of stolen days between!

Dreams of dark, of northern rivers,
   And the pass still packed with snow
(For the months are stubborn givers
   Where the spring-run salmon show),
Where the North-East storms and blusters,
   Yet the courting grouse cock swanks
And in shy and starry clusters,
Peeps the primrose on the banks!

Dreams – a flow of crystal wanders
  'Neath the high, wind-haunted chalk,
And the captious pounder ponders
  And the dry-fly pundits stalk;
And an inn there is at even
  Where the brothers sit confessed
Of the Orkneys to Loch Leven,
  From Loch Leven to the Test!

Dreams, where Thames the old slow speeding,
  Glides through lilac'd hours and gay,
Where the ten pound trout was feeding
  (So you're told!) but yesterday;
Where you check your leisured homing
  (Empty creeled!) to stand and hear
Philomela in the gloaming
  Call the waiting summer near!

Dreams of leisure, dreams of pleasure,
  Dreams that crowd their radiant rout
With the mayfly's mazy measure,
  And a carnival of trout.
Where the cuckoo calls uncaring
  Down the endless afternoon
And the dog-rose twines his fairing
  On the bonny brows of June!

While the rivers do not falter
  But run downward to the main,
While the changing seasons alter
  And the swallow comes again,

While the tadpole to the frog grows
  And the acorn to the tree,
Shall the primrose and the dog-rose
  Bind the golden hours for me!

Anon 1920

Rainbow

Why should our members grouse about
That splendid fish the Rainbow trout
To me, for all it's little whims
It is the noblest fish that swims
I know it wanders quite a bit
But why the Devil shouldn't it?
Cruising, for instance, up the Bends
To see the World, and meet its friends
Making at times a playful rise
It gives the members exercise
If, when in true Olympic style
You've chased it over half a mile
It makes a sudden homeward tack
Or rises just behind your back
Then hurries off to base again,
You've had your fun – so why complain?

Hunting a quarry of that sort
Is not a sedentary sport.
I know the purists always frown
On any trout that isn't brown
And furthermore go on to say
In their authoritative way
(Which means of course you wouldn't know,
You silly ignorant so and so)
'It's not a trout it's just a char'
That shows what purists really are
For called by any other name
It's just as beautiful and game
It feeds (on nothing) all day long
Nor waits for any dinner gong
Whereas its cousin Fario
Its nose will very seldom show
Till stimulated by a rise
Of different sorts of water flies,

To show how people's views can vary
Our honorary secretary
Who personally was known as quite
A violent anti Rainbowite
Or never to have cast a fly
That wasn't absolutely dry
Yesterday found his iron will
Defeated by the lust to kill
And with a nymph, well under water,
Achieved a pretty wholesale slaughter.
So let us hope, at last that this is
The end of both his prejudices
And that last evening he came back
(With six large Rainbows in a sack)
A Nympho-Rainbow-Maniac.

Colonel Pryor from THE HOUGHTON CLUB FISHING BOOK *1954*
(Quoted by Mick Lunn in A PARTICULAR LUNN)

Heavenly Record

Upon a river-bank serene,
A fisher sat where all was green
– and looked it.

He waited till the lights grew dim,
He saw a fish, or the fish saw him,
– and hooked it.

He took with high erected comb,
The fish, or else the story home,
– and cooked it.

Recording angels by his bed,
Weighed all that he had done, or said,
– and booked it.

J.S. Watson

Envoi

'Well I'm –!'

G. E. M. SKUES

Mr Theodore Castwell, having devoted a long, strenuous and not unenjoyable life to hunting to their doom innumerable salmon, trout and grayling in many quarters of the globe, and having gained much credit among his fellows for his many ingenious improvements in rods, flies and tackle employed for that end, in the fullness of time died and was taken to his own place.

St Peter looked up from a draft balance-sheet at the entry of the attendant angel.

'A gentleman giving the name of Castwell. Says he is a fisherman, your Holiness, and has "Fly-Fishers' Club, London," on his card.'

'Hm-hm,' says St Peter. 'Fetch me the ledger with his account.'

St Peter perused it.

'Hm-hm,' said Peter. 'Show him in.'

Mr Castwell entered cheerfully and offered a cordial right hand to St Peter.

'As a brother of the angle –' he began.

'Hm-hm,' said St Peter.

'I am sure I shall not appeal to you in vain for special consideration in connection with the quarters to be assigned to me here.'

'Hm-hm,' said St Peter. 'I have been looking at your account from below.'

'Nothing wrong with it, I hope,' said Mr Castwell.

'Hm-hm,' said St Peter. 'I have seen worse. What sort of quarters would you like?'

'Well,' said Mr Castwell. 'Do you think you could manage something in the way of a country cottage of the Test Valley type, with modern conveniences and, say, three-quarters of a mile of one of those pleasant chalk-streams, clear as crystal, which proceed from out the throne, attached?'

'Well, yes,' said St Peter. 'I think we can manage that for you. Then what about your gear? You must have left your fly-rods and tackle down below. I see you prefer a light split cane of nine foot or so, with appropriate fittings. I will indent upon the Works Department for what you require, including a supply of flies. I think you will approve of our dressers' productions. Then you will want a keeper to attend you.'

'Thanks awfully, your Holiness,' said Mr Castwell. 'That will be first-rate. To tell you the truth, from the Revelations I read, I was inclined to fear that I might be just a teeny-weeny bit bored in heaven.'

'In H – hm-hm,' said St Peter, checking himself.

It was not long before Mr Castwell found himself alongside an enchantingly beautiful clear chalk-stream, some fifteen yards wide, swarming with fine trout feeding greedily; and presently the attendant angel assigned to him had handed him the daintiest, most exquisite, light split cane rod conceivable – perfectly balanced with reel and line – with a beautifully damped tapered cast of incredible fineness and strength – and a box of flies of such marvellous tying, as to be almost mistakable for the natural insects they were to simulate.

Mr Castwell scooped up a natural fly from the water, matched it perfectly from the fly-box, and knelt down to cast to a riser putting up just under a tussock ten yards or so above him. The fly lit like gossamer, six inches above the last ring; and next moment the rod was making the curve of beauty. Presently, after an exciting battle, the keeper netted out a beauty of about two and a half pounds.

'Heavens!' cried Mr Castwell. 'This is something like.'

'I am sure his Holiness will be pleased to hear it,' said the keeper.

Mr Castwell prepared to move upstream to the next riser when he became aware that another trout had taken up the position of that which he had just landed, and was rising. 'Just look at that,' he said, dropping instantaneously to his knee and drawing off some line. A moment later an accurate fly fell just above the neb of the fish, and instantly Mr Castwell engaged in battle with another lusty fish. All went well, and presently the landing-net received its two and a half pounds.

'A very pretty brace,' said Mr Castwell, preparing to move on to the next of the string of busy nebs which he had observed putting up round the bend. As he approached the tussock, however, he became aware that the place from which he had just extracted so satisfactory a brace was already occupied by another busy feeder.

'Well, I'm damned!' cried Mr Castwell. 'Do you see that?'

'Yes, sir,' said the keeper.

The chance of extracting three successive trout from the same spot was too attractive to be forgone, and once more Mr Castwell knelt down and delivered a perfect cast to the spot. Instantly it was accepted and battle was joined. All held, and presently a third gleaming trout joined his brethren in the creel.

Mr Castwell turned joyfully to approach the next riser round the bend. Judge, however, his surprise to find that once more the pit beneath the tussock was occupied by a rising trout, apparently of much the same size as the others.

'Heavens!' exclaimed Mr Castwell. 'Was there ever anything like it?'

'No, sir,' said the keeper.

'Look here,' said he to the keeper, 'I think I really must give this chap a miss and pass on to the next.'

'Sorry! It can't be done, sir. His Holiness would not like it.'

'Well, if that's really so,' said Mr Castwell, and knelt reluctantly to his task.

Several hours later he was still casting to the same tussock.

'How long is this confounded rise going to last?' inquired Mr Castwell. 'I suppose it will stop soon?'

'No, sir,' said the keeper.

'What, isn't there a slack hour in the afternoon?'

'No afternoon, sir.'

'What? Then what about the evening rise?'

'No evening, sir,' said the keeper.

'Well, I shall knock off now. I must have had about thirty brace from that corner.'

'Beg pardon, sir, but his Holiness would not like that.'

'What?' said Mr Castwell. 'Mayn't I even stop at night?'

'No night here, sir,' said the keeper.

'Then do you mean that I have got to go on catching these damned two and a half pounders at this corner for ever and ever?'

The keeper nodded.

'Hell!' said Mr Castwell.

'Yes,' said his keeper.

from SIDE-LINES, SIDE-LIGHTS AND REFLECTIONS *1932*

Acknowledgements

Acknowledgements and thanks are due to the following authors and publishers for the use of copyright material: Storm Jameson for the English translation of 'Two Friends' (A.A. Knopf, London, 1928; Katharine Whitehorn for 'Fish out of Water' from *Roundabout* (Methuen, 1962); both reprinted by permission of A.D. Peters & Co.; and also by permission of the same, 'Elmbury Memories' from *Portrait of Elmbury* by the late John Moore (Collins, 1945); H.E. Bates for 'The Little Fishes' from *Sugar for the Horse* (Michael Joseph, 1957); the Trustees of the Nevil Shute Norway Estate, William Heinemann Ltd and William Morrow and Company, Inc. for 'Coldstone Mill' by Nevil Shute from *Pastoral*. (Copyright © 1944 by William Morrow and Company, Inc., London and New York.); Sven Berlin and J.M. Dent & Sons Ltd. for 'The Sacrifice' from *Jonah's Dream* (Phoenix House, 1964); the Executors and Trustees of the estate of the late Roland Pertwee for 'The River God', first published in England in the 1930s (date unknown); Henry Williamson and Faber & Faber Ltd for 'Tide-Head' from *Salar the Salmon* (1935); H.A. Manhood for 'The Lake of the Red Trout' from *Crack of Whips* (Cape, 1934); Commander C. F. Walker, RN(Retd) for 'Fly Nomenclature', first published in *Salmon and Trout Magazine* (September 1963); Daniel Farson for 'French Interlude' from *Going Fishing* by the late Negley Farson (Country Life, 1942); the successors of Nicholas Kaye Ltd for 'The Fishing Hotel' from *Torridge Fishery* by the late L. R. N. Gray (1957); Denys Watkins-Pitchford for 'Record-Breaker' by Brian Vesey-Fitzgerald; also for 'Rudd and Tench Records' by the Rev. E. C. Alston, first published as 'Rev. Alston's Record Tench'; also for 'A Warwickshire Trout' by 'B.B.' from 'Fisherman's Folly' (an unpublished MS.), all first published in *The Fisherman's Bedside Book* by 'B.B.' (Eyre & Spottiswoode, 1945); E. L. Matthews and Paulton House Publications for 'A Tale of Two Boxes', first published in *Creel* (December 1965); Sir Robert Bruce Lockhart, KCMG and Putnam & Co. Ltd for 'By Foreign Streams' from *My Rod, My Comfort* (1949); Richard Walker and McGibbon & Kee Ltd for 'The Record Carp' from *Still Water Angling* (1953), first published in *Anglers' News*, September/October, 1952; William B. Currie and Hutchinson for 'Europe's Biggest Grayling' from *Game Fishing* (Stanley Paul, 1962); Macmillan & Co. Ltd for 'A February Pike' from *An Angler's Hours* by H.T. Sheringham (1905); Frederick J. Wagstaffe and the Editor of *Fishing* (Angling Times Ltd) for 'Pike of the Reservoirs', first published in *Fishing* (October 1966); the Executors and Trustees of the late Mrs Joan Sparks for 'The Roach-Fishers' from *At the Tail of the Weir* by Patrick R. Chalmers (Philip Allan, 1932);

Oxford University Press for 'The Anglers at Home' from *The Arte of Angling* by an anonymous author (1577), reprinted from the facsimile edition (ed. G.E. Bentley, 1956) of the unique printed copy in the Library of the Friends of Princeton University; Harold W. McCormick, Sidgwick & Jackson Ltd and Chilton & Co. (Philadelphia, USA) for 'The Heaviest Rod-caught Fish' from *Shadows in the Sea* (Sidgwick & Jackson, 1963); Clive Gammon for 'The Haven' from *A Tide of Fish* (Heinemann, 1962); Lady Hills for 'The Evening Rise' and 'The Charm of Old Rivers' both from *A Summer on the Test* by John Waller Hills (Geoffrey Bles, 1924); the Owner of the Copyright for 'The Skill of the Fisherman' from *A Humble Fisherman* by Morley Roberts (Grayson & Grayson, 1932); Herbert Jenkins Ltd for 'Tussle with a Salmo-Ferox' from *In Scotland with a Fishing Rod* by R. Macdonald Robertson (1935); and for 'Whose Trout?' and 'Shocks and a Lesson', both from *Itchen Memories* by G.E.M. Skues (1951); Thomas Nelson & Sons Ltd for 'Dry Fly on the Earn' from *The Path by the Water* by A.R.B. Haldane (1944); Brigadier Sir Alan Durand for 'Scottish Memories' from *Wanderings with a Fly-Rod* by Sir Edward Durand (Herbert Jenkins, 1938); the Owner of the Copyright for 'Dry Fly Fishing' and 'Refreshing Pleasure' from *Fly Fishing* (Dent, 1899), and 'Earthly Paradise' from *Fallodon Papers* (1926), all by Viscount Grey of Fallodon; Commander V.J. Robinson for 'When all else Failed', first published as 'The Garden Ranger's Day' in *The Field* (18-11-1965); Max Christensen for 'Christmas in Tasmania', first published in *Journal of the Flyfishers' Club* (Winter 1965); Chatto & Windus (Educational) Ltd, for 'The Finest Trout in the River' from *Where the Bright Waters Meet* by Harry Plunkett Greene (Philip Allan, 1924); the Blunden Estate and Sidgwick & Jackson Ltd for 'The Pike' from *The Waggoner and other Poems* (1920) by Edmund Blunden; the Editor of *Journal of the Flyfisher's Club* for 'The Cream of It' by an anonymous poet (1920); Andre Simon and the Wine and Food Society for 'The Prickly Cohort' from *Wine and Food* (1955) by Kenneth Mansfield; Seeley, Service & Co. Ltd for 'Well I'm – !' from *Side-Lines, Side Lights and Reflections* by G.E.M. Skues (1932); Mick Lunn and Unwin Hyman Ltd for 'Basic Rules' from *A Particular Lunn* (1990); the Owners of the Copyright for 'Broadbill Swordfish' from *Tales of the Angler's Eldorado, New Zealand* (1926) by Zane Grey; Chris Ogborne for 'A Blagdon Day' from *Blagdon* (1985); 'Moc' Morgan for 'Buzz and Kick' from *The Complete Fly Fisher*, edited by Peter Lapsley (1990); Bernard Venables for 'The Fisherman in Winter' from *Mr Crabtree Goes Fishing* (1989); William Humphrey and Chatto & Windus for 'The Superfish' from *My Moby Dick* (1979); the Hemingway Estate and Jonathan Cape for 'The Old Man's Great Fish' from *The Old Man and the Sea* by Ernest Hemingway (1952); Cassell and Trevor Housby for 'Conger, Tope and Bass' from *Successful Sea Angling* (1990); Fred J. Taylor and Richard Walker for the latter's *Tench Methods* quoted in the former's *Fishing for Fun* (1979); Bob Church for 'Grafham: Britain's Greatest' from *Stillwater Trout Fisheries* (1976); Robin Mulholland and the Crowood Press for the 'Virtues of Grayling' by Robin Mulholland, from *Grayling: the Fourth Game Fish*, edited by Ronald Broughton (1989);

and the Owners of the Copyright for W.B. Yeats's poem *The Wild Swans at Coole* (1919).

The Publishers would also like to thank the Editor of *Anglers' Annual* (The Heathcock Press Ltd), the Editor of *Angling* (City Magazines Ltd) and the authors, respectively, for permission to reprint the following articles:

(From *Anglers' Annual*) 'The Evolution of Fly-Fishing Philosophy in France' by Major O.W.A. Kite (1965); 'The Art of the Tiddler' by F. W. Holiday (1963); 'Anglers' Weather' by David Bowen, FR MetS (1965); 'The Chub beneath the Bridge' by Peter Ward (1967); and 'Salmon through the Looking Glass' by Arthur Oglesby (1967).

(From *Angling*) 'A Tench called Diana' by Donald Cameron (September 1960); 'Finding those 10lb Tench' by John Ellis and Maurice Ingham (June 1963); 'The Trout's Sister' by the Rev. Frederick E. Mold (November 1962); 'I want *Fun* in my Pike-Fishing' by Fred J. Taylor (February 1962); 'Barbel by Sight and Sound' by Peter Stone (November 1962); 'Sharks from the Shore' by Jack Shine (February 1964); 'Bass over Splaugh Rock' by Des Brennan (June 1963); and 'The Sport that Died' by Eric Horsfall Turner (October 1961).

In addition, the Editor would like to thank John Davison, editor of the *Grayling Society's Journal*, and Sidney Vines for their many helpful suggestions.

Finally, the Publishers wish to point out that though they have made every effort to trace all copyright holders for permission to include their pieces in this anthology, they have not always been successful. They apologize to those whose names have been omitted and for any errors that may have occurred in the form of acknowledgement.

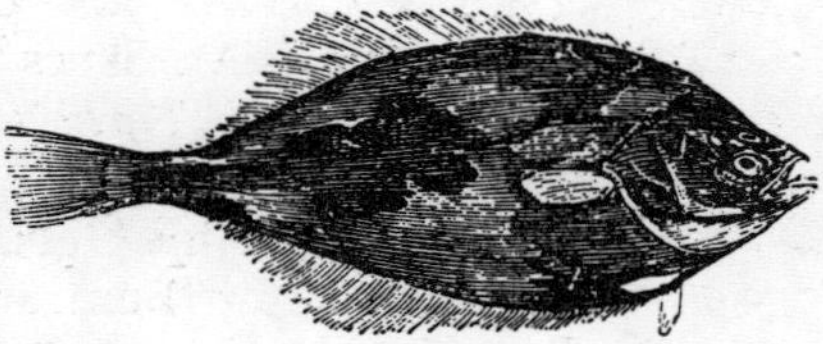